KINGDOM

OF

REBELS AND THORNS

KINGDOM

OF

REBELS AND THORNS

THE AERMIAN FUEDS
1 & 2

FROST KAY

KINGDOM OF REBELS AND THORNS

For information on reproducing sections of this book or sales of this book go to:
WWW.FROSTKAY.NET

Cover by Covers by Combs
Interior formatting by We Got You Covered Book Design
Copy Editing by Madeline Dyer
Proofreading by Holmes Edits

ALSO BY FROST KAY

TWISTED KINGDOMS
FAIRYTALE RETELLING

The Hunt

The Rook

The Heir

The Beast

DRAGON ISLE WARS
FANTASY ROMANCE

Court of Dragons

DOMINION OF ASH
POST APOCALYPTIC FANTASY ROMANCE

The Stain

The Tainted

The Exiled

The Fallout

The Chosen

MIXOLOGISTS & PIRATES
SCI-FI ROMANCE

Amber Vial

Emerald Bane

Scarlet Venom

Cyan Toxin

Onyx Elixir

Indigo Alloy

ALIENS & ALCHEMISTS
SCI-FI ROMANCE

Pirates, Princes, and Payback

Alphas, Airships, and Assassins

THE AERMIAN FEUDS
DARK FANTASY ROMANCE

Rebel's Blade

Crown's Shield

Siren's Lure

Enemy's Queen

King's Warrior

Warlord's Shadow

Spy's Mask

Court's Fool

To my mama: thank you for always telling me
that I could do anything I set my mind to.

I LOVE YOU.

PART ONE

THE REBEL'S BLADE

PROLOGUE

———⊷∘⟨⟨⟨∘⊶———

THIS WAS IT.

Escape was impossible and death inevitable.

Leering men surrounded her; the stench of their rotting teeth and filthy clothing assaulted her senses. Black spots dotted her vision as she struggled to maintain consciousness. She couldn't let herself slip away, though, or think of what they'd do if she did.

Sage had been trained for this sort of thing, had been told pain was in the mind and, while she could push *some* of it away, her body was only so strong. It was impossible to remain unaffected. She blinked, clearing the tears and blood from her eyes, only to catch the dark, empty ones of her captor studying her with amusement, seeming to enjoy her every wince or whimper. Biting the inside of her cheek, she steeled herself; she would not give him the satisfaction.

If by some miracle she made it through this alive, he was on her list.

Her body screamed in pain as someone pushed her forward, her toes skimming the floor seeking purchase. Her hands, slick with sweat, slipped from the chains, shifting the entirety of her weight onto her manacled wrists. The metal bit into her abused flesh, though she had thankfully lost feeling in them some time ago. Tremors now wracked her nearly naked body.

How much longer could she hold on?

She peered at the ringleader, a sadistic man named Serge. He appeared to be moving his lips, yet all she heard was the high-pitched ringing in her ears. The edges of her vision blurred, and every sound seemed distorted—almost as if she was underwater. She would die here and her family would never know where to find her. Bitterness and regret then filled her. She should have killed the crown prince when she had the chance. This was his doing, she knew it. If she made it out alive, she would bring Aermia down around his ears.

ONE

KING MARQ

THE TOES OF HIS BOOTS hovered over the air. Marq stood on the ledge of a massive open window and gazed down at the waves crashing into the jagged cliffs below. The wind whistled softly, carrying the scent of salt and seaweed through the window. It caressed his face, ruffling his charcoal-colored woolen cloak. Gulls cried over each other amid the roar of waves and the sharp voices of the fishmongers' wives as they haggled prices. Despite this cacophony of noise, it was peaceful here. Pulling his gaze from the boiling sea below, he turned his attention to the port, its ships decorating the harbor, bobbing like toys. Fishermen, merchants and traders marched to and fro like ants.

He sighed. His wife had loved walking in the market, always looking for new treasures or herbs to bring home. Her eyes would round and light up with excitement over some trinket. The woman had also harbored a deep love for the sea. A soft smile brightened his features thinking of the first time he saw her. He had turned into a bumbling idiot. He had taken a walk below the castle at low tide, as was his custom, and had reveled in the quiet time to think.

When he'd caught sight of her, it stopped him in his tracks. She was completely oblivious to the world, with her arms thrown high and her palms facing the sky—almost like she was worshiping the sun. As she tilted her face to its rays, her midnight hair cascaded down her back, kissing the waves as they lapped just above her knees, her dress fluidly twirling about her legs. He had seen nothing more beautiful. As a boy, his nana used to tell him stories of sea nymphs and Sirenidae, and he wondered, could she be one of them? He was afraid she would disappear if he looked away even for a second.

Then she'd dropped her chin, running her fingers along the frothy waves, a tiny smirk playing along her mouth.

That's peculiar, he had thought, *what's she smirking about?*

His eyes snapped from her full pink lips to soft purple eyes. All he could do was gape. Purple eyes? Incredible.

"You know that's considered rude; to stare in most places." She had grinned at him expectantly, yet he still hadn't moved a muscle. He couldn't. Rolling her eyes at him, she had gestured for him to come closer. "Come introduce yourself."

He recalled how he had wanted to run to her, but that wouldn't do. He was a prince, and princes were dignified, so instead he had collected himself and strode toward her, attempting an air of confidence. But it was just his luck that on the first step he'd caught his boot on a rock, stumbling and flailing his arms as he attempted to catch his balance. However, he had instead somehow entangled his feet in seaweed, landing on his stomach with a face full of sand.

Curses and sand had spewed out of his mouth. Marq growled and clenched his jaw, the sand crunching between his teeth.

"Figures," he grumbled to himself. "There goes any chance of wooing her."

Female laughter, interspersed with an occasional wheeze, had then tickled his ears, bringing his attention back to the woman. He'd been so embarrassed that he had rolled over and threw an arm over his face. Perhaps if he couldn't see her, then she couldn't see him. If only life worked that way.

A cool drop of water had plopped onto his face. *What the devil was that?* Moving his arm, he'd squinted up at the purple-eyed beauty who was at that very moment leaning over him. His heart stuttered, which surprised him. *Is it supposed to do that?*

She had shoved her hand out at him, laughter dancing in those unusual eyes of hers. "I'm Ivy," she had stated. "You should have seen my fall in the forest last week. I tripped on nothing, nothing at all. You figure out how that happened. I can tell you one thing, it was not pretty!" she'd continued.

He'd blinked. She talked fast. Marq didn't think she had taken a breath.

She'd grabbed his hand and pulled him up, "Here, let me help you up!" Her impish grin had enchanted him, making him feel right at home. She'd changed his life that day, for in her he had found something he didn't even know he needed.

The vivid memory faded, and the present came creeping back in. Marq's gaze once again sought the waves below. Without Ivy, he was weary of his empty life. The passing of time had not diminished his ache for her. And as each day passed, his memories of her faded bit by bit. He couldn't remember the sound of her voice anymore and it killed him. Self-loathing bubbled up at his uselessness; he didn't recognize himself anymore. Thirty years of love and memories haunted him every day.

Again, the waves seemed to beckon him. He knew it would be easy to take just one step. If he was a weaker man, perhaps he might have. He scoffed, thinking the ocean would likely just spit him back up.

He pondered what the future would hold: how was he to die? Would he go to sleep one day never to wake up? Or would he instead bleed out on a battlefield somewhere, sword in hand? How would he be remembered?

The quiet scuff of a boot roused him from his morbid reverie, and he internally groaned. Lord save him from one of his son's 'interventions'.

Without turning around, he asked, "To what do I owe the pleasure of your visit, son? Decided to check up on your old man, have you?" Ivy had called her father 'old man', and the memory brought a smile to his face.

He already knew what his son Tehl would say, so he shook his head, instead answering his own question. "No, I think not." He reached out and rapped his knuckles on the window frame. "I highly doubt this is a social visit as it's been a while since you last visited me." His eldest son was pragmatic and logical, putting duty before all else. If he were visiting, then it had to do with Aermian business.

Marq turned to study his oldest boy. A strong, azure gaze met his own. He supposed Tehl was not so much a boy anymore.

"What is it you need, son?"

Tehl was casually leaning his broad shoulders against the cold stone wall, one black brow arched, the spitting image of his mother. At least Marq could have a little piece of Ivy in his son, he mused. He had grown into a handsome man. Maybe one day he would get some adorable grandbabies out of him. Ivy had always wanted to be a grandmother. He rubbed his chest; perhaps, if he rubbed hard enough some of the terrible grief could depart and he'd no longer feel like someone was squeezing the life from his body. Marq shoved down the pain and focused on his son.

"You must have heard about the revolts. Are you having trouble pinning down the leaders? If it isn't handled soon, it will turn into civil war," he commented.

"You know of the recent revolts?" Tehl asked.

Marq released a heavy sigh. "It's of no consequence. Tehl, get on with it. I haven't seen you in three weeks, and I am not getting any younger. I know you have no desire to see me, as you've made clear, so you must need something. Am I wrong?" His son's expressionless face stared back at him, mute. He grimaced, pressing the heels of his hands to his weary eyes. Sometimes his son made rocks seem downright chatty.

"I am surprised you're not out patrolling the city or chasing skirts. That seems to be your only pastime these days, other than avoiding me," he muttered.

Tehl scoffed, pushing off the wall. His son strolled over to his side and peered out the window. "No, that's Samuel's job, not mine. He chases enough women for the both of us." Tehl's lips pulled down. "I don't chase. If I want one, I say something and either the female accepts or declines. I don't have the time for chasing." Tehl's hands fluttered in the air. His son's dark blue eyes focused back on him after a moment. "I have too many responsibilities to engage in something so frivolous. *Your* responsibilities," Tehl added, his tone bitter.

Marq shook his head. "Your mother would be disgusted to see your brother's treatment of women. I only wish one of you would finally pick one, then I might at the very least have grandchildren to keep me occupied." He and Ivy had always liked the idea of being grandparents. Maybe they would fill the blasted hole in his chest, he thought.

Sadly though, Marq didn't expect that to happen soon. Sam loved all women so much it seemed he felt no desire to settle down with any one woman, while Tehl was too busy trying to save the world to notice anyone at all.

"Your mother always wanted you to find someone that made you happy," he hinted.

"You don't know how Mum would feel, because she isn't here," Tehl remarked, as if he were speaking of the weather.

Marq gasped, the barb stealing the breath from his lungs. In fact, it would have been less painful if Tehl had punched him in the face.

His son's face fell, remorse evident. "Forgive me. That was uncalled for." Tehl's gaze dropped to his cloak, and he added, "But she is gone and you need to let her go."

"I will never let your mother go. A companion like her is rare, and I can only hope you might one day find what I had in your mum. If you're ever fortunate enough to find a woman like her, you'll understand," Marq said, gruffly.

His son stared, his eyes narrowed in disbelief. "What you had only happens in fairy tales." Tehl's face pinched. "And look at what her death has done to you. You're unable to even care for yourself, much less Aermia. You are wasting away. I can't even recall the last time you left the castle walls. Our people are starving, and why? Because it seems you're incapable of halting this steady descent of yours. The Scythians steal into our kingdom to despoil the land, burn our crops. Aermians are disappearing along the border."

Marq's eyes widened. "Scythians?" he repeated, trying to make sense of his son's words. Over the last nine hundred years, a few outcasts of the Scythians kingdom had sought refuge, but they kept to themselves. He shuddered, thinking of the warriors—more monster than man—that they created. He scrutinized his son. "What do you mean by Scythian?"

"Exactly what I said. It wasn't the rebels causing the trouble along the border, it was Scythia."

"You have confirmation?"

"Yes, there were survivors this time." Tehl's face hardened. "If you can call them that. They will be scarred for life, children." Pain filled his son's eyes. "Our kingdom needs you, but you sit in this godforsaken tower and do nothing."

Having vented his frustration, Tehl's shoulders slumped. The pain and anger his son was struggling with became evident with his every word. Marq felt it as if it were his own. Did Tehl not understand how much he was trying, fighting every day? His only companions of late were sadness, guilt, and anger.

"Don't take that tone with me, son. You cannot fathom how it has been, having lost the woman who owned my soul. She was my helper, friend, and companion. My other half. When she died, it may as well have been me," he replied. Every word was a slash to his tortured soul.

"I understand that you miss Mum, but…" Tehl trailed off, his head cocked as he seemed to take note of his father's belt, his eyes narrowing.

Marq looked down, attempting to discover what had caught his son's attention. Before he could discern anything, Tehl reached out and snatched the dagger from under his cloak. Marq gritted his teeth and tilted his head toward the open rafters of the great stone ceiling above. Lord give him patience. "Why did you do that?"

Tehl ignored his question, instead replying with one of his own. "What is this?"

Marq observed his son run a careful finger along the edge of the blade, wondering what in the world he was going on about. "What does it look like, son? I am certain you're in full possession of your wits?" he inquired, exasperation coloring his words.

Tehl's face was impassive even as his hand clenched the hilt of the blade. That one display of emotion was enough to make Marq scrutinize his son. His son rarely showed emotion of any kind. Why was he so furious?

"You *know* you're not allowed any weapons in your possession," Tehl hissed.

Ah, he thought. *So that's what this is about.*

Tehl was worried he might hurt himself again. There had been one instance following Ivy's death he had cut himself. He had been numb, unable to feel a single thing—not anger, not guilt, nor joy. He couldn't even cry. What sort of human being was he, to be incapable of mourning his loved ones? And even as he made that miniscule cut in his own flesh, there'd been no pain. He'd still felt nothing.

"I have always carried a blade," Marq reasoned, attempting to placate his son. "This is not unusual. In fact, it is essential for protection."

"I am trying to protect you from yourself."

That stung. "It was only the one instance, son, we'd barely buried her, but I am in no such danger now," he reasoned. "I have no wish to die."

"Death is a weak man's tactic to escape problems. You, as the king, ought to be stronger than that. No person should hold that much power over you."

Those words pained him but, as they weren't unfounded, he could not fault his son for them. "Then you ought to understand that it is only for protection. You shouldn't worry."

Tehl glanced away from him in disgust. "I can't save you from yourself, and I'm done trying. Mope around your little fortress, lose yourself in your precious memories, or drink yourself into oblivion. Hell, you can sit in this tower and rot, or jump out the damned window if that's preferable. I am not your guardian." Black smudges rested beneath his son's eyes. He looked exhausted. Tehl sighed, "And you were correct in guessing this was not a social visit, as enlightening as it has been. It seems Sam and his sneaks have found new leads on the rebellion leaders. My men and I will investigate. We will find them soon."

"Always the dutiful son, aren't you?" Marq asked, not expecting an answer. His son kept himself so engrossed in his duties to Aermia that his life was slipping past him and he didn't even see it. Tehl needed someone to shock him out of his rut, this relentless routine he kept up. "You need a wife." The accompanying look of absolute horror on his son's face made him chuckle. Biting back a grin, he continued, "You need someone to help you. It's time to find a woman."

"A woman?" Tehl repeated, stunned. His face soured, disgust evident as he stared at Marq, his arms crossed. It was rather akin to the look his son had given when he was little and had wanted pudding but received spinach instead.

"I don't need a wife. I have a higher chance of being struck by lightning than being married." Tehl appeared thoughtful. "If I took a mistress, would that appease you?"

Marq scowled at his eldest son. "No! That would be disgraceful."

Tehl's lips twitched.

Realization dawned: his son was teasing him. His scowl deepened. It seemed sons were more trouble than they were worth. Why couldn't Ivy have given him daughters? He crossed his arms and his scowl morphed into a smirk. "You may joke now, but just you wait. At your age, I had rather the same attitude, but I received a large slice of humble pie." Tehl looked at him as he continued: "Your mother."

Tehl paled and backed away as if he had some disease. "I have to go. Take care of yourself, father. The next time we meet, I will have good news about the rebellion." With that, his son turned on his heel and left the chamber.

That boy was headstrong, yet Marq knew he would make an exceptional king. He knew it. He slumped against the stone wall. It seemed their conversation had taken a lot out of him. He hadn't experienced that many emotions in a long time. And yet…maybe things were looking up for him. As soon as he had thought it, he winced. Hope was a dangerous thing.

TWO ⊙

TEHL

———⟨○⟨⟩○⟩———

THE KING WAS LIVING IN the past. It seemed like he wanted to lose himself in his memories and never come back. Tehl tucked his father's dagger into a sheath at his waist, moving down the corridor.

Where does he keep getting these weapons?

He needed to increase the security on the armory. You would think someone who wasn't lucid more than half the time would lose some of their cunning, but not his father. One thing he could say, it seemed King Marq did not dull with age.

Tehl scanned the chilly hallway that led to the part of the castle his father inhabited. He shuddered, it unnerved him. Between the dim lantern light, the chill from the drab, gray stone, and the puddles of darkness, it felt like something out of one of the horror stories Sam would read to him. Goosebumps broke out on his arms and the hair on the back of his neck prickled. He hated it up here.

Light winked at him from the bottom of the stairway, and Tehl picked up his speed, ready to leave the gloom behind him. He stepped into the bright hallway, glad to have left behind the dreary turrets. How could his father stand it? He resided in the darkest, ugliest part of the castle, and Tehl couldn't see why.

Tehl loved their castle. It was a true feat of architecture, having been built from the stone bluff on which it rested. White marble columns stretched toward the high, arched ceiling where shimmering gold stars twinkled in the sunlight as it streamed through the windows. It danced over the stained glass, casting murals of colored images onto the smooth white walls. The kaleidoscope of colors helped to soothe his frayed nerves after the depressing conversation he'd had with his father.

He reluctantly turned from the peaceful scenes as he caught sight of a familiar head of curly, golden hair.

"Samuel," Tehl shouted. "Are the Elite ready for our stroll through the Sanee?"

Sam glanced over his shoulder with an innocent smile that made Tehl pause. There was nothing innocent about Sam. That look boded mischief. He eyed his brother, wondering what he was up to.

His brother turned with militant perfection and executed a courtly bow. "Why yes, my lord. Everything is almost in place, my worshipfulness."

A deep sigh slipped out of him. "Dear God, Sam, cut it out. I can't take any of your teasing this early in the morning." He needed a drink of something strong to cope with Sam at the moment.

His brother's face morphed into a blinding smile of white teeth, which only irritated him further. It was too early to have that much energy.

"Well, I knew you were off tracking down Father Dearest earlier, so I figured you would need something to brighten your day. It seems I was not far off. I'm sure I saw a dark cloud hovering over you as you approached. Quit being so serious and angry. We have to be on our best behavior enough as it is. Smile, live a little."

Tehl frowned. "I smile," he argued. Perhaps not as often as Sam, but he wasn't droll all the time. It wasn't in his nature to be as carefree as Sam.

Or rather, he mused, *as carefree as Sam pretends to be.*

"You do enough of that for the both of us," Tehl retorted. "Do you ever take *anything* seriously?"

"Not if I don't have to. That's something *you* do for the both of us, brother," Sam joked, slapping him on the back.

In spite of himself, one side of Tehl's mouth tipped up. As the second son, his brother had always been granted so much more freedom. While Sam ran through the palace, wailing like a banshee, playing pirates or dragons, Tehl had to sit quietly, listening to his father and his advisers. After a time, though, Sam ended up sneaking in, choosing to sit with him through all the long boring talks. It bonded them. Samuel didn't need to sit there, and yet he did, so Tehl wouldn't be miserable. Tehl couldn't even imagine not having his brother around.

Besides their behavioral differences, they were also like the sun and the moon in appearance. Their only shared feature was their eyes. They had the same deep sapphire eyes, so dark they made the midnight sky green with envy. The striking eyes were framed with such thick dark lashes that his mum had always been envious.

But that was where their similarities ended, for Sam was light to his dark. Sam's curly blond hair, sunny disposition, and boyish smile had an endless stream of women falling at his feet throughout the years, while he'd had a much harder time of it, even with his exotic looks. Despite what some people said, it seemed personality made quite the difference.

Tehl flicked his eyes upward to his own unruly black waves. He had his mum's hair, so dark it almost seemed highlighted with blue. His strong jawline, high cheekbones, and dimples all came from his father, though. Tehl smiled as he remembered his mother telling him they were his father's secret weapon. Dimples—who would have thought women loved them so much? A secret weapon, yes, but one would have to smile for you to see them. His smile dimmed. After conversing with him, women would run for the hills. So he chose not to say anything. You can't embarrass yourself if you don't speak. He didn't feel comfortable talking to strangers anyway. Tehl was the 'serious' one to Sam's 'fun-loving' personality. He didn't have time to chase women; his duty demanded too much attention.

Tehl eyed his brother, contemplating the difference between the man he knew Sam to be and the persona he encouraged. While Sam held the title of Elite Commander, it was Gavriel, their cousin, who fulfilled the duties, although this was not due to any negligence on Sam's part. Rather, it served a purpose for his brother's true talents: information acquisition and manipulation. A more befitting title might have been spymaster, he was possibly the most qualified man to have ever played that role. He had a million different faces for the myriads of circumstances in which he found himself. He was a master of disguise.

However, Tehl thought, *Sam doesn't have the weight of starving, angry people on his shoulders, nor the threat of revolt, war, and invasion looming over him.*

Just contemplating it was enough to give him a throbbing headache and send his heart pounding. Because his people were unaware of the true extent of his father's deterioration, it was impossible for them to understand how Tehl was floundering in a vain attempt to remedy everything unaided.

The sound of Sam's voice penetrated his reverie. "Sorry?" he said, blinking to clear his thoughts.

"You still in there?" Sam teased, knocking the side of Tehl's head. "You didn't hear a word I said, did you? Perhaps you were dreaming of that sweet little thing vying for your attention last night? She was gorgeous and curvy in all the right places!" Sam waved his hands in the shape of an hourglass and waggled his eyebrows.

Tehl cringed at the memory. The harpy had thrown herself at him, despite his obvious lack of interest, finding a miraculous number of opportunities to do so again and again throughout the evening. Vain was an understatement.

"For hell's sake Sam, get your mind out of the gutter. She was pretty until she opened her mouth." Tehl shuddered. "When she smiled at me, it was like looking at a leviathan. She seems needy and manipulative, and I have no desire for her to sink her claws into me. Also," he continued, wrinkling his nose, "she had so much rose oil on her I could barely breathe. I haven't survived elite training, battles, and assassination attempts only to die by stupid rose perfume. I don't care if she is Jaren's daughter, I won't spend another evening with her."

Sam tilted his head, thinking. "It would be rather poetic, wouldn't it? To die by a rose? Just imagine the tragic retelling: oh, poor Crown Prince Tehl Ramses perished, not by the sword, but because he suffocated by a set of rose-oil-saturated breasts!" Unable to keep a straight face, Sam let out a snigger.

"Not on your life," he muttered darkly. "I'm grabbing my cloak and then I will meet you on the city streets."

Sam's face sobered for a moment. "Be careful. I still don't know what it is we're dealing with. I know it is to be an exchange, but I'm unsure how many parties will be involved. Keep your eyes and ears open—though I will stay near you most of the time." His brother paused, his eyes glittering in challenge. "Let's see if you can locate me among the crowd this time." Sam then swaggered off toward the armory.

Tehl once again continued down the corridors of the castle, noting again how much things had changed since his mother died. It seemed all the vibrancy and warmth left with her and now, despite the impressive architecture, the place felt empty and hollow. The flowers had all but disappeared and the cheerful tapestries replaced with dull, muted ones.

He planned to change that, though. And it wasn't the castle alone which required restoration. The kingdom did as well. It had been three years since the last festival. This year would be different. Aermia needed something to look forward to, and he would give it to them.

As he pondered these hopeful changes, he couldn't help the frustration which also came. Whenever he thought of the changes his mum's death had wrought, anger seemed to bubble up at the injustice of what he had been dealt. Not only had he lost his mother, but in the aftermath, he'd lost his father and his youth. And if that wasn't enough, now he had a rebellion on his hands.

He ground his teeth, exasperated with the shortsightedness of those responsible for its incitement. They were ignorant of the havoc and grief their rebellion brought on Aermia and her inhabitants. Shaking his head, he attempted to clear his thoughts. Maybe today would be the day he received answers. Tehl clasped his woolen cloak, slipped on his hood, and departed the palace, completely unnoticed.

THREE

SAGE

SETTING ASIDE HER TOOLS, SAGE stretched her cramped fingers. She loved creating new pieces, but setting a couple hundred black seed pearls was not her idea of fun. She stood as she placed her hands on her hips and arched her back, sighing with satisfaction. Being hunched over for so long had made her feel like she'd never be able to stand straight again. She limped over to the window and attempted to rub the feeling back into her stiff legs. Sage poked her head out to gauge the time and noted that the sun was high in the sky. She needed to hurry up.

Sage set about gathering up her tools from where she'd left them. The sweltering heat from the forge made her hair stick to her damp neck as she meticulously placed her tools in their proper place. She valued the heavy fall of coffee-colored hair plaited down her back, but days like today made her want to hack it all off. She swiped at the sweat on her brow with the back of her hand and appraised the broad sword she'd painstakingly created.

The sword was beautiful; too extravagant for her own taste, but a creation to be proud of.

Sage lifted the sword and placed two fingers under the hilt, testing the balance. She knew the balance was perfect, but she still checked it every time out of habit. It sat still and straight atop her fingers, neither end outweighing the other. The light caught its finely sharpened double edge, gleaming wickedly. She drew her thumb gently across the blade's length and watched with satisfaction as the line of blood appeared there.

Perfect, utterly perfect, she thought, *and made by a woman to boot.*

Sage sighed, content, knowing if she and her family were frugal, the coin this brought would keep them fed for a good, long while. They'd need it, too. Fine swords were not in high demand anymore. Ever since the Sickness had swept through the land, many swordsmiths moved on, seeking greener pastures in which to ply their trade. She was thankful Colm Blackwell, her papa, had made a name for himself prior to the devastation. They still received commissions from all regions of Aermia due to his renown, albeit less frequently. Their faithful customers and their referrals had kept them afloat. Without them, she'd no clue what they'd have done, and although Sage wished she could forge fine art more often, few requests such as this came.

Holding it before her, she again examined the blade, and a triumphant grin spread across her face, as she let herself admire this deadly weapon she herself had forged. It was truly a work of art. A black dragon adorned the pommel, its sapphire eyes glittering up at her. The dragon's tail circled up the hilt, and the dragon appeared to be perched there observing the world. The black seed pearls used for scales added luster to the fearsome beast's hide. She'd outdone herself, and it would fetch a hefty price from whatever nobleman commissioned it.

As a young girl, Sage had always been fascinated with swords and the forge. It was incredible to her that her papa started with a boring lump of metal and could create something useful, beautiful, or deadly. While her brothers, Seb and Zeke, chased each other with sticks, she grew up always by her papa's side. Her mum always tried to get her interested in things more appropriate for a girl of her age, yet Sage always conveniently lost her dolls and sewing needles, instead ending up back in the forge. Her papa took to calling her 'his little shadow.' This began her long journey in learning how to forge weapons.

As she grew, he was always willing to pause and teach her things here and there. One day, he handed her a wooden sword, and she remembered looking at it unimpressed. Chuckling at the look she gave him, he patted her head and told her a secret that day. One couldn't know how to craft a fine sword if they didn't know how to use one, and use it well. He'd then tapped the wooden sword and said this was where she had to start.

At the tender age of five, he'd trained her in sword wielding, and Sage loved every moment. Even when her arms quivered and her body screamed, she was powerful. As she grew, so did the swords her papa made for her. When she came of age, he'd allowed her to fulfill the duties of an apprentice, despite her mum's chagrin. Her mum was disappointed she didn't have lady-like aspirations, yet her mum accepted it and loved her no less.

Over the next five years, she'd worked hard in her father's forge, perfecting her skills. No one ever suspected it was Sage who made their swords and not the famed Colm. Men were fickle that way. They ate up her work, but if word ever spread that a woman had made them, her swords would be considered unsuitable for a warrior. It was rubbish. She loved designing new pieces. Being the secret designer didn't bother her if it meant she could keep doing what she loved.

Their business had continued to flourish until the queen died. While their king mourned the loss of his beloved, the kingdom slowly deteriorated in his absence. Bandits attacked the outskirts of Aermia, burning crops, and pillaging villages. Business slowed for their finer work, so they adapted and changed the focus of their wares to tools and farming equipment. Though it lacked the complexity and challenge she craved, Sage knew it put food in their bellies, something few people had.

When her papa became ill, it was by far the worst thing they'd faced. The Sickness started slowly, but eventually he began to waste away. It attacked his lungs, weakening him and stealing away his energy. Her heart broke to see him so ravaged. Their roles reversed after that. Sage ran the smith while he, instead, sat watching her. He and her mum took care of the customers, while she continued to work in the back. She was exhausted at the end of the day, but still thankful that her labor prevented them from sleeping with hollow stomachs and kept a roof above their heads.

It was these circumstances that culminated in a decision which altered her life over the past year. With just one meeting, her entire life changed.

The day was like any other. She'd hiked to her favorite spot, a hidden meadow, and there she practiced her swordplay, as like every other morning. In the middle of an intricate set of steps, the forest stilled. Halting, she listened. Not one sound could be heard. Even the trees were silent, unnaturally so. Sage scanned the forest while spinning in a circle. She kept her sword angled in front of her, ready to defend herself. The hair on the back of her neck prickled; she was being watched.

Just come and get me.

"I know you're there. Show yourself," she commanded.

A figure emerged from the forest, approaching at an almost leisurely pace, gliding silently in her direction. He was tall, with a warrior's build, his dark cloak flowing behind him. His arms were loose at his sides, completely at ease, yet she didn't doubt for a second he was dangerous. She'd bet her family's smithy on it. No one glided without extensive combat training.

She peered at his cloak again, noting the green color. Camouflage, that was brilliant. Sage lifted her sword, warning him to stop. Despite the ten feet between them, a trickle of unease slithered down her spine. He wasn't a typical thief, but something else entirely. The deep cowl of his hood prevented her seeing his eyes, but she still sensed him measuring her as she took his measure. Unease crept over her as she waited for his next move.

"Little one, I am not here to harm you," he rumbled softly. His voice was deep and smooth like whiskey, with a hint of a growl.

"Says the wolf to the lamb," she retorted, her gaze never wavering.

One side of his lips pulled up. "You are right to be cautious of men in the woods. It's not safe for you to be here alone. You should be in your home where you belong," he admonished.

Sage bristled and squared her shoulders. What right did he have to tell her what to do? "You are neither my father, nor brother, nor husband. You've no right telling me where I should be. It's you who is not safe. Leave my meadow."

"You and your family have suffered much," he stated. "We have been studying you for some time, Sage. Your skills would prove useful for Aermia, to heal her and protect her."

Her guard went up. *What was he about? Was this a trap?*

Sage glanced around the meadow searching for others, chills skating down her arms, her unease tripling. "You have been watching my family and me?"

she probed, licking her dry lips. Time to go. But first, she needed to shift his focus off her. "Who is this 'we'?" she questioned, stepping toward the forest.

He dismissed her question and answered with one of his. "What do you see as you walk through the city?"

What an odd question. "I don't understand what you are looking for," Sage replied steadily. Another step closer to her escape.

"Our people go hungry while our land's dying. Meanwhile, trouble stirs along our Scythian border. No doubt you've heard whispers of those disappearing along it, though none know for sure why or where they've vanished." He paused, considering for a moment. "Are you aware that this most likely means they've been taken? Why would someone steal another person?"

"No," she breathed, not hiding her shock or disgust. Stars above, he was talking of slaves. Being torn from your home and forced to God-knows-where sent a chill up her spine. Scythians were the stuff of nightmares, barbaric and ruthless, with no shred of conscience. History books from every nation corroborated the fact that they hated outsiders, as well as anyone who didn't fit the model of 'perfection' to which they aspired. A 'perfect' Scythian had yet to cross the Mort Wall in the last five hundred years, not since the Nagalian Purge. Why would they steal people?

"And how long do you say this has been going on?" Sage inquired, her suspicion clear, all the while edging toward the forest border.

"The reports of missing Aermians go back the last four years, as far as we understand. The commander has sent a few soldiers, but the pathetic attempts always come to nothing." Controlled anger laced his words.

It seemed he wasn't so calm and collected. That told her he most likely believed what he was telling her. Sage pursed her lips, trying to discern if he was being truthful. He didn't come by her on accident; he sought her out for a reason. Sage's instincts told her he was dangerous, but she didn't think he was interested in harming her. He also had shown no signs he was touched in the head. So what did he want?

Sage gave him a hard stare and spoke her mind. "What do you want from me?"

"Change. You'd be a great asset to the restoration of Aermia and its people."

"An asset?" she scoffed, how impersonal. Whoever he was working with viewed people as tools and not individuals. "An asset to whom?" she drew out the question, staring unflinchingly at him, awaiting his answer. There were only five more feet until the forest edge, and she fought to keep from sprinting into the woods. Something told her he would be onto her before she could scream, even if she made a run for it.

"The rebellion." Noting her position, he angled his body toward her. "I will not hurt you, but if you run I will catch you."

Sage froze, not so much from his threat as the phrase he'd just thrown out there. The word echoed in her mind, yet he had said it like it was of no consequence, as if it didn't have the potential to change everything in her life.

Rebellion.

She had heard whispers over the years, but had never given it another thought. It had always been young hotheads spouting off treasonous nonsense, acting like that made them heroes of some sort. But never had she seen actual proof of an organized rebellion. That would be a HUGE secret. The rebellion would have to be well trained or very new. Sage scrutinized the mystery man and highly doubted he was wet behind the ears.

This is what their king had driven his people to: treasonous meetings in the woods. The king's grief superseded the needs of his people. Aermia was rotting from the inside out. Why had no one stepped up? It wasn't as if he didn't have two sons that could at least have tried to fill his place, his sons' inaction made them as guilty. The time for mourning had passed.

Now was the time to fight.

If she joined the rebellion, she could make a difference, but she also wasn't naïve. Sage wasn't about to commit to something until she had all the facts. That meant knowing those she was dealing with.

She tilted her head, considering. She could lose everything by agreeing. If caught by the Crown, she'd be tried as a traitor and hung. That would leave her family helpless and destitute. She couldn't be the only one with something to lose—he needed to have a stake in this too. Her heart raced as she decided. "I don't make deals with strangers. Show me your face and actual evidence that what you say is true. Then we'll talk."

From beneath his hood sounded a rumbling chuckle. Goosebumps ran down her arms. If his looks matched his laugh, she was in real trouble. Sage held her breath as he reached up and pulled his hood off, revealing a mane of black hair.

No. Not quite black, she thought, *rather a deep red.*

It reminded her of a dark wine. Not once in her lifetime had she ever seen hair that color before. He also had a strong chin, and thick eyebrows accentuated unique eyes the color of citrine, so bright they looked like liquid gold. A thin scar ran from the end of his right brow, passing dangerously close to his eye, and ending at his chin. She realized he was quite an attractive man, despite the scar. In fact, the scar added to his dangerous air.

"What do you expect from me and when do I get to meet your 'we'?" she asked, eyebrows lifted.

"Soon," he said, and a dazzling smile transformed his rugged face. He was beautiful in a wild sort of way. "I will be in touch, little one, then all your questions will be answered." He bowed, then turned to walk away.

Swamp apples. That wasn't an answer, and he never gave her his name. "That's not good enough! I'm not going into this blind. I need a name!" Sage shouted at his back.

He looked over his shoulder and locked onto her with his odd, mesmerizing eyes. For a moment, they stared at each other, until he winked and broke the spell. "Rafe. I'll be seeing you soon."

She let the memory fade away as she stared down at the broadsword still carefully clutched in her hands. Lifting a hand, Sage rubbed at her temple, glancing out the window. Realizing just how much time had passed while she was daydreaming, she let a curse slip out. She should have left a quarter of an hour ago. Sage placed the sword in its bed of velvet and rushed to grab her black cloak from the wall.

Opening the door which connected their home and the forge, she called out, "Mum, I'm slipping out. I will bring back meat if I can find anything edible at the market. If not, it will be fish."

"Be safe, my love. We will hold down the fort," her mother trilled back and then decided she needed admonishment. "Try not to get your clothes so filthy this time. It took hours to get the stench out of them last time."

Sage looked at her collection of blades, snatching her favorite and attaching its sheath to her waist. With sarcasm evident in every word, she retorted, "Yes mum, you know how I strive to get pushed into puddles if only just to spite you."

"Don't get sassy with me, Little Miss, and try to be home before dark please."

Sage smiled at her mum's words and tone. "I will. If not, don't worry. I can always spend the night with Elle and be home early in the morning." Sage poked her head out the door, scanning left and right. People milled along the lane, but it seemed no one paid her any attention, so she casually meandered into the flow of people. If she didn't hurry, Rafe was sure to wring her neck.

F·OUR

TEHL

SANEE WAS ONCE A THRIVING, beautiful city. Now it was rotting. In every direction, buildings were adorned with decaying wood and chipped paint. Porches sagged and troughs had green algae growing in them. Rotting fish permeated the air. His city desperately needed care. It was disintegrating before his eyes, but he didn't know how he could stop its decline.

Oddly enough, in spite of the smell, a sense of peace enveloped him as he walked down the open lane. The familiar sound of pots clanking, donkeys braying, and the crashing of the waves on the shore surrounded him. Tehl preferred this to the whispers and delicate giggles of court. The symphony of sounds reminded him of trips to the market with his mum as a boy, and he still found that comforting.

Once he looked closely, though, noting the state of his people, his small moment of peace left him. He had always known the merchants to be jovial, and perhaps plump, yet now they were thin and haggard, ghosts of their former prosperities.

The further he trudged into the city, the more depressed he became. The people in the fishing district were the worst. Their hollow eyes tracked his movements, and the looks they were giving him made his skin crawl. Tehl clenched his hand around the sword hilt each time he met any pair of eyes that seemed hostile. Perhaps the warning in his gaze would discourage them from trying anything.

Beggars littered the streets. There hadn't been half this many a couple months ago. It was the children who caught his attention. Most of them sat on crates and bins, staring listlessly at the filth-strewn streets. Where were their parents? Their thin little bodies made him ashamed of what he had left at the table this morning. As soon as he returned to the palace, he would put something in motion to care for the children. It was appalling how long it took to build up a successful kingdom—yet how quickly it seemed to fall around your ears.

He spotted Garreth casually leaning against a post, supposedly dozing, so Tehl moved on, noting familiar faces as he went. Tehl looked to the left and glimpsed a familiar set of eyes beneath a straw hat. Gavriel. He looked so different that if it wasn't for his cousin being a mere eight feet away, he might not have spotted him. It was incredible how the Elite blended in. Samuel and Gavriel's training had paid off.

Scanning the vicinity, Tehl paused when a small, faint carving caught his eye. A wooden door showed a rough version of his family crest: a black dragon spewing flames. Rather than clutching the sword in its claws, however, they had depicted the dragon with the sword piercing its heart. His brows lifted, surprised at the boldness displayed by whoever had the audacity to openly mock the Crown. He committed the symbol to memory and noted the sign hanging above the door which read *Cobbler*.

How original of them.

So, the shoemaker was a resistance sympathizer. Though he doubted the man knew anything useful, he made a mental note to have Sam investigate.

Tehl glanced at the sky and blew out a frustrated breath when he realized he'd already wasted a considerable amount of time wandering the streets. He'd be cutting it close. As he navigated the streets and alleyways, darting around horse droppings and the occasional puddle, he kept his eyes and ears open, picking up on snatches of conversation. It both irked and baffled him how little the people understood current events. His brother had hoped to nip this kind of talk in the bud but gossip remained unconquerable. Hearing their hushed conversations of so-called heroic deeds, he scoffed. Heroic, his ass. Try self-serving.

People were so careless. If he were so inclined, they would be tried for treason and their whole family would lose everything, all because of a casual conversation. He smiled to himself as he noted with interest that at least one Elite had slipped into each group.

He put the thoughts aside; gossip was the least of today's worries. The current priority was catching any of the rebel leaders. The capture of even one of their high-ranking officers could be the break he needed, and it would be an enormous step in the right direction. He rather hoped they'd put up a good fight, though. He'd been itching to brawl for some time.

Tehl arrived at their exchange location, Lavender Alley, and examined his surroundings with distaste. You'd think a street named Lavender would at least have the decency to smell as delightfully as it was named, but no. Death and decay filled the air, and he didn't want to know where it was coming from.

As he moved farther into the dank alley, the stone cobbles beneath his boots were black and slippery, and he spotted red beady eyes peering at him from the shadows. Long little pink tails and whiskered noses stuck out of every nook and cranny.

Rats.

God, he hated rats. They were so vile. It was all he could do not to stumble when one darted past his foot.

Do not slip and fall, because: One, the rats will eat you, and Two, you will catch a disease, and die a horrible death before you even make it back to the palace.

With these gems rattling around in his head, he pressed forward.

To his left, there was a perfect hiding place. He cautiously made his way to it and faded into the small dark space between the stone walls. Somehow, the smell became stronger here. What was that anyway? Tehl tried not to breathe through his nose, but it seemed to slither into his mouth and squat on his tongue. While trying to keep from gagging, he jerked a cloth up over his mouth and nose. He may have experienced nasty things in his life, but this was one of the worst.

It seemed fitting that the rebellion would pick this place. Rats enjoying the company of other rats.

A moment later, movement left of his shoulder alerted him to another. Surveying the shadows, he noticed little whiskers twitching at him from a hole in the wall a mere six inches away.

Damn! Nothing went his way today.

Tehl tried not to move, calming his rapid breathing. Tehl never panicked in dangerous situations. Yet throw in one stupid little rodent, and it was all he could do not to flail his arms and take off running.

He steeled himself. Mind over matter. Logically, he knew that he was way bigger than a rat and he needed to calm the hell down. Just when he gained control, it began creeping toward him.

Gritting his teeth, he hissed at the rat. "Psst...get out of here!"

The furry menace would not be deterred. It scampered right onto his cloak, pausing briefly to sniff it. He hoped he smelled so offensive the whiskers would be singed right off its dingy face. But he had never had good luck. The rat continued crawling across his shoulder, sniffing here or there.

Don't get comfy, he thought to it. His cloak would *not* become its next home.

A flutter of activity distracted him from the creature invading his space. Two cloaked figures approached from the dead end of the alley.

Where did they come from?

It was a dead end. Something exchanged hands, and words were spoken in hushed tones, much too soft to pick up. He strained his ears, trying to catch their conversation, but his mind went blank when a tiny nose nuzzled his neck. He shuddered.

Disgusting.

Needle-like claws scratched along his neck as whiskers tickled his ear. It was imperative that he remained stock-still. *Stay calm, stay calm, stay calm,* he chanted in his mind.

If any of the Elite—or my brother—hear of this, I'll never hear the end of it.

He realized he'd been so preoccupied by the nasty vermin making its new home at his neck, he'd missed the meeting. One figure disappeared into the dark while the other cloaked figure paused for a moment, and then started toward him, taking soundless steps on the diseased cobblestones.

The little bastard then sniffed his ear again. Goosebumps broke out on his neck, and he shivered. Abruptly, sharp pain exploded from his ear. The little bugger bit him! Pain and heat radiated around his ear, down his neck, and across his cheek. Tehl shook his head once, dislodging the fiend from his ear and hissed out a breath. *Stars above, that hurt.*

At the sound, the rebel making his way toward him paused. The figure cocked his head as if listening.

Tehl forced himself to hold his breath, praying that his position hadn't been compromised. He focused on blending in.

Be one with the stone, be one with the blasted stone.

The rebel wasn't very tall or broad shouldered, petite even, childlike. His thoughts screeched to a halt. The rebellion wouldn't use children…would they? The idea made him sick. The figure before him could easily be a boy of thirteen or fourteen, and the more he turned it over in his mind, the more it made sense. What a perfect way to pass messages. No one ever paid much attention to where children ran off to, and no one would suspect a child as a rebel informant. It'd be brilliant if it wasn't so disgusting. If that *was* the case, which he suspected it was, he'd have to be very careful. He could never hurt a child.

He inched his hand into his cloak, clutching his dagger. Maybe he could instead scare the youth into doing what he wanted. All he needed to do was convince the child that he himself was not the enemy.

The cloaked rebel scanned the alley. After a moment, the young rebel began moving toward him again, ignorant of the danger lurking in the shadows. His whole body tensed. He didn't want to threaten the boy but he wasn't sure he had any other choice. If he fought, he risked injuring the child.

As the rebel passed, he stepped behind him, wrapping his right arm around the rebel's neck and pulling upward in warning. His other wrapped around the boy's ribs and pressed the tip of his dagger against the rebel as he whispered, "You will come calm and quietly or things will not be looking good for you."

"My coins are hanging from my belt on the right side," the rebel replied in a higher register. "Take them and leave."

The boy's reply surprised him, for the child's voice never trembled or wavered. He must be brave or stupid to not have any fear with a blade involved.

"I do not want your coins, son. What I need is information. You can help me with that. After what I observed, I think you may be the one to get me what I need. What do you know of the rebellion?"

The rebel stiffened, shaking his head in an emphatic *no.* "Don't involve me in your treasonous affairs with talks of rebellion. People are hung for less, and

I'd rather not be found guilty by association. I want no trouble." Conviction rang in his voice.

Had Tehl not seen the exchange himself moments before, he was sure he would've been inclined to believe the boy. His lips thinned. "Lying to a new friend makes a horrible first impression." Tehl pushed aside the boy's cloak with his own dagger, revealing a shiny blade. "I doubt you'll be needing this. I would hate for you to hurt yourself…or me," he said, relieving the boy of the dagger.

"I'm *not* your friend," the rebel hissed.

The boy was angry. No one enjoyed being powerless.

"Release me," growled the rebel.

At that inopportune moment, little whiskers poked the back of his neck. With all the excitement, Tehl had forgotten about that fuzzy tyrant taking up residence in the hood of his cloak. Momentarily surprised, he loosened his grip around the rebel's ribs, and that was all the opening the boy needed. He thrust his hips backward, knocking Tehl off balance, and ducked his chin, escaping Tehl's hold.

For a second, Tehl only gaped at his empty arms. How had that happened? The boy attempted to flee, slipping and sliding along the cobbles. Tehl scrambled after the boy. "Oh no you don't!"

The rebel was quick, but Tehl had longer legs. He reached out, grabbing a handful of his cloak and yanked the boy back. All the frantic movements were enough to dislodge the rat from his cloak and send it sailing through the air, after which it landed in a dank puddle of sludge with a splat.

Serves the menace right, he thought.

The boy twisted and tugged on his own cloak as he tried to dislodge it from Tehl's fingers. A chuckle slipped out. Like he'd make it that easy for him. The boy growled and stopped tugging.

The blow came before he could block it. A foot clipped him hard enough on the chin that his teeth clacked together. Copper flooded his mouth. Damn it, he had bitten his cheek. Tehl spat blood on to the ground and wiped the back of his arm across his mouth, appraising the boy. He grudgingly admitted that it was a perfect round-house kick and said so.

"Are you hungry for more?" was the arrogant reply.

Tehl managed to stop himself from rolling his eyes. With a mouth like that, he wondered how many fights the boy got himself into. He watched as the rebel shifted sideways to defend himself. Tehl eyed the boy's form and adjusted his stance even while he sighed. He didn't want to play this game with a child. He tried to stamp down his frustration with the boy and imagined what Sam would say in his position. "Cease and there will be no repercussions. I will not harm you."

A disbelieving laugh burst out of the lad. "You held me at knife point, so excuse me if I don't believe the words spewing from your lying trap."

"If you don't come willingly, things will get rough. I promise you, I won't be the only one bleeding." He bared his bloody teeth. The hood of the young rebel's cloak slipped, revealing part of a smirk. Tehl narrowed his eyes at the cocky boy in front of him. He was much too confident for his own good and someone needed to knock him down a peg or two…though for a lad he sure had odd-shaped lips.

The boy's smirk grew into a full-blown smile, showing all his straight white teeth. "I would love to see you try," he taunted, launching into a sweeping kick.

Tehl stepped to the side, avoiding the kick and onto the lad's cloak as it brushed past him. The boy turned around trapping himself in his own cloak. Tehl seized him by the shirt and pulled him up onto his toes. "Listen here you little cur! Stop this before you get hurt. What would your father say if he saw you?"

The child's smile turned into a sneer, "I wouldn't know. He left my mum before I was born."

Pity pricked Tehl—until a fist drove into his ribs. He tightened his grip on the boy as his breath whooshed out of him. Fine. If the lad was hankering for a fight, then he'd get one. Tehl jammed a knee into the boy's lower stomach. The young rebel bent toward him, letting out a groan of pain, and a sliver of guilt bubbled up at the sound. It faded though, as the boy jerked his head up and knocked him in the face. Pain exploded from his nose, his eyes watering. He glimpsed thinned lips before small forearms wedged in between his and smashed outwards breaking his grip.

The young rebel ducked out of his range to assess him, and Tehl knew the exact moment the boy decided to go on the offensive, starting with a swift jab. Instinctively, Tehl lifted his forearm to block the blow though he noted for someone so small, the lad had a lot of power. He could give it no more thought, though, as the rebel continued his assault by twisting his hips and throwing a cross punch followed by an uppercut. He blocked each blow with ease, his training paying off. The rebel then hesitated a second, and it was all the opening he needed.

Tehl threw two hooks, putting his body weight into them, yet the lad deftly blocked both blows. And when he jerked his knee upward, the boy curled forward, avoiding his knee, dancing out of his reach. He was impressed; few men his own weight could hold their own against him. He was quicker than Tehl, and he knew how to use that to his advantage. The rebel lashed out with a couple kicks that he swatted away. It took a moment, but Tehl detected a pattern in the boy's movements. He'd first dance in to trade a few blows, before slipping out of his reach and attacking with a few kicks, and it was a good strategy. The fluid way the boy moved suggested that he had training. He needed a good grip on him. But for some odd reason, he was enjoying himself.

He followed the boy's movements, expecting his next kick. Sure enough, the rebel attempted to sidekick him. Tehl caught the lad's leg, grabbed the front of his shirt, and pushed him backward into the stone wall, pinning him there.

"You had enough yet, son?"

The answer he received was a snarl and a head to the face, followed by a sickening crack, and pain blasted through his face. Warm liquid gushed down his lips and chin, dripping onto his chest. His nose was broken!

Through his blurry eyes, he could see the boy's mouth grinning at him, smug.

"You sure you had enough?" the young rebel mocked. He didn't know when to stop. The boy tried to head-butt him again, but his elbow blocked the boy's head. The young rebel's head snapped back into the stone wall behind him with a sharp cry.

Damn, he was a little too rough with the child. He spun the dazed boy around to face the wall, so he could inspect the wound and bind the boy's hands. He couldn't analyze it because of the hood, but although blood seeped through it, it was not at an alarming rate. Messy but not too bad. The lad would live.

Blinking his eyes to rid himself of the tears his injury brought, he searched for a length of rope to bind the boy.

When that was done, Tehl then cautiously ran his hands inside the boy's cloak, looking for weapons; he didn't feel like getting stabbed. One dagger at the waist.

The boy slumped against the wall. He didn't want the boy concussed. Tehl jostled the boy. "Stay awake. You will need to be examined by a healer. You hit your head pretty hard." He turned the boy back around and used the wall to help hold the youth up.

"I didn't hit my head. You pushed my head into a stone wall," the boy slurred, but somehow still managed a dry tone.

Tehl still hadn't seen the lad's face. It was disrespectful to wear your hood up when someone was talking to you. He reached over and grasped the boy's hood. The boy struggled weakly against him.

"Hold still," he admonished, "I only want to see your face."

At first nothing made sense. What was going on? He expected the round face of a young boy, but an angel stood before him instead. Big emerald eyes glared up at him, framed by long black lashes.

A woman.

FİVE

TEHL

HE STARED AND GAPED LIKE an idiot.

The boy was a woman.

Tehl leaned closer.

Yep, still a woman.

Wait. The rebellion was using women?

"Get off me!" she yelled, startling him.

He was so close to her, he felt the woman vibrate with anger, yet despite all the blood and yowling, he was entranced. He stared, mapping out high cheekbones, a heart-shaped face, and creamy skin. Somehow one of his hands reached out to touch her smooth skin only to have her teeth snap at him, trying to remove one of his fingers. Tehl looked aghast at the offending appendage. When had it moved?

"Don't touch me!" she screeched.

He focused back on the wriggling woman he was pressed against; his brain finally caught up with his eyes. "You're a woman?" Tehl asked, stupidly.

"Last time I checked," she retorted, hotly. A mocking smile spread across her face. "Not so quick, are you? Let me repeat it for you. I am a woman," she drew out, lengthening the word, so it sounded like *woooomaaan*. "How is that broken nose treating you?" she taunted.

"About as well as yours," he baited, tweaking her button nose.

Her big green eyes immediately welled up. Crystal tears glistened on her black lashes. Tehl frowned, feeling like a beast. Why did he do that? An apology was on the tip of his tongue, until saliva exploded across his face. There was nothing more disrespectful than being spat upon. It was not only disgusting but degrading. As Tehl had already been bitten by a rat and his nose broken. Why not add being spit on to the list?

Meticulously, he wiped the blood and spit from his chin, all the while keeping her pinned, and by the time he finished, he had calmed down.

"I have never met anyone stupid enough to spit on me," he said, appraising her. "You don't realize the danger you put yourself in. Lawfully, I have every right to kill you."

Tehl met her green eyes and lifted his hand, wrapping it firmly around her delicate neck. He squeezed once for emphasis. Her face never wavered from the bland, bored expression she was wearing, but the swift staccato of her pulse under his thumb told another story. She pretended she wasn't afraid, but her pulse announced her a liar.

She took shallow breaths, her gaze never wavering from his. "You don't want to hurt me. You held yourself back. Several times you could have hurt me, but you blocked instead of striking. Also, you pulled your punches. That leads me to the conclusion you need me. I will bet my mum's ruby necklace you won't kill me." She looked up at him with a calculating glint in her eyes. "Your threats don't scare me."

What an interesting female—so unlike the women of his court. "Everyone fears something," he reasoned. "Are you sure death doesn't scare you? What if I squeezed my hand, cutting off your air?"

She didn't so much as twitch.

"Pain for long periods of time?"

Her impassive mask still didn't alter.

"The death or torture of a loved one?"

Still nothing.

Tehl was impressed; most men would have panicked by now. He moved his thumb across her pulse, causing her to jolt. He did it again, and she hissed at him. *Why did she react to that?* She didn't like him touching her at all, but it wasn't just because of the skin-on-skin contact. It was the *type* of contact.

A plan formed in his mind, but he wasn't sure he could pull it off as he had never been much of a womanizer.

"You sure are a pretty little thing. So much beauty hidden under that cloak." He locked eyes with her before raking his eyes down her generous curves. Her attire surprised him. She was wearing brown leather trousers, a linen shirt, and a leather vest. He lazily stared at her leather trousers. No wonder women weren't allowed to wear trousers. The way they hugged her hips and thighs was indecent. She was gorgeous. Too bad she was a traitor.

Tehl had to fight his scowl. He needed to maintain his persona, but it was unfair—she was so beautiful. It was just wrong. She should instead have had the common decency to have some gross imperfection. He swallowed the lump in his throat and made a show of ogling her body. Humiliation, anger, and a touch of fear bled through her impenetrable mask.

"*Tsk tsk*, a woman wearing trousers… So naughty," Tehl drawled. "It sends the wrong message to men around you, my dear. It gives them ideas."

In increments, he closed the remaining distance between the two of them, invading her space. He lifted one finger and skimmed it lightly around the shell of her ear and down her neck, touching the v of her cleavage—all the while looking into her eyes. Hers widened, and her heart picked up speed as she panicked.

"GET OFF ME, YOU PIG! DON'T TOUCH ME! HELP! HELP! HELP!" she yelled, her green eyes wild.

He craned his neck toward the entrance of the alley. People scurried by, but no one stopped. Cowards. Tehl looked back to the frantic woman struggling in his arms. He needed her information. She could lie all she wanted, but he had seen the exchange with his own eyes. She hadn't reacted to any of his other forms of intimidation. He would have to scare her into giving it up.

He'd never forced a woman and he never would. Just the idea made him sick to his stomach. But she didn't know him. Tehl's heart was heavy with the knowledge of what he had to do. He morphed his face into a leer and flashed her a lascivious grin. Tehl tightened his grip on her neck and pressed his large body harder into her, sandwiching her between the wall and himself.

He planted his lips softly along the column of her neck, allowing a low hum to escape. A small whimper escaped her lips. Tehl clenched his jaw, disgusted with himself, and forced out the words lodged in his throat. "I could have you here, and now, no one would look twice," he crooned into her ear.

Her breath quickened, and her heart raced against his chest. He felt like a total lecher and a creep. At that moment, he was. Tehl turned his head and skimmed her jaw with the tip of his nose. She smelled like cinnamon. Why did she smell like cinnamon?

He shook himself out of his stupor and focused on the task at hand. "This is what you will do." He nuzzled her once more, and then leaned back, placing a finger beneath her chin, forcing her eyes to meet his. Her glassy green eyes brimmed with tears almost crumbling his resolve. Tehl hardened his heart against her and gazed at her evenly. "You will come along like a good little girl, quiet and docile. No more kicking, screaming, or head-butting. If you do that, then I won't leave you damaged and broken in this hellhole."

She jerked her chin out of his grasp and looked away. Why did acting like a monster get things done? The world should not be like this. Sometimes, like now, he felt so dirty and low.

"Do you accept?" He purred in her ear, hoping she didn't call his bluff.

She trembled in his grasp and dipped her chin once. That was what he was looking for. Tehl released her face and moved his beaten body back a hair, just enough for her to take deep breaths without their chests touching.

She shivered, but fire still glinted in her eyes. She would cause him more trouble, despite what she'd told him. He grabbed her biceps and pulled her from the wall to the center of the alley.

"How can I trust you won't hurt me if I do as you ask?" she demanded, eyes filled with hate.

She deserved reassurance, and he could give her that much. Tehl looked down at her, "I give you my word you won't be hurt when I take you to the palace."

She barked out a laugh while a tear trekked a path down her dirty cheek. "You're a liar and a lecher." She looked at him, disgusted. "If you take me, you won't like the outcome. Someone will miss me; you can bet on that. I promise you will regret the day you were born because my brothers, crooked as they may be, will hunt you down."

He forced a chuckle since, even tied up and helpless, she was making threats. Raising his eyebrows, he smiled. "You're not in a position to be making threats. Threatening your future king is hazardous for your health."

Her reaction did not disappoint. She stilled, and what color she had, drained from her face. He slipped his hands up her arms and settled them on her shoulders. "I imagine you are quite attached to your neck, and so am I, if I am honest." She shuddered at his comment. "So pipe down," he added.

"You disgust me," she spat and wrinkled her nose at him, like he smelled offensive. Thinking about it, he probably did. This whole situation had him sweating like a pig.

"Your father has left us all to starve. I *had* hoped his son would make a better king, but here the crown prince stands, threatening to rape me if I don't give him information on something that I am not part of." She leaned toward him, anger sparkling in her eyes. "Your mother was an amazing woman. If she saw you today, she would be appalled!"

She flinched back, closing her eyes, when he lifted his hand toward her. He watched as she swallowed thickly. Did she think he would hit her? He frowned. He would never hit a woman. She was right, though. His mother would be ashamed if she could see him frightening the poor girl.

"You know nothing about my m-mother—" he stuttered as her lips parted on a breath, capturing his attention. He knew he shouldn't, but he couldn't help himself. He grabbed her face and gently brushed his thumb across her bottom lip. They were so smooth and soft.

What was wrong with him?

Tehl went to withdraw his thumb when she lunged at him, biting his finger. He cursed and ripped his thumb out of her mouth, shaking his hand. "Gods, woman, why would you do that?" Tehl inspected the small wound. There were actually teeth marks.

Her eyes popped open, and she grinned at him. She arched an eyebrow at him and howled with laughter. What was so funny? Was it the blow to the head affecting her? Was she touched in the head?

"What's wrong with you?" he asked, perplexed.

"Why *wouldn't* I bite you is the question."

He was not going there; he deserved it. Her information would be worth all the pain. Tehl eyed his feisty captive. They had wasted enough time and needed to leave. The mutinous look on her face promised a fight. He needed to take her by surprise. Tehl struck and slung her over his shoulder before she knew what happened. He grunted as a sharp pain shot through it and down his arm, making his hand tingle. When had he injured it?

From her new position, she let out an undignified little shriek that gave way to cursing. His lips curled at her creative verbiage.

She thrashed, making it difficult to keep a hold on her. Nothing about today would be easy. He lifted a hand and swatted her on the butt. "Knock it off, or I will end up dropping you on your head. If you hadn't tried to escape, I would've let you walk. You and I both know you won't be reasonable." More curses floated his way. Guess that was his answer.

He gingerly picked his way to the entrance of the alley, keeping his eyes on the treacherous cobbles beneath his feet. A burning pain in the middle of his back jerked him from his thoughts. He'd only experienced pain like that once before in his life, and it came from a very nasty horse.

"Did you just bite me?" he growled, incredulous.

"You took all my weapons and tied my hands. What was I supposed to do?" she mumbled into his back.

The bloody woman had bitten him.

"Lord, you're more harpy than woman!"

"If you let me go, you'd never have to deal with me again," she reasoned, her tone syrupy sweet though she was anything but.

"I thought women were sweet and gentle," he wondered out loud. "What kind of woman are you, anyway? Running around in trousers? What ever happened to being a lady?"

"Never said I was a lady."

He snickered. She was right there. "Well, with a vocabulary like yours, you could make sailors blush."

Having reached the end of the alley, he scanned the busy intersection, searching for his men. A familiar laugh drew his attention to a group sitting on barrels, playing dice. His brother's blue eyes met his. Tehl jerked his chin, signaling it was time to go.

Sam stood with a flourish, tipping his hat to his dice buddies, and meandered over to them.

"Did you get what we came for?" Sam assessed the bundle draped over Tehl's shoulder and glanced back at him with confusion. "It's smaller than I expected."

"I assure you we got *more* than we bargained for." He said wryly. "Look for yourself."

Sam walked around and lifted the woman's face and then bit out an oath.

"My God, Tehl, what are you doing with a woman?! Did you do that to her face?" Then in a soft tone he added, "Are you all right, sweetheart?"

Tehl felt her shake her head: no. *Ah, here comes the sob story.*

"That precious woman," Tehl interjected, "is the rebel you sent me after, and she gave as good as she got."

"No, I am not all right," she cried over him. "This man has threatened to hurt my family or torture me if I don't give him information. But I don't know what he is talking about," she sobbed into his back. "I want to go home! Please help me! Don't let him take me," she pleaded rather loudly.

What a world class performance.

Sam walked back around and eyed her hog-tied hands, then lifted his gaze to Tehl's. "What's your name sweetheart?" Sam asked.

"It's…it's Ruby," she stammered out.

He had broken her nose, threatened her, and had basically accosted her, yet she didn't shed a blooming tear until the end, and he suspected it was more from anger than pain. Now she was a completely different creature. Apparently, besides fighting like a she-demon and cursing like a sailor, she was also an actress.

He opened his mouth in defense, but closed it as he caught sight of Sam's face. His brother was not buying it. Sam quirked up one side of his mouth and raised an eyebrow. There was no fooling Sam. An amazing actor she may be, but he was sure his brother was an even better one. He was not the spymaster for nothing.

Sam made a show of studying her bound wrists. "What happened to your hands, darling? They have cuts all over them!" he probed as he ran a finger over her bloody knuckles.

"I was trying to protect myself from him." She sniffed.

Tehl distinctly remembered it was she who had first attacked. *He* had done everything in his power to keep them from fighting.

Sam lingered on her hands a moment longer and then continued to investigate. "Did you not have a weapon to protect yourself?"

"I did! But he disarmed me," she wailed, her whole body shuddering with her cries.

Unbelievable. "Her blade is in my belt."

Sam reached into his cloak and plucked her dagger from his waist, inspecting it. He ran his finger along the detail of the worn hilt and circled back to her, remarking on the blade. "What a unique dagger. It's well made. Why, the attention to detail is stunning! How did you come by it?"

She sucked in a breath, trying to control her crying. "I took it from someone."

"Now, I don't believe that." Tehl heard the triumph in Sam's voice. "Because I have also seen daggers like this on all the other rebels I've come across. You are not what you seem, darling. Only one thing's certain: you are a traitor to the Crown and dangerous."

The wailing and sobbing stopped. "You learn to be tough when you live on the streets. Why don't you come closer and I will show you how dangerous I can be?"

"No thank you. I like all my body parts just the way they are. Now that's all squared away, Ruby, we can get you settled in your new abode!"

"Hell no!" she screeched at Sam, struggling again.

"Would you please do something about that?" Tehl complained, trying to keep the bothersome wench in his arms. "My ears are about to bleed from all this shrieking."

The girl sneezed and then demanded, "What did you blow in my face?"

Sam ignored her question and sauntered back into view, brushing his hands off. His brother winked at him and patted one of the many pouches he always carried at his waist. Tehl would bet his next pair of boots it was Ashwanganda powder.

"How much longer does she have?" he asked in a low voice.

"What! What was that? Did you poison me? Put me down!" Even as her yelling continued, her body went limp. "Oh God, you drugged me. You are both going to regret..." She trailed off like she'd forgotten what she was talking about.

And she probably had, courtesy of the Ashwanganda.

She pressed her face into his back and rubbed her cheek against it. "You have hard muscles, like a rock," she said in a sing-song voice.

Sam smirked at him. "Not one word, Sam. Not one word."

"*Sam*. What a nice name," she chirped. "Is it short for Samuel? That is a strong, handsome name," she slurred while poking him in the back with her nose. "I want a nap; I am so tired."

She would give him whiplash with her quick subject changes. Her body finally succumbed to the sedative and went limp against him. For someone so tiny, she had weight to her. Tehl carefully pulled her off his shoulder and into his arms, tucking one arm beneath her knees and one around her shoulders.

Sam stepped closer, inspecting her face. "She is a beauty underneath all the blood, bruises, and grime."

Tehl's stomach soured. He was the cause of each cut and bruise marring her relaxed features. His brother cleared his throat and Tehl raised his eyes to Sam's face. He lifted an eyebrow in question and, after a beat, asked, "Well, what is it? Why are you staring?"

Sam flashed a blinding grin, "Seems you're studying her a little closely, brother," he drawled. "Me thinks you might like her."

Tehl scoffed at this ridiculous accusation. He'd only just met the woman. Pretty she may be, but she was also a criminal.

"You know me better than that, Sam. The fairer sex only cause trouble." His gaze bounced to her, then settled back on his brother. "I feel bad I hurt her. Look at her bloody face. No woman, no matter how trying they are, deserves the beating she received."

"Why is she so battered?"

He cleared his throat. "I thought she was a man."

Sam scoffed. "She doesn't look like a man. Your eyesight needs checking."

"She disguised herself," Tehl defended.

Sam studied her face first, then his. "She isn't the only one with a few marks. She put up a hell of a fight."

"That she did." His eyebrows furrowed. "The moves she executed weren't anything she'd have learned on the street. She had training. I've never come across her fighting style before. If she'd had her blade, I'm sure I'd have come out of this with a stab wound or two."

"I thought only men did the stabbing," his brother deadpanned.

Of course, Sam would make an inappropriate joke right now.

Tehl grunted and shot his brother a crooked grin. "There's something wrong with your mind.

Sam's serious face shifted to a mischievous grin. "What can I say? It's a gift."

"Not a gift I want." It still boggled his mind that they were from the same parents when they were so different. "I still say you were adopted."

"Oh! You always say the nicest things," Sam tittered, sending him a coy smile that disturbed him.

Gavriel approached them, tipping his straw hat back to reveal an amused grin. "You never cease to surprise me, Sam."

"Whatever do you mean, cousin?"

Gav rolled his eyes at Sam's innocent expression. "I hate to break up this entertaining exchange, but people are getting restless." Gav nodded toward the girl. "We need to leave before the urchin wakes up."

Tehl surveyed the people surrounding them. Most were casting scared and nervous glances in their direction. A few young men stood grouped together, glaring their way. The last thing they needed was the hotheads starting a fight.

"Lead on, then."

Sam slapped him on the shoulder, gave a short nod to Gavriel who turned, making eye contact with their men among the crowd. Simultaneously, the Elite gathered in loose formation around them. Gav nodded once more, and they began their journey home. Although Tehl noted several concerned looks thrown at the unconscious girl being carried like a sack of potatoes, no one dared approach.

Tehl turned his attention to the man at his side. Gavriel's eyes never stayed in one place. They were always sharp, ever alert to potential dangers. Gav was an interesting study in contradictions. He was a soldier through and through, but he also had immense talents in healing and the sciences. There was none more fierce on the battlefield, yet he never lost his temper and he had a compassionate heart.

Tehl considered Gav a brother, for his cousin had been raised with them since childhood. Gav also favored his mother's side of the family, so the black hair, straight nose, and wide shoulders meant he resembled Tehl more than his actual brother. But Gav inherited what he didn't: the amethyst-colored eyes that ran in his mum's side of the family.

Tehl squinted at the ridiculous thing atop his cousin's head. Gav had yet to rid himself of the absurd straw hat adorning his head like a giant bird's nest. He couldn't help but stare. His cousin's unusual-colored eyes flickered over to him, and a small smile touched Gav's mouth.

"Staring into my eyes, cousin?" Gav teased. "And so intense... If I didn't know any better, I'd think you were mooning over me."

Sam sniggered at this comment.

"Have you *ever* seen me moon over someone?" Tehl asked with a grin, only half serious, scouting the area, noting anyone who looked suspicious. You could never be too careful.

"Honestly? You don't know how to moon, neither can you woo, seduce, nor charm anyone."

Tehl considered that for a moment. There was truth to that. His people skills were abhorrent. He didn't know whether he was insulted or impressed his cousin knew him so well, so Tehl settled on narrowing his eyes and glaring. Gav shrugged a shoulder and continued his survey of their surroundings.

"Hey now," Sam broke in, "no need to point out the obvious. He needs a little training from yours truly." Sam pointed to himself.

Now they were ganging up on him.

Tehl glanced at the Elite who were pretending they weren't listening in. Nosy bastards. He shifted the girl in his arms. "I am the only one with a woman in his arms."

Sam choked out a laugh and held up a finger. "But you had to render her unconscious to get her to stay with you so...she doesn't count. If you would listen to my advice more women would stick around."

Tehl attempted to infuse some of Sam's attitude in his voice and failed. "I don't need any of that. All I have to do is snap my fingers and they come running." He sounded like an idiot.

"Right," Sam drew the word out. "Because that's how women desire to be spoken to: I am man, I drag you by hair to cave, you like." Sam dropped his shoulders like a wild man, grunting.

A short laugh burst out of Gav. "That doesn't work in real life, although if it did, it would be heaven, pure heaven," Gav replied with a twinkle in his eye. "Life would be so much simpler."

"Ah don't lie, you haven't taken a woman to bed since your wife passed," Tehl stated, looking down at the sleeping woman in his arms. Silence greeted him. He whipped his head up, eyes darting between Sam and Gav.

Both his brother and cousin were looking at him, silent. His eyes continued to bounce back and forth between them as he tried to figure out what he'd said wrong. He'd stated the absolute truth. Gavriel didn't care about women anymore. After his wife died, it was like the fairer sex didn't even exist to him. They might flirt and smile, but he never noticed. When propositioned, it seemed to shock him, almost like he had no clue why they would be interested.

Tehl opened his mouth, preparing to ask what he had done, when Sam cut in.

"Are you incapable of watching what comes out of your mouth? Why would you say that to Gav?" Sam hissed, anger evident. "You will have some serious issues as king if you can't learn to be more diplomatic and at least a little sensitive."

Tehl grimaced as he took in the pain Gav was trying, but failing, to hide. It clicked then why his words upset his cousin. He cursed his ignorance. Gavriel still missed Emma, so the subject was a painful wound which his words had scraped open again.

"I'm sorry Gav," he offered, remorse coloring the words. "I know how much you loved Emma. We all miss her and wish she was still here." Tehl cleared his throat to get rid of the large lump lodged there.

All three of them grew up with Emma and loved her dearly. They all met her one day as children. She was working in the stables at the time, and he remembered how she threatened each one of them with the loss of a limb if they *ever* hurt one of 'her' horses. After that, they'd grown attached to the fiery girl. She may have been plain in appearance, but the light she had inside shone so bright that all who knew her thought her lovely. It was Gavriel she had adored, though, from the very moment she laid eyes on him. The law for royalty to marry common blood had worked out for them. Everything had been right...until her accident. It broke them all when she died. It was devastating to lose Queen Ivy and Emma so close together.

Gav gave him a sad smile, which spoke in itself of his immense loss. The hurt his friend was experiencing pained him, adding to the weight he already bore.

"I miss her, Tehl. She was it for me. And you're right, there are no other women and there won't ever be." He took a deep breath and glared at the cobbles beneath their feet. "I can't believe Emma left me alone to care for the child. A little girl no less! I know nothing about her care. She...she needs her mother. And so do I." All three fell silent when Gav's voice broke.

Isa. Gavriel's child. He couldn't remember the last time he saw the little girl. Tehl sent Gav a curious look. "When did you see Isa last?"

Gav tilted his head back, staring at the sky. "It's been six months since I've been to my keep." He paused. "I need to take a leave soon and go visit."

"Six months, Gav? You haven't seen Isa in *six months*?" Tehl asked, shifting the unconscious woman in his arms. If it had been him, he was sure he wouldn't want to miss a single moment with his daughter, all the more so had she lost her mother.

"You're missing everything! Your keep is only a two-hour ride from here." Sam's censure was loud and clear.

Gav turned back to them. "Don't judge me, Sam," he said evenly. "You don't understand how hard it is to go back there. It kills me. Everything there reminds me of Emma, most of all Isa."

That Tehl related to. Didn't the palace feel empty and desolate without his mum? He couldn't imagine losing a spouse. An idea then struck Tehl. Why none of them had considered it baffled him.

"You could bring her here to live. Then you could spend time with her without all the haunting memories of your home." The more he pondered it, the more Tehl liked that idea. He would love to have his little cousin close by, perhaps it would even soothe his own heart's wounds.

Gav looked at him thoughtfully. "That's a good suggestion; I will consider it. My only worry is removing her from somewhere she's already familiar with. Her mum's death has confused her enough as it is."

Sam speared Gavriel with a serious look. "I bet she is more confused that she's lost you *as well* as her mum."

Gavriel's shoulders slumped, and silence descended on them as they each drifted off into their own thoughts. Just thinking about sweet little Isa made him feel lighter, more buoyant. She had been a precious baby girl with big violet eyes like her papa and unruly red hair like her mum. He didn't want a wife, but he liked children. Would they look like him? He shook his head at the thoughts he had no time for and headed toward the dungeon on the west side of his castle.

It was time to show the rebel her new home.

SIX

TEHL

AS TEHL APPROACHED THE DOOR, two guards saluted and opened it for him. When he crossed the threshold, a flutter of movement had him glancing down at his unconscious captive to find green eyes scrutinizing him.

"It's awake," he called to his brother and cousin.

"And it has a name," she snapped. "What did you do? I still can't feel my arms or legs…" Seeming to realize she was still in his arms, she demanded, "Put. Me. DOWN. You have no right to hold me."

Gav's eyebrows rose to his hairline. "Correct me if I am wrong, but I was under the impression that attacking the crown prince is against the law." Gavriel stared, daring her to argue with him. She glared at all of them as they continued their descent.

"Well, I didn't know he was the crown prince." She huffed out an annoyed breath. "I thought he was a thief and I was protecting myself. Why aren't my legs working?" she asked again.

If only it was her mouth she couldn't feel. "It will wear off with no permanent damage," he supplied, hoping it would quiet her.

"I am so grateful there will be no permanent damage, my prince," she mocked, lip curling.

What a terribly vexing wench. If she wanted to irritate him then he'd return

47

the favor. Tehl squeezed her against his chest, lowering his head. A low hum rumbled in his throat as he grazed her temple with the tip of his nose.

"I like the way you say 'my prince.' Say it again for me." Tehl lifted his head and took in her reaction. Her face was pinched and her lips clamped shut so tightly they were turning white.

Well that shut her up.

A smile played about his mouth as he continued, "Shall we go and explore your new home then, my love?"

"I'd be delighted, my pet," she hissed through clenched teeth.

"Pet... Interesting word choice. What do you think about that, Sam?"

His brother glanced over, biting back a grin. "There are so many things I could say, but alas—" Sam sighed. "I suppose I shall control myself."

Gav scoffed, "There's a first time for everything."

The girl's brows wrinkled in confusion. "What's wrong with the word 'pet'?"

Tehl arched a brow. "Would you like me to show you?"

Her face cleared as understanding dawned and her eyes widened in horror. She lifted her chin. "Not on your life."

The little rebel stiffened in his arms as Sam coughed—a lame attempt to cover his snicker.

Having reached the base of the stairs, they approached a sturdy-looking desk where the Keeper was scribbling away furiously, their boots splashing in shallow pools covering the stone floor.

The Keeper, an older man by the name of Jeffry had a wicked sense of humor and Tehl considered him a close friend. The man had a scruffy gray and white beard, and deep wrinkles bracketed his charcoal eyes. As he was rarely outdoors, his skin was so pale he almost resembled a specter.

At their approach, he abandoned his scratching, meeting Tehl's eyes, before sliding his gaze to the woman in his arms. He sat back and laced his fingers across his stomach as they stopped before his desk.

Tehl gave the older man a warm smile and lifted the girl in his arms. "I have a new one for you, Jeffry."

Jeffry's gaze settled back on his new prisoner, and he quirked an eyebrow in question. "Well, isn't this a surprise," Jeffry commented, staring at Sage with interest. "I don't believe I've had the pleasure of housing a woman down here.

It's a delight to meet you, missy." Jeffry stood as he spoke, his chair creaking. He reached over his wooden desk and gently patted the woman's arm.

He then pinned Tehl with his off-putting eyes. "You're positive you've got the right one? This isn't fit for women."

"She's the rebel we were after this morning. You can imagine my surprise as well when I realized it was she we came for."

Jeffry continued to eye him and then addressed the girl. "Are you dangerous, little miss?"

"Come nearer, and I'll show you," the rebel purred.

Jeffry grinned. "Well. This shall be interesting, my dear. Welcome." He then opened one tome atop his desk and dragged a finger down the page.

"Jacque," Jeffry called, lifting his head. "Please put her in cell two-zero-eight." He rubbed his silver eyebrows and inquired: "What was your name, miss? It's imperative I keep my records well organized and up to date. I'm sure you understand."

The rebel stayed silent.

"It's Ruby," Sam offered.

The Keeper jotted down her name and swept his arm in a grand gesture toward the sharp-faced Jacque. "Jacque will show you to your new home! Be seeing you soon, my dear." The Keeper then ridiculously fluttered his fingers at Ruby as Tehl departed with her.

Jacque peeled himself from the wall, moving past them as the stoic guard led them deeper into the dungeon.

"I am not your 'dear'!" Ruby called over his shoulder.

"Always a pleasure," the old man called back, adding to himself, "She is delightful. Absolutely delightful."

Tehl allowed himself a small smile at Jeffry's antics. He was eccentric, but he was a hard worker and extremely loyal. The Keeper had been one of his father's closest companions. Jeffry was present at both princes' births. The Keeper had sat with his father outside their mother's chamber, helping to calm him while he awaited his sons. Previously a member of the Elite under King Marq, his age had eventually prevented him from fulfilling his duties. Although he could have retired to his keep, he instead opted to continue his service to the Crown here saying that although he wasn't as able as he was in his youth, he still had a lot to offer. And he was right. The Keeper was one of the few he considered family.

Tehl watched as the girl absorbed her new surroundings. Iron bars and mossy stone encased them. Each cell was small, sparse, and drab; either cloaked in shadow or shrouded with complete darkness. Some cells boasted a window, but that was not necessarily a blessing. Hearing the crashing waves outside and knowing freedom was so close yet unattainable seemed like another kind of torture. It was a depressing place to spend one's time.

Jacque had stopped ahead of them and was unlocking a cell, swinging open the door with a screech. A rusted two-zero-eight hung above the door, and Tehl gauged its interior dimensions at around nine feet by nine. Its only contents were an old cot and a bucket in one corner. In the center of the floor, emitting a putrid stench, was a sturdy metal grate.

Tehl stepped through the doorway, carrying the small rebel like a bride over a threshold. Her eyes found his, pleading with him not to cage her in here. A flicker of uncertainty gave him pause.

What if I'm wrong?

He mentally slapped himself for these thoughts. No matter the lies she spouted, it did nothing to change what he'd seen with own eyes; she was a rebel supporter.

He strolled in and unceremoniously deposited her on the cot, quickly exiting the cell. He allowed the cell door to shut behind him, ringing with a sense of finality, before turning around.

Tehl stood with the three men, rolling his shoulders, and shook out his arms as a million pinpricks traveled down them. They had fallen asleep holding her for so long. The men regarded the motionless woman, waiting, but she only stared at the ceiling blankly. Tehl had expected a lot more shrieking and cursing based on her prior behavior, but she stayed silent.

He gripped the iron bars and cleared his throat. Her green eyes dispassionately wandered to his chest, lacking their previous fire. Why wasn't she looking him in the eye? "Ruby, I would think long and hard about your life choices. If you help us, things will be a lot easier for you. If not..." He paused long enough for her to meet his eyes. "There will be consequences for your actions."

She stared at him stonily. "You promised not to hurt me. Are you so dishonorable to go back on your word?" Her gaze drifted over the other men. "You ought to be ashamed of yourselves, taking part in this madness. Do you take pleasure in his unjust actions and threats?"

None of them responded to her bait. The girl's attention then swung back to him. As he suspected, she was quite the actress. Here she was trying to manipulate them from her cell. Tehl detested lying, and it was all she'd done since first opening her big mouth. Had she been honest, even once, things might have been different.

"The devil's in the details, love." Her eyes narrowed. "I said no harm would come to you *when* I took you to the palace, not *while* you're *staying* here."

"Staying?" She let out an unladylike snort. "You talk as if I'm some honored guest and not a prisoner trapped in the dark belly of your home."

"It's rather like we're living together. Don't most men keep their mistresses hidden?" Tehl needled.

Her pale cheeks colored to an alarming shade of red, her ire raised. She closed her eyes and blew out a breath, dismissing them. Her impassive mask slid back in place.

"Be seeing you soon."

Still nothing.

She was in her own little world. He would need to make it difficult for her to ignore him at their next interaction.

Tehl pushed off the bars, nodding to Jacque. The wiry guard took the lead, guiding them through the dungeon. Its design ensured those attempting escape would have a hard time accomplishing the feat, most likely losing their way among its various twists and turns. Gavriel's steps echoed behind him, yet his brother's steps were noticeably absent. Sam moved like a griffin in the darkness, silent and predatory. When they reached Jeffry's desk, Jacque strolled to his usual position behind it, leaning against the wall.

Tehl nodded to them both before heading back up the stairway. He needed to get away. The rebel wench was still messing with his mind. Pushing up the stairs, he broke into a run, thighs burning as he burst through the door like the devil was on his tail. In the dim courtyard, his breath seesawed out of his chest.

Why can't things be black and white? He hated gray areas.

Sam and Gav caught up with him, faces showing their confusion. Odd, since nothing surprised Sam anymore. What had he done wrong this time?

"Why are you looking at me like that?"

Sam opened and closed his mouth a couple times before saying anything. "I'm not sure where to start." His brother sighed, covering his face with his large hand, and glanced at his cousin. "Do you want to go first, or shall I?"

Gav grunted. "You."

Sam held up one finger. "First, I have never heard you call a woman 'my love'. Not in jest and not in seriousness. Brother, you hardly even *talk* to women, let alone bestow an endearment." Sam shook his head. "Of course you'd start with our minx of a prisoner, who is guilty as sin."

He gave his brother a blank look. "I meant nothing by it. I was only trying to irritate her."

Sam looked at him skeptically, holding up a second finger. "Second, did I or did I not hear you flirt with her?" He turned to Gav for confirmation.

"Yep, that happened," Gav drawled.

Tehl blinked. "No, I didn't." What were they talking about?

"I've only heard you use innuendo a handful of times our entire lives, and I have *never* seen you flirt, not even once." Gav grimaced. "It was odd."

"Ass." Not his best retort.

"No more than you were today," Gav quipped.

"Touché," Tehl conceded.

"Third," Sam interjected, holding up three fingers, "you were acting out of character. Why were you playing the lecher? *None of us* have touched a woman without invitation. Why would you make her think such?"

"She wasn't afraid," Tehl explained. "She wouldn't stop fighting me, though I tried everything. I tried to be peaceful and speak with her. When that didn't work, I threatened her and her loved ones, but still *nothing*. I had to do something." Both men were visibly upset by his explanation. He pointed a finger, first to Sam, then Gav. "Don't you two give me those looks and don't be hypocrites. I've observed both of you interrogate, and I know some of the things you've said or done because you understood it necessary for *them* to cooperate."

Sam opened his mouth, but the look on Tehl's face must have made his brother reconsider his comment.

"No, Sam. She is *still* our enemy, regardless of her gender. Everything she represents threatens our families and the safety of the people in our kingdom. I did what I had to. I used what scared her to our advantage."

"So, you're saying you want us to threaten to ravish her?"

His brother locked eyes with him. Sam was serious. It was times like these when he remembered just how dangerous Sam could be. He would do anything to protect Aermia and its people.

"No, Sam." Frustrated, Tehl kicked a rock with the toe of his boot. "I scared her by crowding her and leering, but that's as far as I want to take it. The entire time, I was only trying to scare her into cooperating, but my stomach churned. When I think about it, I feel sick," he confessed. Her terrified eyes flashed through his mind. Boredom, shock, irritation—yes, all of those. But never fear. He lifted his head and stared at the inner wall, eyes distant. "We don't need to give the rebels any more reasons to hate us. We may need that information, but not enough to incite a riot over our tactics."

"You think that could happen?" Gav asked.

"I do. I have never met a woman with skills like hers. No doubt someone will miss her and perhaps already has. I think it wise for one of us to always have an eye on her. We need to make certain none of the men cross a line they shouldn't."

Both nodded in agreement.

"It's what makes us different from the criminals; we have honor and we have morals." Gav then turned his head and stared pointedly at Sam. "Well, at least some of us have morals."

Sam stared right back and, to Tehl's shock and amusement, a slight blush crept up his cheeks. "Hey now, I have morals. I do my duty as commander, I am excellent at being sneaky, I treat women right, and I *always* respected my mother." Sam crossed his arms, mock-glaring at them both.

"I think you and I have a very different view of morals, my friend," Gav said lightly, regarding the guards moving through the training yard and barracks.

Sam retorted something, but their voices soon faded to a dull buzz as he tuned them out. The sun had already begun its descent behind the palace, throwing jagged shadows across the courtyard. Nothing had gone as planned today and while his head throbbed, his entire body was a giant bruise.

He tuned back into their conversation, looking their way. Apparently, they were still bickering about morals with Sam losing. The corner of his mouth lifted as he listened to them. They argued like an old married couple.

"So…," he began, raising his voice so they'd hear him over their debate. They both paused, looking at him expectantly. "I will go and get cleaned up. In the meantime, I'll leave Jeffry to take care of that Ruby girl until we're ready for her interrogation." He turned his back to them, already starting toward the palace when Sam's words stopped him.

"You mean the rebel, right?" Sam asked.

Tehl's brow furrowed. *What?* He peered over his shoulder. "That's what I said."

"No, you said Ruby."

"That's her name, is it not?" Tehl intoned. A flicker of annoyance ran through him at the delay of his warm bath. "Out with it, Sam."

"In using her name, you're establishing a connection to her." Sam gave him a searching look. "She's nothing but a wealth of information. An asset. A prisoner. Maybe you need to keep your distance."

He didn't care if Sam handled this. That meant one less thing on his list to take care of. "If that's what you think is best, Commander," Tehl murmured, emphasizing Sam's title. He shifted impatiently from one foot to another. "Are we done?"

"Yeah, we are. Go take a bath. Lord! You reek. I can smell you from here." Sam wrinkled his nose. "What in God's name did you get into, anyway?"

Tehl sent a rude gesture Sam's way, nodded to Gav, and made his way back to the palace.

SEVEN

SAM

"HE DOESN'T KNOW WHAT HE is getting into with that woman," Gav declared as they watched Tehl limp his way to the palace. "She's a distraction he doesn't need."

Sam couldn't agree more; the girl was heaps of trouble wrapped in a tantalizing package, one that even his brother had noticed.

"She's dangerous, that one, and in more ways than I can count. Tonight, I'll be having a little chat with her to get a feel for what we're working with here. I have a feeling she isn't the type to break easily. It'll take just the right touch."

Gav turned his startling purple eyes on him. "If you hurt her, he will be livid," Gav admonished him. "If you don't tread carefully, this will come back on us, you understand that?"

Sam nodded, but Gav's words rankled. He wasn't a bumbling idiot or wet behind the ears. Sam clasped his hands to his chest and smirked at his cousin. "I don't know what you're talking about. Women love me! She'll be putty in my hands in no time." He pasted on a smug grin full of male confidence.

"She's not your typical woman. I bet she will see through anything you throw her way."

"We shall see about that, we shall see. Care to bet on it?"

Gav rolled his eyes and followed Tehl's example, heading back to the palace.

Sam rubbed his hands together. He eagerly anticipated this new challenge. Puzzles were his specialty, and Ruby was a puzzle that could solve more than a few of their problems.

EİGHT

SAGE

THE CLANK OF THE CLOSING door reverberated in her mind. Any freedom had left through it.

Sage was trapped in a stone box.

A wet stone box.

What to do now? Her thoughts whirled at a frantic pace, flipping through ideas. She squeezed her eyes shut, trying to regain her cool. She could only thank the stars she had nothing condemning on her when she was taken.

When the prince first grabbed her, she had thought he was an everyday pickpocket. Sage wasn't even concerned; it wasn't until he'd started in about information she felt something was amiss. After that, it became clear she needed to escape. And yet, despite her vast skill set, there was only so much she could do against a man who outweighed her with a hundred pounds of muscle.

She hadn't doubted herself before, often going head-to-head with men in training. Sage never needed to, she always succeeded. Dueling with the prince, though, gave her a little more perspective. It also bruised her ego. Rafe had told her there would always be someone who was more skilled, better trained, or stronger than her. The key, however, was to be more *prepared* than your opponent in those instances and she had met no one who fell into that category until today.

Sage opened her eyes and stared at the drab ceiling above her. If the crown prince had his way, she would become well acquainted with this cell. And yet...she had been so captured by his dark blue eyes, she'd stared into them several times. The crown prince was dangerously handsome. Wide shoulders, broad muscled chest, and dimples...the dang dimples. Such a shame his insides didn't match his exterior.

Even thinking of his behavior made her shudder. He was more animal than man. Sage couldn't imagine what would happen if he ascended the throne. It was a frightening thought.

Sage closed her eyes and exhaled a long sigh, realizing she couldn't even wiggle. She'd humiliated the prince. He wasn't likely to let it go. Men were fragile creatures when it came to their egos, so he would come for her; it was only the matter of *when*. What was their plan? That question concerned her. She cringed, remembering his nose running along her neck. Her heart pounded, breath seizing, as the unpleasant memory flashed in her mind.

Calm down, she commanded herself, *he's not even here.*

She took a measured breath through her nose and held it, letting it out slowly to release some of her tension and continued until her heart had slowed.

After a time, feeling crept back into her digits and Sage tried to move her feet and hands. The best she could manage was a slight wiggling of her toes and fingers. Sage clenched her jaw, frustrated at being so vulnerable. She hated it.

What drug had they used? She hoped it wouldn't have any permanent effects. Sage knew they probably wanted her undamaged. But one could never be too sure. The Crown was dangerous. Most likely they needed her healthy, so they'd have a better chance of getting her to talk. It was a brilliant move, but it wouldn't work on her. They hadn't been trained by Rafe. He had shown her that pain was in the mind. Now, for the most part, she could turn it off. Despite this, a million what-ifs played out in her mind.

Focus Sage. Focus on what's most important.

Trust. She needed to trust the training she'd received, she could get through this. Her first task was to stop worrying and assess the situation. What resources were at her disposal? Sage flopped her head to the side, scrutinizing her temporary home.

Just terrific.

Her surroundings were depressing. Green lichen covered the damp gray stone walls and ceiling. A large grate in the center of the floor emitted a foul odor, and a faint gurgling sounded below it. A lone, wooden bucket sat in one corner, most likely to piss in. Her fingers twitched against the rickety old cot, she was surprised it hadn't collapsed beneath her.

Having completed the first step, she moved on to the second. Find a weapon. She could probably pull apart the cot and make a pike or club of sorts. Sage chuckled darkly. She didn't need a weapon, she *was* one.

Sage moved on and assessed her cage again, this time searching for any weaknesses. A tiny window faced the sea, gracing the room with a small beam of sunlight. There was no way she would fit. And even if she could, she would have to figure out how to deal with the five-hundred-foot drop into the sea below. Her gaze dropped to the grate—that, as well, was too small.

Last, Sage examined the iron bars making up the door and one wall. Stupid things didn't even have the decency to sport a rusty spot or two. The damn thing looked impenetrable, and it heightened her frustration. She wouldn't be breaking out tonight.

Pinpricks rushed up her arms causing her hands to clench. Relief swept through her at the movement. Finally, she was regaining mobility, and as soon as she recovered full movement, she'd do a more thorough inspection of her cell.

Time crawled as she waited for more feeling to return in her extremities, counting the stones in her ceiling. How much time had passed? Minutes? Hours? Sage had no clue. After a time, her rambling thoughts were interrupted when a horrendous throbbing began in her head and pulsed along her body. The drug had been a blessing in disguise as it had been blocking all her pain. Sage rolled her neck but, rather than helping, dizziness assaulted her.

Get up, Sage. You need to get up.

After a couple tries, she managed to sit, the room spinning around her. She braced a hand on the stone wall when nausea slammed into her. Saliva flooded her mouth just before she heaved until her stomach was empty.

Once her stomach settled, she tried lifting her head again. Even the small movement was painful now that she wasn't focused on throwing up. Sage gingerly touched her bruised face, trying to map out her injuries. When she brushed the bridge of her nose, she cringed. It was swollen and crooked.

"Well, that's just great. A broken nose," she muttered to the empty room.

She continued her exploration, discovering a bruised cheekbone, a cut in her eyebrow, and a fat lip. She ran a hand along the back of her head and jerked in pain. Sage examined her hand: blood stained her fingertips. That explained the dizzy spells.

Gritting her teeth, she continued, next probing her ribs with her bloody fingers. Each time she pressed down, her breath whooshed out as the pain struck anew. Sage blew out a relieved breath. If she had broken them, she wouldn't have been able to sit. She grasped her linen shirt and pulled it up over her shoulders with painstaking slowness. Sage ripped her threadbare cloak into strips and bound her ribs. By the time she finished, she was aching everywhere and more than irritable. To make things worse, the cold air on her bare skin had her shivering. Sage squinted at her shirt and hesitated, cringing at the idea of trying to put it back on.

She still needed to straighten her nose though. No reason to stain her shirt even worse than it already was. Both feet dropped to the floor as she straightened. Sage blew out a deep breath trying to psyche herself up for what she had to do.

On the count of three, one, two, three!

Grasping her nose, she simultaneously pulled up on the bridge and down on the tip of her nose. Tears washed down her face as white spots danced across her vision.

Hot liquid dripped down and mingled with her tears, painting the stone floor with crimson spots. Sage tilted her head back and reminded herself to control the pain. If she focused hard enough on her anchor, her family, Sage could turn it off.

What would they do when she didn't show up? How would they run the forge?

They would search, but it wouldn't matter. They'd find no trace of her. The Elite were too careful to leave evidence of an abduction and with her disguise, no one would have recognized her. Dying her hair black with squid ink turned out to be a good move. Even if her parents asked someone who had seen the Elite haul her away, their description of her wouldn't match her parents'. They wouldn't connect a black-haired boy with a brunette woman. Thank God she'd also given the Elite an alias. Now they couldn't track down her family. From this point on she *was* Ruby.

The faint sound of shuffling steps sounded from the corridor. Sage pushed through the pain and donned her shirt, only able to finish enough buttons to keep it closed.

The whisper of leather against stone drew nearer to her cell. Sage straightened, patiently awaiting whomever was paying her a visit. Sage clenched her hands, preparing for a fight.

To her surprise, the old man from the desk came into view. Sage noticed again his striking coloring. She couldn't decide if it was attractive or off-putting.

He stopped in front of her cell, watching her through the bars. There was something about his eyes that disturbed her, and she tried not to squirm under his intense gaze. She opted instead to stare right back.

Without thinking, she blurted, "Do you ever scare yourself when you glance in the mirror?" Sage lifted a hand to cover her mouth. *Why did she say that?* She had to get it together; she needed to sell her act.

An amused grin peeked out from his wiry, gray beard, his eyes twinkling with mirth. He clasped his hands behind his back and straightened. "Can't say that I have. Sure as hell have scared others, though. It's one of my preferred pastimes." Glee was apparent in his voice.

"Well, that's comforting," she grumbled. "What do you want? If you've come to scare or intimidate me, you'll be disappointed. I don't do frightened very well. I leave that to the high-class ladies."

Jeffry, Sage remembered his name, took two shuffling steps closer to the iron bars.

Why is he shuffling like an old man?

She'd bet her finest pair of daggers that those shuffling steps were all for show. Her lips fought a smile. She wasn't the only one playing games.

She circled her hand once for him to continue; yet he remained silent, giving her a look she didn't quite understand. If he thought he was going to unnerve her by staring, he was sorely mistaken. Her green eyes stayed focused on his metallic ones as she stared back in a silent challenge.

He gave her a toothy smile full of white teeth and cocked his head. His eyes traced her face and body. "Underneath all that grime and blood, my dear, I believe you are quite the stunner."

She sucked her cheeks in, trying to reign in her anger at being ogled so openly. She pushed down the anger, slipping into character. Sage batted her lashes and fluttered her bloody fingers at him like she had seen the strumpets do.

"I can stun you all right," she purred in a smoky tone. "If you come and join me, I'll show you how much." She winked, saucily.

His smile widened.

"I bet." He shook his head at her, amused. "Trouble, that's what you are. Pure trouble." He chuckled and then continued, "The princes won't know what to do with you, that's for sure. It will be enjoyable to watch."

"I don't even know what I'm doing here. Surely the princes won't hurt me?"

"You aren't getting any information from me, missy. I wanted to see how you were settling in."

She scoffed. "Every man who's ever said he wanted to make sure a woman was 'settling in' wanted much more than that. I know how this particular drama ends."

The old man gurgled. Was he dying? He tipped forward and slapped the bars, startling Sage. Lifting his head, he wiped tears from the corners of his eyes. Her concern melted into irritation. He was laughing at her!

He eventually caught his breath and looked her dead in the eye. "Aye, missy, you're a beautiful woman, one many men would want." Pointing to his chest, he continued: "But this old man has no desire for you. I already have a wonderful woman waiting at home for me." He eyed her again and shook his head. "For heaven's sake. I have granddaughters your age! Every time I look at you, I only see them." He sobered, his previous carefree persona melting away. "Listen, tonight will be rough. I have strict instructions you're to receive no food, water, nor blankets, so prepare yourself my dear. Tonight is your first night in purgatory. Good night."

She watched him shuffle like an invalid until he'd disappeared around the corner. Sage couldn't help but roll her eyes at the whole shuffling bit. She would eat her shirt if he wasn't in better shape than most men half his age.

Sage dismissed him from her mind and focused on her newly discovered predicament. No blankets? She eyed the window. It might be her salvation during the day, but it would mean her death during the night. She fingered the remains of her threadbare cloak. Were they trying to kill her or did they enjoy others suffering? Sage would figure something out; she had to.

NINE

TEHL

AS TEHL MADE HIS WAY toward the infirmary, Sam's words replayed over and over in his head.

You're connecting with her.

Sit this one out.

Tehl didn't necessarily agree with Sam, but his brother understood emotions better than he did. That little spitfire may be a huge part of his problems, but she could very well be the solution.

Ruby. The name just didn't match the impression she'd left. When he'd discovered that cloak had been hiding a beautiful woman, he'd barely covered his astonishment. And it was still difficult to reconcile the fierce opponent she had been with the stunning girl before him. But her face didn't fool him. She was tough and bloodthirsty.

Who could have trained her? No one learnt to fight like that overnight, yet he didn't know of any masters willing to take on female apprentices. Skills like hers only came with grueling years of training and dedication. It must have been in secret or he'd have heard tell of her. So the question was, how did she acquire such skills? Why hide them? To have any chance at uncovering her identity, they'd first need to find her master.

Reaching the infirmary, Tehl headed through the open door to Jacob, the palace's most-prized healer: *the* Healer. The older man had held the position since well before either prince had been born. He stood now with his glasses low on his nose, squinting at herbs. Without thinking, Tehl tossed himself onto one of the many pristine cots, hissing in a breath when his ribs protested the rough treatment.

That girl sure didn't pull her punches.

The pungent scents of basil and lemon permeated the room, causing his nose to twitch. Absentmindedly, he rubbed it as Jacob completed whatever he was working on. Jacob scrubbed his hands, turning as he dried them. He paused as he took in Tehl's injuries, his thick spectacles magnifying the coppery-hazel of his eyes. He smiled crookedly. "What happened this time?" He moved closer to Tehl, examining his face. "You've been beaten to a bloody pulp." His owl-like gaze awaited an explanation.

Tehl grunted. "A woman." He watched the other man attempt to contain his obvious amusement, even while he continued cataloging injuries.

"You win some, you lose some, I suppose. Not *all* women fall at the feet of royalty, my lord."

"You're hilarious," Tehl deadpanned. "I'm worn out and desperately in need of a bath. Would you make this quick?"

Jacob leaned closer, sniffing. "You're correct there, my lord."

Tehl rolled his eyes. He appreciated his old friend's sense of humor, but he had other priorities—his swollen nose for instance. Pointing to it, he told the Healer, "You will need to reset my nose. She might have broken a couple of my ribs, but I'm still fairly mobile, so they're more than likely only bruised."

Jacob's eyebrows furrowed as he drew closer and probed the bridge of Tehl's nose. The Healer clucked his tongue. "Your nose *is* broken. Let's take care of that before I examine anything else. On three, I will straighten it. One, two—"

Pain exploded in his face. Tehl glared through his watery eyes. "What happened to three?"

"It sets better if you aren't expecting it. Stop whining. It's not like this is your first time experiencing a broken nose," Jacob chided.

"Still hurts."

The Healer ignored him. "Lift your shirt."

When Tehl painstakingly lifted his shirt over his head, he heard a familiar voice say.

"It's fun to get a little rough, but your little woman may have taken it a bit too far."

He deposited his dirty shirt on the clean cot next to him and lifted his head to scowl at Sam and Gav.

"What?" His brother raised his hands in mock innocence.

Tehl disregarded the pair, turning back to Jacob who was still inspecting his body.

"A woman. She must be some kind of hellcat."

Tehl frowned as he noted the glimmer of awe evident in Jacob's voice.

"And you should see her! She is a curvy little pixie," Gav put in. "You'd never think she had it in her."

Tehl's head whipped around, glaring at the obvious admiration in Gav's words.

Eyes glinting, Sam chided, "Add to that the fact he had at least seventy-five pounds on her, yet she *still* beat him bloody. Brother, you've let yourself go. If you were in better shape that woman couldn't have bested you."

Tehl rolled his eyes, refusing to dignify his brother's ribbing with a response. He knew Sam's comments were good natured though, so he wasn't bothered overmuch.

Ignoring his irksome brother and cousin, Tehl focused instead on Jacob's movements as he cleaned each injury. At some point, Jacob had stopped trying to maintain his blank face; he was now smiling broadly.

Tehl cleared his throat. "Found something amusing, have you?"

"I have, thank you. I had thought, as you got older, these crazy injuries would eventually lessen, but *it seems*—" Jacob paused mid-sentence, examining his back. "Did she *bite* you?!"

Tehl glanced up in time to see Sam and Gav trade glances. Sam vaulted over the cot for a better look. His three friends peered at the circular welt on his back. The silence shattered as both Sam and Gav burst into peals of laughter. Tehl narrowed his eyes at Jacob, who was chuckling underneath his breath.

"It's not that bad," he mumbled, creating another round of laughter behind him.

"Sam look! You can see all her bitty teeth marks!" Gav chortled.

"I'm all for a well-placed bite on occasion, and we've all marked our territory at times, but brother? That's just brutal." Sam plopped down next to him, jarring the cot and, subsequently, his ribs. Tehl sucked in a shaky breath only to have it whoosh out of him when Sam bumped him with his shoulder. "However did you come by it?" Sam probed, brimming with curiosity.

He sighed, knowing his brother wouldn't leave the subject alone without the full story. "When I threw the blasted woman over my shoulder, she attempted escape by any means possible, thus the biting."

After staring for a beat, Sam shook his head and stood, twisting from side to side as he tried to work out the stiffness. "Sitting on barrels all day has left its mark. My back's all kinked," he sighed, adding, "What I wouldn't give for a hot bath right now."

Tehl shot his brother a dirty look. "Yeah...because sitting all day is just *so* hard on your body," he said sardonically, thinking of every ache afflicting his pummeled body.

Jacob noticed the blood on his shoulder and mangled ear. "Bloody hell, Tehl! How'd you come by this?"

"A damn rat bit me."

Gav's brows furrowed, and his cousin opened and closed his mouth several times, but Sam spoke up first. "How did that even happen? What was a *rat* doing on your shoulder?"

"It's a long story." Tehl was not keen on doling out an explanation; exhaustion was riding him hard. He closed his eyes as Jacob continued his ministrations, smearing smelly stuff on his neck and inspecting his lip. Jacob pulled it down, and checked Tehl's gums, letting out a resigned sigh when he'd finished. "I'll need to stitch it. Your teeth have cut clean through." Uncorking an amber bottle, he portioned some of the liquid in a cup and on a rag, handing Tehl the bottle afterward. "Take a couple swigs. It will help clean the wound and numb some of the pain."

Tehl brought the bottle to his lips and took a healthy gulp, before Jacob swiped the outside of his lip with the whiskey-soaked rag. The liquid burned a hot trail down his throat and warmed his belly. The Healer threaded a needle, ready to stitch the botched lip. He cringed. He'd always hated this part. People were *not* meant to be stabbed with sharp objects.

"This will sting."

Gav shifted closer, watching Jacob with interest. Without looking away, he addressed Tehl. "So you're telling me you were bitten by a rat *and* a woman, got your nose broken, had your lip busted, and are suffering bruised ribs, all from a pint-sized woman?"

Tehl huffed. "She's tougher than she looks."

Sam nodded. "My plan *was* to let her stew, maybe a couple of days, then I'd work my charm on her." Sam smirked. "But now I can't bear to wait that long. I believe I'll collect all the information we need by the end of the week."

If anyone could accomplish that, it was Sam. Tehl was sure his brother could charm the knickers off a nun. "Good. The sooner the better, honestly."

Jacob leaned over to retrieve a small pair of clippers and cut the string that was tugging Tehl's lip.

"There you go. I put in ten stitches but it should heal quickly. Try not to agitate it, though, by rubbing your tongue along it." Jacob picked up a couple herbal packets from his desk and made a few notations. He handed them to Tehl, motioning to the green. "Mix those into your wine tonight before bed and they'll reduce some of your pain." He pointed to the purple herbs. "Use the lavender in your bath. It will help you relax and, hopefully, fall asleep. You'll need the rest. Also, when you're done with your bath, wrap your ribs with that gauze. If you need anything, you know where to find me." Jacob gathered his remaining herbs and ambled toward the door. He stopped in the doorway, and smirked over his shoulder. "If you need anyone to teach you what *proper* foreplay with a lady is, I suppose I'd be willing to help you out." He winked and slipped through the door.

Tehl's jaw dropped in horror.

"Did he give us love advice?" Sam grinned through his own shock. "I want to be him when I grow up."

Tehl squeezed his eyes closed, attempting to erase the image that had sprung in his mind. Putting that aside, he steeled himself for the laborious trek ahead to get to his rooms. Tehl slid off the cot and shrugged his shirt back on, ignoring the buttons for now.

Gav rocked forward onto the balls of his feet and clapped his hands. "Well...," he drew out, "after that remark, I need a drink. Want to join me?"

Sam rubbed his hands together in anticipation. "Yeah, I'm coming. And maybe, while we are at it, we can scare up some enjoyable company of the female persuasion." Gav smiled at Sam's antics and moved toward the door. Sam looked to Tehl expectantly.

He clasped his brother on the shoulder once with a slight smile. "No, you go. I need to clean up, so I'll catch up with you in the morning. Also, I need you to get any information you can on Ruby and report it as soon as possible."

The three flights of stairs leading to his quarters just about killed him. When he finally reached his own floor, he paused to catch his breath. Tehl leaned against the wall while listening for the sounds of anyone approaching. God help him if anyone caught him slumping against the wall like an invalid.

Once his body let him breathe again, he covered the remaining twenty feet to his room and went straight to his bathing area. To his delight, steam was already wafting from a hot bath that had been prepped before his arrival. He stripped and dumped the herbs in the tub. Tehl lowered himself in and sighed as the warm water enveloped him. Immediately, his muscles relaxed.

Best part of life right here.

Tehl closed his eyes and drifted off. The next thing he knew, he was choking on water. He jerked up, sluicing water everywhere as he coughed. Time to get out. Clumsily, he climbed out of the tub, still sputtering on water. He wiped the water from his eyes and peered blearily around his room. Why did his bed seem so damn far away?

He stumbled back to his main quarters and collapsed onto the bed, still soaked. He thought about what his mother would say if she knew he had climbed into bed while wet. She would have skinned him alive and fussed over the state of him, the mattress, and the sheets. He could imagine her scolding him saying, "You'll catch your death, you silly boy!"

He smiled and floated away into the recesses of his mind. His thoughts turned to a raven-haired beauty. *Why did she intrigue him?* Trouble. She was only trouble, he reminded his sleepy self. He closed his eyes and dreamt about warrior angels with green eyes.

TEN

TEHL

TEHL CRACKED HIS EYES OPEN and blinked to clear the sleep from his eyes. How did he get to bed? He sat up; the blankets fell to his waist, exposing his skin to the chill of the morning air. The last thing he remembered was being in the bath. At least he didn't drown. Rolling his head back and forth, he took stock of how he was feeling: sore, but much better than yesterday. His stomach rumbled, reminding him he'd missed dinner last night.

Tehl threw on some leather breeches, a linen shirt, and a dark blue, velvet vest. He may be royal, but he would not primp and dress up. He ran his hands through his disheveled hair, not looking at the mirror, and rushed down to the dining room.

Gav was munching on a piece of toast while reading something, and Sam was digging into his mountain of food. "So much for manners," Tehl commented dryly.

Gav grunted, and Sam didn't spare him a glance, too intent on his horde. A servant placed a plate in front of him with everything he loved. The delicious smell of baked hot cakes, eggs, and buttery goodness teased his nose. His mouth watered, taking in the deliciousness laid before him. Tehl ignored everything but his food and dove right in.

His mountain of food speedily disappeared, much to his disappointment. Tehl took the last bite of his last hot cake, savoring the taste as it melted in his mouth. Opening his eyes, he looked down the table toward Gav, who was reading while sipping his coffee. Tehl flicked his eyes to Sam, who sat across from him. Sam had his head tilted back against the chair with his eyes closed.

"Rough night, Sam?" His brother didn't move or respond. "I know you're not asleep. If I hadn't seen you destroy half this table of food five minutes ago, I might have believed it."

"Give me a moment," Sam grouched, glaring at him.

"Out too late last night?" Tehl smirked. "That's what happens when you are chasing women."

"If that's what he was doing, he sure as hell would be in a better mood," Gav remarked from behind his book.

His brother leaned his head back and closed his eyes and muttered, "It *had* to be a woman!"

"What do you mean by that?" Tehl asked, curious.

"What I meant was *that woman* has caused a ruckus already. Most of the Elite and Guard saw us bring her in yesterday, so naturally they were curious. Last night, a group went to investigate. She goaded them into a fight and they opened her cell."

"Did she escape?" Tehl growled.

"No, they kept her caged, but she took out five of our men last night! *Five*, with no weapons. Unbelievable! I slept down there to make sure no other men attempted to satisfy their curiosity," he shouted.

"She took out five of our men?"

"Well, she didn't kill them if that's what you're wondering," his brother snapped. "She rendered them unconscious and then stole their clothes."

Gav spewed his coffee and hacked. Tehl slapped him on the back and turned to Sam. His lips twitched at the irate coffee-covered man.

"Great," Sam blew out. "I am done with this day and it only just began."

"Why did she steal their clothes?" Gav sputtered, between coughs.

Sam stabbed a finger at Tehl. "He told Jeffry she wasn't to have any food, water, or blankets until he said so. I guess she figured she would help herself to their clothes to keep warm. She deserved them if she took down five guards."

Tehl smiled down into his cup of coffee while listening to his brother rant. "One little woman did all that? I am surprised she got the best of your guards.

It seems they need better training," he needled.

Sam stood, knocking his chair back. His brother placed his hands on the table and leaned forward. "That is no woman! She is a damn warrior disguised as an angel!" Sucking in a deep breath, he continued. "We have a problem if all the rebels have received the same training as the woman. Ruby was seventy pounds lighter than those men, and she *still* got the best of them. We don't know what we are dealing with. They aren't a handful of unhappy farmers. The resistance is organized and trained. They pose a real threat."

Tehl turned this over in his mind. Ruby had surprised him with her prowess in battle. Were there other women who were trained? What was the rebellion planning? Her information was vital.

"We need her information, sooner rather than later. You need to break her. We need the resistance taken care of. They don't understand the severity of our situation or who is knocking at our borders," Tehl said, gravely.

Sam looked him dead in the eye, "I will pay our lovely captive a visit this morning to see how well she slept. You'll have what you need in the next couple of days, my lord." Sam bowed and stomped from the room.

"She wound him up. I don't think I have seen him lose his temper like that in a couple years. I forgot that he even had one," drawled Gav, still sipping on his coffee. "If he interrogates her when he's angry, she could manipulate him."

"He is the best at what he does, he won't go in blind," Tehl defended. "He won't let her manipulate him."

"Women are different creatures than men. They play by a different set of rules. She will be more difficult than Sam expects."

"Would you like to deal with her?"

Gav shook his head. "Not particularly, but it would be better with both of us there."

"Then your main priority is to deal with Sam and Ruby."

Gav stood and set his coffee down. "It's been an eventful morning. I will apprise you of the situation later," he said, tossing the words over his shoulder. His cousin strolled out of the room like he had all the time in the world.

Time…that was the one thing Tehl didn't have. Hopefully they would get what they needed today.

ELEVEN

SAGE

SAGE'S EYES FLICKERED OPEN AS light filtered through the window, dancing across her eyelids. The window allowed just enough light to warm a small portion of the otherwise icy floor.

Sage cursed, irritation and alarm surging through her. She'd fallen asleep without realizing it. Last night had been rough.

She shivered in the damp cold. It seemed her recent wardrobe additions were not enough to ward off the chill, but the memory of their acquisition had her smiling in spite of herself. She'd mopped the floor with those idiots, and stealing their uniforms for warmth was icing on the cake. When their commander arrived after the fact, his expression had been priceless. Sage smirked. She couldn't wait to tell Rafe.

As terrifying as it had been initially when the men came for her, she'd enjoyed putting them in their place. It was an image she wouldn't soon forget; the Elite sprawled across the floor, naked.

The commander, or Prince Samuel, had retrieved his men with muttered curses, all the while attempting to burn a hole in her head with a dark glare. As he left, she'd heard him bellowing at Jeffry; he was obviously displeased. Her glee was short-lived, though, when he camped outside her cell shortly thereafter. The cursed man had stayed all night. Unlike her, the cold stone didn't seem to bother him at all for he began snoring as soon as he lay down.

Sage had stayed awake, knowing she couldn't allow herself to be so vulnerable in his presence.

In the middle of the night, she'd glanced to where he'd been sleeping to find he was now watching her. Not to be cowed, she'd stared right back, watching him watch her, neither of them speaking a word. For hours, they'd stayed that way, until the fingers of dawn trickled through the window. He'd then silently rolled up his pallet and disappeared down the corridor. Sighing in relief, Sage had leaned her head against the wall, only for a second, and that was the last thing she remembered.

How could she be so careless?

Sage shifted and winced with the movement. Pain coursed through her, reminding her how bruised her entire body was. She unclenched her hands and noted they looked a little blue. It was stinking cold down here. Sage scooted into the sunlight, exhaling a happy sigh as sunlight warmed her back. Stars above, she hated being cold. Sage took a slow breath in and closed her eyes.

"Enjoying yourself, I see."

She stiffened at his voice, but wouldn't give him the satisfaction of seeing her discomfort. Her eyes snapped open as she stared unflinchingly at the commander standing before her cell. He moved like a damned cat, quickly and quietly, nothing to warn her of his approach.

"Jumpy, are we?" he mused, leaning a shoulder against her cell. "Never fear, I don't bite too hard…not unless you ask me to that is."

Oh, he was the epitome of arrogance. It was even in his posture, his stance. But there was also a cunning glint to his eyes, and that gave her pause. She'd have to tread carefully with this one. Rumors were circulating about the young commander; he was cunning, ruthless, an incredible strategist, and an accomplished womanizer. A deadly combination, for sure.

Two could play his game, though, and she doubted he'd ever encountered an opponent of her level. The 'helpless, innocent woman' wouldn't work; she'd blown that cover to smithereens after taking out his men. The trollop however…now that had potential. She mentally grimaced at the idea of pulling it off though.

Seductress, how unoriginal, though simple at least. Men. All you need is a little skin and they become so stupid.

Preparing herself, she lowered her lashes and peered through them with a smile.

Let the games begin.

She uncoiled from the floor and arched her back to allow the sun to halo her figure. She watched as his eyes skimmed her curves.

Bait set.

Sage unbraided her hair and ran her fingers through the raven tresses like she'd seen the women of the night do. Her silky waves cascaded down her back.

"See something you like?" The words were ash on her tongue, though she maintained the façade.

"Quite a few things, actually," he crooned back.

"Oh?" she inquired, letting a sensuous smile slide across her lips. Hips swaying, she sidled close to the bars, pausing just out of reach. Sage gestured lightly to his face and quirked a brow. "And how did you come by that scar?" She took one step closer and pointed to his face again, making sure to cock one hip.

Meeting her eyes, he grinned broadly. "Boys being boys, we engaged in a fierce snowball fight but, sadly, the losing team felt it necessary to pack theirs with stones."

Well, that was an unexpected response.

The commander extended his arm in between the bars, brushed a piece of hair from her shoulder, and traced a line of scar tissue at her collarbone. Every fiber of her being rebelled against his touch, and she clenched her teeth to keep from shoving him away.

"And how did *you* come by *this scar?*"

She debated lying and yet...perhaps a little truth would keep him talking. "Boys will be boys. I guess we have something in common. Whenever the boys played at swordplay, I wanted to join. So, one time they gave me one of their wooden swords but ganged up on me. I walloped them but one managed to crack me on the collarbone, gifting me this little token." After falling quiet, Sage brushed her fingers down his temple, tracing his scar. His breath hitched at her contact, and she inwardly grinned, satisfied that things were so far going as planned.

"It only adds to your beauty," he breathed, slipping his hand from her collarbone and into her hair. She looked from the scar to his eyes and froze. His clear blue eyes were frosty. Unease crept up her spine. His actions and words didn't match the ice in his eyes. Sage tried to slip back and out of reach, but his hand tightened just as quickly.

"Where are you going? Why don't we keep discussing your childhood? I'm very keen to learn all about you."

She tugged harder only to be pulled roughly against the bars. What an idiot she was; she should've known better. Sage had meant to play him, but he'd turned it around and played her even better. She'd sauntered right into his web thinking she was the spider, not the fly. Rafe would rebuke her for such an idiotic mistake.

Prince Samuel leaned toward her. "First rule of hand-to-hand combat: never allow your enemy to get a good hold on you."

She grinned, feigning confidence. "It seems we've reached an impasse. You have to open the door to get to me." Her grin shifted to a feral smile. "And when you do, I can fight and maybe I will end up with your clothes to keep me warm as well."

His eyes gleamed and a wicked smile split his handsome face. "Gav, stop lurking and help me. That's what you're here for." A tall violet-eyed man emerged from the darkened hallway to the left.

How long has he been there?

These two men moved like blasted wraiths.

"Open the door and cuff her, please."

The other man opened the door to her cell and moved toward her. Fighting, Sage clawed at the commander's arm, but his grip stayed fast. She went limp, hoping her dead weight would catch him off balance and give her a chance. Instead, the commander reacted not at all, and it accomplished nothing, except for ripping a few hairs from her neck.

"Stop fighting. If you don't, you'll just hurt yourself further," the other man growled from behind her. Sage could not let them pin her. She shot her foot back, connecting with his shin. He grunted in pain but wrestled her arms behind her back, and she writhed against both men, angering her damaged ribs. Before she knew it, cool metal clasped her wrists and closed with a faint click. Cuffs. She tugged a few times against the metal restraints but nothing.

She was well and truly caught.

"If you stop pulling at the restraints, you'll spare yourself bruised and bleeding wrists," the one called Gav warned. His touch was firm but not unkind. He moved to her side and leaned against the bars, staring down at her.

She couldn't stop staring at the unique coloring of his irises.

Purple eyes? Who had purple eyes?

"You have the most incredible eyes," Sage blurted. Her face heated. *Where the hell had that come from?* Heavens above, she needed to get a grip.

His eyes widened, crinkling at the corners. The commander's snickering caught her attention as she faced forward.

"Ah, damn. And here I thought you fancied me." Prince Samuel's knowing smirk infuriated her. She would wipe that smug expression right off his face as soon as she had the chance.

Sage gave up her pathetic role as seductress and allowed her disgust to manifest itself. "I wouldn't fancy you if you were the last man in the whole of Aermia. I'd venture to say you're more a woman than I am. How much time do you spend before your looking glass?" She mirrored his smirk.

His smile dropped. Leisurely, his eyes skimmed her face and hair. "You're not wrong, but perhaps next time you're attempting to seduce someone, you ought to glance in the mirror yourself. Dirt, blood, and bruises provide little appeal."

Her cheeks burned once again for it was true, she was a mess. Sage had been so focused on escaping she hadn't considered the state of her face. Prince Samuel let go of her, and Gav gripped her bicep, moving her toward the cell opening.

"Where are you taking me?" she demanded.

"You'll just have to see," was Samuel's flippant response.

Again, she threw herself to the floor, but Gav's grip didn't budge. He hauled her up, giving her a stern look. "Ruby, are you going to fight us the entire way?" Gav looked quite exasperated.

Her fake name surprised her for a moment, but recovering she hissed at him. "Until my last breath."

The two men exchanged looks. The purple-eyed man slid his hand underneath her armpits, and the commander reached for her legs. She got in one good kick before her legs were secured and she was suspended midair. She bucked, but it helped her not at all.

Prince Samuel jerked his chin toward the other man, and they began to move. She registered pain in almost every part of her body. How would she escape now?

There was one thing she hadn't tried, distasteful as it was. It was a last resort, but there was no honor in being dead.

So, she screamed.

At the top of her lungs.

Men rushed from the dark corners of their cells to their doors and began bellowing at the commander and his man. A chorus of shouts—*"Leave her alone!"* and *"Don't touch her!"* and *"Let her go!"*—filled the corridor, repeating over and over, but neither man was even phased. They ignored the prisoners' clamoring and continued. When they stopped at a dark chamber, her heart pounded in her chest. Chains clanked, and cool metal embraced one of her wrists. Sage yanked on her other arm and swung wildly. A large calloused hand caught her wrist and returned it to its shackle. Samuel dropped her feet, and she stumbled back into the stone wall.

She blinked several times, hoping her eyes would adjust to the dark. She heard the strike of flint and soon a flare of light burst from the lone lantern stationed on a sturdy-looking table. The floor beneath it was stained a dark brown.

Huh? She thought, *Why is the—*

Suddenly everything clicked.

Blood and lots of it. Blood stained the floor and table.

Bile burned its way up her throat, and she forced it down.

How many people were hurt in this room?

She tore her eyes from the stain and noticed a pristine porcelain cup placed upon the filthy surface. It was filled to the brim with some sort of golden, frothy liquid. A scent like apple pie wafted over and teased her nose, sweet and crisp. She knew it had to be drugged but her body didn't seem to care, her mouth watered.

When was the last time she had a drink? Yesterday morning? Was this one of their tortures?

Sage forced her eyes away from the cup and back at her two jailers. They stood shoulder to shoulder watching her. Why was everyone always staring at her? She was so sick and tired of being stared at. She wasn't an animal in a menagerie. "Well, gentleman? Get on with it already."

"Are you done with all that screeching?" the commander inquired, tugging on his ear. "Damn, woman. My ears are still ringing."

She would have found it funny if he didn't have her in chains. "I suppose… for the time being anyway."

Prince Samuel gestured to the cup. "Would you like some?"

"No, thank you."

"But Gavriel made it especially for you."

Sage scoffed. "I'm sure."

The commander retrieved the cup and sniffed it. With a shrug, he took a couple of sips.

Well it's not poisoned at least.

Looking back at her over its rim, he asked, "So? Would you like some?"

Is this a test? she wondered. *What reaction was he looking for? Best to not appear too eager.*

Sage raised her eyes from the cup and noticed his grin. It made her want to punch it right off his stupid, smug face.

"No, thank you. I wouldn't want anything that's touched your lips to come into contact with mine. I don't know where they've been," she sneered. His grin widened. Why was he still smiling?

"You should ask your mother since they kept her busy all last night."

Her jaw dropped and she stared at him.

"Wha—what?!" Sage sputtered.

His sapphire eyes crinkled in amusement. "What is it, Ruby? Cat got your tongue?"

This was the man everyone feared? "Did you—" she paused, incredulous, "Did you just joke about bedding my mum?"

His smile now reached epic proportions. "Let me assure you, there was little sleeping involved."

Sage once again sputtered and gaped like a fish.

"Oh, come on," he teased, "You've got to admit, you walked right into that one."

She gave Gav a disbelieving look and frowned. "*This* is the man with whom the king has entrusted Aermia's safety? Is this a joke or something?" she continued, shocked. "This is ridiculous. I must have died. Only in hell would someone joke about tumbling my mum."

"You're not dead," Gavriel stated. "But you might be soon if you don't drink what Commander Samuel is offering you. You need liquids."

"What is it?"

Samuel approached her and placed the cup to her lips.

"It's cider, plain and simple. Now open."

Sage eyed the concoction, but couldn't detect anything because of her damn broken nose. The commander had already taken a sip yet he appeared to be fine, so she opened her mouth. More gently than she expected, he poured the brew down, and it slipped refreshingly down her throat, coating her taste buds with its sweet and tangy flavor. Sage closed her eyes and savored it. Her parched throat rejoiced, and she gulped down as much as possible. In her haste, a portion of the precious liquid spilled, dribbling down her chin.

"Slow down or you'll end up throwing it all up," Samuel chided.

He tipped the cup up and she got every last drop. Opening her eyes, she stared curiously back at him. His famed midnight eyes matched his brother's but there was something about the commander's that intrigued her. His eyes were prettier than his brother's and probably held more secrets, too.

Wait, what? Why was she even thinking about this?

She blinked once slowly and took stock of her body. She felt giddy, yet a part of her registered that this wasn't normal.

"What did you put in my drink?"

"We put nothing in it."

"Liar," she retorted.

It wasn't possible, for her body was going soft on her. The commander returned the cup to its table and faced her. Both men seemed to be waiting for something. She looked to Gav. He looked like he was carved from stone. Why was he so serious all of a sudden? It struck her as funny and a giggle burst out of her. Oh dear, that was not a good sign. She needed to reel it in.

"What's happening?"

"Gavriel has a sort of talent with chemistry. He discovered a manner of fermenting an apple, which alters its reaction in our body. Gav has a special name for it, but I always forget. But, anyway, after experimenting we've found that when administered in the right proportions it acts as a truth serum."

She couldn't feel her face well, but Sage was sure her eyebrows were raised. They had to be joking. There was no such thing. "You're lying. I'm positive nothing like that exists."

Think, Sage, Think!

Were they just trying to mess with her head? She needed to focus on her training. Closing her eyes, she repeated what Rafe had taught her.

Be the lie.

Live the lie.

She was not Sage. She was Ruby.

Vaguely, she registered Samuel speaking. Sage opened her eyes. "What's that, handsome?" she asked with another giggle.

"What's your real name?" the commander--or rather, as she liked to think of him, *the prince*—asked.

"Ruby. Like the gem, you know? All shiny and red. My mother used to have a necklace with rubies all in it." Leaning forward, she strained against the chain and whispered, "But it wasn't hers. She stole it!"

"Where is your mother now then, Ruby?"

"Oh, she died a while ago, when the Sickness came through. I don't miss her much, though. She said I was old enough to take care of myself anyway. My brothers were just lazy bags of bones, but not me. When she kicked me out, I learned to fend for myself. On the streets, I toughened up real quick and learned how to fight dirty." She smiled. "You might have seen some of my work on the crown prince's back?"

"And what of your brothers?"

Sage shook her head trying to clear the fog blanketing her mind. She needed to focus on her story if she wanted to make it out of this alive. "Filthy pirates is what they are. I haven't seen them in ages," she slurred. "Dirty rotten thieves, I tell you. They're not important." Her body tingled, so warm all over.

"And what part do you play in the resistance?"

She sniggered, "Resistance? Darling, I know nothing about that. Gossip on the streets spreads like fire in a drought. If there was a resistance, I would have heard about it already. There's no such thing."

Samuel pulled her dagger out of a sheath at his waist and laid it on the table. "Then why did you have this?"

Sage peeked over at the dagger. "Seriously? Is that what all this is about? A silly dagger? I'll give it to ya straight then. I filched it off of an unsuspecting idiot about six months ago. Don't know who he was, though, and honestly, I don't even remember what he looked like either."

The two men in front of her blurred together into one: a curly blond-haired man with purple eyes. The cuffs at her wrists chafed.

Damn! They're so itchy.

She pulled and tugged at them.

"So, you're telling me you stole this, and it's not yours?"

Her head lulled to the side. She blinked, and there were two men again. "It's mine now. Do I look like I could afford something of that quality?"

Neither man said a word in response as the room spun, making her stomach lurch. Her eyelids drooped as her mouth slackened. This was not good; she'd never eat apple anything ever again.

"Sam? She's going to pass out," muttered Gav.

Samuel leaned closer, looking her over, and swore. "How much was in that cup?"

"Enough to make her talk."

Sage was numb. She felt nothing and crashed onto her knees, held upright only by the metal at her wrists.

How peculiar...

A strange euphoria spread through her as warm liquid ran down her arms. The dark one wrapped a strong arm around her waist, hoisting her up as the blond one with the devastating smile unlocked her wrists.

Maybe they'll stop itching now.

Her head flopped against Gav's shoulder, and she stared blearily at him. He was a stunning man. She kissed his neck and breathed in his leather and musk scent. Sage looked up into his unique eyes when he stiffened. "You really do have the most beautiful eyes. I think we would have gorgeous babies."

Surprise flashed on his face just before it blurred. Then everything went black.

TWELVE

TEHL

WHEN WILL THIS DAY END?

Demari, the Aermian steward, was currently droning on about expenses for the Midsummer Festival. The budget was already set. Why were they still discussing it? It was times like these that he felt his mother's loss; this had always been her forte.

"Your Highness?"

Tehl snapped out of his thoughts. "Yes, Demari?"

"What colors would you like us to use in the decorations?" His thin steward stared at him, awaiting an answer along with twenty other sets of eyes.

"Colors?" Tehl grimaced and addressed the small crowd. "I don't care, do what you will. I already approved the budget, so if you have questions, ask Demari and he can assist you." The thin and graying steward then smiled at the rest of the household servants. "That will be all." They bowed and scurried after Demari.

It had been such a long day. He'd been sitting in the wooden chair for so long he'd begun to ache. Tehl was inclined to just eat in the private dining room as it was much more comfortable, however, he hadn't eaten with the court in three days, so he'd have to brave the shark-infested waters.

He should've gone to bed; there was absolutely nothing worth his time or attention in this room. Sam and Gav never showed up for dinner, so Tehl found himself surrounded with less than ideal dinner companions. Men and women alike, engaging in droll and vapid conversation. Looking down the table, it seemed only feathers were visible. The reason women dressed to resemble distorted birds eluded him. Where they'd gotten the idea that it was somehow appealing to men remained an even greater mystery.

A hand on his arm forced his attention back to the lady seated at his side. She was leaning toward him with a dress cut so low, he was worried her breasts might actually tumble out of it. Her face wore a practiced smile as her lashes fluttered, her peacock-feathered hairpiece tickling his face. Tehl leaned back and pasted on a smile although the feathers put him in mind of strange antennae. It was ridiculous.

"Your Highness, I had heard tell that you bested a nefarious foe yesterday, and that you fought valiantly despite having sustained injuries. I wanted to be certain you weren't permanently harmed in any way, and should you require anything at all, I would be more than willing to provide assistance." A seductive smile slipped across her face as she stroked his arm and leaned even closer, if that was possible. "I hate to think you might suffer in any way." More eye-batting.

His jaw slackened. Could she possibly be saying what he thought she was saying? He swept his gaze down the table and spotted her father giving him a disturbing smile.

"She is an expert caregiver. I'm sure she'd be at your disposal any time you need."

Was she being thrown at him by *her father*? The Aermian nobility knew the old laws; he'd only marry a commoner which meant this man was, what? Offering his own daughter as a mistress to the crown prince? Filled with revulsion, Tehl's eyes darted back to the girl who continued to eye him. If he ever had a daughter, he wouldn't let a man near her without honorable intentions. And even then, no guarantees. He neither understood nor wanted anything to do with such a dishonorable man.

He covered her hand with his and whispered, "I very much appreciate your concern, but I am well-cared-for by our healers. Good evening." Tehl shoved back his chair and fled, more than happy to leave the sniveling court behind.

When he returned to his chambers, a fire was already crackling in the hearth. He fell more than sat on his bed and painstakingly pulled off his boots, followed by his vest and shirt, tossing them all into a corner. Raising his eyes to the mirror across the room, he warily took stock of his reflection. Well hell, he looked terrible. His skin was black and blue in multiple spots, and the bite on his shoulder looked pretty damn ugly.

A knock sounded at his chamber door, interrupting his thoughts. "Enter," he called.

Sam and Gav entered, looking just as ragged as he did. "Get anything out of her?" Tehl asked, exhausted.

They traded looks before responding. Not a good sign. Sam sat on the corner of Tehl's dresser and propped a leg up. "You first, Gav. I feel like I've talked enough today. Your turn."

Gav grimaced, brushing imaginary lint from his sleeve.

"Not well?" Tehl guessed.

"Your brother used his usual charm, and she played right into him." Gav's expression remained solemn. "She fought us the entire way afterward, and we had to chain her. She'd taken neither food nor water, as per your orders, so Sam offered my ester cider, which she wanted not as she assumed it to be poisoned, but long story short: Sam tried it first, and she was thirsty enough to drink the whole cup."

"You used the serum then? And how did it go? Did it work?" Excitement raced through him. The serum Gav created was a stroke of genius; they'd managed to get even the toughest of men to blubber out their life stories with it.

"Well..." Gavriel seemed unwilling to continue so Sam interrupted:

"It didn't work."

Gav glared at his cousin. "Hey! What happened to me telling the story?"

Sam shrugged. "You were taking too long."

"Wait," Tehl cut in. "What do you mean 'it didn't work'? It's worked on everyone we've tested it on so far."

"Well, I'm sorry to inform you, it didn't work on Miss Ruby." Sam pulled a face. "I drugged her out of her mind, but she never once stumbled or slipped."

"Then what was her story?"

"She said her mother named her Ruby after some necklace she'd stolen. Later, her mum threw her out on the street where she's been supposedly living ever since. She also said her mother is dead and that her brothers are now pirates, and she stole the dagger from a random man about six months ago," Sam finished with a strong dose of skepticism.

"So, why don't you believe her, Sam?" Tehl asked.

Sam stood and began pacing. "First, she doesn't look like a 'Ruby'. I mean she's not even a redhead!"

Sometimes he couldn't follow his brother's logic. Tehl glanced to Gav and his cousin rolled his eyes. "What does red hair have to do with it?"

Sam tossed his hands in the air. "Everything and nothing. I guess that's beside the point, so let's leave it for now. Did either of you notice how her words would change as she spoke? She constantly shifts from proper, educated speech to slang. When I spoke of how the ester was distilled, she had no difficulty following. A child who grew up on the streets, uneducated, would've had more questions and general confusion." Sam paused, considering. "I also found it interesting that she didn't divulge information unless prompted. Generally, after administering the ester, we can't get them to shut up, but not so with this girl. Not once did I have to redirect the conversation."

Tehl looked to Gav for confirmation. "Do you agree?"

"Unfortunately, I do. I've no idea how she lied to us, but I'm certain she did," Gav bit out.

The room fell silent as each contemplated the implications of this.

"How long was your interrogation?" Tehl asked.

"Until she lost consciousness," Sam deadpanned.

"Why the hell did she pass out?" Tehl growled. "That's not even supposed to happen."

"Ask our brooding alchemist."

Tehl arched a midnight eyebrow at his cousin. Gav folded his arms and returned their looks with a scowl. "It was a bit of an overdose. I made adjustments for her smaller size, but somehow it was still too much."

Shrugging, he added, "She's slept the rest of the day, but at least she didn't die or anything."

"I am greatly pleased to hear you didn't kill our solitary tie to the resistance," Tehl said dryly. "So, what now?"

Gav glanced between the two brothers. "It pains me to say this, but I think there may be continued benefit in restrictions on food and water. I'm not interested in hurting the woman, however, I'm also hoping two days of isolation might provide the incentive for her to be more forthcoming."

Tehl looked to Sam. "What do you think? This is, after all, your area or expertise."

Sam shook his head. "Honestly? She'll be a problem no matter what, but I believe Gav's suggestion has merit. She seems to come alive with company so isolation may just do the trick."

"It's settled then. Keep an eye on her, but without her knowledge. Stay out of sight. First, though, go and rest, both of you. You're dead on your feet."

Mumbling their farewells, each departed for his own chamber as Tehl watched the flames dance in the hearth, soothed by the comforting sounds of crackling wood. After a moment, he stripped himself of any remaining clothing and fell into bed with a sigh. Tomorrow would be a better day.

It was too much to hope this day would be an improvement from the last. He'd barely finished breakfast and he already had a list of issues demanding his attention. When he said he didn't care how the festival came together, it seemed no one listened. Who gave a rat's ass if the linens were white or ivory? He certainly didn't. And who knew that the colors in his theme had the potential to either elevate or offend various nobles? What a crock. If a color scheme offended you, then you really had no business representing a kingdom.

In addition to this, it seemed every invitation required his personal signature. After the first hundred, his hand cramped. Shaking it out, he glared at the sea of invitations still taunting him. Groaning, he laid his head on the desk. Was this what his life had come to? Picking colors and signing invitations? He would complete the invitations, and with efficiency, but he briefly allowed himself a moment to indulge in a bit of wallowing.

Suddenly, his door burst open. The noise startled him enough that the pen in his hand scratched a hole in one of his pristine invitations.

"Damn it," he growled, glaring up at the intruder. "Ever heard of knocking? Look what you made me do!" Tehl waved the ink-marred invitation before his brother. "It's ruined. Now I'll have to sign another of these stupid things. I'm going to be here forever."

Oddly enough, Sam had not interrupted his invitation tirade and allowed him to finish before speaking.

"I am sorry, my prince, but I have urgent news."

Tehl sat up taller. His brother rarely used his title and usually only to tease him or when addressing him on matters of great importance. "What is it?"

"I've just received word that the Scythians have broken their borders and attacked. This time, however, they did not return to their own borders, and have instead set up camp in Silva."

All color drained from Tehl's face. "What of the people?"

"They took care of anyone capable of resisting and enslaved the rest. If those captives cross their border, there's no chance of recovery. As Silva's a farming community, no garrison is stationed there. What would you have me do?"

Tehl's fists clenched, his voice hard. "It seems they're looking for war. I will not allow my people to suffer and die in Scythia. What are the enemy numbers?"

"My current information says around twenty-five soldiers."

"Gather a company from the Elite, and we can depart immediately."

Sam shook his head. "I believe we would be better off if you stayed. We ought not risk both of our country's princes at once. If things go south, we need someone to handle things here."

Tehl shot up and placed both hands on the desk. "I understand your concerns, but these are my people and they need me. My place is not sitting here, waiting. I will fight for them, you know this."

Sam studied him and nodded. "I will ready the men."

"Please saddle Wraith."

"It will be done."

Spinning on his heel, Sam departed. Tehl stared after him, trying to calm the fury that had overtaken him. It was the Scythians. He loathed any dealing with the damned kingdom. They were barbaric warmongers. Dark eyes, dark hair, and olive skin characterized the entire nation, not because of some geographic isolation but rather owing to their disturbing practice of removing any born who did not fit the established standard. Even contemplating it had Tehl's stomach turning sour.

He strode to the armory, determined to strike fear into their dark hearts. No one attacked his people and got away with it.

THIRTEEN

TEHL

AS THE COMPANY MADE THEIR way to the border, Tehl observed the passing countryside with appreciation. The rolling fields had always enchanted him as a boy whenever they rode this way. The golden wheat gleamed and swayed in the wind, almost as if it waved a greeting as they galloped by.

His eyes wandered to his brother riding beside him. He looked to be made of stone, his expression severe and his jaw set. It was hard to believe this was the same man with whom he'd joked and teased the previous night.

"Are you going to stare at me the entire way?" Sam asked without even sparing a glance in Tehl's direction.

"I wasn't staring at you," he fibbed.

"Sure you were." Though he continued to scrutinize the landscape, the corners of Sam's lips tipped ever so slightly heavenward.

Mollified at having achieved at least a little reaction, Tehl changed the subject.

"How long 'til we arrive?" It had been a long time since he was near Silva.

Sam squinted at the sun and then to the forest. "We have a couple hours until we get into position, but it will be dark before we reach the trees. After that, it will be slow going once we enter the forest." Sam's voice drifted over the thunder of hooves toward Tehl.

Tehl nodded and focused back on the trail ahead.

When they finally reached the forest boundary, only a sliver of the sun remained over the western mountains. Sam slowed his mount and raised a fist, signaling all to slow their approach. The company followed at a trot as he led them to a small creek and dismounted, gesturing for the Elite to follow suit.

As Tehl swung off Wraith, he was stopped short by a sharp pain in his calf. *Damn leg cramps.*

Carefully, he flexed his foot back and forth until the pain subsided. Stepping from his horse, Tehl stretched, clicking his neck and back.

Sam, noticing Tehl's discomfort, sauntered over with a grin. "Stiff, brother?"

"I'm sure that's what Daisy asked you last night," Tehl shot back.

Sam whistled. "Two innuendos in a week. I think I might finally be rubbing off on you."

"Let's hope not," Tehl retorted, attempting to gnaw a hunk of dried venison.

Sam grimaced. "That's disgusting! For God's sake, close your mouth. Our tutors beat matters of etiquette into us, so how is it you've retained such an awful set of manners?"

Tehl responded by opening his mouth and displaying more chewed food. "Does it look like there's anyone to impress out here? I'm pretty sure the men and the horses don't care, so I'll eat however I damn well please." He finished his tirade by shooting a meat-filled grin in Sam's direction and, though he obviously fought it, his brother's lip still twitched. He loved that about Sam; no matter their situation, he never lost his sense of humor.

Sam rifled through his saddlebags, eventually producing a canteen, which they shared, the cool water refreshing them after their hard ride. Tehl closed his eyes and inhaled deeply, enjoying the crispness of the evening air, but paused when something familiar tickled his nose, stirring up childhood memories. Glancing around, he noticed the forest floor was littered with little herbs. With a soft smile, he bent down, skimming his fingers across the ruffled leaf. Lemon balm. His mum had always kept it in her solar, so wherever she went, the scent clung to her skin and garments. Sam squatted next to him, mirroring his smile. Tehl broke off a leaf and passed it to his brother. Sam rubbed the leaf and brought it to his nose.

"Smells like Mum."

Tehl nodded, no other words needed. He leaned back and stared at the night sky. A few stars had appeared, shining like diamonds on blue silk. In the distance, he could see the fields of wheat had softened from the brilliant gold of day to a soft silver in the waning light.

Sam too peered up at the sky and muttered, "It's time. I'd prefer to have the moon for a bit of light but we'd best head out now." Standing, he commanded the company: "Prepare to depart."

Sam eyed his men with pride as they followed his orders with efficiency, each checking their tack and gear before mounting up. They were ready within moments.

"Listen up," Sam called. "You all know how many lives depend on the success of this mission, so I'm sure I need not tell you how essential a soundless approach is. Be alert. It's going to be a tedious few hours, so prepare yourselves."

Sam then kneed his mount forward, approaching the tree line.

Tehl noted that, in the faded light, the shadows of the forest seemed a bit sinister. As a boy, he always treasured this forest; the trees stretched their limbs over him like giant protectors. Tonight, though, they seemed more like reapers, limbs reaching to steal your life from your body.

Sam raised a hand and motioned, signaling the company forward. Tehl directed Wraith beneath the leafy canopy and tried to shrug off the feeling of foreboding creeping over him. They would do their best and hopefully it'd be enough.

Wraith sensed his unease and tossed his head, sidestepping, so Tehl forced himself to relax. Unclenching his hands, he tried to shake the tension from them and ran a soothing hand along Wraith's glossy neck.

Ahead, Sam stopped, raising a fist. Everyone froze, scanning the darkened woods around them. Silently, Sam dismounted.

"The village is not far from here. The Scythians are camped out in the town's center with the survivors being held slightly north in an old silo." Sam's eyes shifted to three men right of Tehl. "Jethro, Garreth, and Sethen: accompany the Crown and make your way toward the prisoners, but be cautious. The Scythians have already made it clear that if any step out of line, the silo will be burnt to the ground along with everyone inside."

Shocked, the Elite whispered curses of outrage to one another.

"Be certain every Scythian is dealt with." Sam looked each man in the eye. "Form your groups. I'll lead from the east, Jaxon from the south and Luchas from the north. Stealth is our ally. Execute this both swiftly and silently, but await my signal to begin our strike on the square. Fight honorably for Aermia's people, and I'll see you all on the other side."

Tehl slipped from Wraith's back and clasped his brother's arm. Sam gave him a crooked grin. "Don't die. I'd really hate to take your place, forced to sit for hours through all those bloody meetings."

Tehl mirrored his brother's grin. "You don't need to worry about me." Releasing his brother, Tehl addressed Jethro, Garreth, and Sethen. "Let's rid ourselves of these animals before they have a chance to hurt anymore of our people." Each nodded, exchanging feral grins, eyes lit in anticipation.

"Let's go."

FOURTEEN

SAGE

SAGE BLINKED AND RUBBED HER eyes, trying to clear the sleep from them, though they felt like a bag of sand had been poured over them. Her tongue, thick and dry, stuck to the roof of her mouth. She lifted her head and surveyed herself but was surprised to see nothing was tying her down. Why weren't her arms and legs moving? Squinting at the stone wall across from her, she tried to remember what had happened. Slowly, little pieces of yesterday resurfaced in her mind. A cup full of apple cider…violet eyes…and blond curls.

They'd drugged her, *again*.

How long had she been out? Minutes? Hours? How much time had she lost? Her breathing picked up as her heart pounded. She was panicking, which was pointless.

Calm down, you're okay.

The drugs were still in effect so it mustn't have been long since they were administered. Hence, they'd likely wear off after a short time; she needed to be patient. Sage dropped her head back on the cot and began counting the gray stones in the ceiling to pass the time. At around stone one hundred and seventy, her eyes became heavy, and she finally dropped off.

Sage jerked awake and bolted upright, painfully jostling her ribs as she did so. The sudden movement also had the dark room spinning around her. Her entire body was sticky and over-warm. Panting, she placed her fist to her mouth, wanting to retch from the various unsavory smells that seemed to be pressing in on her. Sage grimaced and leaned against the wall, the cool stone bringing relief to the heat in her feverish skin.

Pale moonlight now shone through the bars of the small window. She'd slept quite a while, but at least it meant the truth serum had worn off. She noticed a small tin cup glinting in the dim lighting, and she remembered how dry her throat was. With a groan, she hoisted herself off the bed and staggered a few steps to pick it up. Her legs shook, threatening to collapse. Sage tried not to spill a drop of the precious liquid as she stumbled back to the bed. She needed a healer.

Just as she was about to bring the cup to her lips, it occurred to her that something could be amiss with it. She sat, debating whether to drink it or not. She swirled the water in the cup and eyed it. Sage dipped one finger into the cup, tasted a drop and then waited.

Nothing.

She didn't know how much time had passed since she drank the cider, but she was definitely suffering the effects of dehydration. She needed to drink this. But was it worth taking the chance of being drugged again? She'd never been helpless before yesterday, and it wasn't a feeling she relished. This time, Sage sniffed the cup, just to see if she detected anything out of the ordinary, but she smelled nothing. Her tests so far didn't mean it was safe to drink, but she couldn't survive without water, so she'd have to take the chance. Sage brought the cup to her parched lips and she took a small sip, letting it wet her mouth and soothe her dry throat. She took another small sip, trying not to gulp it all down at once. She decided it was enough for now and hid the now half-empty cup beneath her cot. Who knew when she would receive more?

Sage's stomach cramped and let out a large growl. It seemed the water had awakened her appetite. When had she eaten last? What day was it?

Don't focus on it, think of something else.

Instead, she tried to recall everything she had told the commander during the drug-induced interrogation. She needed to keep her story straight or they'd hang her with it. The memory of it was still a blur, but Sage was fairly certain she hadn't revealed anything important.

A frigid breeze floated off the ocean and through her cell window, caressing her overheated skin. The room was freezing, but she felt as if she was sitting beneath the sun. Her linen shirt clung to her skin in a sticky mess. Was this an after-effect of the concoction they'd given her? Or was she actually ill? Sage examined her wrists. Already, they were swollen and tender to the touch. Angry red lines mapped her wrists. Sage winced. She didn't doubt an infection was starting.

Her head pounded like someone had kicked it, so, rubbing her temples, she lay on her side, cradling her head in one arm. Hopefully, with a little rest, she would sleep off the pain. Vaguely, she was aware of metal clanging nearby, but didn't rouse enough to open her eyes. Damn noisy prisoners.

Out of nowhere, a strong hand covered her mouth while other hands clasped her ankles, sufficiently rousing her from her daze. Her eyes flew open, and she found herself surrounded by four strangers. She tried to jerk from their grasp but, in her current state, was too weak to accomplish anything. The man whose hand enveloped her face yanked her head back with her hair, bringing her to him. His rancid breath washed over her as he leaned closer. "You sure are a pretty little thing underneath all those bruises, aren't ya?"

She glared at him and bit down as hard as she could. He yanked his hand back, cursing her. "Vicious little wench!" he spat.

She bared her teeth in response.

"Get her up, and quickly. I have pressing matters to attend to," remarked a tall man with a haughty voice.

Sage bucked her hips, trying to dislodge the bruising fingers pressed into her skin, until a massive fist hammered into the side of her face. Tears pricked her eyes as everything blurred and darkness swirled around her. Sage shook her head, trying to focus, but only succeeded in nauseating herself.

Tight metal cuffs encased her wrists, and her body swung through the air. Sage's ribs screamed as someone wrenched her arms above her head. Her body dropped painfully, the restraints biting into her already sensitive wrists. Her toes brushed the floor as she scrambled for purchase.

Sage dropped her chin to her chest, heaving in a breath as she tried not to retch. She stared at the grate below her and thought grimly that it wasn't for waste but to wash away the crimes of this room.

Shiny, brown leather boots interrupted her study of the floor. Sage lifted her head and met the eyes of the man who was no doubt her executioner. His primary characteristic was his unusual height—he had to be at least five inches over six feet. Apart from that, though, he seemed rather ordinary: brown hair, brown eyes. Utterly forgettable. Not what she'd pictured death to look like.

"What do you want from me?" she croaked. "I've already told Commander Samuel everything." Sweat dripped from her temples into her eyes.

"The commander didn't think you were entirely honest with him, so here I am." He stepped up to her with cold eyes and fingered her sweat-soaked shirt. He watched her face as he languidly slid his hand from her ribs to the hollow of her waist and then to her hip. Her blood froze in her veins as a cruel smile crossed his face.

"Men's clothing? Interesting choice. So improper. You have to know the ideas you inspire when you showcase your body in such a manner." He squeezed her hip. "I am sure your mother wouldn't approve."

"I wouldn't know, she's dead," she replied.

"Now, now. Let's not lie to each other. Wouldn't want to start our relationship with lies, would we?"

He dropped his hand, reaching for the blade sheath at his waist. Her eyes tracked his movements as he removed the knife from its sheath. She would stay calm. She would not allow them the satisfaction of breaking her. He brought the blade to her face and scraped the sharp edge to where her pulse hammered in her neck.

"Let's start this again, shall we? My name is Serge. I will ask you a question. You will answer me—truthfully, I might add—or there will be consequences."

Sage tried to remain as still as possible. One flick of his wrist and she would bleed out in seconds.

"What is your name?"

"M-my name is Ruby." She held her breath, awaiting his next move.

He lifted his lips in a mocking smile and replied sarcastically, "I appreciate your honesty."

He moved his dagger from her neck to the opening of her linen shirt, catching it with the blade. He flicked his wrist, and her shirt fluttered open. Embarrassment and rage battled inside her, but she stamped both emotions down. If she gave them one inkling of her feelings, she knew they'd run with it. She could show no fear.

Sage raised her chin and gave Serge her haughtiest and most disdainful look.

"Oh! I can be so clumsy sometimes," he whispered. Leering, he leaned forward and placed the knife tip between her leather trousers and hip. With another tug, it cut through them like butter and they fell flimsily to the floor. Even the pain radiating through her body wasn't enough to distract her from the embarrassment of being stripped in front of four men. Their eyes crawled over her skin like insects, leaving goosebumps in their wake. Sage focused on a stone behind him and steeled herself. She would *not* show fear.

The tall man pushed away the shirt from her stomach with the tip of his dagger and seemed to survey each mark or bruise marring her torso.

"The crown prince knows how to punch. A pity that your beauty had to be marred by his hands." He grinned, which only made him look more deranged, and clapped his hands once. "Next question, what do you do for the resistance?"

"I've already said I don't know what you're talking about. I didn't even know about the resistance until the commander spoke with me. What would the resistance want with an orphan? I don't have any skills to offer."

"Not quite what I was looking for."

He ran his eyes down her legs and back up her thighs. He caressed the front of her legs with his rough fingers, and she couldn't contain a shudder of revulsion.

Serge raised his eyebrows. "This appears to be the only spot untouched. Probably the best place to leave my mark." Lazily, he slashed along the front of her left thigh. Pain exploded in her leg, and she hissed out a breath but maintained a blank face.

He cocked his head with a smirk. "I do enjoy symmetry."

After a moment, the pain in her leg worsened, burning like hell. Her whole body trembled, and she bit back a whimper as blood dripped down her leg.

Time passed, and Serge continued his line of questioning. He also proved to be a sadistic bastard. Sage drifted in and out of consciousness until a sharp crack across her face whipped her head to the side, her face throbbing in time with her heartbeat. Serge grabbed her hair and yanked back her head, and his other hand wrapped around her neck with a squeeze.

"No falling asleep on me, dear."

"I am no one's 'dear'," she choked out, her swollen lips making speech difficult.

"Your fire is incredible," Serge mused, "and I rather enjoy the idea of breaking you. Perhaps I'll keep you around as a mistress."

"Not on your life," she spat vehemently, throwing every last bit of energy she had into the words. "I would die first." His smile dropped as hers appeared.

"That can be arranged, *dear*," he sneered, tightening his grip on her neck.

Sage tried to suck in a breath, but none came. She would die after all. She hoped her family would be okay without her.

Her thoughts were interrupted when someone shouted, and suddenly, the pressure on her neck disappeared. She sucked in a breath—only to cough so hard she was sure her lungs were coming out.

Someone wrapped their arms around her waist and lifted her off her wrists. Like a fire, pain consumed her entire body. She opened her mouth to cry out, but only choked on it, instead emitting a shaky wheeze. The fetters were peeled from her wrists and her arms flopped limply to her side.

What was happening? Sage peered up and saw amid the swirling room two spots of violet. "Gav?" she coughed out. Did she already die?

The purple eyes stared down at her, concerned, and a deep voice pleaded with her to stay awake. "Ruby? Keep your eyes open for me, darling."

He gently pushed her bloody hair from her face and gave her a gentle smile. The purple eyes left her and the voice snapped at someone else. Another voice answered just as sharply, and that voice too seemed familiar, only at the moment she couldn't place it.

A ghoulish figure appeared above her. A specter with silvery hair, gray eyes, and a myriad of wrinkles.

She must have died. Nobody looking like that would exist in this world.

The voices seemed to urge her to do something, but she couldn't understand what. Their words faded as her pulse pounded and lights dotted her vision, followed by darkness. Smiling, she gave into the blessed void of nothingness.

FİFTEEN

TEHL

TEHL SAT, WATCHİNG AS THE sun peaked over the horizon. As its rays shed a dusky light on the ashen silo before him, his thoughts returned to the events that had transpired the night before…

Initially, all had gone smoothly. They'd been well prepared. Between Jethro, Garreth, Sethen, and himself, they'd managed to subdue the Scythian guards. It happened with such unusual ease that it both surprised and troubled him.

He was not prepared, however, for what greeted him as they broke open the silo. Tehl had halted as the stenches of urine, body odor, and blood assaulted him. Filthy women, children, and the elderly trembled on the ground, terror evident in their eyes. The children whimpered, hiding themselves within the skirts of their mothers. All bore evidence of the Scythian's cruelty, each one bruised and battered. His heart broke within his chest, simultaneously growing hot with rage. They would not get away with committing such atrocities.

"Peace," he whispered. "We mean you no harm. We are here to free you from this prison. My men and I are removing the Scythians to ensure your safety." At his words, some burst into tears while others seemed to say prayers under their breaths.

"Safety?" an incredulous voice cut through the air.

Tehl searched the group of villagers for the owner of the voice. He stopped when he saw a young woman kneeling with two small children. She stood to face him with narrowed eyes. She was a tiny thing; he doubted the top of her head reached even his shoulder, yet her chin jutted out defiantly and her fists clenched. She was the owner of the angry voice.

"Does it look like we're safe?" she hissed, gesturing to the people. "Where were *you* two days ago? *You* let this happen, *you...*" She swallowed and continued roughly: "*You* let our loved ones die."

An older woman placed a hand on the girl's shoulder. "Dear one, don't blame these men. That's simply not fair. They didn't harm us. They are here to help."

Lips tight with anger, the young woman shook her head and stabbed a finger at him. "No! What isn't fair is that our king didn't protect us! And now? Now our families are gone forever." She blinked rapidly, fighting back tears, and glared.

"I am sorry for your loss," Tehl offered, hating how generic his words sounded. He meant it, every word.

She dropped her head. "That won't bring them back." The young woman sucked in a breath and pinned him with eyes full of unshed tears. "Finish this," she growled. "Not one of them deserves to live."

"Never fear on that account, lady. It will be done." Tehl's promise was sincere and deadly.

She'd studied him a moment and dipped her chin in dismissal. The young woman scooped up the little ones at her feet and buried her face in the downy fuzz blanketing their heads.

Tehl had grappled with himself. He wanted to rage through the village, destroying anything Scythian he could get his hands on. Turning to his men, he registered his own shock and anger mirrored in their faces—clearly, they too were struggling with this.

He had turned back to the villagers and offered the group a smile meant to inspire confidence. "Stay here until we come for you and don't worry; you're safe now."

An unladylike snort exploded out of the young woman. Her blue-gray eyes locked onto him. "Mmhmm. Because we have been *so* safe here previously!" she mumbled. "Are you really going to leave us defenseless? Without even weapons?"

Tehl reached into his boot. Plucking out a dagger, he held the hilt out to her. "You do know how to use one of these?"

She scowled at him as she passed one child to the elderly woman beside her. "I am well acquainted with daggers, thank you."

"Good. Do you require anything else, my lady?"

She ran her finger along the blade and a ghost of a smile touched her lips. "No, that will be all, I'm sure."

A smile tugged at his lips. She was feisty, in a way, reminding him a bit of Sam. "What's your name?"

"Jasmine, my lord," she tacked on the title with a bow, or as much of one as she could execute with a small child on her hip. It seemed her anger toward him had waned, a little.

Sethen stepped inside. "The commander has signaled."

Tehl jerked his chin at Jasmine. "Protect your people." Her eyes widened as he spun on his heel and moved from the doorway.

Jethro brushed his dirty blond hair from his eyes and whispered, "They're southeast of the center. We need to move if we want to catch them."

Their group rushed through the village, stepping over fallen Scythians at every turn. His brother had obviously moved quickly. Stealthily as well—there'd been no sounds of battle. As they approached the town's center they halted, remaining hidden in the shadows while Jethro called out a signal. Some of his tension left his body when they heard his brother's answering call.

As Tehl and his men approached the fire-lit square, he saw five Scythians kneeling on the ground before his brother, surrounded by the Elite. Samuel, who had been pacing, paused when he caught sight of them and then strolled up to Tehl, feigning casualty. His tension returned, followed by a healthy dose of adrenaline. Something was wrong.

"We have a problem."

A short statement—and not one that boded well.

"There are Scythians in the trees across the river, over the Mort Wall, observing us, yet so far they have done nothing to come to the aid of their kin." His brother jerked his head toward their captives. "I can't put my finger on it, but something is wrong. They were defeated far too easily."

That gave Tehl a real pause. Scythians were notorious for fighting until death rather than be taken captive. Their soldiers were not trained to be passive. He squinted over Sam's shoulder at the brawny group of warriors, their dark eyes staring back seemingly void of all emotion. His brother was right, something was amiss in this situation.

"A trap?"

"No," Sam said in a low tone. "The area has been scouted and there are no others. It seems those watching from the Scythian riverside are alone."

Tehl scanned the dense forest for any hint of the soldiers his brother spoke of but could detect no signs of movement, not until the moonlight caught the tip of an arrow. Why hadn't they attacked? He and his men were within the archer's range. What were they waiting for?

Tehl caught his brother's eye and spoke under his breath. "Maybe we should give them a show and draw them out?"

Sam nodded, and Tehl stalked toward the line of warriors, halting just before them. They were truly giants of men. He himself was a tall man, but a few of them topped him by five inches. In addition, each man wore his long black hair exactly the same: knotted back with bone and feathers. The skin of their faces was so flawless it seemed unreal, almost like they'd been hewn from stone.

Unnatural.

Tehl suppressed a shudder. It was actually what led to Scythia's exile from the rest of the world: an unhealthy obsession with perfection—more specifically the perfect warrior—and these statues, kneeling dark-eyed and motionless before him, served as proof that their obsession had not been abandoned.

He moved down the row inspecting each man, noting the swirling designs painted on their skin and their multiple piercings. Coming upon the last one though, Tehl froze.

Not a man. A woman.

Beneath the myriad of scrawling designs, her bronze skin glistened in the firelight. She dropped her head, sending her midnight braid slithering down her back. Tehl stepped closer and grabbed hold of it, giving it a rough tug.

Her face tipped upward, exposing blank, black eyes tipped up at the corners. He'd never before seen a Scythian woman. He understood them to be guarded jealously by their men. Her face sported sharp, high cheekbones with arched brows and a pouty lower lip. She was a beautiful woman, no doubt about it.

"They're sending women to do warriors' work now?"

Silence met his question.

No response, not even a flicker in her eyes.

Tehl lifted his eyes to the forest, he shouted across the river. "There is no need for hiding. We are warriors, not spies. Tell me, where is your honor?" He dropped the woman's braid, holding his breath. Would they take the bait? His eyes darted to the woman and again to the riverside. Eight warriors had emerged from the forest and now stood on the riverbank. An enormous warrior stood at the forefront, regarding them steadily, his black hair hanging down his bare chest.

"Have you nothing to say?" Tehl asked, lifting a brow.

The massive warrior took a step forward and spoke, his deep, accented voice rumbling across the river. "What would you have me say? I was rather enjoying the little show. Don't stop on our account."

'Don't stop on our account.' That statement alone revealed quite a bit. They were unconcerned with his treatment of their captive kin. So why were they here? Tehl's mind ran several scenarios but none seemed to fit.

His brother cleared his throat. "I wasn't aware it was a show we put on." Sam turned and addressed the captured warriors. "You hear that? They care nothing for you. Your own brethren would stand by while you die and enjoy it."

"In death there is honor," was her short reply.

His brother cocked his head, studying the female Scythian and Tehl wondered what he was about. Sam sauntered over to cup her chin, tilting her face first to the left, then to the right.

"Women—always more emotional creatures. You can't even beat it out of them," he spoke just loud enough for his words to carry across the river. "Isn't she beautiful, brother? And so exotic! Look at those cheekbones and plush lips. She could make a man very happy." Sam's gaze skated down her leather breastplate and rested on her flared hips. "And those hips!" Sam whistled. "Perfect for having children. Maybe I should take her as my layman."

Foreign curses and growled threats erupted around them.

Tehl grinned to himself. Leave it to Sam. His brother was playing on the enemy's purist beliefs, for Scythians were sickened more by 'mixed breeding', as they called it, than by death. The man had a devious mind.

Brilliant. Absolutely brilliant.

"I think she could bear you many strong sons," he agreed in a casual tone, as though speaking of the weather. "You and I both know you'd benefit from a few spare heirs."

Finally, the large warrior spoke up. "These men do not concern me, but they chose to cross the Mort Wall and have broken our law. They are now criminals, so I leave their lives in your hands, but we deal differently with our women. Give her to me, and we will depart from Aermia."

Lies. "You mean to tell me the warlord of Scythia had no knowledge of this attack?" Tehl asked, his voice hard.

"This was not sanctioned."

Tehl didn't believe him for one second; they'd been pillaging Aermian lands for months and it was not the work of a ragtag band of thieves, either. Each attack had been executed with military precision. Obviously, they weren't simply thieves and murderers, but liars as well.

"I think not." Sam's smile was frosty. "The woman is mine now. I will release the other warriors, and if they make it across the river tied up, they're yours to deal with."

Samuel nodded to his men and, brusquely, the Elite hefted up the warriors one by one, pushing them into the flowing water. The first immediately sank without resurfacing. The other three labored across, and the first to reach the bank struggled to his feet only to be struck with an arrow to the chest. Tehl's breath whistled out of him as the other two met the same fate.

"Well that's *one* way to deal with disobedience," Sam remarked, disinterestedly.

The warrior shrugged a shoulder. "If they were caught, they're not worthy, anyway. However, it is in your best interest to release the girl, so I suggest you do so."

Sam shook his head with an arrogant smile.

The warrior nodded curtly. "So be it."

They melted back into the forest as silently as they had appeared. He scrutinized them as they disappeared, the warrior's parting words ringing in Tehl's head. They bore a note of finality, of warning: tonight's actions would bring consequences. But what was done, was done. They'd have to deal with whatever came of it later.

Sam squatted next to him, facing the woman. "You're important; care to enlighten me as to why?" he asked.

She set her jaw and stared through his brother.

"Yeah, I figured as much." Sam looked to Sethen and Garreth. "She is now your responsibility. Make sure she is not harmed and cannot escape." His brother turned back to the woman and trailed a finger down her cheek. "How do you fit into the puzzle, my dear?"

The Scythian woman jerked her face away and continued to ignore him.

Tehl blinked, having been pulled from the previous night's memory by the snapping of a branch. Looking up, he saw the fiery woman from the silo pushing through the tall grass. She reached where he was sitting, and she slumped onto a nearby fallen log. The girl pulled his blade from a sheath at her waist and held it out to him.

"No, keep it." he muttered, returning his attention to the village. She neither spoke nor made a move to leave. Curious, Tehl glanced at her from the corner of his eye, only to catch her staring at him.

"What?" he asked, irritated by the intrusion; he'd been enjoying the silence.

"Thank you. I mean, for the blade... I have never owned anything so fine." She opened her mouth to continue before closing it again. After a pause, she sucked in a deep breath, continuing, "Look. I am sorry for the way I spoke to you last night, my lord. Had I had known it was the crown prince to whom I spoke, I would have shown more respect." She again paused. "No, that's a lie. I'd have spoken the same way, but I have been informed there could be dire consequences if I don't apologize, so..." She trailed off and shrugged.

His lips twitched at her rather blunt confession.

"There will be no punishment, Jasmine. You were upset and angry." He allowed his amusement to bleed into his voice as he spoke. "The Crown can spare you, this time at least."

Her shoulders slumped, and her breath whooshed out. "Oh. Good then. I...I have to think about more than myself now."

He remembered the two small children clinging to her the night before. "You lost your husband?" He winced at how tactless that sounded.

Sorrow shrouded her features. "No." She shook her head. "I lost my brother and his wife, my only living relatives. So their twins are mine now."

"How old are they?"

"They just turned two years. I doubt they will remember anything of their parents when they're grown, only my stories of them."

Tehl sympathized; he of all people knew how painful it was to lose family. She pushed her dark brown hair from her face with a watery smile. His eyes narrowed as he scanned her face, realization dawning. Her skin hardly creased, even when smiling. She must be very young. Not much younger than himself. "Exactly how old are *you*? Your face, it's smooth. You can't be over twenty years."

"Has anyone ever told you how blunt you are?" He shrugged, and she sniggered. "I will be nineteen years next week."

She was too young to raise babes alone. How would they survive the winter? Did she even have a place to live? Tehl decided he would arrange matters so that the little family would be taken care of. As he thought, he turned his gaze back to Silva, making a mental list of all the things the villagers would need to rebuild. The remaining farmers and his Elite were already working to clean up the damage. As usual, Sam stood in the middle of it, heading the efforts. His brother looked up and caught his eye. He handed off his shovel and strode their way.

It was time to get to work. Tehl stood stiffly and offered a hand to Jasmine.

"Thank you, my lord." Taking his hand, she stood, groaning and rolling her neck. She spared him a glance and a quick smile before focusing on Sam's approaching figure. "Quite the old pair we make."

Sam's smile widened as he glanced from his brother to Jasmine, eyes lighting up at the sight of her. "And who might this lovely woman be?" Sam flirted with a wink.

Her soft smile dissolved into a scowl.

Samuel took her hand and kissed her knuckles. "I am happy to make your acquaintance, fair lady. I am Commander Samuel of the Elite. And you are?"

Jasmine jerked her hand from his and wiped it on her skirt, disgusted, muttering something about slobber. Tehl smirked at his brother's odd expression. He couldn't tell if Sam was amused or offended by her reaction.

"It's not that easy to scrub me from your skin, my lady," Samuel teased. Jasmine simply raised her eyes and glared.

Her temper rose, and Tehl's smile widened. Jasmine would put Sam in his place, he could tell. And boy, did she not disappoint.

"I would appreciate it if you kept your hands, and lips, to yourself. Please refrain from touching my person in any way," Jasmine fumed. "I am sure this comes as a shock, but not all women appreciate your kind of attention."

Well, that *was* a first. He'd never seen Sam shot down. One point to Jasmine.

Sam brushed it off, though, dismissing Jasmine. "We relocated the people of Silva because of the burned homes. I plan on leaving a few Elite here until the Guard arrives to help with rebuilding. The Mort Wall has weakened, it'd be prudent to establish a post here; thus, Silva will always be protected."

Tehl was about to reply when Jasmine muttered, "Because you did such an amazing job before…"

Sam stiffened and gave the girl a cold look. "You know nothing of war, little girl. I suggest you gaze around your Scythian-free home before casting judgments."

Jasmine flushed with anger. "You know what I see? Loss. Loss of my family, my friends, and my life; and all because you didn't protect us. Our homes were burned to the ground while we were beaten and starved. I lost every member of my family, save the twins, becoming a mother in one night. And you," she seethed, "let the brutes responsible go free."

Samuel's face softened. "They died. Nothing is more final than that. Those Scythians departed from this world; they can't hurt anyone anymore."

"They should have suffered, just like the rest of us have. We will feel the effects of their attack for years." She stepped forward and poked Samuel in the chest. "That is on you!"

"What you're feeling will also pass." Sam's gaze held compassion.

She dropped her eyes and turned her back on him. Jasmine stepped forward and curtsied deeply. "Thank you for the gift. I won't forget your kindness and help." She pushed passed Sam and hustled toward the village square.

Samuel frowned after her. "You never told me your name," Sam shouted. His brother could never leave well enough alone.

Jasmine peeked over her shoulder. "You don't need it."

Tehl turned toward him, a smug grin plastered on his face. "You know what? I don't think she liked you, Sam."

His brother was still watching the young woman walk away. He ran a frustrated hand through his blond curls, but quickly shifted, sending a cocky smile his brother's way. "She experienced something horrific. It wasn't me."

Tehl glanced at the petite brunette now smiling at Jaxon. "No, that woman despises you. She didn't act that way toward me or Jaxon." He pointed out Jaxon smiling as Jasmine giggled.

Sam's face darkened as he spied the exchange. When he noticed Tehl's interest, his face blanked. "She has horrible taste in men, especially if she had this remarkable specimen," he said, motioning from his shoulder to his toes, "before her and still chose Jaxon."

He rolled his eyes at his little brother and shook his head. His eyes swept over the ruined village once more, the smile falling from his face, now sobered. "What happened last night...," he paused, gathering his thoughts. "Something was not right, Sam. No one has ever taken one of them prisoner. *No one,* Sam. It doesn't feel right."

Sam nodded as Tehl spoke. "I've been thinking the same thing. We may have had the element of surprise, but that doesn't account for them laying their weapons down. Neither did they resist nor speak when we restrained them. I had been prepared for some kind of trap, but then nothing happened. When we discovered the warriors across the river, I thought for sure they'd ambush us and that perhaps that was the plan all along." His brother stared at the log behind him in thought. "Yet, all they did was stand there! It makes little sense. Who sits back and watches their kin get dragged away? Also, those warriors didn't even care, and that is dangerous. Why would they only react to my taunt to their woman?" Sam paced as he continued to work through his thoughts. He covered his face with a hand and took a deep breath through his nose and paused. After a moment, he dropped his hand in frustration. "We've more questions now than we did prior!"

Tehl waited for Sam to finish venting his frustration. Sam barked out a harsh laugh as he stabbed a finger Tehl's way. "And the nerve! You and I both know those warriors weren't rogue. Scythia sent them here for a purpose, I just don't know why. Another damn piece of the puzzle missing," Sam huffed.

"We will figure it out," Tehl replied, placing a hand on his brother's shoulder. "At least we have someone that might shed more light on the situation in Scythia. You got her to respond to you last night; you can do so again. But currently there are other pressing needs. These people need our immediate care and focus."

Sam sighed and nodded. "It would be best if we left two teams here for rebuilding and protection until the Guard arrive." He eyed the surrounding destruction as they returned to the village.

"What of their thane?" Tehl asked.

"They have no protector or keep near. They have always reported to Sanee."

"What?" Tehl frowned. Without a thane, or a post, the people of Silva were left vulnerable. They needed the protection more than any other area, as they were right on the Scythian border. Tehl glared at the destroyed homes; every time he felt he'd gotten his feet under him, something set him off balance again. "Gather those set to return with us and inform them we depart in half an hour."

Sam nodded once and strode toward the Elite, already barking out orders. Tehl rolled his kinked neck. It was no wonder his father was driven mad after his mother died. Running a kingdom by yourself was difficult. He had a rebellion to deal with, a Midsummer Festival to plan, and Scythians breathing down his neck. Tehl sighed and straightened up. He could do this. He would do this. He just needed to take it one day at a time.

SİXTEEN

TEHL

WHEN THE TALL GRAY TURRETS came into view, Tehl breathed out a sigh of relief. Between his lack of sleep and hours of hard riding, he was sufficiently worn out. It seemed like he'd only blinked and they'd arrived at the inner courtyards. He rubbed his eyes hard. Had he fallen asleep? No, he didn't think so, but he sure didn't remember the last leg of their journey. Tehl brought Wraith to a halt and dropped to the ground. The moment his feet hit the dirt, he groaned—everything in his body seemed to ache. Ruefully, he stretched his lower extremities, chiding himself. He needed to ride more often. He'd been spending too much time in the city.

Leaning against the saddle, he gingerly ran a hand down Wraith's sweaty neck, whispering praise to the exhausted beast. Wraith cocked an ear, listening as his master spoke. Tehl stroked the downy nose softly and stumbled back a step as Wraith bumped him in the chest with it.

"I know buddy, time to cool down, but don't worry, afterward it'll be oats and carrots for you." Tehl could have sworn Wraith smiled in response. With a smile of his own, he gave a farewell pat to the horse as a young stable boy sporting an unruly mop of orange hair collected the reins and led him away.

Tehl glanced back to the company and saw his brother discretely issuing instructions to Garreth and Jethro, after which two Elite came and collected the Scythian woman, no doubt carting her off to the dungeon.

Returning to Tehl's side, Sam gave him a brief report. "Everything is being taken care of, my lord. Supplies and men are already on their way to Silva. We'll attempt to obtain whatever we can from the female warrior. I'll update you in the morning with anything we learn over the course of tonight."

Tehl nodded. He was more than ready to rid himself of his armor and be done with this day.

He returned to the castle. The lanterns lining its interior walls scattered distorted shadows along the dimly lit corridors and illuminated a figure approaching him from the far end of the hall. It wasn't until the figure neared that he noticed a familiar set of purple eyes. Gavriel. His cousin met him in the middle. Tehl clapped a hand on his cousin's shoulder in greeting and motioned for him to follow.

"Walk with me." Together, they moved toward the royal wing. "How have the last two days gone? Have you survived court in my absence?"

Gavriel grimaced. "Barely. I don't envy you or your lot in life. I can't fathom how you listen to your officials drone on about such droll things all day, nor the bickering nobles I had to dine with two nights in a row. Don't even get me started on some of the crazy women…"

Tehl smirked at the disturbed look Gav shot him. As he jogged up the stairs, he taunted, "What? You couldn't handle all those ladies vying for your attention?"

"If you could even call them ladies. Several bore a stronger resemblance to bloodhounds than women. I had to scrub twice to get the feeling of wandering hands off me." He shuddered.

Tehl barked out a laugh. "No need to worry, I won't subject you to that again any time soon." As they arrived at his chamber, Tehl turned his head, ready to bid Gavriel goodnight, but caught a whiff of himself. Oh boy, he stunk. "Sam and I will update you in the morning, and I'd appreciate a report from you as well, but for now I think a bath is my top priority."

The smile fell from Gav's face. "Actually, there are things that require your attention immediately, as in tonight."

Tehl tensed. Turning back to his cousin, he inquired, "What does it pertain to?"

"The rebel in the dungeon."

Tehl perked up. Perhaps the woman broke. He smiled. "Did she give you the information we need?"

"*No, but...*"

"Then it's not important; if it can't wait, speak with Sam. I have had a long day. We'll speak in the morning."

Gav's face hardened. "There's been an incident with the girl, Ruby: she's sick. She needs a healer."

"She can have one when she answers our questions," Tehl retorted.

"Tehl, it's serious."

The stress of the last several days combined with his desperate need for sleep increased his frustration. Tehl glared at his cousin and spoke harshly. "If that's the case, then it should be easy to make her a deal. She gives us what we need in exchange for a healer. She is a prisoner, not a guest. My orders stand. No bread and just enough water to keep her sustained! Is that all?"

Gav picked an imaginary piece of lint off his shirt and looked up at him, his purple eyes simmering with anger. "Yes, that is all, *Your Highness.*"

His anger melted away with his cousin's mild answer. Shame and embarrassment pricked him over his outburst. As Gavriel sketched a bow and stalked away, he called out to him. "Gav...I'm sorry, but we need her talking—and soon."

His cousin glowered over his shoulder. "If she dies, it will be on your head. Will you be able to shoulder that? I know you. You would never forgive yourself."

Tehl blew out a frustrated breath as he moved into his room. Thinking on his words, guilt pricked him. Gav had a good heart and was only being a decent human being. He didn't deserve such treatment.

His chamberlain entered, distracting him from his thoughts, and began divesting him of his chain mail and leathers. After everything had been removed, he rolled his shoulders, relishing how light he was without them.

"Would you like me to ready a bath for you, Your Highness?" the chamberlain inquired.

Tehl knew he needed one, but figured he was so exhausted that he'd probably fall asleep and drown in the tub. "No, that will be all."

The chamberlain bowed and then departed. Tehl looked across the room to the mirror; his face and clothing were streaked with dirt, ash, and sweat. His eyes were bloodshot and turning a hideous shade of blue-green. He trudged over to the washbasin and began scrubbing all the skin he could reach. Once he'd completed that, he peeled off the rest of his soiled clothing, leaving a trail to the bed. His eyes burned as he closed them. All his worries and responsibilities could wait for tomorrow. Time for blessed sleep.

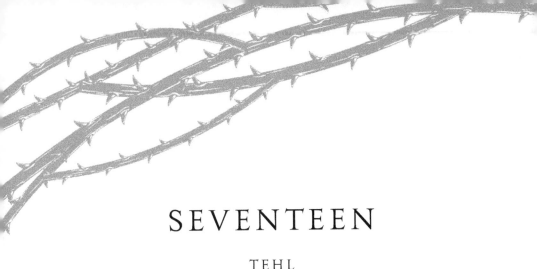

SEVENTEEN

TEHL

THE FAINT LIGHT OF DAWN painted the ceiling in a soft buttery yellow, rousing the crown prince from his bed. Goosebumps appeared on his arms and torso the moment his feet touched the icy stone floor. He rubbed his tired eyes, wishing he could slip back into bed and stay there. Tehl shuffled to the window and squinted as he watched the new day dawn. He had a mountain of things to do, but before anything else, he needed to deal with the rebel.

Tehl abandoned the peaceful picture his window offered him. It was time to get moving. He threw on a clean pair of trousers and a linen shirt, stumbling as he tried to pull on his boots. He opened his door as quietly as possible and peeked out, glancing down the hall in both directions. Pleased to find it empty, he gave a smile, nodding to the guards stationed at his door, and slipped away. The last thing he needed was to be waylaid. He snaked through the corridors, hoping to remain unnoticed, and exited through the east entrance. The sun caressed his face and he closed his eyes, taking a moment to savor its warmth. The metal ring of swords pulled him from his trance. Tehl opened his eyes and cocked his head, watching Samuel beat Jaxon into submission. Both men had discarded their shirts, skin covered with dirt. Noticing his brother watching, Sam shot him a grin. "Coming to practice, brother?"

"Not this morning. I have other duties demanding my attention."

"If you need my help, you know where I am." Sam winked and turned back to Jaxon.

Tehl dismissed his brother and strode to the dungeon entrance. The guards stationed there snapped to attention with a bow. He dipped his head in acknowledgment and continued down the stairs to the bowels of the castle. Jeffry was slumped at his desk, stroking his mustache, obviously deep in thought. His eyes lifted to Tehl, bitterness filling his face.

Tehl's brows furrowed as he stopped before the old man's desk. "Is everything all right, Jeffry?" The Keeper's scowl deepened. Multiple emotions flickered on the older man's face until it settled into a mix of disappointment and distaste. Confusion swirled through him. What had he done to deserve that look?

"My lord, I have always supported your father, yourself, and your brother because your family has always been honorable and just. You know I consider you part of my family."

"Thank you, Jeffry. You have been faithful in your service and a wonderful friend to my father. My brother and I consider you family as well."

"I'm afraid I hadn't finished, son."

Tehl straightened at Jeffry's bluntness. The Keeper pierced him with another dissatisfied look. What could have upset him to such a degree? He had never been one to take offense easily in the past. Tehl opened his mouth to ask, when Jeffry cut in.

"May I speak plainly?"

Despite the awkward tension between them, a smile crept onto Tehl's face. He'd never known his old friend to speak in any other way. Jeffry was a blunt man.

"You always have before. Even if I said 'no', I doubt that would keep you from telling me, anyway."

Jeffry cracked a brief, crooked smile but quickly sobered. "What you are doing with that woman is wrong, sire. She has caused no trouble, and from my brief talks with her, she is a lovely young woman."

Tehl sent Jeffry an incredulous look and chuckled. He hooked his thumb over his shoulder pointing down the hall. "Are we speaking of the same woman? You don't mean the vicious viper Sam and I brought in here?"

Jeffry straightened and stood up to his full five-foot seven-inch frame. The older man placed his gnarled hands on his desk and leaned forward. "She shouldn't be here."

Tehl couldn't believe it, she had Jeffry fooled. Gavriel was all up in arms over her needing medical care last night. What sort of spell had she cast over everyone while he was away?

By now, more than a bit annoyed, Tehl stared at Jeffry and inquired, "I understand you disagree and your opinion is noted. However, have my instructions been followed?"

Jeffry stiffened at the dismissal but nodded.

"Just rations of food and water? No blankets? No care as I requested?"

"Yes, we have followed your commands to the letter, my lord."

"Then I appreciate your devotion to your responsibilities despite your personal feelings. Now though, I must see if I can glean any information from our captive." He gave Jeffry a short nod and strode with determination to the cells. He'd only made it three steps when Jeffry spoke from behind him.

"I doubt you'll get anything from her."

Tehl looked over his shoulder with a chilling smile. "I'm sure I'll find a way."

As he continued down the dank hallway, his mind turned over the odd conversation. Jeffry had never been disappointed in him, and he didn't like that he seemed to be now. Curses and pleas were shouted to him as he wound his way toward the woman's cell. He passed one cell only to pause and back up.

The Scythian woman.

She sat in the dead center of her cell staring at nothing. Tehl scrutinized her for a moment, waiting for some reaction to his presence. Nothing. Not even a glance. Wherever she had buried herself within her mind, it was effective. She wasn't mentally present.

Tehl shook his head and moved on. A conundrum, that's what she was. But he would leave the figuring out to Sam; his brother salivated over puzzles, so it made sense to trust him with this one.

At the end of the dim hallway, he veered left and a familiar figure came into view. Gav was asleep against the wall not fifteen paces away. Why was his cousin sleeping down here? Was he that worried?

"He has quite the hero complex, doesn't he?" a low voice whispered in his ear.

Years of training kept Tehl from flinching, and he knew his brother was the only one who still surprised him. He rolled his eyes and turned as Sam emerged from the darkened area between two lanterns. "Was that really necessary?" Tehl quipped.

Sam smiled. "Someone has to keep you on your toes, and I need to keep up on my sneaking skills, so it's dual purpose. Looks like you might need to brush up on your spying skills though."

"That would be nice, but I doubt my advisers will let me out of the castle so soon after being gone for a couple days." Tehl eyed Gav's prone figure and then back to Sam. "Do you have any idea what he's been up to? Did he speak with you at all last night?"

Sam shook his head. "I haven't spoken to him since before we left. I was just as eager as you to speak with dear Ruby this fine morning."

His cousin finally stirred and then hefted his large frame off the ground. Despite the weak lighting, Tehl was able to detect dark smudges under Gav's eyes. When had he slept a full night? The extra responsibilities were taxing everyone, and he now felt even worse about their previous conversation. Tehl opened his mouth to apologize, but Gav held up a hand.

"Your prisoner awaits you," Gav said flatly.

Damn. In letting his temper get the best of him, he'd really mucked things up last night. Tehl sighed. It wasn't the place for apologies; he'd have to make amends later.

Tehl stepped up to the cell bars, his nose wrinkling at the smell. It smelled worse than a healer's tent on a battlefield. Tehl examined the small form in the middle of the floor. She lay curled on her side with her back facing them. As she shifted, she disturbed the faded black cloak covering her, revealing a naked thigh. Tehl froze, his brain scrambling for some explanation. The last he had heard, she'd stolen some clothing from the Guard, so how was she naked now?

His head whipped to the side, meeting Gavriel's gaze. "Where are her trousers?" he asked sharply.

"Destroyed," Gav bit out, his body rigid.

Tehl's eyes returned to the pale bruised leg. "How?"

"Ask her yourself, sire."

Tehl clenched his jaw at the sneer in his cousin's voice and cleared his throat. "Time to get up."

The wench didn't move, she ignored him.

He raised his voice. "Answer me, rebel."

Again, she didn't acknowledge him, but continued to lie there. Tehl gritted his teeth and leaned forward, the cold metal biting into his hands as he squeezed the bars. "Listen here, Ruby, you will answer your crown prince and show some respect!"

A third time, she ignored him.

"Unlock it," he demanded to no one in particular.

Sam stepped forward and placed the key in the lock and turned it. Tehl wrenched open the door and prowled around her body, stumbling as he caught sight of her face. It was almost unrecognizable. Her face was purple and swollen, the creases of her lids barely visible. Dried blood had clumped her black locks into snarls around her face.

Tehl leaned over and lifted the cloak, sucking in a sharp breath at her state. Everywhere he looked, her skin was mottled with bruises. She was too pale, almost translucent. His eyes tripped over her torn shirt and bare legs, cataloguing all the cuts that crisscrossed her thighs. Her blood was smeared over her body like a garish painting. He paused at the tourniquet tied around her left thigh.

Thank God someone had done at least that much.

Tehl swallowed thickly and lowered himself to a squat. Her hands were resting limply by her head, wrists oozing blood and yellow pus onto the stone beneath her.

"Gav, *what happened?*" he whispered, his voice hoarse, his eyes on her mutilated wrists.

"One captain took it upon himself to make sure she was interrogated."

Bile burned his throat. He couldn't believe it was one of his own men who did this. Shame and rage filled him. Tehl tore his eyes from the broken girl and stared at his cousin with accusation. "And where were you?"

His cousin's face hardened. "I was taking care of the kingdom as you were hunting Scythians like you commanded me to, my lord."

Tehl grunted, knowing he was being unfair, and turned back to the girl.

He reached out and gently brushed the damaged skin around her wrist, still in shock. "All this from her bindings?"

Gav took a deep breath and shook his head. "When Jeffry and I came upon her, they'd already stripped her. She got those because they'd hung her from the ceiling by her wrists. Tehl..." He paused, swallowing. "There was so much blood. I didn't know if she was alive when I pulled her down."

Tehl lifted his hand and placed it on her forehead. She was burning up; a light sheen of sweat dampened her temples and her swollen face. He smoothed her hair from her face and glanced down at her bare thighs. His stomach rolled, and his breath seized. He had to ask. "Was she..." Tehl stuttered, "um, violated?"

Tehl held his breath as he awaited his cousin's response. Gav's expression promised death. The floor dropped out from under him. It had happened under his roof, so *he* was accountable. Prisoner or not, she was still his responsibility and never did he intend *that* sort of interrogation. There were some lines you just didn't cross.

"No," Gavriel growled, passed clenched teeth. "I arrived in time, but that doesn't mean she's unscathed. Take a closer look at her bruises."

He peered at her and reached for her leg. Her body was a map of injuries. Tehl traced one and familiarity struck him. He looked between his hand and the mark.

Handprints.

They were bloody handprints.

Disgust washed over him; such treatment... How could it have happened under his watch? "Why hasn't she been treated then?" he hissed, glaring at her offending bruises. Perhaps if he stared hard enough, he could singe them from her skin altogether.

"Because you ordered me not to. I did what I could for her without committing insubordination."

Gavriel's words cut him like a knife. His anger gave way to a heavier burden—soul-crushing guilt. She was going to die. He'd seen fevers like hers before; it'd be a miracle if she made it another night. While he was sleeping soundly in his bed, she'd lain, dying, on a cold, stone floor. A wet, rattling cough brought his attention back to the pitiful creature before him.

Tehl leaned over her and shook her once. "Ruby?" She moaned and began to shiver, but didn't wake. "Sam!" he called without taking his eyes off her. "Get her to a healer."

Sam moved into the cell and knelt by her side. He placed his fingers above her collarbone and leaned over her. He placed his ear near her mouth and listened. After a moment, he rose, regret evident in his eyes. "Tehl, I honestly don't think she'll make it. Her lungs are filled with fluid—whether from the fever or blood from internal damage, I'm not certain."

He should have listened to Gav. Because of his foolishness, the girl would die. "We need a healer. We have to try."

Sam shook his head at him. "It's too late, brother. We can only make her comfortable."

Tehl understood, but he wouldn't accept it. There had to be something, anything. A hand squeezed his shoulder. Gavriel. His cousin no doubt blamed him, yet he still offered comfort, though he deserved none.

"Where do you want her moved?" Gav reached down to pick Ruby up.

Something about Gav holding her made him bristle. Tehl brushed aside Gav's hands and scooped her up into his own arms. He cradled the frail body against him and stood. He all but ran from the cell, leaving his brother and cousin behind.

Sam caught up first. "What do you plan on doing for her? You can't care for her, Tehl. Pass her to me, and I will see that she is cared for."

He tightened his grip and picked up his pace. "It's my fault she is in this state, so she's now my responsibility." When the Keeper came into view, he realized he now understood exactly why Jeffry had been so disgusted. Tehl spared him a glance as he passed. "You were right, old man."

Tehl shot up the stairs, trying not to jostle the girl too much. He burst out of the dungeon, and in the morning light, she looked even worse. She needed Jacob right now.

He ran.

Several servants jumped out of his way as he barreled toward the infirmary. It would be all over the palace that he was running through the castle with a naked woman in his arms, but at the moment, he didn't care. All that mattered was getting to the healer in time.

She let out a wet cough and shivered in his arms as Tehl slammed into the infirmary, Sam and Gav right on his tail. Seeing their urgency, Jacob jumped to his feet, rushing to his side before he could blink. The Healer's eyes widened. "What happened here?" Jacob asked clinically.

"Interrogation."

Jacob's face darkened. "Place her on this cot." He motioned with his chin to the right. "Is this your hellcat?"

"Yes," Sam answered, looking lost.

Tehl placed her with care on the cot while Gav cradled her head and Sam pulled a sheet over her exposed legs. After placing a hand on her forehead, Jacob listened carefully to her breathing. "I will do all that I can, but I am not sure if she will survive. The state of her lungs alone…" He shook his head. "I need to strip her and assess injuries. Get out."

Tehl stared down at the shivering girl. She didn't look anything like she had when he met her. She was so vulnerable. "If she recovers, I want her placed in one of the guest quarters." He ignored the looks he received and focused on the Healer rushing around the rebel.

"I don't think that is wise or particularly safe. She may be helpless now, but she is still dangerous. You would put anyone who has to deal with her at risk."

He knew the risks. "I'm aware of that, but I don't care right now. It's largely my fault she is dying, and I need to right this wrong. I'd prefer her warm and comfortable when she awakens. We will deal with the danger she poses *if* she survives."

Sam pinched the bridge of his nose. "Well, I guess we'll need guards stationed at the infirmary. We don't know what her reaction will be should she regain consciousness." Sam grinned at Jacob. "We wouldn't want anything bad to happen to the good Healer here."

Jacob glared at Sam. "This is not the time, or place, for jesting." Censure and urgency filled the Healer's voice. "Leave, and please find Mira and send her in. Time is of the essence!"

"Of course."

Sam turned on his heel and swept out the door after Gav. Tehl spared the broken girl a parting glance.

Please make it.

EIGHTEEN

SAGE

SAGE FLOATED IN A VAST sea that burned hot and cold. One moment she was hot and uncomfortable, the next, so cold it felt like she'd been stabbed with a thousand needles. Fingers of mist ran through her hair, whispering words she couldn't understand. Sage sighed, content, thinking the mist must have been a gift from above. But then it shifted, creeping over her body, filling her nose and mouth, stealing her air. She was suffocating. Her body began to sink, and colors swirled above her tauntingly as she slipped farther and farther below the surface.

She was going to die.

A gruff voice called to her from the darkness, whispering that he would make everything right, that he would take care of her. She smiled to herself. It'd be nice to have someone take care of her for a change.

Fire pulsed through her veins and she cried out. She was burning! She writhed in pain, unable to pull away from the heat overtaking her body.

Again, the gruff voice spoke. "We need to get her into the tub. Her fever is too high. Fetch more snow from the ice cellar!" Then it softened, and she felt a gentle pressure somewhere on her arm, steadying her. "Be still, Ruby. We're going to cool you down." The voice commanded.

Needles pricked her all over once more, and someone screamed. Who in bloody hell was screaming? She ached for silence, for some reprieve from her torture. *Leave me alone! I'm tired. I'm done. Let me go!*

"Please... Let me die...," Sage pleaded aloud with the darkness.

The gruff voice spoke again. "No. You will not die, Ruby. Do you understand me? Not on my watch."

Irritation filled her. Even now, in death, would they give her no peace?

Sage smiled when the darkness finally surged forward, beckoning. She welcomed it with a gentle sigh, gratefully sinking into its cool embrace.

Darkness gave way to light. The flames were gone, but now ice froze her blood. Her teeth clacked together as she shook uncontrollably. Had she died? Why was it so cold? Perhaps everything would go numb soon. Sage opened her eyes and tried to make sense of the myriad of colors flooding her vision. After a moment, the pair of hazel eyes peering down at her with concern came into focus.

"Ruby, dearest, can you hear me? Ruby?" She recognized the gruff voice. She sighed when he put a hand to her cheek; it was a blessedly warm appendage. Like a flower to the sun, she tried turning toward him, wanting to soak up the heat he gave off, but for some reason she couldn't move. She tried to speak, but the shivers wracking her body made it difficult. If she could just tell him she was cold, perhaps he'd warm her up.

"C-c-c-col-d-d-d."

His eyes snapped to the other side of room. "Mira, I need you to climb into bed with her. She needs your body heat. She is shivering far too much for my liking. It would be best if you stripped. I will step out of the room."

Sage registered a soft rustling before a big ball of warmth wrapped itself around her. She pressed her nose into it and sighed. Warm at last.

"I have you, love. That's right, snuggle in nice and close. I will keep you warm," a soft voice crooned.

Then the voice sang to her:

Lullaby, and goodnight, my sweet, the skies are dark but the stars are bright,
May the moon's silvery beams bring you endless sweet dreams.
Close your eyes and slip into your rest, may these dark hours keep you close and

give you peace.

Dream until the sky's bright with dawn. Lullaby and goodnight, my sweet, I'll protect you from harm, and you'll wake in my arms.

Finally, warm and at peace, Sage floated away to the tune of the melody.

NINETEEN

TEHL

TEHL SAT IN HIS CHAMBER, mesmerized by the dancing flames in the hearth, mulling over recent events. Two days had passed since he'd left Ruby to Jacob's care. He had thrown himself into his duties with uncommon gusto, even giving attention to the details of the Midsummer Festival, selecting decor and pouring over guest lists with enough zeal that even Demari was satisfied. Sam and Gav checked on the rebel daily, bringing back to him bad news each time. She wasn't breathing well, and her fever raged on. And that wasn't the only bad news.

Word had spread that he'd been seen sprinting through the castle holding a mostly-naked woman. By the next night, he'd had several men congratulate him at dinner on his new mistress. When Tehl denied having a mistress, the men had laughed, giving him knowing looks. His blunt words and adamant refusal only piqued their curiosity. Still, gossip was hardly the worst of his problems.

Of primary concern was his war council; they were divided. Half supported a preemptive strike on Scythia while the other half wanted to pretend they posed no threat at all—yet neither was a viable option. He'd listened to them debate for hours over whether to take action. Ultimately however, Aermia would not win a war with Scythia while they continued to battle the civil unrest within their own country. They needed to unite their people first; only then they could deal with Scythia. Tehl had said so, though the mention of the rebellion was most unwelcome to those who preferred to disregard its existence.

Tehl snorted. Stubborn fools. Still, their dissent mattered little at the moment; he had the final say. He knew Scythia would attack; it was only a matter of when. Sam hoped it to be immediate. Tehl didn't put his stock in hope, however; he put it in preparations. For that reason, Tehl had already started work on potential battle plans, although it felt odd to be planning war in one room and a festival in the other. He wondered if one would interfere with the other. Would they already be at war in a month's time? And if so, would they survive it? Would there be time for the festival? It had been too long since his people had had something to celebrate. As frivolous as it seemed, he knew they needed this reprieve from their sufferings. He shook his head and stretched, weary of his thoughts.

He felt restless. Maybe he just needed exercise. Tehl lifted himself from his large wing-backed chair, his boots making a soft thud as he crossed the plush rugs of his room. The castle was silent, peaceful. He wandered down the hallways and stairs, pondering little and important matters alike. Servants scurried to and fro, bowing as he passed, then hurrying on, absorbed in their tasks.

Eventually he found himself in the hallway leading to the infirmary. He figured he'd end up here at some point. Time to check on the little rebel. Both guards bowed before one opened the door for him to enter. As soon as he stepped into the sweltering infirmary, his nose was assaulted with eucalyptus. Sweat collected on his brow and between his shoulder blades.

His gaze swept over the room. The girl's cot had been moved, and it now sat close to a roaring fire. Jacob sat, sound asleep, in a rocking chair next to the fire. The older man's shirt was soaked clean through with sweat, a soft snore escaping him. He moved closer but pulled up short when he noticed a blond head alongside the dark one.

What the devil?

A few more steps and Tehl stood before the cot, staring into a pair of tired blue eyes. She stared back, surprised by his presence, but spoke not a word. His eyes slid along the black-haired rebel curled up next to her, clinging to her almost like a barnacle. Her swollen face was pressed into the blonde's neck, an arm slung across her chest. He watched as the blonde's surprise gave way to curiosity. It seemed they both had questions.

"What's all this?" he asked softly.

"She was too cold. We tried everything else to bring her temperature up, so Jacob asked me to lie near her, share my body heat. It's working. She finally stopped shivering about an hour ago."

"Do you know who she is?" Tehl asked, wondering if she knew the risk she took.

She nodded once. "Jacob told me before we put her in the tub. People overtaken with fever often put up a fight when we put them in the ice." She shrugged. "So it was a good thing I was forewarned; I would never have thought someone so tiny could fight like that! Rather like a lioness. It took both guards, Jacob, *and* myself just to hold her down."

This woman understood the rebel was dangerous *and* a traitor, yet she didn't hesitate to use her own body heat to keep her alive. It was a noble and courageous thing to do, and he respected her for it. "What's your name?" Having forgotten to whisper, Jacob stirred at the sound of his voice, though he didn't awaken.

"Shhh...," the young healer chastised, glancing to Jacob with concern. "He only fell asleep a few minutes ago, and it's the first opportunity he's had since she arrived." She turned back to him and stilled as if just remembering to whom it was she was spoke. "Forgive me, my lord, I was thoughtless when I spoke." She paused. "My name is Mira."

He waved off her apology. "There is nothing to forgive. Mira, you only spoke out of concern for Jacob, and I could never find fault in that."

"What did you do for me, dearie?" Jacob's gruff voice asked, still rough from sleep.

"She was taking care of you." Tehl gave Mira a smile, which she returned with a crooked one.

Jacob reached over, affectionately patting Mira's hand. His hand drifted to touch the rebel woman's forehead, absentmindedly stroking her tangled hair from her face.

"How's she doing?" Tehl inquired.

Jacob took off his spectacles and tried to clean them on his sweaty shirt, only to grimace when he examined them in the firelight. He'd streaked sweat all over them. The Healer plopped his glasses in his lap and squinted up at

Tehl. "Bad news is that the infection has a firm hold on her lungs. The good news is her fever is dropping. She is not in immediate danger, but her lungs are still a serious concern. If the fluid doesn't clear, she could easily die."

Tehl grimly regarded the source of his guilt. "Is there anything I can do?" She looked so frail.

"No, there is not." He heard the old man sigh. "In her sleep, she's been asking for her mum and papa."

Tehl's head snapped to Jacob. "Has she said anything else?"

Jeffry shook his head before Tehl finished. "Nothing but whimpers. When we put her in the ice bath, she started screaming and thrashing." Jacob's face pinched inward. "And she was begging me to let her die. She was out of it though, the fever-induced delirium. If she survives, I doubt she'll remember any of this." As Jacob finished, his shoulders slumped, clearly exhausted.

Mira untangled her arm from the girl and touched Jacob's hand. "You have done all you can for her and given her your best. We both have. But now it's up to her to keep fighting, and the herbs we've administered will help her do that. Why don't you go and find a bed for a couple hours? I'll stay here and send for you if anything changes."

Mira's actions warmed Tehl's heart. She was just as worn out as Jacob, but was still trying to care for the older man. The Healer opened his mouth to argue when Tehl cut him off. "Go and get some rest, friend. I will watch over both girls for the next few hours while you rest. When you come back refreshed, you will be more ready to tackle her sickness."

Jacob stared at him a moment, his tiredness apparent. After a beat, he nodded and hefted himself out of the rocking chair. He shuffled out, touching the girl's forehead and Mira's shoulder as he passed, murmuring goodnight.

Tehl moved to the abandoned rocking chair and took Jacob's place. Sitting this close to the fire had raised his temperature by several degrees he was sure. He only hoped he wouldn't suffocate. He tugged on his collar. It was much too hot for his leather vest. Tehl decided he was better off without it and undid the buttons and peeled it off. Next, he loosened the strings on his shirt, but froze when a feminine throat cleared. He lifted his eyes to the twinkling blue ones now staring at his chest. It was his turn to clear his throat.

She lifted her eyes, amusement plain on her face. He fumbled, attempting to re-lace his shirt in embarrassment.

"No need to lace up on my account. It *is* bloody hot in here. I bet those leather pants are cooking you alive."

He dropped his laces and looked at her. "Don't you worry about your reputation, though? Here you are alone in a room with a half-dressed man; if someone saw us, your reputation would be ruined."

She chuckled, her shoulder shaking with her laughter. Why was that so funny? Most women would be anxious right now.

When she caught sight of the look on his face, she choked back her laughter with a smile. "My reputation was ruined long ago when I started working here with Jacob. Heaven forbid a young woman work near an older man. Do you know that most people think I'm his mistress?" She paused. "If you're worried about propriety, those hulking guards can serve as chaperones. No one's virtue is endangered." Mirth colored her words.

Mira spoke straight with him. She didn't play coy or use double meanings, leaving him to guess at her words. He liked that. "Mira, I think we'll be great friends."

Pink touched her cheeks. He couldn't tell if it was from the dizzying heat or his words, but one thing was sure: she was exhausted, and dark smudges lined her drooping lids.

"Why don't you sleep for a bit? I will watch over the both of you until Jacob returns."

She looked at him with hope. "Truly? That would be heaven. I haven't slept either. If her breathing gets more labored, or there are any other changes, don't hesitate to wake me. Please and thank you." She paused. "Oh, and don't forget to stoke the fire." Another pause. "My lord," she tacked on.

"I'll take care of it. Now sleep."

Mira rearranged herself, checking the girl's temperature and adjusting the blanket to cover them both. As soon as she closed her eyes, she was asleep, emitting a soft buzz from her nose that made him grin. Tehl settled into the rocking chair, closing his own eyes. It was sure to be a long night.

The heat slowly lulled him to sleep. He dozed until a rustling disturbed him. Tehl yawned and scooted to the edge of his chair, focusing on the two sleeping girls. The rebel had kicked their blankets off and was now shivering, little goosebumps running up her arms. The pathetic whimper that passed her lips had Tehl frowning. Mira, even in her sleep, scooted over and threw a leg over the girl, but her shivering kept on.

Tehl got up and began laying more wood over the coals. He then crept over to the cot, pulling the blankets up over both girls. Finally, the combination of the stoked fire and the blanket slowed Ruby's shivering considerably. He settled back into the chair, its dark wood creaking as it bore his full weight. He leaned forward, placing his elbows on his knees and his chin in his hands, keeping an eye on the rebel.

His eyes traced a small patch of light freckles on her button nose. Her long, dark lashes rested on her pale cheeks, showcasing the black bags and bruises beneath them. Her dark hair lay across her chin and hung off the cot in tangled, sweaty strands. A pained moan reached his ears, and he found himself reaching out to soothe her, gently removing the hair from her clammy face, smoothing it behind one ear.

He wasn't much familiar with comforting someone, but he remembered how his mother would softly draw on his face whenever he was ill. As a child, he had loved it. He started tracing the rebel's arched eyebrows down to her cheekbones, then her chin. He avoided the broken nose and bruises. Tehl continued this way until she stopped shuddering. As Tehl pulled away, she turned her face into his hand, her lips resting against his palm.

"… Don't leave me papa. I hurt all over."

Her innocent plea made his heart clench. He heard her mumble something else and leaned closer to hear. Tehl caressed her cheekbone with his thumb and whispered, "I won't leave you, love."

Her lips formed part of a smile as she exhaled a soft, "love you, papa," and then she was once again dead to the world.

Her soft utterance was so different from his first impression of her. She didn't seem like a ruthless traitor. Was she perhaps coerced into this? Even with these thoughts spiraling, he knew it was largely wishful thinking on his part. She was guilty. A rebel.

He shouldn't have checked on her. Something about her was alluring to him whether he wanted it to be or not. His brother was right in his observations— Tehl couldn't think clearly around this girl.

She was a potential informant and that had to be the end of it. Even so, he never moved his hand from her face.

Much later, a deep cough roused him. Tehl raised his head from where it had been resting on the girl's cot. He stared in horror as he realized that during the night, he somehow ended up holding her hand. He jerked his hand away and looked toward the door. Jacob was watching the scene with a keen look.

"What?" Tehl mouthed, trying not to wake either girl.

"Nothing, my lord. You took very good care of our girls last night. Thank you."

Jacob walked briskly over and elbowed him out of the way. He placed a hand on the rebel's forehead and smiled, relieved. "Her fever broke." His soft tone had Mira stirring, but not enough to wake her. Jacob moved away, waving for him to follow. "The danger is mostly gone now that the fever's gone. I think she will survive."

Tehl stopped to study the older man. "How soon do you think Sam will be able to speak with her again?"

Jacob frowned, his face darkening briefly, but he quickly smoothed it to a thoughtful expression. "It depends on her recovery and willingness to fight. It's possible she will be physically recovered in two to three weeks' time, my lord. Mentally, though? I have no idea."

Tehl took that in stride. "She will fight. It seems it's a favorite pastime for her." Tehl looked back to the sleeping forms. "Please keep Sam or Gavriel informed of her progress."

"As you wish." Jacob bowed.

Leaving her this time was just as difficult as it had been the previous time; he wouldn't visit her again. Sam would have to be the one who discovered her secrets. She called out for her papa, saying that she loved him. Under the influence of the truth serum, she had shared a different story.

Secrets. It seemed she had many. Tehl hoped that she could start talking and help them before it was too late.

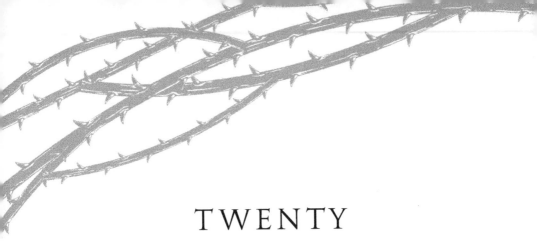

TWENTY

SAGE

HERBS HAD TEASED HER NOSE before she was fully awake. Now, clean white walls glared at her, and Sage squinted, eyes watering as she tried to makes sense of her surroundings. A roaring fire was going next to the cot upon which she was lying, and an empty rocking chair sat nearby.

Memories assaulted her.

Burning.

Drowning.

A gruff voice.

She needed to stop passing out.

Sage drew in a sharp breath, causing her lungs to seize. She gasped, and a burst of harsh rattling coughs racked her body. Each cough sent pain pulsing through her, making her wish she could sink back into oblivion. Slight pressure shifted on her abdomen, startling her. Sage lifted her head, squinting at the arm slung over her waist, a *very* female arm. Her gaze followed the petite arm to the young woman plastered to her side. Puzzled, she admired the heavy golden braid draped across her arm, tracing it back to its owner. Surprised blue eyes stared back at Sage.

"Who in the hell are you?" Sage blurted. "And why are you in my bed?"

The last thing she remembered was someone taking her cuffs off before darkness had swallowed her. The blonde shifted and Sage was suddenly aware of how closely they were tangled together. A blush crept up her neck and onto her cheeks. The woman laid a hand on her forehead and, if Sage hadn't been so tired, she would have jerked from her touch despite the fact it was impersonal.

"Ah. Your fever broke in the night." Relief was clear in the young woman's voice. "To answer your other question, I'm Mira."

Sage pursed her lips, squinting at the girl. "Still doesn't explain why you're clinging to me like a lover."

Mira scooted back, smiling at her, displaying not a shred of embarrassment. She waved a hand, indicating their surroundings. "This is the infirmary; you were brought to us delirious with fever. We used an ice bath several times to drop your fever, but by the time your fever dropped a few degrees, you were shaking uncontrollably. We covered you and placed you next to the fire, but it wasn't enough." Mira shrugged. "The only other option was for me to crawl into bed with you in order for you to benefit from my body heat."

Sage appreciated that she kept her explanation succinct and clinical, but she still had so many questions. First, though, she took stock of the woman next to her; it was obvious from her posture and the dark rings under her eyes that she'd hardly slept. The fact that she had been caring for Sage in spite of this meant she owed this woman a great debt of gratitude.

"Thank you." Sage patted Mira's hand. "I'm sure I don't know everything you've done for me, but from the circles under your eyes, I know it couldn't have been easy. I'm grateful to you." Mira smiled back at her, accepting her thanks with a quick dip of her chin.

Sage scanned the room, noting any exits and various things she might use as weapons should the need arise. A fire poker lay within a few feet of her. Excellent. She dropped her gaze to her hands, playing with a loose blanket thread to feign nonchalance. "How did I end up here?" Sage peered up through her lashes at the young woman.

Mira's lips parted, but then she hesitated, as if searching for the right words. It was interesting that she felt the need to censor her explanation. What didn't she want Sage to know? The young healer was most likely a wealth of information, so she'd need to be nice and put the woman at ease. She gave Mira a sheepish smile and noted the girl's posture relax. Perfect.

"Sorry for all the questions, I am just so confused."

She spoke the truth. It baffled her that she'd been placed here, in this warm room, rather than her frigid and dingy cell. So far, they had drugged, starved, and tortured her. Why bring her to an infirmary then? Suddenly, it hit her. It was her information they were after, information she couldn't provide if she was dead.

Sage winced and rubbed her temples as a throbbing pain started behind her eyes. She needed to put those somewhat depressing thoughts aside and focus on what was now her top priority: recovery.

She'd never get out of here alive in this condition.

A harsh and rattling coughing fit seized Sage. Immediately, Mira hopped up, fetching her a glass of water. The healer cradled her head and brought the cup to Sage's cracked lips, carefully pouring the soothing liquid down her parched throat. Sage grumbled an incoherent complaint when, all too quickly, Mira pulled it away.

"If I give you any more, you might retch," Mira explained. "You need that to stay in your stomach."

The young healer turned and placed the glass on the bedside desk before speaking. "Though accompanied by his cousin and brother, it was the crown prince himself who carried you up here to be treated. That was three days ago."

The crown prince's dirty hands were on her? She recoiled at the thought. She was also concerned; that kind of attention was dangerous. What had she done to warrant it? She needed to be out of here sooner rather than later. After wiping any hint of her thoughts from her face, she faced Mira and inquired, "How long will I be here?" Hopefully she'd be allowed to stay in the infirmary until her escape. Just the thought of moving had her aching.

Slipping a simple woolen gown over her shift, Mira spoke, "Until you're healed enough so we can safely move you to another room."

"Another room?" Sage probed.

A male voice spoke from behind, startling her. "Indeed, young Ruby. Once you're more stable, we can move you to a more comfortable space for the duration of your recovery." An older man stood close to where she was sitting, grinning down at her. "Orders from the crown prince himself."

It took everything inside her not to recoil at his words. Why would the crown prince want her to be comfortable? She studied the older man as he came closer, placing two fingers on the inside of her wrist. His hands were calloused but gentle. Like many of his profession, he seemed a kind sort of person. Nevertheless, she had to fight the impulse to yank back her arm and move away. He released her hand and leaned over her body, peering into her eyes, and this time Sage shrunk back, snapping, "Does no one in this infirmary understand the concept of personal space?" She swallowed, trying to mask her unease with irritation.

Sympathy shone in his eyes as he straightened. "Healers are curious by nature. We dedicate our lives to discovering better ways to mend and heal—and doing that means getting close and personal. Had the lovely Mira here not been willing to invade your 'personal space,' I don't believe you would be with us now."

Sage cringed at how ungrateful that sounded. She offered him a quick smile and rushed to explain. "I meant no offense and deeply appreciate what you both have done for me. I was a bit disoriented and a little surprised at finding myself in a bed, let alone with another person sharing it. And then to have a man touch me who I don't know. It's…off-putting."

He bobbed his head in understanding. "I can't imagine what you are going through, my dear. The state you were brought in…," he trailed off, swallowing. "It was inhuman. Mira and I did our best to care for you. We were at your side every moment. You were never left alone." The kindness in his gaze almost undid her. He understood her panic at being left unprotected, especially after what she'd suffered. "Also, my name is Jacob." He gave a courtly bow and popped up, quite spry for someone his age.

Sage forced a wobbly smile on her face and lifted her shaky hand in the air for him to take it. "My name is Ruby. It's a pleasure to meet you." A flash of disappointment flicked across his face, but it was gone before she could even be sure she'd seen it. He was all smiles as he kissed the back of her hand like a gentleman.

"Quite the manners, my lady," the Healer remarked.

She tugged her hand from his and examined her nails. "I figured it was only fitting after that gracious bow. And I am no lady, only a girl from the streets," Sage wheezed, already short of breath. It felt like someone had put a wet cloth over her mouth and was forcing her to breathe through it. She began hacking anew, squeezing her eyes shut as tears leaked down her cheeks from the force of coughing.

"Take a deep breath, my girl. It will help," Jacob's low voice coaxed. The smell of lavender, eucalyptus, and mint saturated the surrounding air. It took several tries for her to take a deep breath, but eventually her lungs loosened allowing her to breathe. She slit her teary eyes and looked up at the tight-lipped Jacob.

"Am I going to die?" she asked bluntly, her heart pounding weakly. She was already exhausted.

The Healer's face was severe as he stared down at her. "I won't pretend that your situation is not serious, but as I told you before, you'll not die under my care."

His words did elicit a faint echo of familiarity, but she couldn't quite place it. Her eyelids drooped, fatigue grasping her in its claws. "How is it possible that I am so tired? Mira told me I have been sleeping for days."

He slumped into the sturdy rocking chair next to her cot. "Your body is trying to heal itself. Sleep is a very good thing, and you'll probably be doing a lot of it this next week. Close your eyes, Ruby. Mira and I will watch over you."

The idea of them watching her as she slept discomfited her, and apprehension crept over her. She'd be so vulnerable. Sage tried to reel in her thoughts and looked between the two healers. She sensed nothing dangerous. For three days, these two had diligently cared for her, and she'd come to no harm at their hands. As much as she hated turning her back on the older man, she wanted to face the door. That way she could see anyone who tried to sneak up on her. Better the devil you know than the devil you don't. She gave Mira a sleepy smile and, after snuggling into the blankets, drifted off.

TWENTY-ONE

SAGE

SAGE'S EYES FLEW OPEN. SOMETHING had awoken her. As the hair on her neck rose, she realized something about her surroundings was different. Firelight writhed with the shadows on the walls in a twisted dance of black and yellow. She looked around and made out the crown of Mira's blond head peeking out of a blanket on the cot next to hers, snoring lightly. Exhaling, Sage tried to calm herself. Nothing was amiss; it had only been a bad dream. She shuddered, forcing the unpleasant images from her mind. She turned and faced the fire, hoping it would drive the chills away. Her eyes drifted to the Healer sitting in the chair, and her heart leapt to her throat.

It wasn't Jacob in the chair.

For a moment, she was paralyzed, but then she was scrambling backward violently, putting as much distance as possible between herself and the strange man. Her legs caught in the blankets, and she stumbled to the floor, coughing as she fell.

The intruder rushed toward her, and a scream caught in her throat as she fought to free herself from the web of bedding. She had to get away! Panicking, Sage pulled herself across the floor, nails clawing at the stone. Large hands gripped her waist, and she cried out; she couldn't go through this again. He needed to stop touching her. Now. Sage raked her hands up his arms and pinched with all her might, drawing blood. "Someone help me!"

she yelled.

Both guards crashed through the door, but her heart sank when they hesitated. They weren't going to help her. Sage's stomach soured; she was going to be sick.

"Vicious little wench! I'm only trying to help," his voice rumbled against her back. "Calm down, it's Sam."

She didn't care who he was, she continued resisting him with all she had. He cursed. An ear-piercing shriek passed her lips as he hauled her up from the floor. He dropped her on the cot, and she stilled, thankful at least that his hands were no longer on her. She opened her eyes and saw it was the young prince standing before her, watching her intently.

Before she knew what she was doing, her fist smashed into his face. His head snapped to the side, and he worked his jaw. Terror filled her, and she was rooted to the spot. What would he do? He swung around, his dark blue eyes meeting hers. Her skin crawled at his nearness so she did the first thing that came to mind: she coughed into his face.

Instantly, he recoiled, his face twisted in disgust. Her victory was short lived, though, as another vicious coughing bout seized her. A dainty hand appeared before her nose with a bottle of scented oil.

"Deep breaths, Ruby, you need to take deep breaths. No need to fear. I won't let anything happen to you," Mira spoke in a calm and encouraging tone, rubbing a soothing hand between her shoulder blades.

Sage did what she was told, never taking her eyes from the enemy. Despite her fear, Mira's comment struck her as funny. What could a petite little woman accomplish against the much larger man? If she had to guess, she'd say he was nearly the same height as his brother, over six feet. Between coughs, she managed a sharp laugh. "Mira." *Wheeze.* "He could do whatever he wanted." Sage looked over her shoulder at the sweet healer and patted her shoulder. "I appreciate the thought, though."

Sage returned her gaze to the dangerous man in their presence. Samuel Ramses. A man of many titles; *Prince Samuel. Commander Samuel.* And then the label known only by a few: *Spymaster Samuel.*

It seemed he was also her jailor, tormentor, and, very likely, the harbinger of her death.

His extended proximity still perturbed her. Since their first encounter, he'd not shown a single genuine emotion. She suspected he was all façade. Even now, he sat casually, but his eyes told a different story. They held a measure of wariness. The spymaster stared back at her, taking in her assessment of him. Hatred rolled through her, bleeding onto her face. "You here for round two?"

A little glimmer of emotion flashed in his eyes, but disappeared just as quickly. "No." He dropped his eyes to the fire next to him.

"Maybe more drugs this time?" Sage snarled. She shouldn't be provoking him, but she couldn't help it. She hated being cornered.

His jaw clenched as he whipped his head her way. "No, I have no intention of drugging you, Ruby. I also have no intention of harming you."

She barked out a laugh. She was tired, cranky, and fed up with being afraid. "'Intention' is an interesting word, is it not? Everyone has good *intentions* until they don't. So forgive me if I don't put stock in anything that comes out of your lying trap," she spat. Mira gasped at her offensive words.

Sage was done with the situation. What game was he playing? Would he hurt Mira, too? She had no doubt that all the men of this place had been born into privilege—spoiled and able to do and take whatever they pleased. Such men had no business wielding power.

"Ruby. You must believe me when I tell you that neither my brother nor myself sanctioned what happened to you."

She allowed her disbelief to show on her face. Was he here to cast off the blame from his family? Why bother? They must want her cooperation badly, she thought.

Furious, her anxiety temporarily evaporated. "How dare you come in here to shirk the blame. You," she spat, pointing a shaking finger at him, "are a liar and a coward." Mira squeezed her shoulder, as if to quiet her, but there was no stopping her now. If she would die, she wasn't going quietly. "If that was the truth, it was still *your* men. You are the one who drugged me so I couldn't protect myself from…" Her voice broke. Tears flooded her eyes. Sage glared through the watery glaze. "You will *never* be absolved of your crimes."

Compassion filled his face.

Disbelief rolled through her—like she would believe he felt remorse over his actions. His emotions weren't genuine, just another mask to get what he wanted. The spymaster reached out to her, and she jerked back, bumping into Mira. "Don't touch me!" she hissed, her lungs tightened painfully as she tried to catch her breath.

"I think it would be best if you left, my prince," Mira stated, not a suggestion but a command.

"I won't leave. I have orders to watch over Ruby and make sure she is protected."

Sage's mind spun. "Protection? Where was your protection when, when…" She stumbled for the right word. "When they stripped me down and used me for their amusement?" she rasped, her face hardening. "Oh, that's right, I needed protection from *you*. So forgive me if I won't count on your protection. None of this is for *my* protection but to make sure your asset doesn't escape your clutches."

The spymaster's face sharpened, and his eyes glistened with anger. "What do you mean they *used you for their own amusement?*" he asked in a deceptively soft voice.

She shivered at his dark tone. Sage knew where his mind had gone with that question. "A man does not have to force himself on a woman to hurt her. Words can cause as much damage as blades and fists. To my knowledge—" Sage choked on the words, not able to force them from her throat. She swallowed and donned her blank mask, her heart beating wildly in her chest. Sage forced herself to look at the young healer for confirmation.

Mira's pale face pinched, and she jerked her head once.

"You don't have that on your conscience…" Sage sneered and turned back at the commander. Pity. Pity was written all over his face. Panic clawed her chest as his blues eyes delved into her, like he saw every inch of pain swirling just beneath her surface, threatening to break through. Sage fisted her hands in her lap, her broken nails digging into her palms. She would not weep in front of him.

"I am so sorry."

Her dam broke.

Grief and shame choked her, sucking the fight right out of her. It was too much; her pain wouldn't be contained any longer. Sparkling drops dripped down her bruised face in rivulets. Sage closed her eyes, shutting out everyone.

She was weak.

Large arms wrapped around her pressing her into a wide hard chest. "Let it all out, darling."

Her breath seized.

He caged her.

Trapped her.

Sage writhed against him. "Get your filthy paws off me!" she screamed, blinded by her tears. He tightened his grip and whispered things she couldn't understand through her panic. The world spun. She couldn't breathe. Her heart would burst. He needed to stop touching her.

"My lord, you are making her worse, please let go of her," Mira pleaded.

"No, Mira, she needs this." His tone of voice brooked no argument. "Let it out, Ruby. It's okay."

No, nothing was okay.

Her enemy held her.

Sage couldn't protect herself.

She was damaged.

Weak.

Sage cried harder, trembling as he held her steady. Something broke open inside her, and she wasn't sure how to put it back together. Samuel's large hand tunneled under her hair and rubbed the back of her skull. Sage cried herself out and hiccupped, her throat raw. She lay limply against the spymaster's wet chest, thoroughly wrung out. It was then she noticed Mira had moved to her other side, tenderly combing her fingers through Sage's hair, singing.

She stared at the fire, wishing she could burn away everything she was feeling. Emptiness and pain were her companions. The spymaster's breath tickled the hair at her crown. She needed him to stop touching her skin. Sage pulled every last drop of strength and courage she possessed and begged. "Please, have mercy, let go of me. Every touch feels like *them*."

"It's okay, Ruby. Those men have been taken care of and they can't hurt you here. We will protect you. My brother has ordered it. If you would prefer me not to be here, I can send Gavriel."

A hazy memory of purple eyes and a man unchaining her resurfaced. Her savior. "I like Gavriel."

A chuckle rumbled in his chest, vibrating her cheek. "Most do; he is a good man."

He gave her a little squeeze, which unsettled her, her skin prickling. She *really* wished he would let her go. If she wasn't so weak from illness, she'd have the strength to make him let go. She hated being weak, but every muscle in her body was tired. Her stomach growled, breaking the silence that had settled upon them.

"It sounds like you're in need of some breakfast." His arms released her and Sage avoided his eyes by scrutinizing the fire. "I know you don't trust me, but please at least trust this will all work out." The spymaster's attention shifted to the young healer. "I will send someone with her breakfast, and Gavriel will stay tonight." He patted her shoulder. "Speedy recovery to you."

Sage shrugged his hand off, ignoring him. He sighed as he stood. She listened as he crossed the room and exited, his footsteps fading down the hall. Sage's eyes returned to Mira. "What'd he mean, breakfast?" she questioned.

"You've slept a full day, it's nearly dawn. The sun should rise any minute."

She had lost an entire day. What day was it? "Where is Jacob?" she wondered out loud.

Mira folded the blankets, placing them on her cot. "Prince Samuel sent him to bed last night before he settled here for the evening. We will move you to your new room today."

She didn't want to leave the infirmary. It was safer here than anywhere else.

Mira continued, "I will stay with you until you're healthy enough to leave."

Equal parts of sadness and jealousy swirled through her at Mira's naïvety. She would never leave this place. Even if she gave up information, the Crown wouldn't think of releasing a valuable asset. Escape was her only option.

Jacob swept in, smelling of herbs and disturbing her thoughts. He stepped in front of the fire, a warm smile on his face. "It's fantastic to see you sitting up by yourself! Progress is a wonderful thing. I have other good news. A chamber is ready for you and Mira to relocate to today." He gestured to the guards standing nearby. "These gentlemen will help move you to your new abode, and Mira will help settle you in. I'll check up on you daily, but Mira will be your support until we can boot that sickness from your lungs. Garreth, if you please, pick up the lovely miss Ruby and follow me."

As the soldier approached, she forced herself to hold her ground and not scramble away. She focused on his face, telling herself over and over that he was not her torturer, though she went rigid the moment his hand touched her.

"Easy there, love," his deep voice whispered. "I am just going to carry you; no harm will befall you. My arms are going underneath your shoulders and knees and that's all; I won't move them."

He plucked her from the cot and cradled her in his arms. Her eyes closed. Even though she chanted in her head that he would not harm her, the terror was still there. She dug deep for some humor in the situation. Sage finally settled on: "I am not your love."

"I suppose not." Despite having her eyes closed, she could hear the smile in his voice.

Her eyelids stayed tightly shut. Sage knew they went up three flights of stairs, made a left turn, and then a right. A door creaked, and she was placed on something soft. By the time she opened her eyes, the guard was already heading out the door, and Jacob and Mira were the room's only other occupants. She cleared her throat. "Thank you."

Just before leaving, the guard looked over his shoulder with a wink. "My pleasure, love." Then the door closed.

"Stubborn man," she grumbled to herself.

Her new cage was stunning, more beautiful than she ever could have expected. She'd been placed on a giant four-poster bed that was crafted from the pale aqua wood of the jardintin tree. They only grew in the coral sands of Blested Beach, and their wood was rare and highly prized. White, gauzy curtains were draped from post to post, floating around the bed. Rich, dark blue carpets covered the stone floor and deep cushioned chairs were scattered around the spacious room in a sea of colors. A large fireplace occupied the wall adjacent her bed, its mantle comprised of purple shells, shimmering abalone, and dainty starfish. Next to the fireplace, two large doors of pale wood overlooked the sea, their tops filled with glass forming a window. Royal blue drapes of brocade bracketed the doors, their base embroidered with exotic fish.

The room embodied opulence.

Sage ran her hand along the crisp white coverlet upon which she sat.

Compared to her pristine surroundings, she looked just like the street rat she professed to be.

"How do you like your new home?" Jacob asked.

"It's gorgeous. I've experienced nothing like it, and there's only one thing that could make it better."

"What would that be my dear?" Jacob asked curiously.

"A bath," she said. Sage glanced at her hands and grimaced. "I feel like I'll leave a trail of filth everywhere I go."

A giggle snuck out of Mira, and she placed a hand across her mouth, attempting to cover it. The sound loosened something in Sage, bringing a genuine smile to her face.

"I am sure you will have to burn this shift," she said, pointing to Sage's sweat covered linen.

The Healer chuckled and nodded his head. "Mira will draw you a bath, and I will let the kitchen know where to send your breakfast. I'll be in tonight to check on you before I find my own bed. Enjoy your day, my dear." Jacob patted her hand and quit the room.

Sage watched as Mira first stoked the fire, then buzzed around the suite, getting things settled. She slumped into the pillows, surprised to see a mosaic on the ceiling. It was a beautiful array of blues, greens, and yellows; it was like she was beneath the sea, looking up at its surface. "So, what do we do now?"

"We get you healthy."

Sage rolled her eyes, then craned her neck to see the blonde. "Yes, I know, but will we be able to leave the room when I can walk?"

Mira's face became guarded.

That was a no.

"It will be some time before you regain your strength. Let's concern ourselves with that when the time comes."

"So basically, no then?"

Mira sent her an apologetic smile and disappeared into the bathroom. "Just wait until you see this bathroom," Mira called, her voice echoing.

She stared at the ceiling, with the sound of running water in the background. Sage had been nowhere with working plumbing. How did it all work? When she took her bath, she would have to inspect the pipes.

Mira bustled out, brushing damp strands from her face. In another setting, she and Mira would have been friends. She was a sweet, caring woman. When the time came to make her escape, she'd do everything in her power to make sure Mira wasn't blamed.

"Bath time?" she asked, excited at the prospect.

Mira grinned at her. "I have no desire to continue dealing with your smell as I try to sleep. It's time to get you washed up."

Sage grinned back at her. Oh yeah. Mira would be a great friend and ally in this horrid place.

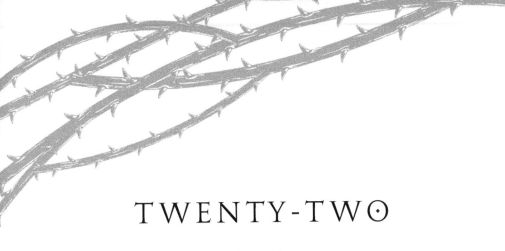

TWENTY-TWO ☉

TEHL

TEHL'S DAYS MELTED INTO EACH other. Each day would start out with monotonous planning for the Midsummer Festival—discussions that would inevitably dissolve into arguments over colors, decorations, or budgets. There was also the usual comment regarding his mother's role in times past, which always frustrated him. Did they not realize he missed her as well? Without fail, he always ended the meetings with a headache—or the impulse to run screaming from the room.

Once *that* nightmare ended, he would be pulled into the war council where again, sensible discussion dissolved into arguments over whose idea should be acted upon. It was ridiculous. They were all suggesting the same thing, just in different ways. It boiled down to this: everyone wanted to either go to war or send spies to Scythia.

However, the moment a man of theirs stepped foot on Scythian soil, it'd be considered an act of war. This point sparked a heated debate among the council, on whether it was worth the risk. Sam believed it was, as did Tehl, though the former worried that, were their spy to be discovered, Scythia would make an immediate retaliatory strike. And, as Sam had yet to extract even a word from the Scythian woman, they didn't have the information needed to make their chances of success feasible. No, they would have to wait to spy on the enemy nation until they had more of an idea of what they'd be getting into once they were over there.

Finally, Tehl ended each day entertaining his court at dinner in the place of his father. The never-ending stream of scantily-clad debutants throwing themselves at him was tiresome. He couldn't quite figure out why they did that squished-lips thing. They resembled fish. When he'd asked Lady Rose about it, her expression of outrage practically singed his hair off. She'd then snapped her fan shut and stomped away in a bustle of rustling skirts; this too, confused him, as it was an honest and impersonal question. He didn't understand why it was so offensive. He would want to know if he was making a face that was so incredibly unattractive.

Ladies of noble birth preened and simpered before him everywhere he went. It perplexed him that they would put themselves in a compromising situation simply to get his attention, since they knew he could marry none of them. The old law dictating Royalty must marry only those of common birth kept Aermia united. Each group would thus be represented by their own member of the monarchy: one for the nobility and one for the citizens.

Even as he made his way from the training area each morning to his personal dining room, young women seemed to stop him at every point. That morning, Tehl tried to be more inconspicuous, hoping to reach breakfast *sometime* before noonday. He scoped out the corridor, searching for any sign of a woman, and saw none, until he spied one of his Elite, Garreth, walking briskly toward him with a young woman in his arms, Mira trailing behind him. The healer gave him a small smile and Garreth nodded respectfully as they passed.

Tehl's breath stilled when he saw the young woman's face. It was the rebel. Her hair tumbled out of its braid and stuck to her damp face. The pallor of her skin made her black hair seem as though it had sucked in all the surrounding color. What struck him most was her face. Her cheeks were sucked in, her brow furrowed, as though she were in terrible agony. Her hands clutched Garreth's tunic so tightly that her knuckles were white.

Garreth jogged up the stairs and vanished from his view. Why was she in so much pain? Where were Garreth and Mira taking her? He needed to ask Sam; his brother always knew what was going on these days.

Tehl jogged to the dining room surprised to find his brother crunching on some bacon there, alone. Tehl had left the training yard before Sam, yet here he sat, already eating. How did he manage it? Tehl shook his head in mirth and flopped down into his chair.

"How did you get here before me? I left before you did. And don't tell me your skills are better than mine." He eyed his brother while snatching up an apple pastry.

Sam cracked a smile and threw one muscular leg over the chair arm. His brother plucked a raspberry off his plate, inspecting it closely. "I *am* better than you, I walked right by you." Sam's familiar blue eyes snapped to his. "You were gawking at Ruby."

Tehl tensed at his brother's comment. "Ruby? On a first name basis, are we? I thought she was an asset, and that we didn't use her name." He sat back and crossed his arms, waiting for his brother's retort.

Sam tossed the berry into his mouth and chewed thoughtfully. "She is not an ordinary asset. With what she has gone through, she deserves to be called by her name. I've been thinking. If we treat her differently, she may become not a prisoner but an ally. We need someone like her. She has surprising battle skills, not to mention a strong will that rivals yours. She could be the key to ending the rebellion, not with brute force, but with us all uniting against Scythia." Sam paused, tapping his finger on his chin. "It would take careful maneuvering."

So that's what this little speech was about: he wanted the rebel to spy for him. "I assume your 'maneuvering' has already begun." A smug smile crept across his brother's face that answered his question. Tehl snagged a fluffy biscuit for himself, buttering its surface thoughtfully.

"So I can thank you for having her moved this morning, I take it?" He watched Sam out of the corner of his eye while drizzling honey on the flakey biscuit.

Sam leaned his head back and steepled his hands underneath his chin. "Her fever broke, so it was time we had her moved somewhere more secure."

Tehl bit into his biscuit and let the sweet and buttery goodness melt in his mouth. A groan slipped out. What did the cook put in these? They were delicious. He examined the golden biscuit as though it would solve the kingdom's problems.

"Trying to get that biscuit to tell you all its secrets, brother?" His brother's voice held laughter. Tehl spared Sam a glance, and his brother wiggled his eyebrows. "Did you even listen to a word I said?"

Tehl smiled sheepishly.

Sam sighed and began muttering to himself. His lips fought a smile; there was nothing more Sam hated than to have to repeat himself. Sam blew out an annoyed breath and continued. "As I was saying…before you and your biscuit got intimately acquainted…I had her moved into one of the smaller suites in our wing."

Tehl spat out his biscuit and watched as it smacked Sam right on the cheek. Sam reached up and brushed the gooey pastry off his face in disgust. His brother meticulously wiped his hand on his napkin and pinned him with a glare. "Now that was just rude," he murmured.

Tehl sniggered at the disgust on his brother's face. The longer he stared at Sam, the funnier it became. Gut-wrenching laughter boomed out of him as Sam's face pinched even more. "Sorry, but it's funny…," he said between peals of laughter.

At that, Sam's irritated expression broke. Before long, his brother was laughing as hard as he was. Tehl took a gasping breath and grinned. "I haven't done something like that since I was a child."

Sam mirrored his grin with a devilish glint in his eye. "It's all right, I will get you back sooner or later," he stated casually.

That remark wiped the smirk from the crown prince's face.

Sam was the master of pranks.

Sam's smile turned predatory, like a leviathan smiling at a seal.

Never show fear.

Tehl straightened his shoulders, feigning confidence. "We'll see about that."

He ran his hand thoughtfully along the dark stubble on his cheek. Sam did nothing without good reason. "So you moved a dangerous rebel into the royal wing, not the guest quarters?"

Sam squinted. "That's what I just said."

Tehl mulled it over. It made sense to keep her close to them so they could watch her. There would be less chance of someone meeting her then. Not to mention if she tried to escape, it would be significantly harder for her to do so. There weren't many rooms available. The only ones were…

His gaze locked with his brothers. "You know how this will look right? An unattached woman living in our wing? Those rooms were used for mistresses in the past and the occasional visiting family member. Everyone knows she's not family."

Sam's lips formed a smirk.

Realization dawned on him. "That's what you want them to assume."

Sam swung his leg to the floor and scooted to the edge of his seat. "Precisely. You were seen running through the palace with a half-naked girl in your arms and your two closest friends trailing you. Rumors are already circling about whom the new mistress belongs to. Many had already tried to get into the infirmary to meet her out of curiosity. This way, no one can get to her except those we allow. Our court assumes she is involved with one of us, so it won't seem odd for her to be staying close by. It is better than the alternative, having any of them knowing the truth," Sam said. "She draws attention everywhere she goes. We need to control how she is perceived by others. People rarely look past the surface. They see what they expect to see. Gav and I have been noted entering at night and leaving the infirmary in the morning. By keeping her inaccessible, it will keep our court guessing and thus focused on the wrong thing."

It was a logical plan. He didn't like her being so close, but it seemed like the best option. The rebel would hate being thought of as his mistress. He liked the idea, but the long-term consequences concerned him. "Her reputation will be ruined," he worried.

Sam scoffed. "Her reputation was ruined when you flashed most of her body to most of the people residing in the castle. There've also been the nightly visits from Gav, you, and me. Not to mention, we don't know who she is. She's in character, a cover. Ruby will cease to exist when she leaves."

"You think she will escape?" Tehl asked.

"It's just a matter of time, Tehl. Be thankful she's as sick as she is. I will keep the Elite on her at all times, but she's good. Once she is healed, there isn't any place that could hold her..." Sam trailed off. "If we can get her on our side, she would make the perfect spy. She's unlike anyone I have come across." Sam's voice was full of awe.

For some reason, that rankled Tehl. He brushed it aside, pinching a grape between his fingers. "Can we turn her?"

Sam considered this for a moment, staring blankly at the wall behind him. "I think so. She is not an anarchist. She legitimately wants to help her kingdom. She's been led to believe the Crown is doing nothing for its people. If we show her what we do and how we are dealing with Scythia, it may soften her enough to give her pause over her chosen ties with those of the rebellion."

Frankly, Tehl had his doubts about anything being able to 'soften' the vivacious girl, but it was worth a try. He shrugged.

Footsteps caught both their attention and a moment later, their cousin came into view. Gav dropped into the chair next to Tehl and began picking out an assortment of fruit, pastries, cheeses, and meats.

"Good morning," Gav said cheerily before digging into the feast before him.

Sam stood and circled his own chair, gripping the top of it. "Good, we are all here. I explained the situation to Tehl, but you need to be informed of the developments." Gav focused his attention on Sam, continuing to shovel eggs into his mouth. "If anyone asks you about your new mistress, be evasive but don't deny that you have one."

Gav paused mid-bite, his eggs slipping from his fork comically. Gav gaped at the two of them. "What new mistress? What the devil are you talking about? I've never had a mistress, and I certainly never will. And why would anyone ask me about it?" Gav spluttered.

Sam winced. "Members of the court, and servants, saw each of us enter the infirmary for the night. They drew their own conclusions. They are not sure which one of us she belongs to. There are some who believe she belongs to *all* of us."

Gavriel set his fork down, his nose flaring as he drew in a deep breath. "You mean to tell me that our court assumed that all three of us had her? Why would you ever tolerate such an obscene conclusion?" Gav's voice dipped down lower.

Tehl held up his hands in innocence. "I have been trying to convince them for the last few days that she is not mine," he said.

Gav pinned Sam with his gaze. "This was your idea?"

"Yes." No remorse.

Gav glowered at his breakfast. "I can understand how this would tactically be the best choice."

Sam beamed. "Thank you, I am glad you see it that way. I—"

"I wasn't finished," Gav cut him off. "This will brand her. You know what they will call her right?" He looked to both of them. "They will consider her a whore. She'll lose any chance of a regular life with a good man."

"I anticipated that. No one has seen her face, nor does anyone know anything about her. Even if any of the information leaks, her name is fake. I searched high and low for information about who she is. I haven't found a single thing about her. When 'Ruby' disappears, so will that reputation."

"What happens if we get her to switch and work with us? She will be seen around the palace," Tehl interjected.

"That's why she is in the royal wing. We can control who sees her. Anyone who saw her face when you took her to the infirmary won't recognize her once she heals. Even since we pulled her from the dungeon, she looks different. Gav, you have seen her. What do you think?"

Tehl glanced over to Gav and watched as he pushed his food around his plate.

"She looks like a different person from when we pulled her from the dungeon, it's true, and she is still covered in cuts and bruises. When she is fully healed, she won't be recognized by anyone except the ones who have had close contact with her—like Jeffry, Jacob, and Mira. Who are the servants that are taking care of her meals and chambers?"

Sam piped up. "I chose a special few who worked with our mother and are discreet. Also, the same four Elite have guarded the infirmary for the last couple of days. They are trustworthy. I have no doubts in their loyalty to us."

"You realize if they think she is one of ours, you must stop entertaining female company. Can you do that?" Gav challenged, a sardonic lift to one eyebrow.

Sam carelessly waved away his question. "It won't be a problem. Besides, even if I still kept my female company, it would keep people guessing. They would wonder if I was just a scoundrel stepping out on my mistress, or if she belonged to one of you." Gav wrinkled his nose and resumed eating. "Any more concerns?" Sam inquired.

Both men grunted 'no', and Gavriel resumed eating. Tehl watched him eat in morbid fascination. Was his cousin chewing his food? He was inhaling it. One moment there was a pile on his plate, and the next, there was none. "Little hungry, cousin?" Tehl teased.

Gav scowled at him and wiped his mouth. "I didn't get to eat dinner last night, and then I practiced with the Elite this morning. Don't judge me, I am starving. At least I don't have honey and biscuit stuck to my face," he retorted sourly.

Tehl brushed his cheek, his fingers sticking to the honey. He viciously scrubbed at it with his palm. "Why didn't you tell me, Sam? You would let me leave like that?"

Sam tugged on his pierced right ear. "I thought it was funny. Gavriel said nothing, either, until you teased him."

Tehl huffed at his brother, dropping his gaze to the table. Sam's plan was reasonable, and it didn't have any holes in it that he saw, but it still didn't sit right with him. He hated the idea of anyone thinking he had a mistress, let alone one he would share with other men. Possessiveness surged through him at the idea. When he found the right woman, he would never share. She would be his and his alone.

Sam strolled to the end of the table and looked out of the window at the cerulean ocean. "Gavriel, I told the girl you would stay with her from now on," he said absently.

Gav cradled the back of his head with his laced fingers. "Why is that? We were taking turns."

"She doesn't like me."

Gav snickered, but turned it into a cough at the black look Sam gave him. "I don't know how that is possible," Gav deadpanned.

"She wants you."

Gav stilled for a moment. "Why?"

"She remembers you pulling her down from the chains. I suppose she associates you with safety. Last night..." Sadness passed over Sam's face. "She was terrified of me when she saw me—she scrambled back so fast, she fell to the floor. She didn't possess enough energy to run, so she crawled away from me. I wanted to rip someone's head off when I left. She is a complete wreck. She needs your calming personality, Gav."

Gavriel's face softened. "I understand. I will watch over her, and who knows. Perhaps she will open up if she feels safe."

"If she sees you as a savior or a friend, she may soften. You are what we need to get her to switch sides or even just act as an intermediate between the Crown and the rebellion. She could stop a civil war." Sam paced as he spoke and then looked straight at Tehl. "I have news you won't be happy about. The captain awaiting judgment for his crimes against Ruby has disappeared."

The silence was deafening. A pin-drop could have been heard.

He got away.

The sick bastard got away.

"Did I hear you correctly?" Gav hissed in his soft, scary voice. Gavriel was about to lose his temper, and it would be a sight to behold. "You let him get away?"

"I didn't *let* him do anything." Sam's voice whipped through the air. "He was publicly stripped of his title and locked in his rooms awaiting judgment." His brother's fists clenched, and small tremors shook his arms. "I visited him this morning to exact some old-fashioned justice after I left that poor girl in the infirmary. But he was gone. My people are searching, but so far there has been nothing."

Tehl's blood boiled. It wasn't Sam's fault. Tehl knew his brother blamed himself. He took a moment and reined in his temper.

His brother's anguished eyes met his as he continued, "I promised her she would be safe from him this morning. That he would be punished."

Serge *would* be punished. Tehl would make sure of it.

Gav rested his elbows on the table and his head in his hands. His shoulders heaved with ragged breaths. Tehl hadn't seen Gav this upset since Emma died.

Tehl gave his cousin a moment to collect himself and centered his attention on Sam. "Use any resources necessary. He needs to be found. He is a danger to Sanee."

"I agree. If you will excuse me, I would like to go hunting myself. I will see you at the war preparation meeting this afternoon." With that, Sam pushed off the wall and stalked toward the exit.

"Brother," he called after him. Sam paused, looking at him expectantly. "When you find him…bring him to me."

Sam gave him a wicked smile and a slight bow. "It will be done, my prince."

"And so the plot thickens," Gav mused. "My question is, why would he run? His punishment would have been severe, but he wouldn't have hung. Serge wasn't known as cowardly, so this doesn't fit with his character. He was of the Guard, not the Elite, so I can't figure out how he made it past them. Most would have been found by Sam's spies by now. It doesn't bode well that they're turning up nothing. We've got to be missing something."

"As much as I would like to pursue it myself, Sam is the best. He will find him." Tehl rapped his knuckles on the table and pushed back his chair. It was time to start his day. He would have to put this aside and trust Sam to do his job.

Tehl scratched the back of his neck, and his nose wrinkled. "I need a bath before I get hounded about the Midsummer Festival. I will meet you at the meeting."

"One thing before you go. Is it necessary I stay with her during the night? Her rooms are close to ours—if anything were to happen, we would hear it."

"I don't need you there for protection; but I do want you there so she can feel safe and secure."

He examined Tehl as he mulled it over. His cousin rolled his neck as he stood. "I understand. I'll do my best." Gav clapped him on the shoulder as he left.

Tehl hoped this went as planned. He was tired of feeling one step behind.

TWENTY-THREE

SAGE

A SALTY SEA BREEZE RUFFLED Sage's hair, loosening strands from her braid. She sat on her balcony, watching the gulls heckle and chase each other playfully. As the cool air kissed her bare arms, it left a trail of goosebumps in its wake. She tightened her shawl about her, enjoying the summer's day.

Mira sat beside her, humming a little tune as she sewed. Over the last few days, she'd established a sort of routine. Gavriel left before she woke each day, so she enjoyed a quiet breakfast with the healer before stepping into her bath. Afterward, Mira would rub her with special oils to help open her lungs while she let her hair dry by the fire. It was around this time that the sweet healer turned evil, forcing Sage to walk the rooms until her legs shook. After this torture, Mira would read to her until lunch, and then they'd eat together. Once Sage had a full belly, she would inevitably fall asleep.

She still wasn't sure if it was due to her body healing itself or Mira slipping something into her tea.

When she woke, Mira would move her out to the balcony, and that was her favorite part of the day.

She had learned a lot about Mira. She'd told her about growing up with her family until she became an orphan at the tender age of eleven. She became a ward of the Crown and ended up in the palace. Jacob's wife had taken notice of her, deciding to take the young girl under her wing. Jacob, too, had opened his arms to her, and together they basically raised Mira. Growing up watching Jacob help people had cultivated within her a desire to help as well, and that's how the little blonde became the only woman healer of their nation.

Mira asked Sage questions here and there, but she never probed. She tried to answer Mira's questions as honestly as possible.

Once the sun began to sink below the horizon, they would move inside and have dinner. Sage would stare into the fire, missing her family and pondering her escape. Once she climbed into bed, Gavriel would magically appear. He was always kind and never made her uncomfortable. Sage didn't love that he stayed the night in her room, but he placed his cot so it sat on the far side of the room. She was also comforted by the fact that she kept a stolen knife stashed beneath her pillow. She would never be helpless again.

Right before she fell asleep, Jacob would shuffle in to check on her. Sage swore he was made of kindness, jokes, and smiles, ever full of exuberance, joy, and just a pinch of mischief.

She could barely make out someone muttering, so she pulled her eyes from the rolling waves, looking instead to the interrupter of her thoughts. "What did you say, Mira?"

Concern marred Mira's face. "I called your name twice before you answered. Are you all right?"

"I am fine." Sage smiled softly. "I was deep in thought, that's all."

"Anything you want to share?"

"Nothing important, just wishful thinking. I am a little stir crazy, and I envy the gulls and their freedom. Sometimes I wish I could fly, too." Sage peered through her lashes at her companion, hopeful. "I am better today. My lungs aren't giving me as much trouble as they have been. I am strong enough for a short walk."

Mira shook her head. "You aren't ready now, but in two or three days you should be. I will talk to Jacob and get his opinion, and perhaps we can go from there. How does that sound?"

Sage pushed down her resentment, knowing her friend was not the true source of it. She forced a smile onto her face. "That sounds reasonable. Thank you, Mira."

Jacob would first talk to the crown prince of her request to get out and walk. Embittered at the level of control that tyrant had over every aspect of her life had her heaving out a frustrated breath.

She returned her gaze to the bobbing ships in the ocean and the oyster fishermen preparing to sail back into the harbor. At that moment, she heard the creak of her door and the heavy tread of boots moving through her room toward them.

"That must be Jacob. I knew he would come early," Mira explained, rolling her eyes. "We're out he—" Mira choked on her own sentence.

Sage glanced at her tongue-tied friend to see what had startled her. Mira hastily dropped her sewing to the ground, sinking into a curtsy. Sage tensed, knowing whoever was approaching was not someone she wanted to see. She hadn't seen Mira that flustered before. Sage focused on the double doors, battling her terror. She would not become a victim. A huge, rugged older man filled her balcony doorway. His steel, dark blue gaze swept over her, pausing on the curtseying healer at his feet.

"Your Majesty, please forgive me!" Mira cried.

Sage's eyes widened, and her heart flew to her throat.

It was the king.

The king.

King Marq.

"It's nothing. Please leave us." His voice was gruff and deep.

Sage shivered and stared pleadingly at the healer, who hadn't taken her eyes from the king since he first stepped foot on the terrace.

"Yes, Your Majesty." Mira stood and met her eyes, flashing her an apologetic smile before scurrying out of the room.

Traitor.

Sage vaguely heard the door close behind Mira as she stared at her friend's empty chair, numbness seeping into her limbs. What did his visit mean? What could he want? She rubbed her eyes and blinked up at him. He still stood on her balcony; she wasn't imagining things.

The king of Aermia was in her room.

He glided confidently from the doorway to the balcony, resting his large, weathered hands on the stone railing. Other than the initial glance, he had yet to look at her.

She couldn't help but stare. He was nothing like she imagined. She'd expected a hunched-over old man, but that couldn't be further from the truth. He stood tall, wrinkles etching his face and silver streaking his blond hair. Tanned, muscular forearms peeped out of his rolled-up sleeves. How similar he and his sons were.

All in all, he was an exceptionally handsome man despite his age. He must have made a striking figure in his youth. Sage had always thought the princes' good looks came from their mother, since her beauty had been famed throughout Aermia, but obviously they took after their father as well.

This was the man that had deserted her country.

He was the traitor.

Sage felt ill. She'd been harboring a glimmer of hope that there was a valid reason for the negligence of their king in his duty toward Aermia, but he stood before her strong and virile, seemingly unscathed by time and illness. He had no more right to rule than she did, despite his royal blood. She checked her growing resentment, fixing her face into a neutral mask.

"Looked your fill yet, darling?"

His softly spoken words snapped her out of her gawking. Painstakingly, she stood and dipped into a wobbly curtsy. "My king, I am sorry if I have given offense. I did not mean to stare, but it is not every day the king himself waltzes into one's rooms." She observed him through her lashes to see if her sly needling bothered him.

His full mouth twitched and a small smile graced his face. "Your rooms? I was under the impression that you were staying in my home."

Arrogant. Like father, like son.

A tart reply was poised on the tip of her tongue when he spun to face her, resting a hip on the sturdy railing. His blue eyes were hauntingly familiar; another trait his sons had inherited. He wiggled his eyebrows, his eyes sparkling.

He was teasing her.

The *king* of Aermia was teasing her.

Well *that* threw her off balance. Her world tipped on its axis. Was this really happening? What was going on?

"Touché, my king," she conceded, dipping her chin once. Her legs quivered, but Sage locked them and stood tall. His gaze ran along the contours of her face. She tensed when his eyes scanned her body, right down to her bare feet peeking out from under her nightgown. Sage shoved aside her anxiety and met his bright blue eyes. They crinkled at the corners as he smiled down at her, his two dimples popping.

He was beautiful, and that was downright offensive.

The king gestured to her feet. "My Ivy always hated wearing shoes, too. She hated the confined dress code. She changed once we married, and it was a damn miracle she wore anything proper to court. She often left her hair unbound, with bits of shell and sea glass woven through it."

Her heart squeezed at the longing she heard in his voice. "She was a lovely woman. The whole kingdom misses her, sire."

The smile on the king's face faded and grief took its place. She fluttered her hands at her side, lost for words.

Weariness weighed on her, and her legs shook with the effort to stay standing. She braced a hand on her chair, gesturing to the empty one next to her. "Would you like to sit down, Your Majesty?"

"Thank you."

Sage waited for him to seat himself and then sank into her own chair, relieved to be off her feet. He didn't speak, merely gazing out at the sea. Awkward minutes passed, and Sage tried not to shift uncomfortably in her seat. She spied on him from the corner of her eye, scrutinizing his profile. From her reports, he was a renowned hermit, so why the visit? Information? More torture? Would he harm her?

Dread trickled down her spine. She was alone with a massive man.

Stupid, stupid, stupid!

She should have strapped on her stolen knife. The bed was too far. Pressure on her balled hand startled her from her frantic thoughts. Her emerald eyes widened as the king's large hand squeezed hers.

"Calm down, darling. I'll not hurt you."

He already had.

The king patted her hand twice before relinquishing it. She watched him rest beside her, his hands laced together over his stomach.

The entire situation was surreal. Here she was attempting to dethrone him, and he sat there like they were bosom buddies.

"With your permission, I would like to be blunt, Your Majesty."

He cocked his head, gray-blond curls tumbling across his forehead. "Be my guest."

"I don't understand what prompted your visit. It's confusing. I am humbled by your presence, but I feel it might be improper for you to be spending your time with a girl from the streets."

Maybe he would take her hint and leave.

"You do realize my wife was a fisherman's daughter?" the king drawled.

"Yes."

"Your station matters not a whit to me. Hard work from both the common and noble classes is what makes Aermia a successful kingdom."

She wasn't expecting that. He would not leave that easily. Time to try another tactic. "I am a thief," Sage challenged.

"That's what I have been told, but I don't believe a word of it."

He smirked at her, and Serge's smirk flashed through her mind. Shivering, she pulled her shawl tighter around her as if it could protect her from the horrible memories.

The king's face pinched as he caught her expression. He faced the ocean and threw his boots onto the balcony edge. Once his gaze moved from her person, the air trapped tightly in her lungs released in a soft hiss.

Sage endeavored to remember what he had said. He didn't believe her. "What do you know about me?"

He tipped his head back, letting out a bark of laughter, the sound of it scattering the gulls in the wind.

"I know the story you told my men and sons: your name is Ruby, your family abandoned you, two of your brothers are pirates, and that you have been living on the streets for some time. You steal to survive, but that's not who you are."

"Who am I?" Sage raised both eyebrows in a mute prompt.

"You are courageous, strong, and kind."

"What?" Suspicion slithered through her. He was up to something.

"You had the opportunity to kill my son and some of the Elite, but you did not. That suggests you're not one to revel in violence," he paused and breathed deeply, "even when you were…I won't say 'interrogated,' because that was not an interrogation. It was a violation…"

He knew? He was the king, of course he knew.

"You never stopped fighting," he continued, steel lacing his tone. "They did not break you, no matter what you may be feeling now."

Her eyes dampened. His sons sanctioned it. The king didn't know.

"Everyone to cross your path has been treated by you with kindness and appreciation. You have not taken advantage of anyone." His faded sapphire eyes flashed to her green ones. "You have a good heart."

He was sincere.

Sage blinked.

The king meant what he said.

Her emotions bounced everywhere. Pain, fear, helplessness, gratitude, shock, and embarrassment flooded her. Her family appreciated her, but no one had ever said something of that magnitude to her. Sage struggled with what she had been told and what she was currently experiencing. "How do you know all of this?"

"I may not be visible but that does not mean I am not around." A sheepish smile crossed his face. "Also, Jeffry and Jacob have always been close friends."

"Jeffry and Jacob?" Sage parroted back. "The Keeper and the Healer?"

His eyes gleamed. "The same. They're twins."

"Really?" In her mind, twins were supposed to look alike. They had a wicked sense of humor in common, but that was pretty much where it ended. "Jacob never said anything."

"Not all of us share everything. I would think that'd be something you'd understand." His solemn eyes rested on her.

"I don't understand what you mean, sire," she fibbed, scrunching her face up in confusion.

He regarded her evenly. "You are an excellent liar."

She kept her body loose and gave him an offended look even as her heart sped up.

The king held up a hand. "In different circumstances, I believe you would be an honest person. From your character, I would stake my life on you protecting someone."

"I think you are seeing things that aren't there, my king. My name is Ruby," she said firmly, turning to admire the setting sun and the kaleidoscope of colors it cast on the evening sky.

"Sure it is, darling," the king retorted.

"I am not your 'darling'," she muttered in a low tone.

The bellowing laughter that burst out of the hulking king suited him. The sound comforted her just as much as it frightened her.

"You are feisty, and I like it. I have enjoyed our time together. I'll be visiting again soon." He nimbly shot out of his chair, hovering next to her. Sage scrambled out of her seat putting a little more distance between them.

"May I?"

She followed his eyes to her hand, where it was fisted in her shawl.

He had asked.

The king of Aermia was asking, not taking. She grudgingly let him lift her shaking hand. He pressed his lips to the back. "Until tomorrow, then."

He spun on his heel, disappearing through the double doors. Sage flopped into her chair and stared, sightless, at the weathered stone beneath her feet. Her head spun. He was nothing like she pictured. She had been told he was a selfish old man, but the man with whom she talked did not seem to be so in any way. Nothing was as it should be these days.

Nothing could have prepared her for this.

Nothing was black and white anymore.

TWENTY-FOUR

SAGE

MIRA RUSHED ONTO THE BALCONY, her skirts rustling with every step, bewilderment evident in her features. Sage was pretty sure her own face mirrored the young healer's.

"Was that truly the king?" Sage had to ask. The answer was obvious, but it seemed so farfetched to think he willingly spent part of his afternoon sitting with her. Mira's head bobbed so emphatically that her blond hair bounced around her face.

Sage blew out a breath, lifting the few stray hairs tickling her face. She opened her mouth but nothing came out. She waved a hand to Mira, as if that could explain everything, and placed her chin in her palm, waiting for Mira to say something.

Mira opened and closed her mouth like a fish. Finally, she settled on, "Are you all right?"

Mira's concern for her warmed Sage's heart. She smiled, grateful to have the healer supporting her. Mira must have had a million questions, yet her first question was on her wellbeing. "I am fine. Confused, but fine. What did I do to warrant his company? Does he visit everyone who enters the infirmary?"

"No," Mira shook her blond head. "I haven't seen him in over a year and I don't understand why he would come to you. He doesn't even show up to welcome important visitors."

Sage arched a brow, and Mira's cheeks pinked at her careless words.

"Not to say you aren't important," Mira rushed out.

Sage attempted to tuck her grin away, but the dismay on Mira's face made her lose it. She sniggered.

Mira chuckled, slapping her on the arm. "You vain thing. I wasn't trying to be mean." Mira took on a curious look. "Indulge me, though. What did the king want?"

"I don't know. We talked little, mostly just staring out at the ocean and listening to its waves. Maybe he just wanted company?" Sage shrugged. "He said he was coming back tomorrow."

"WHAT?" Mira screeched.

Sage pulled on her ears playfully. "Ladies are capable of such sounds?"

Mira didn't smile.

Her smile dropped. "What? What's wrong?"

Mira stood up and paced the small space. "Does this look like it's fit to entertain the king?" She gestured to the worn but clean chairs on which they were sitting.

"He didn't seem to mind when he was here," Sage interjected. "I doubt his focus was on the furniture."

Mira mumbled to herself, counting on one hand.

"What are you doing?"

"I am making a list. There is a lot to be done before he returns tomorrow…"

Mira spouted off a long list of things to be changed or accomplished before the king's following visit. It was spoken so quickly that Sage caught only a few of her self-imposed tasks: scrub the stone, new furniture, food, waitstaff. Sage shook her head. Mira was overthinking it.

Sage hoisted herself out of her chair and into the healer's path. She grasped Mira's biceps, shaking her once. "Listen. Calm down. I have a feeling that wouldn't please him at all."

Mira opened her mouth to argue, but Sage cut her off. "I'm sure you know much more about palace etiquette than someone such as myself, but I got the impression he enjoyed the simplicity of today. Little is needed. From what I gathered, he has been seen little these last few years. He obviously wants to be left alone, so no waitstaff. I agree on the refreshments, though. It's a wonderful idea, as men can *always* eat."

The blonde pursed her lips as she contemplated. "Men do love food," she finally conceded. Mira noted the setting sun and hustled her back into their suite. "Let's start a fire and get you all toasty."

Sage closed the doors to the balcony, drawing the heavy curtains across the windows, and clambered into the enormous bed. She quaked underneath the covers while Mira coaxed the fire back to life. Sage ground her teeth together in frustration. It wasn't even that cold outside and yet she shivered like it was the middle of winter. She owed Mira her life.

"Thank you, Mira."

"It's nothing, Ruby."

Sage was really starting to hate that name. She wished she could give Mira her real name. It seemed like ages since she was truly herself.

Her mind flitted to her family. What were they doing at this moment? Had they stopped searching for her? Tears pricked her eyes as she thought of the fear and pain her family must be experiencing. She had disappeared from their lives over two weeks ago. Sage needed to keep focused on regaining her health; she would not break down. She had to keep up this pretense until she managed escape. Sage shoved down her sadness and turned her thoughts to the day's unusual visit. No matter how charming the king was, his visits didn't bode well for her.

"Mira?"

"What is it?" Mira sat on the bed next to her.

Sage swallowed hard, hoping this gamble would pay off. "I am worried about the attention this will bring me if others know about the king's visits. I feel like it'd be best if we kept everything discreet."

Mira studied her face and clasped her hand. "I agree. When the king left, he demanded the guards' silence, but not mine. However, I see the wisdom in keeping silent, so I shall. Gavriel reports back to the princes, though, so we need to be careful to leave out any mention of his visits in the evenings."

"You would do that for me?"

"I would do it for both of you. You may be just what the king needs right now." Mira stood and moved toward the door. "I'll go and find us some dinner."

"This means a lot to me. I won't ever forget your kindness, Mira," Sage said with sincerity, every word from her heart.

Mira winked over her shoulder, exiting the chamber. "Next time, you can take care of me when I'm ill."

Guilt coursed through her, knowing she wouldn't be here when Mira got sick. Hopefully, she would be far away and could leave this all behind her, but something told Sage that leaving Mira would be much harder than she'd initially imagined.

Knuckles wrapped on the door as it swung open.

"That was quick, Mira. Did you run all..." Sage sat up, surprised.

Gavriel strolled through the door, his black hair windswept, his violet eyes warm.

She twisted to the windows, noting the faint light filtering through them. "You're early."

A spark of anxiety crept up on her. She had never been alone with him before. Why the change? Sage swallowed and tried to be rational. Gavriel hadn't hurt her. He'd always been kind. He saved her.

Gav wouldn't hurt her.

"Well, I had little to do this evening, and I wanted to escape dining with the court. Thus, I decided to beg for sanctuary." He cast her a sheepish grin.

"By all means, enter and enjoy the comfort of my Crown-appointed abode." Sage gestured to the opulent suite.

Gavriel jostled something under his arm while he moved to his cot, his back to her. She peeked out of the corner of her eye, covertly examining the parcel.

"Would you like to see what it is I brought you?" he said, not turning around.

How did he know she was looking? He must have eyes on the back of his head, just like her mother.

"I would," she said. "I must admit my curiosity is piqued."

Avoiding any sudden movements, he made his way over to her, a spring in his step, placing the parcel on her bed.

If any other man had done so, she'd have scampered away, but there was something so soothing about Gavriel. This man could have left her to die, but he didn't. He chose to help her. She had nothing to fear from him.

Carefully, she unwrapped the parcel. Inside, she found a stunning chessboard. "A game?"

She tipped her head up staring into his gorgeous violet eyes. *The man had no right to look that devastatingly handsome.*

"I beg your pardon?"

"What?" She blinked.

He rubbed his nose, flashing her a shy smile. "Um...about my eyes."

Sage squished her eyes close, mortified. Of all the things to say out loud. A nervous chuckle escaped her. "Oh, hell, I can't believe I said that out loud." She wanted to bang her head against the wall.

He waved a hand at her as if to wash away her embarrassment.

"It's true, though. You are gorgeous. I have never seen eyes like yours before."

Seriously.

Someone needed to bind her mouth shut.

It was his turn to give her an embarrassed smile. "Why, thank you."

"But I can't accept this," Sage sighed dramatically. "What would your court think of you bringing a thief gifts? It simply isn't done!"

"I'll just tell them that my eyes didn't woo you, so I had to bring you gifts to capture your heart," he teased.

The awkwardness melted away with their combined laughter.

Gavriel bowed to her. "So, my lady, would you like to play a game of chess with me?"

"Of course, my lord, that sounds positively delightful!" she simpered. A smile played about his lips as he set up the board.

That started what was to become a nightly tradition of theirs. They gossiped, laughed, and teased Mira, whose frequent response was a playful scowl over the top of her book.

But Sage still dreaded going to bed. Everyone settled down and fell into an easy sleep, save her. She would stare at the ceiling, willing herself to stay awake, until sleep claimed her anyway.

Nightmares assaulted her.

Sharp blades. Terror. Leering faces. Torn clothing. Humiliation. Pain. Rough, bruising hands. Helplessness. Shame.

The first time, she woke up screaming, Gav had his arms wrapped tightly around her. Mira was whispering, but Sage didn't understand what she was saying.

There was only terror.

And hysteria.

Gavriel rocked her, his lips on her temple, murmuring to her she was safe. Eventually, the hysteria turned into soul-shattering sobs. Gav's arms were no longer a cage but a sanctuary, and so she snuggled into them, crying herself asleep.

The next day, she was so embarrassed that she avoided any eye contact with Gav at all, but the stubborn man wouldn't let her get away with it.

Three little words.

You're not alone.

It turned out that Gav, too, suffered from nightmares because of his wife's accident. He wished someone had been there to comfort him on those nights. Gav brushed the hair from her face, just like her father always had. "There is no reason to be embarrassed, Ruby. What happened to you was traumatic, and it's okay to be vulnerable sometimes. I can help fight your demons."

Sage teared up with his compassionate promise. She never expected to have someone care for her in the palace of all places. She couldn't believe how lucky she was to have gained two such devoted friends. Mira and Gavriel were something special. She wished she could take them with her when the time came for her to depart.

TWENTY-FÍVE

SAGE

BETWEEN HER AFTERNOON VISITS WITH the king and Gavriel's company in the evenings, Sage's days were more diverting and seemed to move a little quicker. Neither man was anything like she'd expected him to be.

She had accepted the king's visits, but still didn't know what to make of them. He insisted she call him Marq, and it was odd using his given name instead of his title. She still expected someone to reprimand her every time she said it.

With each day she spent with him, it became increasingly evident that something wasn't right. Some days, he was teeming with energy and stories. Others, he stared morosely out to sea, like he had nothing to live for. Sage didn't know which persona she would greet each day. Marq lost track of time and memories. It frustrated him when he recovered from one of his episodes.

It was heartbreaking to watch. He may have been physically strong, but his mental state was deteriorating. The king hadn't abandoned Aermia like she had been led to believe; he was sick, but not in the usual way. Whatever it was, it could not be seen or examined. From the stories he told, however, she realized how much he loved his people. It was sad that he had not the capabilities to even care for himself, let alone a kingdom.

How had his sons kept his current state a secret for so long? How would the rebellion use that information? That question plagued her. She didn't know what she would do with the information. Despite her best efforts, the king had grown on her. He didn't deserve what they had planned for him. It wasn't a crime to grow older. Sage still didn't care for his sons, but she had softened toward Marq. She didn't know what to do. She needed to think.

And think she did.

Sage had been trapped in her suite for two weeks. She needed to get out, even if it was only a walk, before she lost her mind.

Her sanctuary was her balcony overlooking the sea.

Sage stretched her poor, abused legs out and propped her feet on the railing. At least they were healing. The sun warmed her deliciously as she plotted how to trick Mira into letting her out.

Any time she brought the idea up, the blond healer would change the subject or make excuses about her health. True, Sage wasn't completely healed, but she knew her own body and she could handle a walk. Her coughing had abated during the day and was now only an issue at night.

"I haven't seen a prettier sight since my dear Ivy," a deep voice purred.

She jerked, but relaxed once she recognized the voice. Sage cracked her eyes open sleepily, wearing a lazy grin. "You are a shameless flirt! What would your sons say if they heard you speaking like that?"

He flashed her a wolfish grin and plopped down in the seat he had adopted for himself. "They would probably be disappointed that I beat them to it." A pause. "Sam would give me his blessing, though, once he stopped nursing his own wounded pride."

A peal of laughter erupted from her, which seemed to please him. His grin deepened. It was good to laugh. Freeing, almost.

"I don't doubt that for one moment. I never know quite what to expect from him." Sage had seen Sam here and there, but he never stayed long, and she appreciated that. He still made her uncomfortable. She didn't think it was the man himself so much as the fact that he was a sizeable man, one who could hurt her if he chose, and it was that which unsettled her.

"I have news which I believe will brighten up your day."

Sage reached out, clasping the king's rough hand. "Just having you here considerably brightens my day, Marq."

"And you call me the flirt," the king said, smoothly. He leaned toward her like he had a secret. "What would you say if I told you I was going to steal you away for a walk?"

Sage squealed, unable to help it. "I would say you were my favorite person in the entire kingdom. Plus, you would save me from an early death of boredom. Please don't be teasing me. My poor heart couldn't handle the disappointment."

"Your wish is my command." Marq sprung up from the chair and held out his arm.

Sage graced him with a blinding smile and allowed him to take her arm. She barely kept from bouncing on her toes. She was to be free, even if it was just for a bit.

Mira and the guards stood outside the door. Various degrees of surprise showed on their faces when she followed in the king's wake. All of them bowed deeply as they passed, and Sage struggled not to pick up her pace. Someone surely would send her back into her gilded cage. A soft, sweet voice made Marq pause. And there it was. Mira.

"Excuse me, Your Majesty, she's not well enough to be out. If she exerts herself too much, it will aggravate her injuries."

The king looked over his shoulder and spoke. "We're not going for a strenuous hike in the mountains, only for a walk. She will lose her damn mind being trapped in those rooms any longer. We both appreciate your concern, and I promise to take good care of her. Good day."

Having dismissed them, the king strode forward with purpose. Sage craned her neck and met Mira's worried blue eyes. "I am all right," she mouthed, smiling encouragingly before facing forward and catching up to His Highness.

"So where are we going?" Sage inquired curiously. If she had been able to skip, she would have.

"It's a surprise."

His face betrayed nothing. Marq led her down the long hallway to the last door on the right. The door swung on silent hinges, revealing another suite as elaborate as hers. She was a little disappointed that she wasn't going for a longer walk, but she figured beggars couldn't be choosers, so she pasted on a smile, appreciative of the king's kindness. Marq glanced at her face and chortled.

"What's so funny?"

He pointed at her face. "The look on your face was priceless. Don't worry, *this* is not your surprise." He turned and walked toward an immense bookcase and pushed a silver-leafed book inward, until there was a faint click. The bookcase rolled to the side, exposing an empty doorway.

Her feet carried her to the king's side. She ran a hand along the stone, looking for the catch. "A secret entrance? Where does it lead?"

"Follow me, and you will find out."

King Marq lit a lantern and began descending the stone steps. Unease crept over her. Was this some kind of trap? It would be foolhardy to blindly trust him. She turned it over in her mind. Had Marq truly wanted to harm her, it was within his power to do so, even more so because their alone time afforded him many opportunities to do whatever he pleased—yet he'd never given her cause for fear. She realized it was more the situation than the man himself that discomfited her, and even that was lessened by the small weight at her ankle. After the king had caught her off guard that first day, Sage had made sure to always have her little knife on her.

"Are you coming?" His words echoed up to her.

Sage stepped into the dark stone stairwell, her decision made. The king waited until she'd reached him before continuing down the spiraling steps. Each of her ragged breaths felt overly loud in the closed space. Time ceased to exist in the shadowy stone staircase. Every once in a while, they passed darkened doorways. When she asked where they led, the only answer she received was, "Here and there."

She shrugged it off; everyone had secrets.

Forest-green lichens crept up the walls the farther they descended. Sage's legs shook with each step, causing her to brace a hand against the wall. Something slimy squished between her fingers and down her hand. Disgusted, Sage jerked her hand back. What was that? She shook her hand, ready to break down and ask how much farther they had to go, but before she got the chance, Marq spoke.

"Watch your step. The stones are quite slippery."

Sage rolled her eyes at his back.

"I saw that," he chided.

What? How could he have seen her face? Spoken like a true parent.

His low chuckle filled the air. "No, I didn't, but I *did* raise two boys."

She smiled at his response. It sounded like something her papa would say. The crashing of waves on stone snagged her attention. She looked around, trying to locate the sound, hope filling her. "Is that what I think it is?" she whispered.

The king looked up at her, eyes glittering with excitement. "Come and see for yourself."

Sage almost fell on her face in her haste to scramble down the remaining stairs. Marq steadied and aided her the next few steps as they entered a cave. Sage stared in awe at the starfish that clung to the cove walls. She had a special fondness for the little sea creatures. Her heart stopped when they wound around a large porous rock and she spotted a rough archway pouring sunlight into the dim hidden cove. Their speed picked up as they burst out of the cave.

Her feet sunk into the damp sand, filling her slippers up. She was on the beach, the bloody beach! She yanked off her slippers and wiggled her toes in the sand, a bright smile lighting her face. The king watched her with a silly smile of his own, taking in each of her expressions.

Joy and appreciation filled her. Momentarily forgetting his station, and her suspicions, she grabbed him in a fierce hug. "Thank you so much!" Sage whispered into his shirt. She stretched up on her toes and kissed his whiskered cheek before stepping out of his arms.

She looked up at him only to see the oddest expression cross his face. Suddenly self-conscious, she dropped her eyes to the golden sand beneath her and took another step back. "Uh…I'm sorry," she mumbled. He had told her to call him Marq, it was true, however, his casual behavior did not negate the fact that he was still their sovereign and *not* her grandfather. She needed to keep that in mind.

"Ruby!" he admonished, his boots entering her view. A large, calloused finger slid under her chin, forcing her to meet his eyes. A wealth of emotions simmered there. "It has been a long time since someone has embraced me with genuine affection. Thank you for such a gift."

His sturdy arms embraced her tenderly. Warmth and affection filled her as she took in his words. Maybe, just maybe, she'd found a kindred spirit in the

Aermian king.

After releasing her, she was shocked to see him plop down in the sand and strip off his boots and stockings. He rolled up his trousers and stood. "Shall we, my darling?"

Sage rolled her eyes at him—she would never break him of that. "Despite that nickname, we shall, my king."

He led them straight to the ocean. Sage lifted her skirt as the warm water raced past her toward the pristine beach. Her eyes closed as she tipped back her face and raised her arms above her head, savoring the sun's warm embrace. The briny sea breeze ruffled her clothing, making the linen slap against her legs. She wished to capture this moment and remember it always. This was freedom. Freedom and peace.

"I love the sea," she said, not opening her eyes. "As a little girl, I always wanted to be of the Sirenidae. My grandmother used to tell me fantastic stories about swimming with them when she was a girl. Do you think the Sirenidae still exist?"

Sage twisted to face the older man, opening her eyes. A mixture of love and wistfulness shone in his face.

"What is it?" It was times like these he would turn inward, shutting everyone out. She gave him an encouraging smile.

"I met Ivy here. She was so beautiful I didn't think her real. I tripped just trying to get to her," he grinned absently at the memory. "She stood exactly as you are now, face to the sun, arms stretched out, the waves caressing her ankles. I thought she was a mirage that would disappear before my eyes." He crossed his arms and kicked at the waves. "The truth was a lot less fantastical. She was the daughter of an oyster fisherman. Tired of waiting for him to return one day, she wandered onto this beach looking for sea turtles. That moment is etched into my memory. She was the most beautiful creature I have ever laid eyes upon."

The love and devotion in his voice brought tears to her eyes. *That* was what love should be like.

"I have never heard that story before. Thank you for sharing it with me. I will cherish it," Sage whispered, meaning every word.

His eyes emptied, the light extinguished. Her heart clenched at his desolate expression. Today was a good day, and she would not let him disappear.

An idea formed and so she plotted. She could be thrown into the dungeon for this, but it would be worth it. Sage swung her foot back and kicked a volley of water over the king. He yelped in surprise, eyes widening. Water dripped from his graying blond curls onto his startled face.

Life flickered back into him, and then there was something in his eyes that gave her pause. Feigning nonchalance, she balanced on the balls of her feet and shrugged one shoulder. "Your face was a little red, I thought you might need to cool off."

There was definitely a deviling gleam in his blue eyes. His face twisted into a mischievous grin, one she had almost certainly seen on Sam's face; like father like son.

"My dear lady, you look overheated yourself. Allow me to refresh you," he growled leaping toward her.

The sand shifted beneath her feet, impeding her escape. A wave of water slapped her in the face, leaving her sputtering.

"That's it! I *will* have my vengeance!" she shouted, flinging saltwater at the ambushing king. Sage only got one good splash in before he struck again, practically drowning her. Sage lifted her hands up in surrender. "I yield, I yield!"

"So, you yield and therefore agree that I am the most skilled water warrior you've yet crossed paths with?" He puffed his chest in mock pride.

She pushed her dripping hair from her face and wiped the saltwater from her stinging eyes. Sage placed her fist over her heart and bowed with a flourish. "I bow to your superior water warrior skills, Your Majesty."

They eyed each other as she stood. The oddity of the situation hit her. If she ever told this story, she was certain no one would believe her.

He chuckled briefly before composing himself. Almost immediately, however, another chuckle escaped. He then pointed to her head. "You seem to have something in your hair."

Sage patted her head and encountered something slimy. Seaweed. She had seaweed in her hair. She looked back at Marq in time to see him struggling to keep a straight face. "Is this funny, sire?"

His lips twitched once before his laughter rumbled out, joined by her own giggles. Once they had both reigned themselves in, she asked, "What would you like to do now, my king?"

"My king? Your Majesty? Sire? We are well past all that. Please, call me Marq, darling."

"I will call you Marq the day you stop calling me your darling, my king."

"Touché." The king dipped his head. Marq straightened and gazed at an outcropping of black porous rocks. "How would you like to go starfish hunting? Ivy was always fond of it."

"That sounds like just what I need this afternoon."

Much to her delight, they found all manner of interesting things. Crabs, starfish, sea anemones, sand dollars, and gorgeous sea glass rested in the tide pools; they found every color of the rainbow. When was the last time she'd laughed and smiled so much?

As the sun sank, they began strolling back to the castle. She tilted her head back and observed the immense gilded prison looming above them. She had half a mind to run screaming in the other direction, but she discarded the idea as soon as it formed. Though frail in mind, the king was strong. In her state, she would make it only a few paces before he caught her.

She glanced his way and caught him studying her in that intense way he was prone to from time to time. She smiled weakly and dropped her eyes. "Is there something on your mind, my king?"

"Did you have a nice time this afternoon?" The vulnerability was clear in his voice and it hurt her heart.

"I can't remember the last time I have enjoyed myself this much." Her honesty surprised herself. "Thank you for such a wonderful adventure this afternoon. I will treasure this memory." And she meant it.

"The same for me, my darling," Marq admitted. "Thank you for humoring an old man."

Sage raised her chin and winked flirtatiously at Marq. Right before her eyes, Marq Ramses, king of Aermia, blushed.

"What is this?" she exclaimed, pointing to his pink cheeks. "Are you blushing, Your Majesty?"

"I don't know what you are referring to. Men don't blush, especially not kings. I must have gotten too much sun."

"As you say, my king." Sage tucked away her grin.

"Your words say one thing but your tone says something very different." He squinted at her. "Don't forget that I've two sons well versed in sarcasm."

"You are quite right."

Her smile dimmed. His two sons. Monsters. Sam no doubt was proficient in the art of sarcasm, the crown prince however... A chill ran down her spine. In her meager experience, he didn't have a humorous bone in his body. Probably no joyful ones either.

The unlikely duo reached the entrance to the stairwell and began their trek up the slick stairs. Every step slurped obnoxiously in the narrow space. Sage wished she had put her slippers back on as the algae and seawater squished between her toes, but it was too late now. She then noticed that Marq had yet to put his boots back on as well. She squared her shoulders. If the king could do it, then so could she.

Sage sent up a quick prayer of thanks when they reached dry stairs. She flexed her toes with each step to alleviate the cramping from trying to keep her balance. The dark algae covering the walls ended at that point too. How odd. "Why does the algae stop here?"

"The tide comes in and fills the stairwell to this point."

Her eyes widened in understanding. She had wondered why they left this passage unprotected, but it made sense. Even the best swimmer couldn't hold his breath long enough to swim up all those stairs once this place flooded. The stairwell seemed to shrink around her, so she picked up her skirts and scampered after the king.

With each step, her breathing sawed in and out. After another couple of flights, her legs quivered with each step, but still she pushed on. Finally, a wracking cough seized her, and she gasped for air.

Marq swung the lantern around. "Are you all right?"

She waved a hand at him and then placed both hands on her knees. "I will be okay," she wheezed. "I need a little break. My legs feel like jelly."

He frowned at her and pursed his lips. "We might have overdone it today. I know a shortcut we can use."

He waited for Sage to catch her breath before starting back up the stairs like a mountain goat. Sage mumbled curses and continued, slogging after him. To her relief, they climbed only fifteen more stairs before he glided into a new tunnel.

Grit and dust stuck to the bottom of her feet as she followed. Beady eyes gleamed at her from the abandoned hallway. She sincerely hoped that whatever happened to live down here left her alone, specifically creatures of the eight-legged variety. She gave each web they passed a wide berth.

King Marq halted as the hallway came to a dead end. He probed the wall until she heard a faint click. Soft light filtered in when the king poked his head out the door, looking left and then right. He waved her forward and shut the door behind her. She memorized their hiding spot with a keen mind.

It was a perfect way to escape.

The king peeked around the corner and then flashed her a smile full of mischief. "It's been years since I snuck around with a young lady. It's clear. Let's make our escape."

They casually wandered from their spot, each mirroring the other's grin. They had only taken a couple steps when a doorway opened, and a sea of men spilled out, spotting them.

TWENTY-SİX

SAGE

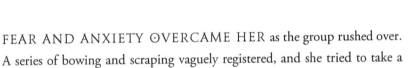

FEAR AND ANXIETY OVERCAME HER as the group rushed over. A series of bowing and scraping vaguely registered, and she tried to take a step back from the king's side. His hand slipped around hers and tightened. Her breathing turned ragged. So many men. She needed to get away. She wasn't safe.

One by one, the pairs of eyes focused on her, making her skin prickle. Each look held its own special horror. She was surrounded. She needed to leave. Sage frantically searched for an escape route when her eyes caught a familiar gaze.

Gavriel.

She barely registered the spymaster standing beside him before focusing on Gav. If she could only get to Gav, she would be safe. She dropped her gaze to her hand in the king's grasp. Her fingers were white. She couldn't feel them. Her eyes dropped farther to her feet, and Sage grimaced at her dirty, bare feet next to the king's hairy ones. What a sight she and the king must make. Both windswept, looking tumbled.

Tumbled.

Oh no.

She tried to slam the door closed on her nightmares but they fought back.

Bile crept up her throat at the memory of grabbing hands. Her vision swam, turning the floor to a puddle of colors. Giant, black blobs entered her line of sight. A large hand stretched toward her, palm up. A buzzing filled her ears, and black spots danced across her eyes.

"My lady, it is so nice to see you again."

Gav. Thank the stars, it was Gav.

Sage blinked as he took her hand and placed a light kiss on the back of it before kissing her cheek. "Take a deep breath, Ruby. These men will not harm you. Sam and I will let nothing bad happen to you," he whispered in her ear. "Breathe, you need to breathe."

Sage's breath rushed out of her at his softly spoken command. She didn't even know she'd been holding her breath. Sage closed her eyes and tried to will the fear away. It didn't abate completely, but with Gav at her side, it was more manageable. She was not the victim. Sage lifted her head in increments until she met his unique eyes.

"You're looking so well, my lady." His gaze swept over her, missing nothing.

"Thank you, my lord. The healers took excellent care of me. The sea breeze and sun were exactly what I needed this afternoon."

"Indeed."

His penetrating look was uncomfortable. She shifted her eyes from his face to Sam's grinning one.

Sam stepped forward and dipped into a courtly bow. "My lady, I praise the stars to be able to see you again so soon."

Whispers erupted around them at his comment. Sam smiled down at her smugly. A glimmer of irritation worked through her. What was he talking about?

Sage pasted on a sweet smile. "If only I could say the same," she mumbled so low that only Sam heard it. His lips twitched at her insult.

Insufferable man.

"The pleasure is all mine, Your Highness," she simpered, sounding like an idiot.

It was as if a silent signal had been given. The surrounding men pushed forward to greet her, her anxiety ratcheting, but as Gav had promised, both Sam and Gav positioned themselves so that none of the men touched her.

"What the devil are you all doing standing in the doorway? Don't you have things to do?" The irate voice carried over the melee.

The crown prince.

Sage cringed and huddled closer to Marq, a small whimper escaping her. A hand tightened on her own, making her realize she hadn't released his hand. She drew strength from the king as the prince's frustrated voice moved toward them.

He was the reason she was left in that cell. His men were the ones who had brutally attacked her. She suffered and had nightmares each night because of him. A spark of rage ignited inside her, burning her dread to ash. She would not cower. Sage dug deep from a place she didn't know she still had. She straightened to her full height, a few inches over five feet, shored her nerves, and cleared all emotion from her face.

The spymaster's watchful eyes intensified, cataloguing each of her movements. That man saw too much. She needed to keep an eye on him, but her thoughts ceased when the crown prince came into view, her breath stuttering as if she'd been kicked in the stomach.

His powerful figure cut a swath through the men. Wide shoulders and a powerful chest led down to sculpted waist and strong thighs.

Imposing. That was the word that came to mind when looking at him. He was taller and stronger than his father.

Sage's eyes snapped back to his face. High cheekbones faded into a hint of dark stubble shading his chiseled jaw. Thick, wavy hair framed piercing eyes. Eyes that were locked on her.

Alluring.

There was something about his inky hair and midnight eyes that appealed to her, though she knew better than to trust that. Beneath that beauty held cruelty, and Sage would never forget that.

His face registered his shock before he schooled his features. He lengthened his stride, stopping mere paces away. Sage locked her shaking knees, attempting to hold onto the anger, which kept her fear at bay, and not scamper away.

"Your Majesty. It is good to see you." He bowed to his father respectfully.

King Marq stepped closer to his eldest son and slapped him on the shoulder, dragging her with him.

"It is good to see you as well, my son. This young lady has been a source of much amusement of late. We had a stimulating afternoon. I haven't truly enjoyed someone's company in far too long." Marq touched her hair, his fingers trailing over the silky strands until they brushed her shoulder.

Her eyes snapped to the king who smirked at his son. What was he doing? He had never touched her like that. Stimulating company? Even to her, those words sounded suggestive. She scanned the group of men, gauging their reactions. Many knowing looks sent their way made her want to puke all over the floor.

Her gaze returned to the crown prince. Anger was plain on his face. Disgust. Sage returned his glare with one of complete indifference, but her mask was cracking. She needed to leave. Now.

The king turned to her like he had read her mind. She gave him a relieved smile when he kissed her hand prettily. He would take her back to the room unscathed.

"Thank you for the wonderful afternoon. I will see you soon, my darling."

What?

Sage blinked and then stared at him in confusion. The king dropped her hand and thrust her into his eldest son's arms. Her whole body froze as the crown prince reflexively caught her, his giant hands wrapping around her biceps. The hair rose on her arms when the prince's thumbs swept across her exposed skin. When would this hell end?

"Please accompany her back to her chamber."

She meant to plead with Marq, but the words stuck in her throat. Sage sent him a pleading look, which he returned with a bright smile before sauntering off with most of the men. He'd left her with the enemy. He'd betrayed her.

Why would he do that?

Fear, betrayal, and confusion tangled inside her. The large body in front of her shifted, causing her to jerk backward and snap out of her thoughts. Her eyes flicked to the man holding her hostage. A cry gurgled in her throat at the anger there.

He released her abruptly and held his elbow out to her stiffly. "If it pleases you, I will escort you back."

Everything screamed at her to run. But to where? She had nowhere to go. Her emerald eyes darted around, taking in the few remaining men who were eyeing her with curiosity. A warm hand settled in the middle of her back.

"Accept his offer, Ruby. It's for your safety," Gav whispered.

Safety? Sage wanted to laugh. She would never be safe with him. She eyed the crown prince's elbow like one would a snake. She didn't want to touch any part of him, but logic filtered through. If she went quietly, maybe she could get away. If she insulted the crown prince in front of witnesses, there would no doubt be consequences.

Sage took one step and paused. Gavriel nudged her in encouragement. She gathered her courage and shuffled to the prince's side. Her fingers rested lightly on his sleeve, his arm hard as ice. "I thank you, my lord."

He drifted forward, Sam and Gav alongside them. Courtiers passed them, tittering and whispering into each other's ears or behind fans. Sage ignored the stares that crawled across her skin. She was led through a twist of hallways and rooms, finally arriving at a grand staircase that split in two. Sage cringed inwardly at having to hike up another set of stairs.

She'd only wanted a walk.

"What was that?" the prince hissed.

"Nothing, sire."

The prince set a grueling pace up the white and gold marble steps. After the first set, her legs trembled so badly that she wobbled and almost tumbled down the stairs. The crown prince cursed, slipping an arm around her back. She would have thrown it off if she could have stayed on her feet. Once again, he picked up his speed, dragging her up two more flights of steps. His grip tightened around her back so that his fingers were brushing against the swell of her right breast.

Her mind flashed back to unwanted caressing hands and cold eyes. She flung herself out of his arms when they hit the landing. Sage lurched to the side, swaying, before she caught her balance and stormed toward her door. She needed a bath. She could still feel his skin against hers.

A large hand slid around her wrist like a manacle. Without thought she lashed out at her attacker, punching. The crown prince caught her fist in his palm, snarling at her.

She tugged on her arms but he held on. "Let go of me!" Frantically, she pulled on both of her hands locked in his grip. He prowled toward her, making her scramble backward. A solid object pressed into her back. A wall.

She was trapped.

Dark blue eyes glared into green ones. "What were you doing with my father?" he snarled.

"None of your business."

The pace of her breathing escalated with his closeness. She had promised herself she would never let herself get in this position again, and yet here she was. She was better than this. Swiftly, she smashed her knee upward, and color drained from the prince's face. Sage pivoted under his arm and swept her leg out, knocking him onto his back. She ripped the knife from her ankle and pounced on him. Sage straddled his chest, her knees pinning his arms, with her knife tip pricking his neck.

"Don't you ever try that with me again! I don't care if you're the next king. If you touch me without my permission, I will kill you! Do you hear me?" she screamed. "I don't care if I swing for this, but I never want to be forced to suffer your touch again! Do you understand me?" she growled, pressing her stolen blade harder into his neck.

"He can't answer with your knife pressed against his neck." Gav's calm voice wrapped around her. "You need to step back, Ruby. I won't let anything happen to you, but you need to let him go."

Gav moved closer, but she never took her eyes off the crown prince. What was she doing? She wasn't an assassin. His midnight eyes tracked the single tear that dripped down her face and plopped onto his cheek.

"No more," she whispered brokenly. She was lifted off him and into Gavriel's arms. Sage looked up, meeting her friend's violet eyes. "Please take me to my room."

Gavriel wrapped her up and led her to her suite. A scratchy voice made her falter.

"I promise."

She looked over her shoulder with a single nod of acknowledgement. "Remember that you do."

Sage wavered when both guards turned to her. She inspected both of them and arranged her face into a weak smile. She knew them. Sage ignored their pity-filled eyes and entered her suite, for once happy to be in her cage.

Mira stood up from her chair, dumping her book on the floor. "You have been gone for hours! Did you overdo it? Why are you wet and dirty? Never mind, I will draw a bath right now."

Sage shrugged out of Gavriel's arms and rushed into Mira's. "Thank you for being a good friend," she whispered into the healer's neck.

Sage dropped her arms and moved to the balcony to watch as the last of the sun's rays faded. Gav and Mira whispered to one another, but her mind was a thousand miles away.

It was time.

Something had caught her attention when she arrived at the door: a guard was twisting his ring on his finger. It caught her attention because it was something she, too, did when deep in thought. The ring's exquisite design intrigued her.

A dragon pierced by its own sword.

So similar to the family crest that you wouldn't notice the detail unless you peered at it closely. Her time in this prison was finished. The rebellion was here.

At last, she would escape.

TWENTY-SEVEN

TEHL

TEHL GLARED AT THE CEILING. He was such an idiot. What was he thinking grabbing her like that? He hadn't thought at all. Tehl blew out a breath as Sam leaned over him, his blond brows wiggling.

"The family jewels still attached brother? They're kind of important, something about heirs…"

"Not sure, Sam. Bruised for sure, though. Would you check on them for me?" he joked through his pain.

Sam's faced soured. "I fear I must decline; I love you, but not that much." His brother held a hand out. "I will, however, help you up. That much I can manage."

Pulling onto his knees, nausea washed over him. Tehl hunched over and heaved. He had never been hit that hard between the legs before. Tehl swiped at the sweat on his forehead before holding his head in his hands.

Rapid footsteps stomped toward them—an angry staccato.

"What the bloody hell were you thinking?" his cousin exploded, shaking a fist at him.

Tehl pushed to his feet, bile burning his throat.

"It's a good thing she kicked you as hard as she did or I would've had a go at you!" Gavriel's eye narrowed on him. "You're damn lucky."

"She has impeccable aim, for sure," Sam piped up, unhelpfully, from the wall.

"Shut your mouth, Sam." Gavriel stabbed a finger Sam's direction. "You're just as guilty for not doing anything!"

"Well, I never!" Sam gasped.

Gav gave Sam a black look then turned his rage back on Tehl. "Did you, or did you not, both ask me to befriend the girl to gain her cooperation?"

"I did," Tehl gritted out.

"With the stunt you pulled, I doubt she would give us a blanket even if we were freezing to death. I have been earning her trust bit by bit, but do you think she will listen to anything I say now?" Gav ran his hands through his hair then stabbed a finger at him. "Not only did you destroy any chance of her working with us, but you frightened her. Ruby has suffered here." Gav's eyes darted between them. "Hell, you both are aware of the nightmares she has every night. I try to calm her, and they've lessened in the last week, but I would bet my horse she has terrors again tonight. *Think* before you act."

Remorse filled Tehl. He had avoided the rebel because of this very problem. He didn't think when he was around her; everything became muddled. "I'm sorry, but imagine my surprise when I spotted her among my advisers in a wet nightdress. She held *my* father's hand as though she did it every night. She looked tumbled, don't deny it." Anger licked at the remorse burning it away. "She should've been in her room."

Gavriel's lips thinned.

Sam sauntered over to them. "What I would like to know is how she's acquainted with our father. Did you see how chummy he was with her? He was smiling at her like he used to before Mum died. How did they meet Gav?"

"I haven't the foggiest. Mira, her healer, was the only other one aware of his visits."

"Visits?" How many times had his father come to her?

"Evidently he snuck in almost two weeks ago and surprised them both. He had the Elite and the healer sworn to secrecy. He's been visiting her for a couple of hours every afternoon."

"Do you mean visiting or *visiting*?" Sam queried.

Tehl stiffened. Had she seduced his father?

"When he introduced her, did his tone imply the latter?" Sam questioned.

Gav shook his head. "No, Ruby spoke to Mira about her afternoons with your father. They talked. Marq told her stories about your mum and the sea. They're companions, nothing more."

"I thought you were getting pretty close to her." Tehl's brows furrowed. "You weren't aware of his visits? Ruby said nothing to you?"

His cousin's jaw clenched. "She never told me, though she had plenty of time. She didn't trust me with this."

"Ruby wasn't sworn to secrecy?" Sam probed.

"The rebel wasn't sworn to secrecy, but she said nothing."

"Why?" Sam asked skeptically. "She could gain many things from her connection to him. It was obvious my father has affection for her. What is she after?"

Gav continued to glare Sam's way. "Ruby's worried the king's attention would bring more of *our* focus." His cousin turned his glare on him. "She didn't want *you* coming to question her."

His own eyes narrowed. "If she hadn't betrayed the Crown, she would have no reason to fear me. My question is this: what does my father want with her? We have no idea what she's fed him or what he's told her. She's dangerous. Sam—" His eyes cut to his brother. "Any new information on her?"

Sam sighed in frustration. "No, no one knows anything. Either that or they're just unwilling to give her up. I have picked up one lead, but it will be a few days before I know anything."

"Okay then. Keep me posted on that. In the meantime, I need to visit our father." Tehl wrinkled his nose. He was not looking forward to that. "Gav, when you asked her to step away, she did because she trusted you." He let his cousin absorb that for a moment before continuing. "She still trusts you, as do I. I need you to continue to keep watch over her."

Gavriel nodded. Tehl next addressed Sam. "I have no clue what you're doing with your sneaks; that's your realm to deal with, but keep an eye out. The rebel's been here for three weeks. Someone will come for her, and soon, I'm sure of it. When they do…," Tehl trailed off, exchanging a knowing smile with his brother. "In the meantime, Sam, I need you to gain an oath of silence from the Elite guarding her door."

"Apparently, they are already excellent at keeping secrets," Gav cut in.

"On that note…" Sam winked and stalked toward the Elite.

Tehl hung his head, staring at the carpets beneath his boots knowing what his cousin would say next. His eyes traced the blue scales of a mermaid woven into the rug, awaiting the inevitable speech.

"This situation could have been avoided."

There it was.

"Damn it, Tehl."

"I don't have eloquent words and manners like you, Gavriel. I may be able to read people, but I'm never sure how I should react to their emotions." He paused, frustrated. "I can't change who I am." He rolled his neck and faced his cousin. "What would you do if you were in my position?"

"You won't like it."

"Still, I want to hear it. If it will help me be a better king for Aermia, then I will do my duty."

"You need a wife." Blunt.

Tehl blinked at him trying to figure out if he heard right. "A wife?" he parroted. What did that have to do with anything?

"Yes, a wife. You need someone to round your sharp edges and make you more approachable. Someone that will complement and enhance your abilities, support you in your role. Plus, the things you hate are all tasks that your mother oversaw. When you marry, your queen will assume those responsibilities." Gav's face morphed into a devilish grin. "She will also help you with the whole heir business. Baby-making is always fun, and I can tell you *that* from experience."

He smirked at Gavriel's last comment. "Heirs?"

Gav's smile widened, and he nodded. "Heirs."

Tehl shook his head at his cousin. "I will consider it. Thank you for your advice."

Tehl patted his cousin on the shoulder and headed down the corridor. Would a woman make that big a difference? Gavriel never gave bad advice and his family had keenly felt the loss of his mum and Emma. Their presence certainly made a difference.

But where would he ever find a bride? He didn't have time to hunt for one. Tehl filed it away for later. He needed to deal with his father.

If he could find him.

Although he'd searched all of his father's usual haunts, he'd yet to encounter him. Marq Ramses had an uncanny ability to disappear when someone was looking for him. Tehl's time had run out. It was time for dinner.

He grudgingly made his way toward the great hall. A loud shriek echoed through the doorway, followed by the buzz of many voices. Tehl hesitated in the doorway, wishing escape was possible. He'd rather eat with the Elite or out in one of the pastures. At least with the animals he could enjoy some measure of peace and quiet.

He braced himself and strode into the great hall with his head high and shoulders back. The sound of a hundred chairs scraping the floor reverberated in the open space.

Made-up faces flashed him painted smiles, their eyes predatory. Men and women dipped in intricate bows and curtsies as he brushed by.

He leapt up the two stairs to the dais and faced his court. "Be seated and enjoy your dinner," he commanded in a loud voice before sitting.

Gav was sitting on his left but Sam's seat was empty. "Figures," he grumbled to himself.

"What was that, Your Highness?" said a young woman, two chairs down.

He looked at her for a moment and then realized his voice had carried farther than intended.

Tehl cleared his throat and sent her a brittle smile. "Nothing, my lady."

She lowered her eyelashes and simpered in her seat. He wanted to roll his eyes at her coy glances. She was anything but bashful. Caeja, councilmen Jaren's daughter, had thrown herself at him many times already; it seemed ridiculous to play shy now. Sam's running theory on their motives was disturbing. His brother figured that, though they knew he couldn't marry them, most of them didn't care. He said they were probably all hoping to get pregnant, so it'd be their child on the throne one day. His nose wrinkled at the idea, and he realized he was still staring at Caeja. Her cheeks pinked, whether from embarrassment or anger he didn't know, but he quickly wiped his face clear of expression.

Tehl focused on his food and only spoke when asked a question. He tried to keep his answers short so that no one drew him into conversation. Once he finished, he sprawled in his chair and watched the delicate political dance around him—every look, laugh, touch, or joke was a means to an end.

His mind drifted back to what Gav had said earlier.

A wife.

She could probably steer through the court waters better than he could. Plus, if he had a wife, maybe some of these women would leave him alone. Tehl almost snorted at the thought.

Yeah, right. The women of his court had no shame.

The more he considered marriage though, the more he liked the idea. His thoughts had already turned to children of late, so if he married soon, it was possible that within the year, he could welcome a child of his own into this world.

Tehl stood and retired for the night, thankful to leave behind the lights, people, and music. In his suite, he paced, restlessness plaguing him. He was too wound up from the day's activities to fall asleep. He needed to spend a while on the ledge.

He brushed aside his tapestry to display a hidden door that complained as he pried it open. He then picked up his lantern and slipped into the black tunnel.

These hidden, dank hallways had always intrigued him, ever since he was a child. He had fond memories of hiding in places where his mum would be, then jumping out to scare her. She would scream, swat him on the shoulder, and kiss his head. Tehl smiled at the memories as he came upon the tiny gray door that led to his sanctuary. He had to hunch over just to fit through. On the other side, a cool sea breeze ruffled his hair as he waited for his eyes to adjust to the dark.

Moonlight glimmered on the black sea, only to be shattered by the frothy white waves and luminescent algae growing on the rocks beneath the surface. He edged along the castle wall to a large ledge that overlooked the sea. It amazed him how the ocean never looked the same. It was always changing, and yet, constant.

He loved this spot. It was the ideal place to sit and ponder life. No one had ever found him here, not even Sam. If they knew about it, they left him alone. Peace. Joy. Contentment. In his mind, that was what his ledge represented.

Closing his eyes, he leaned his head against the stone wall behind him. Little bats called to each other in the night, bringing a smile to his face. Many abhorred the small creatures of the night, but Tehl had grown fond of them over the years since they'd made their nests beneath his ledge. He left them in peace, and they left him in peace.

A pebble skittered across the stone, and his eyes popped open at the disturbance. He jolted when he recognized his father squeezing himself through the little door.

Marq Ramses skirted along the wall and plopped down beside his son. Tehl gawked at his father, bewildered. The king never failed to surprise him.

He hadn't wanted to be found earlier, so why was his father seeking him out?

Marq's lips quirked upward. Without looking at him, his father murmured, "I wanted to join you. And, as for not wanting to be found, well…I am always around, you just need to search harder."

He blinked at his father, realizing that he had spoken his thoughts aloud. Tehl shook his head and turned back to the frothy black waves. He had a million questions for his father, but they could wait. Now was the time for peace. They sat in companionable silence for some time, the ocean waves lapping below.

"Your mum used to sit out here."

Tehl shifted, glimpsing his father from the corner of his eye. His expression was so bittersweet that he ached for his mum.

"Any time she felt overwhelmed or tried to work through a problem, she would sit here, sometimes for hours. I always worried about her falling, but she'd just pat my cheek and tell me to stop being such a worry wart." His father smiled. "Then she had you and your brother. From the day she held you in her arms, things changed for her. She was still herself, but much more cautious; she had her precious boys to care for. Then, one day, you discovered this ledge."

"I thought I was the first and only one to discover it."

The king shook his head. "This was your mother's place well before it was yours. I have lived here my entire life, yet I never knew it existed—not before her. She was in the palace but a week before she discovered it." He fluttered his hand out, encompassing the cove. "Your mum was so afraid when she realized you'd found her cove. She wanted to forbid you from ever coming back; that's how scared she was. She was worried you'd hurt yourself or fall."

His father clasped him on the shoulder. "I stood up for you. A person needs a place to decompress, especially a prince. I also reminded your mum I never forbade her to come here, though I, too, always worried." Laughter rumbled deep in his father's chest. "I received a nasty look for that one, let me tell you. She pursed her pretty little lips like she'd eaten a hundred lemons. After a while though, she nodded her head and dropped the subject. But later, I noticed a pattern. Every time you disappeared, so would she. So one day I followed her. It turned out, she had snuck down the stairway behind you, and there she sat, watching you from the stairs. She understood you needed your time, but she also wanted to make sure you were safeguarded." His father's eyes crinkled. "Thus, I retraced my steps and never mentioned it."

Tehl swallowed around the large lump in his throat. "She watched over me *every time?*"

His father nodded. "You were never alone. She loved you with everything she had and hoped to protect you as much as possible from the world. She was a wonderful mother. The kingdom is a darker place without her," he choked out, pain in his eyes.

Tehl gave his father some privacy, returning his gaze to the inky sea. Why would someone subject himself to that kind of pain? Having that sort of love could destroy a person, so he wanted no part of it. He wanted a companion, but not for love. There was too much risk in that. His mind drifted to the rebel, her clinging to his father for dear life. It seemed his father might have a new ladylove. What was his father thinking? She was a traitor, not to mention too young for the king.

Way too young.

She had to be near *his* age. It was absurd.

"What were you doing with that girl today, father? She was in a nightdress— hardly the proper attire to entertain the king," he demanded.

His father scrutinized him, but Tehl kept his face serene, letting his father examine him.

"Son, no matter how mildly you spoke those words, it reeked of jealousy. Does Ruby interest you?"

"Answering my question with a question, that's telling in itself. As for your question, no, I don't have a claim on the girl, nor do I want one. Why are you taken with that slip of a girl? She's nothing compared to mum."

His mum was tall with lithe grace and ethereal beauty, whereas the girl was short, all curves and mystery. Her emerald green eyes flashed through his mind. He'd never seen prettier eyes. Tehl frowned at his thoughts and glowered at the waves. Nothing about her should appeal to him at all.

Tehl turned his frustration on his father. "Again, why were you parading your indiscretion around today?"

Silence answered him.

"Mum would be disgusted with your behavior. She hated men who took mistresses." Tehl laughed without humor. "But who am I to tell you how to treat your light-skirts? Do you even know who you hopped into bed with?"

The look on his father's face had cowed many a man, but not Tehl. He kept his gaze steady. His father drew in a deep breath and let it out again, speaking between clenched teeth. "Firstly, 'that girl' has a name. Learn it and give her some damn respect. She is no light-skirt. She's as beautiful as your mother, both inside and out. That being said, I have never replaced your mother and wouldn't even think of doing so with someone at least half my age, no matter how charming she may be. Even *if* she was my mistress," the king growled, "it would be no concern of yours. I am the king and can do as I damn well please. I am not required to dole out explanations to you. You, on the other hand, have much to answer for."

"What?" He was working himself to the bone to keep Aermia from falling to pieces. What complaint could his father have?

"That poor creature has been locked up for weeks because of you. My only motive today was to give her an afternoon of happiness, as is my right."

Was his father that naïve?

"You realize she is deceiving you?" Tehl asked incredulously.

"No more than anyone else."

She had his father fooled.

He replayed his father's words when something dawned on him. "How did you know I had her locked up?"

The king's face seemed to say, '*Seriously?*' "I've been the king longer than you've been alive. I can still keep track of what goes on in my home, even if I am not always a part of it."

Tehl pinched the bridge of his nose. He came to this spot for peace, but all he was getting was a headache. "So you're telling me it doesn't matter to you that she's a traitor to the Crown, and in league with the rebellion? She's dangerous and yet you'd let her go free?"

"Ruby's not free. She is up in her suite at this very moment."

"That is not the point! She could have escaped today!" His voice rose with each word. "She is all we have to help us settle this rebellion before it turns to civil war. To mention nothing of the fact that, with Scythia practically knocking at our door, discontent is the *last* thing we need right now! I don't understand why you would take the risk. She is trouble! Trouble crammed into an alluring package."

A smug smile crept up his father's face.

"Stop looking at me like that. Any man would notice," Tehl muttered.

"You would need to be dead not to notice." His father winked. "And yes, to answer your question, I knew she was with the rebellion. My curiosity was piqued after speaking with Jeffry."

Tehl winced. Her time in the dungeon wasn't something he wished on anyone. "I..." He paused, at a loss for words. "I am responsible for what happened. What befell her shouldn't have happened."

A large hand rested on his neck. "We can do only so much, son. Our people choose to obey us. When they don't, we must deal with the consequences of their actions as justly as we can. That being said—" His father's tone turned to ice. "The man responsible ought to die."

That was one thing they agreed upon. "I couldn't agree more, and when we find him, which we will, he will regret ever touching her."

Tehl leaned his head against the wall, watching the billowy silver clouds drift across the darkened sky. The bloodthirsty part of him was excited to find Serge and finish this business. Another part of him, however, couldn't stop focusing on the beguiling yet irritating rebel currently locked in his home.

"What do you think of her?" He cracked one eye open and glanced at his father. "You must like her if you visit her every day."

His father stared out at the ocean. He was quiet for so long Tehl thought perhaps he wouldn't answer.

"She isn't what I'd expected," was the soft reply. "Ruby has been puzzling and interesting, because although she did hide things from me, she was also completely honest about others. She has shown courage, kindness, strength, and compassion. I was also surprised to find she actually wants the best for our people and truly cares for them as a whole." His father met his eyes. "She's not the enemy. Mark my words, she could give you what you need and more."

Tehl leaned forward and clasped his hands loosely between his knees. "Did you learn anything useful from her?"

"Nothing she didn't want me to." The king smirked. "She has just as many faces as Sam. She has been well trained; I hope that whoever she is working with will negotiate, as they're sure to be a formidable enemy."

"If she is anything like Sam we need to proceed with extreme caution. Her betrayal could ruin Aermia."

"I consider myself a good judge of character and my gut says, given the opportunity, she would do what is best for the people, no matter the 'side' she is on at the time. We must show her that ours is the best for Aermia."

"Gav is working on it as we speak. She doesn't care for Sam, though, and she *loathes* me."

His father cocked his head in a silent question.

Tehl straightened his back and then stared anywhere but at his father. "I handled her roughly, threatened her family, and threatened to ravish her before we imprisoned her."

At his father's sharp inhale, he faltered before soldiering on. "Then I ordered limited food and water. I forgot about her when I went to the border after the Scythian invasion. When we arrived home, she had already been attacked. She believes I set those men on her." He put a hand over his mouth and mumbled, "I even ended up backing her against a wall when she tried to walk away from me today. I didn't know I had much of a temper until I met her." Tehl threw a rock, irked. "On top of all that, Gav tells me I need a wife, which after planning the Midsummer Festival, I am inclined to agree with."

The lullaby of the night descended after his statement. Waves thundered below, harmonizing with the soft fluttering of bat wings and his father's quiet breaths.

"It sounds like a lot of upheaval."

Acceptance.

There was no judgment or condemnation in his father's tone. Tehl slumped against the stone wall, the tension leaving his body.

"A wife? I swear you told me there would never be one a couple of weeks ago."

"Circumstances change, father. I can't do this by myself. I need help. Sam and Gav are doing what they can, but I need a consort."

His father nodded in understanding. "I know what you mean. After your mother died…I just couldn't. Still can't. I am sorry I'm not what you need."

The king aged before his eyes. Tehl's heart ached at the change. Part of Marq Ramses had died along with his wife, leaving only a glimmer of the man he grew up with. This broken man had taken over his father after his mother's death.

His father levered himself up and looked down on him, infinite sadness sucking the life from the blue eyes so like his own. "I will do my best to help when you need me. Good night, son."

The king picked his way across the rocky ledge to the door way.

I need you now was on the tip of his tongue but he bit back the words. For a while tonight, before he'd slipped into melancholy, his father had been his old self. It was as if the king was in a deep hole and Tehl had no idea how to dig him out.

He tilted his head back and gazed at the luminous stars above him. They winked like fireflies in a darkened meadow. A wife. He wondered again where he was going to find one. His brother was right; he lacked social skills. He had the constitution of a bear some days, so who would want to live with that? He needed to make it happen.

TWENTY-EİGHT

SAGE

SAGE SAT ON THE FLOOR, staring into the crackling fire before her. She ran her hands through the luxurious carpets, her mind running a mile a minute. She'd now been in the castle over three weeks. Her eyes slid to her companions: Mira was rocking in her chair, reading about some herb, and Gav sat on his cot writing letters. She was going to leave them; she had to.

She looked to the two people who had taken such good care of her; as unlikely as it had seemed, the three of them had become good friends. A rebel, a healer, and a prince. Sage smirked. It sounded like the beginning of a bad joke. Her smile faded a touch as guilt stabbed her. She had to leave them.

Gav looked up from his furious scratching with an easy smile, meeting her eyes. Her own smile froze on her face. She dropped her eyes so his probing ones couldn't read her thoughts.

She was a liar.

A fake.

Sage felt sick.

She was a traitor of the highest order.

They had been nothing but kind. She had to figure out how to leave without implicating either of them. The Elite rebel with the ring would start his shift early the next morning, so she had until dawn for her goodbyes.

Her thoughts moved to the sleeping draught she'd stashed in her dress.

When she was moved to this room, Mira had dosed her with the sleeping draught to ease her pain and help her sleep. The problem was that once she took it, she couldn't wake up from the nightmares, so she hated taking it. Each day, when Mira was using the privy, she would pour some into a different bottle and dilute the one that Mira was using. The pain was worse, but it was worth it if it meant waking from her terrible dreams.

A soft sigh drew her attention to Mira, slumped in her chair, looking exhausted. A surge of affection bubbled inside her for the sweet woman who had pulled her from the edge of death.

Gav set aside his correspondence and stood, gesturing to the chessboard.

"Would you like to play?"

She smirked at him. "Are you ready to lose again?"

Gav scoffed, eyes twinkling. "A woman has never beaten me." He puffed up his chest, strutted over to the wall, and struck a pose.

She giggled at Gav's uncharacteristic playfulness. A petite snort caught her attention, and she stared at Mira, eyes wide. The poor girl covered her face in embarrassment, unable to completely cover her beet-red cheeks. Mira attempted to hold in her laughter, but the harder she tried, the worse her little snorts became.

Sage jabbed a finger at her friend, laughter spilling out of her. "What," she gasped, "was *that?*"

Mira shook her head, blond hair covering her face like a curtain, lamenting, "I try to control it, but sometimes it simply will *not* be controlled!"

"Do not worry, my lady, your secret is safe with me." Gav sent Mira a friendly smile, along with a wink, and patted her on the shoulder like a man. He flopped down onto the other end of the bed and set up the board.

Sage stood up and stretched her hands above her head with a soft groan, arching her back like a cat. "I am in the mood for some lavender mint tea. Would either of you like some?"

She made her way over to the hutch upon which sat the honey, tea, and an assortment of cookies and cakes, all the while praying they both said 'yes'. She closed her eyes in relief as a chorus of yesses sounded behind her.

Slouching, she pulled out her draught from her gaping dress. She was thankful that it was sweet; mixed with the tea and honey they wouldn't taste it. She put a couple teaspoons of tea leaves into each cup, as well as a few drops of the draught, then slipped the small bottle back in her bodice.

"Honey?"

Please want honey, please want honey, please want honey, she chanted in her head. A masculine and feminine 'yes', Sage thanked the stars.

Sage spooned some into each cup, and then moved to the pot hanging over the fire and carefully poured water into each cup, stirring them until the tea was so fragrant her mouth watered. She handed one to Mira and then Gav. As they lifted the tea to their lips, she had a sudden urge to snatch the cups away or knock them to the floor. Instead, she stifled the feeling and sipped at her own tea, silent.

"Thank you, Ruby, I needed this. It's delicious." Gavriel's smile skewered her heart.

Mira mumbled her thanks as well and settled back into her rocking chair with her book.

"Shall we?" Sage pointed to the game.

Gav lay on his side, smiling impishly. That was her answer. Sage rolled her eyes and chose black, even though it meant she'd given away the first move. She studied his move and countered.

When she looked up from the board, Gav was studying her, intensely. Her heart stuttered, and her palms began to sweat. Did he suspect her betrayal?

Be calm, he can't know.

"I am sorry for what happened today with the crown prince. He meant no harm."

She wasn't expecting that.

Gav moved his next piece and captured her rook. "He may be rough around the edges, but he is actually a good person. Tehl will make a powerful king."

Rage and bitterness welled inside her. Sage wanted to ignore his comment, to act like she hadn't heard his words, but she couldn't. "You mean to tell me," she said through gritted teeth, "that the man who threatened to ravage me, hurt my family, starved me, and then had me attacked is a good person? Forgive me if I don't agree."

"He never had you attacked," Gav replied, his voice soft.

"No." Sage cut him off, slashing a hand through the air. "Do not defend him. I don't want to hear it. Even *if* he didn't sanction it, it still happened under *his* roof by *his* men. How can he expect to rule a kingdom if he can't control what happens in his own home?"

"I understand, but he isn't—"

Heat filled her cheeks as frustration built up inside her. How could Gav defend such a monster? Tears tracked a path down her cheeks as Sage dropped her blurry eyes to the game board, trying to get a hold of herself.

"You *know* how I suffer at night," she whispered. "Nothing would ever convince me he is a good man. The crown prince is a pretty monster who holds too much power." Sage moved a piece and balled her hands into tight fists.

Gav's tanned hand touched hers softly, imparting comfort. She squeezed his hand once, then swiped at her tears. She met his grave eyes with a watery smile. "I understand that you owe your loyalty to your cousin and that you love him. You are a wonderful person, Gavriel. You see the best in people, but we can't agree on this subject. It's best for you and I if you don't mention him."

He released an aggravated sigh and held up one hand. "One more thing, then I will let it rest. Just remember to never judge a book by its cover. You might be surprised by what you find inside."

"You're right." She paused waiting for him to look up at her. When his eyes met hers, she murmured, "His cover is exquisite, but I have seen what is inside. It's a nightmare. Like I said before, he's a beautiful monster."

Gav blanched at her statement but recovered. She knew she was being harsh, but it was the truth, and he needed to hear it. Focusing back on the board, he moved a piece, and she looked down to find he had her king trapped.

"How did you do that," she muttered.

"With lots of diversions," he teased.

Sage glared at him and swatted his shoulder, her grin undermining its effect. This was her last night with them and she wouldn't ruin it. A thump drew their attention to Mira. She had fallen sound asleep in her chair, her book askew on the floor.

Gav shook his head and looked back at her. "I guess it is time for bed."

"That it is." She stood and curtsied. "I concede to your excellent strategizing skills, my lord."

Sage picked up Mira's book as Gavriel put away the game.

"Mira, love, we need to get you to bed," Sage crooned.

Mira growled something unintelligible and snuggled further into the chair. Tenderly, Sage pushed her friend's fine blond hair from her face. She would most likely never see this woman again. She swallowed, a lump forming in her throat. "Gav," she called. "I will need you to carry her to bed. She won't get out of this chair herself."

Gav chuckled, hoisting Mira out of the chair like she weighed nothing. Gently, he lowered her friend into the bed. Sage nudged him out of the way, tucking her in. She placed a small kiss on Mira's forehead and whispered, "Good night, sweet girl."

Sage crept from the side of the bed, turning to the fire. Gav stood, watching her haloed by firelight. His dark form glided to her. Sage squeaked when his muscular arms engulfed her suddenly. One of his hands slid into her hair, pressing her face against his firm chest.

"I am sorry I brought my cousin up and that it upset you so. I'll try not to do so again."

Her mouth parted in surprise as his lips touched the crown of her head. Sage tipped her head back, staring into his glittering eyes full of affection. It killed her knowing they would be on opposite sides come tomorrow. She lifted onto her toes to press a delicate kiss on his cheek. "Thank you for being what I need you to be." She cradled his cheek and Gav's eyes closed as he leaned into her palm. "Your wife was a lucky woman." Sage meant every word.

His throat convulsed, and he released a shuddering breath. Sage rubbed her thumb along his cheekbone once more before releasing him. She stepped from the circle of his arms, moving away. Gavriel's hand gripped hers, halting her. Sage examined her small hand in his, running her eyes from his muscular arm to his wide shoulders and, finally, to stare at his profile.

"Thank you." His voice was gruff. "Ruby, I..." Anguish and confusion was clear in his voice.

"You have a lot to offer, brother." His head snapped to her at the endearment. "Most of us miss *someone* and we all have to learn to let go. One day you will be able to move from the guilt. And maybe you will find someone again."

His dear purple eyes swept across her face as if he was searching for something.

She drew in a breath, squeezing his hand. "I am not that someone, Gav. I am, however, your friend. Just as you are mine." She gave him a small smile.

He mulled that over for a bit, eventually returning her smile. "That you are. I suppose you're right, sis."

His returning her endearment filled her with joy. 'Brother' and 'sister' were the highest honor you could bestow upon someone other than blood kin. With those titles, you claimed them as a companion for life. Sage's smile spread so wide that her cheeks hurt, Gav's expression mirroring hers.

"Not that I haven't enjoyed our heart-to-heart, but I really ought to head to bed," she hinted.

Sage let go of his hand, and he ruffled her hair as he walked to his own cot. She scowled at him, placing her hands on her hips. "None of that, though!"

"Not a chance, sis. We're siblings now. That's just what we do."

"Out!" Sage stabbed a finger at the door.

Gav winked and left the room, still smirking.

Sage changed her dress in a rush, switching it for one of Mira's plain ones. She then clambered into bed, pulling the covers to her chin. A few minutes passed before Gav snuck back to his cot. Blankets rustled as he tried to find a comfortable position.

"Good night, Gav."

"Night, Ruby."

Shame washed over her at the use of her fake name. They had practically adopted each other, yet he didn't even know her. She was a fraud, a fake. She wished she could tell him, but it was too dangerous now. It wasn't just about her. If she said anything, it would endanger both her family and friends.

She didn't want to leave without giving him something honest, though.

"Gav?" she whispered to the dark.

"Yeah," he groggily replied.

"My brothers used to call me 'Sai' when I was little. You're welcome to call me that."

The room was quiet, save Mira's soft breaths and the crackle of the fire. Had he fallen asleep?

"Sai it is then, dear sister. What is it short for?"

"It's not, just a nickname," Sage evaded.

"Okay. Sweet dreams, Sai," Gav slurred.

It wasn't long before loud snores came from Gav's cot. Sage stared at the ceiling for another hour before deciding to test the depth of her friends' slumber. Sage jumped off the bed and stomped to the bathroom. Nothing. She grabbed the cold doorknob and slammed the heavy bathroom door. The sharp noise thundered through the room. Still nothing. They didn't even stir.

Sage trudged back to bed feeling equal parts of triumphant and somber. She would be free in a matter of hours, but would leave behind friends she had come to treasure. Someday she would try to find a way to make it right between them.

Sage slipped back into bed and forced her eyes closed. Her perspective had changed with her time here. Not everything about the Crown was evil and there were no absolutes. The crown prince was still an arrogant brute, it was true, but she had softened toward everyone else, even the king. Her heart clenched at the thought of Marq. She would protect him. The older man had suffered enough. With that thought, she drifted off.

Light knocking at the door roused her. She eyed her companions, still sleeping soundly, and snuck from bed. Carefully, Sage pried the door open. The Elite from the previous day stood before her.

"There's not much time, we have to move now. I take it you took care of your companions?" he asked in a hushed voice.

She nodded once, taking a final peek at her cherished friends. Now that it was here, the thought of escape was bittersweet. Hopefully they would understand her actions. Sage closed the door and looked to the guard expectantly.

He shoved a worn, brown cloak and cane into her arms. "Put the cloak on and use it to conceal the cane."

Sage regarded the two Elite sleeping on either side of her door. "Did you expose yourself?" she asked, clasping the cloak. She tucked the cane away, awaiting his answer.

"No, but the night is still young." He gestured to the sleeping Elite. "I had them drugged."

She smirked up at him. "Great spies think alike."

An amused grin played at his mouth as they slipped silently down the corridor. With each twist and turn, room or staircase, Sage catalogued everything. She had seen little of the castle apart from her suite and the infirmary. She filed each detail away so she could create a map later.

Her partner paused to scan the large, open hallway before them. When he was sure the coast was clear, he waved her forward. As they moved through the main corridor, she spied the doorway leading to the courtyard and her heartbeat sped up. Sage's pace picked up, exceeding her guide's. Her breath whooshed out at the sight of a dark blue sky and twinkling stars. A hand snatched her cloak, stopping her in her tracks.

"Slow down," the Elite admonished. "Pull your hood up around your face and lean on the cane like you're aged. Make sure your braid is hidden, as it would give us away immediately."

She did as he said, hunching over, and hobbling outside.

"Old mother, let me help you."

He lifted her other hand up and placed it into the crook of his elbow. The pace was excruciatingly slow; the sky was already starting to lighten. They needed to move. Should she make a run for it? Her comrade tightened his grip on her hand as if he had guessed her thoughts.

Finally, they reached the gate. They were going to make it.

"What are you doing up this early?" The voice shattered the quiet of the early morning. "I thought the Elite usually slept in 'til the sun was high in the sky."

Her muscles coiled, preparing to sprint. Sage had come this far. She was not going back.

"I am helping the old mother to the gate."

The guard on the wall above them smiled. "Will you need any assistance outside the gate, old mother?" he inquired kindly.

In the scratchiest voice, Sage uttered, "No, young man, but thank you for your kind offer. These old bones aren't as young as they used to be, but I can still get myself around. A good day to you."

Her partner waved to the guard as they began their painstaking shuffle through the gate and into Sanee. With the tall, gray stone walls behind her, joy and elation filled her. She longed to sprint and stretch her legs. But soon. Very soon. For the next half hour, they wound down the hill and into the city.

The rebel moved her into a shadowy alley. "Rafe expects you. Goodbye, Blade." He sketched a bow and disappeared from sight.

Sage shook her head at the nickname. Rafe called her the rebellion's blade only once! And for some reason, it stuck.

She ditched the cane and straightened, rubbing her smarting back. She desperately wanted to see her family, but she knew she needed to find Rafe first. Time to find out what they'd all been up to this last month.

TWENTY-NINE

TEHL

TEHL STARED WITH NARROWED EYES at the many papers littering his desk. No matter what he did, it seemed like they multiplied every time he blinked. This had to be the worst of his responsibilities, the paperwork. It always came in unrelenting waves. He picked up a petition that had something to do with the Midsummer Festival. Tehl read the same line five times before dropping it onto his desk and slumping into his seat with his eyes closed.

He had slept fitfully the previous night, spending most of it just staring at the ceiling. His conversation with his father kept running over and over in his mind. Nothing seemed clear, but one thing stood out to him. As much as he was loath to admit it, he was in the wrong when it came to the girl. His handling of the situation from beginning to end had been a long series of mistakes. Which meant he had to apologize. To a rebel. To a traitor. His day couldn't get much worse.

His back pinched, interrupting his thoughts. He'd sat on that ledge for so long that his whole body ached. Maybe he was just getting old. He snorted and raised his arms above his head, stretching from left to right. A groan of pleasure escaped him and he wondered why stretching felt so good. Hell if he knew, but he was pleased his back had lessened its throbbing.

Tehl straightened and assessed the mountain of documents before him. He needed to get someone to help him in here.

The emerging sunrise poured light into the room, warming him. Tehl yawned loudly and blinked to clear his watering eyes. He needed to stop moping around and get down to business. He eyed the stack of letters concerning the festival like how a mouse eyes a snake. Before he could do anything with them, a quick rap sounded on the door. Damn, they found him already. He would hang himself if he had to discuss anything even remotely connected with decor.

"Enter," he called gruffly.

Sam, Gav, and Mira, the blond healer, entered his office. Tehl's smile dissolved at the distraught look on Mira's face. She looked like someone died. His eyes bounced to Sam, his brother meticulously straightening his shirt. Gav's face was beet-red. Something was wrong.

"What happened?"

No one answered him at first, and his eyes snapped back to Mira. She twisted her hands in her skirt, staring at her feet with tears dripping quietly down her face. The room was still and tense, and his heart pounded wildly as several thoughts flashed through his mind.

"Is it," he croaked, and then cleared his throat. "Is it father?"

"No." Nothing else. Sam's tone was emotionless.

What the hell happened? Tehl stood up and leaned on his desk. "Stars above! Someone tell me what is going on before I go mad."

"She's gone."

Two words only.

Two words that froze him.

There was no doubt in his mind who *she* was. "Do you know where she went?" he rasped.

Sam shook his head, obviously irritated. It was the first expression he had shown since walking through the door. "We don't. The Guard stationed at the gate did not see her leave. She could still be here in the castle, but I doubt it. Someone with her training and skills would be long gone by now. If you like, we will still search the palace, but it will take a couple days to search the grounds, too," his brother huffed. "The only thing we know for sure is she had help."

Tehl stared down at his piles of papers. She was gone. His chance to prevent a civil war, peacefully, was gone.

In an uncharacteristic display of anger, he shoved himself to his feet and threw everything off his desk. Breathing hard, he looked down at the clean wooden surface. He needed to reel it in; anger solved nothing. How did she get past Gav?

Tehl zeroed in on Gav. "How did you let this happen?" he snarled.

Gav's fists clenched and small tremors rocked his forearms. "I did everything you asked," he hissed.

Oh hell. Tehl took a step back. His cousin was beyond angry, furious even. If Gav hissed, it was time to walk the other way. His cousin hadn't been this temperamental since he was a boy, barely on the cusp of manhood.

"I stayed with her since day one." Gav stabbed a finger at him. "I slept in her room *every* night, cared for her, befriended her, and watched over her. I even let others assume she was my mistress, all to protect her! Don't you dare put this on me!"

Gavriel was right.

Tehl held up a hand. "I am sorry for implying that this is your fault. It's not. Thank you. This hasn't been easy on you."

He walked around the desk and leaned against it, crossing his arms. Mira still hadn't looked up from the floor.

"Mira," Tehl called, trying to blot out the anger in his voice. "How did she escape?"

She peeked at him with tear filled eyes. "I don't know. She gave no hint she would be leaving."

"Was there anything unusual about last night?"

"No, not at all. It was like any other night, we ate, spent time by the fire, and I read while Gav and Ruby played chess. At some point, I fell asleep and Ruby tucked me in."

"Sai," Gav cut in.

"What?" Mira's face scrunched in confusion.

"*Sai.* Before bed she told me to call her Sai."

Tehl cocked his head and studied his cousin. Gav shifted and pinked a little bit. Interesting. That was not typical behavior. "What about you?"

"We talked while we played our game. Then we tucked Mira into bed. She hugged me, kissed me on the cheek, and, uh, called me brother. Then we went to bed."

His brain snagged on kiss. Why the hell was she kissing Gavriel? Was she trying to seduce him?

"Don't give me that look, Tehl. It wasn't like that."

Tehl wiped away whatever look was currently displaying his emotions.

"What was it like then?" Sam challenged. "She has only wanted you. Yesterday, she was close to murdering Tehl, but you talked her down. Please explain that. Exactly how close are you two?"

Mira glared at Sam. "Your tone makes it sound like they were having some clandestine affair. I've been present the whole time. Nothing of that sort ever happened." Her eyes flickered to Gav, then back to Sam. "She was comfortable with Gavriel, because he took care of her and soothed her at night when she'd wake from the night terrors *your* men inspired," she accused, furious.

Her narrowed eyes pierced him in his spot, "As for you, she might still be here if it weren't for you. She was shaken after that stunt you pulled yesterday. Most of her experience at this castle has been a nightmare. What made you think she would change her mind and stay here to help you?"

All three men stared at the normally meek woman. She had a little fire in her. It took a moment for her anger to die out. Her eyes widened, and she sunk down into a deep curtsy. "Forgive my strong words, Your Highnesses."

Tehl liked Mira, she was an intriguing blend of meekness and steel.

"Mira, there's nothing to forgive. But satisfy my curiosity, how do you know we need her help?"

She quirked an eyebrow. "Just because I am a woman, it does not mean I can't see or hear. You've not been as quiet and discreet in my presence as you perhaps thought. But I've kept your secrets, and I will continue to do so."

"Thank you, Mira. If we need you further, I will send for you. Have a wonderful day."

Her gaze narrowed at his dismissal, but she only gave a slight nod, curtsying before she left, the door clicking shut behind her.

"We need her to be found, but use discretion. I doubt anything will turn up, but without her, drastic measures will need to be taken when dealing with the rebellion." Tehl sighed. "Most importantly, we need to find who helped her. Her escape means that there are spies among us, in our home even. The rebellion leaders are not stupid. If they were willing to give up that knowledge just to free her, she is even more important than we guessed. Did she say what Sai stood for?"

"No, she didn't, though I asked, but she avoided the question. She trusted me and that's the only reason she gave me her nickname. I think she wanted me to have a real piece of her as a parting gift. I should have seen it." Gav rubbed a hand across his forehead in agitation. "She called me 'brother'," Gav mumbled to himself.

Sam stepped to Gav's side and clasped him on the shoulder. "She's a spy, most of what she said to you was probably fiction. She needed your trust."

Gav shook his head. "I am not naïve. Some of what she told me wasn't real, but I feel she told me as much of the truth as she could, given the circumstances. She wasn't playing a game. She meant it." Gav gazed at him steadily. "I returned her sentiment. I called her my sister."

Tehl's eyes bulged out of his head. Gav was willing to admit deep affection for her, and considered her a member of their family even. He couldn't believe it.

"Truly?"

"I did. I spent almost a month with her. I helped nurse her back to health and held her in the middle of the night. You made me her guardian, and I took the responsibility seriously. How could you expect me not to get attached? She also cherishes Mira, though. If Sai returns, it will be for her. We'll need to keep eyes on her."

"Is Mira a threat? Would she help Ruby or Sai—whoever she is?" Tehl asked frankly.

"No, she would not betray the Crown, she is loyal. What I meant is that if Sai got hurt or in trouble, she would go to Mira, and Mira would help her."

Tehl straightened, moving to the window. "We don't have time to search for her this week. In seven days, the Midsummer Festival will start. Nobility will arrive from all over Aermia and," he hesitated, "I received word that a Methian prince will join us for the festival."

Sam and Gavriel gaped at him.

Sam recovered first. "They haven't visited our kingdom in almost one hundred years, Tehl. Why now? A coincidence? I think not." Sam asked, always pragmatic, "Do you think this bodes ill for us?"

"I can only guess. We treat them like guests, but we watch them like enemies. We need every available member of the Elite at our disposal this week. Sam, I need you to use some of your people to search for the girl. If you don't find her in the next two days, hold off the search until after the festival has finished. We have too many things pulling at our attention as it is. Hopefully, we'll come out of this unmolested."

"Well, I certainly want to be molested by many pretty women." Sam's eyes gleamed.

"Really, Sam? At a time like this?"

Samuel held his arms out in a what-can-you-do gesture. "Brother, you left yourself wide open. I mean, who uses the word 'molested' anymore? Why not 'unscathed' or 'unharmed'?"

"Whatever," Tehl grouched. "Don't you have some information-gathering and rebel-catching to do?"

Sam's lips spread into a mischievous smile. "I do, my lord. I will attend to my duties immediately. Good day, sire." Sam clicked his heels together and swept from the room.

"He has style. And he always manages to find the humor in a situation," his cousin remarked. Gav stared out the window for a moment and then surprised him, "I decided to move my daughter here, so I have some arrangements to make, but if you need me, all you need to do is ask."

"That is the best news I've had in weeks!" He grinned at the thought of having their miniature relative running around the castle. "When should we expect her?"

"Within the next couple of weeks. Do you need me for anything else?"

Tehl glanced back at the obscene pile of papers and back to his cousin, a silent plea in his eyes.

"Not going to happen, Tehl. I will see you at dinner." Gav backed out of the room, a crooked smile on his face.

"Respect. Does no one show the Crown respect these days?" Tehl asked himself.

Gav chuckled, closing the door. Tehl glanced distastefully at the pile of correspondence, making no move to touch the letters. Stalling. That's what he was doing, stalling. He sank into his chair and began organizing the papers. He definitely would need coffee to get through all this.

THIRTY

SAGE

SHE ROAMED THE CITY, TURNING down random streets and alleyways to be certain there was no one following her. Sage peeked around a building and down the lane, spotting only a fisherman, a handful of washwomen, and a stumbling drunk. The washwomen seemed to be getting an early start to the day's activities while the man was no doubt sobering up from an already-forgotten night.

The smell of freshly-baked bread teased her nose. Sage's stomach rumble loudly, and she winced; sneaking around was pointless if her stomach gave her away. She needed food.

Sage tugged on her cloak, double-checking its hood was well in place. She took a last glance behind her, scanning the alley. Blessedly, still no signs of pursuit. She entered the lane, seamlessly blending into the group of washerwomen.

Her eyes darted left and right, searching for signs of danger. When the Crown came looking for her, and she was sure they would, they'd be looking for a woman on her own. They'd probably not take notice of the lowly washerwomen. People often saw only what they expected to see.

Whenever one of the women would look her way, she would give them a polite smile—friendly enough that they wouldn't think her rude, but not warm enough to invite conversation. Together, they meandered down the slick cobbled road when a familiar sight greeted her.

A dreary, worn-down fishing shack. It blended well alongside the various other dilapidated structures. To anybody looking, it was a typical lower-class home, but it actually held many important secrets. A sense of excitement overcame her, and she barely kept her feet from sprinting toward it. Instead, she discreetly separated herself from the group, approaching the battered edifice. Sage slipped into the narrow space between her gray shanty and another hole parading as a home. She scraped her hand against the rotting wood until she met with a rickety door in need of a new fresco. Sage shoved on the door until it swung inward on soundless hinges. She stepped in, shutting it behind her.

She blinked several times as her eyes adjusted to the dark interior. It smelled like dust and molding cloth. Old furniture and faded carpets were haphazardly strewn about the space. As she stepped into the kitchen, she noted the lack of dirt on the floor. Sage tiptoed into a spacious pantry and, again, shut the door behind her.

She probed the wall and found the catch, hidden behind ancient jars of peaches and pickled herrings. A soft click sounded, and a hidden door sprung open. A proud grin curled her lips as she entered. The door was pure genius; no one looked for a door that was a part of the actual shelving.

Sage hunched over, creeping into the bitty space. The door swung shut on its own, trapping her in the dark. She took a calming breath and walked forward four steps. Lifting her hands in front of her, she reached for the spiral staircase hidden there. Cool iron touched her fingertips. Sage shuffled until her slippers met the unyielding metal stairway. She glided down the stairs without hesitation, missing not a step. She reached the bottom and strode directly forward, the placement of her feet exact. The place was rigged with traps; one wrong step and you would find yourself in a pit of jagged rocks. A door met her hand, and she rapped once, paused, and then knocked again three times swiftly and two times slowly.

She hadn't minded the dark before, but something about standing in it now had sweat breaking out on the back of her neck. The inky darkness pressed into her, and an onslaught of dark memories washed over her, making her gasp. Chains. Brown eyes. Pain. Fear.

Sage clenched her eyes closed and tried to slow her breathing as her anxiety rose. "You are not there. This is not that place. No one can hurt you. You are free," she whispered to herself, trying to keep the panic at bay.

"Pass phrase," a deep voice demanded from behind the wooden door.

An image of a blade pressing along her torso flashed behind her closed lids. Sage braced both hands on the thick door to keep upright. She panted heavily as she fought the urge to run up the stairs in search of comforting light. She took a shallow breath, and managed to say, "It's Blade."

"That's not possible," the voice argued.

Irritation combined with her terror caused her to lash out, kicking at the door. "God damn it, Hayjen! Open the bloody door!" She was teetering on the edge of hysteria.

The door yanked open, and she stumbled forward into the arms of a giant man. Already feeling trapped in the darkness, the sudden contact from this man had her entire body trembling.

He needed to stop touching her. *Now.*

Instinctually, Sage slammed her knee up into his groin, and he doubled over in pain. She twisted and stabbed her elbow into his face, his head snapping back. Sage planted her foot on his stomach kicking him into the wall.

"What the bloomin' hell was that for?" he wheezed, his large body sliding down the wall.

It was like she was trapped inside herself as she watched herself attack this man for no reason. The sound of his voice penetrated her panic, ringing with familiarity. She had attacked her friend. Hesitantly, she rose from her defensive crouch, taking a tentative step toward him.

"Hayjen?" she whispered.

Her old friend glared at her from his spot on the floor. "Sweetheart, who else could it possibly be?" he lisped through his newly acquired split lip.

She squatted in front of him, staying out of reach, and offered a sincere apology. "It has been a rough couple of weeks. I am so sorry."

"Where have you been? You just disappeared one day. We searched, but no one discovered any hint as to your whereabouts." He scanned her from head to toe, snagging on her wrist. Self-consciously, she pulled her sleeve down, and his ice blue eyes snapped to hers. "Where did that come from?" he barked out the words, his voice menacing.

For a split second, a horrid flashback was her reality, and she again experienced the pressure of the chains and the warmth of her own blood dripping down her body. She shuddered, shaking her head to dislodge the memory, and forced herself to meet his penetrating gaze. "That's what I need to discuss with Rafe. Can you take me to him?"

Hayjen scrutinized her for another moment before grunting. Sage took that as a 'yes' and stood, stiffly offering her hand to the bear of a man. His meaty hand clasped hers as she hauled him to his feet. Sage made to release his hand but his tightened around hers.

"One minute," he mumbled.

She trembled in his grip when he lifted her hand to his face. She bit her cheek, mortified with her own weakness. Hayjen would never hurt her, yet here she was cowering like he was an enemy. It sickened her.

Lightly, he drew a finger along the uneven skin that had finally begun to heal. "You will carry these scars for the rest of your life, and I am sorry for it. But you aren't the only one." He dropped her hand and pushed up his shirt sleeves, displaying thick wrists bearing scars remarkably similar to her own. Her eyes sought his, and she saw just how much he understood her pain. No pity, but respect. They shared a special kind of camaraderie born from their fellow suffering and survival.

"Rafe will not like it." Hayjen nodded to her wrists. "He has been in a foul mood of late."

The comment made Sage crack a smile; his anger was legendary. Rafe didn't lose his temper often, but when he did, it was a sight to behold. The man's wrath could make a Nagalian sand storm seem like a small burst of wind. Hayjen gestured for her to follow and began navigating the winding corridors.

For anyone who didn't know their way around, it was a disorienting labyrinth of tunnels. Every once in a while, her nose would catch the scent of sea salt on a draft. Some of the tunnels connected with the ocean; an easy escape if the location was compromised. She would take the leviathan—the giant carnivorous fish—over the Elite any day.

She winced at her disingenuous thoughts. If she'd learned one thing during her "stay" at the castle, it was that nothing was black and white. Not everyone had been horrible, and she had been surprised with the kindness displayed to her. Stealing away without saying goodbye to Mira, Gav, and the king pained her.

Angry male voices carried from down the corridor, spiking her pulse. She shoved down her agitation as well as the accompanying guilt. It was something she'd have to deal with later. Hayjen swung to his right through a doorway and stepped to the side as she breached the doorway.

The scene they came upon as they entered astonished her. There had to be at least twenty-five men crammed into the tiny space. Rafe had his back to her and was listening to a thin older man named Mason, who was waving his hands wildly as he tried to get his point across. People were talking over one another, and stabbing fingers at each other.

What's going on?

All the loud male voices unnerved her, and goosebumps broke out on her arms. Sage rubbed them vigorously trying to rid herself of the sensation. No one had yet noticed her. She took a deep breath and crossed her arms to hide their shaking and fortified herself for what she knew needed to be done. Sage struck a casual pose on the wall, and projected her voice, using the smokiest tone she could manage: "Gentlemen! Gentlemen! This is no way to act in the presence of a lady. Have you all forgotten your manners while I've been away?"

Silence descended and twenty-five heads swiveled her way. The quiet was deafening. Her heart beat frantically in her chest, and nausea tried to overwhelm her, but Sage pushed through it, focusing on Rafe's back so she wouldn't have to look into all those eyes and panic.

The rebellion's leader tensed, and he turned to face her. His luminescent amber eyes zeroed in on her, a wealth of emotion displayed there. Looking at him, she had a sudden realization. After everything that had happened the last few weeks, she had expected him to appear different in some way, because she felt so different herself. Yet here he was, looking exactly the same. Seeing his long scar and unruly wine-colored hair, exactly as she remembered it, comforted her somehow.

She was home.

"Little one," he breathed out the fond nickname. Her heart flew to her throat as he rushed up to her and swept her into his arms. His familiar spicy scent washed over her as he hugged her tighter.

This was as close to family she'd been in almost a month. "My family?" she choked into his chest.

"They have been taken care of. They never stopped searching for you. Every time they posted a drawing of you, we had to pull it down. We didn't want the Crown getting anywhere close to them."

Grateful tears ran down her face and onto his shirt. He had protected her family, keeping them safe when she could not. She was safe. She was *finally* safe.

"Let it out, little one. Let it out. I have you," Rafe soothed.

She was only vaguely aware that she started crying. She'd held in so many of her emotions for so long that there was no stopping it. Everything she'd bottled up came out in a rush. After a bit, she pulled back and looked into Rafe's face, the sight so dear to her. He clasped her cheeks with large hands and brushed away any evidence of her tears.

"You're safe now." He leaned down and pressed a tender kiss to the crown of her head, tucking her tightly against his chest once again, like he was afraid she would slip away. A soothing rumble began in his chest, relaxing her.

A stray thought popped into her head. Did grown men purr? Was that what he was doing? She would have to ask her mum about it later.

Rafe lifted her, squeezing tighter, and she raised her head from his shoulder, looking to the silent group of men. Sage stared into their faces, embarrassment colored her cheeks. Maybe she could take a page from Sam's book and use humor to cut the awkwardness. She crossed her eyes and gave them a silly grin. Most returned it with one of their own.

Mission accomplished.

She tapped Rafe on the shoulder to put her down when she spotted a familiar pair of eyes. Her whole body froze as she continued to stare into the eyes of the person who featured in her nightmares every night. Sage would never forget him: the monster masquerading as a man.

She could barely breathe. A dull roar sounded in her ears, her head fuzzy. The walls closed in on her. As her feet touched the ground, the breath rushed out of her. She couldn't see him any longer but she swore she still felt him, if that was even possible. What was he doing here? Panting, she tried to pull herself together.

"What's wrong? You need to take another breath. You're shaking."

The shaking didn't stop though. It only worsened.

Hayjen stepped up next to her and pulled her sleeves up to display her injuries. "This might have something to do with the way she is reacting."

Sage stared down at her wrists, eyes stinging, ashamed of the scars but too panicked to do anything about it. A hand tilted her chin up, and she met burning amber eyes. "Are there more?"

She closed her eyes and dug for courage. Sage took a breath and looked Rafe straight in the face. "Yes, there are many more." She wet her lips before continuing. "You have a spy in your midst."

Genuine shocked crossed both men's faces. "Who?" Rafe demanded.

"Serge," she took a breath and continued in a hushed tone: "That was the name he went by. The plain fellow. Brown hair, brown eyes, incredibly tall. He is staring at us now. He was a captain of the Guard at the palace." Her voice never wavered or cracked. A small success.

Rafe spun, pointing at the culprit. "Is that the man you saw?"

Her eyes flew to him, a scant fifteen feet away, not able to turn her gaze away. Terror filled her. Rafe snapped his fingers in front of her face, and she blinked, looking back at him.

"He is not a spy, Sage. He works for us. We planted him in the Guard so we'd have eyes inside the dungeon and on the spymaster. He gave us the information on your whereabouts so we could get you out. His name is Rhys."

"Us?" Sage mumbled to herself. Rhys. The name was familiar, but she'd never met the elusive member of the rebellion's circle. He had been on an assignment since she joined. The room blurred, and the ground heaved beneath her feet. She stumbled back, into Rafe. Everything was off kilter. Serge was a spy. "*You* sent him?"

"Yes," he drawled.

Her gaze bounced from Rafe to Serge—or Rhys, or whatever his name was. Something broke inside her. Anger and hate warred with her terror before the former overcame the latter. Determination filled her. They were separated only by a round table. He was so close, a wicked smile adorning his face. It didn't matter whom he'd sided with. He was a horrible human being, and he should never be allowed to harm anyone else. She would make sure of it.

Sage snatched Rafe's dagger from his waist and spun out of his arms. She launched herself onto the table, sprinting toward the man who'd haunted her. Only a couple more feet and she'd reach him. Strong hands grasped her ankles, yanking her feet out from under her. She threw the blade with a feral cry as she crashed down into the table. Her elbow smarted, but she didn't care. Her eyes never left the monster bleeding in front of her.

She missed.

She'd missed his heart and had struck his shoulder.

Sage fought to move forward, but was wrenched across the wooden table by powerful arms. The whole room erupted into a chorus of shouts as men rushed to help their downed man. Sage struggled harder, but no matter what she did, the arms circling her would not let go.

Desperation filled her. "You sick, twisted piece of garbage! You are the evil in our world!" Rafe had moved a step back from the table, so, seeing an opening, Sage lifted her legs and pushed off the table trying to knock him off her. "Mark my words, you wretch! You'll die!" she screamed.

"Stop!" Rafe bellowed in her ear.

"Never," she promised. "Put me down. That animal doesn't deserve to live."

"I don't think so. Not after the stunt you just pulled. Why would you attack one of our brothers?"

She stilled, disgusted with his word choice. "Brother?" Her icy voice was deadly calm. The venomous tone caught the attention of those closest to them. "Brother?" Sage hissed again. "Do brothers chain their families to the ceiling? Or torture them for hours? Or...," she swallowed bile and continued, "or try to rape their sisters?"

Rafe's arms had slackened at her last statement. Sage used his shock to her advantage and tucked her chin, pushing his forearm over her head in one swift motion. In less than five seconds, she was out of his hold and backing away. "*You*! You sent him to me."

Rafe's face was filled with pity. She didn't need his pity. Sage shook her head, her long braid whipping around her head. This was his fault. Betrayed emerald eyes met remorse-filled amber ones. The entire time she'd been blaming the Crown for her suffering, it wasn't the Crown's doing after all; it was her own so-called brotherhood.

"I was keeping my cover! Someone had to interrogate you, and I was protecting you from much worse things. The Crown is corrupt, so stop being so ungrateful for what I did for the cause." After he'd finished, his face contorted in pain, bringing her a small amount of satisfaction.

"You! Shut your damn mouth!" Rafe thundered, sending a deadly glare Rhys's way.

His voice sent shivers along her flesh. Sage sucked in a breath and stared down her personal demon, numbness settling over her. "You almost killed me," she said, her tone flat. "I'm sure I could do without your special form of protection. The Crown protected me, not you. If *this* is what you all are—" She waved a hand, indicating the remaining men. "If *this* is how you operate, I want no part in it. The princes' rule is a far cry above anything you lot would accomplish."

"Then the rumors are true, you are a whore. Mistress to the king, the princes, or perhaps all of them, at least from what I'm told," Rhys sneered.

Suddenly, the anger was back, and she saw red as she sprung toward the snake spouting lies, but a solid arm wrapped around her middle. She looked into the ice blue eyes. Hayjen. She dropped her eyes and stared straight ahead, frustrated that she was stalled once again.

Hayjen leaned down to her ear, whispering, "It is not the right time. We *will* take care of him, I vow it. But it must be when the time is right. Don't let him get to you now. Take a deep breath and match your breathing to mine."

Trusting him, she tried to do as he said, breathing in time with him.

The viper on the ground smirked at her as someone tended to his wound. "Never fear, though, you won't be required to entertain the old man for secrets, not anymore. Instead, you can be the instrument we need. Poetic justice if you ask me. He won't ever see it coming from his lover."

"What is he talking about?" she questioned Hayjen.

"He's talking about the king's assassination on the night of the Midsummer Festival. They plan to use you to get it done."

Her gaze clashed with Rafe's. "Regicide? *That's* your plan?" She looked around the room, but most of the men avoided eye contact. Cowards. "We are supposed to be trying to help the people! We're not assassins. This is wrong, and you ought to know that. We can't build our regime on the blood of the royal family!"

"It will be done," Rafe stated, his voice ringing with finality. "We voted, and the decision was made. It will happen with or without your help."

She snarled at him and squeezed Hayjen's arm, willing him to let her go. How could they do this? Her friend released her, and she stalked over to Rafe, staring into his rugged face. She searched his eyes, but all she saw was determination. She was so confused. How could he sanction this?

"This is wrong," she whispered, for his ears only. "You know it is."

His jaw tightened, but he gave no answer. It seemed he was unwilling to change from this terrible course.

Disappointment filled her. It was not supposed to be like this. She had thought them her friends, her family even, yet if she didn't do something, they would kill another of her friends. Her mind reeled.

Sage realized she had only one choice.

Perhaps if she accepted, she would have a chance at thwarting their plan. "I will go along with this, but once it's done, I am out. I never want to see you again." She squeezed her eyes shut. After a beat, she opened them, looking up at Rafe with all the condemnation in her soul. "You make me sick."

She turned on her heel and stormed from the room, a symphony of male voices shouting behind her. She wound through the narrow tunnels until she came to a stairway. The dimly lit walls felt like they were closing in on her. She had to get out.

She sprinted up the dirty steps and burst into a dim cave echoing with the sounds of thundering waves. Sage's breaths came in sharp pants, the sea breeze doing nothing for her rising nausea. She leaned over, braced her hands on her knees, and began heaving. The cave spun around her and somehow, she ended up on her hands and knees as she continued retching, her stomach emptying completely before it subsided.

Weakly, she wiped her hand across her mouth and focused on getting up off the ground. Large hands gripped her waist, startling her, and a piercing scream tore from her throat. A spicy scent tickled her nose. Rafe. It was only Rafe. Despite what her mind knew, in her current state, her body still recoiled. She slapped his hands away and spun to face him. She eyed his casual stance and took a couple wary steps back, never taking her eyes from him.

"Are you all right?" his deep voice rumbled.

What a dumb question. Why would she be all right?

She couldn't bear the sight of him. He made her ill. Tears flooded her eyes, and she had to suck her lips into her mouth to keep them from trembling. He had betrayed her, more than anyone she'd ever known. It would have been less painful had he physically stabbed her. She examined her ruined slippers, trying to get her reaction under control.

"Sage, I—"

"Don't!" Sage cut him off. "Nothing you say justifies what just happened." She pointed to the stairwell. "You are supposed to be a protector. Our way of life isn't that safe, but I didn't expect that the danger would come from you!" She spat the words out. "You sent him to me, that nightmare…that monster! He's wicked and soulless! His acts would haunt even the strongest of men."

Rafe held his hands out before her. "I didn't know," Rafe pleaded. "We weren't aware of what he'd done. Justice will be served."

"You did nothing in there, Rafe! Nothing! I haven't been able to sleep a full night in almost a month because of what he did. Are those the type of people we are working with? That man should be dead or, at the very least, rotting in a dungeon."

"He will be dealt with, I promise, little one." As Rafe took a step closer, she took a matching step back. His hands closed into fists at his sides. "I will not hurt you."

"You already have." His face fell, but she continued. "But it won't happen again." She dusted off Mira's old dress and switched the subject. "You really plan to kill the king?"

Rafe turned to the waves crashing against the black rocks below them. "It needs to be done. Have you forgotten all he has done to Aermia and its people?"

"I have not." She knew all too well how much the people were suffering. "That doesn't make it right, though."

"Have you been compromised, Sage?" Rafe turned, his eyes hard, probing. It was as if he wanted to see into her mind, searching for secrets.

"No, I have not."

"Then how is it," he said, taking a slow step toward her, "that you went from hating him four weeks ago to defending him now?" He took another step, and another, until he was only a foot away, his gaze intense. She didn't move. She would be damned if he cowed her. "Does he have some sway over you? You need to tell me the truth, Sage, and I will not judge you for anything you might have done to stay safe. I understand what it is like, living among the enemy. Are any of the rumors true?"

It took her a second to figure out what he was implying. Sage slapped him hard across the face, fueled by righteous indignation. "How dare you!" she hissed. "I would never do that! I am no whore," she sneered, "and you know nothing."

Rafe never flinched, his amber eyes serious. A red imprint shone in his cheek.

That must have stung like the devil.

A slight growl rumbled in his chest, and he finally succeeded in intimidating her. There was always something wild about Rafe. Primitive almost. Restrained aggression. She took a step back.

"Well then, little one, explain it to me. If you hold no affection for the king, what changed your mind?"

Should she tell him about the king's mind? Would it convince him to stay the rebellion's hand? It was a gamble but it could save Marq's life. "He's sick."

Rafe snorted. "Well then, it will be easier to get rid of him."

Sage looked at him in horror. "That's not what I meant." She tapped her head. "He's sick in here. He is not mentally all there."

"How would you know this? My best spies can't get close to him." His dark brows arched in question.

Sage debated telling him about Marq's visits but knew gossip would reach his ears sooner or later, so she might as well use the information to her advantage. "He visited me every day."

"Why?" he barked.

"Honestly? I think he was lonely, and curious about me as well. They may not have had proof, but they suspected me of working with the rebellion. However, he always treated me with kindness and respect. When he was lucid, I could see what made him such a good ruler. I agree with you, he shouldn't being 'ruling'. But it's not *him* we should worry about, it's the princes. They are smart and powerful. *They* have the ability to see through your plans." She paused. "That's why it won't work. If they saw me, I'd be locked up before I uttered 'swamp apples'."

Rafe cocked his head, a sly smile on his face. "They won't be able to touch you, Sage."

"How do you mean?"

"I meant what I said. You will go as my consort to the festival."

Why did he have to speak in riddles?

"Out with it, Rafe." She was tired of talking to him. All she wanted to do was get home and see her family.

"You will go as my escort to the festival, and they will have no choice but to leave you alone." He paused. "I am going as the Methian prince."

What? The Methians hadn't visited in years. Had he lost his mind? That would never work.

Rafe continued: "The Methians accepted an invitation to the festivities this year. They would have arrived in time for only the last couple days of the festival, but something will happen on their journey and we will go in their place. The Crown won't dare touch you if you're with me. They wouldn't dare offend the Methians."

She tried to poke holes in his plan, but nothing came to mind. "What happens to their real prince and his entourage? Are you going to murder them as well? The Methians have always been known for their prowess in battle. They won't go down without a fight."

Rafe clasped his hands behind his back and looked down at her. "It is nothing to concern yourself with. It has been taken care of."

Sage dropped her chin, bitterness welling inside her. She hated not having the full plan. It was something they commonly did after all—if no one person had all the information, the entire plan could never be given up. She understood this, but it still rankled.

All at once, exhaustion hit her. The day had barely begun, but it already felt like a lifetime had passed since she'd played chess with Gav. She was done right now. "I need to see my family." She turned her back on him, moving toward the ascending staircase.

"You will be debriefed in a couple of days. Later this week, I will send someone to measure you for your costume for the festival. Be ready."

Not a question, a demand. Sage looked over her shoulder and lied to Rafe for the first time since meeting him. "I gave you my word, and I meant it. The king is sick, and maybe you're right, it might be a blessing to put him out of his misery. I'll be ready when you come for me. Just know that I meant what I said, I am truly done after this. You will leave me and my family alone henceforth."

Rafe sighed. "Little one…"

"Those are my terms if you want my cooperation. I want your word."

Rafe stared at her and nodded once. "I promise."

"Thank you." With that, Sage turned her back on one of people she had thought of as a true friend.

THIRTY·ONE

SAGE

SAGE HIKED UP THE STAIRS, feeling pinpricks of guilt with every step. She hated that she had to lie to Rafe. She'd accompany him to the festival, but that was it. She would not harm the king. It was a line she wouldn't cross. She needed to warn one of the princes, or even Mira, if she could only get to them.

She reached a platform with the ladder at its end and began ascending its rungs. Hand over hand, she climbed until she reached a hatch. Shoving it up and open, sunlight poured in, and she was momentarily blinded. Its rays warmed her, driving away the damp chill from the cave. She hauled herself into the brightly-lit space: a small tool shed in the fishing district. Sage glanced through its windows and checked for anyone watching that might spot her exit. No one; the coast was clear. She pulled her hood up and began moving through the outer rim of the district. It still amazed her how extensive this tunnel system was; she had moved underground about a mile from start to finish. The vast combination of caves and tunnels was an excellent asset to the rebellion, one they frequently made use of.

Sage picked up her pace as she wound through alleys and markets. The closer she got to home, the more she wanted to run. When their smithy finally came into view, her heart galloped wildly. She had been dreaming about coming back for weeks, and now she couldn't believe she was here at long last. Unseen, she slipped to the back of the forge. The heat was staggering when she entered the room, but even that felt like home. Her poor papa was sitting on a bench, hunched over a dagger, inspecting it.

"Papa?" she called.

His faded eyes wandered to her and froze. He rubbed his eyes and blinked several times. "Sage, my little shadow, please be here. Please be real."

His plea just about broke her heart. "Papa, it's me. I'm really here." It killed her that he thought she was nothing more than a figment of his imagination. Sage rushed to him and fell to her knees in front of him. "Papa, I made it home," she croaked, wrapping her arms around his middle.

A large hand settled on the back of her head and stroked her hair, the comforting gesture breaking loose a sob she didn't know she'd been holding in.

"My sweet girl, my sweet, sweet girl. My baby girl." His voice cracked with emotion. "I am so happy you are here. What happened? Are you all right? We never stopped looking for you. We knew you didn't elope. But it was as if you'd vanished into thin air. Where have you been?"

She looked up into his anguished face. He had aged so much in a month. His hair looked grayer, his green eyes a little duller, black bags circling them. He tenderly wiped her tears away, which only made her sob harder. She hadn't thought she'd ever see him again, she realized. It was hard to believe she'd made it home.

He gave her a warm smile and crushed her against his chest, speaking softly. "Shhhh…it will all be okay," he crooned into her hair. He rocked her until her tears ran out and her hiccups had all but stopped. She took one more sniff of his smoky shirt before sitting back on her heels.

"Where have you been?" he asked again, his eyes grave.

Sage dropped her gaze to his boots. "I've been very ill and have been healing for the past couple of weeks. The healers didn't think I would survive. I would have come home as soon as I woke, but I was so weak." Sage paused, debating how much she should reveal.

"Is there nothing you can tell me?"

Her papa knew her well.

"I was being held captive. I am so sorry for the pain I've caused, but no, it would endanger you all if I say more. The less you're privy to, the better."

"Can you at least tell me who took you and why?"

Sage stared at his top button, deciding. He needed to understand the threat to their family. "The Crown took me, because they thought I was associated with the rebellion."

He slipped a finger under her chin and lifted her head, so she had to meet his eyes. "And are you?"

She closed her eyes for a moment and swallowed hard. She would never lie to her papa. Just as quietly as he asked, she answered, "Yes." She refused to open her eyes and see his reaction, so afraid he would be disappointed with her.

"Open your eyes, my sweet girl."

She cracked them and breathed a sigh of relief. It was only love on his face.

"Sage, I know you would do nothing to harm our family. You have more kindness, love, and compassion than most people of my acquaintance. I am sure whatever you did, you did it because you care about our people and this nation. I can't find any fault in that. I just want you to stay safe."

"Me too, Papa. I have one more loose end to tie up, but then I will be done with it all. I promise."

He studied her for a moment and then kissed her forehead. "Okay, if that is what you want."

"It is," she said with conviction. "It's not what I imagined it to be. Nothing is as clear as I once thought." Sage paused before changing the subject. "Is Mum inside?"

He shook his head, "No, she is at the market. She will be home later and so will your brothers. Why don't you go rest until then?"

"I am fine, Papa," she argued. "I can help you with whatever you need." She looked at the scattered projects around him.

"No. You are so pale, I am surprised you haven't passed out. You need your rest. Plus, if your mum found out, she'd have my neck," he said dryly. He hefted himself from the bench and lifted Sage to her feet. His arms engulfed her in another bone-crushing embrace. "I love you so much."

"I love you, too, Papa."

He released her and shuffled into their home. She followed and noted that everything *looked* the same, but *felt* so completely different. Her papa opened the door to her room, and she glided through it, stopping in the center to examine everything. Not one item was out of place, and not even a speck of dust had come to rest on the furniture.

"Your mum said you would return, despite what everyone else said. She wanted to make sure it was ready for you when you did." He clasped his hands and scrutinized her. "Do you need anything?"

"No, Papa. Just some rest."

He patted her arm and then departed, closing the door behind him. Sage kicked off her soiled slippers and collapsed onto her bed. It was a lot lumpier than the luxurious one she'd had at the palace, but this one was familiar, home. For the first time in weeks, she truly felt safe. The last thing she saw before closing her eyes were the faded yellow stars on her ceiling, stars her mum had painted long ago. As soon as she shut her eyes, she was asleep.

Sage jolted awake, breathing hard, a dagger in her hand. Her whole body was covered in a thin film of sweat. She registered a touch on her arm and quickly placed the blade's tip on the offending hand in warning.

"It's okay, love. Shhhhhhh... It's just me, put the dagger down. You're safe. You've no need to be afraid." Her mother's voice carried to her through the darkness.

Sage trembled as her eyes adjusted to the dark. "Mum?" She turned in the direction of gentle voice. A small pool of moonlight highlighted Gwen's cheekbones and dark eyes. "Are you really here? I'm not dreaming?"

"Yeah, baby." Her mum's hand stroked her hair as she spoke. "You were having a nightmare... I came in when I heard you. Sage." Her voice broke. "Love, I am so happy you're home. I've missed you so much. We looked, and looked, and looked, but there was no trace of you." Glimmering tears spilled down her mum's cheeks.

Sage dropped the dagger. "I am so sorry, Mum." And she truly was.

"Papa told me what the two of you discussed earlier. I am so relieved that you're safe. We are so thankful to have you home. I love you so much, baby."

She pulled Sage into her arms and hugged her like she'd never let go. Her mum gave the best hugs. They were love, warmth, and comfort all rolled into one. Gwen released her, pushing Sage's midnight hair from her face, running a hand down a dyed lock.

"I was surprised to see a black head sleeping in this bed rather than the little brown one I've always known," she whispered, a smile in her voice. Gwen dropped her hand and looked straight into Sage's eyes. She could tell her mum was fighting to keep her emotions off her face.

"Sage," she said, her voice quiet but firm. "I put you in your nightdress so you'd not sleep in those dirty clothes." Her mum paused. "I saw them."

Her heart sank. Sage made it a point not to look closely at the marks on her body...the brands of her humiliation. She couldn't shake the sense of powerlessness that they inflicted. She hated that her mum had seen them. It was something she'd hoped to never discuss, because the shame just about choked the life out of her. She ought to say something, but she just...she just couldn't. She occupied her hands by smoothing imaginary wrinkles on the bed, searching for something to say.

"Sage, look at me."

Her eyes raised, and Sage saw more compassion and love in her mum's expression than she could handle. "I know you must have questions, but I...I *can't* do this right now. If I do, the nightmares will be..." Trailing off, she reached out and clasped her mum's hand as a tear dripped down her face. It gutted her that, in hurting her, Serge had also hurt her mum. "Please, Mum. I love you, and I promise that, when I can, I will come to you."

Gwen nodded and cupped her cheek. "Okay, love. I understand. I...I have seen nothing like that before. I can't imagine what must have taken place and how bad it must have been for you..." Her mum choked on a sob. "Oh, my sweet girl, if you need me at all, you have only to ask."

Sage's smile wobbled as fatigue crept back into her body. Her room didn't seem so comfortable now that it was cloaked in darkness and shadows. She didn't want to be alone; gulping down her pride, she gave her mum a beseeching look. "Mum, would you stay here with me?"

Her mum answered by crawling into bed. Sage stared at her, her eyes and heart filling with gratitude.

"Nothing will hurt you. Your papa, brothers, and I will all care for you." Her mum patted the bed and Sage scooted down, facing her. She ran her fingers through Sage's hair, singing a gentle lullaby like she had done when her daughter was just a little girl. She closed her eyes and drifted off to the comfort of her mum's clear notes sweeping through the air.

The next day was spent lazing about with her family. She played games with her brothers, helped her father finish a few projects, and picked flowers with her mum. They studiously ignored the fact that she'd been taken captive, and it wasn't until later that night, as the two of them washed dishes, that her mum even broached the subject of her disappearance.

Laying down the pot she'd been scrubbing on, her mum touched her arm. Sage set her rag down and steeled herself for the conversation that would happen.

Gwen's smile was warm, though there was sadness in her eyes. "We are so happy to have you home. There aren't enough words to express how thankful we are." Her mum looked down at the floor, deep in thought. She took a fortifying breath and looked up, her hazel eyes peering into Sage's face. "There have been rumors since you disappeared. *We* knew you would never run away or elope, but honestly? That's what most are assuming, that you're compromised." Her mum didn't soften the blow. "Brace yourself for some backlash from all this. It's unfair and cruel, but there is nothing we can do except push through it."

"Who's saying I'm not compromised?" Sage bit out.

Even though she had suspected something like that would be the case, the reality of it still hit her hard. Sage had been kidnapped, attacked, and humiliated, yet she would have to bear the disdain, as if it was her fault. Even if she left the rebellion, the consequences of that situation could affect the rest of her life. The joke was on her. She had escaped, but she wasn't free.

The expression on her mum's face made her wince. The last thing she wanted was to hurt her. Chagrined that'd she'd allowed her bitterness to seep into this conversation with her mum, she immediately moved forward and clasped her mum soapy hands. "I am sorry. I didn't mean that, I'm still adjusting to everything. I want to work through it, but for now, let's be done with this." Sage pecked her mum on the cheek and turned to the large wooden table, and began to scrub viciously.

Her mum's gaze was heavy on her back, and Sage prayed that she would just let the subject drop. When the water sloshed in the sink behind her, she exhaled a sigh of relief.

As they continued their chores, Sage couldn't help the fat tear that plopped onto the table as she scrubbed. She wanted a family. She wanted a husband who would love her in the same way her father loved her mum. Now though, she had lost any chance of that. Her chances died the day she got caught in that alley. This was the only time she would mourn for that future. She was the one who'd decided to join the rebellion, knowing full well there could be consequences. Now she had to live with them. As soon as the tears stopped, she wiped them away, as if they'd never been there. If only other things were so simple to remedy.

THİRTY-TWO ⊙

SAGE

SAGE SPENT THE REST OF the week attempting to regain a sense of normalcy in her life. She helped her father in the forge during the day and celebrated the Midsummer Festival at night. The first time she left the house, their neighbors and friends refused to look at her, sneering and gossiping behind her back, but by the end of the first week, their fascination had dwindled. Whispers still followed in her wake, but she had at least a little reprieve from the open censure she'd received initially.

There were only a few interruptions to her life. At one point, Rafe dropped her a mixture with which she could remove much of the squid ink from her hair. The first time she looked in the mirror and saw her own brunette hair, she felt more grounded, like she was a step closer to her true self. A couple days later, a seamstress swept in, took measurements for her costume for the festival's finale, and then bustled right back out. Apart from that one instance, she mostly ignored the rebellion and the plans for assassination until the last day arrived, and then her panic set in. She still hadn't figured out how she would save the king, but she had to try. When her costume arrived, Sage placed it on her bed and her mother, catching sight of it, sat down heavily, her jaw slack.

Sage understood the reaction. Never in her life had she seen something so fine. It must have cost a fortune. Every year prior, she'd gone as a maid of the sea, or something else similar, but the magnificent costume wasn't something she could have imagined, even in her wildest dreams.

The bustier was a pale and shimmering aquamarine silk. Tiny, dyed seed pearls accented the edge of the cups forming intricate waves. Two delicate ties wound around the neck, the material fading from soft aquamarine to a silver that was almost white. On the ends of the straps dangled white, blue, silver, and green shells, pearls, and sea glass. A finely woven, silver net lay next to it on the bed, glimmering like early morning dew on a spider's web.

What was that for? It certainly wouldn't cover much.

Moving on, she examined the skirt. The shimmering transparent silk was hand-painted with every hue of blue and green found in the ocean. Each individual thin strip of the skirt started off pale, but intensified to a much deeper color as it reached the bottom. She couldn't help herself; she ran her hand along the symphony of colors, her eyes widening as she realized the colors weren't woven together. Each sliver of color was a separate piece of material! She raised the skirt, examining and watching it undulate before her. It reminded her of a jellyfish gliding in the ocean. Even though the length of the skirt seemed modest, her legs would peep out with every move.

She shook her head and carefully laid it back down. She turned around to her mum. "I can't wear that."

Gwen stared at her for a beat, then back to the garment. Her mum's lips pursed, and she looked back at Sage. "It's not *so* bad…" she trailed off.

Sage snorted. "My legs, midriff, and entire back will be on display. It will only give more fodder for the gossip mill, Mum. I don't want to humiliate Papa and you."

Her mum smiled wryly as she crossed the room, approaching Sage. "I won't pretend that I don't wish there was a lot more fabric to the dress, but you and I both know that with where you're going, it will help you fit right in." Her mum's hazel eyes met hers. "This is a disguise, love. You won't humiliate us. You will look regal in that dress. It's fit for a queen. All we want is for you to come home safe to us. That's it. If this disguise is what's required for that to happen, then so be it."

Sage searched her mum's eyes for any doubts or condemnation, but she found nothing. Sagging with relief, she returned her gaze to the dress. "Quite the disguise," she muttered to herself.

Gwen rubbed her hands together. "Let's get started then."

By the time her mum finished with her hair and some minimal cosmetics, her back and butt were smarting. Sage had forgotten how much time it took to get ready for such a fancy affair. She stood up with a groan, twisting from left to right to sooth her aching back. "Ugh...I am *so* old."

Her mum's response was a slap on the butt as she chuckled. "You're not old until you have grown children, love. Now strip and hold still while we get that thing on you and get it all arranged."

Sage did as she was commanded, ridding herself of the much humbler garments she usually wore. Her mother's sharp inhale had her eyes snapping to her face, but she was busy with the skirt. "Everything okay?" she inquired.

"Mmhmm."

She eyed her mum curiously. How odd. She shrugged it off and stepped into the skirt aided by her mum. The silk kissed her legs as it moved, tickling her skin. She giggled, reaching down to scratch her calf. Her mum smiled, twirling her finger at Sage, indicating she should turn around. Sage plucked the bustier from the bed and held it in place. Her mum brushed her hair aside and tied the straps around her neck and back. It pushed her chest up so high, she thought her breasts would smother her. There were no hiding those.

"Oh, let me fetch the sandals and jewelry." Her mum bustled from the room and Sage turned, viewing herself in the mirror.

The woman staring back looked nothing like her. The colors complimented her green eyes so well that they sparkled like emerald jewels. The stark contrast of white starfish combs made her brown hair seem even darker. She would never be tiny and delicate because of the physical work she did in the forge, but her voluptuous chest, tiny waist, and curvy hips made up well for her muscular arms and broad shoulders.

She stepped closer to the mirror, and all her joy drained right out of her. Faint pink lines marred the otherwise smooth skin on her stomach. Sage bit her lip and pushed her left leg out to examine the damage. One of the ragged lines was so long it wrapped completely around her thigh. She reached down to touch it, and the scars on her wrists glared up at her.

She was ruined. There was no way she could wear this to the palace.

A sudden noise startled her into looking up and she caught her mother's gaze in the mirror. Sage couldn't mask the pain that shone in her eyes. Her mum placed the jeweled sandals and a pile of jewelry on the bed next to her, coming to stand behind her. Clasping her arms, she soothed, "You are enchanting, baby." Her mum reached down and caressed her wrist. "Everyone has scars, love. Some wear theirs on the inside, and some bear them on the outside. But you know what? Those that allow the world to see their scars and move forward are the bravest and best of us. That is true courage."

Sage teared up, touched by her mum's simple words. Gwen squeezed her wrist once and reached down to the pile of treasure lying on her bed. She picked out two wide silver cuffs with seahorses and a few pearls on them. "As you know, your father made these for me when we were betrothed. They are not as fine as what you are wearing, but I guessed you might like them. Then you will carry a piece of your family with you and help you take courage."

"I would be honored to wear them," Sage choked out.

Her mum clasped them on her wrist and, although they didn't completely cover the scars, they did help her feel less self-conscious. Sage reached down and fingered the large scar that ran diagonally across her abdomen. "Is there anything we can do to cover this?"

Gwen scrunched up her nose, deep in thought. A smile broke out on her face. "I have an idea."

She gingerly picked up the fine silver netting and set to work. Right below the tie on her right shoulder her mum pinned the netting, draping it to the center of her chest, and pinned it there with a pearl. She then draped it down Sage's stomach and tied it in an intricate knot, attaching it to her left hip but allowing the rest of the material to drape down. She'd worked a miracle in a matter of moments! Her scars were now much less visible. She felt more comfortable having a little more covering.

"Well? What do you think?" her mum asked enthusiastically, her words coming out in rush.

"It's so beautiful, Mum. Thank you."

Her mum beamed at her and retrieved the sandals. "Your carriage should be here any moment. Let's get these sandals on."

Her mum was still fussing over her when the carriage arrived. After what seemed like forever, she was ready and putting on her finest cloak. Just before departing, she placed her leg on the bed and methodically placed her daggers into their thigh sheaths. She then dropped her skirts and swished around, eyeing herself in the mirror. Even with all the slits, you couldn't spot her weapons. She grinned at the expression on her mum's face and hugged her goodbye. "Mum. I have to be prepared. Don't worry too much. I love you, and I will be home later tonight."

Her mother clutched her hand. "You better be, love. I will rip Sanee apart looking for you if you disappear on us again." Her mum's face was serious. Sage didn't doubt for a second she really would do just that.

"I promise, Mum."

She dropped her mum's hands and exited her room. Her father sat on a bench by the front door, his green eyes crinkling when he spotted her. "You are lovely."

She stretched up on her tiptoes and kissed him on the cheek. "Thank you, Papa."

He touched her cheek and affectionately rubbed his thumb along her cheekbone. "Keep your head and be cautious."

"I will."

Her father opened the door, and she peeked out, surveying the area. No one was paying them any heed. A cloaked man emerged and opened the carriage door, and so, sparing a last glance to her parents, she slipped into the carriage. She shot a quick glance to the man holding the door and amber eyes peered in at her.

She sat quickly, with Rafe entering right behind her. He tapped the ceiling, and the carriage lurched forward. She tilted her head away from the window, hiding her face. Instead of moving into the city they traveled deeper into the country, entering a copse of trees, which hid another carriage. Rafe hopped out of their carriage and opened the door of the one alongside, holding out his hand to her. "My lady."

Sage took the hand he offered, stepped down, and then right back up into the other conveyance. As soon as they were both inside, the driver started back toward Sanee. "Smart," she mused, watching the sun set on the horizon. "Hiding the Methian's carriage out here and conveying us to it from within the city? Good move, especially since no one will note an unmarked carriage heading to the country. Very clever, Rafe. "

"I thought you might like that, little one." She could hear the smile in his voice.

He had no right to call her that anymore. He had betrayed her. "I am not your 'little one', my lord. If you recall, I am a lady of station."

She frowned at him when he merely chuckled. "Forgive me, my lady, I meant no offense by it." Another more muffled snigger followed his comment.

There was no way they could keep up this ruse, especially in front of actual dignitaries. "They will throw us out or lock us up as soon as we speak. You know that right?"

"I think not." Rafe was silent for a moment. "How do you like your costume?"

She pushed back her hood and glared at him. "It is beautiful to be sure, but it's also entirely inappropriate."

Rafe flipped his hood down as well, leaning toward her. "It's more modest than what you will see there, I give you my word. And," he enunciated, "it is entirely appropriate for someone of your station." He shifted in his seat and then asked, almost self-consciously, "Did you truly dislike it?"

She smiled and patted his leg. "It is incredible. I have never seen painted silk like this. The colors are unreal. The fabric-maker must have been quite skilled. It's as if he took the sea and imprinted onto the material. I reckon I'll never see the seamstress again, but make sure she knows she did a fantastic job." She paused. "And Rafe? Thank you."

He nodded once, looking out the window. As they entered the city and made their way up the hill, Sage drew her hood to once again cover her face. Ahead of them was the palace, and unease rolled through her even looking at it. She still had no clue how she could save the king. Lost in her thoughts, she didn't realize they'd already covered the distance. It wasn't until the carriage stopped that she looked up, a million butterflies taking flight in her stomach. She swallowed back the nausea that accompanied them and took several shallow breaths in an effort to alleviate her anxiety. Salty air wafted through the door as Rafe held a hand out to her. Her eyes bounced from his outstretched palm to him and back again.

Get it together! she scolded herself.

Sage grasped his hand and gracefully descended the stairs, murmuring a soft, "Thank you, Your Highness."

Rafe bowed and tucked her hand into his arm, leading her up the steps and into the palace foyer. Well-dressed servants were directing people here and there. Voices and soft music echoed from her left. A servant bowed to Rafe and guided them to the anteroom outside of the ballroom. As she moved, the shells, sea glass, and pearls hanging from the back of her top tinkled in a melody of sound.

Sage murmured a quiet, "Thank you," as the servant divested her of her cloak. As she straightened her netting and brushed her skirt out, a choking sound caught her attention. Sage glanced to Rafe as he sidled closer to her, looking utterly transfixed. "Little one," his voice deepened. "There just aren't words. You are breath-taking."

A blush crept up her neck and into her cheeks. She tugged at her cuffs, self-conscious. His hand reached down and touched the edge of her scarred wrist peeking out from underneath the cuff. She grimaced. He missed nothing.

"Are there more?" he whispered.

She eyed the servants milling around them and bobbed her head once.

He stiffened. "We will talk about this later."

Sage batted her eyelashes at him. "No, we won't, Your Highness. I'm done." She placed her hand in the crook of his arm and faced toward the herald. Rafe's gaze burned into her until their names were called. They both straightened as the door opened. She pasted a demure smile on her face.

Into the dragons' nest we go.

THIRTY-THREE

TEHL

HIS HEAD WAS POUNDING.

Adjusting his crown, Tehl moved the blasted starfish, so it'd stop poking him in the ear. Slowly, he stretched his neck and scanned the sea of costumed people. The air buzzed with excitement. Tehl wished he had their energy. For him, this week had been brutal. Between getting ready for tonight, leading each festivity every day, and the late nights and early mornings that were usual to festivities, he was already dead on his feet.

He shifted in his chair and peered at his brother. Sam was eyeing a pretty redhead across the way, winking at her before moving onto catch the eye of another young woman. Same old Sam.

Catching his expression, his brother shrugged and gave him a smirk before turning to lazily glass the room. "Don't give me that look. It's my responsibility to have enough fun for the both of us. You obviously look like you'd rather be anywhere else."

Tehl frowned and tugged at his costume. Generally, he didn't mind being bare-chested, but here it left him feeling like he was being hunted, surrounded by leviathans. Sam had no problem with being ogled though. It seemed like his goal was to show as much skin as possible. "Are you aiming to add more women to your harem with that getup?" Tehl quipped.

"God, I'd better." Sam grinned, a wicked gleam in his eye.

One of the noble families made their way toward the dais to pay their respects. If it hadn't been for the constant greeting from guests, he'd likely be asleep in the chair. Tehl straightened, swapping pleasantries. Their youngest son, perhaps three by the looks of him, was scowling and tugging on his own costume. The poor little guy looked as miserable as Tehl felt, so he searched a nearby platter for something to improve the little man's night. As he did so, he heard Sam and a duchess chattering about the lovely decorations.

Good. After all the stupid work I put into picking them out, they should *be impressed.*

He spied a lemon tartlet that might tempt the boy. Plucking it from the platter, he stepped down to the duke and his family. Each bowed or curtsied, and the little one wobbled, frowning at the floor.

"What is your name, young man?"

Big brown eyes peered at him from a round face. "Xavie, my prince." The duke cleared his throat and the little boy's eyes darted to his father. The duke smiled, puffing out his chest a little so Xavie straightened and puffed out his chest. "I mean *Xzavier*, my lord."

Tehl bit back a smile at how the boy had tried to deepen his voice. "Is it uncomfortable to be a lion, Xzavier?"

Xavie scratched at his neck where the scruff must have tickled him. "Well… it itches like the dickens," he spouted, pulling on it.

"Xzavier!" his mum scolded. "Where did you learn that phrase?"

The little boy slid a glance to the duke before looking quickly to the floor. The duke smashed his lips together to keep from laughing while his wife blushed and discreetly swatted him on the arm.

Tehl focused back on the Xzavier. "My costume is bothering me, too. You know what helps me get through it?"

"What?" he asked curiously.

"Sweet treats," he replied, offering the lemon tart to the boy. He swore Xavie's eyes widened to twice their usual size and glazed over. Chubby little fingers reached for it, but then hesitated.

"Go on," Tehl reassured, "it's for you."

The little fingers swiftly plucked it from his hand, cradling it in his little palms like the most precious of treasures. "Thank you!" He squealed, rushing to show his mum his newfound prize. She wiggled her brows at him, enjoying his enthusiasm. Tehl stood, grinning down at the little Xavie who returned it tenfold. After the duke and duchess had withdrawn, Tehl padded up the steps to the dais, returning to his seat.

Sam clasped him on the shoulder. "Well done, brother. You notice the needs of others, it will make you a good ruler one day."

Tehl shrugged off the compliment and focused on the people milling about.

"The Methians have yet to arrive." He had awaited them all week. They had received word there had been a delay due to weather, so he had no clue when to expect them, and that put him on edge.

"Crown Prince Rafeth of Methi and Lady Salbei," the Herald's voice echoed.

"Well, well. Speak of the devil," Sam whispered.

Tehl scrutinized the couple descending the staircase into his ballroom. The prince was a tall, muscled man with wide shoulders and a trim waist. A long scar ran from his eyebrow to his chin, giving him a dark, dangerous air. The prince ran a hand through his rakish hair, the glossy auburn waves, so dark they were almost black. Numerous pairs of female eyes tracked his approach.

"Damn," Sam whispered, "there goes half my harem."

If he wasn't so tense, he would have laughed at his brother's woe-begotten tone. Tehl turned his attention to the woman who accompanied the Methian prince.

A sirenidae.

Tehl barely managed not to gape.

A damn sirenidae sent from the sea to tempt him.

A sea of blue and green showcased her fine figure, her nipped-in waist and flaring hips accentuated by her seductive skirt. As she glided down the stairs, it undulated like the sea itself. Every step she took provided tantalizing glimpses of her legs. Her shiny, dark brown hair caressed her chest and fell a couple inches above her navel. His gaze dropped to her petite sandaled feet; even those were attractive. He had to give it to the Methian prince; he sure knew how to pick women.

"My God," Sam breathed. "I would sell my soul for one night with that stunning creature."

For once, Tehl completely agreed with his brother. If only she would lift her head. He slid his gaze back to the Methian prince who was currently staring at him as he whispered something in her ear. Their gazes locked, his eyes feral as he glared at Tehl.

Point taken, she was his.

Sam's sharp inhale caught his attention. He looked to Sam with raised brows.

"Bloody hell," Sam cursed. Sam glanced at him and then back to the approaching couple, so Tehl, too, turned his attention back to the foreigners when a pair of striking emerald green eyes met his boldly.

Familiar eyes—nothing foreign about them.

Recognition dawned. He blinked a couple times to make sure he was seeing clearly.

It was the rebel. *She* was the Methian prince's companion.

What the hell? How was she acquainted with the Methian prince? Was she their spy or was she spying on him as well? Questions popped up in his mind, one after another but, with some effort, he pushed his questions aside. Now was not the time.

Let the games begin.

They stopped at the foot of the dais, and the room quieted as whispers circulated around them. Tehl stood and nodded his head to the other prince. "Welcome to my home, Your Majesty. I am glad you have traveled safely to our kingdom. I hope you shall enjoy your stay with us."

Prince Rafeth bowed. "I thank you for your invitation. We were happy to receive it and be afforded the opportunity to visit your beautiful kingdom."

Tehl caught sight of Gavriel on his left. His cousin stood stock-still, staring at his supposed friend, the mysterious Sai. She stared back at him with not even a glimmer of recognition.

The prince's eyes narrowed at his interest, but he swept his arm out to introduce the woman. "Let me introduce Lady Salbei, my companion."

She smiled at them and dropped her gaze to the floor, shyly. Oh, she was good. That girl didn't have a shy bone in her body. She executed a perfect curtsey and hovered there.

Sam slipped down the stairs to lift her from the ground. He picked up her hand and kissed it. "My pleasure to meet you, my lady," he mumbled against her skin, oozing charm.

"The pleasure is all mine," she purred back, dark lashes fluttering.

Sam winked at her, and Rafeth shifted closer to her side. The prince was not stupid; he knew when another man was trying to encroach on his territory. His brother needed to be careful this time. Tehl, however, needed to play host.

"We would be delighted if you would sit at our table and enjoy refreshments. One of my servants will direct you." A servant appeared at their side and bowed low.

The prince nodded graciously. "We will humbly accept your invitation." He turned and offered his elbow to the rebel at his side. "My lady."

Tehl sat on his throne and took their measure as they followed the servant to the courtyard. He about swallowed his tongue at the naked skin bared to his eyes. Her back was completely bare save four delicate ties holding her top together. Her hips swayed as she walked, leaving a trail of drooling men in her wake.

"What an interesting twist," Sam murmured. "Who knew she cleaned up so well? You know, I like my women devious… If I could just sneak her away from the prince…," his brother trailed off, probably thinking of a way to steal her virtue. "Do you think he knows?"

"Knows what?" Tehl asked quietly.

"Who she is."

"I couldn't say," Tehl said. "I don't know what to think. In the last month of trying, we still have learned nothing about her. We already knew she wasn't some street rat, but it appears she's the Methian prince's companion."

"She is not someone new to him, either," his brother remarked in a low tone. "I could tell from the way they moved together, and his reaction to your stare and my wink. Their relationship is real."

"Is she a spy for the Methians? Or is she a plant for the rebellion?" he asked under his breath.

Sam's lips tipped up. "It's a mystery I intend to untangle. I will keep our new guests occupied." Sam sauntered down the stairs, smiling and winking at female passersby. No matter their age, they blushed and smiled back.

Tehl ignored his brother's antics and looked to his cousin. Gav seemed rooted to the same spot, scowling at the floor.

"She didn't even acknowledge me," Gav gritted out, looking up at him with fire in his eyes. "Never once did her expression flicker. I even questioned my own eyes for a second until I spotted the scars."

"Scars?" He hadn't noticed any scars.

Gav scoffed at him. "Of course you didn't notice them. You were too busy ogling her, right along with most other men in this room."

Tehl shot him a dirty look but quickly smoothed it when their exchange garnered attention. "We will figure this out. Sam is gathering information as we speak."

Gavriel snorted. "Maybe halfway to helping her out of her skirt."

Tehl brushed that comment away, along with the accompanying uncomfortable stab of jealousy. A servant entered, bowing before him. "Dinner is ready, Your Majesty."

Tehl descended the stairs, the crowd parting for him, bowing as he walked by. Swiftly, he made his way outside and toward a table that was raised above the rest. Reaching it, he turned to face the crowd below him. He picked up a goblet of wine and raised it to the people. "Good people of Aermia, I stand before you, in the king's stead, to start the festivities this eve. I am not one for speeches, so…" He paused and smiled. "Let the festivities begin!"

The crowd roared back at him as he set his goblet down, and music filled the air. He surveyed the jovial crowd as they *oohed* and *ahhed* over all the work that had gone into tonight; His staff had done well. There were candles in little glass jars hung on ropes high above their heads. They winked in the darkening sky like stars. Large, dark blue lanterns sat on carved wooden columns, illuminating the area in soft light. Exotic orchids perfumed the air, spicy and sweet.

Soon though, other scents filled the air, those of roasted meat, herbed bread, and rich gravy. Hordes of his staff moved into the courtyard and up to his table, laying out a beautiful banquet.

"Thank you," he said to those working around him.

Despite his hunger, he focused on the people surrounding him. There were a couple of his advisers, some visiting nobility, Gavriel, Sam, the Methian prince, and the rebel. He still couldn't get any name to stick to her. Rebel?

Ruby? Sai? Lady Salbei? Who was she?

His companions for the evening gazed at him expectantly. "Please sit. Prince Rafeth, Lady Salbei, it would please me greatly to have you dine with me." He gestured to the seats on his right.

Rather than place himself between her and Tehl, Prince Rafeth guided Lady Salbei to the seat next to him, which he thought odd. He glanced at Sam from the corner of his eye, noting that his eyes narrowed ever so slightly. His brother had noted it as well. Sam and Gav sat on his left and across from the foreign prince.

Tehl took a bite of the roasted rosemary red potatoes, savoring the herbed butter. He swallowed and looked at the prince. "With everything that befell you on your journey I'm glad you've made it here unscathed."

"It's fortunate we made it here at all. We kept getting delayed. Once we made it past your border, however, it was nothing but smooth sailing."

"Do you sail?" Tehl asked, trying to keep the conversation flowing. "I would love to hear about your homeland."

"I enjoy sailing every once in a while." The prince gestured toward the sea. "Our sea is nothing like yours, the water is gray and turbulent most of the time. Our forests are our real source of pride. There are trees as far as the eye can see, and everything is lush and green. To those unfamiliar, I've heard seeing it for the first time seems unreal. The lakes are so clear you can spot fish swimming at thirty feet down."

"How do you farm?" Gav asked, intrigued.

The prince twisted his wine goblet between his fingers. "We have areas that have been cleared over the years, usually near lakes and springs, and that's where we grow our food."

"What about cities?" Sam probed.

The prince watched Sam for a moment before he answered. "We, of course, have cities, but not where you would expect them."

Tehl tucked his grin away, knowing that answer would bother Sam.

"Where?" Sam asked, his curiosity shining through.

Rafeth caught the twitch of Tehl's lips and shot him a grin before turning back to Sam. "Our cities are in the mountains themselves."

"You mean *in* the mountains?" Sam asked, incredulous. "That would take years of work."

Rafeth shrugged, "You're not wrong. Our homes were carved out of the mountains hundreds of years ago."

Sam gaped at him for a moment before recovering. "How interesting."

Gav's voice whipped through the air. "My lady, where are you from?"

Lady Salbei smiled at Gav, eyes bright. "I am from Aermia."

"How did you ever come to meet Prince Rafeth?" Gav pressed.

She looked up at the Methian prince with a sweet smile. He picked her hand up and kissed it. "Would you like to tell the story, little one, or shall I?"

The rebel blushed, turning back to the table.

She had to be the best actress Tehl had ever met.

She blushed on command.

Incredible.

"I lived in a little village along the Methian border in the providence of Challaraies. My parents died when I was quite young and my grams raised me. She lived in a cottage about a mile outside of the village, too far to run for help if we needed it. So we needed to protect ourselves." She paused taking a breath. "Grams's father had been in the Guard most of his life and was stationed in this little village. Over time, he married and had three daughters. He decided just because he had girls didn't mean they didn't need to have skills, so he taught them how to use a sword and bow. Grams passed it on, teaching me what she could."

She cleared her throat and the Methian prince handed her his goblet. "Thank you," she smiled gratefully at him. She took a quick sip and resumed her story. "Growing up, I loved being able to use both a sword and bow. But the sword was always my favorite."

Her eyes sparkled at the shocked older men at the end of the table. "I practiced every day and loved every moment. As I grew, I had to take on more responsibilities, because it got to be too much for Grams. One day when I was about twelve, I was exploring and I found the most beautiful meadow with a gurgling spring. It was clearer than anything I had ever seen and so full of fish. From then on, I hiked there every day. I would set up my fishing nets and then work with my sword. Years passed, and that meadow became my second home. I even made friends with the local animals." She smirked at them. "But that is a story for another time."

She picked up her story, but he wasn't paying attention her words, only to where her hand unconsciously ran along the edge of her costume, where pearls met lovely skin. He jerked his gaze away and scowled. What was wrong with him?

Tehl glanced around the table and smirked. He wasn't the only one. The other men were just as entranced as he had been. The Methian prince's eyes were locked on her, full of banked desire. He looked at her almost coveting, like she was his most prized treasure. She noticed none of it though, so lost in her story. Tehl tuned back in.

"The forest stilled, silent." She dropped her hand, and the men held their breath, eyes focused on her. "I knew I wasn't alone. I scanned my surroundings trying to figure out where it was coming from. The hair on the back of my neck stood up, because I could feel that something watched. I clapped and hollered, but still nothing, so I knew it couldn't have been a bear. I thought perhaps my stalker was of the feline variety."

Curses sounded around the table, and she grinned slyly at them. "Despite my best efforts, I found nothing. So I braced myself for an attack. Finally, when I couldn't handle the silence any longer, I shouted, 'I know you're there, so come out and face me.' To my surprise, it was a man who stepped out." Tehl looked from the prince to her.

Prince Rafeth chuckled. "Her swordplay was a thing of beauty. Every move was like water, such fluidity I hadn't seen in a very long time. Not to mention she herself was stunning, so fierce but so tiny. One of the first things out of my mouth was 'little one'. It popped out before thinking about it."

She shook her head ruefully. "Needless to say, I was not pleased with his appearance, nor his nickname, so I commanded him to leave my meadow. But all he did was laugh and said it was not my meadow, but his."

"You were on Methian land?" a baron asked from the end of the table.

"She was," Prince Rafeth replied.

"All those years I had been fishing and hunting on their land." She smiled sheepishly.

The Methian prince ran his thumb along the top of her hand and sent her a secret smile. He didn't like how Rafeth looked at her. Tehl frowned at himself. It must be residual guilt from the events several weeks before. He shook it off and focused back on the couple.

"It wasn't long before his visits became a regular event. We even began to train together. I learned a lot from him." She smiled at the Methian prince with true admiration.

She was a good actress, he would grant her that, but the emotion shining through was real. Their affection for each other was a reality. And the way the prince touched her, both with possession and interest…that was *definitely* real.

"Is that how you came by your scars?" Gav questioned looking her straight in the eyes.

The table stilled, silent as most of the men glared at Gavriel. Tehl couldn't believe his cousin would ask that. Why would he make her relive that?

Sam even looked taken aback by Gav's question. If looks could kill, Gav would be dead. The Methian prince had retribution written across his face as his hand clenched the rebel's. She looked over at the prince and gave him a small smile before cocking her head, staring evenly at Gav.

With intent, she untangled her hand from the prince and calmly removed each one of her cuffs laying them side-by-side on the table. She placed both hands on the table for all the men to see. "That's what torture looks like, my lords," she said in a low tone. She looked each man in the eye until she lifted her wrists up in front of her face and twisted them. "This is what happens when bad men have power."

She stood up and brushed aside the delicate silver netting hiding her navel. A six-inch scar marred the smooth skin. "I was hung from a ceiling and then cut for their amusement." She dropped the netting back in place and lifted her sandaled foot to the arm of the chair. Her skirt rippled away leaving her calf and thigh exposed. A map of cuts wrapped from the outside to the inside.

It wasn't the first time Tehl seen them, but it still sickened him. The rebel had experienced many horrors in his dungeon. A slight tremor ran through her arm as she ran her finger along a few of the scars.

"Was justice served?" one of his advisers growled.

She paused and looked down the table at his adviser, sending him a vicious smile. "Not yet. But it will be."

The Methian prince's eyes were focused on her scarred thigh. "My lady, perhaps showing all your scars off at the table isn't the best of manners."

She dropped her foot and didn't spare the prince any attention. The rebel stared at Gav. "I am sorry if I have embarrassed you, my lord, but beastly questions call for beastly actions."

Immediately, he could see the guilt in Gavriel's face. Standing abruptly, he bowed to her. "Forgive me, my lady. It was unseemly and unfeeling of me."

The rebel clasped her simple silver cuffs on her wrists and pieced Gav with her gaze. "Nothing to forgive, my lord." She squared her shoulders and curtsied to Tehl. "I shall go and freshen up. If you will excuse me, my lords." She swept down the stairs like a queen, head held high.

Tehl scooted his chair back, ready to go after her. "I believe apologies need to be made to your lady. Enjoy your dinner." He strode away before anyone could argue.

Again, the dancing crowd parted for him as he tried to catch up to her. Her skirt waved and taunted him as she turned a corner ahead of him. She was going the opposite way of the powder rooms. He stalked her down a couple hallways until he figured out where she was going. He cut through one office and ended up right behind her. "My la…"

She gasped and spun with a kick. Reflexively, he caught her leg and jerked her against him. She flailed backward, toppling them into the wall.

His face was smashed into her neck, and her hair tickled his nose. Her pulse raced against his lips. He tried to move his right hand, but her hair caught in his rings, not to mention it was sandwiched between the stone wall and the curve of her lower back. The more he moved, the more tangled it seem to get. She hissed out a pained breath when he accidentally yanked on her hair. "Sorry," he mumbled. He focused on his other hand and found it still clenching her thigh. "If I let you go, will you hit me?"

"Yes," she spat. Her words held much vehemence, and she ruffled the hair at the top of his head.

"Okay then. Until you calm down, this is where you will stay." Tehl spread his fingers and widened his grip on her thigh. Soft skin pressed into his calloused hand. Were all women this soft? And where was that cinnamon smell coming from?

Hunting for it, he ran his nose along the column of her neck. The aroma was stronger behind her ear, intoxicating. His mouth watered. Tehl wanted to run his tongue along her tender throat. His hand shifted on her thigh, and his thumb met the end of her sheathed blade. Tehl snapped back to reality. She wasn't just a warm, soft body; she was dangerous. He scowled at the faint tremors wracking her body.

"P—please, don't touch me," she stuttered out.

Guilt flooded him at what she must be experiencing with him practically mauling her. But then anger burned through his veins, overriding the guilt.

She was the one who attacked him.

She was the one creeping around his home.

She was the traitor.

He opened his mouth, and drunken voices nearing made both of them squint down the corridor. Tehl dropped her leg, jerking back, only to drag her with him.

"Let go," she seethed, pulling away from him.

"I am stuck," he growled right back at her, trying to untangle himself from her hair.

"Oh, God," she whispered. He looked away from the knot of her hair in his rings to see the color had drained out of her face. "No one can find us like this. It would humiliate Rafe." Her eyes darted left and then right. "There's nowhere to go." Her eyes darted rapidly from Tehl, to the wall, and back to the approaching voices. "We need to distract them." Her brow furrowed and then blanked as her tremors worsened. "You need to embrace me."

"What?" How would that solve any of their problems? They would be found no matter what. That would make him appear like he was seducing the Methian prince's woman.

"Listen to them. They're drunk. They won't remember anything come morning, or even in a matter of minutes. Plus, you can hide my face that way."

His face soured.

"Believe me." She glared up at him, eyes full of hate. "I don't want any part of you touching me. Do you have any better ideas?" Hope shone in her eyes.

He didn't—there was no escape, and they were out of time. He grabbed the back of her head with his tangled hand and her hip with his other.

"Take a step back."

"What?"

"We don't have time to argue. Move."

The rebel glared, and pressed back against the wall.

"Now, shift to the side."

Her eyes narrowed to slits. "No."

Tehl ground his teeth. "This was your idea," he reminded, "I am not the villain here, I'm trying to shield you."

She hesitated for a moment and then reluctantly obeyed. He leaned into her and placed his forearm against the wall, blocking anyone's view of her face from the hallway. Her body shuddered against his as a group of rowdy men rounded the corner.

Their slurred voices made her shudder harder. Her eyes were glazed over, like she was somewhere else. Tehl looked at the frightened creature before him, pity filling him. Softly, he pulled a couple locks of her tangled hair forward and stroked it.

"I will not hurt you, and I won't let any of those men hurt you, either. It will be okay," he soothed. Her eyes locked on his, filled with fright. "Shhh... it's all right, love." He let go of her hair and cupped her cheek. "Trust me." That seemed to get to her. She blinked a couple times and then snorted.

Well, at least he had broken through her terror.

She darted a glance to the loud group of men who were making crude comments and then back to his face, panic in her eyes. He watched her solemnly as he ran his thumb across her bottom lip coaxing her mouth open. Small panicked breaths puffed out of her lips, but at least it didn't sound like she would pass out anymore.

He tipped her chin up and rested his forehead against hers. "I am going to kiss you, so don't stab me," he warned her. He sure didn't want her to start screaming and have those men think he was assaulting the Methian prince's lady.

Ever so careful, he brushed his lips along hers once, twice, and then just pressed them there, staring into her wide green eyes. She stiffened further; even her lips were hard against his. He moved his head back and narrowed his eyes at her. "You need to kiss me back, so they don't think I'm ravaging you in the hallway."

Her hands shook as they crept up his chest and hesitantly sunk into his hair. Her nails scraped against his scalp, sending shivers down his spine. He tilted her head back and nuzzled her cheek, running his lips along her cheekbone, gently across her lower lip, and up her other cheek.

He inhaled a deep breath of cinnamon and was surprised when her hold tightened on him, just a bit, guiding him back to her lips. A soft kiss danced across his lips, fleetingly. She tilted her head and pressed her curves against him in a way that made his hands want to wander, but the reminder of the daggers hidden on her person, and his own beliefs kept them in place.

Tehl held her against the wall and angled her head so he could get better access, her breath catching in astonishment. He couldn't get enough of her taste, or the feel of her in his arms. He wanted more.

Tehl slid his lips sensuously against her full ones, over and over, trying to coax her into opening. When that didn't work, he traced his tongue along her bow of her top lip to her plush bottom one. That got a response out of her. She pulled on his hair, and he groaned, beseeching her for entrance. Pain exploded on his bottom lip. He jerked back and glowered at her. She'd bitten him.

Whispering wrenched his attention from the woman is his arms. He eyed with disdain the lewd inebriated men blatantly staring. When they recognized his face, theirs paled, all bravado forgotten. "Forgive us, Your Highness," they chorused.

"Leave us," he commanded, his tone icy.

There was a flurry of clumsy bowing and drunken scrambling down the corridor. Her small hand slipped to his bare chest and pushed hard. Tehl stumbled back a few steps and a sharp cry sprang from her lips. His body missed being pressed against her already. He glared at her, pushing aside his ridiculous response to their kiss.

Tehl raised an eyebrow. "Didn't think that through did you, my lady?"

She straightened her skirt and looked up at him with fury-filled eyes. "It worked perfectly. I didn't want you to be touching my person anymore and you are not," she said primly. "I count that a success."

Tehl rolled his eyes and tried to untangle her hair from his person. "Are you going to tell me what you are doing wandering around here?"

THIRTY-FOUR

SAGE

SAGE STILLED. EVERYTHING SHE HAD rehearsed flew right out of her mind. It was all she could do not to throw him off of her when he pressed closer. It felt just as when Serge, or should she say Rhys, had his hands all over her. She shuddered and focused back on the irritated prince in front of her.

She watched his large fingers fumble with unknotting her hair from his rings, and she blew out a breath at his incompetence. Sage pushed his hand away.

"By all means, take the lead," he said sarcastically.

Sage bit back her retort, knowing she needed him to listen to her. Her skin prickled from his gaze. There was nothing she wanted more than to disappear from this place and never set eyes on the crown prince ever again. She focused on unwinding the hair and was blunt. "Marq is in danger. Someone will try to kill him tonight."

He inhaled sharply. Sage didn't lift her eyes from her task, worried that her anxiety would get the best of her. Was he shocked that she used his father's name or that he was in danger?

"Who?" His voice was bland.

Was his tone a good sign or bad?

Her muscles coiled, and she casually slipped into a defensive position. She took a deep breath. "Me."

Silence.

Sage looked into his eyes as emotions crossed his face: shock, concern, fear, anger.

"I never planned on hurting him, nor will I in the future. He was nothing but gracious and kind." Sage glanced down and stared at his sandaled feet. "He doesn't deserve to die for being sick," she whispered. She lifted her head and met his hard eyes. They looked like chips of sapphires, frigid but beautiful. "I couldn't care less what happens to you, but I will not let harm come to your father."

Questions poured out from him in a frustrated rush. "How did you come by this information? Who sent you? Why would they send you if you will not harm him?"

All logical questions, but she would only actually answer the last one. She grimaced as she yanked the last of her hair from his rings and straightened. She stepped back, out of his reach, and his eyes tracked the movement knowingly.

"It is none of your business who I am, or whom I am working with." His face flushed with anger. Time for her to get to the point. "Logically," she began, "I was the best choice. Your father is a known hermit, yet he visited me every day for weeks. They figured we had a special relationship and that he would seek me out tonight." The words were bitter on her tongue.

The crown prince crossed his arms, thoughtful. "They intended to send you back into the arms of your enemy? I assume they know what happened, so if they still sent you, that in itself is telling. What noble masters you serve."

Her heart clenched—that was exactly what her so-called brothers did. Rafe sat downstairs, celebrating, all the while knowing what he had sent her to do.

"Can't you see how wrong that is?"

The sympathy in his tone surprised and almost undid her. Sage blinked hard and got a hold of herself. The crown prince paced in front of her as she stared at the floor. "You're right."

His pacing stopped, so she pressed on, "My own so-called brothers were willing to send me back here, despite everything that took place. I only want what is best for Aermia, bloodshed and death is not the answer. They didn't listen, though. If I didn't take the job, someone else would have. At least this way I can protect him."

"How do you plan to do that? If you don't try, someone will replace you, Ruby." He paused. "Or Salbei or whatever your name is."

"You can call me Sai," she offered.

"God save me from spies," he muttered as he spun and crossed his arms, muscles bulging. Sage eyed him warily, balancing on the balls of her feet. He was a big man, but she was faster. She'd outrun him if necessary.

"I don't trust you, but I can see that, for once, you are being honest. Your affection for my father is obvious, so tell me, what do you plan to do?"

This time she paced, the only sound the whispering of the silk swishing along her legs. "You need to stage an attack."

The crown prince regarded her shrewdly. "You want me to pretend there was an attack on my father?" He threw his hands in the air. "Are you out of your mind? I have the Methian prince sitting in my courtyard along with hundreds of people. Do you know how will they react? The kind of chaos that would ensue?"

"I didn't mean to make a huge scene. I'll return to the table. A while later you can rush through the crowd and get Sam and Gav's attention, the three of you leaving early. Most of them still suspect you have a mistress upstairs you're not sharing with the world. To others watching, it might look like more than it is," she hinted.

"You are being watched?"

"Yes," she admitted.

The crown prince let out a harsh laugh. "I can't believe I am going along with this, but I honestly can't see any other option if we're out of time. I will not take a chance with my father's life."

"Then I will leave you to it. You have much to accomplish with little time. Good evening." She backed away until she reached another corridor.

"If you are betraying me in any way, you will never see the light of a day again," he uttered, menace clear.

Her heart sped up at the threat, but she gave him her back, anyway. She was not a coward.

Pausing, Sage considered him over her shoulder and winked. "You would have to find me first." She sprinted down the hall and rounded another corner before slowing down, once again resuming Lady Salbei's persona. She neared the courtyard and sent up a prayer. Stars above, let this plan work.

The plan worked.

She returned to the table to be greeted by many admirers. It made her uncomfortable but she was still flabbergasted at how a little flash of skin and a sad story could turn some of the gruffest men into a puddle of goo.

Rafe seemed to be enjoying himself more since she returned, holding her hand, kissing her temple, or stroking her arm. She was impressed with his acting abilities. If she hadn't known any better, she would have thought him truly besotted with her.

A little after midnight, the crown prince came thundering through the crowd. Even though Sage despised everything about him, he was still a thing to behold. His black hair shone underneath a silver crown and she couldn't help but notice the hungry looks women gave him, their eyes devouring his bare chest and arms. He powered up to their table and nodded to his guests. He whispered in Gavriel's ear and then Sam's.

Sam stood and roamed over to her side, a smile creeping across his face that would make any woman's knees weak. He lifted her hand and gave it a lingering kiss. Completely inappropriate and completely Sam.

"It has been a pleasure to bask in your presence, my lady," he whispered across her flesh. "I cannot wait for us to get better acquainted."

Sage barely stopped herself from rolling her eyes and wiping her hand on her skirt. A low grumble came from Rafe that put a sly smile on Sam's face. Sam looked at her, his eyes smoldering. "Until we meet again, my sweet."

The three royals bid everyone good night. She studied Rafe out of the corner of her eye as he scrutinized their departure. His amber eyes caught hers, a strange glint in them. "My lady, I believe it is time I retire for the night." A sensuous smile slipped across his lips. "The journey and all of this excitement must have tired you as well."

She faked a yawn behind her hand. Rafe raised himself out of his chair and offered his hand to her. Sage smiled at him and let him help her up. She bid all the gentlemen goodnight when a gruff voice from the end of the table piped up. She zeroed in on the older man with the ruddy complexion and wiry gray hair.

"My lady, if I might be so bold as to say so, to my old eyes your scars enhance your beauty." Everyone's attention at the table concentrate on him. The older man straightened in his chair and sent her a kind smile. "They show your courage, bravery, honor, and willingness to fight back. Fierceness is a fine quality in a woman." His gaze ran over Rafe, evaluating him, before his faded gray eyes moved back to her. "If you ever find yourself in need of a husband, feel free to call upon me."

Sage's cheeks heated with his remark, though she knew the comment was good-natured. She smiled her first real smile of the night and dipped her head to him. "I will keep that in mind."

Rafe's tensed next to her. "She will not find herself in that position, though, I assure you," he said stiffly. Sniggers turned into coughs when he turned his glare on everyone. She had to stifle one herself and look away from the older man's twinkling eyes. Rafe bid them goodnight and rushed them toward the castle. He beckoned a servant who helped them locate their rooms.

When they first arrived at their guest quarters, the comfortable rooms made her feel right at home, but only for a moment. She quickly brushed it off, keeping in mind to whom these rooms belonged.

A large bed with luxurious carpets and tapestries adorned the walls and floor. The warm hearth invited her closer, so she stared at the flames, waiting for Rafe to start asking questions. She heard him flip the lock and then he was beside her, staring with her into the flames.

"Is it done?" he asked in a low tone.

"Yes." Simple. To the point. It *was* done, though not what he expected. However, there was finality in her actions; what she had done could not be reversed.

Rafe turned and stared at her profile. She stood still, trying not to fidget. She hoped he couldn't read on her face what she had done. What was he looking for? How was she supposed to act after killing someone? Sage decided numb seemed like a good place to start so she tried to emulate it.

"How are you?"

She kept her face expressionless, but inside she raged.

How was she?

Really?

He wanted to know how she was after stealing an innocent man's life? What an inconsiderate and stupid question.

She twisted her neck and stared at him. "I feel nothing."

"Oh, little one. I wish I could take this burden from you." Rafe reached out and cupped her face with one hand. She almost flinched but stayed still. His amber eyes filled with anguish at her expression, and he pulled her into his arms.

She held herself stiff and kept focused on the dancing flames. "How soon are we to leave?" she asked flatly.

Rafe's hands continued to rub tiny circles on her lower back. "I have a messenger delivering a missive in a couple hours that will imply I need to return to my kingdom immediately." His hands slowly skated up her back to her shoulders.

Her eyes flew to his when he caressed the nape of her neck. His eyes probed her like he was trying to figure out a puzzle. The color of his eyes still startled her sometimes, like tonight. The amber almost glowed in the firelight. His thumbs rubbed across her collarbones, sending goosebumps along her arms. She pretended she didn't notice his attention tracking the little bumps.

"You looked ethereal tonight. I couldn't have imagined something more beautiful, even had I tried. It was like the sea had conjured you to tempt me to her depths. You caught the eyes of most of the men tonight."

"Wasn't that the idea?"

Rafe chuckled darkly. "That was the general idea, right up until I saw the way you looked when you took off your cloak. I thought by the end of tonight that I might have to fight off those princes and the older man at the end of the table." He smiled at her, smug. "But they all knew you were mine. No one would take a Methian prince's woman."

Now that got a reaction out of her. Her eyes jolted to his, her eyebrows creasing. "You played your part well, possessive lover and all. But Lady Salbei isn't yours, because she doesn't exist, and as you know, I belong to no one." Sage brushed his hands off her and began to walk away.

"What did the crown prince say to you?"

Sage halted and squinted at him over her shoulder. "I only spoke with him at the table. What are you talking about?"

"He said he would find you and apologize for what happened at dinner."

Sage feigned surprise. "Well, he never found me." Rafe nodded, believing her lie. "I am tired. Wake me when we are to leave."

When the missive came, leaving was easier than she expected. They made their apologies to some of the advisers and to Gavriel. He kept casting looks at her that reeked of betrayal, and it ate at her heart. Rafe said their goodbyes and hastily moved her to their carriage but Sage looked over her shoulder and caught Gav's eyes. Just before disappearing into the dark carriage she looked at him directly, mouthing, *Forgive me, brother.*

The returning ride was the same as their initial departure. They rode far into the country, switched carriages and began their ride back to the city. She stared at the moonlit grasses, moving like ocean waves in the gentle breeze. "Where is the other carriage going?" she questioned.

"It will pick up the real prince and take him back to Methi where he won't remember a thing."

She ignored Rafe the rest of the ride and pondered the choices she had made since she joined the rebellion. Whether right or wrong, she had certainly grown wiser because of it.

Before she knew it, they were in front of her home. She straightened her cowl and peered at Rafe from underneath it, her eyes straining to pick him out in the dark. Sage reached across the gap between them and grasped his hand.

"Thank you for the training you gave me. I will always be thankful for what you taught me, but this is the last time we'll see each other. I am done, Rafe."

"You're sure this is what you want, little one?" His face was grim.

"Yes." Her tone brooked no argument.

He caressed her palm and his hood dipped. "If that is what you want, then fine. But this won't be the last time I see you."

Sage stared him down. "Yes. It will," she said sternly. "Any association with you puts my family in danger. I am not willing to risk it anymore. That's what

I mean when I say we are done."

His betrayal had cut her deeply. She would never let someone use her to hurt someone else. She swallowed thickly and let loose the words he needed to hear. "I thought you were my friend, Rafe. But friends don't send their loved one back into a hell from which they escaped, nor do they sanction murder for the greater good. They don't send people to torture them and then protect the wrong doers."

Rafe growled.

Sage held up a hand. "I am done." She stood up and tipped back his hood, exposing his magnetic eyes. She kissed his scar and whispered a farewell against his cheek before leaving him to the darkness.

THIRTY-FIVE

TEHL

TEHL TRIED TO WORK OUT the kink in his shoulder, slowly rotating it in a wide arch. The last day of the festival was a far cry from what he'd planned for. He hadn't slept at all the previous night.

Why was it so much harder to stage an attempted poisoning and subsequent rescue than to actually poison someone and then rescue them?

Despite all the revelry followed by hard work and the plotting the night before, he had responsibilities to take care of, so he couldn't let his exhaustion keep him from them. He rubbed at his shoulder, thinking of the new developments this morning. The Methian prince and the mysterious Sai had crossed the border into their own kingdom early this morning, and Tehl still didn't know what to think about it. She'd slipped through their fingers yet again. Although she'd made the right choice last night, she still was no friend of the Crown. She was still a traitor. There were just too many questions surrounding the entire situation. Reaching any concrete conclusions was difficult with the little information they had, and trying to piece it together was already giving him a headache. Sam was the spy, not him.

"Getting old, brother?" Sam's words interrupted his thoughts.

Speak of the devil and he will find you. Tehl spun to his brother as he stretched his shoulder once more. "Not any more so than you. Didn't I just hear you complaining in the ring? Something about needing beauty sleep?"

Tehl quipped.

Sam shrugged, sending him an unrepentant grin. He ran a hand through his blond curls. "I understand you have a busy day before you, but I need to pick up my armor this morning, and I thought perhaps you'd like to join me?"

He couldn't remember the last time he wandered the city with his brother, not for any duty but just for the pure joy of it. A boyish smile formed as he contemplated the idea, and Sam's smile mirrored Tehl's once he agreed. His brother gestured to a cloak lying on the fence encompassing the training ground.

"Prepared, were we?" Tehl joked, retrieving the items.

"Hopeful. And, of course, *always* prepared," came Sam's glib reply.

They both slid their hoods up and snuck out of the courtyard, entering Sanee. For a while, they wandered around, without real purpose, picking up smoked fish here and a pastry there. It was relaxing for Tehl to simply be, to enjoy the moment of complete freedom with his brother. They stopped by a seamstress, picking up some new linen shirts, and then went to a cobbler for new boots. They found new tack for Sam's horse as well as other random things that interested them. Tehl also enjoyed watching Sam interact with people, smiling and laughing, asking after their children and grandchildren.

As they left the last little shop, Tehl studied his brother. "I've enjoyed this, but I have to ask, why are we making these purchases in Sanee when we employ people at the palace to do all of these things?"

Sam shrugged and looked down the lane. "True, but these people need it more."

That struck Tehl.

He had always been proud of his brother, but never before seen the true depths of his generosity and foresight. Samuel cared for the people as much as he did. "How long have you been doing this?"

"Since I was a boy, probably around sixteen, so maybe nine years. Mum always said to help when we saw a need. At first, I tried to give them money, but they would often donate it to the poor, despite needing it themselves." Sam shrugged. "So I came up with another idea. They wouldn't turn down work, so I began commissioning the things I needed from them."

"Do they know who you are?"

"No, just a wealthy nobleman. The people around the fishing district rarely mingle with those living near the castle. It's been easy to keep my identity a secret."

Tehl liked the idea. "I might follow your example."

Sam smiled. "It only makes sense that you, like everyone else, would want to imitate me."

He rolled his eyes at the cocky reply and gave his brother's shoulder a shove. "Do you have everything you need?"

"One more stop, and then we can head home. I commissioned a sword." Sam's eyes widened with excitement. "I am close with the family that runs the forge. Years ago, I actually ran around with the smith's sons causing mischief until they began to work on merchant ships."

Only his brother would have a secret identity and secret set of friends. "Will we meet them today?"

Sam shook his head. "No, they'll be working, but you'll get to meet Colm, their father."

His brother led him down a couple dirt lanes to a forge at the edge of the city where they entered a storefront. Inside, a middle-aged man was cleaning blades and displaying them. Sam greeted the older man with a hug and began chatting.

Tehl glanced around at the odd collection of things: axles for wagons, horseshoes, and axes interspersed with short blades, and swords of various lengths and styles. His brother's yip of excitement peaked his curiosity. He abandoned the daggers he'd been examining and moved to Sam's side.

The older man held out a broadsword that awed Tehl in its beauty. The magnificent blade had been crafted with Aermia's symbol perched on its hilt. The fierce black dragon draped itself around it, sapphires glittered for its eyes and the scales shone like obsidian. Tehl leaned closer.

Black seed pearls, how clever.

Sam reverently took the sword and placed two fingers underneath the hilt to test it. The balance was perfect.

Sam handed it to him, smiling giddily. "She is one of a kind, is she not?" his brother asked, his blue eyes gleaming. "Colm, you've outdone yourself."

Tehl gently touched his finger to the edge and a drop of blood welled instantly. Tehl grinned at the smith. "I suddenly find myself in need of a sword as well."

"Thank you." The smith held his hand out. "The name's Colm Blackwell. Any friend of Sam's is welcome here."

"I'm his brother," Tehl tipped his head toward Sam.

The smith smiled. "So you're the illusive brother, the one with the 'serious side'."

Tehl shrugged, his lips tipping up.

"Sam, would you like this wrapped?" Colm held his hand out for the sword. Tehl placed the stunning sword in the man's hands.

"Yes, please. And I have to say. I've seen your work over the years, but this is truly something else. The craftsmanship, the attention to detail, and the artistry are each remarkable. The dragon looks so lifelike, I feel like he might fly away any moment," Sam flattered.

Tehl smiled at the older man and gave him a nod of respect. "Your craftsmanship is unique. I have seen nothing like it. You do your trade proud."

Colm paused and studied them thoughtfully. "I've known you a long time Sam, so humor me for a moment. What is your opinion on women working in a trade?"

Sam's brows furrowed for a moment before clearing as he seemed to reach some understanding. "If they can accomplish the task, why should they not be able to do what they want?"

Tehl contemplated the cogs working in Sam's brain and tried to identify the reason for the change in subject.

The swordsmith turned his attention on him. "And what of you?"

Tehl cocked his head, wondering what the man was getting at, but answered anyway. "Women are the stronger of the two sexes. They give life and deal with us on a daily basis."

Colm laughed at that for a moment before sobering. "Sam, I am sure the boys have told you that Sage helps me in the forge."

"Indeed."

"Well, in reality, she does more that assist me. I cannot take credit for your sword," he said in a low tone. "My daughter created it."

Tehl looked at the man and then to his brother. Sam blinked a couple of times, then a slow smile bloomed on his face. "Is Sage here? After all these years, I still haven't met her. Are you hiding her or something?"

The swordsmith smirked. "Any man who knew you would hide their daughter."

Sam chuckled, but didn't deny it. "Why keep her talents a secret, though?"

"Most men think their sword will be defective, weak, or worthless if crafted by a woman." Colm's face hardened.

"What rubbish," Sam added.

"Damn straight. She is the best swordsmith in all Aermia. We receive commissions from all over and great swordsmen now wield some of the best blades, all made by a woman."

"Can we meet her? I would love to pay my compliments to her in person, and of course, satisfy my curiosity."

Colm grinned at that. "You have an overabundance of curiosity. Sage," he hollered. "Would you please come help me for a moment?"

"Mmhmmm..." a feminine voice sounded from the back.

Tehl and Sam's attention focused on the light steps heading their way. The curtain pulled back, announcing a curvy brunette's entrance. Her head was down as she brushed her skirt off.

"What did you need, Papa—" Her question cut off when she looked up, eyes locking with Tehl.

Bright green eyes.

The rebel.

She was right under their noses the whole time.

Finally, a true name. Not the rebel, Ruby, Lady Salbei, or the mysterious Sai.

Sage.

It fitted her.

Tehl stepped next to Sam as they both stared her down.

"Why hello, Sage," Sam purred.

PART TWO
THE CROWN'S SHIELD

PROLOGUE

LIFE WAS CRUEL.

Men were evil.

And hope was lost.

But sometimes, just sometimes, there was a glimmer of something good. Something so sweet that it made all the wrongs, the hurts, the pains, and the nightmares fade just a little.

Sometimes they come in unexpected ways from unexpected people.

Sage's came from a source she'd have never guessed.

Her enemies.

ONE

SAGE

SAGE SQUEEZED HER EYES SHUT and reopened them, though it did nothing to change the scene before her. Her mind was reeling, this couldn't be happening. She couldn't be seeing who she thought she was... She blinked a couple more times.

Swamp apples. Still there.

Two royal figures stood before her, blue eyes staring, one in anger, and one in calculation. Her fingers went numb, and a high-pitched ringing filled her ears.

They were here.

The princes of Aermia were actually here. In *her* family's forge.

Sweat dripped down her spine.

How did they find her? No one had followed Rafe and herself as they made their way home from the festival last night, she had been sure of it. So *how* had they done it then?

She jumped as she felt a touch on her arm. Anxious, her eyes jumped to the one touching her but she relaxed as she met the gaze of her father. It was only her papa.

His eyes narrowed at her. "Sage? Are you all right?"

She nodded slowly and gave him a weak smile, deliberately ignoring the two men boring holes into her head with their eyeballs. "What can I help you with, Papa?"

Her papa grinned. "Actually, I have someone I want you to meet." He wrapped an arm around her and looked toward Sam. "Sage, I would like to introduce you to Samuel."

For a beat, Sage simply stared at the spymaster before her father began again: "This is the Sam your brothers got into so much mischief with over the years."

She started at his words. *Him?* Stars above, it couldn't be true. Life couldn't be that cruel, could it? Apparently, it could.

"It was he who commissioned the dragon sword."

Her gaze dropped to the sword in question. The great dragon broadsword she now held in her hands. Sage then glared at the sword, feeling oddly betrayed, as every foul word she'd ever learned ran through her mind. Of all the bad luck in the world, why did nothing ever go as it was supposed to?

The spymaster cleared his throat, pulling her from her thoughts. As she raised her eyes to his, he arched a brow. "I'm happy to meet you at last. Zeke and Seb have spoken of you so much that I almost feel like I know you."

Sage pulled in a breath and sent him a brittle smile. "I feel exactly the same way."

Sam leaned forward, not breaking her gaze. "The sword's perfect. I've never seen its equal. It's truly a stunning weapon. How long was your apprenticeship?"

Sage hesitated. Sam knew her family, but she didn't know what her brothers had divulged to the spymaster all these years, and she had no desire to give him any *more* information.

Before she had a chance to reply, her father spoke up.

"Actually, she never left my side, even as a little one." Her papa squeezed her. "I used to call her 'my little shadow'. Every time I stepped back, it was onto little toes. Her brothers had no interest in it, so, much to the chagrin of her mother, I trained her instead. Now, here she is: the most talented swordsmith in all of Aermia." Her father's face beamed with pride.

"Indeed," Sam remarked.

"Indeed," Sage mumbled. More like unfortunate.

Sam smiled. "How fortuitous it is to meet you in person." His smiled widened. "Beauty and talent. I believe Colm and your brothers have been hiding you from me?"

"Damn straight," her papa added.

Her eyes flickered to the crown prince's and she registered the barely-masked hostility there. It was time to go.

"Well, it was lovely meeting you." She smiled at Sam. "And thank you for your compliments. I hope the sword serves you well, however, the forge doesn't run itself, so if you will excuse me." As Sage turned away she tried to decide her next move. Should she run to the meadow? Or perhaps go and find Rafe?

"I would like to commission a few pieces."

Sage spun around when the voice cracked through the air like a whip. "I'll be honest, seeing my brother with such a beautiful blade has me a bit envious."

The dark tone sent a shiver down her spine.

Even though she'd warned the princes of the plot to kill the king, they were still her enemies. Their games weren't over: it was just the beginning.

Sage cringed and turned toward Sam, clenching her hands in her skirt to keep them from trembling. Looking at him again she realized that, unfortunately, he was still one of the most beautiful men she had ever seen. Wavy blue-black hair, sapphire eyes framed with long, dark lashes. The full mouth highlighted by strong cheekbones and a defined jaw. She couldn't believe she had kissed that mouth just last night. She shivered. Though it hadn't been the worst thing to ever happen to her, it wasn't something she wanted to repeat any time soon. Sage blinked. Why was she even thinking about that? Stupid prince.

He shifted and her gaze was drawn up from his lips to his eyes. His eyes held no warmth. Sam smirked while standing next to Tehl and her impassive mask began to crack. Her emotions were all over the place. She needed to rein herself in. But when her father clapped his hands together, she just about jumped out of her skin. She'd almost forgotten he was there.

"Well, I still have a little work to do, so I will let you two work out the details. But it was great seeing you, Sam. Stay for dinner?"

"I would love to, but I'm afraid I've got to get back to work."

"That's too bad, son. Perhaps next time."

She caught her father's sleeve as he turned and gave him a pleading look. "Papa, do you think it wise to leave me here unchaperoned?" She kept her voice low.

He eyed her and then the two royals, patting her hand absently. "I will only be in the forge and can see you the whole time." He turned his gaze toward her. "So have no fear, love." He raised his voice so that Sam could hear him. "I have known Samuel for many years. He would never do anything improper in my forge or make my daughter uncomfortable." The words were friendly but also held a clear warning.

Sam dipped his head, smiling boyishly. "As you say, Master Blackwell. You know, I feel as though Sage is my sister already."

Her papa acknowledged Sam with a quirk of his lips before moving back to his workbench. Sage stared after him, feeling like she'd just been left to drown in a river. Her father simply smiled encouragingly before turning away, whistling a lilting tune as he departed.

Sage swallowed hard, locking her knees to stop their shaking. She wouldn't let them detect the fear in her, so she gathered her courage. Grabbing paper and quill, she placed them on the counter before the two princes. The salty smell of sweat caught her nose. Hers or theirs? She had no clue. Steeling herself she asked, "So what would you like?"

Silence followed her question, yet she refused to look up at them. She waited them out a bit but still they said nothing.

"My lords?" she prodded.

When each remained silent she forced her eyes from her paper, eyebrows raised in a mute prompt. Sage found herself under intense scrutiny by both sets of calculating blue eyes. Her stomach clenched.

Suddenly, Tehl smiled fiercely, teeth gleaming. "I think I would like something similar to my brother's. The dragon seems lifelike, which I approve of, but I'd rather you leave off all those pearls and sapphires. Maybe substitute obsidian and black diamonds."

Of course, he wants a black sword, she thought, *it'll match his black heart.*

Sage mulled it over. It would be harder to get the obsidian and black diamonds but it was definitely possible. She grinned evilly as she thought of how much she could charge him. Her father may not have understood whom he'd been dealing with, but she most certainly did.

"It will take time to track down the stones you desire, but we can do it. Of course, you will need to pay upfront; twelve gold marks." Sage smirked when the crown prince's eyes widened just a fraction.

Sam spoke up first. "Come now. I only paid three for mine. His stones can't be *that* costly." Sam gave her a lazy smile as he tried to bargain. "Surely you can give us a deal, I mean we're practically family."

"You are." Sage pointed her pen at Sam before stabbing it toward his brother. "He's not. That's my price so take it or leave it."

Sam sniggered when the crown prince glowered at her before speaking. "I guess I'll need to borrow some gold, brother."

Pulling a bag from his waist, Sam set the coins on the counter.

Sage merely smiled, feigning innocence. "Is there anything else you need?" She kept her tone sweet even as she felt giddy inside. Were she to be locked up today, her family would still be taken care of for a long time.

"As a matter of fact, there is." Sam placed a dagger in front of her. "Something like this."

As she caught sight of it, the blood drained from her face. A rebel blade. More specifically *her* rebel blade. As her gaze snapped to Sam, she caught him taking in her reaction with interest.

So then, what now? Would he punish her family? The spymaster seemed to know she had created the dagger and had no doubt seen others like it on the other rebels. He now had proof she wasn't only a spy, but the rebellion's weapon supplier to a point. She wouldn't be going back to the dungeon, she would hang.

Her eyes darted to her papa, whistling away and working, oblivious to the danger she'd put them in, before returning to the two royals.

Carefully, she pushed the dagger back toward them. "I'm afraid that is an outdated design. Can I interest you in something else instead?"

She hoped they understood the translation: she didn't work for the rebellion anymore.

Sam's brow furrowed at her words before he cleared his expression. He plucked her dagger from the counter and slipped it back into the sheath at his waist. "Nope, I believe I have everything I need then. How about you, brother?"

She couldn't help darting a glance toward Tehl, but her breath stuttered to a halt when she met his angry eyes. He leaned closer, feigning interest in a dagger on display, but Sage held her ground, refusing to be intimidated. She froze, however, when she felt his breath caress her temple.

"There is only one thing I require here and none of it was forged with metal. So far it has eluded me, but I believe very soon it will be within my grasp." He paused before continuing, "There is nowhere to run, Sage."

Her eyes flew back to Tehl's. Seeing the determination on his face she knew she needed to leave. *Now*. She had planned on never seeing Rafe again but at this point she had no choice. This wasn't just about her own safety anymore.

By then he'd withdrawn from her space, though he continued watching her intently. She smiled grimly and placed each hand on a displayed dagger.

"Only over your dead body," she hissed. He would never find her again and he would never hurt her family. Of that she would be certain.

Both men tensed at her threat and her smile turned deadly. At least they understood that danger was imminent.

"Papa," she called, never taking her eyes from them. Sage heard him as he hoisted himself up to stroll over to her. When he reached her she continued, "I find myself quite fatigued." She then handed him the sheaf of paper with the crown prince's specifications. "Would you mind finishing up?" Sage broke the staring contest she'd been entertaining with the two men so she could meet her papa's worried green eyes.

"Oh, love, I'm sorry. Do you need anything?"

A warm smile split her face as she felt the concern in her papa's voice. "No, no. I'm sure it's just too much dancing last night." Kissing her papa's whiskered cheek she spared the royals a last glance. "It was lovely meeting you, Sam." She hoped to never see him again.

Sam smiled like he knew exactly what she was thinking, which ratcheted her anxiety up a notch. "We'll be seeing you soon then."

Sage turned and forced herself to keep a sedate pace as she departed, until she entered her home. Closing the kitchen door, she then picked up her skirts and ran, revealing the leather pants she always wore beneath them. She vaulted over the table bench and burst into the living room, startling her mum.

"My stars, Sage! You scared me half to death." Her mum took in her facial expression and jumped to her feet. "What is it, love?"

Sage opened her mouth and floundered. What could she say? That she had put them all in grave danger? That she would most likely be hung? That she had let them down? She waved her hands and bolted to her room with her mum on her heels. Sage rushed around the room, ripping her rucksack from a chest at the base of her bed.

"Dear? You are scaring me. You need to calm down and talk to me."

Sage spun to face her mum. "They found me, Mum. I was so careful not to lead them to your door, to put any of you in danger. But of all the wretched luck in the world…" Sage sunk her fingers into her hair.

Her mum pulled her hands away from her tangles and held them. "Take a breath, you need to calm down. I need to understand what is going on if I'm going to help you."

"I don't have time," Sage cried in dismay.

"The quicker you talk, the faster I can help."

Her mum's stern tone penetrated the sea of panic she was swimming in. Her vision blurred as she looked into mum's face, her hazel eyes full of concern. She sat heavily on her bed, pulling her mum with her. "I only wanted to help our people, to make Aermia a better place. I was tired of all the sickness and poverty. Our people were crying out to the Crown but all they received was apathy… I mean, Aermian women on the border are being *taken*. By Scythia!"

"What?" her mum gasped.

"Mum, I was offered a way to help. A way to make Aermia better. I wanted to make it better."

"The rebellion." It was a statement, not a question.

She tipped her head back, gazing at the faded yellow stars painted on her ceiling. "Eventually I was caught. It was the Elite, more particularly it was the crown prince and the commander."

"They are the ones who marked you?" Her mum asked, her voice infused with both anger and sorrow.

"Not by their hand. It happened in the dungeon by their men. When they found me I was on death's door so they brought me to a skilled healer and had me looked after as I healed. I didn't understand why they cared at the time. I figured it was because they wanted information. But I have since learned the man who did this wasn't theirs. He was *from* the rebellion." She barely choked out the last sentence.

A sob broke free from her mum's lips. "Oh, my poor baby."

Sage wanted to mourn too, but she also knew they didn't have time, not now. She swallowed her pain and continued. "It broke me, Mum. Last night was my last night. I told them I was done with it." She paused. "Do you remember the dragon broadsword that I made?"

Her mum's brow wrinkled. "Yes."

Sage barked out a humorless chuckle. "It turns out it wasn't for a regular run of the mill noble. No, it was for a prince, the commander who, it turns out, is intimately connected with our family. Papa wanted us to meet, so he introduced us."

"The Crown's never commissioned any pieces from your father."

Sage smiled sadly. "They have, and my identity is no longer a secret."

Her mother's face tightened in anger. "I can't believe your father did that. How do we know the commander?"

She swallowed, her eyes watering, her mum loved Sam. "It's Sam, Mum. Zeke and Seb's friend, Sam."

"No," her mum breathed. "It can't be."

Sage's heart squeezed. "Of all the rotten luck in the world, right?"

Her mum trembled. "He's been visiting since he was a boy, your brothers love him!" She straightened her spine and lifted her chin. "No one hurts my children. You're right; you need to leave. Immediately." Her mum stood and, in a flurry of swishing skirts, began stuffing things into her pack. "I have a friend who can offer a haven—even your father is not aware of her." She paused. "Is Sam still here?"

"They were when I came inside so I assume so."

"Okay. Give me one moment." Her mum rushed out the door while Sage ripped off her skirts and packed all of her trousers in the sack. She also strapped on as many blades as possible, along with her sword. Hastily, Gwen bustled back in and pushed bread, dried fruit, and jerky into her bag as well.

"This may not last long, but my friend will take care of you before you run out." Her mum also pressed a letter into her hand. "There are directions in here. I will come to you when it is safe, but you need to go now. I could still hear your father talking with them so I will go and say hello. Perhaps I can keep them preoccupied for a while longer."

Sage bit the inside of her cheek, trying to keep from crying, and hugged her mum fiercely. "You'll talk to Papa, right? And tell him I love him?"

Her mum pushed back and cupped her cheeks. "Of course, sweet girl. We will always keep you safe. We all love you so very much, you know that." Sage threw on her cloak and strapped on the sack, eyes watering. She cocked a hip and smiled through her tears. "So…how do I look?"

Gwen grinned back at her. "Improper as ever."

Her heart lightened at her mum's statement. She would be okay. Things would get better. They had to for she would make it so. Sage clambered into the windowsill and swung her legs over the edge. Turning back, she peeked from under her hood, blowing a kiss at her mum.

"Goodbye. I love you."

Her mum scowled for a beat but it soon morphed into a smile. "Never goodbye, love, because I will see you soon. Be safe, tell Lil hello, and that I'll visit soon." She paused. "Remember, Sage, never to judge."

Sage's questioning expression seemed to make her mum's smile widen. Shrugging it off, Sage waved, dropping to the ground on silent feet. There wasn't much to keep her covered, and it was at least twenty-five paces until the homes started. Probably best to sneak into the forest until the homes were a bit closer together.

She kept low to the ground, waiting and watching for movement. Nothing. Her heart pounded as she sprinted through the open before she disappeared into the forest. She heaved a deep breath, only slightly relieved. She was safe for the moment.

Opening the letter, she read the directions. Her mum's friend lived in the fishing district. It was actually close to one of the rebel's bases so she could use one of their tunnels to keep hidden as she made her way there. Shoving the letter into her vest, she began weaving through the forest, feeling calmer almost immediately. There was something about the mixture of vegetation, freshly turned soil, and damp wood that soothed her soul. She breathed deeply, reveling in the cleansing air. If only she could stay here and pretend the outside world did not exist. Mulling it over, she decided she would gladly become a hermit.

A whiff of freshly baked bread floated on the breeze and quickly shattered her daydream of disappearing into the forest. She scanned the modest stone homes that had slowly crept toward the forest's edge. In one, a mother gestured furiously as her son with a loaf of bread. The next, a young woman vigorously washed clothing while humming a familiar tune. Sage continued to move along the tree line, searching for an exit. Unfortunately, it seemed like everyone was home today. Finally, she spotted the perfect place to slip into the city.

The home was clean but in clear need of maintenance. An old man slept in a rocking chair on his back porch, a threadbare blanket covering his slumbering form. Sage paused, observing the place for a few moments, searching for anyone else who might be in the house or the one next to it, yet all remained silent.

She crept from her hiding place to the house in a matter of seconds where she cautiously peeked between the wooden shutters. The home appeared sparse, a stone fireplace dominating the wall across from her, with a worn chair in one corner and a small side table holding a couple of well-loved books. The kitchen was part of the same room, though all that occupied it was a sturdy table and a single chair. She doubled checked, but saw neither pantry nor food lying about. Where was the old man's family?

For some reason, it made her heart hurt knowing he could be all alone in the world. Sage dropped her sack and pulled out the food her mum sent with her. It wasn't much, but it was all she had to give. She slipped back to the porch and eyed the sagging stairs. There was no way she could sneak up those—they'd give her away immediately. Ignoring them, she placed a knee on the porch. She leaned closer to the old man's feet and placed the food beside his chair. Soundlessly, she shifted back and slipped quietly between the empty homes, moving in the direction of the fishing district.

TWO⊙

TEHL

SHOCK PULSED THROUGH HIM EVEN after she'd left. They had actually found her and not only that, but they even knew her true identity *and* her family. She was completely different from when he saw her the night before, less exotic, less refined. Yet she was just as beautiful. When he initially caught sight of her, he'd felt inclined to haul her over his shoulder and lock her up so he and his brother could finally extract some answers from her, and he'd been about to do so when Sam had slid him that look.

He wasn't sure the reasoning behind his brother's decision to let her walk away, but Sam always had a plan. The man had more information, and secrets, than anyone he'd ever met… Except, perhaps, for the rebel girl. She might be the exception.

He pulled himself from his thoughts when he heard the click of a shutting door.

Was she coming back out?

Her excuse of illness was one of the oldest tricks in the book, and it was surprising her father hadn't seen through it.

When he glanced up he noticed an older woman emerging from the curtain. She pushed some silver-streaked hair from the hazel eyes bracketed by fine lines, probably from smiling too often, as it seemed to suit her. She skimmed her eyes over him but lit up with joy as she spotted Sam.

"Samuel!" she exclaimed and rushed toward them. "It has been too long, my boy." She hugged Sam and then planted a kiss on his cheek.

"Gwen, dearest, your beauty has faded not a bit. Colm is one lucky man." Sam grasped her hand, placing a quick kiss on the back of it.

She swatted Sam's shoulder, her lips quirking. "Some things never change, do they? I was hoping you might have finally found a woman to settle you."

"I'm afraid the only woman in my life is my duties, and she's all I've got room for. She's a hard mistress, demanding all my time and energy, so I fear I would have nothing left to give a young woman. For you, however, I think I would make an exception."

Tehl barely kept from rolling his eyes at his brother's antics. Sam couldn't help himself, he just *had* to flirt with anyone that was female.

"Hey, now," Colm scolded, though good-naturedly.

Tehl took the moment to study the older swordmaker while his brother distracted the lady. The older man was a complicated mixture of opposites. He was tall and wide-shouldered, with massive hands, yet his clothes hung loose and his face was gaunt. The size of his clothes bespoke a time of good health and what was most likely considerable strength. Tehl watched as the swordsmith's hands shook slightly while he worked. What had happened to him? Was he sick?

"Forgive me for being so rude but, who is your companion?"

Tehl discarded his musings and turned to the woman who was now appraising him. Her smile was friendly, but her eyes were shrewd. As she looked him up and down, the corner of her lips pinched slightly.

Interesting, he thought.

It appeared she didn't like him though he'd yet to speak a word. *Like mother, like*

daughter.

"I am Tehl, my lady." He inclined his head, respectfully addressing the older woman.

"Forget all the formal nonsense. A friend of Sam's is a friend of the family's. Call me Gwen." She brushed her hands against her skirt and looked between Sam and himself. "Would the two of you like to stay for dinner?"

"Colm invited us already, and I do wish we could stay Gwen, but I fear that business waits for no man. Thank you for the offer. However, we really ought to be going."

"That's too bad. Perhaps next time?"

"Next time of course." Though Sam smiled, his expression held a hint of disappointment. "We will be back for the blade in a couple weeks."

"Definitely. Will Zeke and Seb be done with their trading then?"

"Actually, they're home now. They're out running errands for me so I'm sure they'll be sad they missed you."

Sam picked up his sword and passed his other packages to his brother. "Tell them not to be strangers." He then gave Gwen a quick hug, and shook hands with Colm, before turning toward the exit. As soon as he'd turned, the smile slid from his brother's face, grim determination replacing the former levity.

"You're *sure* you don't have time to stay?" Gwen called lightly.

Something in the tone of her question felt off, and Tehl's brows furrowed.

Sam pasted the smile back on his face and tossed over his shoulder, "I am afraid not, dearest, but next time for sure." Sam waved to the couple once more, and they meandered away until they were out of sight from their home. He picked up his pace, urging his brother, "We need to hurry, she's running; I know it. Gwen was trying to stall us." A bitterness had seeped into his words with the last sentence.

"I thought the same thing. I knew something was off when she smiled at me with her lips but it didn't match her eyes." Sam didn't often show his true feelings but Tehl could feel the frustration pouring off his brother. "What's wrong?"

"I have known them for years, Tehl, years. You have no idea how many times I snuck over there to visit their sons, Seb and Zeke. I never met Sage. She was younger and always by their father's side. Neither of the boys had an interest in the forge. I can only guess what Sage told her mother, but my friendship with them just ended. Instead of being honest with me, Gwen shut me out and protected Sage."

"That is, I believe, what mothers are *supposed* to do," Tehl drawled. Odd that it was him making this observation to his brother when it was usually the other way around.

"Believe me, I know. I just..." Sam stopped, searching the surrounding area and running a hand through his hair. "I wish things were different. Everything is so damn tangled." Sam squinted at the forest and changed the subject. "She couldn't move into the city from this direction. If she had, we would have seen her. If I was her, I would have slipped into the trees to sneak along so I could enter the city near the fishing district. The homes butt up against the forest there so it'd be an easier transition for her." Sam met his eyes as he made his way quickly back. "We have to hustle if we want any hope of catching up with her. If we lose her this time I doubt we'll ever discover her again. Our only chance to quell the rebellion peacefully will disappear with her."

Tehl nodded and quickened his pace to match his brothers. They jogged down the lane scanning the area. "We could have avoided hunting her down if you had let me take her at the forge," Tehl pointed out, baiting him. "I understand that you're friends with her family, but this isn't about one family, it's about a nation of people."

Sam scoffed.

Tehl smiled at his brother. Sam loved to tell others why he was right, and Tehl had deliberately created the perfect opening.

"First, we want her to come willingly."

His lips twitched. Hook, line, and sinker.

"As we have seen in the last month, she won't give us a damn thing if we push. We don't want to be seen as the evil ones. If you had taken Sage from her home, we would've become evil, and she would have resisted us with everything she had," Sam continued in a lofty, lecturing tone. "But now, she will run to someone she trusts, someone who can protect her and who is potentially very dangerous."

Tehl let out a snort. So that was it. His brother was brilliant. "The rebellion. She is running to someone in the rebellion."

Sam grinned, huffing out a breath. "Exactly. Two birds, one stone."

They slowed when they reached the end of the forest, and a small cluster of homes gave way to the bustling city's edge, families filling the streets, going about their daily business. Sam paused at an abandoned barrel and dumped his packages into it. Tehl raised a brow. Was he really going to leave his goods in that barrel? Sam saw the question on his face and smiled.

"I can't track a rebel spy if I am weighed down by loot. That girl is fast!

Plus, no one is looking to steal from an old barrel, so I doubt anything will happen to it. Stop scowling and blend in, damn it! You keep an eye on the south, and I'll watch the north."

Tehl pulled his hood to more fully shadow his face and scanned the road. Children sat in the dirt, etching games into it with little rocks. Others chased each other or hung onto the edges of their mums' skirts as the women gossiped and shopped. He couldn't help the smile on his face when a baby boy picked up a rock and began gnawing on it, behind his mum's back. His little face sagged in relief with each bite. The little one must be getting teeth. He pulled his gaze from the baby and studied the surrounding people. Tehl inspected each person carefully, even the young men. The first time he had met Sage she was posing as a boy so she could very well be doing so now.

"There," Sam breathed.

Tehl shuffled sideways to where his brother looked. There she was, moving out from between two homes and into the lane. She then flittered from one group of people to the next, looking for all the world like she belonged in each. It was fascinating.

Sam sprawled lazily next to him, groaning about a headache. Sage's head swiveled in their direction. She spotted Sam and appeared to dismiss him before moving down the dirt road. His brother was right. People saw mostly what they expected to see.

Sam straightened and paused next to him. "Shall we investigate a bit?" Excitement gleamed in his brother's blue eyes.

Tehl nodded, gesturing ahead of him. "Lead the way."

Sam's eyes flicked to his boots. "Do try to be quiet, we don't want her to know we are coming."

Tehl glared at Sam. "But of course. Anything that you command, Mighty Lord of The Sneaks."

Sam scratched his chin with a satisfied smirk. "You know, I have always wanted to hear someone say that. Though, admittedly, I'd always hoped it would come from someone of the female persuasion."

Tehl scoffed and kept close behind. They followed Sage at a distance as she made an odd series of twists and turns.

"She's coming to a dead end," Sam whispered, but, when they turned the corner, she was gone.

"Bloody hell," Sam said.

He searched along the street but she was not there. A flicker of movement drew his eyes up. Tehl blinked. She was running across the roof of an alehouse.

"Sam."

"I see her. We need to split up or she'll spot us coming."

He waited for Sam to get a good ten paces ahead before he made a show of sedately meandering down the cobbled street. Her fluid jumps and quick steps made it easy to keep his attention on her. Every movement was precise and athletic, never stumbling or slowing down. He'd have to pick up his pace to keep her in his sight, but, just as he had the thought, his breathing stuttered as she hurled herself across a large gap between buildings. Her dark cloak floated behind her, suspended in the air, until her fingers caught the edge of the roof. Bracing her feet against the building she twisted, and, with her back to the wall, noiselessly dropped to the ground.

He had never seen anything like it.

"I want her. Do you think she'd marry me?" Sam whispered heavily in his ear.

Only years of practice kept him from jumping at the sudden proximity of his brother. Damn his brother and his eternal sneaking. "Was that necessary?" he asked harshly.

Sam shouldered next to him as Sage slipped down the alley. "No, I find it enjoyable, so I wouldn't expect it to stop any time soon. Also, you probably would have heard me if you weren't watching her quite so closely." Sam hitched a thumb over his shoulder. "You passed me a couple buildings back and never even noticed. Not that I can blame you… That woman…" Sam groaned. "Beauty, grace, cunning…and those moves! I bet she's flexible—"

Tehl slapped his brother on the back of the head. "Don't even think about it."

Sam scowled, rubbing the back of his head. "Why ever not? Do you like her?"

Tehl returned Sam's scowl. "No. But it does seem disrespectful to talk about her like that when she is your friend's *daughter*," he defended, stepping down the alley, little shanties popping up in the small areas between buildings.

The closer they moved toward the ocean, the poorer the area became. Rusted metal roofs sat atop cheap wooden homes.

"She is skilled though," Sam commented. "If it was anyone other than us, she would have lost any tails long ago."

Tehl agreed. With all the twists and turns, ups and downs, it was hard to keep track of her. He had no clue where they actually were in the fishing district except that the sea was nearby, and he only knew that because he heard the thundering of waves and the smell of seaweed.

They continued on until a break in the endless maze of shoddy homes gave way to the open expanse of sea cliffs. Where was she going to go now?

"She has nowhere left to go." Sam said, obviously perplexed.

The rebel hastily glanced left and right, before sauntering toward a large outcrop of rocks near the cliff's edge.

"She better not shimmy down those rocks. If she does, I'll be very put out," his brother complained.

Sage moved around the rocks and out of sight. Tehl sighed and abandoned their hiding place. Both brothers approached cautiously, keeping an eye on their surroundings, as they slipped around the rocks.

Rocks.

There was not a blooming thing but rocks.

Sam padded to the edge and peeked over. "Nothing. That's odd." Sam turned and scrutinized the rocks. "She can't have disappeared into thin air."

"Maybe it is another of her skills," Tehl said. "Women are tricky like that."

Sam snorted. "*Now* you make a joke?"

Tehl examined the area closely before answering. "It seems to always work for you. I thought I would give it a try."

Sam snarked something back, but Tehl missed it as something caught his eye. There was something unnatural about the moss between two boulders. He approached it and bent down, running his hand along the moss, when his finger snagged on wood. A trapdoor. "I guess I was wrong, Sam. It isn't one of her tricks after all." He felt along it until he encountered a cool metal ring. Tehl pulled it up carefully, so as not to alert anyone who might be below them, but the door moved with ease, gliding along on well-oiled hinges.

Sam squatted next to him. "Well, I've always wanted to go searching for booty by the sea."

Tehl rolled his eyes and swung his legs into the hole, then rolled to his belly grasping the edge with his hands until his boots met a firm ladder. One rung at a time, he lowered himself into the opening, Sam following behind. His brother then closed the hatch, catapulting them into darkness. In the pitch black, they moved steadily, deeper down the chasm. After a few moments, Tehl's eyes sufficiently adjusted so he was able to see a soft light filtering in from the bottom.

Tehl stepped to the side when his boot touched the damp stone floor. He took in the crude porous archway that led to an uneven stone tunnel. The sound of crashing waves echoed around him, making it seem like they were surrounded by water.

Sam brushed his hands off and took in their surroundings as well. "Intriguing," was all he said before continuing down the corridor.

Suddenly, a piercing scream sliced through the air, making his blood freeze. Both brothers slid hidden blades from their stashes and sprinted toward the tortured scream. They burst into a giant cavern with a small opening to the sea. Tehl dismissed the surrounding area, focusing on Sage, who was folded in a man's arms. The man growled and faced them. Just when Tehl thought things couldn't get any worse, they did.

It was the Methi prince.

THREE

SAGE

HER HEART GALLOPED IN HER chest. She had been moving so fast that, when Rafe had reached out and grabbed her, an embarrassing shriek had burst from her. Terror filled her for a moment, wrenching her back into her nightmare, and, before she knew what was happening, Rafe had pulled her into his arms and had held her growling. The menacing sound triggered another spike of fear. Sage pushed against his chest, a whimper escaping. She needed to be free, she couldn't breathe.

"I think the lady would like you to release her," a dark, velvety voice commented. Her eyes closed at the familiar voice. Could she never escape him? *How* did he find her? Rafe's arms tightened, trapping her hands between them.

"It seems to me that she was running from you. She reeks of terror. I'm sure that's your doing. She has nothing to fear from me, I would never harm her."

Except that he already had. Sage pushed once more, but he didn't budge.

Rafe continued, "You need to leave me and mine alone."

She lifted her chin and glared up at Rafe. She wasn't anything to him.

"I hate to intrude, Your Highness," the spymaster broke in, "but you have yet to let her speak for herself. From the way you are holding her, I doubt she can even breathe."

And that was how the crown prince found her. Sam. The man of a million faces and lady friends, the spymaster of Aermia. Rafe peered down into her

294

damp eyes and loosened his hold a little.

"Are you all right, little one?" he asked rubbing his thumb along her cheekbone.

Sage jerked her face back. "I will be once you let me go."

Hurt and something else flashed across his face before his arms slipped away. She took a large step back and angled herself, keeping all three men in view. The crown prince studied her, no sign of the anger and shock he wore an hour ago. Her eyes turned to the golden prince. Sam appraised her with a lazy air, while his eyes wandered up her body, making her feel naked. She glared at him when he met her gaze and merely winked.

Damn rogue.

Rafe stiffened, his hands caressed the forearm length daggers strapped on each of his thighs. "Keep your greedy eyes off her. She is not yours to gaze upon."

Sage debated between knocking Rafe on the head or smirking at Sam, but one thing was for sure, the situation was about to explode. Her gaze bounced from one man to the other, pausing on Sam. A devilish twinkle entered his eyes that made her cringe and want to hide. She had been on the receiving end of that twinkle and she'd ended up drugged out of her mind.

"Your behavior is shocking, Your Highness. It was my understanding that women don't belong to anyone but themselves." Sam quipped.

"She's mine."

The dark possessiveness in Rafe's voice made the hair on the back of Sage's neck stand up. She touched her knives and took another step back. "I am no one's, Rafe. Not the rebellion's, not the Crown's."

Rafe turned his glare on her. "No matter what you choose, you will always be mine. *My* family, *mine* to protect."

She looked away from him and locked eyes with the crown prince. He stood silently next to his brother, simply absorbing the situation. Sage wondered if he stayed silent because when he spoke he tended to offend people, or if he truly just had little to say.

Tehl's deep eyes released her and shifted to Rafe. "What is your part in this, Methian? Are you aware of Sage's loyalties?" The crown prince studied Rafe. "She's working with the rebellion. So either Methi's supporting the rebellion or you're a fraud."

"Little one? They have your name?" Rafe hissed, never taking his eyes off the two royals.

Her jaw tensed at the accusation in his tone. It wasn't like she gave it to them.

"We do." Sam rested one shoulder against the rough cavern wall, looking casual. "Sage and I have an interesting history, I grew up with her brothers. Imagine my surprise when I went to collect my sword from Colm this morning, and he introduced me to his elusive daughter." Rafe cursed, causing the spymaster's smile to widen. "I must have been standing under a lucky star, my sword and the lady I have been searching for, all under one roof."

Her breath stuttered. She had heard Zeke and Seb speak about their adventures with Sam over the years. She would never have guessed the outcome of their friendship would be what lead to her hanging. How much did Sam know about her family? Even if she ran, her family wouldn't be able to escape. Sage was well and truly trapped. She only had one option left: to bargain. "What do you want, Sam?" she asked, defeated.

"The safety of Aermia," Tehl cut in, his voice echoing like thunder in the small cave. "We want a peaceful resolution between us and the rebellion, no bloodshed. I want to discover why Scythians are stealing our women, and I want to know what the hell you're doing with a Methian prince, if he even is one."

"That was a lot of wants, brother," Sam remarked off-handedly.

"Shut up, Sam. No one asked you."

"I think her question was for me."

"Nobody cares what you think."

Sage gaped at the two royals. She'd seen this side of Sam, but she hadn't seen so much as a glimmer of humor from the crown prince. Shaking off her shock, she scrutinized the men. "You still didn't tell me what you want from me."

"We want you to be the liaison," Sam proposed.

A liaison?

Between the Crown and the rebellion," he continued. "There is no need to fight. I am sure we can come to an understanding if everyone can be reasonable."

Her eyes widened as his words sunk in. An ambassador? Maybe she could protect her family if she accepted. Sage blinked and her vision was blocked by a large back. How did Rafe move like that?

"You want to *use* her?"

Sage shifted to the side and peeked around him.

"You mean like you? You had the power to help her escape our dungeon." Sam chuckled at Rafe's silence. "Come now, don't pretend like you don't have spies inside the palace. That's just insulting. You left her there with strangers, for a month, so she could give you information."

"You know nothing," he hissed.

"No, I know everything." The humor faded from Sam's eyes. "Including who sanctioned my father's assassination attempt." Rafe stilled. The spymaster held up his hands. "Keep your shirt on, I am not threatening Sage. Despite her best efforts, my father lived."

Rafe's gaze prickled, but Sage ignored it, staring at Sam's exposed collarbone, hoping to hide the deceit written on her soul. She had betrayed the Crown by joining the rebellion, and she had betrayed the rebellion by colluding with the Crown.

She was a traitor to both.

No one should trust her.

"I spent enough time around her," Sam continued, "to know she would have never agreed with that decision. She isn't a murderer, but you tried to make her into one." The spymaster's eyes hardened. "I hold you accountable. You stood by her side last night and let her leave. You are the guilty one. How could you encourage her to do that? To do that to your own family? You and I already carry the burden of death but if she'd taken his life, the Sage you supposedly love would cease to be, we both know it."

Rafe was breathing hard next to her by the time the spymaster finished his tirade. His wide, leather-clad chest heaved like he had just run a race. He inhaled a final, shuddering breath and stilled. Sage shuffled to the side, farther still, studying his profile. His face was blank. Her heart shrank a little. After everything Sam said, never once did he defend himself or capitulate. Rafe thought he was right.

She shook her head, placing her hand across her mouth. To a certain point, she'd understood no one person was greater than their goal, but she never expected Rafe would be the one to demand her sacrifice, forcing her to give up her morality and soul for the rebellion. Except for the crashing waves, silence descended upon the empty cavern, the air thick with regret and pain.

Sage continued to stare at Rafe's profile, her decision made. She couldn't return to the rebellion or forget the responsibility she had toward the people. She stared at the flame of a flickering lantern as she came to terms with her future. Could she do it? Could she deal with the rebellion and the Crown *and* still be fair? Would they hang her if she refused? Her eyes dropped to the crown prince, fatigue riding her. "What would happen if I declined being your ambassador?"

"Then we'd find another way."

That surprised her. Her eyes narrowed. Where were the threats?

The crown prince added, "But Sam, Gavriel, and I believe you would be the best option to avoid bloodshed."

Again, he surprised her.

"You would leave her and her family alone?" Rafe asked, skepticism coloring his tone.

"I have known her family for almost ten years. I have no desire to see any of them hurt." Sam met her gaze. "But if you choose to help, I will send Jacob to your father."

Her world spun. Jacob was the finest healer in Aermia. Her father had been sick for so long, but a healer of Jacob's caliber wasn't within reach for them. It would mean everything for their family if he could be healed.

"You would let her father suffer, knowing he is sick, if she doesn't agree?" Rafe questioned.

"No."

Her eyes jerked to the crown prince.

"We will send Jacob, regardless. Sam was trying to sweeten you up to the idea. Jacob will do whatever he can for your father. But if you say yes, you will help thousands of innocent people, *our* people."

Thousands. How many would suffer if there was a civil war? If she joined the rebellion to help the people of Aermia, if she agreed, she could save lives. Sage turned to Rafe and scanned his face, looking for a trace of his thoughts. He stepped closer, weapons glinting. A little sliver of fear wormed through her. Sage locked her knees to keep from taking a step back. Her nose flared, as anger surged hot on the heels of her fear, why did her body keep failing her?

Some of her tension melted away at the tender look Rafe gave her.

"Little one, I sympathize with how much you desire your father to be healthy. You want to help the people but this..." Rafe paused and watched the royals over her shoulder for a moment. He looked down, citrine eyes warm, and clasped her hands. "I don't trust them, but you will help many by accepting their offer. You are familiar with the Crown and the rebellion, you can make it right for the both of us, and so many others."

Sage studied him then turned back to the royals. Dark blue eyes latched onto her green ones.

"You have suffered more in our home in the last month than I suspect you have suffered in your life. If you decide to be our ambassador, we will protect you." She watched his Adam's apple bob and his jaw tighten. "You don't believe us, but we did not sanction your attack. Despite what I may have threatened you with, I would never treat a woman that way. I take responsibility for my men's actions."

A lump formed in her throat at the sincerity of his apology. She wanted to believe he wouldn't hurt her, but no man was trustworthy except her papa... and Gav. She still didn't like the crown prince, but she wasn't heartless. He didn't deserve to carry the guilt of her attack.

"He wasn't your man; he was the rebellion's." Both royals straightened, rage distorting their faces.

"Serge was a rebellion spy?" the crown prince snarled.

She nodded, bile creeping up her throat at the memory of his smug smile. She swallowed hard when the crown prince's glacial gaze snapped to Rafe.

"You sent your own men to harm her? Was it a test to see if she would give up information? To see if she would hold up under pressure?" he spat, stepping forward, Sam at his side.

Rafe matched the brothers' steps, vibrating from head to toe. "Never," he growled. "That animal did what he did for his own sick pleasure. Mark my word, soon he will painfully disappear from this world."

That was news to her. Rafe scolded her for stabbing him.

"He is not dead?" Sam asked in interest. "I am surprised that you've not already taken care of him. Did he not betray one of your own?"

Rafe glared. "We don't execute someone unless there is evidence and witnesses." Rafe spared her a look before going on. "It was her word against his."

"Were the myriad of scars not proof enough?" the crown prince bit out.

"No, they were not."

Sage's throat tightened.

"She greeted him by stabbing him through the shoulder."

Sam smiled darkly at her. "You stabbed him?"

"I threw my blade when someone yanked my feet out from under me." Sage clenched her hands, feeling angry all over again. "If it hadn't been for that, he wouldn't be around to hurt anyone else."

"A woman after my own heart."

"Indeed." Sage shared a sharp smile with the spymaster.

"It was because of that." Rafe pointed at her face, frustrated. "No one understood why she was attacking him. She outright tried to kill him in front of a roomful of men. To them, it looked like she was acting without provocation, like she..." He hesitated before soldiering on, "Like she was broken, not fit to lead."

Hurt stabbed her as tears burned at the back of her eyes. The rebellion circle thought she was crazy. They didn't believe Serge, or Rhys, or whatever should be held accountable for the trauma he'd inflicted. "Was there a trial this week?" she demanded. Rafe's serious expression told her everything.

"Yes. The decision was passed that since there were no witnesses to validate either of your claims, Rhys would go free."

Her stomach dropped. How could they allow this? They were letting him go. A deranged maniac. Why would they doubt her? Did anyone fight for her? Why wasn't she told?

"Sage," Rafe called to her, pulling her out of her thoughts. "He has been part of the circle for a long time. He had sway, and I had to stand by their decision for the moment." A predatory smile graced his handsome face. "But he will not walk this earth much longer. *No one* hurts my family. He will wish for death."

Her breath caught at the promise of vengeance in Rafe's eyes. That man would never hurt her or anyone else again, she was sure of it.

"I would like to see your technique or maybe try a few of my own. One for each inflicted on her," Sam offered, his tone flat.

"Don't forget the broken bones and bruises," the crown prince added heatedly. "He ought to pay for those as well."

Rafe regarded them before a vicious smile spread across his face. "I may require your expertise."

The royals mirrored his feral smile, dark promises filling their eyes. All three of them were in agreement: the crown prince, the commander and the spymaster, and the rebellion leader. If she hadn't been in the same room, she would have never believed it. *This* brought them together?

Rafe stalked toward the royals with feline grace, halting in front of them, looking like a warrior pirate. His hands flexed at his sides once before he shoved his hand out. The crown prince glanced at her once before stepping forward and clasping Rafe's forearm. Rafe looked over his shoulder and tipped his head to the side, beckoning her.

Sage steeled herself and glided to Rafe's side. She looked from one prince to the other. This was her last chance to back out, but she was never one to back down from her duty. She thrust her arm out for Sam to take. Sam quirked a smile at her and clasped her arm.

"It will be a pleasure working with you, my lady."

"We will see," she said, making his smile widen.

Sage forced herself to turn to the crown prince. She willed herself not to shake when she reached out to him. With care, he clasped her arm, long fingers overlapping. He stared down at her with solemn eyes. "Thank you for your sacrifice."

"If she is harmed in any way, mentally, emotionally, or physically, our agreement will be void and you will have war," Rafe threatened from her side.

The crown prince's dark sapphire eyes dropped hers and stalked to the large man at her side. His voice dropped low, deadly. "Agreed. If she is harmed by anyone in the rebellion again, I will burn it down to the ground."

She blinked up at Tehl, shocked at the threat. Apparently, her value as an asset had increased more than she realized. His thumb caressed her arm, and she shifted awkwardly. He hadn't let go. Sage pulled her hand from his grasp, feeling uncomfortable. Time to get down to business.

"It is time for you both to leave. I will arrange a meeting in six days at a location of my choosing." Sage said as she scanned all three men, hoping she didn't sound as inexperienced as she was. "Each of you will meet with whomever you need to. You will only bring six men with you to the meeting in six days' time. Demands will be exchanged, and we can meet three days later for negotiations. Any objections?" Silence met her question. "Good, then it's set. I will see you all in six days' time. Good day." She nodded and turned on her heel.

"I would speak with you before you leave, little one."

She flashed Rafe a sharp smile, knowing what he wanted to talk about. It wasn't going to happen. "And I you, but I have somewhere I need to be. So if you will all excuse me." Sage reached her bag and picked it up, then retreated, forcing her steps to slow so she wasn't seen running toward her escape.

"How will we contact you?" Sam asked.

Sage peeked over her shoulder. "I will find you."

Time to disappear.

F·OUR

SAGE

⟐∘⟦⟧∘⟐

ONCE OUT OF SIGHT, SAGE sprinted down the stairs, needing to
get away. Her boots pounded against the dirt floor, padding a loud rhythm
as she sped from one tunnel to the next. She burst into an intersection of six
openings, ducking into the second one on her right without hesitation. She
had to get ahead of Rafe; he had a peculiar way of finding her whenever she
least wanted to be found.

The floor gently sloped downward, fading from dirt to wet sand. The rough
stone walls surrounding her were covered with seaweed, little sea creatures,
and moisture. She shivered as the ceiling dripped cool water onto the top
of her head and down her neck. Pushing her brown hair from her face, she
sloshed through puddles to the mouth of the tunnel. Passing through it, she
was momentarily blinded by the sun's brightness. When her vision cleared,
her breath caught at the view before her.

Nothing surpassed the turquoise waters of the Thalassian Sea. The ocean
glimmered in the light like a million aquamarine pebbles covered its surface.
Its waves called to her. She would kill for a swim right now, to explore the
treasures under the surface. Sage sighed. She didn't have time for that.

Reluctantly, she peeled herself away from the enticing ocean and scanned
the surrounding bay. Ships rolled in the blue-green waves, hulls towering
above her. Those moored where the bay met open ocean were actually

rebellion supporters. It was brilliant, really, for if anyone left through this doorway it just looked like they had exited in one of the vessels.

Sage eyed the slippery steps carved into the cliffs. They looked awfully slick. With care, she crept up the steps, testing each ledge before placing her weight on it. Finally, she reached the wooden dock; its wood creaked beneath her as she stepped from the stone staircase. People milled about, and she heaved a sigh of relief when the merchants ordering about their workers didn't spare her a glance.

She lifted a hand, shading her eyes from the brightness of the sun, scouring the ships for the Sirenidae. Her eyes landed on an old but well-kept vessel where 'Sirenidae' had been painted in pale green, contrasting the dark wood of its hull.

Gotcha.

Sage meandered among the workers, blending seamlessly and arrived at the massive ship in no time. Oddly enough, there weren't many people around the ship. Where were all its sailors? Unease crept over her, but she steeled herself. She trusted her mum. Gripping the rope rails, Sage marched across the ramp with the churning ocean below, hoping her hosts would not stab her for trespassing on their vessel.

When her feet met the deck, she peered around curiously. The ship was clean and its wooden deck well oiled, practically gleaming in the sun. Large white sails billowed in the breeze, reminding her of her mother doing laundry on sunny days.

Someone takes pride in their work.

A whisper of leather against wood caught her attention, and she focused on the shadowy cove obscuring the new arrival. Sage shifted on her feet and ran a reassuring finger along the blade at her waist. "Sorry to board your ship unannounced, but I mean you no harm," she called out. "I seek refuge, and it was my mum that sent me. She said your captain could provide shelter."

"Blade?" a familiar voice asked gruffly. "What in the blazes are you doing here?" Hayjen stepped forward, his ice-blue eyes regarding her.

"Hayjen?" How did her mum know Hayjen?

"Your mum sent you?"

Sage thought about not answering him for a moment, but she trusted

Hayjen as well as her mum. "Yes. Gwen Blackwell." When his face didn't show any sign of recognition, she questioned the directions. Maybe she read them wrong. "I have a letter," she explained, pulling it from inside her vest.

Hayjen's lips pursed before he replied. "I will speak with the captain." Her friend turned back and left, leaving her standing alone on the deck.

Sage frowned. Well. That was odd. Questions swirled through her mind but they would apparently have to wait. She leaned her back against the mast and soaked up the warming rays. If she wasn't careful, she would fall asleep right where she stood.

After a time, her eyes peeled open at the sound of Hayjen's approaching feet. He smiled, his eyes crinkling at the corners. The tension in her shoulders relaxed, this Hayjen was familiar.

"She will see you now."

Now that sparked her interest. A woman captain. You didn't hear about one of those every day. Women could work in any trade but it was still usually frowned upon if she worked in a position or trade dominated by the male gender.

Sage returned Hayjen's smile and followed him down a narrow hallway that smelled of orange oil. They paused at an ornate door painted with swirling colors, and Hayjen knocked twice before opening the door for her. She skirted around him and waited for him to follow, but he simply winked and closed the door. She hadn't expected that.

Sage turned and took in the chamber. A pale blue wooden desk stood in front of three large, clear glass panes that formed a bay window with a plush window seat. Bracketing each side of the window were two massive bookshelves full of colorful books. She found herself gravitating toward them, running a finger along a red leather spine.

"Do you like them?" a husky female voice murmured.

She smiled at the books. Sage had known the other woman was watching her. "They are lovely," she commented. "You have quite an amazing collection. Some of these look to be hundreds of years old." Sage turned to greet the woman but jolted when she met a magenta gaze. She stared blatantly, not able to help herself. She had never seen eyes that color, *ever*. Someone had invented small colored lenses that could be placed in the eyes to change the color, but this was something else, it was obviously natural—and yet it seemed unnatural.

Sage blinked when the captain arched a delicate white brow and pushed her hip off the opposite bookcase. She moved like water, smooth and flowing. She sat on the edge of the pale blue desk and adjusted the emerald silk scarf wrapped around her head and neck, covering damp hair that was seeping through. The scarf dripped down onto unique clothing. Neither buttons nor stitches adorned them. Everything seemed knotted or tied, yet it somehow created a form-fitting dress. A long pale foot dangled from the desk. Sage pulled her gaze from the interesting dress to meet the woman's dancing eyes.

The captain gestured to her eyes. "You will not ask about them?"

Sage quirked her lips at the candidness. "My mum taught me not to ask questions that were rude, and as that would be in that category, I will refrain. But what I am curious about is how you know Hayjen."

The woman smiled at her. "I was a pirate, and he happened to be one of the goods I was stealing, but that's a long story for another time."

Was she joking or serious? Before Sage figured it out, the captain spoke again.

"I've been waiting a long time to meet you, Sage Blackwell. Your mother and I are very old friends."

"Really?" Sage cocked her head to the side, curious, as the woman looked to be only a handful of years older than herself. "This is the first time I am hearing about you," Sage replied carefully.

"No need to beat around the bush, *ma fleur*."

Sage hesitated a moment before continuing. "My mum is a proper woman, and you look anything but proper. No offense."

A smoky chuckle emerged from the woman. "None taken." She smiled with warmth at Sage. "You have spirit which I presume you get from your mum, but your lovely eyes must be from Colm."

Well then. The woman wasn't lying after all.

The captain shifted on the desk and faced her. "And, to answer your question, your mum and I grew up together, but because of some, shall we say, *unsavory* acquaintances, we had to part ways. We still write letters and every once in a while she steals away to see me, but it's not as often as we would like." The woman's voice turned serious. "Your disappearance just about killed her."

Sage's eyes widened, and the captain's smile sharpened. "There are few things I cannot discover. She came to me but even I could not find you and that is saying something. All Hayjen discovered was that you were on an assignment but we both knew that wasn't the case with Rafe riled up. So that narrowed it down to one man who possessed the skills necessary to make you disappear so entirely."

"Sam," Sage breathed. How was this woman associated with the rebellion? And who was she?

A bitter smile marred the captain's stunning face. "That boy." She shook her head. "Knows more tricks than a whore. He concealed you well."

Sage frowned at the glimmer of respect she saw in the captain's eyes. Whose side was she on then? "If you guessed where I was why didn't you tell my mother? Or even Hayjen? He thought I was dead," Sage questioned.

"Your family would have gotten themselves killed with that information. I was protecting them, even if I couldn't protect you. I knew I could trust Rafe to do that."

Anger and hurt seeped into Sage's blood. "He's a pretty poor protector. I want nothing to do with him or his other aspirations."

"So you're not with the rebellion any longer?"

Sage studied the captain's eyes. Admitting she was part of the rebellion was dangerous. "Rafe is no longer part of my life," she replied cryptically.

"Interesting. What made you want to leave?"

"Not everything is black and white."

"True, but something must have set you off."

"I'm not blind anymore. There are no absolutes when it comes to people. I believe in certain ideals but prefer to go about it in a different manner than certain others."

"How very insightful for someone so young."

Sage snorted. "I am hardly young. Mum has been chomping at the bit to marry me off." She looked down at a scar peeking out from her sleeve. "But I have survived things that have changed my view of the world. Sometimes the enemy isn't someone far off, but a brother wearing a friendly mask."

"All scars heal, *ma petite fleur*."

Sage's lips twisted. "Some take longer than others." She lifted her eyes and forced a weak smile. "I am in need of sanctuary for a little over a week. I'm willing to work and help here in exchange for you harboring me."

The exotic woman dipped her head. "Done. You will be treated as if you were my own. I have watched over you since you were a child. I look forward to spending time with you." Her magenta eyes flashed. "No one will take you from here. You are safe and protected."

"Hayjen?" she questioned, feeling bad she even asked. Sage didn't want Rafe to know where she was. She had enough to deal with at the moment.

"He will be silent. He is, after all, my husband. We will both protect you."

Sage froze. Hayjen was married? She'd have to come back to that later. "The leader of the rebellion has an uncanny ability to…"

The captain slashed her hand through the air. "That predator will not find you here. Even if he did, he would never set a foot on my ship."

Sage had heard no one call Rafe a predator before, but the description aptly fit. There was something raw and primal about him, a wild danger, like if you got to close you could be bitten. Sage reeled in her thoughts and bowed to the captain. "Thank you for your hospitality, if there is anything I can do to repay you Ms…" She trailed off realizing the captain never gave her name.

The captain leapt from the desk and dipped into an elaborate bow, displaying all sorts of pale skin. "Lilja Femi, at your service."

Sage catalogued the many weapons strapped to the exotic-looking goddess bowing before her. Lilja's scarf slipped from her head exposing wet silvery hair, and her neck! Sage's breath froze at what she spotted: three slits flared slightly with each of Captain Femi's breaths. The captain stood and met her eyes, her gaze inciting a challenge. Sage quickly schooled her features, hiding her fear, and forced her hand from the dagger at her hips.

"Breathe, *ma fleur*, I will not hurt you," Lilja coaxed.

Sage forced a breath in and out. Her mind scrambled. It couldn't be. They weren't real, and, even if they were, they'd supposedly disappeared a thousand years ago. So long ago, in fact, that they'd become a legend, a fable in stories.

"Sirenidae," Sage whispered. The proof was evident. Her mum had sent her to a damn Sirenidae, a living, breathing—sort-of—Sirenidae. This is what she must have meant about not being quick to judge. In all the old stories, Sirenidae were believed to be beguiling, deadly creatures, though so beautiful your eyes would bleed.

Yet, growing up, her mum had never told the stories that way. She'd always painted them as heroes, fierce and kind. Now, Sage understood why. Her mum was hiding a Sirenidae! Sage's fear spiked again. She was standing in a room with one of the most dangerous races ever. The fifth race existed.

The Sirenidae lived.

Sage let out a shaky breath and said the only thing she could think of. "Do you have a tail?"

FIVE

TEHL

HE COCKED HIS HEAD AND watched the mysterious man track Sage's departure, a wealth of feeling in Rafe's eyes as he watched the girl. How close were they? After she'd gone, the man in question turned to them with outright disdain and disgust evident on his face. Tehl was sure his own expression mirrored the rebellion leader's. He didn't want to work with him; the man was a traitor and a liar.

"Are we going to glare at each other all day or get down to business?" Sam drawled.

Rafe's lip curled as he continued to stare at them with those eerie eyes. There was something off-putting about the man's gaze but he'd be damned if he let the other man realize it. Tehl straightened and stared right back. The rebellion leader's lips twitched slightly, like he was holding back a smile.

"Since the two of you are *still* staring, I will start."

Sam pushed from the wall, breaking their stare-off. His brother was up to something. A million questions lurked in his Sam's eyes, despite the carelessness of his expression.

"What is your name?" Sam asked. "We are working together now so that makes us friends."

Tehl snorted but kept silent, waiting for the rebellion leader to answer.

"My name is Rafe."

Sam blinked. "You don't expect me to believe you used your own name last night. You are a better spy than that."

Rafe shrugged, quirking his lips. "Believe what you want to believe, but maybe because I used my name I am the best spy, it keeps you guessing."

Sam mirrored the rebellion leader's smile.

Games. It was always games with these damn spies. Why couldn't anyone just say what they meant? If someone didn't give a straight answer, they'd be here all day. "Are we going to have problems with the Methians?" Tehl inserted.

"No, you will not."

"Are you sure?"

Rafe crossed his arms. "They received your invitation but declined. One of my men intercepted it, and we forged a different one."

"The seal?" Sam asked.

"Borrowed."

"And when the Methians hear that their prince was visiting?" Tehl quipped. They did not need a war with Methi.

"Aermia won't be blamed. The Methi prince will want you to search for the imposter but you won't find him on account of the fact that you're now working with him. Your alliance with Methi is secure."

It was like he took the thoughts right out of Tehl's head. That made him scowl. He didn't like anyone guessing his thoughts. "I don't like you." The words popped out of him. Sam gave him a look of exasperation while a deep chuckle trickled out of Rafe.

"The feeling is mutual, prince. While I would rather rip you from the throne, this way will be a bit less bloody and better for Aermia."

Amber eyes met his, and an understanding passed between them. Both had an interest in Aermia and believed they were helping the people. Grudgingly, Tehl dipped his head in acknowledgment. He would play nice for his people, but it didn't mean he had to like the man.

"You have a few of my people in your dungeon. I want them released."

The corners of Tehl's lips lifted. Negotiations. He could negotiate. "Agreed, if all assassination attempts on my father's life stop now."

"Agreed."

"If one of your people steps out of line and harms my family, I will obliterate the rebellion. It will make what the Scythians did to the Nagalians look like child's play. No one touches my family," Tehl threatened, letting his darker side peak out. A glimmer of respect resonated in Rafe's golden eyes. Bloodthirsty bastard.

"No need for threats, prince. I take my vows seriously. I keep my word." Rafe's eyes darkened, looking almost predatory. The rebellion leader lazily caressed a razor-thin blade strapped to his leather-clad thigh. "But, if one hair is harmed on Sage's head there will be nothing left of your family or its legacy. The kingdoms will forget you ever existed. She is one of the very few reasons I agreed to this."

Tehl studied the posture of the rebellion leader with curiosity. Everything about him bespoke aggression and possessiveness when he spoke of the young woman. Huh. Sage, that petite and devious emerald-eyed nymph was the key to keeping this hothead restrained. He would not forget that little tidbit.

"Her safety is already one of our top priorities," Sam assured the rebellion leader. "We will treat her as one of our own, even provide her with her own room."

Rafe eyed his brother. "Be sure that you do." His threat was clearly implied. "She will not stay at the palace. She will return to where she belongs."

Sam smiled, a sly twinkle in his eye. "And she belongs here, with you?"

That struck a nerve. Rafe's jaw tightened as his eyes glittered with anger. "Yes, here, with her family and me."

"I have spent limited time with the wench, but from my experience I can tell you that no one commands her, not even you. If she stays in the palace it will be at her own behest, not yours nor mine," Tehl spoke, eyeing the man across from him.

"You deny my request?" Rafe bit out, his face turning red.

"I am denying you nothing," Tehl replied. "She is not yours to speak for. She is not your mother, sister, wife, or betrothed. You have no claim on her."

Fascinated, Tehl watched the man's face turn purple. He didn't know that could happen. That had to be unhealthy.

"*She's mine.*"

The words slid along Tehl's skin, full of menace. Tehl opened his mouth with a retort when Sam stepped between them, raising his hands up.

"By all legal and familial accounts, she belongs to no one." Sam paused when the rebellion leader hissed out a breath. "But, if that is a deal breaker for you, you can put it in your list of demands."

The large man deflated like a puffer fish before Tehl's eyes. His brother always knew what to say.

"That is, once you discuss it with the lovely aforementioned female."

And then Sam had to ruin it.

"Fine," Rafe huffed, looking between Sam and Tehl. "Leave the same way you entered, and be quick about it. I'd like you gone so no one stumbles upon you before I've had time to break the news."

Tehl raised an eyebrow at the arrogant tone.

Rafe ignored him and continued, "I will see you in six days." The rebellion leader turned and strode for the door.

"You would turn your back to your enemy?" Sam called.

Rafe craned his neck and smirked at them. "You would be dead before you tried anything. Plus, we aren't enemies, are we?"

Tehl's lips curled at his comment while Sam sputtered. He liked when people were straightforward. They were unwilling allies who would sooner stab each other, but strange circumstances set them together.

Tehl moved back into the tunnel with Sam prowling after him.

"Well that was interesting."

"An understatement for sure, brother."

Tehl ran his hand along the wall, working his way toward the ladder in the tunnel's dim light.

"Aren't you the least bit curious about what other things are hidden down here?" Sam asked.

His brother's curiosity was insatiable. Sam would have spies crawling through these tunnels by nightfall. "Not even a bit. I am sure you will have discovered everything there is to know in a matter of hours though," Tehl replied wryly.

"Damn straight," Sam exhaled.

They were both silent, lost in their own thoughts as they returned to the palace. It amazed Tehl how much could change in just a couple of hours. They discovered the rebel woman and her identity. They found out Sam had grown up with her brothers, and Tehl himself had just made a deal with the rebellion. In two weeks' time, the threat of civil war could be over, though he knew things were never that easy.

Various officials and a few of his advisers swarmed him with lists of tasks and questions as soon as he walked through the door. Sam smiled at him and waved, slinking away, the traitor.

After approving the week's menu and a series of visitor requests, he finally made it to his office. Tehl glanced at the sun, realizing it was already time to meet with his war council. What would his council's reaction be to the deal he'd just struck? He straightened a crooked paper on his desk, briefly rethinking his decision but there was no going back. It was done. Nothing he could do now.

He shook his head at himself and abandoned the peace of his office a little early, determined to be the first one in the war council's chamber. He avoided most of the people in the palace halls and slipped into the large, open space. The ceiling curved up, forming a dome with a glass window at its center. His boots echoed on the stone floor with each step of his approach to the round table at the far end.

The dark wooden table stood on a slightly raised dais and was one of the few pieces the palace boasted that was over a thousand years old. Tehl stepped up to his seat and ran his palm along its surface. How many kings and princes had conducted war meetings here?

"Finished watching me, Sam?" he called to his brother, lurking in the shadows.

His brother's baritone chuckle filled the air, echoing around them. "Here, I thought you had lost all of your observational prowess. When did you spot me?"

He glanced at Sam as his brother detached from the side of a bookcase. "I never saw you." He tapped his ear. "The bookcase gave you away. The wood groaned."

"Damn." Sam looked accusingly at the bookshelf. "Traitor," he muttered, under his breath.

Tehl dropped his head, concealing his smile at Sam's antics. He never failed to amuse him. "Is there a reason you were lurking around the war room, brother?" Tehl sank into his chair.

Sam shrugged. "Nothing new, I wanted to listen to any gossip. You know our advisers are as bad as old women. Nothing stays a secret with them."

"Isn't that the truth?"

Samuel strolled to Tehl's side, sprawling into the chair on his right. "How do you want to approach this meeting then? It has the potential to go quite badly."

"There is no need to bring up your past with Sage's family." Tehl stared absently at Sam's glinting earring and continued. "No one in the meeting will know anything about her, save Gav, yourself and I—but I say we tell the truth. That you had some key information which led the rebel to consider working with us instead of against us and that she has negotiated a meeting where we will hopefully do just that."

Sam turned his shrewd gaze from his own boot to Tehl's face. "Do you think it wise to mention that the rebel is a woman?"

Tehl mulled it over for a moment. He knew that some may not trust or respect anything she said just because of her gender and a couple of them had met her last night at the festival. He wouldn't be able to hide her though. "They will meet her eventually, some met her last night and you know as well as I that she has won most of the old men over already."

"True, the use of her injuries was truly masterful. I wouldn't have been able to execute it any better."

"You mean her performance?" he questioned.

"Yes. By her little act she stirred their sympathy, righteous anger, sense of justice, protectiveness, and a hint of lust. Most of them are already wrapped around her finger." Sam sniggered. "I bet most of them would offer for her if they found out she wasn't already spoken for by Rafe. Not that the rebellion leader knows it."

"He is quite covetous of her, isn't he?" Tehl still didn't care for her, but he couldn't deny her beauty or the appeal of her strength.

"He is more than that, brother. That man loves her. If he feels she is threatened at all then we will have some serious problems on our hands."

Tehl sat forward and shot Sam a look before watching the door swing open. "That is why this meeting is important. We need them all to be on our side."

"Precisely."

Both brothers watched as the men filtered in, taking their places. Jaren was the last to arrive. The orange-haired man sauntered into the room as if he owned the place. Tehl couldn't stand the man. When he wasn't looking down on everyone, obviously viewing them as incompetent duds, he was throwing his daughter, Caeja, at Tehl, no doubt hoping for a royal connection.

Jaren lowered himself in his chair and looked around the table. "I hope I am not too late."

Tehl never rolled his eyes at anyone besides his brother, but, at that comment, he almost did. Jaren purposely came in late simply to gain attention. Tehl ignored him and stood. "There have been developments in the last twenty-four hours that will affect how we deal with the rebellion." He gestured to Sam. "Commander Samuel will share with you what he has discovered." Sam stood and bowed to Tehl.

Tehl sat in his chair, nodding for Sam to begin.

"We have been trying to hunt down members in the rebellion."

"Not that it has been fruitful," Garreth interrupted. "I have come up empty-handed every time."

"True," Sam said, placing his hands on the table, "until now."

A series of rumbles and questions erupted.

Sam raised a hand, and the room quieted, faint echoes bouncing around them. "Over a month ago, I received a missive detailing an information exchange that was to happen. I investigated, and, to my surprise, it was accurate. The rebel was caught and brought back to the dungeon."

"Why weren't we made aware of this?" asked the balding Lelbiel. He was a sharp, portly man, but extremely knowledgeable when it came to organizing anything.

"Because there was no information at the time. We interrogated the rebel intensely but they would not break."

"I am sure if you had given me an hour with him, he would have been singing a different tune," Zachael, the combat master, remarked. Tehl didn't doubt it. Zachael knew more about combat and painful uses of pressure points than anyone.

"This situation was…delicate. It required a certain touch." Sam's face hardened. "Some took it upon themselves to interrogate the rebel without our knowledge or permission. When we were informed, the rebel was near death. It was luck they survived."

"How bad was the damage?" questioned the grizzled William.

Tehl eyed the older man with a crazy head of gray hair. The man was an animal when it came to any form of battle on horseflesh. The night of the festival, he had told Sage her scars were a thing of beauty. Tehl was sure that when William figured out who the rebel was, he would be on their side.

"Broken ribs, nose, too many cuts and lacerations to count, bruises, dehydration, and starvation. Also an infection that caused a fever, and fluid in the lungs."

Tehl watched his advisors' eyes widen at the severity of the injuries Sam was listing. "Let it be known that the men who disobeyed me were punished severely. They are no longer with the Guard and are barred from the palace."

Shock radiated through the men. The punishment had been harsh.

"Surely that was a little bit heavy-handed. It was a rebel, after all, a traitor. I am sure those men only wanted to please you as do we all," murmured Jaren, slick as oil.

"Their punishment was hardly sufficient, I assure you."

All the attention focused on Gavriel, who had thus far been observing the table in silence. "They didn't do it for the Crown. They did it for their own sick pleasure and the thrill they received from having power over another person."

Jaren eyed Gav with distaste before dismissing him, looking back at him with a fake smile on his face. "My mistake, my lord."

"So this rebel recovered and agreed to work with us? *Against* the rebellion?" Garreth asked, knowing full well who Sage was. He was the one to carry her to her room when she left the infirmary.

"With time, we were able to reverse some of the indoctrinating that had been taught."

"So we have a spy in the midst of the rebellion?" Jeb inquired, a quiet man with black hair peppered with gray. He had more knowledge about Aermia—how? Geography? Their history? Legally?—and the surrounding three kingdoms than probably all the people of Sanee combined.

"No. We have an liason," Sam answered.

"You want us to work *with* the rebellion?" Jaren asked incredulously. "That's ridiculous. They are traitors and deserve death."

Tehl ground his teeth to keep from shouting at the idiotic man.

"You would rather we attacked our own people?" William retorted.

Jaren glared at William for a moment before turning his eyes on him. "They are not our people when they are opposing us, they are our enemies."

"They're not our enemies if they will work with us," Sam drawled.

Jaren opened his mouth then wisely shut it when all eyes moved to him, his face turning the color of his hair.

"Have you contacted the leaders of the rebellion then?" Gavriel prodded.

"We have," Sam continued, "and they will negotiate. They are not some group of disgruntled ragtag farmers. They are organized, they are armed, and they have a vast network of supporters. If they attacked right now we could overtake them, but only at significant cost to ourselves and great loss of life." Sam gazed around the table. "If we allow ourselves to be embroiled in a civil war, the Scythians will take Aermia. That is something none of us wants. Our kingdom needs to be united in strength before we can deal with anything that Scythia throws at us."

"What is in it for them?" Lelbiel asked.

"They don't want bloodshed either. We are not yet sure what they want. We are to meet in six days and exchange demands; three days after that, we can begin negotiations."

"You trust this liaison?" Jaren prodded.

Tehl stood and stared the table down. "Yes, I do. Some of you met the rebel last night."

A few confused looks were passed around but a pair of clear gray eyes met him in understanding. William obviously knew whom he was talking about.

"So when do we get to meet this liaison?" Jeb asked.

"You will meet her at the exchange," Sam replied.

All sound ceased in the room. Various expressions of surprise and shock moved over each man's face. Slowly understanding dawned. A series of curses and movements exploded in the room. Each man shouting over the top of one another.

"A woman?" hissed Jaren.

"A woman liaison, how quaint... and exceedingly unusual," remarked Lelbiel.

"It's never been done before," stated Jeb.

Tehl waited for a while, until they got themselves together before nodding for Sam to continue.

"Yes, a woman. An *important* woman," his brother emphasized. "She is high in the chain of the rebellion's command and well loved by them. She will be highly useful to us."

"A woman?" Garreth muttered, as if he wasn't in on the secret. "It's bloody brilliant! No wonder we haven't been able to find their messengers. Women have circles that men never enter. Imagine the network of spies you could form with someone planted among them."

Sam grinned at the Elite captain. "I was thinking the same thing."

"A moment," Zachael growled. All the men looked at the wrathful dark man, vibrating with anger. "Do you mean to tell me that the Guard you removed beat this woman?"

"Yes."

Disgust and rage raced across the combat master's face before he released a breath. He looked Tehl in the eye before bowing his head in shame. "Forgive me, I had no knowledge of their actions."

"You are not accountable for their disobedience. You train the men well, it is their decision to follow your commands as well as mine."

Zachael lifted his head, guilt still weighing down his shoulders.

"Such a trauma can break the mind even if the body heals. I trust your word that she will make a trustworthy ambassador." Jeb hesitated. "But is she prepared for this responsibility?"

"You tell me. Did lady Salbei seem like a weak, unhinged woman last night?" Tehl leaned back in his chair to watch the show.

Half the men gaped at him from the table. It made him want to smirk at their open mouths. They looked like fish.

William smiled at him. "The enchanting siren from last night is to be our ambassador?"

"Indeed, she is," Sam replied.

Jaren's eyes flashed with outrage. *Here we go.*

"You knew she was a rebel last night, and yet you did not think it was pertinent information to tell us?" Jaren haughtily demanded. "How do you know she wasn't the one to try to assassinate the king?"

"Your crown prince does not have to explain anything to you, Jaren," Gavriel spoke up, coldly. "I would rethink the tone you were using with your future king."

Jaren glared at Gavriel for a moment before reining himself in. He gave Gavriel a thin-lipped smile before turning to Tehl. "Excuse my tone, I meant no offense. I was surprised—that was all."

Zachael and William coughed at his lie. Tehl's lips twitched in humor. He despised Jaren, but he was a necessary evil. The man was filthy rich and had a brilliant mind. "These are extraordinary circumstances we are all having to adjust to," he said graciously. Sam gave him a look like he approved, so he must have said it in a politically correct manner.

"The scars?" Lelbiel asked.

Tehl understood what he was getting at. He was sure none of the men in this room would forget her display any time soon: creamy thighs and—

A chair screeching cut his thoughts off.

Zachael pushed his chair back and placed his hand heavily on the old round table. "We did that?" he choked out.

Grim faces surrounded the table, even Jaren looked disgusted.

"No," Garreth interjected. He was next to the combat master. "Sick men did that."

Murmurs of agreement sounded around the table.

"If I remember correctly—" William paused. "She said the captors hadn't been punished."

Tehl eyed the wily old fox with appreciation. Nothing slipped by that man. "The men were punished except for the leader, he escaped. He has been apprehended by the rebellion."

"Are they going to hand him over?" Garreth asked, curiously.

A vicious grin touched Tehl's face. "I asked, but they kindly refused. I doubt we will see Serge again."

"And you are okay with that?" Jaren questioned.

Tehl pinned him with his gaze, his smile widening. "I am more than okay with justice, especially when I sanction it. Anything else, Jaren?"

Jaren swallowed hard. "No, my lord."

Tehl tipped his head. "Very well then. We have six days until we exchange our list of demands. We will meet here in three days and discuss what those will be. Think about it in the next couple days. I don't want to bicker about it for hours. Good day."

His advisors stood at his dismissal and bowed before streaming out of the room, leaving Sam, Gav, and himself as its only occupants. "That went better than I thought it would."

Gav bobbed his head. "It worked in our favor that she was at the festival last night. Her scars had already made an impression."

"You're right. She was a human being already, not some faceless female rebel." Tehl squinted at his cousin. "You're sounding like Sam."

"Hey now," Gav protested.

Sam sniffed. "Eh hem. Everyone wants to be like me."

Tehl exchanged looks with Gav before they both snickered. "You keep believing that if it makes you sleep at night, brother."

"I will tell you what makes me sleep at night. This pretty little blonde..."

"That's enough of that." Tehl cringed. "I don't need those images in my mind." Sam had already scarred him enough.

Sam smirked. "I will *always* want those images in my mind."

Gavriel shook his head. "You understand nothing until you have a wife. Come to me after being married a couple years and then we can swap stories."

Sam looked intently at his cousin, looking intrigued. "Really?"

Smug satisfaction filled Gav's face. "Indeed."

Tehl stretched and stepped off his raised chair. "This has been informative, but I have a date with Damari." Today they were going over the treasury books. He loved pouring over the books. Numbers always made sense. They never changed, and, if something was wrong, it was because there was a mistake somewhere.

"Run off to your accounting then." Sam wrinkled his nose. "I will make inquiries and discover what our various advisors think we should demand."

"No rest for the wicked," Tehl called over his shoulder, heading toward the door.

"I will hold your compliments close to my heart, you know."

"You do that," he retorted, leaving the war room.

SIX

SAGE

IT HAD BEEN THREE DAYS, and Sage still had difficulty grasping the fact that she lodged on a *Sirenidae* vessel. Not only that, but though it'd been mere weeks, it seemed as though her entire world had been flipped on its axis:

The Aermian king wasn't evil.

The rebellion wasn't perfect.

A race thought to have disappeared fifteen hundred years ago somehow still existed.

It was enough to have anyone's head spinning.

Sage mindlessly peered at the glistening waves as they lapped against the hull, fascinated that, despite the movement, its waters were clear as glass. She marveled as little schools of fish darted around below, shimmering purple and silver in the sun. She cringed, though, when it served as a reminder of the abrupt question she'd carelessly blurted to her host, and she had to fight the impulse to bang her head against the quarterdeck. Thankfully, Lilja had only laughed instead of seeing fit to drown her. The unusual captain had then slapped her on the arm and showed her to her quarters.

Sage leaned her elbows on the railing, deciding tonight she would finally ask about the Sirenidae. For the last couple of days, she had found herself staring at Captain Femi's scarf, curious about the gills she knew it hid. She had been sorely tempted to ask at the time but quickly decided it was better to wait for the right moment. Since then, Sage had been filling her time by helping Lilja, doing whatever was needed.

There'd been a few instances where she'd thought of sneaking from the ship to her family's smithy, just to see if they needed her, but reason always prevailed. It was too much of a risk, for she knew both Sam and Rafe would have her home watched, hoping to catch her doing just that. Also, she was certain she had seen Rafe skulking about the docks shortly after her arrival. That man was an expert tracker, so it was best not to tempt fate.

As she sat, silent in her contemplation, the sun slowly sunk below the horizon, streaking the sky in shades of gold, orange, red and pink. Abandoning her perch, she skipped down the stairs and onto the deck. Sure-footed, Sage moved to the opposite side and down into the galley, and her stomach growled as the savory smells of herbs and warm bread greeted her.

Lilja smiled and waved her forward. Sage stepped up the table, watching as Lilja added spices to what seemed to be a stew. "What can I do to help, captain?"

The captain flashed her a smile, pointing to the bread and vegetables. "Could you cut those for me?"

Sage plucked a heavy blade from a wooden block and began doing so. "It smells delicious," she remarked, glancing at the stew, and paused. It was almost the same color as Lilja's eyes. "It's an...unusual color though."

"A question but not a question. I find you refreshing, Sage."

Sage's brows wrinkled.

The captain tossed her a wry look before continuing to stir her soup. "It's apparent you are filled with curiosity, and yet you have not asked me a single question."

It was true. She was brimming with a million questions, but she also didn't know what sort of burdens came with the answers. Sometimes it was best to remain ignorant. "On some occasions, it's safer to keep your questions to yourself."

Lilja considered her for a moment before setting her spoon down. "True, but without questions how would one learn? Knowledge is power."

"It also means danger," Sage answered, not looking up from chopping her sea onion.

"Another wise answer for one so young."

"You age quickly when your innocence is stripped from you," Sage replied, keeping her cuts in perfect, even slices. She may be young but she felt like she'd aged years in the last month.

"You have suffered many things, *ma fleur*."

A pale hand settled on hers, ceasing her cutting. Sage lifted her gaze to Lilja's and saw in her unusually-colored eyes that the captain understood what she was suffering. Sage dropped her eyes back to the onion, waiting for her to speak.

"It will pass with time, love. You have strength beyond anything you can imagine." The captain removed her hand and paused. "So to answer your question-not-question. I muddle a special seaweed into the soup, and that's why it turns that color."

Sage appreciated the change in subject. Her time in the dungeon wasn't something she wanted to think of; she dreamed of it often enough each night. Hayjen and Lilja had burst into her room the first night thinking she was being murdered, but she'd only been screaming in her sleep, and poor Hayjen had received a blow to the face when he woke her. She still prickled with guilt whenever she thought of it. She'd been so out of sorts she hadn't known what was real or what was the dream.

"Where do you find the seaweed?"

"It grows about three hundred arm-lengths below the ocean's surface."

Sage's eyes rounded. That was incredible. She had never heard of anyone being able to dive that deep. Maybe asking a few questions wouldn't be too offensive. "That must be an interesting trip," she ventured, tipping her vegetables into the soup.

"It is unlike anything you can imagine."

"As a little girl I always wanted to be a Sirenidae," Sage remarked off-handedly, scrubbing the sharp blade in a wash bin. "I've always loved swimming, and I feel like the ocean is my second home."

"There are so many treasures down there. It is truly a completely different world."

Sage wiped the blade dry and placed it back on the wooden block, turning to Lilja. As she again eyed the woman's scarf she fought her nerves, jerking her chin toward the royal blue material concealing the mysterious white hair and gills. "How do those work?"

White teeth flashed at her in a deep smile. Lilja brushed away the scarf and drew a long pale finger down the side of her bare neck. "They filter the oxygen from the water, and my body keeps the oxygen and injects it into my blood while forcing out the water."

Her brows furrowed. "Oxygen?"

"Air."

What a perplexing thought. But fish had to breathe some way so she supposed it sort of made sense. "I didn't know there was air in the water."

Captain Femi gestured for her to sit at the table. "It is all part of science."

Sage pierced her with a serious look and sat slowly, thinking. No one practiced science after the Scythians did what they did. Everyone lived and used what they could from nature. Science had caused the Nagalians' genocide and no one wanted that again.

"Don't give me that look, *ma fleur*. I will not turn into a murdering barbarian before you." Captain Femi's eyes glinted. "Remember: knowledge is power."

"Indeed." Sage cocked her head, studying the woman across from her. "How are you still alive? Sirenidae are now just myths."

"Through secrecy, deception, and cunning."

Sage didn't doubt that. "Do others exist?"

Lilja lifted her scarf and patted it into place without looking away. "That is a secret I can not give you, but our race will never die off."

Sage respected her answer and moved on. "Are the stories true? Do you drag men into the ocean and drown them?"

Lilja stared off, like she was seeing something else. "That is one fable that sprung up after we disappeared. During the Nagalian purge, we did wage war from the sea and drowned our enemies. But we never did it as sport, as the fables say, it was against the law."

"Whose law?"

Lilja's gaze sharpened. "The king's."

"Are you speaking of Poseidon?"

"The one and only."

Her mum had told her stories about the unearthly ruler of the Sirenidae.

"Did he have magenta eyes and white hair as well? Is that a racial trait?" she asked curiously.

Lilja smiled. "The silvery-white hair is a Sirenidae trait. We are born deep in the ocean where the sunlight doesn't reach, so we have no color in our hair." Captain Femi gestured to her eyes. "As for the unusual color, they change once we eat the rose seaweed. It has properties that enhance our vision, enabling us to see in the ocean's depths."

"So you weren't born with pink eyes?"

"No, my eyes were a lilac color. They fade back if I'm unable to regularly eat rose seaweed."

"Does the sun affect your hair?"

Lilja shook her head. "No, I've spent too much time in the sea. Between the lack of sunlight and the salt, it is permanently colorless."

"What would happen if a Sirenidae was born on land?"

"They would look like anyone else."

So they could blend in. "What about the gills?"

Captain Femi laughed. "If I stay out of the sea, they seal shut until I swim and need them again."

Sage opened her mouth to ask another question but paused when Hayjen stormed in, wearing a blustery expression. Her burly friend halted at the edge of the table, scrutinizing her. Sage glanced to Lilja, the captain's face sobering as she eyed her husband warily.

Sage's heart flew to her throat. Something bad had happened. "Are my family okay?" she asked, her tone sharp.

Hayjen's blue eyes softened a touch. "Your family's fine, Sage. I checked on them myself today." He blew out an irritated breath. "Rafe called a meeting of the rebellion. It is to be in less than half an hour."

Sage pondered that for a moment. "Why is this the first time I am hearing about it?"

Hayjen's nostrils flared. "It's my belief he intended to exclude Sage."

A small noise of outrage escaped Lilja.

Frustration bubbled under Sage's skin. What game was he playing? She had every right to be there. She'd certainly earned it. Was she now the enemy because she was a liaison? She was merely seeking the best outcome for *all* citizens of Aermia. "I will have to sample some of your fabulous soup later, I'm afraid. It seems I have business to take care of."

Capitan Femi cocked her head, eyes twinkling. "Give them hell, *ma fleur*. Show them what you are made of."

The look in Hayjen's ice blue eyes stopped her. "Rhys will be there."

Every muscle in her body tensed at his name. Nightmarish images flashed through her mind and she bowed forward, clutching the end of the table, her fingers turning white as the wood bit into her flesh. She let go the breath she'd been holding and tried to regulate her breathing.

Could she handle seeing him again?

She barely registered the scraping of a chair when an elegant pale hand entered her view. Sage focused on the hand settling on her own. The slight pressure caused her to glance up into magenta eyes filled with understanding but no pity.

"There is no shame in weakness. There's strength in knowing your limitations, but this is not one of your limitations, Sage. You are better than that animal. You know he will never hurt you again. The strength of your inner person shines brighter than the dawn's first rays. He has no power over you. You are not in that dungeon, you are here with Hayjen and I. He will be by your side in place of your family. You have allies. You are *not* alone." Warm hands cupped her cheeks. "You will never be alone. Dig deep, and use all that anger and desire for vengeance to do something good. Use it to protect your people."

Sage's eyes blurred, and she dropped her eyes to Lilja's chin. She needed those words. "I want him dead," she whispered, speaking the ugly truth out loud. "I know I shouldn't feel that way; it's wrong. But he haunts me every time I sleep. I am so tired, Lilja, worn out. Why is that monster free?" She lifted her watery eyes back to Lilja's.

"Everyone is punished for their actions one way or another. I don't care what the rebellion decided. He will be held accountable for his actions, mark my words, *ma fleur*." Her eyes darted to Sage's emerald ones. "Can you do this?"

She pulled in a stuttering breath and nodded yes. She would not let her fear rule her. Lilja's hands dropped from her face while Sage blinked back her tears. She sucked her lip in and bit it. She would let no one keep her from this meeting.

She twisted her head back to Hayjen. "Are you ready?"

He walked around the table and wrapped both Lilja and Sage in his burly arms. "I am. Everything will be all right. I will never leave your side." He dropped a kiss on top of the Captain's head, releasing them. "We will be home in a couple hours, my love."

Sage trailed him before glancing over her shoulder at Lilja. "Do you want to come with us?"

Captain Femi snorted and waved her off. "Those men would run for the hills if they met me. I would be a distraction more than anything. Watch that man of yours, he has quite the reflexes. I doubt you will escape him easily tonight. Keep your wits about you."

Now it was Sage's turn to snort. "Never lost my wits to a man yet."

She jogged up the two stairs and across the shadowy deck. Reaching the rail, she swung her leg over and shimmied down the rope ladder. At the bottom, Hayjen reached for her and pulled her to the dock.

"Are you ready to face the beasts?"

Determination filled her, and she used it to force back some of her fears. "Indeed."

Hayjen grunted and began a clipped pace along the dock that had quieted. Most of the laborers had gone to their homes or ships by now, yet it was still early enough that they hadn't drunk enough to be noisily inebriated. Hayjen led her to the same tunnel she'd escaped from and Sage dropped down, noting the water was three inches higher than the last time she'd done this.

Her friend noted. "The tide is coming in. We will have to take a different route home."

Home.

That word resonated with her.

Where was home?

It wasn't safe for her family or her to stay with them anymore. Much to her chagrin, the palace had started to feel like home. There was also Lilja and Hayjen. She felt safe with them. They expected nothing from her, but offered her everything. Where did she belong? Where was home?

Hayjen took the lead, and Sage followed in his wake, each tunnel blending into the next in her mind. He hesitated outside a thick wooden door, looking to her before opening it. She shored her defenses and nodded, so her friend soundlessly pushed it open and entered. She hung back for a moment, taking a deep breath. A chorus of masculine salutations greeted Hayjen. Sage then stepped forward into the room and met seven narrowed gazes.

Silence.

Sage had to fight her panic at being the subject of so many male stares, but it was time to play at being collected and unaffected.

She smiled warmly at the room, avoiding a pair of muddy brown eyes glaring daggers at her. She kicked the door, and it thudded shut behind her. She then glided to Hayjen as he pulled out a chair. Pulling in a shallow breath through her nose, she sat, placing her hands on the worn table.

"Good evening, gentlemen." She peeked up at them from underneath her lashes and gave them a soft smile. The stern faces melted into more welcoming expressions. Bitterness welled inside her at how easily they were manipulated. Rafe had taught her well.

"Why is she here?"

Sage covered her flinch and kept her serene mask in place at his voice.

He couldn't hurt her here.

Hayjen's hand settled on her knee in silent support. She maintained her smile as she faced down her own personal demon. Rhys looked the same to her, completely unremarkable except for his height. Nothing to indicate the sadistic monster living inside him. And here she was, sitting at the same table like everything was okay. His eyes roved over her, causing bile to burn her throat. Everything in her body revolted against the lecherous glint in his eyes.

A low growl emanated across from her, snapping her out of trance.

Sage pasted a bland smile on her face and clenched her hands to stop them from trembling. "I am part of the rebellion circle, am I not?" She couldn't stand looking at him anymore so she looked into each face around the table, skipping over Rafe.

"Of course you are, dear," spoke up Mason from her right.

She gave him a kind smile. He was an older man with a fierce love for his family. "How is your daughter doing? I heard you have a new grandbaby to love."

His moss green eyes lit up with joy. "The wee babe is doing well."

"I am happy to hear it."

"I am glad as well that your family is doing well, Mason. But maybe we should focus on the task at hand." Rafe's low, baritone washed over her, irritation coloring his tone.

Sage slid her eyes to the mountain of a man staring her down. Rafe's amber eyes bored holes into her. She felt like prey just before it was pounced upon. He was obviously not happy with her. He broke their stare down and swept the table with his gaze, her breath rushing out once she was no longer the subject of his scrutiny.

Finally, he started to speak. "There has been a development that is beneficial to the rebellion."

Sage held her breath as the circle of men leaned forward.

"Thanks to Sage's negotiating skills, we have a meeting with the Crown."

Sage noted the various expressions of shock and revulsion that crossed their faces. Sputters of indignation and curses exploded around the table.

"What do you mean by that?" demanded Noah, a merchant with a heart of gold and a shrewd mind for numbers.

"He means—" Rhys's insidious voice cut through the din, "—that the princes' whore used her wiles on Rafe and the princes of Aremia."

Goosebumps rose on Sage's arms as his eyes brushed over her skin.

"What did you do to get them to agree to such a farce?" Rhys continued.

Sage clenched her teeth so hard her jaw ached. She refused to look at him, focusing instead on Hayjen's face. She would not dignify that with an answer. *Breathe in and out. He cannot hurt you,* she chanted to herself.

"That is enough young man," Mason chastised from the end of the table.

Her eyes darted to the stern older man. His eyes flicked to hers briefly, softening a touch. Sage was grateful to him for sticking up for her when no one else did.

"She must be something special to keep the attention of that many men." Rhys released a loud groan that made her stomach heavy, and saliva fill her mouth. "I overheard she could do this one thing with her..."

"Enough!" Rafe snarled, a low growl rumbling out of him.

Sage flinched in her seat, eyes snapping to the seething man across from her. The hair on her arms stood up at the sound he'd made. Lilja was right: he was a predator. Everything about him screamed danger from head to toe; black leather and numerous weapons were strapped all over his muscular frame. His eyes glinted with rage, burning an intense gold. She'd begun trembling again but stilled as Hayjen put pressure on her knee, letting her know he was there for her.

"Don't you ever speak about Sage that way or you will find yourself with more than a shoulder wound!" Danger was woven into each of Rafe's words.

"Is that a threat?" Rhys questioned, a small tremor in his voice.

The corner of Sage's mouth twitched. It seemed even monsters were afraid of Rafe.

"It is a *promise.*" The rebellion leader's lips twisted into a sinister smile. Sage would hate to be on the receiving end of such a look. Rafe eyed each man before pausing on her for a moment. "We do not speak about our comrades in this way. Even if the lies Rhys is spouting were true, we all understand there's a heavy price to be paid to accomplish our goals. We do what we need to in order to survive."

"I thought you were done after your assignment, Sage?" Madden, who had been quiet up until this point, asked.

Sage ripped her gaze from Rafe and held Madden's hazel eyes with hers, flashing him a rueful smile. "As did I, but life has a funny way of playing tricks on you."

"So what of this meeting?" Hayjen rumbled from her side, taking the attention off her. "How does a meeting with the Crown benefit us?"

"We have had information that the Scythians are mobilizing their warriors. One can only guess what they are up to but…"

"War." Madden supplied, not looking surprised.

Rafe nodded. "We believe so, yes."

"But why now?" Badiah asked, confusion clear on his slender face. "They've been silent since the construction of the Mort Wall and that was a good two hundred years ago. It's always been their pattern to *send away* their unwanted kin. Now they're *taking* people? *Our* people?" He shook his head. "It makes no sense. They hate outsiders and anything that doesn't meet their ridiculous notion of perfection. This does not bode well for any of us."

"Which means we can't afford a civil war," Sage supplied.

Badiah eyed her as if he was reading the thoughts in her head. "You mean for us seek a treaty with the Crown."

"What?" Madden asked, incredulously. "We can't trust them as far as we can throw them! Is *that* the source of your Scythian information?"

"No, it is not." Rafe didn't elaborate.

"We have the advantage," cried Rhys, shooting to his feet, his chair falling to the dirt floor with a dull thwap. Sage tensed but maintained her calm facade. "We are so close to starting a new regime. Have you all forgotten about why we are here in the first place? Our families are starving, our crops are dying, and our people are now being stolen! Where has the Crown been all this time? What have they been doing? Hiding in the stone palace, doing nothing. Meanwhile we suffer."

Mason eyed Rhys skeptically before glancing to Rafe. "We sanctioned the assassination of the king not even two weeks ago. It seems naïve to think the princes would forgive such an act and now seek peace between us."

"You have never steered us wrong, Rafe," Badiah cut in. "But none of us are infallible. Are you certain this isn't a trap of some kind?"

"It isn't," Sage murmured. Suddenly, she was the center of attention. Sage forced false bravado into her voice, raising her chin. "During my time at the palace they tried to recruit me, and so I listened, and I learned from the things they were willing to share as they attempted to win me over. The king was a wealth of information." Her face hardened. "The Scythians *will* strike. If we do not unite as a kingdom, they will destroy us and swarm Aermia like locusts. There will be nothing of us left to rule." She let them mull that over before continuing. "Our goal is to save the innocent lives, to give them a better life, to give them a voice. This is our chance to do just that but without the bloodshed. No one need die. We still have control. Arrangements have been made to exchange demands three days from now. You have until then to decide what you want."

"The decision has been made?" Madden growled.

"Yes, it has." Rafe deliberately rose from his seat, muscles bunching with the controlled movement, and crossed bulging arms over his wide chest. "This will greatly aid our cause. Now, it is up to you to decide what we need from this."

"How does Sage fit into this?" Hayjen asked, shifting in his chair.

"She will be our liaison. She knows the rebellion and the Crown. Sage is perfect for the job."

She doubted that.

"If she is supposed to be the liaison then what is she doing here?" Madden asked. "This doesn't seem very neutral of her."

Sage tried to not be offended, but she was. She had done everything they had ever asked of her.

"I agree."

She gasped, looking up into Rafe's serious face. He stared back without emotion. Betrayal burned through her. He planned on kicking her out. Sage looked around the table hoping to see someone disagree with him, but from their blank faces she knew they agreed with him. Her gaze trailed back to Rafe. For a moment, she had thought that maybe she could trust him, but, once again, he'd betrayed her. She didn't even know him anymore. Her thoughts must have shown on her face because his eyebrows creased and his face fell, ever so slightly.

"Little one..." he murmured softly.

Sage shoved down her own personal feelings and maneuvered her face back into her mask. She pulled her hands from the table and reached down to squeeze Hayjen's hand, and then scooted out her wooden chair, her heart hollow. She'd spent years of her life with these men. She'd trained, schemed, fought, and laughed with them. Yet as she stood, it was like they were strangers to her. They had sanctioned regicide, sent a monster to hurt her and then protected him, and now, they had cast her out. She was done.

"Well then, gentlemen. Be wise in your choices, you have the chance to heal Aermia. Don't be foolish or hotheaded in this." Her features hardened. "If anyone of you try something stupid at the exchange, it will mean the obliteration of the rebellion and all the resulting bloodshed will be on your head. Don't overestimate yourselves, and don't underestimate the Crown." She bared her teeth at Rafe and took perverse joy in how his fists tightened in response. Someone wasn't happy. "I wish you all the best." She touched Hayjen's shoulder, signaling him to stay, before striding out of the room as if it had been her choice.

As soon as the door thudded behind her, she fled. She suspected Rafe wouldn't be far behind.

SEVEN

SAGE

SHE HASTENED THROUGH THE LABYRINTH of tunnels, twisting left and right until she finally spotted the dock. Her breath heaved in and out of her chest as she paused and admired the sparkling stars in the colorless night sky. They winked at her like gems haphazardly strewn across a bed of midnight silk. The sounds of bawdy sailor songs filled the air, merchants and corsairs alike already deep in their cups.

She startled as a large man crashed into a crate before slumping onto the wooden deck and laughing, obviously inebriated. Sage crept around him, picking up her pace as she headed to the Sirenidae vessel. A wooden ladder dangled against the ship's hull, and Sage eyed it with skepticism. There had to be at least four feet between the ship and the dock so it'd be a stretch to reach it. She pursed her lips.

Would it be better to call for Lilja's help?

Nope. She could make it, but she couldn't hesitate.

Sage backtracked a few paces, focusing on the ladder as it swayed in the light breeze. She loosened her arms and released a deep breath before pushing off the balls of her feet and sprinting to the dock's edge. Her muscles coiled and sprung as she pushed from the wooden surface and she caught hold of the rope, her momentum crashing her into the wooden hull and nearly knocking her senseless. Her feet dangled below her, and she scrambled to get her feet onto a rung. Her right boot finally caught the ladder, and she made quick work of climbing it, vaulting over the rail as soon as she'd reached it. She allowed herself a satisfied smile at the fact that she'd made the leap despite being so short.

"For a moment, I thought you would not make it, *ma fleur*. Quite agile, aren't you?"

Sage didn't take her eyes from the dock below even though she hadn't heard Lilja's approach. "You watched me the whole time but didn't offer help?"

A husky laugh reached her ears. "You didn't need my assistance. Besides, it was amusing."

Sage rolled her eyes and peered into the inky corner Lilja was lurking in. "And if I hadn't been able to make it?"

Captain Femi waved her hand and uncoiled from the barrel she was sitting on. "You would've gotten a little wet. It might even have done you some good. After all, the ocean contains healing properties that aren't found anywhere else in the world." The captain sauntered to her side and ran a hand down her brown locks as if she'd been doing it all of Sage's life, scrutinizing Sage's face. "What has you so riled up, child? And where is Hayjen? He was not to leave your side."

"I was relieved of my position among the circle." The words felt like ash on her tongue. She swallowed hard, feeling bitterness well in her. "I am the best asset they have and a wealth of information, yet they threw me away like I meant nothing." She dropped Lilja's knowing gaze turning back to the rail. Little lights bobbed along the ships, illuminating a series of card games, storytelling, and cleaning. "I fit nowhere," she found herself saying. "I have no home. The Crown doesn't trust me because I am part of the rebellion, and the rebellion doesn't trust me because I was imprisoned for so long with the Crown. Neither wants *me*, but both want something *from me*. I only have value in what I can give them, not as a person." She blew out an angry breath, glancing at Lilja. "What rubs me is that I thought Rafe, of all people, would stick with me, that he was my friend. But he is nothing but a pretender. He cast me out today."

Captain Femi hissed. "Aye, you need to beware of that one. You couldn't find a more pigheaded man if you tried."

That perked her interest. "You know him?"

Lilja's eyes shuttered but her smile was sharp and knowing. "I know of him. That man is about as flexible as a hundred-year-old oak tree. He may be wise but he's stuck in his ways. By the time he figures you out, it will be too late."

Sage's brows furrowed. What was she talking about? "Too late?"

"To correct his mistakes, *ma fleur*." Lilja brushed a hand along her cheek and yawned. "It is time for me to find my bed. Don't worry about the ladder, Hayjen will pull it up when he comes home. Goodnight, love."

Sage smiled at the quirky female and whispered a soft goodnight as Captain Femi glided across the deck, her skirts swishing seductively behind her. She shook her head and claimed Lilja's abandoned spot. Weariness filled her, making her ache for her own bed, but she didn't want to miss Hayjen so she'd just have to keep her vigil.

A whisper of sound had her eyes springing open as she observed Hayjen heaving himself over the rail in the dim moonlight. As he pulled up the ladder, Lilja slipped into view, wearing a translucent robe that was most indecent. Sage blushed and averted her eyes, instead stretching the crick her neck. Hayjen glanced over the ship's side and jerked his head to his wife. She froze for a beat before stomping over to the rail and glaring down at the dock.

"You are not welcome here," Lilja glowered. The captain's white waves slipped from the emerald silk scarf wrapped around her hair, displaying her face. Danger carved her face into sharp planes that could cut glass.

Something about the captain's look and her tone made the hair on Sage's arms stand up. One thing was apparent, she never wanted to be on Lilja's bad side.

Sage leaned forward to listen, shivering when a menacing growl rose from the dock.

"You will not hide from me what is mine!" That made her spine stiffen, she knew that voice.

"There is nothing on this ship that belongs to you, I can assure you of that."

"Come now, Lilja, you and I both know you harbor what is not yours."

Captain Femi tossed her head and glanced to Sage's shadowy corner before glaring back down. "Leave. There is nothing here for you."

"I will have what I came for. Do not make me come and retrieve her."

Lilja's face hardened into angry lines. She leaned over the rail, her silvery hair making her seem almost ethereal in the moonlight. "You set one foot on my ship, and I will drag you to the bottom of the ocean and watch with glee as you drown."

The malice in Lilja's voice shocked Sage. There was a danger lurking in her new friend that she had heretofore never witnessed. Perhaps some of the myths were true after all.

When Hayjen placed a large hand on her shoulder, the currently ferocious woman turned to him. Whatever she read on his face seemed to calm her. She smiled up at her husband and placed a quick kiss on his hand before turning to Rafe. "My threat stands."

Sage finally stood and strode to her friends, staring down at the handsome man seething below her. His eyes flashed to hers, roving her face.

"Sage."

In that single syllable, he had infused a wealth of meaning. She reached over and pried one of the captain's hands from the railing. "It's okay. Why don't you go back to bed and I will handle our unwelcome guest?"

Lilja searched her eyes before nodding. She spared one last glare at Rafe before turning on her heel and striding to her chamber. One side of Hayjen's lips turned up, before he whispered, "Don't let him step foot on this ship. Heaven knows I can't control her if he does."

Sage returned his smile before turning back to their audience. Rafe stayed quiet as Hayjen's footsteps faded away, gazing intently into her eyes as if trying to peer into her soul.

"Little one... "

Sage stiffened at the endearment, her lips pinching. "What do you want, Rafe?" she barked.

He scanned her face before he spoke. "I want many things, but, first, you need to return to those who love you."

"Home?" she scoffed. "I can't *go* home, Rafe. I need to keep my family as far from this as possible. You know that. A treaty hasn't been signed. I won't put them in any more danger than they are in already."

"I didn't mean to your parents' home." A pause. "I meant mine."

Sage gaped. *His* home?

"I will have you protected the entire time."

"From the rebellion?"

"Yes," he drew out.

"The same rebellion that cast me out for having the unlucky happenstance of being caught and tortured by the Crown?" she hissed. "The same rebellion that sent a monster to check on me but did the opposite, damaging me in a way that will never heal? The same men I thought to be my brothers in arms but who kept that monster in their midst, even letting him decide what's best for our people?" Sage seethed with righteous indignation. "The same rebellion that commissioned me to murder our king? *That* rebellion?"

"You weren't cast out…"

She slashed a hand through the air. "That is exactly what happened! You sanctioned it! You sought me out in the woods. You offered me a chance to help protect people, yet the men you are working with have done the hurting."

"No one is perfect, Blade."

Oh, he'd used her nickname—something he only did when *really* pissed. Well good. Maybe he would now feel a fraction of the turmoil she was feeling. "You're right, but I refuse to be blinded by honey-coated words meant only to incite loyalty." She stabbed a finger down at him. "I have had a few weeks to think on our first conversation in the cave. I was too distressed after my escape and dealing with that low life to notice, but I remember your face. You weren't shocked when I told you of the king's illness. And I very well know that you never agree to something you don't know inside and out. You *already knew*," she accused. He didn't drop her gaze or look ashamed. Disgust filled her. "You were willing to sacrifice an innocent old man for what you wanted."

"No one is innocent."

"You're right." She stared pointedly at him.

Rafe cursed and threw his hands in the air. "He wants to die, Sage. The old man misses his wife, he can't function. It would be a kindness to put him down."

Revulsion filled her. "Like a lame animal? Are even listening to yourself?

Who made you the judge?"

"You are still young, little one, and naïve. We're at war."

"What war?" she cried, flinging her arms out wide. "There is no war, save the one you're trying to create!" His condescension made her blood boil. "Don't you dare patronize me! My youth was ripped from me in that cell. Don't you dare call me naïve after what I have seen and experienced."

His face dropped, and he raised his hands, attempting to placate her. "It's not my intention to argue with you."

"No," she said hollowly. "You came to cage me."

His hands curled into fists, his face turning red. "Why are you being so difficult? I can see Lilja's influence already. I should have stolen you away earlier."

"Excuse me?!" she growled, rage pulsing through her. Sage leaned over the rail, glaring furiously. "Lilja has been nothing but kind and honest, unlike you. I am where I want to be, I am not leaving!"

"Oh, yes, you are," he retorted. Rafe sprung from the deck and slammed a blade into the side of ship.

"What the bloody hell? Lilja is going to skin you," Sage yelled.

"If she can catch me," he grunted, climbing the side of the ship. Her eyes widened and she took a step back as Rafe cleared the railing in no time. He crouched there, eyes brimming with a tumult of emotions.

Stars above, he was angry.

"I will not leave you here."

He reached for her arm, but she pulled just out of his grasp.

Rafe's eyes hardened. "Do not make this difficult. I will protect my family. You're part of it."

Her chin jutted out. She was *not* leaving with him. "Family don't betray each other. I am nothing to you."

His jaw clenched before he shifted onto the balls of his feet. "No, you are everything."

A moment of clarity hit her.

He wasn't going to take no for an answer. She would have to out maneuver him. Rafe would never hurt her intentionally, but he wouldn't give up. Time to put her skills into action. She would have to fool the master.

Sage softened her face a little and stared at him with resignation and exhaustion. She didn't have to fake being tired, she really was. "I am tired, Rafe. I haven't slept a full night in ages."

He reached a hand out and cupped her cheek, his palm rough but gentle. "I know, little one, I will you keep you safe so you can sleep."

She swayed into his body, placing a hand on his chest. "Will you protect me from my monsters?"

A small smile flashed in the dark, breaking what was left of her heart. "Always, little one, always."

Sage smiled back, steeling herself, and then shoved with all her might, ducking down to avoid his grasping hands. Startled amber eyes met hers just before he disappeared, a loud splash sounding below. She peered over the rail at Rafe as he flailed in the water. He sputtered and kicked to the wooden dock, heaving himself up as water pooled beneath him.

"Sage," he bellowed.

She grinned impishly at him and waved, ignoring her churning stomach. "I will send a message on the day of the exchange with a location. If you come up here uninvited again, I will have Lilja take you for a swim." Incense filled her nose just before Captain Femi appeared at her side.

"And it would be a pleasure," the Sirenidae purred.

Rafe looked between them, his fury mounting the longer they stared at each other. He stabbed a finger at her. "We will talk about this Sage Blackwell." He straightened his soggy leather vest then turned, prowling down the dock.

Sage released a breath she hadn't been aware she was holding. She felt so many emotions that she couldn't differentiate them anymore. She swallowed and pushed Rafe from her mind. There were too many things to deal with, and his obvious control issues were at the bottom of the list. She glanced at Lilja from the corner of her eye. The captain was still squinting in the direction Rafe had gone when she spoke. "Did you enjoy the show?"

"There's been more excitement around here in the last three days than the last three years combined." The sound of Hayjen's deep voice rumbled from a nearby alcove.

Sage rolled her eyes and hid a smile. Privacy? More like the illusion of. "Eavesdropping?" she hummed.

Lilja quirked a white brow, a smile on her lips and her eyes bright. "Of course we were spying, as if we would truly leave you alone with that bully. For a moment, I thought he would snatch you from my ship and abscond with you into the night. You're lucky you're so quick." The Sirenidae sniggered. "The look on his face when you pushed him will provide me with amusement for years to come."

Sage turned to rest a hip on the rail, trying to figure out the woman next to her. Lilja spoke of Rafe as if they knew each other intimately. "How do you know him? Is he a former lover?"

Lilja choked and shook her head so furiously her white waves flipped around her. "Stars above, no. Let's just say he and I have run in the same circles over the years, and I don't approve of his highhanded ways."

Sage snorted. "Highhanded is a mild term. Do you truly dislike him?" Despite his obvious failings, Sage still felt he had a good heart.

Captain Femi's magenta eyes caught hers. "No, he wants good things. I just disagree on how he gets them."

Hayjen popped out of his darkened corner to join their conversation. He wrapped his arms around his tall wife and grinned broadly over her head. "He has a will as strong as Lil's, and she doesn't like when someone challenges her."

Lilja scowled and swatted at his arm. "Not true."

Hayjen peered down at his wife, a silly grin on his face. "You and I both know it's the truth." Before she could argue, he swept her into his arms. "Now, my contrary wife, it is exceedingly late, and well past my bedtime." He lifted his eyes from his wife to Sage. "Time for you to seek your bed as well, I believe."

Sage scoffed at him. "When did you become my keeper?"

Hayjen grumbled under his breath like he was prone to. He shifted Lilja in his arms and stared up at the stars. "Lord save me from feisty women."

Lilja touched his face. "Ah, but you love it."

His lips tugged up at the corners before he addressed Sage. "Well... I am a glutton for punishment. I only meant that you might be tired as well. I know you didn't sleep last night."

She smiled sheepishly and bid the couple goodnight. Sage paused by her door, watching Hayjen cart away the giggling Lilja. A stab of envy struck her at their companionship. She hoped someday she would have that. Sighing, she slipped into her room, most likely for another night of nightmares.

Over the course of the next few days, Sage continued helping Lilja and furthering her own training. Captain Femi was a wonderful sparring partner. The woman's movements were smooth and fluid, yet quick as a viper. Training aboard the ship added another element of difficulty. The dipping and swaying of the vessel caused her to stumble a time or two, but over time it improved her balance.

The day of the exchange arrived speedily. She sent messages to both the Crown and the rebellion with the meeting location, praying that Lilja's contacts proved trustworthy.

Sage had encountered and persuaded a merchant to lease the entire space of his home for a few hours. Calling him a merchant was a perhaps bit of a stretch as he was more pirate than anything, but she didn't care. She was most likely living with pirates. If Lilja was a legitimate trader she'd eat her own hat.

The home she'd secured suited her purposes well. It was neutral territory with plenty of escape routes. The peaked roof was perfect for surveying the surrounding area. It also boasted a hidden trapdoor between the chimney and tallest peak, making it easy to lurk in the rafters of the house.

Sage perched in the rafter with the hatch slightly raised, peeking out of the trapdoor. She scanned the street below with interest. She had been sure to arrive early specifically so she could observe the interactions between the Crown and the rebellion before she made her entrance. She was still piqued by the fact the rebellion's demands had not been revealed to her. Over the last three days she had tried needle it out of Hayjen, but it seemed that the man was skilled in avoidance and, occasionally, in disappearing into thin air.

A laugh drew her attention. A blond deckhand was chatting up a washer girl. Her eyes narrowed on the familiar frame.

Sam.

If he hadn't laughed she wouldn't have known it was him. That man was certainly good at what he did. She snorted. But he was always chasing women.

If Sam was nearby it meant his group had already arrived as well.

Sage clicked the trapdoor shut and waited in the darkened beams for her guests to enter. A door creaked open. She watched with interest as a cloaked figure slipped into the room and searched it. After a moment, he threw back his hood and whistled softly. His disheveled dirty blond hair almost covered his eyes. Sage scrutinized him. He was familiar, but she just couldn't place him. He moved to one side of the room and waited.

The door creaked open again and a heavy tread moved across the wooden floor as Hayjen entered her line of vision. He stopped across the room from the cloaked man. "So, they sent us in first?" The blond remarked while chuckling. "Either they trust us implicitly, or we're expendable."

She could see Hayjen's lips crack a smile. "No doubt the latter," he joked.

Both men turned to the door when it opened, both cataloguing the newcomers. A man with black and silver peppered hair glided into the room. Sage would bet her best blade he was an assassin by trade or, at least, exceptionally skilled in combat. The man trailing behind him was someone familiar. It was the older gentleman that had said her scars were beautiful the night of the banquet. They both moved to the blond's side, assessing Hayjen.

Light footsteps slipped into the home, adding Badiah to the mix. The slender man perched on a chair next to Hayjen making him appear like a child when contrasted with the other man's hulking frame. Sage smiled. None of them would suspect the small man's skill with daggers and hand-to-hand combat was perhaps unparalleled. Badiah was deliberately using his short stature to his advantage; no doubt the other men would underestimate him. She held in a snigger. Badiah wasn't anywhere near as mild and delicate as he was portraying.

"God damned pirates," exploded a voice behind the door as it was flung open. Noah. He never changed, he still couldn't whisper.

"For all that is holy, lower your voice, Noah," Madden grumped behind him. "You could wake my dead mother with your bellow."

Both men quieted as they got a good look at the room. "Well, isn't this a regular old tea party? Crumpets anyone? I heard that's what the Crown's lackeys eat these days," Noah taunted.

Sage pursed her lips, searching the Crown's representatives for trouble.

She slowly exhaled when she found none. Noah couldn't be more contrary if he tried.

Sage cocked her head when she heard the back door open beneath her. Mason strode into the room followed by a large figure hovering in the doorway, but, before she could examine him, her eyes snapped to the opposite door as it opened as well. Three more cloaked figures entered and paused, watching the man below her. One of the three threw back his hood, exposing blond curls, stepping into the room. "Well isn't this a happy occasion," Sam cried gaily.

"Really?" Gavriel's smooth voice chastised.

Her heart clenched. Gavriel. She hadn't seen him since she left him behind at the festival. The look on his face still haunted her. Sage shook her head and focused back on the events playing out below.

Sam's eyes swept the room and up into the rafters. She stilled, knowing her cloak hid everything but her eyes. His eyes narrowed into a squint, then a small smile tugged at his lips. That was the moment he spotted her.

Damn the spymaster.

She placed a finger to her lips, and he dismissed her immediately. None of the other men had noticed her yet.

Idiots.

What she did notice was that the two figures in the opposing doorways still stared at each other.

"Your Highness," Rafe intoned below her.

The crown prince nodded to the rebellion leader. "Rafe."

The room crackled with anticipation and tension. Both men went to stand with their representatives. Twelve men in one room. Both sides distrustful, looking like they'd rather be anywhere else. Madden whispered something, and the black-haired man she had labeled as dangerous narrowed his eyes.

"Where is our liaison?" the gray-haired man asked.

"She is not yours," Noah corrected blandly. "That's the purpose of an liaison, is it not?"

Madden rolled his eyes even as Sam smirked.

Sage didn't feel ready to leave the safety of her hiding spot, but she focused on the fact that she had numerous escape routes. None of these men could cage her again. It was time to get things started before there was any bloodshed.

Sage shifted on the balls of her feet and dropped from her perch to the floor, landing in a crouch. She lifted her head, considering the room. Weapons glinted in almost everyone's hands.

She smiled and straightened lazily, projecting confidence. "You called, and I answered." Sage sauntered toward the middle of the room, keeping her back to the front door. Men stared at her from both sides, a range of expressions on their faces. The blond man's mouth was still hanging open. She slipped to his side and placed her finger under his chin, closing his mouth, and fought the temptation to wipe her hand off after touching him. Instead, Sage winked at him, her heart thudding. "If you leave that open long enough it could stay that way."

She moved forward to stand next to the dark one. She cocked her head to the side to give him the impression she was sizing him up even though she already had. "You," she murmured, watching him tense, "are someone everyone should be afraid of."

He stared down at her with banked intrigue. "And are you afraid of me?" he asked just as softly.

"No," she answered, realizing it was true. The two of them were similar. It was the ones who hid what they were you had to watch out for. "There are worse things in the world than you."

"A realist?" the dark man mused. "A pleasure to meet you, my lady. I am Zachael." He bowed from the waist.

"Charmed." She dipped her head in acknowledgement, gliding down the middle of the men.

"My offer is still open," the grizzled older man remarked from her left. Rafe hissed from his side on her right. "Still spoken for I see," he added, lightly.

"I wasn't spoken for then, neither am I now."

The older man arched an eyebrow as the room went completely silent.

Sage shrugged and shot Gavriel a real smile before spinning around to face the room again, her cloak sweeping the floor. "Let's not dawdle. Please hand over your demands."

Mason and the older gentleman stepped forward and each handed her a scroll. She glanced at the scrolls, butterflies fluttering in her stomach. This determined their futures. Sage lifted her head and handed each gentleman the opposite side's proper scroll. There. It was done.

She copied the smile her mum used when she was proud of her children. "Now, that wasn't so hard was it? We will meet in six days at a location of my choosing. Once negotiations begin, they will not end until an agreement is made. Think wisely, gentlemen. As for today, if I find out that anyone was followed," she looked pointedly at Sam, who flashed her an innocent smile. "There will be consequences." She jerked her chin toward Zachael. "If you think he is dangerous, you don't want to see me angry."

She turned to her former comrades. "That goes for you as well. No threats, no tricks, no violence. If I catch wind of any of shenanigans, I have a friend who is fond of tying a barrel to one's boots and dropping that individual off the dock to see how long he can hold his breath. Understood?" she barked.

The group of men straightened under her unflinching regard.

"I have things to attend to. Good day."

Sage spun, taking a few steps, sprinted to an older chair, using it to vault herself up and into the beams. She pulled herself up and looked down at the curious faces below her. She allowed a grin touch her face. "Be safe, gentlemen," Sage imparted as she escaped through the hatch up onto the roof. She ran sure-footedly across the roof and leapt to the next roof, rolling out of her landing. She popped up and sprinted across. They wouldn't be able to follow her this way. Only six more days until the future of Aermia would be decided. Hopefully, they wouldn't all kill each other.

Not likely.

EİGHT

TEHL

HE GAPED AT THE TRAPDOOR like a fool. She had catapulted herself off a chair and into the rafters, then disappeared. Sage somehow still surprised him.

"What a woman," Sam muttered. "Did you see how she twisted her body and pulled herself up? Imagine what she could do…"

"If you value your life, you will not finish that thought," warned the giant across from them. His glacial eyes stared daggers at Tehl's brother but that was not the person his brother needed to worry about. It was the golden eyes that had locked onto Sam with such malice it had him elbowing his brother in the side.

Sam glanced first to him and then to Rafe. His brother's smile dropped to a scowl. "Your minds are filled with filth. Before you so rudely cut me off, I was going to say imagine what she could do for the Elite."

Tehl schooled his face. He was sure that wasn't what Sam would have said. What made him wary was that Rafe's amber eyes still hadn't moved from his brother. Stars above, they didn't need any fights. He shuffled to the side, blocking his brother. Tehl crossed his arms as aggressive eyes snapped to his face. "Do we have a problem?" he asked, feigning boredom. Rafe could try to intimidate him all he wanted, but it wouldn't accomplish anything.

Rafe blinked and then relaxed. "No, we do not."

"We will see you in six days then."

Tehl nodded, signaling that it was time to leave. Zachael, Garreth, William, and Gavriel circled Sam and himself. They quickly parted ways with the rebels and quietly chatted about inconsequential things on the way back home. He itched to know what was held in the scroll, but it would have to wait until they arrived.

"What do you mean they want representation on the council?" Jaren barked.

The bickering and arguing had started as soon as the demands were read:

1. Money sent to the families who'd lost their loved ones or homes to the Scythians.

2. Any service provided by a rebellion member would receive compensation.

3. Lower taxes.

4. Restoration on the Mort wall.

5. No seizure of rebellion weapons and assets.

6. A rebellion member has the choice to accept an assignment or decline without punishment.

7. All previous unlawful acts pardoned.

8. Equal representation of the rebellion on the council.

"It means exactly what the letter says, Jaren." William retorted.

Jaren threw his hand in the air. "This is ridiculous! Why are we negotiating with them?" He leaned forward in his chair with a gleam in his eye that Tehl didn't care for. "We have access to something they care about." He paused. "The rebel woman."

The whole table of men stared at him.

"We do," Gavriel said, carefully, his violet eyes shuttered.

"She is a bargaining piece. If we captured her, we would force their hand. Not to mention we'd have knowledge of their main base."

"It's not a bad idea, in theory, but the consequences would be heavy," Jeb, the strategist, inserted.

Tehl kept the bored expression on his face, waving away Jaren's idea. "It's an option, but the whole point of this treaty is to avoid bloodshed. No doubt if we pursued this course many lives would be lost. The matter is closed. The rebel woman won't be harmed or touched." His voice rang through the room. Some looked ready to argue. Time to change the subject. "Which of these are reasonable to you?"

"Home reconstruction and monies for the families is doable," Lelbiel answered. "I can check with Demari, but I'm certain we can afford it."

"Good." Tehl thought so too. "Next."

"Compensation for the rebel members," Garreth added. "We're paid a wage for our service to the Crown. It's logical for them to receive it as well." The blond man hesitated a moment. "I think they also should have a say in assignments. They aren't part of the Guard or Elite. The rebels aren't soldiers. They are not bound like we are."

Zachael eyed Garreth, then bowed his head in agreement. "I agree, we do not want unwilling men. That only leads to danger, confusion, and, possibly, dissention."

"Two down. What else?" Tehl asked.

"I don't think they all should be pardoned just because their leaders made a treaty with us," William stated. "I believe in actions speaking louder than words. Hard work deserves rewards, so they must work with us, help us; only then will they receive pardon. "

"I couldn't agree more." Tehl liked that idea. No charity. You work for your privileges.

"The restoration of the Mort Wall is not possible." Jeb looked around the table. "The time, labor, and assets it would take to fix it are unreasonable. A project on that scale isn't possible. It would take years. The Mort Wall is more memorial than protection anyway. Not to mention it would put our laborers near the Scythians. We would knowingly put them in danger and possibly even lose them to their raids."

Tehl thought about the Mort Wall. It had been built after the last war with Scythia, hundreds of years ago, after the Nagalians' genocide. Shortly thereafter, a deadly plague spread throughout the Scythian people with rumors that it had something to do with their questionable use of science but little more was known. What they did know was that the wall went up to keep the Scythians out, and all the danger they presented. But now it was mostly rubble.

"It's a waste of time and resources," Sam put in. "I say we veto that one."

"Agreed." Tehl looked at Jaren, who was examining the wood grain of the table. "What of the taxes, Jaren?"

"We can't lower them." Jaren winced. "I wish we could, but there isn't a way. The taxes are levied based on what a household *can* pay, not everyone pays the same thing. We are not out of line. It been a rough couple of years for everyone." Jaren slumped into his chair looking like he'd aged ten years.

"Thank you, Jaren, moving on."

"The weapons," Zachael spoke up. "We need them. It would save money if we were spared the necessity of forging more by using the rebellion's weapons. We'd be that much closer to being prepared for a Scythian attack."

"That could kill two birds with one stone," Lelbiel commented.

"All right." Tehl swept the table looking for someone brave enough to bring up the final point, representation on their council.

Gavriel stood and placed his hands behind his back. "I think that having their men on our council would round us out and give us a fresh perspective. Many of us don't live among the people or make a living in the city. The only information we receive is secondhand. It could prove to be both informative and helpful to us to know what the people are thinking."

"Once a traitor, always a traitor," Jaren muttered.

Lelbiel nodded in agreement.

All eyes turned to him in question. Tehl didn't like the idea of Rafe having a seat of power because his motives were still questionable. The men in the room all had their flaws, but they were trustworthy. Out of all the rebellion's demands, this one seemed like it would be their most important, it would no doubt be non-negotiable. His personal feelings aside, it would actually be a smart move. No one from the rebellion could cry foul because they would have representation and therefore be a part of the decisions. Tehl didn't like it, but he would do it for the people of Aermia. And they could no doubt work around it, should the need arise.

Tehl cracked his neck and straightened in his chair. "We will grant them this request in exchange for their weapons. I also would prefer not to have them on our council but it matters not what I want, but what is best for

Aermia." He met each man's eyes. "We are bound by duty." Solemn nods followed his statement.

"And if they choose women?" William proposed, a sly glint in his eyes.

"Perhaps you don't recall in your old age, William, but my mother was part of this council. We wouldn't dream of treating the fairer sex any differently than one of you." Sam's teeth gleamed white against his tan face.

William sat back, satisfied, while the rest of his council seemed to ponder the last statement. Tehl knew what old William was thinking. No doubt Sage would be among those chosen. He would never be rid of her unless she resigned. That thought perked him up as she would no doubt detest being so near him. She was bound to disappear after a short while. That was what she was best at.

Lelbiel pulled the smaller letter Sage had slipped to Garreth and examined it. Lelbiel's eyes narrowed, pinching at the corner before he smiled. "It seems that the lady liaison didn't restrict the number of men this time to six. You can bring your full council, and an addition of four Elite. It's interesting that she wouldn't allow you to bring protection the first time but now she will allow it. I wonder what that means?"

Zachael snickered. "It means she expects violence. She is warning us to prepare for the negotiation."

"Indeed," Sam mused at his side.

Tehl stood, staring at the room. "Unless something comes up in the next six days, we have no reason to meet. If you need me, request an audience." With his dismissal, chairs screeched across the floor as his advisors stood and bowed. One by one they left the room.

That had been easier than he thought. Out of the corner of his eye he caught Sam frowning, and a faint wrinkle appeared in between his golden blond eyebrows. "Something on your mind?"

Sam peered at him, blue eyes full of calculation. "Sage allowed us four Elite and your full council. She expects mischief." His brother blew out a frustrated breath. "I hate not knowing the location. I can't scout or place any sneaks."

Tehl's mouth twitched from the effort to keep a smile from his face. "I believe that is the reason she did it this way," he deadpanned.

Sam's eyes narrowed. "Stop making fun of me, this is serious. Your life is going to be in danger."

That sobered him. "We need to be prepared then."

The next six days sped by in a flurry of day-to-day activities and training with the Elite every chance he got. Sam was right, he'd gotten soft spending so much time in the palace. Every night he fell into bed, aching and exhausted, but content.

The missive arrived early that morning announcing the time and place of the meeting. When night fell, all of his men were armed to the teeth. They were to meet at a pub between the fishing district and merchant district. Tehl and his twelve men set out in pairs to Sanee, it was less conspicuous that way. Sam paired with Garreth and disappeared in the blink of an eye.

Zachael walked beside him, assessing every person as well as their surroundings for any potential threats to his person. They wound through the city in companionable silence. Zachael didn't talk for the sake of talking, and Tehl appreciated that about his combat master.

After a while, Tehl at last spotted the pub. It was ordinary, but, after a second look, he noted that the quality of the craftsmanship stood out. It had a thick wooden door framed by two small windows with iron welded in patterns across it.

"Smart," Zachael commented. "The windows look like art, but they're built for protection."

The pair moved up three stone steps and onto the deck. Zachael reached for the door only to have it jerked back from his grip. The light haloed the alluring curves of a woman with shocking silvery white hair.

"Please come in."

Her smoky voice draped over him. The woman was dressed most unusually with fabric draped here and there to cover her body. Was it one piece? He wanted to roll his eyes, thinking how Sam would love to investigate such a type of dress. The purple scarf wrapped around her head emphasized her shocking magenta eyes. A knowing smirk played along her lips while she watched him gawk at her.

Tehl flashed her an apologetic smile before muttering a speedy, "Thank you."

A black curse tore his attention from the unusual female he'd been examining. Tehl quickly snagged Zachael's arm just before he lunged forward.

"Let me go. I've a traitor to deal with." The weapons master snarled quietly.

Tehl scanned the room and stiffened as he spotted the source of Zachael's anger.

Serge.

The smug bastard was leaning against the bar sipping a brew, watching Zachael with obvious amusement. Tehl wanted to rip the man's heart out, but he also knew now was not the time. He reeled in his friend, whispering harshly in Zachael's ear. "Now is not the time, old friend. He *will* get what he deserves in time."

Zachael nodded that he heard Tehl but didn't drop his eyes from the traitor lounging ten feet away. Tehl turned away from Serge when the man waved at them lazily. Two long narrow tables sat in the room with an open space in the middle. Men lounged around the room but there was a definite division between the two groups. Tehl nodded to Rafe when he caught the rebellion leader's eyes.

Tehl stood behind an empty chair at the odd table, waiting for the meeting to begin. A hush fell over the room as light steps echoed from a hallway intersecting the bar. Sage glided into the room in a pair of skin-tight black leather breeches, a white linen shirt, and a snug green vest, making the most of her every curve. She smiled at the group, stopping in the center of the room, demanding every man's attention.

She cocked a hip and ran her hand over a dagger sheathed to her arm. Sage looked up from underneath her lashes and spun in a slow circle inspecting the men. Tehl straightened when her gaze ran over him before moving on. The wench was bold, he would give her that.

"As you can see, I am armed." She gestured to the dagger on her arm and smiled. "But that's my prerogative being the liaison." She lifted her chin. "Captain Femi and Hayjen will collect your weapons."

Protests broke out. She raised her hand, and the room quieted. "This is a peace meeting, you will not need them." Her face hardened. "If you keep a weapon and use it, there will be consequences." Her harsh gaze swept over the room. "Captain Femi knows of some unique ways to punish. I believe one of her favorites is to drop you in leviathan-infested waters and see if you can swim back to shore."

Utter silence filled the room. Leviathans were nasty creatures. The vicious creatures were similar to dolphins, but that's where all similarities ended. They had row after row of sharp teeth, and a love of flesh that made any man shudder.

She quirked a grin at Zachael. "That is if she gets to you before me. There is a reason they call me Blade."

Dark chuckles rumbled through the rebellion's men causing Sage to smile.

She clapped her hands together. "This is how we will proceed. I will flip a coin, whomever wins gets to start the negotiations. Please pass Captain Femi and Hayjen your weapons and we can proceed."

The weapons collection was a slow-going process. Every man boasted a sword and daggers. Sam grumbled the entire time while stripping his off beside him. Sage winked at his brother before barking at Madden about a dagger in his boot.

Tehl removed his weapons, this time ignoring the exotic woman. He couldn't keep his gaze from the green-eyed vixen running the meeting. Despite her bold act, he noted how uncomfortable she was with all the men. Every so often her hands would shake. He pulled his eyes from her as the last person was relieved of their weapons.

Rafe.

Apparently the man carried an entire armory with him.

The giant man, Hayjen, gestured to the wicked looking daggers strapped to both legs. Rafe shook his head, staring straight at Sage. Her face was cool as she strode across the room, stopping in front of the rebellion leader.

"Is there a problem, gentlemen?"

"He won't hand over his blades," Hayjen explained.

Tehl leaned forward in his seat along with the rest of the room. How would she deal with the defiant rebellion leader?

Sage peered up at Rafe, tension in her whole body. "You need to hand over your weapons, there are no exceptions."

Rafe's eyes trailed over her face as he unbuckled the belt that held them in place. "These blades are special. The only hands to touch them are myself and my family." Rafe gathered the daggers and held them out to Sage.

Sam chuckled under his breath. "The smooth bastard. He is claiming her in front of all these men so they know she is close to him. Conniving, but effective."

Only her back was visible, but she didn't move to take them.

"Only you can keep them." Rafe rumbled.

Irritation nipped at him for Sage. Of all the times to try something, the rebellion leader had to do it now. He must be desperate. The thought made his lips curl. She must have been avoiding Rafe. That put a full-blown smile on his face as the captain relieved him and his men of their weapons.

With reluctant fingers, Sage plucked the daggers from his grasp, avoiding touching him, Tehl noted, before she dumped them onto a chest behind the bar. His brother sniggered. Rafe may have been trying to make a point, but hers sounded loud and clear.

"Will the leaders please join me?" Sage asked.

Tehl strode to her side, Rafe on the other.

"Coral for rebellion, dragon for Crown." She flipped the coin, the dragon landed face up. They both nodded to each other and moved to their seats.

"The Crown begins. Please take your seat. Remember not to shout, all your concerns will be heard. No one leaves until an agreement has been struck. This gets decided tonight." She bowed. "For Aermia."

A chorus of *Aermias* thundered through the room. Captain Femi placed two cushioned chairs at the head of the room. Both women sat and looked at Tehl. He placed his elbows on the table and eyed the men across from him. "We have read your demands, and this is what we can offer: payment and support to the families that have been affected by the Scythian attacks. You are not part of our army so you can choose to accept or decline any assignment. You will also receive wages for any assignment you carry out." Murmurs of triumph reached his ears.

Don't get too excited, he thought. "Punishment for unlawful actions will be removed with an exception." He met Serge's brown eyes. "You must work off your debts by accepting work with the Crown. If you don't contribute to the peace and betterment of Aermia, you live your life in the dungeon. Last, we can offer four places on my council." Tehl sat back and waited.

"What of the other demands?" Rafe asked.

"Not possible," Sam replied. "Taxes are based on what each family makes, the food shortage was not caused by taxes, it was caused by Scythians."

Roars of outrage erupted around the rebellion leader. He raised his hand, never taking his eyes off them. "And the others?"

"The Mort Wall," Jeb supplied. "The wall is a symbol, not protection. It would be a costly, colossal waste of time and resources. Scythia has been raiding our borders for a year now, for no reason we have discovered. If we embarked on such a thing, it would put more people in danger."

"War with Scythia is imminent, we need your weapons. That is one of our demands," Zachael added, bluntly.

Sage stood. "The Crown has made their offer, what say you, rebels?"

"We will supply men for the war with Scythia. We will share our expertise on training. As for the weapons, we will part with some, but not all. Once we sign the agreement, there will be peace, anyone who acts is on their own and subject to your laws."

Reasonably, they agreed to meet four out of six of the Crown's demands.

"And the others?" William asked, echoing Rafe.

The rebellion leader zeroed in on William, dripping aggression. "We will not impart all the names of our members and put their families in danger." His amber eyes pierced Sam next. "I will not contribute to your sneaks. I will not put them in your hands, just for you to send them into Scythia never to return."

"What do you suggest? Let all the traitors go free?" Jaren cut in. "Can you assure us that your people are completely loyal to you?" Jaren waved his hand. "And this new venture?"

"We're not thrilled to be getting into bed with the Crown," the mouthy man from last time supplied. "But we are loyal to Rafe. He has never led us wrong."

Sage stood again. "Are these terms agreeable to you, prince?"

"They are," he supplied. "Jaren's concerns are valid. To the Crown, you are traitors. If they are willing to betray their kingdom, what is stopping them from betraying you?" He stared evenly at Rafe. "If we don't have their names we can't keep an eye on them to make sure they are behaving as law abiding citizens."

"I can see your point," Rafe conceded. "I will check on them and will take along another person."

Jaren opened his mouth to say something when Rafe cut him a look. His advisor snapped his mouth shut.

"This person will be someone whom we both trust." Rafe's gaze slid to Sage. "Our lady liaison."

"I am sorry, but I will not be available. My place is with my family," she replied, firmly locking gazes with the rebellion leader.

"This is important to both the Crown and the rebellion. Could you not care for this *and* your family for the sake of peace?" An older man with moss-colored eyes asked Sage.

Her eyes softened at the old man's expression. She let loose a sigh, defeated. "I accept then. Are the terms laid out by the Crown acceptable to the rebellion?"

"All but the number of weapons. We will not part with all of them."

"That is up to neither of you," Sage interrupted. "I know I am the neutral party but this concerns me."

"How does this concern you?" Garreth asked.

She smiled wickedly. "Because they are mine. I made them."

Surprise flashed across several faces. Not everyone knew who she was.

"I will give three quarters of the weapons to the Crown, and the rest I will keep. Did you get all of that Captain Femi?"

The exotic woman lifted her white head from her record. "Indeed. Continue on."

"So this leads us to the final agenda. Who will join the Crown's council?"

"Hayjen, Madden, Sage, and myself," Rafe supplied.

"I see an issue here." Serge's voice carried through the room. He stood up, a stupid smile on his face making Tehl want to punch him. "Having members on the council is fine and all, but we will still have less representatives than the Crown."

Every word out of his mouth made Tehl's hackles rise.

Serge moved to the bar and leaned against it. "What is the council? They are advisors. They may advise, but they have no real power." Serge stabbed a finger at him. "He still makes the final decision. The council is a farce in its actual power of execution. The only way the people would have real say is if we had equal representation."

Rafe glowered at Serge. "What is the meaning of this, Rhys?"

Rhys, so that was his name. Tehl filed that away. Rhys was going somewhere dark, deep, and miserable.

"The Crown is trying to trick us."

What was that leach getting at?

"How dare you!" thundered Jaren as he stood up. "We are extending mercy to you traitorous lot." Zachael grabbed Jaren by the shirt and yanked him back down into his chair, hissing something into his ear.

"You see?" Rhys said, smugness in his tone. "They feel like we are below them, untrustworthy. They will never respect us, despite having a place among them."

Men nodded their heads in agreement.

Tehl saw what was happening. Rhys was trying to sabotage the peace treaty, but why? It didn't make sense. Did he loathe the Crown so much? He had served in the Guard for over four years. Was it because they stripped him of his title? Revenge?

"We need someone to check his power," Rhys continued. "Someone who will stand against him and hold their own. Someone who shares his power."

More men were nodding and shouting encouragements while Rafe looked like he was ready to blow.

"And how would you do that?" the rebellion leader questioned tightly.

Tehl wanted to know that too.

"By uniting the rebellion and Crown permanently." Rhys gave Tehl an arrogant look. "We know of someone who isn't afraid of you. Someone of strong moral character, who stands up for the weak and has a strong sense of duty. Someone who challenges you."

Rhys breached the distance between Sage and himself. Rafe, Gavriel, Sam, and Tehl surged to their feet as she paled and leaned away from him. She stilled when he ran a finger down her white cheek. Captain Femi hissed and slapped his hand away. Rhys smiled down at Sage then rolled his shoulders and faced the room.

"The rebellion wants equal representation."

"What exactly do you propose?" Gavriel asked, rage in his voice.

Rhys smiled directly at him. *That monster should be locked up, not conducting a negotiation.*

"I propose a union between the Crown and the rebellion: matrimony."

Tehl's breath stilled.

No.

"Between the crown prince and the rebellion's blade, Sage."

NINE

TEHL

PANDEMONIUM BROKE OUT IN THE room. The rebels were cheering, and his advisors were cursing and shouting at each other. He blocked everyone else out and focused on Rafe, Rhys, and Sage. Rhys looked extremely pleased with himself. One glance at the rebellion leader, and Tehl knew he was one second away from murder. Last there was Sage. Her face was blank. Not one glimmer of emotion even in her eyes. Why wasn't she reacting? Something wasn't right.

"Are you okay?" he mouthed. Nothing. Captain Femi was stroking her brown hair and whispering to her. "Is she okay?" he asked louder, his voice carrying over the din. Captain Femi's pursed lips thinned in answer. He didn't care for Sage, she was a thorn in his side, but he didn't want to see her hurt.

Gavriel pushed through the men and knelt in front of her knees. His cousin took her hand in his and spoke to her. Still nothing. Tehl couldn't hear Gav's words but he could see him pleading with her, trying to coax her out of her mind.

"This is how you lead your rebellion?" Zachael bellowed. "You wouldn't know your head from your ass. Get your dogs in line, or I will do it for you."

Rafe stilled. He swiveled his neck to stare at Zachael. "What did you say?" Rafe rumbled.

Zachael leaned over the thin table. "I said: get your dogs in line, or I will do

362

it for you. Control them. That's your responsibility."

The room quieted at the challenge.

"I control nothing. I direct them, but they have a choice. That's the difference between the Crown and the rebellion. The Crown forces and takes. We each choose and give. We work as a group, no one has the ultimate power. Which is why Sage will not marry the Crown, she will not be forced into anything."

"Rafe is right," an older man inserted. "We make the decision together." The older man shot Rhys a thoughtful look. "But Rhys is right. We need someone to check the Crown's power. I propose the rebellion vote. Those in favor of Rhys's demand?"

A myriad of hands rose, except for the old man, Hayjen, and Rafe. Bloody hell. They would demand he marry the rebel woman.

"It's settled," the old man said reluctantly. "You marry her or there will be civil war."

Tehl's brain scrambled to catch up to what was going on. This couldn't be happening.

Sam cursed. "Be reasonable. Surely, you wouldn't subject Sage to a lifetime of misery?"

The old man stared at Sage with sad eyes. "She is a good girl. Sage does what is necessary and needed. She has a good heart. She will do this for Aermia, for the rebellion, and for her family."

Tehl's men looked at him, waiting for him to give the signal to leave, but he couldn't move.

"This is extortion," Jeb muttered.

And it was.

He had to choose between his happiness and the welfare of Aermia. Tehl had spoken about finding a wife weeks ago, but this wasn't how he wanted to obtain one. He had planned on picking out a mousy woman to bless him with children then stay out of the way. Tehl never wanted what his parents had. Love was dangerous, but this was something else. He would be tied to a woman who hated him. His life would be hell. Tehl doubted she would let him touch her, but that was a necessity for heirs. Was he selfish enough to say no? He thought about all the men who would die in a civil war and the possibility of Scythia invading Aermia. Blood would run through the streets.

Bitterness filled him. He didn't have a choice. Duty above all.

"You're not considering this, right?" Sam asked pulling him from his thoughts.

Tehl tipped his head back, a bitter laugh spilling out of him. "There's nothing to consider, I am surprised you even asked."

Sam regarded him for a moment. "I wasn't asking you as your tactician, or as your duty as the crown's shield, but as your brother."

"There's no choice, and you know it."

His men circled around him wearing grim faces. "There hasn't been an arranged marriage ever in our history, my lord," Jeb remarked. "That's what makes the monarchy so strong, a strong marriage based on love."

"They would have to keep it a secret," Garreth said. "If the people found out it was arranged, they would lose confidence in the Crown. We need their support now more than ever. If you decide on this, you both must act like you love each other anytime you aren't alone. Can you live like that?"

"He will have to," Jarren despaired. "That's a hard life, sire."

They all knew that if he refused, many lives would be lost. He couldn't live with that on his conscience. His mother told him that with privilege and power also came responsibility, duty. He had a responsibility to his people. He rose from the chair on wooden legs, his men fanning around him. Tehl met Rafe's angry eyes.

"Is this really what you want?" Tehl was sure that Rafe understood what he was asking. Would he let Sage go for the sake of his lofty principles? The rebellion leader's hands clenched so tightly his fist turned a splotchy white.

"It has been decided."

Tehl felt oddly detached when he spoke. "Very well, I will take her as my wife. But I have a few demands of my own." He glared at all the men across from him. "Firstly, since you hold personal choice so dear to you, you will extend the same freedom to Sage."

"Done," piped up the old man.

No one disagreed.

"Secondly, none of you will ever have contact with her again except for the old man, Hayjen, and Rafe. You have used her over and over as a sacrificial lamb." The hothead, next to the old man, sputtered. Tehl ignored him, letting menace seep into his voice. "You sanctioned the death of my father and sent her back to the place where she was tortured and almost died. Again, you offer her, damning her to a fate that will kill her every day." Most of the men shied away from his piercing gaze like cowards. "She is to be nothing to you. She will not be your blade anymore, but my future queen, my consort. I will make this simple. If you even breathe in her direction, you will disappear." And he meant it. "She has three days to come to me, willingly." He peered at Captain Femi, hovering protectively by the girl's side. "Will you ensure this will be done?"

Captain Femi scrutinized him for a moment before bowing her head. "It will be done."

"Make sure she knows what she is getting herself into. Our people need harmony. She must play a role when we're not alone. It won't be an easy life." He hesitated a moment before voicing what needed to be said. "I am the crown prince, so heirs are a necessity. I will have children, several of them. Make sure she knows this is a requirement." Tehl spared one last glare for the group. "We're done here."

Captain Femi stood, leaving Sage with Gavriel. She flowed toward him, carrying the treaty she had been working on all evening. She smoothed it out on the table and held a quill out to him. Tehl looked over it, making sure nothing they'd discussed was missing or additional points added, before stroking his name across the parchment. The woman relieved him of the quill and blew on the ink. With care, she picked it up and placed it before the rebellion leader. He carefully read over it, allowing a few of his men to do the same. Once he received their nods, he scratched his name down.

It was done. Peace was secure even as his own life and peace was signed away.

Gavriel stood from his crouch. "My lord, I request to stay as protection for your betrothed."

Tehl hid his flinch.

His betrothed.

He would be married, but to someone who'd rather eat glass than share a room with him, much less a bed. Tehl nodded his permission and strode toward the door, ready to escape.

"Betrothed?" a feminine voice accused.

Tehl halted in his tracks and spun to meet horror-filled green eyes. She darted glances around the room, panic evident in her movements. Her eyes stopped on Rafe. "What have you done?" she whispered.

"Forgive me, little one."

There was so much pain in those four little words.

Betrayal and rage filled her face, warring with one another. She jerked to her feet. "I will never be yours, I will die first!" she spat.

Taking everyone by surprise, she leapt over her chair and sprinted the opposite way down the hall she entered from. Gavriel scrambled after her, shooting him an upset look.

He now knew for sure what she thought of him. Tehl may have secured peace for Aermia, but make no mistake, he had just started a war all the same.

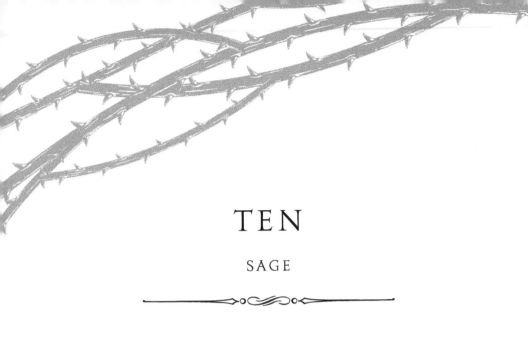

TEN

SAGE

ESCAPE.

Escape.

Escape.

The hallway seemed to stretch forever ahead of her; no matter how fast she ran, the walls still pressed inward. Sage couldn't breathe. It was like a giant hand had reached inside her chest to squeeze her lungs until there was nothing but panic and pain. Her boot caught a rug, and she stumbled, slamming her hip into a table she hadn't spotted. The pain was acute, but it actually helped her regain focus. Heavy footsteps pounded in her direction. Terror filled her. No doubt the monster was coming for her again.

Sage knocked over the small table behind her and sprinted through the exit. Hopefully that would slow him down. She burst outside and the dark of night engulfed her. Normally, she welcomed it, but tonight the tendrils of darkness were clawing at her, trying to pull her apart and feed her to the nightmare. Her surroundings blurred as she tried to escape the nightmare behind her.

She registered only snatches of the startled faces she passed as she ran for her life. She slowed ever so slightly when she gained a moment of clarity. Did she even know where she running to? Home? No, she would lead the monster there, and that wasn't an option. The hair on her arms rose. He was hunting her, she felt it in her bones. Shuddering, she picked up her pace and soon she could see the glimmering waves of the bay.

Lilja's ship.

Safety. She needed to reach the ship, there she would be safe.

As Sage cut through the fisherman shacks, the sound of her boots on the wooden dock soothed her frantic heart; she would make it. A manic smile had just split her face when an arm caught her waist, jerking her back. Terror filled her once again.

He had found her.

Sage screamed, but a large hand hastily clamped over her mouth, her screams muffled. She flailed and struggled, but it did nothing to loosen his grip. Nor could she hinder his progress as he dragged her away.

She sucked in huge breaths through her nose, tears blurred her vision as panic overwhelmed her. As the world around her began to fade away, Sage absently concluded that perhaps death wouldn't be so bad. One thing was sure, she was taking her monster down with her. His harsh breaths touched her neck, making her shiver, not in revulsion, but in anticipation of her next move. He would hurt no one ever again.

"Sage! It's me."

She frantically searched for the source of that familiar voice. Maybe she would have help after all. Sage increased her struggles.

"Sis, it's okay. Calm down. I've got you. You need to stop screaming." The hand released her mouth.

Gav? Where was Gav? Who was screaming? A high-pitched ringing filled her ears, along with the wailing of a dying animal.

"Sis, it's Gavriel. You're safe. No one is going to hurt you." The hands holding her, shook her roughly. "Sage! You need to calm down. I will never let anyone touch you."

Confusion filled her. Was that dying sound coming from her? Sage sucked in a hiccupping breath, her throat burning. Did Gavriel slay her monster?

"Sage, love, there is no monster. Just me."

Without her permission, her whole body sagged against his. She tried to command her it to move, but it simply wouldn't cooperate. He shifted her around so she was facing him, her head against his chest. Her eyes latched onto his. He had saved her once again, even after her deception. More tears poured down her face as gut-wrenching sobs tore out of her. Gav crushed her even tighter to his chest, cooing soft words of comfort. In her distress, she barely registered that, at some point, they had returned to the Sirenidae vessel, and she vaguely registered being placed in a soft bed. Desperately, she clung to the man who'd slain her monster and held back the nightmares. "Please," she begged, "please don't leave me alone."

"I won't. I won't." Calloused hands pulled the covers up to her chin and then a heavy weight settled next to her, gathering her into his arms. In the security of his hold, she finally calmed and darkness claimed her.

The next day's weather matched her mood.

She stood, watching, as a storm rolled in from the south. Gray clouds adorned the sky, the water shifting from its usual brilliant turquoise to a murky blue-gray. The ship bobbed with a bit more ferocity as the waves rocked her to and fro. Drifting, just like her. Last night had not gone at all as she'd imagined. She wished she could erase it from her memory.

When Rhys had touched her, it was like he'd stolen her will. She had frozen, as if she was locked in her own body, watching everything play out. No matter how much she railed from the inside, beating against the walls of her mind, she couldn't break through. She couldn't even lift her hand to swat away his disgusting fingers as he caressed her cheek. Even when a concerned and familiar gaze met her own, his violet eyes pleading with her to respond, she could not do so. She could see mouths moving, as if speaking, but no sound reached her ears. What were they saying? What did they want? Why weren't they disposing of that disgusting wretch?

Sage shivered and scrubbed at her cheek with her palms, as if the action could erase the memory of his touch. She tipped her head back, looking from the swirling sea to birds moving about the sky. They seemed playful, dipping and gliding on the wind, utterly free. She wanted that. But it seemed that she would never be free.

The previous day was still a blur, save the memory of intense terror and her own need to flee. How she had arrived at the dock was a mystery to her. By her sore body, she guessed she had sprinted the whole way. When Gavriel had grabbed her she'd been prepared to die. She was so tired of fighting the nightmares, night after night, never getting more than a handful of sleep. Sage was fairly certain Rhys would kill her, and the thought had been strangely relieving. She had been ready for death, to finally be at peace. In the light of day, now that she was capable of rational thought, she couldn't believe how selfish that thought had been. How could she even think it? It would gut her entire family. They had suffered so much already.

She dropped her elbows to the rail and placed her chin in her hands as she turned her thoughts to Gavriel and the role he'd played in events. She grimaced at her vague recollection of clinging to him as she sobbed her heart out and begged him not to leave her. When she'd woken this morning, her hands had been wound into his shirt, crushing the fabric with her fingers. He had kept his word and stayed. Dark smudges had bruised the area underneath his eyes.

I did that, she'd thought.

She'd released him and crept out, leaving him snoring in her bed, grimacing at what a needy fool she must have seemed to him.

A crash and heavy footsteps made her glance over her shoulder, and a very disheveled Gavriel stumbled out of the hallway and onto the deck. He urgently scanned the area, his eyes panicked, but he calmed as soon as he spotted her. He paused to brush his shirt out and strode to her side, mimicking her pose. Gav didn't speak; rather, he simply watched the ocean, waiting. She examined him from the corner of her eye. His black, wavy hair, so much like the crown prince's, stirred in the ocean breeze, slipping around his square jaw. She had left him without even a goodbye. He must be so angry with her, but even so, he'd protected her. She owed him an apology.

Sage traced the grain of the wood beneath her arms for a moment, preparing herself for the biggest apology of her life. "I'm sorry," was all she got out. She wanted to bang her head on the rail. He deserved better, but she could find no words to make what she'd done okay. Her mouth parted, ready to grovel, when he spoke.

"What are you sorry for, Sage?" He turned to the side, propping a hip against the rail, and stared down at her.

She didn't feel ready to handle the disappointment and accusation no doubt written on his face, but she steeled herself; she was no coward. She slowly turned and, with great difficulty, raised her eyes from his bare feet to the open collar of his shirt, pausing there, still struggling to meet his eyes.

His hand cupped her chin. "Sis? You need to look at me."

Tears pricked her eyes as she met his warm gaze. He had called her 'sis'—he still used the endearment. When she had called him her brother, she had not been acting. She had meant it, and she knew he had too. She bit her quivering bottom lip. Sage had never felt like she was much of a crier, but in the last two months she had cried more than she ever had in her entire life.

"Gavriel, I am so sorry I didn't say goodbye. I needed to go. I couldn't stay locked up like that indefinitely...and I didn't want to be used."

His face pinched. "You thought I was using you?"

She blanched. "No. I just meant that I understood why you were saying certain things. You wanted to turn me into a Crown sympathizer, but I couldn't give you want you wanted. Our friendship was real, I know that, but in the back of my mind I couldn't be sure if part of you was still befriending me because you wanted something from me." She looked away as he dropped her chin. "I was an intelligence officer for the rebellion. In order to get what we need, it sometimes means lying or even becoming someone else. I wasn't sure if you were doing the same. I hoped not, but...we do things for our family that we might never do for others."

"It wasn't fake."

Sage met his eyes. "I know. It became painfully clear to me when I saw the look of betrayal on your face that night of the Midsummer Festival." She exhaled a disgusted breath. "That was supposed to be my last night."

"You helped the Crown."

She smiled ruefully. "No, I helped Marq. Murder is never the solution. He may be sick, but he's a wonderful old man with a good heart, he didn't deserve what they had planned for him. I had no choice but to accept the assignment. It was the only way I could protect him."

"And you did, despite the danger to yourself."

Sage shrugged. "It was supposed to be my last night with the rebellion anyway. I'd already decided that, although I believed in the cause, I couldn't work with them if the end was accomplished through such methods." She snorted. "Not that it mattered. I ended up in the middle of it anyway, despite my best efforts to escape."

"Why did you agree to be the liaison?"

Sage raised an incredulous eyebrow. "Do you really think I had a choice? I had led the crown prince and his spymaster to the rebellion, even if unintentionally. Many people I knew and had worked with could have died because of my mistake. I did what I had to do to ensure their safety." She placed a hand over her heart. "I believe in what the rebellion wants for Aermia, I too love her people. I joined for the chance to help restore our lands, to create a better life for so many innocents, and to help protect them. And, now, serving as the liaison, I can continue to do so, only this way we may spare the lives of so many on both sides."

"And now the rebellion is asking something more from you." Her eyes widened at the bitterness in his words, and she simply stared while his eyes searched her face. "Do you remember much of last night?"

She looked away, gripping the railing so tightly her fingers ached. "Most, until Rhys touched me." She forced out between clenched teeth. "I only have pieces of the rest." A pause. "Thank you for your support and help last night." She flicked her eyes to the side, smiling at him briefly. "The meeting did not go as I..." She halted when a sudden flash of the previous evening formed in a picture in her mind. The crown prince speaking to Lilja, discussing the need for children.

Their children.

His and hers.

Sage gasped and stumbled back from Gavriel.

Marriage, that was the bargain. The rebellion had sold her to the Crown for power. Rafe had sold her. She was chattel, no better than a whore. A warm womb to grow more princes.

"No." Her friend's eyes widened at the vehemence in her voice. "I *won't* do it. I don't care if he's not the devil I thought he was at first! He still is an arrogant, thoughtless pig. I will never wed him. He will *never* touch me."

Gavriel's face cooled during her tirade. "He is still your crown prince, and, as such, you should accord him with due respect when speaking of him."

She let loose a harsh laugh. "He will receive my respect when he damn well earns it. From the moment I met him, he has threatened to harm me. In his home, I was starved, left without adequate clothing, drugged twice, tortured, and... " Her throat clogged, but she pressed on. "...and my innocence was almost stolen. He has bullied and yelled. I was his prisoner for weeks! So excuse me if I'm not singing his praises, my lord." She spat the words.

"You leave out all the positive things you experienced. Perhaps you should meditate on those as well." He shook his head, frustrated. After a moment, his face cleared. "Whether you accept it or not, your rebellion used you as a pawn, *not us*. They were the ones demanding you marry Tehl; it was not our idea. It was *our* crown prince who made certain to set up stipulations for your benefit, not his, because your people did not seem to see fit to do so. The rebellion promised war if he did not do what they asked, and so he thought, not of himself, but of others. Do you think he wants you for a wife any more than you want him for a husband?"

That pierced her. She was broken, used up. No man would want her.

"Instead of grabbing you and taking you back to the palace where you would have no choice, he gave you three days to decide. It is in your hands, not his. Tehl gave you that. Your crown prince gave you the option of freedom, not Rafe, or the rebellion. Just Tehl." Gavriel's chest heaved, and he ruffled his midnight hair in agitation before picking back up. "Those men you call friends sold you while you were defenseless. Tehl stood up for you. If you return to the palace, none of those men will see you again."

Sage gasped at that. How dare the crown prince dictate whom she saw? "He will never tell me how to run my life."

Gav's face reddened. "He wasn't trying to control you, but protect you from your betrayers," he hissed.

Sage wanted to scream. She stepped closer to Gav, not quite knowing what she would do, when a musical voice called across the deck to them.

"You have had your say, my lord. Maybe it is time for you to leave her to my care. Your prince left it to me to be certain she was apprised of the previous night's events."

Gavriel's eyes left her to stare at the woman behind her. He sucked in a breath before looking back down at her. "I have been stationed here for your protection for the next three days. If you need me simply call for me."

He dipped his chin and stalked toward the ramp. Even with all the anger and confusion swirling around her, she didn't want them to part ways angry at each other. "Gav," she called. He peered over his shoulder at her. "Thank you for everything. You have gone well beyond what is necessary."

"I am always here for you," he said, just before he disappeared.

Lilja sidled over, ogling Gav as he placed himself on a barrel overlooking the sea and the Sirenidae. "Such a handsome man, that one. Such unique eyes."

"You're one to talk," Sage remarked.

The aforementioned magenta eyes turned back to her, somber. "We have serious matters to discuss, *ma fleur*. Let's go to the kitchen, and I will make us some tea and biscuits."

Lilja took Sage's cold hand and drew her into the warm kitchen, sitting her down on one of many luxurious pillows in the corner. She closed her eyes, listening as her friend bustled around the area. Before she knew it, a cup of something hot that smelled like lavender and chocolate was pressed into her hands. Sage sniffed as something sweet tantalized her nose. She cracked her eyes, squinting suspiciously at Lilja.

"It's just a little lavender oil, nothing which could affect you adversely." Lilja *tsked*. "So untrusting."

"Well, events these past two months have given me good reason to be," Sage retorted. She leaned into the pillow and relaxed, listening to Lilja hum and cook. The swish of her skirt alerted her to Captain Femi at her side. Her exotic friend folded herself gracefully onto the pillow across from her, examining her.

"He shouldn't have touched you." Lilja's eyes darkened. "You were fine until that cur dared to touch your cheek. If Gavriel hadn't pushed him out of the way, I was planning on grabbing one of Rafe's Griffin blades and stabbing that man." Her lips pursed. "Yet you froze, gone from the world. What happened?"

Sage looked down into her tea. "Terror. And memories. I was trapped."

Lilja touched her foot in comfort. "Are you ready to discuss what happened last night?"

Sage's face hardened. "I don't think I need to hear anything from you."

Lilja gave her a stubborn look. "You will listen to what I have to say." They glared at each other in stony silence before the captain continued. "The treaty was signed by both sides last night, but it hinges on your decision. Hayjen informed me that your marriage to the prince had not been contained in the original list of demands from the rebellion. They believe that the advisors don't hold real power, and, to an extent, this is true, but I don't feel a forced marriage is a good solution. Unfortunately, it's not my decision. It's important to note that the every representative from their side voted for it, save Rafe and Mason." Lilja frowned. "Rafe wants you for himself, you know. Hence the little display with the Griffin blades."

Sage dropped her eyes, glaring at the floor. "I know."

Lilja's laugh rippled through the room. "Indeed you do. That was abundantly clear when you plopped his blades onto the bar without a care. It was an excellent move, but I am afraid we're digressing." Lilja sighed. "I observed the crown prince wrestle with his decision before he agreed to their demand regarding you. Despite his ire at having been put in the situation, he made efforts to protect you. He required that you might be given time to choose—three days—and if you acquiesce, none of rebellion circle are to have contact with you again. This was not high-handed, you know. It prevents them from using or hurting you again." Lilja sent her a severe look. "The crown prince also didn't want you to go into it blind. If you marry him, it will not be an easy life. You will be on display, your life will not be your own."

A harsh chuckle burst out of Sage. "Has it ever?"

Lilja's mouth turned down, but she continued. "The kings and queens of the past have always been bound by love which foments mutual respect and loyalty for one another. Your marriage won't be based on that, you will have to try to succeed without it. For a large part of this, you may need to live a ruse. Any moment you are not alone you will have to play the part, you must pretend to love the crown prince. You know the nation requires heirs as well. It would be your duty to give them to him."

Sage blanched, horror choking her. Heirs? Never. Mutiny must have shown on her face because Lilja gave her a stern look. "He entrusted me with this information. The prince did not want you agreeing to this treaty blind. There is a huge responsibility set on you both."

"I won't do it."

"Then many will die."

Sage blinked at her friend, hurt. "I thought you cared about me. You agree with them? You support this"

Lilja shook her head fiercely. "You misunderstand me. I would spirit you away tonight if you wanted, but you need to consider the cost. Can you live with the civil war that will spring up when you say no? Some could, but I doubt you are one of them. You have a strong sense of duty and love for people. Every person that died in the rebellion, you would feel personally."

"So you would condemn me to life in a gilded cage? I've been a sword maker's daughter, a peasant, an officer of the rebellion even. I am not a princess. I am not a queen."

"All of those things will make you a brilliant queen. Just think about it."

"I don't need to, I don't want it." Having to spend the rest of her life with the crown prince made her want to throw up.

"In three days, if you want out, I will protect you, but think carefully until then." Captain Femi rolled onto her knees and kissed her forehead. The Sirenidae sauntered to the oven, pulling out the buttery biscuits.

Sage's decision would affect everyone in their kingdom. Lilja was right when she'd said Sage would feel each death keenly if she refused. *Could* she live with that? An unreasonable part of her said she could, but she knew herself better. Loneliness and uncertainty filled her. What was she doing? She needed someone to support her, someone to talk to. "I need my mum."

Lilja flashed a smile over her shoulder. "Done. I've already sent for her."

Her mum's arms felt wonderful around her. She wasn't a little girl anymore, but there was something comforting about being hugged by her mum. What would happen to her family if she married? Sage shoved the thought away and enjoyed the day with Lilja and her mum. They regaled her with stories of their youth. Sage was still curious how they met, but they skirted around that story with skill that would make the spymaster proud. Sage laughed until her belly cramped. But when the sun set, so did her happy mood. Her mum would go back to the family, and she would stay here.

"Love, I know you have a lot on your mind, but I wanted to let you know that your papa and myself love you so much, and we are so proud of you. We raised you to be strong, independent, hardworking, kind, and loving. You are all those things and more." Her mum softly brushed her cheek. "You have taken care of us for so long. You have a weighty decision to make, but we don't want you to base it on us. You have done enough." Her mum's eyes grew damp. "I wanted to thank you for the doctor. Jacob has been a miracle. Papa is already doing better."

So they'd kept their promise. "They already sent Jacob to you?"

Her mum smiled. "He has been visiting every other day for two weeks."

Sage hadn't expected that. The Crown had kept their word. "After everything I went through, Mum, I knew I wouldn't find a fabulous match, but I hoped to find someone who would love me like you and Papa love each other. If I choose this life, I will never have that. My life will belong to someone else." She shuddered. "I am required to give him heirs, and I don't think I can do that."

"We will support you in whatever decision you make, baby girl. Never sell yourself short." Her mum wiggled her eyebrows. "From my understanding, you have yet to give him *your* demands."

Sage smiled. Her mum was brilliant. She crushed her mother against her, trying to memorize how it was to hug her. "I love you, Mum."

"And I you, daughter."

Her mum said her goodbyes, and Hayjen escorted her home. Sage waved to Lilja and slipped into her room. She ended up staring at the ceiling most of the night arguing with herself, trying to rationalize saying no. By the time morning came, exhaustion plagued her, but knew she had no choice.

She had to marry Tehl.

ELEVEN

SAGE

SAGE STOMPED ACROSS THE DECK to the captain's cabin. She felt ready to tear apart the world. Was there no justice in the land?

Roughly, she banged on the door. Hayjen yanked open the door, blinking furiously, his enormous torso on display along with bare feet and loosely-laced breeches. She winced, feeling badly for waking him, but grateful she hadn't been subjected to the sight of Lilja's naked body. Sage studiously stared at his collarbone, embarrassed. "I am sorry to wake you, but I will need you to arrange a meeting with the circle for this evening."

Hayjen smiled, his ice blue eyes sparkling. "Raising a little hell, are we?"

Sage's smile was wicked. "Indeed." She nodded and spun on her heel, concluding that she would spend the day however she pleased. Soon, her life would belong to someone else; she had to make the most of the time that was hers.

She spent most of the day lying in the sun and gossiping with Lilja. The highlight of their time together was when the two of them went for a swim. It was pure joy to spend time with sea creatures and experience the ocean the way Lilja experienced it, beneath its surface. Living as a part of it. Then, as soon as Sage would lose her breath, the captain would shoot them to the surface. Again and again, they dove. It was another world, entirely foreign yet wondrous. The only time she'd been alarmed was when a pair of leviathans became curious about them, even following them around for a time. Lilja had assured her they wouldn't attack, but Sage's heart still pumped frantically when one bumped her with his smooth snout. Later, when her lungs could take no more, they made their way back to the Sirenidae and dried in the sun, napping wherever they fancied.

Sage flopped her head to the side, smiling drowsily at Captain Femi. When was the last time she'd had such a peaceful day? "Thank you for today. I suspect I'll not have many more days like this in the future."

Lilja's smile dimmed. "Always find time for days like today. You will always be welcome here you know."

Sage snatched her hand and squeezed. "I will visit." Sage scanned Lilja's face, noting again the absence of the fine lines found in her mum's face. "Why do you look so much younger than my mum? You're the same age." She'd been wanting to ask it for so long.

Sadness tinged Captain Femi's features. "I am actually older than your mum. It is a Sirenidae trait. The sea rejuvenates us and so does a certain algae that grows deep in the ocean. We live longer lives."

"Hayjen?" she asked.

Lilja smiled. "He looks younger than he is."

Now that surprised her. "Is he Sirenidae too?"

"No, but the algae heals and restores the human body."

Sage mulled that over. It must be a well-kept secret. The Sirenidae would no doubt be hunted if word spread. "That is dangerous information."

"It is. And, as queen, you will handle such information."

She froze, and then forced her body to relax. "I will be queen in name only."

"Only if you allow it."

She smiled weakly before standing up, noting the hour. "We will see. For now, it's time to wreak havoc."

Rafe's voice carried through the thick door, and her ire increased, fueling the sense of betrayal she already felt. Sage smiled to herself. She would go down fighting. She kicked the door open with the heel of her boot and sauntered in. Startled eyes snapped to her as she gave them a sharp smile, stopping at the end of their table. She had their attention. "Good evening, *brothers*," she said, a hard edge to her voice. "Sacrificing virgins, are we?"

Everyone flinched save Hayjen, who was grinning like a loon, and Rafe, who looked like he wanted to leap over the table and throttle her. She noted that the monster wasn't at the table… She hoped maybe someone had stabbed him. Brushing aside her morbid thoughts, she focused on the table of traitors before her.

"Sage—" Mason started but cut off when her angry eyes landed on him.

"I joined the rebellion to help our people. I believed you were my brothers in arms, but there have been several times now that you have betrayed me." Sage jabbed a finger at the empty spot. "That man is despicable, yet you turned a blind eye to his crimes and blamed me for protecting myself. You are corrupt."

"How dare you…" Madden began.

"Yes, I dare," Sage shouted over him. "You lot sanctioned the king's murder! Not only that, but you sent *me* to do it! And you knew what going back there would be like for me!"

"If it was so wrong, why agree to be a part of the assassination then?" Noah questioned.

She smiled, baring her teeth. "Of course I agreed, I could never let you hurt someone I love. Had I refused you would've only sent someone else. How could I protect him if I wasn't there?"

The room stilled, the air thick with tension.

"What?" Rafe grated out.

Sage met his furious eyes, her own gaze unwavering. It hurt when someone deceived you, she knew that. "It's not pleasant, is it? To wonder what other secrets have been kept from you? What things were real and what was fake?" His jaw tensed. She smiled at the table. "No matter what the rebellion meant to me, I will never compromise my own honor or morals. Not for you. Not for anyone."

"So you didn't make an attempt on the king's life?" Badiah asked, incredulous.

Her lips twitched. "I attempted, just not very well."

"You lied to us?" Mason inquired in a hurt tone.

"Traitors don't belong in the circle," Madden snarked.

She laughed humorlessly. "I agree." She met his stare squarely, and, after a moment, he dropped his eyes. "I relinquish my place in your circle. Never will I work with or for you again. I hope never to see your faces again, which will most likely be the case as you've already sold me off."

Mason and Noah's faces blanched.

Her smile turned grim. "I was vulnerable the night of the treaty, it was obvious—but, rather than having a care for me, you made your grab for power. You used me to get your own way, without even bothering to get my consent, as if I were merely a bag of goods to exchange. You disgust me." She sucked in a breath, trying to control her rolling emotions. She met each of their gazes, one by one. "You got what you wanted. I will marry the prince." A stunned silence followed her statement. "This is goodbye, gentlemen. The crown prince made himself clear. If any of you seek me out, you will be harshly dealt with. You're wretched, but I don't wish for you to be harmed, so listen. You *will* honor the treaty, or I will personally hunt you down." Sage lifted a brow. "And I know all of your tricks. Don't forget why you've called me the rebel's blade." After issuing her threat, she confidently sauntered from the room, though her heart beat furiously in her chest. A giant roar came from behind her and Sage's eyes widened, the back of her neck prickling. One of Rafe's famous tempers was about to ensue.

"SAGE!"

Sage picked up her feet, full out running down the tunnels.

"Don't you dare run from me!" he shouted.

Her breath caught at how close he sounded. Damn, he was fast! She rounded a corner and sprinted toward an intersection of many tunnels, but she skidded to a stop when Rafe stepped into the middle, not even ten paces away.

How did he do that? Sage blinked, quickly scanning the tunnels. He must have shortcuts. "What do you want?" she bit out.

His chest heaved violently while he watched her. "What are you thinking?"

"That I only have one more evening of freedom before I am chained to my enemy because of you. Excuse me." She straightened, as if to walk around him. "I don't intend to spend it with *you*."

He took one step forward, and she countered it, watching him warily. He cocked his head in an almost canine way, studying each move as she made it. It was creepy. Something in her eyes must have given away her thoughts because he raised his arms carefully, like he was trying to calm a skittish horse.

"It was taken out of my hands. They outvoted me. But all of that is unimportant." He squared his shoulders, holding his hand out for her to take. "You don't have to marry that toad. I can take you away from here. To freedom. Come with me to Methi."

She paused, her brows wrinkling in confusion. What was he talking about? "Methi?"

He took a step closer "Yes, my homeland. I can protect you. We can take care of your family. Just say yes, and I will take care of everything."

Homeland? How could that be? He wasn't Aermian? "What are you talking about? You're from Methi?" Sage accused, her mind scrambling to catch up.

"I am."

Sage gaped. Who *was* this man? "But why lie?"

Rafe exhaled a frustrated breath. "There are many things I need to tell you, but for now just know that I was sent here to help. I came to make Aermia stronger."

"Make Aermia stronger? You're a damn Methi spy leading *our* rebellion!"

"You're making it sound worse than it is. If Aermia is weak, they would open a path for the Scythians. We could not allow the fate of Negali to become ours."

Her mind reeled, but at the same time, many things clicked into place. That's why he'd been so sure Methi wouldn't retaliate when he'd impersonated their prince. It had, no doubt, already been sanctioned. They had sent spies to Aermia to cause mischief. His style of combat was so unique, unlike anyone she'd ever seen, and, in her innocence, she chalked it up to not being well traveled. But they had all been merely pawns. Had Rafe ever cared for Aermia or its people? She placed a hand against the stone wall to keep herself upright. This secret impacted everything. "And what of Aermia?" She eyed his outstretched hand mere paces from her.

He shrugged, as if this wasn't any of his concern. "They can fend for themselves. The crown prince isn't a complete moron. The treaty was signed, so the rebellion has to uphold it." He took a step closer. "Aermia has been solidified now. There is no chance for civil war."

"You're the one who stirred up the rebellion in the first place! We wouldn't have to deal with the threat of civil war if it wasn't for your meddling."

He waved away her statement. "The people were working themselves up to it already. I only shaped the outcome so that it could lead to something successful. It worked out for everyone."

Rage choked her. Worked out well for *everyone*? Her face heated. It most certainly did not work out well for *her*. This man was not the man she had come to know, love, and trust. Every time he opened his mouth, he unlocked another great secret. Did he know how to speak truth? What was she to believe? Sage stood upright, lifting her chin in challenge. "You're a liar."

"I am a spy."

No remorse. Like everything he had done was justified. It wasn't. Not everything was black and white, but right and wrong still mattered. Sage stormed forward and shoved past him. A large hand gripped her wrist, a deep growl emanating from him. Sage halted, her hair lifting on the back of her neck at the menacing sound. Sucking in a deep breath, she faced the beast of a man, ready to defend herself. She caught a brief glimpse of pain etched into his face, just before Rafe dropped to his knees and wrapped his muscled arms around her. Sage tensed as he curled his back, resting his forehead below her breasts.

"Please, please, forgive me. I have been trying to protect my people, help Aermia, and protect you as well. It's too much. I can't control everything, no matter how much I try. Sage, I am so sorry."

It was surreal to have the man she'd always viewed as her mentor kneeling at her feet, begging for forgiveness, his voice full of remorse. His actions would affect the rest of her life and others' lives too. Rafe had lied to her from the beginning, while she had gulped it all down, never doubting for a moment. Sure, she understood he kept things from her—that was a necessity of the life they had chosen. But she never dreamed everything she had grown to love about him would be a complete lie. Could she forgive him for what had taken place? Maybe a year ago, she may have. However, she was, in many ways, a different person now. She hesitantly lifted a hand, running it through his dark wine-colored hair. Her hand looked so small and pale in contrast.

Sage's eyes widened as a gentle purr vibrated against her stomach. "What is that?" she whispered.

"It means I love you," he mumbled into her vest.

Sage froze, her hand clutching his hair. How dare he say that after everything! No, he didn't mean it, he couldn't.

Rafe lifted his head and gazed up at her, golden eyes gleaming. Carefully, he untangled her hand and stood, slipping his hands along her waist. She braced her hands against his strong chest, squeezing her eyes shut. A sob tried to escape, but she pinched her lips. Why was he doing this now? Everything was so messed up. He dropped his forehead to hers, soft breath puffing into her face.

"I have adored you ever since I saw you in the forest practicing swordplay, each of your movements graceful and smooth. I almost believed you to be Methian until I caught sight of those stunning green of your eyes." He moved, his nose grazing her temple, ruffling the hair there. "You were mine from the beginning."

Her breath whooshed out of her when he tipped her chin up. Sage opened her eyes to meet the serious gaze searching hers with an intensity she'd never before experienced from him nor anyone else. Rafe must have found what he was looking for because he closed the distance, and pressed his lips against hers.

This wasn't happening.

She kept her lips still as he gently explored, holding her breath. When she couldn't hold it anymore, her lips parted as she exhaled. Rafe's arms tightened around her, pressing her along his hard body. She jerked back when he nipped her bottom lip. Rafe rumbled his displeasure and opened his liquid golden eyes.

"Finally, you're mine," he sighed, a gorgeous smile lighting his face, and puckering his scar. "Mine. My companion, my mate, after all these years," he murmured, a look of wonder on his face.

Sage struggled to form a complete thought with the whirlwind of emotions battling inside her, she felt like a ship in a storm. She wanted to cry, scream, punch, and hug him all at once but she was still hung up on the word 'mate'. What an old-fashioned word for spouse. She wasn't ready to be anyone's *mate*, and yet she already had a betrothed. Despite all the deceit and anger swirling inside, she couldn't dismiss him. Sage wanted to say ugly things and hurt him as he had hurt her, but she wouldn't. This would be the last time they would see each other. She had to send him away with peace between them.

Sage hesitated a moment before cupping his cheeks. He tilted his face into her touch then turned his face, kissing her palm tenderly. She swallowed her emotions and focused on the man gazing at her in adoration. "Rafe." She paused, licking her lips, him following the movement with heat in his eyes. Fear spiked through her at the look, but she tamped it down and focused on what she had to say. How was she going to let him down without hurting him? "I... I forgive you, but that doesn't change the fact that if I do not marry the crown prince, there will be civil war." Sage dropped her hands and pulled his from around her waist. She clutched them to her chest and kissed each hand. "I am not your mate." She gave him gave him a pleading look. "Even if I had the choice, I wouldn't marry. Marriage needs honesty, and you have proven yourself not capable of it. You're a stranger to me." She gentled her words by squeezing his hands.

Sage braced herself when Rafe stilled, all warmth evaporating, his face looking like it was carved from stone. "You are. You belong to only me. I know it." His tone brooked no argument.

Her lips thinned while she attempted to control her frustration. "I am not, nor will I ever be, yours. You cannot own someone. They have to give themselves to you, and you give yourself in return. I am sorry." The sadness in her heart made it hard to speak. She dropped his hands and stretched to her tiptoes, kissing his stubbled cheek, which still hadn't so much as twitched. "Forgive me," she whispered, sparing him a final glance before stepping around him, eyes burning with unshed tears.

His hand wrapped around her bicep, halting her. "Please, I didn't mean it," he whispered in a broken voice.

Sage looked down at his overlapping fingers, then her eyes trailed up to his anguished face. "I understand that you are, but I can't right now. Please let go." When he didn't move she added, "don't make me fight you, Rafe. Let us part with peace between us."

She watched as his eyes seemed to ice over and he looked fierce once again. "I will never let go of my mate. What is it really?" he said coldly. "Are you anxious to run back to the royals' beds? The three princes seem to hold more affection for you than seems ordinary."

His accusation pierced her, and any remorse she felt for hurting him evaporated. Sage wrenched out of his hold and slapped him with everything she had. Her hand pulsed as she pulled back, pain radiating up her arm. Rafe touched his face, abandoning his stone impression, regret softening his face. Sage tucked her hurt hand against her belly and stabbed her other hand at him.

"You *know* those rumors to be false. How dare you! You may have sold me to the Crown, but I am not a whore. How dare you speak in such a way!" She glared at him, a tear slipping down her face. "You can only belong to someone if you give yourself to them, I never did, Rafe."

"But you've always been mine."

"What does 'mine' even mean? Yours to play with? Manipulate? Train? Lie to? Sell? What Rafe? What?"

A vicious growl rumbled out of him. "Just *mine*. Mine to protect, possess, love, and care for."

"Why would I trust you with any of those things after what you have done?" Sage swallowed hard. "You've hurt me deeper than anyone has. You claim to love me, to want to protect and care for me? But Rafe, you broke me," she whispered. "*You* broke me, no one else."

Understanding dawned, and shame blanketed his face. He heaved, clutching his stomach like she'd kicked him, and stumbled to the wall, leaning heavily against it. Rafe gurgled twice trying to speak, but it was like words were stuck in the back of his throat. "Breezes of old, what have I done?" he choked out. "Forgive me, little one. I—I failed you."

Once again, he dropped to his knees. But this time it didn't look like he would get up. He looked as broken on the outside as Sage felt on the inside.

She swallowed and shook her head. How could she forgive him? How many times must she turn the other cheek just for him to stab her again? But the broken man on the floor tugged at her heart. Anger stirred in her gut as guilt still managed to prick her conscience over his feelings. "In time, perhaps," she muttered woodenly. "But I can't deal with you right now. Goodbye, Rafe." She spun, half running to get away.

"I love you, little one. I'm so sorry." His strangled voice echoed behind her.

Sage pushed herself harder, hoping to outrun the pain, guilt, hate, and love swirling inside her.

Once she hit ground level, Sage wove through the streets of Sanee toward the castle. The closer she got, the sicker she became. She couldn't trust Rafe not to disappear with her in the night, and she didn't trust that one of the rebellion wouldn't try to have her killed or detained until the three days were up. To go back home, or even to the Sirenidae, would place those she loved in much danger. She slowed her pace and let herself finally process all the feelings she'd held back until now, the tears pouring down her face. Tucking her mussed hair beneath her cloak, she pulled the hood up, wanting to mourn the loss of her freedom with a measure of privacy. She mourned the loss of a life she always thought she could have, the trust and friendship she'd lost with Rafe, and, throughout this whole ordeal, the loss of her very self somewhere along the way. The betrayal, the rejection, every tumultuous feeling in her heart broke free. She wandered around, letting herself settle and trying to get herself together. When finally she'd found a measure of peace, her last tear dry, she'd neared the castle's outer wall. As she approached, it felt very much like she was walking to her execution. It was then that Lilja materialized at her side. No doubt the Sirenidae had been following her for some time.

"Heading in early?"

"No other choice."

"Come back with Hayjen and I for the night, or, if you need, we could set sail, perhaps spirit you away from here for now."

Her heart squeezed at the sincerity and concern she detected in Lilja's voice. She didn't know what she did to deserve such a wonderful friend, but was certainly grateful for Lilja's support. "Thank you, but no." She smiled softly. "I have made my choices, and they all lead me here. I cannot let others suffer when it's within my power to prevent it, nor can I continue to sacrifice the safety of my family for my own freedom, no matter how I long for it."

"Difficult as this may be, I hope you know: you *are* making a wise decision, *ma fleur*."

Sage nodded, swallowed, and stepped through the gate. Her heart raced as they passed through the second gate and into the courtyard. She spotted the Elite training on her right, and she watched briefly, before a familiar head of salt and pepper hair caught her attention. She meandered toward the training yard, pressing past several Elite who sent questioning glances her way. Pretending not to notice, she leaned against the fence to watch the sparring. Zachael slammed his sword into his opponent, twisting and striking with a speed that made her smile. Finally, the older man placed the tip of a dagger underneath the younger man's chin. The young soldier nodded, and the combat master removed the dagger from the man's throat. He glanced her way, and she registered surprise on his tanned face. Apparently he wasn't expecting her. Sage forced a grin. "Is that all you've got, old man?" A sea of eyes turned to her, the attention prickling uncomfortably under her skin. She suppressed the desire to run away, panicked, and lifted her chin.

His eyes sparkled as he placed the tip of his sword in the dirt. "Old man? Who, exactly, are you talking to, Sage? I don't see anyone of that description here."

"That last trick an infant could have executed." Male sniggers surrounded them. Lilja muttered something about picking a fight and being upset, but she ignored it for now. "Plus, that's not how you handle a sword."

"Why don't you show me how it's done, little miss?"

The sniggers stopped at the combat masters taunt. She smiled inwardly at the looks of interest from the elite. She may have to put on a false front in every other area of her life right up until she died but this was one place she would never have to. Clambering up the fence, she swung a leg over and dropped into the practice ring.

"Daggers or swords?" she questioned.

"Both?"

This time, her grin was genuine. Daggers were unquestionably her favorite blades. Zachael returned her grin with a wicked smile, though it was not unfriendly, and she decided then that she would like this man. Maybe she would spend her time here, training with the Elite. It would certainly be both beneficial and enjoyable. She pulled her own sword from its scabbard, excitement bubbling inside her for the first time in a long while. She clenched her teeth together to keep them from chattering. It was an odd thing that always happened, that and her blood sang just before she sparred. Sage loved a good bout. She stepped toward the combat master and allowed herself another smirk.

"I hope you're prepared to lose."

The older man grinned. "En garde."

TWELVE

TEHL

HE FINALLY FINISHED UP THE stacks of necessary paperwork to restore the homes destroyed by the Scythian raids. Tehl sighed and sat back, trying to work out the kinks in his spine as he admired the pink evening sky. Sunsets were his favorite.

A knock sounded at the door, interrupting his moment of peace.

"Enter."

Sam sauntered in, a smile plastered on his face in a way that put him on edge. That particular smile never boded well.

"I have some interesting news."

"Oh?" he asked, warily.

His brother's smile widened. "It seems your betrothed is putting Zachael through his paces."

Tehl blinked. Betrothed? So she had arrived then? She actually came? Mixed feelings of anxiety and relief warred within him. There wouldn't be a civil war, but it meant fighting his own mini-war at home, one he must battle alone while seeming at peace in public. Sam's words finally registered in his mind, distracting him from the depressing direction of his thoughts. Paces? "She's doing what?"

"She's annihilating him. Come and see for yourself."

Tehl stood, rushing toward the door, but just as suddenly, jerked to a stop before actually going through it. Once he was on the other side of that door, everything would change.

Sam bumped his shoulder, studying him with serious eyes.

"Are you prepared for this? From this moment on, things can never go back to they are now." He paused. "You know I will be by your side. I will support you every step of the way in this…and I'll do the same for Sage."

Surprised, Tehl stared at his brother with raised brows.

Sam rolled his eyes. "Don't give me that look. You don't have to leave your home, friends, family, and everything familiar behind. You were born into this life. As a matter of fact, it's all you know, yet despite this, it's still difficult at times. She's being thrown into this mess without any preparation and very little understanding."

Tehl nodded, acknowledging his brother's point. He couldn't begrudge her the support she would obviously need. Ruling was no cakewalk; it was a grueling set of ever-present responsibilities and burdens. He straightened his spin and stepped forward. Time to move ahead.

He shoved the door open, moving down the stairs and through the castle with Sam trailing behind him, silently. Tehl strode into the training yard but quickly halted to marvel at the match taking place in the ring. Sage and Zachael were engaged in a deadly dance: twisting, spinning, lunging, and blocking so fluidly that a surge of pride welled up within him. He may not have asked for this bride, but Sage had potential to be a remarkable queen. She was ferociously beautiful with sweat beading her brow and a slight smile touching her lips, her sword flashing. For the first time since Tehl had met her, she looked truly exquisite; she looked free.

"My god," Sam breathed. "You're marrying a damn warrior goddess. I think I've got betrothal envy."

Tehl snorted, never taking his eyes off the green-eyed woman currently out maneuvering his combat master. "You love too many women."

"I would be a one-woman man for her."

He winced as Zachael landed a heavy blow, knocking her to her knees, but in response, she swept his legs out from underneath him. The combat master crashed to the ground in a cloud of dust. Before he could rise, she touched both her dagger and sword to the man's neck.

"Yield."

Tehl tried not to gape when his combat master broke into the largest grin he had ever witnessed on the older man's face.

"Well done, missy, it has been a long time since someone could best me."

Sage threw her head back and laughed, the joyful sound putting smiles on the faces of all in the area. Tehl hung back, still observing, as the Elite moved in on her. One helped her up from the ground, another flirted, and yet another one inquired about her blades. Shortly, though, she shied away from them, the genuineness of her smile bleeding away as it turned forced.

"You better go claim your betrothed before another attempts to steal her away." Sam clasped him on the shoulder. "Ready yourself, brother. You need to play a ridiculously besotted version of yourself. Everyone knows you're awkward."

Tehl flashed Sam a filthy look and marched toward his men as they circled Sage. One caught his gaze and bowed before moving. In the blink of an eye, the others followed suit, and he found himself standing before her. Sage blinked repeatedly, her hands tightened on her dagger. Warily, he closed the distance between them. Before he could second guess himself, or give her the opportunity to stab him, he wrapped his arms around her hips, lifting her so they were the same height. Gazing into her startled eyes, he pressed a chaste kiss to her mouth. It wasn't even a kiss, rather it was simply a pressing together of mouths. She dipped her head so her loose hair curtained around their faces. Sage slipped her arms around his neck, never looking away, and her eyes narrowed. Her expression promised retribution. He scowled back. He hadn't even really kissed her.

Whistles and crass jokes interrupted their stare off. Tehl pulled back and slowly lowered her to the ground, like he was reluctant to let her go. In reality, he was only hoping her arms could stay where they were so he'd know she wasn't grabbing her weapons.

She dropped her gaze, now staring at his wrinkled shirt. He ran his hands down her arms to cup her elbows, wishing he could see her face. If he could see her face, he could anticipate her next move. Her body tensed under his hands, and she tilted her head just enough so that the flat line of her mouth was visible. So concerned about selling his performance, he didn't think about how she would react. If she didn't wipe the rage off her face, everything would be ruined before it even started. He leaned down to her ear. "Smile, darling."

Sage darted a quick glance to the Elite but wiped all expression from her face when she seemed to spot something. Tehl followed her line of sight to the exotic woman from the treatise meeting, Captain Femi. The white-haired captain gazed back evenly at the girl. They stared at each other as if in silent conversation.

Sage's eyes shuttered as she turned back to him. He could tell she reeled in her anger, and then she slipped into character.

"I came early. I hope that's all right." She peered up at him through her lashes, placing a hand on his chest. "I just couldn't stay parted from you," she murmured with a sly smile.

Tehl blinked at her, coughing once. She was good when she wanted to be. "This is where you belong." She blinked at him and raised an eyebrow.

Heat scorched the back of his neck. *That was the best he could come up with?* He wanted to bang his head on the fence. Tehl slid one hand to the back of her neck and licked his lips. Maybe he should just kiss her again and stop making an ass of himself.

Something flashed through her eyes when he leaned toward her. Then the world tilted, and his breath was knocked out of him. Tehl blinked, disoriented. How had that happened? A smug feminine face entered his vision as she squatted beside him, her hand still on his wheezing chest.

"My prince," she cooed. "I think you need to keep your hands to yourself. We are yet to be married. What would your people think of such displays of affection?"

Tehl growled at her, his lungs screaming. His focus shifted to the Elite leaning closer to catch every word. Gossip whores. Sometimes, his men were worse than the old biddies of his court.

Zachael stepped next to him, teeth flashing in an amused grin. "You need practice, my prince. She swept your feet clean out from under you well before you knew what was happening."

"She tends to do that," Tehl remarked in a dry tone.

Sage brushed her chestnut hair from her face as she stood. Tehl waited to see if she would extend her hand. When you knocked someone down during a bout, it was good sportsmanship to help them up. A moment passed and another. Well, he had his answer. He started to sit when she shoved her hand into his face. Tehl eyed it like it was a snake. Would she help him up or try to drop him again?

Her hand wiggled in front of his face impatiently. An idea took root in his mind that made him want to grin. It was time to channel his brother. He grasped her hand and jerked it, pulling her off her feet. She stumbled and fell onto his chest in a heap. A bitty growl bubbled from her throat. Check mate. "My lady, I am not concerned about what anyone thinks." She struggled to stand, but he kept her still, banding his arms around her waist. Raising his voice, he asked, "I assure you that most of the surrounding men are green with envy, am I right?"

A chorus male agreement thundered around them

"Let go, my lord, you are causing a scene," she hissed between clenched teeth.

"This is entertaining, but you have yet to introduce her to the men," Zachael commented.

Sage flashed the combat master a thankful smile even as Tehl scowled, making the men around him chuckle. Tehl kept an arm around her small waist and stood, facing his men. She tried to escape, but he linked their fingers and squeezed her hand. Sage halted her wriggling and stood placidly before him. Her hand felt oddly small in his. When was the last time he'd held hands with a woman? Even though her fingers were delicate, there were calluses on them. At least she was a hard worker. Tehl cleared his throat and raised their linked hands. "Men! Meet my betrothed."

Ear-rupturing shouts and congratulations were flung their way. Sage stilled, her fingers tightening when his men circled them. Tehl felt her shudder when Garreth kissed her free hand, murmuring his congratulations. He met his brother's eyes, darting a glance to the overwhelmed female beside him.

Sam eyed her and shoved everyone aside. "You came home at last! I always wanted a sister to bother. Think of the trouble we can cause." Sam grinned wickedly.

Some of her unease slipped away as Sam approached. Tehl noted her lips twitching, like she was fighting a smile.

"Come give me a hug, sister." Sam held his arms out.

Sage tugged her hand from his and tapped the arm circling her waist. Tehl released her, grinning at the way she stared his brother down.

"I would rather eat coral."

Stubborn wench. At least it was directed at someone other than him this time.

Much laughter and teasing erupted around them. Sam pouted for a moment, pretending to be heartbroken. Sage raised a winged brow at his attempt to sway her. Finally, dropping all pretenses, he lunged for Sage, taking her by surprise. A startled yelp burst out of her when he swung her into his arms like a bride. "You and I both know how dull my brother can be. Why don't we settle you in and see what mischief we can cause?"

"I know exactly what kind of mischief you cause, and I want no part of it."

Sam winked at him and marched toward the castle. "How would you know?"

Tehl sniggered as his unlikely betrothed struggled with Sam, starting in on a huffy rant. "I heard all kinds of stories from Zeke and Seb about…" Her voice faded out as they disappeared through the castle doors. He glanced at the captain as she untangled herself from one of his men, heading in the direction Sam had taken Sage.

That was his cue to leave. "I better rescue my bride before my brother tries to steal her from me."

He said it only half joking. Tehl saluted Zachael and trotted after them. When he found Sam, his brother was whispering something in Sage's ear. She went rigid in his brother's arms and glanced over Sam's shoulder at him.

"We have much to discuss." Sage said.

Tehl nodded. "In private."

He jogged up the stairs, preparing himself for the battle ahead. They arrived at his study more quickly than he would have liked. He held the door open until all three filed in after him. Tehl shut the door and locked it before turning around.

Sage wiggled out of Sam's arms, almost landing on her face in the process.

"Don't be an idiot," Sam scolded. "I wouldn't hurt you."

"I didn't want you touching me and look! Now you are not," she retorted.

"Mission accomplished." She turned to him. "As for you, my lord, don't you ever put your slobbering lips on me again without my consent."

Slobbering lips? Hardly. "If I was slobbering on you, you would feel it. I am sure nuns have experienced more passionate kisses than what I gave you. You can't even call that a kiss."

He ran his hands through his hair and shot Captain Femi a look. Did the woman wear nothing but bright colors? Just gazing at her hurt his eyes. "You explained everything to her?"

"Yes."

Tehl turned back to Sage.

The rebel.

Also his betrothed. That was odd.

"I did what I had to. It was only to keep our secret. I was *not* making any advances. You know as well as I do that I needed to make them believe we're in love. Not sure if we did, but at least *I* did my best." He took in her crossed arms, cocked hip, and agitated expression. She wasn't happy to be here. "Have you come of your own free will?" The question lingered in the air.

Her jaw tightened, and she nodded once. "Yes." She lifted her eyes from the floor and met his gaze head on. "No one forced me. The thought went through my mind to run."

He appreciated her frankness. "I understand."

"No, you do not." A shrug. "But I could never condemn our people that way. If this prevents bloodshed then I am duty bound." A sardonic smile twisted her pink lips. "In my line of work I have become well acquainted with acting. We both have our respective roles, but I would appreciate it if you warn me before you touch me, though it would be better if you didn't have to touch me at all," she added.

His head whipped to the captain. Sage didn't sound like she had been apprised of all his stipulations. "All?"

"All," Captain Femi replied tersely.

He blew out a breath. They needed to speak about heirs. It wasn't a conversation he wanted to have, but he was never one to beat around the bush. "And what of heirs?" Tehl's stomach clenched at the horror that passed over Sage's face leaving her ashen.

She gulped and threw her shoulders back. "As the crown prince, I understand the need for heirs to secure the throne. I thought of a solution that will suit both of us."

"Okay," he drew out, not knowing where she was going.

"I don't care for you and you don't care for me. You shall not be receiving heirs from me. I would rather stab you than share your bed."

That pricked his masculine pride, but Tehl pushed it aside.

"That would make for interesting bed sport," Sam joked.

"Imbecile," Captain Femi muttered. Sam merely smirked, taunting her.

Tehl ignored them both, still trying to figure out what she was talking about. She wouldn't have his children? He fought an odd sense of rejection and disappointment as he stepped toward her. Why was she even here if she wasn't planning on cooperating? "That was one of my stipulations to the ridiculous demands of *your* rebellion. I will *not* be denied children," he warned. He'd always wanted a big family, and he loved having a brother. Tehl would compromise on many things but not this. He braced himself for a fight when her chin jutted out.

"You shall not be denied children, my lord. You may have as many children as you desire, but they won't be coming from my womb. I suggest you keep a mistress."

Sam whistled.

Captain Femi cursed up a storm.

And Tehl stared at her in confusion. "I beg your pardon?" He must have heard her wrong. "You can't be serious." But from the expression on her face perhaps she was. She wasn't his first choice to share a bed with either, but it was just something they both would have to deal with. He actually felt a little insulted. "I have never kept a mistress, and I will never keep one," he stated firmly. "It would shame you, not to mention my entire family line, if I did such a thing. Plus, it would easily undermine our ruse of love." He stared at her. "And even were I to do as you wish, they wouldn't be legitimate. Your plan will not work."

"Have me declared barren."

Tehl froze. That was one of the most humiliating things you could do to a woman. He would never do that. She'd rather be humiliated before the entire kingdom to escape his affections? He did not really desire a love match, having seen the devastation it caused his father when they lost their mother, but he had hoped to at least like, or have a friendship with, the woman he would spend the rest of his life with. They were to raise a family together after all.

"That way it would not bring any reproach on you or the Crown," Sage continued, excitement in her voice. "I imagine your advisers would urge you to take a mistress."

Captain Femi gasped. "Sage, no. This is a very serious decision. Just because you don't want to have children now, doesn't mean you won't."

"I want children, just not his."

That was a punch to the gut.

Silence engulfed the room, and his pulse pounded in his ears. Tehl had never been so insulted in his life. She wanted children but not his? His hackles rose. Whose children did she mean to have? Did she expect him to let her have lovers? Because that would *not* happen. He may not have chosen her, but stars above, they were stuck together. No one would touch his wife. If she wanted children, he would damn well give them to her. He was done. She wasn't thinking clearly, even her friend saw it. "This is not something you can negotiate. It has been written into the treaty. Are you willing to break it and cause civil war?"

"The rebellion had their demands, the Crown had theirs, you had yours, but I did not," Sage seethed, her hands shaking. "While I was being touched by the monster whom Sam promised to take care of, you and Rafe were haggling over my sale. You had no right!"

"It was not like that." His voice rose. "That rat changed the demands and your leader backed them."

She visibly flinched, hurt pinching her face. He needed to calm down. She was as much a victim here as he was. Tehl swallowed the angry words on the tip of his tongue. "I made the best of the situation. I did not snatch you up and lock you in a tower like an evil villain. I gave you a choice unlike your comrades."

"Some choice," she scoffed, tugging on her loose braid. "Marry you and lend you my womb, or live my life and let innocents die. I joined the rebellion to *prevent* loss of life. It wasn't much of a choice in reality," Sage mumbled, staring at the wall above his head.

"And that's why you'll make a good queen."

Her eyes shot to his, her face showcasing her shock. The words had accidentally tumbled out of his mouth, but they were true. She would be a troublesome and cantankerous wife but she cared for his people. Ever since he met her she'd proven to be loyal and hardworking for those she loved—both were fine qualities for a queen.

"I don't want it. I am a sword maker, not royalty."

"That makes you a perfect candidate for the job, Sage," Captain Femi spoke up. "Your humility, sense of duty, and compassion will be what it takes to make you a capable ruler."

"Indeed," Sam agreed.

His betrothed looked around the room and finally settled her eyes on him.

"We were thrown into this mess, both of us. We're bound; there is no escape for either one of us." He stated the facts bluntly. It was better to be honest than play games. "You and I are alike in this. We share that strong sense of duty." Tehl opened his mouth to continue but closed it. What he needed to say had to be said in private. He looked to the captain and his brother. "Leave us."

Captain Femi ignored him and looked to Sage who nodded her consent. Sam unlocked the door and opened it for the tall woman. "My lady."

Tehl watched them leave and gazed at the door after it shut. "I noticed how you trembled when the Elite surrounded us earlier," he began, turning his attention from the door to Sage's apprehensive eyes. "Gavriel told me of your nightmares. I watched you at both meetings. You can put on a fairly flawless mask, but I still saw your terror, though you tried to bury it deep, at being around all the men, even ones with whom you seemed to be familiar."

"What of it?"

He had to tread carefully here. "You fear me."

Her cheeks reddened at his comment. Apparently, that was the wrong thing to say. Sage's eyes narrowed into a glare.

He rushed on to avoid another argument. "Not in the instance you fear my actions but my touch. You reacted that way with any man who touched you, even Rafe. But know this, I will not force myself on you for children." His eyes scanned her face. "Honestly, you may be lovely but a woman who loathes me has no appeal."

A tremulous smile touched her mouth. "Agreed, my lord."

Stars above, something they agreed on. "I don't plan on having children soon. I don't want to bring a child into a world with the threat of war looming. It'll be years before I want them." Now it was time to see if she would compromise. "It's wrong to have a mistress and you know it. The sanctity of marriage is precious. And I won't tell the world you are barren to save face. I understand you need time to heal from what happened. Would you be willing to give me children if we waited?" Tehl held his breath.

She bowed her head, then her gaze returned to his face. "Would you let me choose when?"

He wanted to say no because he didn't trust her. If he gave her that power, she could push off children for forever. But they needed to work together if they would survive this marriage. He needed to give her a little trust, maybe then she would return the favor. "My offer is five years." Tehl watched her throat bob.

"That is acceptable to me... Maybe then my skin won't crawl at the thought." She tacked on.

Tehl's mind flashed back to their kiss in the hallway, at the Midsummer Festival. Heat stirred in his veins, surprising him. A cinnamon smell teased his nose. How did she still smell like cinnamon when she was sweaty? He shook himself and got back to the matter at hand. "Was it so terrible at the festival?"

"I was playing a role, that was different," she huffed.

"Truly?"

"Truly," she echoed.

"Let's try something. Slip into your role."

"What?" she stammered as Tehl strolled toward her, giving her time to step away or tell him to stop. She didn't, but he noted she shifted onto the balls of her feet, slightly at an angle, a defensive pose. Her distrustful look brought a genuine smile to his face. He slowed in front of her and held his hands out for her to take. She was in control, she had the choice to accept or decline. Sage reminded him of a skittish foal, untrusting and wary, not that he would ever tell her that. She would probably punch him in the face. His smile widened. What would his court think about his warrior woman? Sage would cause quite a stir, he was sure of it.

She only hesitated a moment before slipping her hands into his. Tehl bit back his smile of triumph. It was a small step, but at least they weren't fighting. Tehl ran his thumbs along the top of her hands. "See, not so bad." She watched his thumbs for a moment before pulling away. He let her go and stepped to his desk, leaning against it. "What do you want, Sage?" If they were open and honest, they could understand exactly what to expect from each other. If they treated this marriage like a business, it meant they could be partners. Not friends, but not enemies either.

"The impossible." Her smile was sad.

"You will be queen eventually, nothing will be out of your reach."

Her smile turned bitter. "Except for freedom." She rolled her neck, closing her eyes. "I want nothing from you, but I find myself asking anyway. My family." She peered at him. "I have been the one running the smithy because of my father's health. He can't do it anymore. By marrying you, I will leave them helpless."

"Your family will be well taken care of. We can move them here."

"What of the forge? That has been in my family for generations. My parents would never leave. They wouldn't be happy here."

"What if we sent someone to work for your father?"

"They wouldn't be able to afford to pay them," Sage whispered. He could see her pride stung admitting it.

"You're entitled to wealth once we marry. Did you not realize this?" Tehl eyed her. Most women he met were very interested in the Crown's wealth, in the jewels. Yet she acted like the thought never crossed her mind.

She glowered at him. "I don't want your gold. My needs are little. If I have food to eat, clothing on my body, and a roof over my head, I am content. I'm not asking for charity. I am asking you for a solution."

Tehl wracked his brain for a moment, pushing his black hair out of his face. "What if I sent an apprentice from the palace to your forge? There are many, and they are not getting as much training as they would at your father's side. They would still be under the Crown's employ, so your father wouldn't need to pay them. We could rotate an apprentice out every half year or so." Something warm seeped through him at the small smile that put on her face.

"That would work." Her lips pursed. "Though I would still like to work in a smith and continue my training."

Tehl could think of many reasons why she shouldn't do either of those things, but by her stance he knew she would not budge on these either. He nodded. "We can make arrangements for you to continue both. Anything else?"

"No."

"I will send for Mira and have her settle you." He clasped his hands. "Just so it doesn't take you by surprise, the betrothal will be announced tonight."

She paled. "So soon?"

"Yes." He grimaced. "The Elite are the worst gossips; I guarantee word has spread already. I need to hunt down my father and somehow convince him to show up and give us his blessing." Tehl grumbled to himself. Finding him would not be an easy task.

"I can do that."

He glanced at her in surprise.

Sage lifted one shoulder. "He visited every day I was here. I think he will find me even before I go looking."

One less thing off his plate. "Thank you." Silence filled the room. Tehl stared at her, not knowing what to say. He was never good with small talk. "Is there anything else you need?"

Sage shook her head. "Nothing that needs fixing now, my prince."

Tehl stood and stretched, aware of Sage's eyes observing him. He ignored her and strode to the door, opening it, revealing a smug looking captain and an irritated Sam. What kind of trouble had his brother gotten into this time? He turned back to his betrothed. "You know the way?"

"Same room?"

He nodded.

"Then, yes, my prince." She brushed past him, ignoring Sam, and continued down the hall.

If she kept referring to him so formally no one would continue to believe them besotted.

"Sage," he called. She stiffened and stopped, regarding him over her shoulder. "Use my name."

"Of course, Tehl."

He liked the way his name sounded when she spoke it. He scowled at the thought. Sage dismissed him and resumed her clipped pace, disappearing from sight with the captain trailing behind.

"She's trouble," his brother remarked.

"Yes." Sage would make his life very interesting.

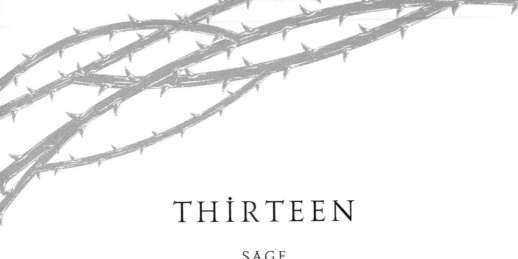

THIRTEEN

SAGE

"YOU KNOW WHERE YOU ARE going, *ma fleur*?" Lilja's ironic words sounded from behind her.

Sage ignored the comment, focusing instead on the stone walls and the lanterns casting flickering shadows across the smooth surfaces. It was odd how soundless her footsteps were in the vast arching hallway. It was almost as if she wasn't really here. The disjointed feeling made her uncomfortable in her own skin. She needed to get out of here.

Sage spotted the staircase to the royal wing and sprinted up, eager to leave the hallway behind. The fist on her lungs eased as she reached the top but the eerie silence of the hall brought the feelings rushing to the forefront as she caught sight of her old door. Goosebumps lifted the hair on her arms.

The door itself may have been unremarkable but that which it represented, at least to her, was highly impactful. It had been her prison of sorts before, but once she entered this time it would start a lifelong sentence. The very thought of being trapped again had sweat pooling between her shoulder blades. Was she really doing this? Could she subject herself to a lifetime of loneliness? The people of court weren't like her. Sage could pretend all she wanted, but she was different, real, common.

What she did for the rebellion and her family shaped her into who she was. Who would she be after abandoning everything she knew? Would Sage still be herself? If she didn't know herself how could she govern others?

Sage panted heavily as her biggest fear rose in her mind. Children. Children needed strong mothers, ones who'd protect them from the world. That wasn't her. Sage knew the truth. She was weak and broken inside. Weak women made for terrible mothers. How could she raise the next rulers of Aermia? Panic clawed at her chest. She wasn't ready. It was too much to ask. Sage had no unearthly clue how to be a princess, queen, or mother. She had no business being here.

"Take a deep breath," Lilja murmured in her lyrical way. "It will be okay. You are not alone."

Sage squeeze her eyes closed. Now was not the time to panic. Opening her eyes, she stared at the ordinary handle for a beat before reaching for it, but her hand stopped, hovering just above it.

Stop being a coward.

Sage clasped the cool metal with determination, pushing it open. The room looked the same. The giant four-poster bed, carved from an aqua colored jardantian tree, still dominated the room. She willed her feet to move and she slowly made it farther in. Each step of her boots sank into the luxurious blue carpets as Sage absently ran her hand along the abalone adorning the mantelpiece. After a moment, she abandoned the fireplace in favor of large windows set into double doors. She pressed her face against the cool glass, trying to get a glimpse of ocean but it was too dark to see much at this hour. The sound of the water crashing on the rocks below still reached her though, and she felt a small measure of comfort. She turned, bracing her back against the door, watching as Lilja took her turn, inspecting the room.

The curious Sirenidae tested out each chair, even remarking on the comfort of each, before standing and moving to investigate the bathing room. Sage watched her friend disappear and waited for the explosion of excitement she knew was coming.

"*Plumbing?!*" Lilja shrieked.

Sage bit back her smile when Captain Femi poked her head out of the bathing room. "I could live in here. I would pay a fortune for the bathing tub alone."

Sage nodded and returned her attention to the large bed, its fluffy white coverlet seeming to beckon. Exhaustion and longing overwhelmed her. All she needed was a nap, then she could start to process everything else. She pushed from the doors and flopped onto the bed, the blanket encasing her face, creating a fluffy cocoon. She lay there, enjoying it, but soon her lungs burned, so she was forced to roll over just so she could breathe. The last time she had been *kept* in this room, it had been her cell. Luxurious to be sure, but a cell nonetheless, and yet here she was again, still a prisoner of sorts but this time she'd chosen the fate.

Lilja's *oohing* and *ahhing* over the bathing space and its luxuries pulled her from her bout of self-pity. There were certainly worse places to be.

A moment later, the door burst open, causing Sage to jump and Lilja to rush over. The room's newest occupant carried with her the scent of herbs and tonics.

Mira.

Sage took a fortifying breath, preparing to grovel. She lifted her arm only to meet a pair of angry blue eyes.

"I'm sorry," Sage blurted the first and only thing she could think to say.

Mira grabbed her arms and yanked her into a hug. "I am nowhere near forgiving you." Mira's arms tightened around her. "But I am so glad you're safe." Mira released her and stepped back to glare at her some more. "I knew you wanted to leave, but I thought you would at least say goodbye before slinking off into the night like a damn thief. You could have trusted me."

Sage swallowed. She should have, she knew that now. "I know, and...I should have. But, at the time, I just didn't want any blame shifting to you for my actions. I said as much of a goodbye as I could without alerting Gav to my plan."

"Was anything you told me true, Ruby?"

"... My name is actually Sage."

"Of course it is." Mira huffed out an angry breath, looking away. "You weren't honest with me. That's not to say I don't understand that you have reasons. I know you had people you were protecting," Mira's face turned red, and Sage could hear the hurt in Mira's voice as she continued. "But color me shocked when my presence was requested to attend you. Why didn't you come to see me as soon as you arrived?"

Sage tugged on her braid, embarrassed and a bit ashamed. "I haven't had a moment. I arrived, was whisked into a meeting, and then immediately sent here to get ready for dinner." Her excuses sounded pathetic, even to her own ears. She should have gone straight down to the infirmary. She shot Lilja a glance, who had made herself comfortable in a chair, both legs thrown over its arm. The captain winked and pretended not to listen. The little eavesdropper was enjoying this.

Sage turned back to the irate healer. "Do you know why I am here?"

Mira's face morphed into amusement. "The current ridiculous rumor is you've been betrothed to the crown prince." Mira sniggered. "I laughed when I first heard it. You detest the crown prince. Of all the men in the world he's the *last*—"

"It's true," Sage choked out.

Mira's jaw unhinged, gaping, but only for a moment before her face blanked. She took a few steps back and sank into her customary chair by the fire. Her blond friend looked to have no words. She opened and closed her mouth several times before she could get anything out.

Sage's stomach churned.

"How?"

Sage paced before the fireplace and began her story, explaining everything from the very beginning. Mira listened carefully, never once interrupting or even questioning. Some parts were ash on her tongue, and she had to muscle through them, the sting of betrayal still somewhat fresh. It was odd recounting everything that had come to pass, but it was also surprisingly freeing. When she finally stopped talking, Sage felt a little lighter.

Mira's eyes dipped to the floor for a moment before returning to Sage's face. "Thank you."

That wasn't the response she'd expected. "For what?"

"Your sacrifice. I know better than most how you feel about the Crown."

Sage turned from Mira's knowing gaze, instead watching Lilja pretend to sleep. "How I feel isn't really important at the moment. There is too much at stake. I have no idea if we'll succeed, and I don't know what I'm doing, but I'm also all the Crown has. If this is our only chance at peace, what choice did I really have?" Sage took a shaky breath, whispering her next words.

"Honestly, after everything that I've been through, it's not as though I have any semblance of appeal." She paused, chewing her lip before continuing. "No respectable man would have wanted me anyway. I should be happy, after all coming here has given me an opportunity. At least now I might have a family of my own."

"How many grandbabies should I expect then?"

Sage yanked out her daggers and pivoted toward the voice. She saw in the corner of her eye that Lilja had done the same, crouching with a long, wicked-looking dagger in one hand. Where had that come from? Sage brushed the thought aside and focused on the person speaking. A section of wall slowly pushed open, revealing the king. He took in their weapons and smiled gaily.

"That's no way to greet family."

Sage gaped as he moved into her room like he owned it. She supposed, technically, he did. "Can I help you, your majesty?"

"Did my ears deceive me, or are you to wed my son?"

Sage floundered for a moment, unable to respond. When she recovered she sent him a scowl. "Were you *listening at my door?*"

"You shouldn't leave the door open, anyone can listen in." Sage mentally rolled her eyes at that. The king continued, "Now, answer the question. Sage, are you betrothed to my son?"

Sage straightened but couldn't meet his eye. She chose to examine the rug instead of Marq. "I am."

Heavy footsteps moved toward her, and brown boots entered her line of vision. A large hand cupped her chin, lifting her face. She met his familiar blue eyes and something about the warmth there had her fighting tears. He searched her face, giving her a sad smile.

"From the Elite, it sounded to be a joyful reunion, but from your face it seems that, for you, at least, this is not a happy occasion." He could not hide his disappointment with this revelation.

Sage forced a smile upon her lips. "We want people to believe it to be."

He studied her, his face sharpened. "You are marrying to protect Aermia, yes?"

She gulped. "Yes."

"That's a weight."

"It is. May I be honest with you, sire?"

"Please."

"I have no desire to be either queen or your son's wife. But I give you my promise that I'll do whatever I can to help the kingdom mend and weather the storms ahead of us."

"And what of my son? Will you do your best to help him as well?"

She met his eyes, the eyes of a concerned father. "I will help him run the kingdom. I will give him children. Don't worry, the royal line will continue."

"That's not what I was talking about. Will you be a good companion, helpmate, and consort?"

"I will advise him to the best of my ability."

"He doesn't need an advisor, he needs a wife."

"The crown prince should have thought about that before he bought me." Sage winced. She knew she sounded unreasonable but she couldn't help what she felt, or change what happened.

Marq's lips thinned. "You feel he bought you?"

"Essentially." She shrugged, looking to Marq hopefully. "I know I am not what you imagined for your son. I am sure he feels the same way, but I'm all that you and our country get." Sage clasped his hands. "As I'm sure you overheard, the lives of many depend upon this. I cannot have the consequences of failure on my conscience; it's why I'm here in the first place. But, in order for this union to succeed, we *need* your permission and blessing. We need your support. The prince told me we have to make the announcement tonight. Would you… Do you think you could come to dinner and be the one to do so? Please?" Sage pleaded.

Marq watched her, an unreadable expression on his face, before pulling her into a gentle embrace. "I can do that, dear. Thank you," the king whispered into her hair.

Sage squeezed him once and stepped back.

"I will leave you so you can make yourself ready then." The older man strode from the room, disappearing as quickly as he'd appeared.

"Stars above." Lilja fanned herself. "He sure is a handsome man for his age."

Mira snorted. "You should see his sons."

Captain Femi flashed the blond healer a smirk. "It's true. They are pretty easy on the eyes."

Sage scoffed. "Beautiful on the outside they may be, but the insides definitely leave something to be desired."

"You better keep that opinion to yourself, lest someone hear you. Don't ruin everything because you can't keep your mouth shut," Lilja chided.

Mira stood, eyeing her leathers with disdain. "You need a bath and change of clothes before you join them."

Sage smiled at the promise of a bath but it fell when she remembered that she'd have to wade into the leviathan-infested waters of court immediately after. Her scowl deepened. Hopefully it wouldn't taint the joy of her bath.

Sage sunk into the deep tub letting the warm water lap at her shoulders, as spicy oil teased her nose. Cinnamon. Her favorite. She tilted her head back, eyes closing, her neck cradled along the tub's edge. She'd needed this.

She could hear Lilja and Mira discussing dresses. Sage liked pretty things, but it still irked her to think that the worth of many extravagant pieces could feed a family for months. She didn't need something that was such a colossal waste of coin.

"Something modest," Sage hollered, and the voices paused as two sets of footsteps moved into the washroom.

"You are now the betrothed of the crown prince thus your dress needs to be impeccable," Mira argued. "Any flaw will give the harpies of his court reason to rip you to shreds. You represent the Crown now."

Sage sniggered. "I don't care what they think. I am not here to impress them, so I will dress as I please. I'm to be the prince's consort, am I not?"

"*You* may not care but in so doing you will make a mockery of the Crown. Is that what you want?"

Mira's harsh words made Sage pry her eyes open. "No," she said, serious now. "But I will not dress in a way that mocks the suffering of our people either. Queen Ivy never wore shoes. I will not shame myself, nor the crown prince, no matter how much I might dislike him. I believe that something both tasteful and simple is not too much to ask."

Lilja shot Mira a look, a small smile on her face. "She sounds like a queen already."

Mira lifted Sage's heavy fall of hair and poured some delicious smelling soap into it, working through the tangles. Sage let out a happy sigh.

"Sage, I wasn't criticizing you but you must remember that how you dress matters from now on. I want to protect you from the judgment you will no doubt face tonight. Many of these women are not kind. Behind pretty little smiles may be a coiled viper."

Sage placed a wet hand on Mira's arm, meeting concerned blue eyes. "I'm aware of what they may be like. But do not fret, I can handle myself. I am not without skills myself when it comes to pretense, and no one here can say anything worse than what many said when I returned home before. Their words only hurt if I let them. I truly don't care what they say, I am here for one purpose and one purpose only and it has nothing to do with them." Sage patted her friend's arm before resuming scrubbing herself. She met Lilja's magenta eyes. "The only dress I have fine enough for tonight is my costume from the Midsummer Festival, and that is inappropriate. What would you suggest I wear?"

Captain Femi entered the room and ran a finger tip along her bathwater. "I sent someone to the Sirenidae for a dress of mine."

Sage eyed her skeptically. They were shaped nothing alike. Lilja was tall and willowy whereas she was short and curvy. How exactly would *that* work?

Captain Femi snorted. "I am a merchant."

"Pirate," Sage teased. In truth, Sage had discovered a few things while staying on the Sirenidae. Lilja was a legitimate business woman, but she also had some *interesting* enterprises on the side. She also had things Sage had never seen before, stuff not of Methian or Aermian origin, and very old.

Captain Femi sniffed but ignored her comment. "I am having dresses brought here for you. They may need to be altered, but I am sure we can find one that fits enough for tonight."

Sage eyed Lilja's colorful outfit, hoping whatever it was wasn't quite so brightly colored.

Lilja caught her expression and swatted the air. "Don't give me that look. Many wish they could wear the colors I do."

Mira squeezed the water from her hair. "They are exotic, but I'm afraid only someone with your coloring can pull off that yellow. It's quite…vivid."

Lilja smirked. "I am sure that, with your golden hair, you could wear it reasonably well."

Mira stood and picked up a towel, beckoning for Sage to get out. She paused for a moment, self-conscious, but steeled herself knowing Mira had already seen her at her worst. She stood, water sluicing down her body, and stepped from the tub as Mira wrapped her in the warm towel. She was led to the vanity to sit as Mira begun working on her hair.

Lilja followed them into the bedroom and met Sage's eyes in the mirror. Sage shivered when she saw the anger plain on her face. "He will pay, *ma fleur*."

She didn't need to ask whom, but, seeing her friend so fierce, she realized the woman could be quite frightening. She imagined this is what the stories referred to when they referred to the Sirenidae as bloodthirsty fighters. She glanced away from Captain Femi into flashing blue eyes and winced when Mira jerked the brush through her hair. Noticing her discomfort, Mira gentled her brushing with an apologetic smile.

"Sorry. I am not a lady's maid, though I am sure you will be assigned someone soon."

Sage gaped at her in horror. "I hope not. I don't have a need for one. I appreciate your help with my hair, but I am capable of washing and dressing myself. It would be a complete waste of a maid's time." She thought for a moment before continuing. "Why would anyone aspire to do such a thing anyway?"

"Mostly it is the distinction that comes with the title. In this case they could boast being entrusted to work with nobility, perhaps even the ruler of our nation, which would no doubt help them in their own pursuits of husbands or networking. Sometimes it is one who has performed their duties well, and they are assigned the task as a reward. A lady's maid isn't nearly so hard as many other positions. There are many reasons, some fine, others less so." Mira started worked more oil into her hair.

Sage didn't want someone she didn't know hanging around all the time. "What about you?"

The blond healer laughed. "I have no desire to ever be a lady's maid. I am a healer through and through. Give me blood and tonics over dresses and hair pins."

Mira finished Sage's hair and stared at it like it was a puzzle. Lilja scooted to the side, bumping Mira out of the way with her hip. "Move, healer, I will take care of this. Hmm..." she mused. "Me. A hairdresser. Who would have thought?"

Sage closed her eyes and let Lilja turn her from the mirror, as she plaited her hair, and Mira applied a few cosmetics to her lips, cheeks, and eyes.

"Not too heavy, please." She hardly wore the stuff, it always melted off in the heat of the forge, so what was the point? Plus, her mum had always said she didn't need it.

A soft knock at the door made her eyes pop open as Mira moved to get it, her skirts rustling. Mira let out a startled squeak and Lilja paused and called, "Hayjen?"

A grunt answered her.

"Please come in."

Hayjen scanned the room and, noting the bed, carefully laid the dresses there, grumbling all the while. "I had to practically fight my way here." He turned, his grumpy face lighting in a tender smile when he spotted his wife. His eyes moved to Sage. "Don't let her fool you, she loves dressing women up." A pause. "You left early." A statement, not a question. "That was wise of you. Rafe was not happy when he returned. Wouldn't happen to know anything about that, would you?"

Sage gave him a hard look, choosing not to dwell on the memory. "I'm afraid I couldn't give him want he wanted."

Hayjen's lips thinned as he leaned against a bed poster. "He is determined."

Her stomach rolled. Sage understood Rafe better than anyone else. "There is nothing to be done."

"Now is not the time to be speaking of such things," Captain Femi chided. "She has enough to deal with tonight."

Hayjen, her long time friend, strode to her side with a smile. He leaned down and pressed his lips to her forehead. "You will make a wonderful princess and, someday, a wonderful queen. Let no one convince you otherwise."

Warmth infused her at the demonstration of affection and his kind words.

He pecked Lilja on the cheek and made his way to the door. "I will stand outside until you ladies are ready."

Lilja finished up Sage's hair and began digging through the beautiful fabrics on the bed, humming as she sorted. The Sirenidae finally settled on an emerald silk dress and shook it out. It was sleeveless with a shallow scoop that cut across the collarbone. It was form-fitting and long enough that it looked like it would probably puddle on the floor. An angled golden sash draped around the hips and fell to the floor. It was simple, but it was also very elegant.

Sage smiled at Lilja. "It's perfect."

She stood and lifted her hands above her head. The smooth fabric glided over her skin like the kiss of a butterfly's wing. Both women tugged gently until it was settled onto her, hugging her body perfectly. Sage marveled at the panels that had been sewn inside so she wouldn't need a bustier. She brushed her hands down the dress, smoothing its fabric, trying not to think about how it clung to her hips and thighs. Sage glanced over her shoulder and released a squeak. The material plunged down, showcasing her back with a sheer material sewn over it with a row of dainty round buttons running down it. The emerald silk pooled at her feet, flowing into a modest train.

It was certainly beautiful, but Sage was slightly aghast. "Who cut out the back of it?"

Mira sniggered.

Sage began to step forward when her dress split along the thigh. She stared at the sash that wasn't a sash. Rather it was part of the dress, sewn to lay over a thigh-high slit. She frowned down at it. "I thought this was supposed to be modest."

"It is. Nothing inappropriate is showing."

Sage gave Lilja a droll look. "Half of it seems to be missing."

Lilja rolled her eyes and tossed her a pair of matching slippers. Sage grinned, stopping to slip them onto her feet.

Gingerly, she lifted the dress and approached the mirror. Her wavy hair was swept back from her face, three braids crossed over the waves, starting from behind one ear and fastened behind the other with gold feather pins. Her waves tumbled down her back in wild array. The stunning green dress made the green of her eyes pop, like gems. Sage stared at her reflection, scrutinizing the woman in front of her. She still looked like herself but more refined. Lilja had certainly outdone herself. She lifted a hand to touch her cheek and stared as it trembled. Lilja shifted to her side, clasping Sage's hand with her own.

"You made a tough choice, *ma fleur*, but it was the right one. You will be okay."

Sage took a breath, trying to release some of her nerves, and smiled at both women. "Thank you, both, so much."

Mira blushed which Sage found entertaining. The healer could sew up all sorts of body parts but as soon as you praised her she couldn't take it and blushed crimson.

Sage lifted her dress and sidled to the door, staring at the handle once again. It was now or never. Gritting her teeth, she yanked it open before she could stop herself and stepped through. Hayjen cocked his head and raised a questioning eyebrow at her determined expression. No doubt she looked exactly as she felt, like a martyr.

"You don't want to know," she grumped.

"Sage, we need to return to the Sirenidae, but I will visit as much as I can. If you need me all you need to do is send for me." Lilja clasped her hands and searched her eyes. "Be brave, *ma fleur*. There is nothing you can't do or accomplish. You are never alone."

Sincerity shown in the captain's exotic eyes. In the short time she had known this strange woman, they'd grown to be good friends. Sage wrapped her arms around her. "Thank you for everything you have done." She leaned back and stepped around to hug Hayjen as well.

"You're not weak, so don't let anyone walk over you. You're their equal, perhaps even their better, in all things," his gruff voice whispered into her hair. His arms tightened for a moment before releasing her. Lilja kissed both her cheeks and then returned to Hayjen's side, clasping his hand.

"We will see you soon," the Sirenidae called, just before strolling down the corridor, her husband in tow.

"They make an interesting pair," Mira remarked.

"That they do."

Mira pushed passed her to the staircase and shot Sage a questioning look. "Are you coming?"

She hadn't moved. Sage shook herself out of her stupor, struggling with the urge to run far, far, away. Mira started down the staircase as soon as Sage reached her. Following behind, Sage took each stair deep in thought. She felt as though every step toward the dining room was one step further away from herself, from her life. Contemplating this, by the time she'd completely descended the two enormous flights, she had come to a realization. The life she felt bleeding away from her, the girl she had been, both had died in that cell somewhere beneath her feet. Ever since then, she had been trying to become that same girl, but she finally understood that it would never happen. She may have the same body, but the passion, the joy, and the hope had been scraped from inside her. Perhaps taking on this role for the Crown wouldn't be so difficult after all, since she was really just a shell anyway.

FOURTEEN

TEHL

TEHL LONGED TO PACE. HE had come into dinner earlier than normal so he could be settled before Sage's arrival. He leaned back and studied the goings on around him. Members of his court flitted about, some laughing, some plotting, some merely enjoying their meals. Tehl took a healthy gulp of his wine and hid his smile behind his cup. He couldn't wait to see the stir his betrothal announcement created.

Soon, Sage would have to deal with all this tedium. There were so many things she could take over; the staffing, the meal plans for the week, planning for visiting nobles and dignitaries, and the blasted letters he both received and sent. And that was only a few of the things he couldn't wait to be rid of. His grin widened at the thought.

"Why are you smiling like a lunatic?" Sam asked while winking at a woman across the room.

"I was thinking about how my betrothal arrangement will benefit me. No more ridiculous tasks that I have very little patience for and even less skill in. Soon all of that, and this, will be her domain." Tehl spoke the words with unadulterated glee.

Sam tilted his head, lips twitching. "I am sure she will *love* that. I imagine she'll work to escape from those duties even more vigorously than you do. But, at least you have time to ease her into everything, the wedding won't be until spring, I imagine. It's a pity though, for, if not, you could get started on that heir-making all the sooner."

Tehl narrowed his eyes at his brother. "It's a little early to be talking of children."

His brother's gaze moved past him and widened. Sam blew out a deep breath, straightening. "It is never too early when you have a woman like that."

Tehl swung around as Sage enter entered the room in a gem-green gown that seemed to flow down and over her curves. It accentuated the shape of her bust, small waist, and flared hips. Her hair was swept away from her face so he could admire her heart-shaped face and green eyes. A small slit gave a preview of a toned, feminine leg every time she stepped.

"You're gaping," Sam muttered.

Tehl snapped his mouth shut as Sage met his eyes, her expression unreadable. Very quickly though, her face morphed, and a happy smile replaced the odd expression, her eyes crinkling in like she was truly happy to see him. If he hadn't known any better, he would have truly believed he'd imagined the change. She was good, he'd give her that.

Tehl stood and began descending the steps, ignoring the myriad of curious eyes on him. His betrothed added extra swing to her hips as she approached and, having reached him, sunk into a deep curtsy before standing proudly before him.

"My lord," she murmured, throatily.

Tehl reached for her hand and placed a kiss on it. "My lady." Her hand twitched in his grasp, the only evidence of her desire to no doubt pull away. He released her hand and placed a hand on her back. Her *scarcely covered* back. He snuck a glance at her attire. Where was the rest of her dress? Tehl offered her his hand to escort her up the dais and eyed her back, displayed for the world to see. There was a piece of fabric but it was so fine and sheer she might as well have worn nothing. There was little he could do about it now, so he tried to dismiss it from his mind. He sat her between his brother and himself while allowing him a moment to survey the reactions of his court.

Astonishment was most prevalent. His advisors gazed at her with curiosity but not anger. Many men looked at Sage with lust in their eyes, but that didn't particularly bother him. She was a beautiful woman; they could look so long as they didn't touch. He cleared his throat, gaining everyone's attention and motioned for the meal to begin. Servants brought out dishes and placed them on the table, serving himself and those around him first, then continuing on down the table. He waited patiently, curious to see who would be the first to start the inquisition.

"Madam, you look ravishing this evening," William complemented, his gray eyes twinkling.

Sage put down her spoon and grinned at the old advisor. "Why, thank you. I do prefer boots and trousers, but a woman likes to dress up every now and again. Makes her feel good."

A few women gasped.

"Boots and trousers?" Jaren's daughter scoffed.

Stars above, he disliked that woman.

"How very vulgar. Truly, you jest?"

Sage snuck a glance at the various people pretending not to listen before answering. "Vulgar? I think not. There is nothing vulgar about hard work is there?" His betrothed gestured to her dress. "How can I clean, or wash, or do anything useful in a dress so fine as this? It would be ruined. And don't you think it would be a shame to damage such a lovely creation?"

Many of the men and even a few women around them chorused their agreement.

"We wouldn't want to ruin something that looked so enticing on your body, would we?" Sam drawled, leaning toward her.

"From what I hear, you rarely leave anything on any woman's body. So, excuse me if I doubt your expertise, my prince," Sage retorted.

A glint entered his brother's eye that Tehl didn't like. "Perhaps you're right. Are you requesting I demonstrate my expertise then?"

Tehl tucked away his smile as everyone leaned forward to hear what Sage would say. She tipped her head back; a peel of laughter escaped her as her hair tumbled down her back. Once she seemed to gain control of herself, she gave his brother an appraising look. "As intriguing as that sounds, I have heard of your exploits, it seems you always come up short. But what would I know of such things?" she asked too innocently.

Sniggers surrounded them at her slight. Sage ignored Sam's gaping reaction and sipped her soup as dainty as any lady, not like she had just insulted Sam's manhood.

Sam recovered quickly, a genuine smile flashing. "Point to you, my lady."

Each question that Sage was asked, she answered in a way that delighted and amused but at the same time gained respect. Several times, Tehl said what seemed to him to be a perfectly logical phrase or response, but, when he received odd looks, Sage would make a comment or joke that would smooth out any conversational hiccups. She was better than some of his dignitaries, a born diplomat. By the close of the meal, she had most of his court enchanted, if not half in love.

"Have I missed dessert?" his father's voice called from behind his chair.

All eyes snapped to the man behind him in surprise. Tehl slid his gaze to Sage, catching her eye. His father had not attended dinner in over a year, no matter how many times Tehl had asked. But one conversation with Sage, and here he was. His gratitude must have shown on his face for she gave him a small nod in response.

His father stepped beside him and clasped his shoulder. "Tonight is a special occasion." His father plucked a goblet from the table and held it aloft. The court followed his example glancing around in confusion. "I am happy to announce tonight the betrothal of my son, Tehl Ramses, to the lovely Sage Blackwell."

The lots were cast. Tehl stood, never taking his eyes from Sage and stretched out his hand to her. She stared at it for a beat before a radiant smile bloomed on her lovely face. Sage slid her hand into his confidently, like a woman in love. Only the tiny quiver of her fingers betrayed her.

Tehl slowly brought her to his side and reached for his own wine. Carefully, he held it to her lips, the ritual a demonstration of their future life; she would share what was his. She sipped it and pulled away, licking her lips. She then reached for her own and smoothly held hers up to him, her fear seeming to have dissipated. He took a healthy gulp and pulled the cup from her hand placing it on the table. He wiggled his lips slightly, trying to prepare her for what was next. They would seal the betrothal with their kiss. He wrapped his hand around her neck, and she shifted on her toes to meet him halfway. Soft, plush lips met his, and he gave her a quick, innocent kiss. The sounds of cheering and applause met his ears. It was done.

She shifted back, smiling at him like she hadn't told him hours ago that she didn't want to have his children largely because she couldn't stand him personally. Tehl needn't have worried about her ability to pull this off, she seemed to be as good as his brother. His father's voice pulled him from his thoughts.

"The happy couple will be married in two weeks' time."

Sage's nails dug into him.

Two weeks. Bloody hell.

Tehl wiped any expression from his face and pasted on his smile. Two weeks. He would have a wife in two weeks. Though her expression remained unchanged he could see that panic filled her eyes, which, thankfully, never left his face. Tehl pulled himself from her and held their entwined hands in the air. More shouts of congratulations and a general feeling of excitement filled the room. He knew it was time to escape because he didn't have the patience to answer everyone's questions, not after what his father had just done.

He put his mouth by Sage's ear. "May I carry you?"

She turned her face, lips resting against his jaw, for all appearances a lover's gesture. "As long as you take me away from here."

Cinnamon wafted from her hair, making him sniff. Where did that damn scent come from? Cinnamon was one of his favorites. Before she changed her mind, he swung her into his arms and carried her away from the chaotic excitement in the dining room. Hoots and hollers followed them, echoing in the spacious hallway. She exhaled a sigh of relief against his collar, causing the hair on the back of his neck to stand up. He rolled his shoulders to rid himself of the feeling. After a few twists and turns, he placed her back on her feet and offered his arm. "May I escort you to your room, my lady?"

She stepped to his side and took his arm, her breast brushing his sleeve, and his body warmed at the contact. Tehl scowled for a moment before smoothing his face into an appropriate expression for strolling with your beloved. It irked him that something so simple affected him. The logical part of his brain told him it was a good thing and that it meant there'd be no issue when they did decide to have children. She was a beautiful woman. He still didn't like it though.

Tehl slowed his gait to match hers as they ascended the staircase. Her legs were so much shorter than his. Again, much to his displeasure, he noticed that with every other step she took, her bare right leg peeked out. "Where did that gown come from?" he asked gruffly, censure in his tone.

Sage kept her eyes on the marble stairs answering. "It was a gift. I came here in a rush so I did not have time to collect my things, and, even if I had, I wouldn't have had something suitable for dinner. The only thing I own that would be fine enough is my costume from the Midsummer Festival. And, somehow, I didn't think you would want me wearing that tonight."

The revealing costume she'd worn popped into his mind. It had been seductive, way too much skin on display. "It would have been inappropriate."

She sniggered. "I thought so too, hence, this gown."

His mind caught on that thought. She wasn't a traditional bride who brought a hope chest with all the things deemed necessary for marriage contained therein. She'd come to the palace with only the clothes on her back. He hadn't spared a thought for what she would wear tonight until she showed up looking like every man's fantasy.

When they turned the corner, entering the royal wing, low and behold, Sam lay in wait for them. Leaning casually against the wall, one boot braced behind him, he was the epitome of casualness.

"How did he arrive so quickly? We left before he did."

Tehl shook his head. "I stopped asking that years ago. I've grown up with him, yet even I don't know all his secrets."

Sam straightened and opened Sage's door for the two of them. She pulled free from Tehl and was across the room before he'd even clicked the door shut behind him. She made it apparent that she didn't want him to touch her, at all. The door opened again, this time admitting his cousin.

"By all means, invite yourself in," Sage replied sarcastically.

Gavriel and Sam both stepped to Tehl's side to watch the strange female pacing across the room. She eyed them unhappily, her dress flaring around her legs with each turn. She was like a caged griffin, regal in her bearing, but dangerous if you moved too close.

Sam was the first to move. He strutted to her bed and plunked down, groaning. "This bed is so comfortable." His brother stretched out his hands behind his head, ankles crossed. The feisty brunette squinted at Samuel and crossed to the opposite side of the bed, scowling at his brother.

Sam gave her an approving smile. "You did well tonight. I don't believe there was a single person in the room who was not at least partially in love with you by the time you left. The only ones who probably shall hate you are those who were hoping to take your place in my brother's bed."

"They can have him," she grumbled. Tehl watched as a calculating gleam entered her eyes as Sam lazed on her bed. "That still doesn't explain why you are now in my bed. Get off."

"It would be my pleasure," Sam purred, the devil in his eyes.

Sage's narrowed dangerously. "I will tie you up and drop you off my balcony if I have to."

Tehl fought a grin. His brother would no doubt have something to say to that.

"Tie me up? I must admit that sounds rather appealing, there are so many options." Sam reached up and caressed the head of the bed. "This would be the perfect bed for…"

A dull thud sounded and suddenly a blade quivered in between Sam's fingers, embedded in the headboard. Sam's face was a mask of shock. Tehl's eyes snapped to the smirking female. He hadn't even seen her throw it. She stepped back from the bed and glided to a nearby chair. With fluid grace she placed her foot on the chair, so reminiscent of the Midsummer Festival's night, when she'd displayed her scars. His betrothed then hitched up her dress exposing a thigh sheath. She plucked two more blades, placing them at a precise angle on the bedside table. She switched legs and pulled three more from another sheath there. Sage dropped her foot, lifting her hands to the flowers in her hair, gently tugging. He then noticed they weren't just hair ornaments but weapons, very long, dangerous-looking needles. She shook out her hair and released a happy sigh. Last but not least, she pulled the fine chain that dropped into her dress and revealed a very pretty looking dagger that dangled on the end. She was a walking armory.

She clasped her hands in front of her. "Now, as I was saying, get off my bed."

Sam obeyed this time, though he took his own sweet time, taking a moment to pry the blade from the bed. His brother *tsked* when he saw the gouge in the beautiful wood. "Look at what you did, Sage. This is jardintin wood."

"You should have gotten out of her bed then," Gavriel replied dryly. His cousin turned his attention to Sage, disapproval on his face. "Did you not even think to warm me when you snuck off the ship today? At first, I panicked because I couldn't find you, but when I discovered Hayjen and Lilja had also disappeared I hoped you were only with them, so I waited, just in case. But none of you returned. I'd just decided to make a search for you when Rafe appeared, very much unhappy." Sage cringed. "That man was beyond angry. He demanded I tell him where his mate went."

Tehl's brows rose at that. Mate?

"I could only guess he somehow meant you so I let him know I hadn't seen you for hours. He stalked off, cursing up a storm. Fortunately, I then spotted Hayjen, and he was able to inform me of your whereabouts. If I hadn't been detained by the rebellion leader, I would still be out there, looking frantically and praying that I wasn't going to happen upon your carcass instead."

"You left Gavriel behind?" Tehl growled.

Sage shot him a mulish look. "He is not my guardian. I can do as I please."

"That may be so," Tehl replied coolly. "But he is also your friend. How could you do that to him?"

His betrothed looked chagrined and held her hands out to Gav. "I am sorry, Gav. I didn't mean to worry you. There were a few things I needed to wrap up tonight. I truly meant to come back though. It's just…" She hesitated. "There were complications."

"Ah. The rebellion leader," Sam deduced. "How long have you been together?"

"Never."

Tehl shifted, arching a brow at her. "You appeared very cozy at the Midsummer Festival. I got the impression you had been together a long time."

"I merely played a role much like I did tonight. We only faked love and affection for each other."

"*He* wasn't acting, sis," Gav spoke up softly. "Every man at the table that night felt his claim on you. Be honest with us. Are you attached to him?"

Sage sunk her fingers in her hair, frustration in the movement. "I have always admired him. Rafe is brave, loyal, intelligent, and kind. I have worked with him closely for over a year. Of course, I was attached to him. He was my mentor… He was my friend."

"Was?" Tehl questioned.

Anger stiffened her body and she glowered. "Yes, *was*. It was he who sent that monster to me, and he was a part of the Circle who also decided to protect him, the very same which almost condemned me for attempted murder." Her body shook, angry tears spilling onto her cheeks. "Then he sold me to a man he knew I loathed, sentencing me to live in the same place where the worst horrors of my life took place. "

"What of our conversation in the cavern? I thought Rafe had plans in order for Rhys."

Sage laughed, slapping her leg like what he said was comical. There wasn't anything funny about what he'd said as far as he knew. He slid a glance to Sam but neither was his brother laughing. Good, he hadn't missed anything, though her behavior remained a mystery.

"You did see him at the negotiation, right?" She raised her hand above her head. "About this tall, utterly ordinary until you see the rot of his demented soul? The man who pawed at me and orchestrated this whole farce?" Another hysterical giggle escaped her. "Mark my words, he will go free. He is rather like the wind. You know, he's there only because you see the effects of his actions, but as soon as you think he's in your grasp, you open your hand to find nothing." Her bleak eyes turned to Sam. "You told me he would be punished and would never hurt anyone else, yet he is, this very day, running around free in Sanee. I stabbed him, trying to free the world from his particulate brand of evil, yet the Circle protected him and blamed me." She then turned to Tehl, accusation in her eyes. "Once again, after your conversation with Rafe, I was relieved that he might disappear from my life, but no. Instead, he is the one who somehow has the power to orchestrate my enslavement to the Crown once again." She chuckled without mirth. "And now his destruction is impossible. If he were to go missing now the rebellion would blame you and all the hotheads itching for a change in government would just use it as an excuse to start their fight back up again."

"We will…" Gavriel started.

"No. She's right," Tehl cut him off, never taking his eyes off Sage. "Our hands are tied at the moment." She deserved to know they would protect her.

Their situation was not ideal, but she would become his family in a matter of weeks. They may not be best friends, but they did want the same thing.

Tehl marched over and knelt in front of her. She had given up much, so he could do this much for her. "In two weeks you will become part of our family. You could have done as you pleased, you owed no loyalty to me, but you did it out of love for my people, and I will not forget that, ever. We are unlikely allies, and now we are to be partners. I promise you this: you will be safe here. I will protect you to the best of my ability, and when the time comes in which I may act without fear of the repercussions you spoke of, then there will be nowhere he can hide. This I vow."

Her green eyes glimmered. It was obvious many emotions roiled around inside her. "I will hold you to that, my lord. The same goes for you, and yours. I'll protect your family to the best of my ability."

She stepped back and shoved her arm toward him, watching him carefully. Tehl clasped her forearm, his fingers overlapping.

"Allies then."

"Yes. Allies," he echoed.

FİFTEEN

SAGE

HER CONVERSATION WITH TEHL THE week prior fueled her anger. Allies, what a joke.

Sage lunged, meeting her opponent's sword with her own. Her muscles strained against the weight of the larger man's brute strength. She bared her teeth at him and spun away, blocking one of his strikes. They circled each other, wary, searching for weaknesses. Sage loved sparring, being as she was so small, she often had to figure out how to take down opponents much larger than she. And when she was able to best them there was nothing so invigorating as that glorious win.

She continued to eye her opponent, trying to anticipate his next move. He was good, she would give him that much, but she knew she was faster. She smiled inwardly. He'd just given himself away with a slight movement of his torso. By the time he'd attacked, she was already in motion, slipping under his guard and knocking him to his knees. She leaned over his shoulder and placed her blade at his throat.

"I yield," he huffed out, black hair shining in the light. His purple eyes peered up at her, crinkling at the corners. "I also had you though."

She sniffed and stepped away, ignoring all the male eyes watching her with interest. Her unladylike pursuits made quite the impression on courtiers and soldiers alike, setting tongues-a-wagging.

"Sage."

Spinning, she caught the rag he'd thrown and wiped her face and neck. It was warm out, already causing sweat to trickle down her spine as well as in between her breasts. That was the worst part about training, the breast sweat. She wrinkled her nose and tugged her leather vest back into place. Most of the time she wore a linen shirt underneath but when sparring on days like today it was much too hot. That left her in trousers, boots, a leather vest, and arm guards. Sage placed the towel on the fence and leaned against it to inspect Gav as he ran a towel over his own face and hair.

"You weren't giving it your all." Irritation colored her voice. "I will not break. I am not made of glass. Again," she demanded, as she pushed off the fence and strode to the center of the ring.

Gav scowled at her but didn't move from his spot. "I understand you will not break but it still feels wrong to spar full force with a woman."

"So you let me win?" Sage clenched her teeth.

Gav looked at her hesitantly. "No, not necessarily…but I could also never hurt you."

"If you will not spar with me, then I will find someone else." She scanned the area locking onto combat master. "Zachael! Would you spar with me?" The combat master grinned at her and moved their way.

"You have been at this for two hours already today. Don't you think you should take a break or finish making plans?" Gav asked.

That had her seeing red. She shoved her sword into her scabbard and stalked to Gavriel. "That's exactly why I am out here, to *escape* wedding plans."

Garreth glanced up from sharpening his sword. "I thought most women loved that sort of thing."

Sage rolled her eyes, placing her hands on her hips. "Do I seem like most women?" The men around her snickered, and she smiled in spite of herself. In the twelve days since she'd arrived, she had trained every morning and afternoon with the Elite. It had taken her a while to get used to being surrounded by men again and several times she'd felt herself start to panic, but Gavriel never left her side and the men never touched her. They were always courteous and respectful. After a week, being around them felt familiar, similar to being around her brothers. If someone pinned or surprised her, she usually had to fight some anxiety, but she managed.

In the beginning, Sage was relieved that the only time she had to interact with the crown prince was for dinner. But as the days wore on, she realized that he had, in fact, abandoned her so that she alone had to manage *all* wedding preparations, and in just two short weeks too. That first day she'd taken Marq to task for announcing their betrothal in such a way. She'd begged him to somehow give them more time, but, despite her pleading, he wouldn't change his mind. She'd seethed at the comments she'd had to bear from the women she was forced to spend time with. Everyone thought she was already carrying the heir as it was the only reason they could think of for such haste. The thought made her nauseous. Thank goodness that wouldn't be for some time.

"You are definitely one of a kind." Zachael's words pulled her from her thoughts.

Murmurs of agreement followed his comment, and she blushed. Sage waved away their words when Gav leveled her with a look and asked, "What is so bad about planning a wedding? My wife loved it."

She turned from his searching eyes to stare at the sky. How could she explain herself without giving away her true feelings, or rather the lack thereof, for the crown prince?

"I wasn't born to this life," Sage whispered. "I always imagined myself marrying behind my family's home in the forest, or maybe in my meadow." She shrugged, trying to cover the emotion rolling in her gut. "I figured I would know each and every face in the crowd and it would be a simple affair. I'd be surrounded by friends and family with the man I loved. I only wanted simple. I still want simple." It was the truth and her dream. She dropped her head and gestured to the palace behind her. "This is anything but." Sage pulled a face. "What is the difference between ivory or eggshell? Anyone?" She spun in a circle and received shrugs. "That's my point. Who cares what color of cream the napkins are? And my betrothed has dumped it all on me."

"He hates it as much as you do. Perhaps he thought you would enjoy it," Garreth tossed in. "But it's all worth it, right? The responsibilities come with the man." Garreth raised a brow, as if daring her to say something to the contrary.

Sage swallowed a bitter retort and spoke sentiments more suited to a woman in love. "He is worth any trial, even suffering through wedding plans." The words were ash on her tongue.

In two days, she would say her vows, promising her life to a man she cared nothing for. Just the thought had her feeling stifled. She needed to get away for a while. "You are probably right." She pasted on a smile and turned on her heel. "I think I'm about done, I need to get out of the sun. Gav, I will meet you here two hours before sunset."

Sage fled the training ground in favor of the palace, slipping into one of its shadowed coves. Gavriel appeared several moments later, striding briskly down the corridor. Once he'd disappeared around the corner, she slipped back outside and snagged an abandoned cloak from the pile with a mental note to return it later.

She needed to see her papa. Her mum visited every day, even her brothers, Zeke and Seb dropped by a time or two, but she had yet to see her father, and she craved his company desperately.

Slipping past the walls was all too easy as no one had noticed her departure. Sage took her time walking to the forge, finding comfort in the familiarity of the town as she meandered from one street to the next. Being so cooped up inside the palace had started to feel unbearable, so, with each step away from it, she could feel her tension falling away.

The hustle and bustle of the community brought a certain amount of solace as well. Grubby children laughingly chased one another, whipping around the scolding merchants and gossiping laundresses, their little bare feet slapping against the ground. Their bright eyes and joyful smiles brought forth one of her own.

Every home and business was familiar, and she felt as though each one she passed was welcoming her home. Sage rounded the final corner, her heart leaping in her throat. Everything looked the same, from the open stall displaying their wares to the scrolling vine shutters decorating the window. Each piece that adorned her family's arched door widened her smile. Every year, she made a flower and presented it as a gift to her mum, and her mum displayed each one with love and pride. Sage flew to her home, kicking up dust behind her. She skidded to a stop when she slipped into the forge, the sweltering heat welcoming her home. Jacob was leaning over her father, checking his chest and both men jerked when they heard her abrupt arrival.

"Papa."

Both adoration and relief were evident on his face as he stood, opening his arms wide and she ran straight to him. He wrapped her in his warm arms, and, immediately, she felt both comforted and safe. Sage grinned against his tunic when she realized that, as she wrapped her own arms round him, his waist seemed to be a bit thicker.

"Sage," his warm voice curled around her. "I am so happy to have you home, love."

Sage couldn't believe the difference in her father. She lifted her head, taking in his altered appearance carefully. His face now had a healthy glow to it, and his cheeks were no longer sharp and gaunt but rounded. Even his breathing seemed less labored.

"Are you well, Papa?"

He cupped her cheek and kissed her on the forehead. "Still a worrier, I see. But yes, love, I am well."

Sage squeezed him once more before throwing her arms round the Healer. "Thank you," she whispered in his ear, a wealth of emotion in those two little words.

He tweaked her nose, his bronze eyes twinkling. "All in a day's work. Think nothing of it." Jacob released her and turned to her father, clasping his hand. "Keep taking the tonic I gave you, and I will visit again in a week."

Jacob retrieved his bag and winked at her before exiting the room. Sage watched the curtain ripple in the wake of Jacob's departure. There was no way to express the depth of her gratitude to the Healer. She hadn't seen her Papa in a month, and it was like looking at a different man. A tiny voice in her head whispered that she was lucky to have been asked to be the liaison for this peace treaty and that here was the silver lining to her storm. Her papa was healing and that made every sacrifice well worth it.

"You're staring at that curtain awfully hard. I assure you it is the same as it has always been."

His poor joke pulled a reluctant smile out of her. She shrugged off her cloak and wiped her forehead, luxuriating in the forge's familiar warmth.

"You are looking well, Papa, and I'm glad of it."

His chest puffed up, preening, his reaction so typically male that she had to bite back another smile.

"The tonics from Jacob have done their job."

"Tonics?" she asked, curious.

Colm's face soured. "Disgusting liquid. But your mum threatened right away to pour them down my gullet if I didn't take them so here I am." He widened his eyes. "She's intimidating when she wants to be."

"Imagine having her as your mum."

"Imagine having her as your wife," he shot back.

They both sniggered and plopped down in a seat. Sage plucked a blade from the stack and began cleaning it out of habit. She had so many things on the tip of her tongue, but each time she opened her mouth they seemed stuck there. Her papa's gaze rested on her but he stayed silent, cleaning blades at her side, waiting for her to speak. They didn't speak for some time, each content to simply spend time together doing the same thing. What was she going to say to him, anyway? That she was sorry for making such a big mistake that tore her from their family? That she couldn't fathom how she would survive the years to come? That the thought of overseeing the palace's day-to-day affairs made her want to jump off a cliff? Where did she even begin?

Her papa's large hand closed over hers, pausing her vigorous scrubbing on a hilt. He uncurled her clenched fingers and took the rag from her. Sage lifted her head and met her papa's gaze, hoping her every emotion wasn't written all over her face.

"What is on your mind, my little shadow?"

She could feel her eyes stinging so she turned away, hoping to stay the flood of tears threatening to spill over. Her mind was a muddle of guilt and anxiety, so many thoughts of 'what if' when it came to both her future and her past. It was enough to drown her, but there was no use crying over something she couldn't change. The course of her life had been set and she needed to just accept it.

"Love, you need to speak to me. I can't read your mind. What's going on?"

"Why haven't you visited me?" she twisted toward him, surprised by her own question. "Mum has visited every day, even Seb and Zeke, but not you. Why? Are you—" She swallowed. "Are you ashamed of me?"

"No," he gasped and scooted next to her, forcing her to meet his eyes. "It wasn't that I didn't want to come and visit, but I know you don't need me there to help you pick out things for the wedding. I also knew you would need to escape all of that at some point and the forge has always been the place for you to do so. Thus, I have waited for you to come here. Now tell me what's on your mind, love. I am listening, and it's obvious you need to get it out."

Sage stared at his dear face, the warmth in his eyes encouraging her to bare her soul, so she did. "I don't know if I can do it, Papa. I could feel confident keeping a small house but not a kingdom. I never wanted to be a lady, and yet that's the role I'll be forced to play *for the rest of my life*. When I think of spending my whole life in that palace it's like I can't breathe. I want to just run away and never look back."

He placed a hand over hers. "Your mum, brothers, and I will pack up right now and flee with you if that's what you need. Just say the word and it will be done. We want to see you happy."

Sage clutched his hand tighter "I know, Papa, but how could I do such a thing when so many would suffer?"

Colm caressed her face. "You have grown into a wonderful woman, Sage, and your heart is filled with more compassion and love than most people's. You have a selfless heart, and I'm proud of you for it."

Sage pressed her face into his hand as if she could soak up his love through her pores. But his words weren't enough to erase the guilt. Sage wasn't selfless, for her accepting the assignment had been with ulterior motives. Primarily, it had been to secure a healer for her father. If she was truly selfless, she would have done anything to help the people, healer or not, and done so without the anger and resentment currently festering inside her.

"He came to see me."

"Rafe?" It was painful to even speak his name.

"No, your betrothed."

She stared at him blankly. The crown prince had done what? "I don't think I heard you right, Papa."

"Your heard me right."

A dull ringing filled ears. Betrothed. Her soon-to-be husband had visited her home. *How dare he come here, what audacity!* She tried to control the rage rising up in her, suppressing it as best she could. "Oh?" she asked mildly, her voice wavering just a bit.

Her papa eyed her expression and began cleaning another blade. "He offered us a place in the palace and to buy our home."

Sage was sure her face was an alarming shade of red. She and Tehl had already spoken on this subject and she *thought* they had already agreed on a solution. "I assume you declined?"

"I did. The forge has been in our family for generations."

"How did he react to that?"

"He offered me a compromise."

"Which was?" Sage asked through clenched teeth.

"He is looking to expand the knowledge of his palace apprentices. The crown prince wants me to train some of them. I agreed." Colm paused his cleaning. "He also left a generous amount of gold for your acquiesce toll."

Acquiesce toll, what a joke. She hadn't acquiesced to anything. The crown prince had well and truly bought her like horseflesh. "Did I fetch a good price at least?" she asked sarcastically.

Her papa snorted. "Your brothers and I had to stash gold in the walls and bury some behind the forge. We have more than we could ever spend in a lifetime." He met her angry eyes. "But you're worth far more than any treasure. No matter how much he left, it would never equal you. Sage, you are precious."

His loving statement soothed and pierced her heart. Even if the only people who valued her for just herself were her family, she could live with that. Many didn't have a loving family. Sage counted herself lucky to have the overwhelming love and support that she did.

"He is nothing like Sam."

She smirked. That was the damn truth.

"He is very serious. He assured me you would be well looked after and want for nothing."

Sage's smile slipped. Materially, she would want nothing, but the one thing she longed for would be out of her grasp forever: her freedom to do as she chose. She forced her lips into a weak smile, just for her papa. She didn't want him worrying. "He will keep his word."

"He will, or he will have your brothers and myself to deal with." Colm chuckled darkly. "I don't care who he is. No one hurts my daughter and gets away with it."

Sage didn't doubt it for a moment. Her papa would go to the ends of the earth to care for his family. Soon she would be part of a new family, though. She stiffened as a thought occurred to her. She would no longer be a Blackwell, but a Ramses, and, for some reason, that angered her. Not only was she going to be assimilated into a new life and family, but she would lose her name too. Sage snatched up a scythe and polished it like she could scrub away all the hurt, anger, and confusion fighting inside her.

She and her father worked in silence until there were no more pieces to polish. Sage stared at the blade in her hand, her reflection distorted in its uneven surface. It felt poetic as it was also a fitting description of her inner self: indistinguishable, distorted, ruined. Sage thrust the blade onto a bed of velvet and quickly stood, stalking to the window. The lush green forest beckoned to her, immense trees standing like soldiers at its border, and she was filled with a longing to visit her meadow. The wind whistled a melancholy melody that spoke to her battered soul. Sage felt her father's eyes on her but she didn't turn. She just soaked up the picturesque scene before her. Her eyes sketched every limb as she tried to imprint each in her mind for she had no idea when she could next visit.

She frowned at the trees when yet another thought occurred to her. For anyone desiring to do so, it would be extremely easy to sneak through the forest to the back of her family's home. The Mort Wall may be miles away but that didn't mean it wasn't within the Scythians' power to make it this far. "Please lock your doors and windows every night, Papa, and never leave Mum alone washing clothes in the back." She tore her eyes from her forest to her father.

Alarm was evident on his face. "It is so dangerous?"

She turned to lean against the window frame. "It may not be now, but it is only a matter of time. Be vigilant."

"Is there nothing you can tell me?"

Sage debated a moment before answering. "People have disappeared, and it has been confirmed that the Scythians are sneaking over the Mort Wall and that, for some reason, they're taking them captive."

"My God," her father whispered. "Do you know what's become of them?"

"We have no idea, but I can only imagine the worst." Looking back outside she grimaced, finally realizing the hour. Gavriel would skin her alive for being late to their training, and he would no doubt lock her up if he knew she'd slipped out for the day.

Her father eyed the fading daylight and stood from his stool. "It's best you be getting back, love. I am sure you are being missed by now."

Sage scoffed, for, in her mind, no one truly missed her. They were just worried about what it would mean if she didn't marry the crown prince. She rushed into her papa's arms, once again surprised at how much stronger he was since the last time she had seen him. "I love you Papa, so much."

"I love you, too." His arms tightened, crushing her against his chest. "I am always here if you need me."

She would miss seeing his twinkling green eyes every day. He always made time for her, treating her with patience and kindness. In her mind, there was no better man.

She inhaled the familiar smoky scent of her father one last time and squeezed her eyes shut to keep more tears from falling. All she had to do was make it out of the forge. He kissed the crown of her head and released her. She stifled a sob when she saw his eyes were damp too.

He cupped her cheeks and smiled. "You are my only daughter, and I don't want to give you up. When you came into this world, you were the most breathtaking baby I ever beheld. I spoke to you, and you turned those big green eyes and looked right at me. At that moment, I was lost to you, I knew you would make my life challenging, but in the best way. I've loved raising you and watching you grow up into a fine woman." He stared into her eyes solemnly. "I know this was not your choice, I want a different future for you from the one you've ended up with." He sucked in a deep breath like he was fortifying himself. "But you will make a fine ruler." A smile. "A warrior queen. You are exactly what Aermia needs right now so never doubt yourself. You have much to offer, don't forget that."

She merely nodded, lips trembling. When she spoke, she could not prevent her voice from cracking with emotion. "Okay, Papa." Sage lifted herself onto her tiptoes and kissed his whiskered cheek. "Love you." She stepped back and strode toward the door.

"I will see you in two days, love."

Her stomach dropped at the reminder.

She peeked over her shoulder with a wobbly smile. "I will be the one in green."

Sage slipped through the curtain and out of the forge, and a cool breeze chilled her warm body. She shivered and set a brisk pace toward the palace as the sun sank below the horizon.

After a time, she halted in her tracks and just let people flow around her. She was already late, someone would have missed her by now, so it mattered little if she was even later. She might as well enjoy her evening. Enticing music drifted from an alehouse across the lane, so Sage stepped from the throng of people into the dim parlor. She scoped the area and moved to an empty table in the corner. When she gestured to the barkeep, a serving wench came quickly over and slapped a mug of warm ale in front of her. Sage flipped her a coin and lifted the tasty brew to her lips. She leaned against the wall, watching the room.

The three-person band in the corner attracted all attention. The music caressed her, soft and seductive, begging her to move with it. Sage gestured to the serving wench for another ale when she'd emptied hers. The place continued to fill with people, each seeking some sort of solace or escape, just like she was. Torches were lit, casting soft light across the room.

Sage brushed off any attempts of conversation by interested men, ignoring the lingering looks she received. She snorted. It was funny that she was a betrothed woman now, not that you would know. She had no cuffs or rings to signify she was already taken. Chuckling, she took a swig of her drink when a large man suddenly plopped down across from her, his hood up.

"Seat's taken," she said gruffly. He didn't move though. She scowled at him and fingered the blade at her thigh. "I am not interested."

"Oh, but I am so interested in you and what exactly it is you're doing." As he said this, he tipped back his hood, revealing golden curls and sapphire eyes.

The damn spymaster had found her.

SİXTEEN

SAM

HE RAISED A BROW, WAITING for her answer.

Sage rolled her eyes and sipped her drink, watching him over the edge of her mug. "I would think it was obvious."

He placed his elbows on the sticky table, squinting at her green eyes. Her pupils were a little larger than normal. He cast a disgusted look around, noting each of the exits just in case. How long had she been in the alehouse? "Are you drunk?"

She glowered at him. "No, that would be dangerous and stupid."

He scoffed. She sat in an alehouse, surrounded by men, many of whom were no doubt criminals, and most of them were eyeing her like they each wanted a bite of her. Not that he could blame them. She certainly was beautiful and she shone brightly in contrast with the tarnished wenches whose breasts were tastelessly falling out of their dresses.

"So is drinking alone when you are the target of so many enemies." His lips thinned in disapproval. "Also, leaving the palace without telling anyone."

Sage grinned at him and lifted her leg onto the bench, placing her half-full mug on her elevated knee. She tossed her brown hair, looking haughty. "Am I supposed to ask for permission? Am I still the Crown's prisoner?"

Sam would never forget how she looked battered and broken in that cell. He'd make sure that never happened to her or anyone ever again who was under their care.

Her grin grew brittle at his silence. "That didn't work out so well for me before. Mark my words, I will never again be held against my will."

She took another sip, her eyes darting over his shoulder. Sage scowled at someone, presumably the oaf who had been ogling her since he walked in. Sam cleared his throat, and her gaze returned to his face.

"You are no one's prisoner."

She sniggered behind her hand. "Mmmhmmm..."

Sage was acting childish. In the time he'd known her, Sam had never experienced this blasé attitude from her, and it irked him. He'd been searching for quite some time, praying no one had stolen her. In the two weeks she'd been at the palace there had already been three attempts on her life which, thankfully, the elite foiled. Sage was being careless with her life and the future of Aermia.

"Did you ever stop to think of the worry you would cause by leaving?"

She let out a charming laugh, causing more than one pair of male eyes to turn her way and linger—not that she appeared to notice. Sam gritted his teeth, wishing she could be more inconspicuous. Sage drained the rest of her drink and slammed the empty mug on the table. "Worry for the Crown, I am sure."

His anger lifted a notch. He snapped his hand out and grabbed her wrist, pulling gently, but firmly, so she leaned over the table. Sam touched her chin, forcing her to meet his eyes. Her careless smile melted and a knowing light entered her eyes that made him uncomfortable.

"I was wondering when you would show yourself."

What was she talking about? "What do you mean?" Sam asked, never taking his eyes from hers.

Sage leaned closer, like she had a secret. "I saw a glimpse of the real spymaster." Her lips turned up into a smug smile. "You can fool everyone else, but you cannot hide from me."

"What am I hiding?" Sam ran his eyes over her features with deliberate slowness, trying to gauge her meaning.

She shrugged, her gaze just as intent. "Anger, pain, guilt; a number of things really. I bet the only people who truly understand you are your cousin and brother, but I doubt either of them knows the true extent of your façade. I think you've worn it so long you don't know yourself what is real and what isn't."

Sam kept his face impassive, despite the fact that her words hit disturbingly close to home. He'd played so many parts over the years, he sometimes felt like he'd lost himself. She was very keen to have noticed, and he idly thought it was a shame she wasn't one of his sneaks. He quickly pulled himself from his thoughts. He wasn't here to have a heart to heart with Sage; he was here to retrieve her.

"Over the last few hours, Tehl, the Elite, and I have searched high and low for you. We were worried that you had been taken or worse. Now you can imagine how I feel finding you, instead, sitting here, drinking in a pub."

Sage's eyes narrowed, and she tugged her arm from his grasp. "Don't you dare judge me. I have done nothing but comply over, and over, giving everything of myself to help everyone around me. So what if I wanted a drink before I shackled myself to a man, a title, and cage I want nothing to do with? It's a very little thing to let me have this small moment to myself."

Sam tensed when silver flashed into her hand. Where in God's name had that blade come from? The longer he spent around Sage, the more intrigued he became. His new sister was a mixture of soft and hard. If only she could get over her aversion to his brother, she had potential to be a fine asset to their kingdom. He snorted. That and if his brother finally learned some tact. It was going to be a long road to success.

She stabbed the blade at him. "I have seen you with new, let us call them *diversions*, every day of the week. You do not get to judge me, or counsel me on my actions and morals. I wanted a chance to think in peace, so I took this chance as it is the only one I shall probably be afforded for some time."

"Yes, but at the expense of others," he retorted.

"That's rich coming from a representative of the Crown. When have you had to make a sacrifice that cost you everything?" Her eyes dropped for a moment before returning to him, filled with ire. "So forgive me if I don't feel bad for taking a couple hours to myself so I could say goodbye to my life and family. After all, I'm *only* continuing yours at the expense of mine."

Sam shot to his feet when she stood from the bench suddenly. The last thing he needed tonight was to hunt her down. Again. Sam scrutinized her as she shifted to the balls of her feet. He was sure he could keep up, but it would be a bloody waste of time. He had several meetings he needed to make tonight so he needed her to come *now*.

"Are you ready then, my lady?"

Sage stared at the back exit for a long moment before tossing a glare his way and stalking to the door, her cloak swirling around her. Sam smiled behind her back. She may be tough on the outside, but she was warm and passionate once you got past her walls. He'd enjoyed making her scowl. They would be great friends; she just didn't know it yet.

SEVENTEEN

TEHL

WHERE THE HELL HAD SHE gone? When her ladies complained that she hadn't shown up for her dress fitting he figured she was out practicing, as was her custom every morning and evening, much to the shock of his court. When Gavriel barged into his study, worried that she didn't show up for her customary bout, he felt behooved to send a few Elite to discreetly search for her. It wasn't until all four Elite showed up empty-handed that he finally got frustrated and, while grumbling under his breath, stomped from the room, determined to find her himself.

His first thought was to visit his father, for he knew they shared an affinity for hiding out whenever there were royal duties to attend to. When he got there, however, he was surprised to learn she hadn't been there all day. Next, he checked the infirmary, but Mira, likewise, had no idea of her whereabouts, and, by then, Tehl had started to actually worry. By a stroke of luck, Jacob overheard Tehl's inquiries and casually mentioned Sage visiting her father. He'd stalked out of the room irritated that she hadn't notified someone of her departure. Was it too much to ask that she use good sense and take measures to protect herself?

He took Sam, Gavriel, and a few Elite to the forge, but yet again she'd evaded him. Even her father, Colm, didn't know where she was, having thought she'd headed home already. Now more concerned, they broke up into three groups, his team searching the fishermans' district. They checked everywhere they could think of, even visiting Captain Femi, but to no avail. By the time they returned to the training yard, Gav's group was already there, still empty-handed.

"Anything?" he growled, already knowing the answer.

"Nothing," Gavriel said tensely. "We need to form a larger search group and soon. Something could have happened."

Tehl nodded and pushed back the thread of panic twisting inside him. Sage was smart. If someone had stolen her, she'd escape. They just needed to find out where to. The Elite surrounded him and someone procured a map and a lantern. His men squatted down next to him as he spread the map across the dirt. He squinted at it. Was she stolen, or did she run? It would narrow their search if they knew if she ran or was taken. He tugged on his hair, frustrated that he didn't know her mind well enough to make a guess. Worried purple eyes caught his attention. Gav was the closest to her. He would know.

Tehl caught Gav's eye and jerked his chin, standing. Once the two of them had walked out of hearing range he turned and looked his cousin straight in the eye. "Is she running?"

Gav blew out a frustrated breath. "No. Sage was upset this morning but she wouldn't leave like this."

"Why was she upset?" He had barely seen her so it couldn't have been his fault at least.

"You dumped the wedding on her."

Tehl blinked at him. "Women love planning weddings. Emma loved it."

Gavriel tossed him a droll look. "Is Sage anything like Emma or even most of the women of your acquaintance?"

"No," Tehl drawled, thinking of her colorful word choices and warrior skills. In all his life, he had never met a woman like her. Her boldness, fortitude, and compassion set her apart from the women he'd been raised with.

"Then why would you think she would enjoy planning a wedding?" Gav lowered his voice. "She's been forced into it with a man she hardly knows nor cares for? I mean, think about it. Do you remember how you felt planning the Midsummer Festival?"

Tehl grimaced. What a bloody nightmare.

"Exactly." Gav pinched the bridge of his nose as he continued, "You had months to plan it. You threw her into this without any prior experience and worse still, your father has given her a scant two weeks to do so. It's an event most of the kingdom will attend so you can see why she'd be, not only upset, but more than a little overwhelmed."

He was an idiot. He'd been so relieved that it was no longer his responsibility that he hadn't stopped to think about how she might feel. Tehl simply assumed she had plenty of help and that it wouldn't be a problem. He sighed. What was done, was done. Now they could only move forward.

Tehl returned to his men, crouching next to Zachael who had joined the group after he'd stepped away with Gav. Zachael sent him a look that promised questions later as Tehl filled him in on their progress so far.

"We searched here and here." Tehl pointed to the fisherman and merchant district. "Gavriel will lead a group south and..." A commotion at the gate drowned out his voice. He stood and caught Sage shoving his brother away from her.

"Who knows where those hands have been so keep them to yourself."

She was safe.

Something loosened in his chest just knowing that, but with the relief came anger. He quickly ran his eyes over her, seeking any sign of abuse, but not a hair was out of place. He found that to be, somehow, both reassuring and frustrating, especially when she unclipped the oversized cloak and sauntered up to Garreth, batting her eyelashes as she spoke.

"I borrowed your cloak this morning, I hope you don't mind." Tehl's jaw clenched when she next lifted her hair up, baring her neck, her back slightly arched. Garreth's eyes very briefly skimmed her curves before snapping to him, a question in his eyes.

Before he could do anything, Sage touched the Elite's arm, effectively returning his attention to her.

What was going on?

"You're not upset, are you?"

"I don't mind, darlin'."

Garreth placed a hand over hers, his thumb running along her skin while the entire group just stared at the spectacle before them. She was flirting with one of his men, *right in front of him.*

What. The. Hell?

A sturdy hand gripped his shoulder. "Calm down, she isn't propositioning him," Sam whispered.

"Like hell she isn't," Tehl ground out. "Where did you find her?"

"In an alehouse."

He saw red.

Tehl considered himself a calm and logical person, but there was something about Sage that made him lose it. Here he had been, worrying over her, searching high and low, just hoping nothing terrible had happened, while she'd actually been out drinking.

"Do you understand what you put me through?" he thundered, without thought.

Sage dropped her hand and turned to him, cocking a hip. "My lord, I went to visit my family."

Tehl jerked forward, out of Sam's grasp. "We searched for you for hours. You left without notifying anyone, leaving your protection behind. Neither your father nor Lilja knew where you had gone."

She smirked.

She bloody smirked at him. Like his words were funny.

"My men wasted their personal time searching for you. Did you want to punish me?"

Her mocking laughter floated over the silent group of men. "Not everything is about you, my lord. I needed to get away and say goodbye to my family. Would you deny me that? Keep me here forever?"

Reason filtered through, causing him to bite his tongue to keep his damning words from spilling out. "No. But your actions put you in danger."

"I wasn't in any danger." She jerked her chin toward the men surrounding their display. "Your men can attest to that."

"You are not infallible; I have had you before."

The expression on her face made him pause.

"You will pay for that comment," Zachael muttered under his breath.

Tehl's brows furrowed in confusion as a round of sniggers erupted around him.

"Not the best choice of words, brother," Sam imparted.

He stiffened, realizing his mistake too late. Sage's face turned an alarming shade of scarlet at the blatant reminder of her capture. Her hands clenched at her sides.

"You've never had me," she emphasized, glowering at the surrounding men who were now trying to disguise their laughs as coughs. "You surprised me one time."

"One time is all it takes. My enemies are your enemies. You can't wander around doing whatever you want, you have responsibilities."

"Responsibilities?" Sage hissed.

Tehl froze. He knew that tone, it was the same one Gav used before he ripped someone's head off. Seething rage.

"You want to speak of *responsibilities*? With *me*?" Her pitch rose, almost screeching.

He wanted to rub his ears, but he didn't think it would go over well. Her arms gestured wildly, a crazed look on her face.

"Where have you been the last week? Not once did you help or give me guidance. I never even *wanted* a big wedding. I'd be fine with a quiet ceremony in a meadow but YOU—" She jabbed a finger at him, eyes blazing. "*YOU* are the royal. We're doing this because of *you* so this should all be on your shoulders, not mine. I will not be your rug or dumping grounds whenever you have undesirable tasks. We will be equals or nothing at all."

"Nothing at all? You are *already* mine, I paid the acquiesce toll not even five days ago. In two days, you will wear my cuffs, my ring. It is already as good as done." The red in her face deepened with every word he spoke. Why was she getting so angry this time? He had merely stated the truth.

"Now you've done it, you bloody idiot," Gavriel whispered.

Tehl spared his cousin an annoyed glance before focusing on the woman spitting fire in front of him. She stormed up to him, stopping two strides away.

"Do you enjoy humiliating me?" Sage spat, her eyes burning.

"What are you talking about?"

"Don't play stupid, Your Highness. Did it ease your conscience to pay my acquiesce toll?" She gestured to her curvy body. "You may have bought me like a whore, but I will never wear your cuffs."

That was downright offensive. He had never treated her like a whore, not once. When he visited her father, he'd been respectful and was trying to do the right thing. This union might not be what either of them had envisioned for their future, but he still wanted to follow the proper protocol pf a groom as best he could. The curious looks from his men were problematic. Sage was *very* close to giving them away.

"Leave us," he bellowed. The Elite bowed and removed themselves, leaving only Garreth, Zachael, Gavriel, and Samuel. Tehl scowled at Sage, every inch of her body radiating defiance. "Are you out of your mind? Do you not recall the need for secrecy?"

"I didn't forget, I just don't care."

That heated his blood. The troublesome wench. "Well you better start caring," he said, through clenched teeth, "we have an agreement."

"We do, but don't you dare tell me how I can react to something. I can say what I want and how I feel. You will not silence me. I have my own mind."

"Even if it reveals us?"

"You mean reveals *you?*" she challenged, tossing her silky brown hair.

Tehl stepped toward her. If Sage made threats, she needed to know he wouldn't back down. He had no problem discussing things or working through problems, but he'd be damned before he was cowed on something this important.

"If you fail to keep your end of the deal, then I will forgo mine. You're the one who asked for time." Tehl wrapped an arm around her waist and pulled her against him, smoothing his hand down her back.

She paled but held her ground, still as stone in his arms, not an ounce of give. "I would kill you first." She twitched, and he felt something sharp pressed against his stomach.

A blade.

Always with a damn blade.

Tehl scowled at her, wondering where she pulled the dagger from without him noticing.

"Listen, and listen well, my lord. I will marry you, but I will never wear your cuffs. I belong to only myself, even if you paid my father more gold than a dragon could horde. You can't buy my loyalty, compliance, or affection."

Her dark green eyes glittered dangerously. "I am to be your wife in name only, we are enemies that happen to have a common enemy, nothing more."

Cuffs. There was that word again. It was the second time she'd mentioned it. When a couple married, tradition mandated that both husband and wife wear cuffs, his on the biceps and hers on the wrists. It was a fitting symbol of them being bound to each other forever. It also served as a sign to others, as well as a reminder to themselves, of their union. Whether she liked it or not, they would be bound to each other in two days.

Tehl studied her, attempting to discern the turbulent thoughts swirling around in her head. His gaze dropped to her wrists, and he stared for a moment before gently sliding his fingers along the twisted flesh. Sage jerked her arm away like his fingers burned her. Was that a reaction to his touch? Or was it born from the things she'd suffered?

He raised his eyes back to her face, and he actually felt pity for her. Her whole body was defensive but behind that he could see there was embarrassment and pain. Tehl kept his face impassive. If she saw his pity, she would only shut down. Instead, Tehl set her away from him and stepped back. As soon as he did so, she flipped her dagger and stowed it in an invisible pocket on her thigh. Momentarily distracted, Tehl leaned closer, intrigued.

Where did it go? Did she have special pockets in her trousers? Tehl shook himself. Thoughts for another time.

"It's perfectly clear you'd rather not wear my cuffs but it doesn't really matter; you must." Tehl held up a hand when her mouth opened. Probably to curse him to the leviathans or something. He brushed his sleeve not meeting her eyes. "Have you not thought about the fact that I will wear yours as well?"

Her mouth opened and closed a couple of times before she huffed out a breath. "I... I hadn't considered it."

Sage's honesty cooled some of the frustration, and he was able to respond more calmly. "Look, we need to learn from each other." Tehl ran a self-conscious hand through his hair, giving her a small smile. "As you have already observed, I am not gifted with words or a great understanding of people. You must tell me what you mean or want, preferably in private, or I won't understand. After what you suffered, I can understand your aversion to something that represents being bound, but keep in mind you're not the only one who is bound in this. You're not alone."

"I don't believe you."

Tehl reined in the spark of anger her stubbornness set off and merely raised a midnight brow. "Have I ever lied to you?"

Sage pursed her lips, squinting at him. After a moment, she turned her head to the side. "No," she mumbled.

"What was that?" Tehl baited.

She finally turned to him, glaring, and crossed her arms. "No," she said, more loudly this time.

"Exactly. Stop treating me like I will stab you in the back every time you turn around. Since you came here, I have put your health and wellbeing above everyone else's whereas *you* have lied repeatedly. Don't punish me for crimes I did not commit." Tehl lifted an arm toward Sam, Gav, Zachael, and Garreth. "And these men have protected you from more than you realize. I would appreciate it if you could keep your disdain for everything about your life to a minimum when in their company. They deserve more."

She studied the group of men. "I understand. I will make an effort not to let my bitterness bite them." She turned back to him, both brows lifted. "My health and wellbeing? If my wellbeing was really your priority you wouldn't have dumped the entire stress of this wedding on my head."

"It was my understanding that women loved that sort of thing." Tehl winced as her scowl deepened. "I have since been informed that you, however, do not share that sentiment."

"Of course not. I mean, would *you* find something like that enjoyable?"

"No, planning the one festival was more than enough for a lifetime." His nose wrinkled in distaste. "It was a nightmare, and I hated every moment."

"Precisely. At least we are in agreement on one thing." Sage twisted her lips. "I will not do the tasks you discard because you can't stand them. We have to do them together, share the burden."

Tehl wanted nothing to do with the celebrations, but what she proposed made sense, it was only fair. Thus, much to his surprise, he reached out and, for the second time in two weeks, shook the hand of his betrothed. And when she didn't jerk out of his grasp immediately, Tehl counted that as a small victory. "Agreed."

She gave a brisk nod and strode away, returning to the four men still waiting for them. Tehl trailed behind, allowing her to speak with his brother before she strolled toward the palace. Tehl arrived at Zachael's side, noting that all the men stared after his betrothed. Sam was obviously both intrigued and a bit lustful, Gavriel was undoubtedly concerned, and Zachael seemed to feel admiration. Tehl, too, watched her disappear and, for the first time, counted himself lucky. She drove him crazy but he could have done a lot worse.

"That one right there is a gem. She may be rough around the edges but she will surprise us all, mark my words," Zachael commented.

"Sage is full of surprises," Sam grouched.

Tehl smiled at his brother's tone. Sam always hated mysteries he couldn't solve and it was obvious that Sage was one of them. She didn't quite fit into any category: rebel, nobility, common, or royal. Sage just was.

EİGHTEEN

SAGE

THE FOLLOWING DAY PASSED IN a flurry of fittings and last minute wedding preparations, such as wine tasting, not that Sage complained. The wine certainly helped when it came to practicing the wedding dance. Normally, she loved dancing but the shrew teaching was a real stickler when it came to form. When Sage finally spied her door late that evening, relief eased some of the tightness in her shoulders; her bed was close.

Sage pushed her door open and shut it, leaning her back against it, tipping her head up. Silence. Sage smiled as she was at last able to enjoy a moment of peace. No judging looks from her ladies in waiting, no instructor correcting her, no one demanding her attention. Just blessed silence. She dropped her head to admire the faint light filtering through the glass doors of her terrace. The sky was clear so the stars on display were breathtaking.

It was at that moment that a most unwelcome thought popped into her head: The next time she gazed at the stars she would be a married woman. She rubbed her arms as a chill ran up her spine at the thought. Her eyes darted to the cold hearth of the fireplace; sitting by the warmth of a fire would feel marvelous.

Sage bolted the door and wove around the furniture, avoiding the areas where darkness clung. She stooped in front of the fireplace and pulled pitched-soaked pine kindling from the basket. She was thankful one of the servants left the kindling, knowing she appreciated her privacy. She strategically placed the kindling in the cold hearth and struck her sulfur match. The spark caught the pine few after a few tries. Carefully she breathed on the precious flames, coaxing them to life. Soon, she had a roaring fire and it chased away the darkness, or most of it anyway. There was still a pool of darkness perched in her chair, which, up until now, she had studiously ignored.

Without turning around she addressed it, "I was wondering when you would show up. What do you want, Methi?"

A deep masculine laugh raised goosebumps on her arms. Sage scowled and rubbed at her arms, irritated that he'd been able to get a rise out of her before even saying a word.

"I was wondering if you had lost some of your edge when you didn't seem to notice me."

"Not at all," she muttered, offended. "I deemed a fire more important than giving you the attention you're seeking." Sage pushed herself up and spun around to face Rafe who was sprawled comfortably in her chair like he owned the place. She'd known he would eventually seek her out, but she still didn't feel ready for it. The lies he'd told her and the sting of his betrayal was not something she was yet able to let go of, nor her confusion over their last meeting. His hatefully spoken words still echoed in her mind, but now was not the time to dwell on those things. She pushed those thoughts aside and stood erect. Looking him in the eye, she said, "You have my attention. What do you want?"

He ran his eyes along her body, and though it was not overly sexual, she could still see heat in his gaze. "You look well."

Sage snorted. She looked horrible. The lack of sleep combined with the exhausting schedule and the palace training had already etched black bags beneath her eyes. "Now, now. We both know you can lie better than that."

His face pinched at her comment, but she wouldn't take it back. These were consequences of his actions and losing her trust was one of them.

Rafe straightened and pushed himself from her chair, making her suddenly very aware of how far she was from the door. She felt a wave of sadness at the fact that she felt the need to be wary around him, but she also knew that, despite her having spent over a year in his company, he was very much a stranger to her.

"I wanted to offer my apologies."

She blinked. That was unexpected.

Rafe inhaled deeply and released his breath through flared nostrils, his eyes solemn. "I was out of line and had no right to say those things to you. I am fully aware that you are not that type of woman. I was angry and upset, but that still doesn't make it right."

Sage nodded. She understood saying something you don't mean in anger. "I understand. Our last conversation was difficult for both of us." That was the truth. Sage understood his duty to protect his own kingdom, and therefor his identity, but it didn't make his dishonesty any less hurtful. The fact was it had been *his* decisions that ultimately led to her torture, as well as being ousted from the rebellion and sold to the Crown. Sage might even have been able to work through these things and forgive him, except she had no idea if the man she thought she knew even existed. She had given everything to Rafe and his rebellion but gained nothing but pain and heartache. The entire situation had left a brand on her heart; she would not make that mistake again anytime soon.

"What are you thinking, little one? I can see the gears of your mind have been set in motion."

Sage returned her focus to Rafe. "I'm wondering if I ever knew you, or if it was all a facade." Her body tensed when he stepped toward her.

Rafe froze at her reaction. A frustrated breath huffed out of him before he began approaching her again, this time holding his hands out to his sides in supplication. "I've been myself with you from the beginning. I *never* changed who I was, and, although there were certain aspects of myself pertaining to my purpose and identity that I didn't tell you, I was *always* real with you."

Sage stared at him, trying to decide if she believed him or not. She supposed it was true, that in all her time with him, their relationship and his treatment of her never changed, so either he was the best actor the kingdom had ever seen, or he was telling the truth. After a beat, she decided. "I believe you."

His shoulders slumped, as if a great weight had finally been lifted off.

"You don't know how glad I am to hear it, little one. I have agonized over this every moment these last weeks. It was all I could do not to come straight here and get you." Rafe ran a hand through his silky hair and shot her a scowl. "Don't think I didn't know you ran straight here."

Sage crossed her arms and glared right back. How dare he! "If I wasn't worried for my safety and that of my family, I wouldn't have *had* to leave early. I just couldn't trust you not to try and spirit me away in the night. I had no choice, thanks to you."

He gave her a rueful smile. "I'll admit that was my plan that first night. Color me surprised when I didn't find you on the Sirenidae."

Sage smirked. "And how did Lilja react to that?"

He mirrored her smirk. "She never knew I came aboard."

Her smile slipped. Lilja's race had some unique qualities, one of which was the ability to hear things that most people couldn't. There wasn't any way he could have slipped aboard unknown without sprouting wings. Her eyes narrowed. "How?"

Rafe smirk grew wider. "You will never know."

Did he do something to her? Sage's brows knit. "You better have not touched them."

Rafe's smile disappeared altogether. "How could you ask such a thing?"

"I don't know you." Sage shrugged. "Just because I believe you didn't lie about *absolutely* everything doesn't mean I can trust you." Pain flickered across his face, and she felt a twinge of guilt, but she immediately stamped it down. She wouldn't allow him to make her feel bad for a situation that he himself had caused. "You didn't answer my question." Sage took a small step back, toward her bed.

"No, I did not hurt them."

She relaxed slightly. Fatigue settled over her like a warm blanket. Sage snuck a glance at the pitch-black sky that seemed to swallow the light of the stars. It was very late. She should be in bed already.

The pop of the fire brought her attention back to her surprising guest and it occurred to her to wonder, *Why was he still here?* He had said his piece. Why hadn't he taken his leave? She heaved out a weary sigh as she moved to pull back the covers of her bed. Propping a hip against the tall bed, she raised her eyebrows expectantly. "Is there something else you need?" She covered her yawn with her hand as best she could, then touched the soft coverlet. "Tomorrow is a big day for me. I need my rest."

Rafe's face darkened and his body tensed, putting her back on alert. She glanced at the bed, trying to gage how quickly she could get to the other side. She had a couple of blades on her, but her stash was at the other side of the room and she would need it if anything happened.

Rafe cocked his head and took a cautious step toward her. "I may have a solution to your problems."

"Problems?" Sage repeated, confused.

"Your marriage to the prince. I've found a way out."

Her eyes widened as wariness turned to a tremulous hope. What was he talking about? There was no way out, the rebellion had made sure of that, hadn't they? "What are you talking about? Are you saying I need not marry tomorrow?" Even as she held her breath for his answer she viciously tried to stomp out that little seed of hope. There was no escape for her, and it would do no good to imagine otherwise.

"No, you will need to marry him."

Sage glared at the rebellion leader. "Why would you get my hopes up?" she barked, her heart picking up speed. For a brief moment, she thought she might have a chance at freedom again. All the worse to realize it was not so.

"I meant what I said. You have to marry the crown prince but when we go to war, and we will, we can fake your death."

Sage blinked, her hand clutching the blanket. Fake her death?

"Before you tell me I am addled, mull it over." Rafe stared at floor and began pacing. "You're known as the rebel's blade and now also as the warrior princess to the court. When Scythia attacks you won't be waiting here, you will be among those fighting. War is chaos. We can make it seem like you fell in battle, which will be glorious and honorable and you would be free of the prince without giving the rebellion cause for retaliation." Rafe paused his pacing to look at her. "You can have the life you always wanted. You can be free of this marble prison."

Her mind scrambled to keep up with the things he was suggesting. War. Chaos. Escape. Freedom. Living her life as she sought, not as someone bid her. But what of her family? "It sounds like you have put a great deal of thought into this, but what of my family? Where would we live? My face will be recognizable."

"You and your family will come home with me, to Methi."

Her jaw slackened. Methi. He wanted to take her to Methi. "As what?" she choked out.

Rafe looked at her with confusion. "What do you mean?"

If her life experience thus far had shown her one thing it was this: everyone wanted something. "What do you expect of me if I accept your help in escaping my nightmare?"

"Nothing," he drawled softly. "I will take care of you like you are my own."

"As your sister? Or like a daughter?" Sage pushed, knowing that was not what he had in mind.

"As my mate."

Mate. There was that odd word for a wife again. Sage shook her head. She would not jump from one man to another. "Would you make me a harlot?"

He looked at her, aghast. "I would never dishonor you that way. We would have a ceremony that combined both our traditions."

"That is not what I meant." She made sure to look him in the eye as she spoke her next words. "Even if I agreed to what you are asking I could never be with you."

The predatory glint in his eyes had her feet moving before she'd consciously decided to do so. The next thing she knew was that she was on the opposite side of the bed with both blades in hand.

Rafe glided to the opposite side and placed his hands on the mattress, leaning forward, his temper only just reined in. "Why," he bit out, "do you keep scorning me? I have offered you exactly what you want. There is no one but yourself keeping you from the life you want." His back heaved as he sucked in a breath before pinning her to the spot with his amber eyes. "I want you above all others."

The sincerity of his words reverberated in her mind and pierced her heart. She looked at him, a sadness shadowing her face. "I could not marry you even if I wanted to, Rafe. Even if we faked my death I would still be married to the crown prince."

"Annulment."

"And if the war doesn't come for years?"

Rafe ran his fingers around one of the post of her bed, then followed her, almost like he was hunting.

"Time doesn't matter. As long as you remain untouched you can go free." He paused, his smile gentle. "You can be free with me."

Her heart squeezed with his words. Everything in her life was out of her control. If she said yes, she would not only be choosing her own path, but that of her family as well. She couldn't leave them, but would they go with her? Would they even want to? Sage wanted to be reckless, throwing caution to the wind just to get out the depressing life she felt was ahead of her, but her head knew better than her heart. Rafe was, in a lot of ways, still very much a stranger, and he had hurt her even more than the Crown at this point in time.

Overcome with exhaustion, she lifted her fists and rubbed at her eyes, being careful not to gouge herself with her daggers. A whisper of sound reached her ears just as big hands wrapped around her wrists. Sage gasped, and his earthy scent filling her lungs.

"This is not a decision to be made lightly little one." He tugged on her hands. "I will wait for your decision."

Sage pulled her hands from his grip and stepped away. She needed to be alone. Everything he was saying and doing was just too much for her to handle, especially tonight. She sheathed her daggers, unlocked the door, and opened it, peering into the hallway outside. Two Elite had posted themselves there. Sage grimaced and briskly nodded at them before stepping into the hallway. Rafe wouldn't go unseen so his presence would no doubt get back to Tehl. Sage levelly met his gaze and gestured down the hall. "Please leave."

His lips thinned and the corners of his eyes pinched, but that was the only indication that he was less than happy with her dismissal. He stalked through the doorway, ignoring the looks of interest and suspicion the Elite were throwing his way. He didn't stop until he was toe to toe with Sage. He cupped her chin and lifted her face, staring into her eyes. "Hold your head high tomorrow, little one. Through your strength, bravery, and honor you have become the savior of kingdoms. People will not understand your sacrifice. Royalty doesn't come from just your bloodline but from your character. You are just as much royalty as the crown prince."

Sage swallowed thickly, tears pricking her eyes, touched by his sudden sincerity. "Thank you," she whispered.

His eyes dipped and Sage turned her face just in time, his lips brushing the corner of her mouth in a kiss. He lingered there.

"What is family for, little one?" He breathed against her skin before pulling back and caressing her jaw. "Until tomorrow."

Sage watched him stride away, disappearing into the shadows of the castle. His black cloak seemed to soak up light. A throat cleared, catching her attention. Sage turned to the Elite guards who wore disapproving looks on their faces. She ignored their looks and stared down the hall. She trained with them, but it didn't mean she owed them any explanation.

A flutter of color flickered down the hall. A familiar head of hair whipped back, disappearing around the corner. Caeja, Jaren's daughter, the harpy mooing over the crown prince. Sage shook her head before trudging back into her room. She closed her door and leaned back against it. It amused her that the vicious noblewoman was spying on her, but it also created a problem.

Sage didn't doubt that by morning everyone would think she was entertaining other men. She could run to Tehl and explain what happened but she was sure he'd approach her about it later. That was the thing about rumors, you could never catch them or control them. She sighed, exhausted. These were all problems for another day.

Closing the door behind her, she stumbled toward her bed, discarding her clothes as she went. She lay down on her side and stared at the crackling fire. By this time tomorrow morning, she would be a princess. A royal. She shivered at the thought and pulled the covers tighter. Her mind and heart were heavy, so she feared she wouldn't be able to rest this night. As it turned out, however, the call of sleep was stronger than the worries of the day. She slipped her hand around a dagger beneath her pillow even as her eyes were drooping. Maybe tonight she wouldn't have nightmares.

NİNETEEN

SAGE

SAGE JERKED AWAKE, DAGGER IN hand, startling the serving women who had bustled into her room. She winced as a couple let out startled shrieks. Sheepishly, she waved her dagger at them, mumbling words of apology. She flopped back onto her bed and just listened, the soothing sounds of the women stoking the fire and preparing a bath relaxing the tenseness of her shoulders. Nightmares had awoken her all through the night. It felt like she hadn't slept a wink.

Today she would marry.

Marry a man she cared nothing for.

She would be royalty.

Trapped.

Morning had come too soon.

That thought had her lungs constricting, and she suddenly felt unable to breathe. She focused on the ceiling above, calming herself by counting in her mind. After what seemed like forever, her breathing slowed and eventually evened out. Everything would be okay.

"What are you still doing abed?" Lilja teased.

Sage turned her head to meet the magenta eyes of her friend and gestured with her dagger. "What does it look like I am doing?"

Her mum, Mira, and Lilja were all gathered by her bed, smiling down at her. Lilja examined her face and cocked a hip. "It rather looks like you got into a fight with a leviathan. That hair."

Sage scowled as she patted her crazy nest of hair. Sometimes it defied nature. Nothing she could do about it.

Her mum slapped Lilja's arm and strode to the bed to sit beside her daughter. She looked down, a soft smile upon her face. "Aren't you ready, love?"

No, she wasn't.

When Sage forced a smile and nodded once, the smile on her mum's face slipped. Apparently, she wasn't as convincing as she thought she was.

Addressing the mass of women gathered to assist her with her preparations, Lilja commanded, "Leave us. We will attend the prince's betrothed. I will send for you when you are needed."

Swiftly they filed out, the soft click of the door signaling their departure. Sage's tension from being watched all the time eased as soon as the room quieted.

Mira plopped down next to her mum and grasped Sage's hand, squeezing once. "Are you hungry?"

That brought a real smile to her face. Mira knew her well. She was always hungry.

Lilja gathered together a few trays and placed them on the enormous bed before stretching out on the other side and raising a brow. "Eat. Now."

"Bossy wench." Sage sat up, searching for something that might go down okay. She finally settled on a flaky pastry dotted with berries and plucked it from the tray.

"That's Captain Femi to you," Lilja sassed.

Sage blew her a kiss before taking a distinctly unladylike bite of her pastry.

"You would think we raised her with no manners," her mum grouched before cracking a smile.

Their jesting finally lightened the atmosphere enough that they were able to pass the rest of the morning in luxury. They ate, drank, and laughed. Sage was lighthearted and relaxed by the time Lilja called back the ladies to assist her in preparing for the ceremony. She was scrubbed and buffed to perfection. By the time they were finished, her skin had a healthy glow and it was softer than it had probably ever been. Her hair even shone with auburn and honey highlights she'd never before noticed.

Lilja rubbed her hands together. "Now we get to the fun part."

Once again, the serving women were ushered out. Sage tipped her head back, allowing her hair to cascade down the back of her chair and onto the floor, and she sighed as her mum and Lilia began carding their fingers through it. Nothing felt better than having someone play with her hair.

Mira shuffled in front of her. "Close your eyes. I'm starting on your cosmetics."

Sage narrowed her eyes. "Nothing extravagant?"

Mira gave her an eye roll and pointed to her own flawless face. "Does mine look extravagant to you? No. All I'm doing is highlighting your features and enhancing your natural beauty. Now, close your eyes."

She obediently closed her eyes but couldn't help mumbling, "Hmph. Everyone is so bossy today," earning some chuckles from her companions. Somewhere between Mira working on her face and the other two working with her hair she drifted off. It wasn't until someone pressed her arm several times that she awoke. She opened her eyes to her mum, who was leaning down to cup her cheek, eyes suspiciously damp.

"You're done, my love. It's time to put your dress on."

Her stomach dropped and her pulse quickened. It was almost time.

Her dress lay across the bed, its fabric spread across the duvet. It was the softest green, almost white, for Aermian brides always wore green on their marriage day. It represented a fresh start, the beginning to a new life.

As Mira lifted the dress, Sage took an unconscious step back. Once she donned it there was no going back.

Mira, Lilja, and her mum all paused, their faces carefully blank.

"Are you all right, *ma fleur*?"

Sage swallowed, nodded, and lifted her arms. The three women helped lift the dress up and over her head. The sleeves slipped down her arms as the dress fell to the floor, caressing her body. Its neck was cut wide to expose her collarbone. Each end edged her shoulders and ran to her elbow where the silky material met lace sleeves. The silhouette followed her curves, flaring slightly at her thighs, like a calla lily. She felt Lilja's cool hands touching the skin of her back, tugging softly to adjust the bustle. All three women stepped back, awed.

Sage shifted, uncomfortable. "How do I look?"

"Like a queen," Mira breathed.

Tears filled her mum's eyes and then spilled over, tracking down her face. "You're beautiful darling. And as regal a bride as ever there was, I'm sure."

Lilja took her hand and led her to the mirror.

Sage gasped. The dress was stunning. The work they'd done on hair and cosmetics was beautiful, but she still couldn't get used to seeing herself like this. It looked like someone had painted a picture of her but enhanced it so that her features seemed more striking and more polished. She grabbed a handful of the dress and turned, eyeing the back. It was open with dainty bows tied in the center to keep the dress in place. Lilja had left her hair loose with a lone braid that started at the crown of her head and wove down behind her ear and under her heavy fall of hair.

She hated it.

Not so much the dress in itself, rather what it meant. She bit the inside of her cheek to hold back the bitter words ready to spill out. Sage flashed her family a grateful smile. Despite her personal feelings she refused to make it harder on them. She met Lilja's eyes and knew by the knowing look that she wasn't fooling her. Lilja touched her hair, offering silent comfort and support.

"Not only stunning on the outside but on the inside as well," her mum murmured from behind her.

Sage turned into her mum's arms and hugged with all her might. "I love you, Mum."

"I love you too, more than you understand." She pulled back and gave her daughter a watery smile. "I should go and find your father. Do you need anything else before I do so?"

"No."

"Okay then. I will see you in a bit my love."

Lilja kissed her cheek and squeezed her hand. "Courage, *ma fleur*."

The two quit the room, leaving only her and Mira, the latter staring at her through the mirror. Her friend looked conflicted as she laced her fingers with Sage's. "I have been with you from the beginning. I know how you feel about Tehl. If you want to leave, I will help you."

Sage froze at the seriousness in both Mira's voice and eyes. Her friend meant it. Mira would risk everything for her. She would lose her life and the only family she ever had to help Sage. Her throat felt thick. She didn't deserve such wonderful friends. She lifted their entwined hands and kissed the back of Mira's. "Thank you for such love, but I am needed here." Despite the brave face she was putting on, she still felt the beginnings of panic setting in. She needed to be alone. "Would you mind giving me a moment to myself?"

Mira nodded. "I will send someone to retrieve you when the ceremony is starting." She then hugged her and disappeared through the door.

Sage turned back to face the mirror. Her mum had spoken true: she did look beautiful. Everything about her shone, except for her eyes. They were dull. Sad.

An ugly sob escaped, her face contorting. Blindly, she clutched the dresser in front of her, leaning heavily against it. She blearily glanced at the cosmetics and jeweled pins scattered atop it as each sob continued to wrack her chest. Why did this happen to her? She wasn't perfect, but she didn't feel like she deserved to be punished for the rest of her life. It was just so unfair. She shoved the items off the dresser, the jeweled pins plinking onto the stone floor. With shuddering breaths, she stumbled to the side table, and, hiking it up carelessly, with shaking hands, she clumsily attempted to attach her thigh sheath. She had to get out of here. Now.

"Do you need a hand?" a deep voice asked.

Sage blinked and looked to the door. Gav and Sam both stood in her room. She tried to rein in the frayed threads of her emotions but it was impossible. She couldn't control anything. Another sob rose, and, in her attempt to stifle it, only accomplished an embarrassing strangled cry. Their figures completely blurred, leaving only fuzzy blob shaped masses. She looked down to her trembling hands. She needed help. There she admitted it. "Please," she cried holding the sheath out.

The blob with golden hair moved to her side and gingerly took it from her, kneeling next her. She tipped her head back, trying to ignore Sam's large hands touching her thigh. Her tears rolled down her cheeks and dropped into the hollows of her ears. Gav moved behind her and wrapped his large arms around her, causing more desperate sobs to slip out.

"Next."

She dropped her leg and lifted the other one to the bed. Sam worked quickly and was standing before her. His deep blue eyes watched her with concern and a deep sorrow that somehow made her only cry harder. Sam stepped forward and wrapped his arms around her too. The tears kept coming. "I don't know if I can do this," she cried over and over again. Both men whispered to her and held her until she'd calmed enough to take gulping breaths.

Lifting her head, she stared at the wet mess she had made of Sam's vest, hiccups jerking her body. His large hands cupped her cheeks and lifted her face. "I am so sorry."

Sage closed her eyes, blocking the pity she saw in his eyes. She'd made a fool out of herself. Why was she so weak? They knew as well as she did that there was no escape for her. She shook her head, fighting off the embarrassment overwhelming her. "No, I am sorry you had to see that."

Sam's rough fingers tenderly brushed away the tears dampening her face. Sage sucked in a stuttering deep breath and forced her eyes open. Sam smiled sadly before looking over the top of her head to Gavriel.

"This is wrong," Gavriel whispered, his breath ruffling her hair.

The spymaster's eyes dropped to hers and she simply stared back at him. In his eyes was a wealth of information. He was truly saddened by the situation but there was nothing to be done. Just as there was nothing to stop the sun from rising each morning, there was nothing that could keep her from marrying the crown prince. Sage nodded once and took a deep breath. She could do this. She had survived so many other things, she would not allow this to break her.

Sage turned to step away from the princes, though Gav's hold tightened a moment before he let her go. She returned to the mirror and examined the damage she had done. Her face was flushed with a map of trails where her tears had fallen. Her eyes were puffy and a shiny clear green. Sage dropped her eyes to smooth out the dress, erasing the wrinkles Sam and Gav had caused. She felt more than saw both men move to stand on either side of her.

Carefully, Sage lifted her face and watched them in the mirror. What did they think of her now?

Gavriel smiled. "You are lovely, Sage."

She gave him a weak smile. "I should with what it cost. I bet I could feed a family for a while if I sold this," she joked.

To her surprise, Sam reached down and clasped her hand, his eyes never leaving her face. "It's not the dress but the woman who wears it. The dress is beautiful but you are what gives it worth."

"It's because of my mother's good looks."

"No," Sam shook his head. "That's not what I meant, and you know it. You're beautiful but it is your inner self that draws people. Your courage, compassion, and love shine, touching everyone around you." He paused. "You know, our mum would have loved you."

Her throat tightened. Where was this coming from? Sage had never seen this side of the spymaster. "I am only doing what anyone else would."

Sam pinned her with a look. "Anyone else would have condemned us to death and ran away. You have gone above and beyond what anyone else would do." Sam turned her from the mirror and knelt in front of her and Gavriel. "From this moment forward, I want you to know you can always come to me for anything. I will support you and love you like my sister, this I promise. And I would like permission to call you such."

Sage gasped and stilled, staring down at the blond prince. She never expected to receive such an oath from *him*. She assumed she would be alone in her gilded cage. Was this a cruel ploy? But as Sage searched his eyes, she found nothing but sincerity and the barest hint of vulnerability. Sam actually meant what he said.

"I would be honored," she whispered.

His radiant smile just about blinded her. "Excellent! I always wanted a sister."

A small chuckle slipped from her. "Just remember that when I am annoying you. Remember, too, that I grew up with two brothers."

Sam sprang up and crushed her against his enormous body. "The same goes for you, sis."

Gavriel cleared his throat breaking up their moment. Sage turned to him, staring into his dear face. He reached out and smoothed her hair from her face. "Do you remember our conversation before you left?"

Sage nodded, guilt pooling in her stomach.

"That was never a ploy to get you to trust me. I meant it then, and I mean it now. Despite the circumstances that brought you here, you are a part of this family, and we take care of our own." Gav held open his arms and she rushed into them. "I am always here for you."

Sage gave him a final squeeze before stepping back to look at both men. Never in a thousand years would she have expected to have two of the princes of Aermia call her family. Sam still threw her off balance, but that was just his personality. "I don't deserve this but I will cherish you both as my brothers, my family."

Twin smiles split their faces, calling one to her own face. Reluctantly, Sage turned back to the mirror and stared again at her reflection. Gav picked up a cloth she had flung to the floor and handed it to her, and, with it, she cleaned up her face. She then fixed the damage to her hair as best she could and squared her shoulders. Now was not the time to be a coward. She gave her word and now she needed to fulfill it. Sage smoothed her dress one last time, turning to her new brothers to inquire of them, "How do I look?"

"Like a queen."

Sam's eyes glinted. "My brother won't be able to stand it when he sees you."

Sage grimaced. "I highly doubt that, but thank you for the compliment."

Gavriel held out his arm. "Are you ready?"

No, she would never be ready but she kept that thought to herself. "Yes."

TWENTY

TEHL

TEHL PACED.

Guilt had his stomach turning. Sage's broken sobs still echoed in his ears. He'd merely gone to see how she fared before the ceremony, to double check that she hadn't run off, and show her his surprise. When he'd reached her chamber though he'd stopped when he saw Sam and Gav standing in the hallway. Neither moved. They just stood there, staring at the closed door, faces bleak. He joined them, leaning close to the door to listen, but when he'd heard the desolate cries emanating from the other side, his own throat had thickened and he couldn't help feeling a little sick. He had leaned forward, resting his forehead against the door, unsure of what he was supposed to do. He couldn't just let her suffer like that but how could he possibly help?

She put on such a tough exterior, despite the fact that she was torn up inside, but he knew she'd never accept comfort from him or want him to see her in such a vulnerable state. Part of him wanted to rush in and wrap his arms around her with an assurance that everything would be okay. But the logical part of him knew he'd more than likely make it worse. A large part of the reason she was so upset was no doubt due to him.

Turning to his cousin and brother, he'd whispered, "Take care of her," before he returned to his own chamber, the burden placed upon them both by their kingdom weighing heavily upon his mind.

Life was simply not fair.

His pacing was abruptly interrupted by the sound of a voice.

"Getting cold feet, my lord?"

He blinked, trying to shake himself from the memory. "No." Tehl tugged at his hair. "Am I doing the right thing?" he blurted.

Zachael studied him for a moment. "Only you can answer that."

Tehl sent him a pleading look. "Please, old friend. Speak your mind. I could use an outsider's input."

The older man exhaled, dropping his eyes to the marble floor. "She has been through much, but she hasn't stopped trying to tough it out. Sometimes, women hold it in for so long they just break down. She will be fine later. I think she just needed to get it out of her system since she probably hasn't done so until now." Zachael met his gaze. "You both need time to adjust. All will be well, Tehl. Be patient."

No. All would not be well for either of them.

The combat master glanced at the window. "It's near time. Ready?"

He pulled in a deep breath and tried to steel himself.

It was time.

Tehl nodded to Zachael and strode through the door, to the courtyard full of people. At his approach, all stood and bowed as hundreds of eyes turned his way, following him as he took his place on the dais beside his waiting father. Carefully, he ordered his features into an appropriately blissful expression for his court and waved to the crowd.

His father shifted closer and asked underneath his breath. "Are you nervous, son?"

Tehl glanced from his father to the Elite mingling among the throng of people. He hadn't been before, but, somehow, his father's words had him starting to be. What if she didn't show up? What if she did? His gut clenched. He shook his head to clear the thought.

Never show any fear, never let them see you sweat.

"Not at all," he answered, infusing it with as much confidence as he could. A deep chuckle had him turning and scowling at the king. "She will be here," he muttered, more to himself than his father.

Tehl turned back to the crowd and fought the intense discomfort he still felt when under the scrutiny of so many people. He never was a people person. He rolled his neck and took to examining the shine of his boots, staring at his warped reflection. Tehl relaxed his clenched jaw and drew in another deep breath. Once this was over things would be better. He would make it so.

Suddenly, the crowds quieted.

She was here.

Abandoning the examination of his boots, he mentally prepared himself and lifted his eyes toward the doors. He could make out Sam and Gav first and then the two brothers of his betrothed, but Sage was thus far unseen. A thread of panic seized him. Where was she?

Music started, and the wall of men parted, and, suddenly, she appeared. Tehl's breath stuttered and he gaped.

From the crown of her head to the tip of her toes she was breathtaking. Her raven mane glistened in the late sunlight, its locks waving in the slight breeze.

"Breath, son."

Tehl let out the breath he'd been holding and snapped his mouth shut. She'd always been attractive but today she seemed ethereal. Her pale green dress made the green of her eyes seem even brighter than ever. He couldn't take his eyes off her.

"Your mother would have loved Sage. Well done, son. Your bride will do Aermia proud."

His bride.

Such a beguiling creature would be his. Tehl stood a little taller as a feeling of satisfaction settled inside him. He watched as she smiled at his people and took in, with wonder, the decorations strewn about the outside garden, creating a version of her meadow, yet she did not meet his eyes. She hadn't even glanced his direction.

Look at me, he thought.

He continued to focus on her, willing her to turn to him. At that moment, her head lifted, like she'd somehow heard him, and their gazes clashed. A jolt went through him at the mix of emotions displayed there.

She dropped her eyes and stopped at the dais, turning to bestow a kiss upon Sam, Gav, and then her brothers. Next, her mum stood and hugged and kissed her. Her father did the same before taking her hand and turning her toward Tehl as he descended the steps, focusing hard on each one so as to not tumble down them like a drunken fool. Colm's serious eyes met Tehl's, an obvious warning in them.

"Are you prepared to bind yourself to my daughter?" he said, somberly.

"I am," Tehl vowed.

Colm studied him for a beat and then placed Sage's small hand in his own. Tehl's fingers wrapped around her dainty hand and he gently led her up the stairs. Sam, Gav, Mira, and Lilja, each a member of the wedding party, followed in their wake. Tehl turned to Sage and reached for her other hand, scowling when he notice he trembled. He glared at the offending appendage, willing it to stop its infernal shaking. He tried clenching his fist, but it was to no avail. Sage too stared for a beat before stretching her hand out instead, a slight tremor evident in hers as well. His eyes snapped to hers and she gave him a wobbly smile, which he returned. It seemed they both were nervous.

"Are you ready?" he whispered.

Her slight smile dropped as she swallowed thickly, and biting her lip, jerked her head up and down. Neither of them were ready, but they were doing the best they could.

"Are you ready, my dear?" his father's deep voice interrupted his thoughts.

Sage turned to his father. "I am."

When she turned back to Tehl, his heart clenched. His people saw a serene bride about to blissfully wed their prince, but they couldn't see her eyes. He, however, did and they were anything but blissful. Depression. Exhaustion. Resignation.

There was no turning back now, their lots were cast.

His father's voice rose, and a hush fell over the crowd. Tehl tuned out his father's words, never taking his eyes from the woman standing before him. Tehl hoped his gaze conveyed to her his commitment to this arrangement of theirs and that somehow it would comfort her, at least slightly. A hand touched his shoulder, breaking his attention from his betrothed. Tehl blinked at his father. "What?"

A laugh burst out of his father followed by many from the crowd. The king smiled and nodded toward Sage. "It's time for the binding."

Tehl tightened his grasp on Sage's hands as she began to pull away. He gave her a stern look before dropping her hands; now was not the time to be having second thoughts.

Sam stepped forward and handed him a silk bag containing a pair of silver cuffs. The silk slid through his fingers while he unwrapped them. Carefully, he extracted the metal bands and stepped up to the rebel, the tips of his boots touching her sandaled feet.

"Do you accept these cuffs of mine and therefore agree to be bound together until we both depart this world?"

Her breaths came in and out in quick succession while she stared at the cuffs in his outstretched hands. Tehl shifted as murmurs rippled through the Crown at her. Silence. Stars above, would she to refuse him? "Sage?"

Her fingers twitched, and she blew out a breath. Sage shoved her arms out baring her wrists but still not meeting his eyes. "I accept."

Relief rushed through him as he hastily placed a silver band on each of her scarred wrists. The cuffs were simple in design: plain metal with small waves etched along the brushed silver edge. It was the simplest cuff ever worn in the Crown's history, but, from what he knew of Sage, he felt they were the most suitable; she wasn't an extravagant woman. Tehl watched her face carefully but she gave nothing away, carefully maintaining a practiced smile. Disappointment pricked him. She didn't want to wear his cuffs, but he hoped she would at least enjoy the design he'd created just for her.

Sage turned to Lilja, who'd stepped up behind her to hand over a roughly woven sack. Sage pulled out a single, larger cuff and turned toward him. His heart stuttered as she stepped closer, her dress rustling. Sage tipped her head back and met his gaze squarely.

"Do you accept this cuff of mine and therefore agree to be bound together until we both depart this world?" Her voice rang out loud and clear among the assembly, giving no evidence of her true emotions.

Tehl searched her face before answering, noting the tightness around her eyes. "I accept."

She reached for his hand and slid her cuff up his arm, her soft fingers teasing his skin. His eyes rested on the cuff adorning his bicep. It was nothing like what he was used to seeing. Most men wore cuffs made of bronze, silver, or gold. But Sage had created something new. The cuff was a series of leather and silver strips woven into a complex braid that was sturdy yet flexible.

"It is done," his father announced. "Please kneel."

Both knelt as his father moved toward them in all his kingly finery, a delicate crown in his grasp. He stood in front of Sage, a tender smile upon his face. "Do you, Sage Blackwell, promise to uphold Aermian law in all your ways, to protect the kingdom with your very life when necessary and to rule with justice?"

Sage lifted her chin and straightened her spine. "Yes."

"I know you will, my dear," he said quietly, for their ears only.

The king then placed upon her head an intricate silver crown embedded with pearls. When his father caressed Sage's cheek before stepping back, Tehl stared in wonderment. His father truly loved his bride.

"Please stand."

Tehl helped Sage to her feet, his own crown feeling heavy upon his head. The king clasped their joined hands, raising them in the air. "Proudly, I present to you the bound Crown Prince Tehl Ramses and his consort, Princess Sage Ramses."

Deafening applause erupted from the Crown. A faint ringing filled Tehl's ears as he beheld the woman beside him who was surveying the cheering crowd with fake enthusiasm.

It was done, he was bound.

A strong sense of satisfaction filled him at the thought. He had a companion and not just any, but one who had just as much at stake. Both of their lives were equally vested in his kingdom's interests. After a moment, she gave him a look from the corner of her eye, a question on her face. He shrugged and smiled, enjoying the shock on her face.

"Now, my son, make your bride yours."

Sage's nails sunk into his hand at his father's words. He barely kept from wincing. Tehl slipped a hand around her waist, pulling her toward him but it was like holding a statue. She didn't give at all. Her wide frightened eyes met his before she slipped a sultry mask into place, stealing the breath from his lungs. Stars above, she was good.

Sage turned to the king and winked. "What if I make him mine?"

His father let loose a booming laugh, gesturing toward Tehl. "By all means."

Sage popped up onto her toes and pressed her lips against his.

Flames.

Bloody hell.

Tehl didn't expect the fire in his veins at her unexpected touch. Heat followed her hands as they skimmed their way up his arms and around his neck, fingers sinking into his hair urging him closer. His thoughts turned to mush when her mouth opened against his. Without her permission, he found his arms snaked around her waist, his hands clutching her dress as he hauled her against him until every inch of them touched. Time seemed to stop as he devoured the promises on her lips. When she finally pulled back, he chased her lips once again only to be thwarted by a finger pressed against his mouth. He blinked a few times, feeling like he'd been awoken from a dream, jolting when he met a pair of very serious green eyes.

Damn.

Any lingering heat in his blood chilled at the carefully composed look on her face as realization dawned.

It was an act.

It was for the crowd.

Tehl cursed his own infernal weakness and fumed. How could his damn body betray him like that? He lowered her to the floor, attempting to compose himself. He was better than this.

Control, Tehl. Control.

The roar of the crowd filled his ears, and Tehl shook his head once before pasting on a smile of his own.

"Are you all right?" Sage muttered.

He grunted. He refused to talk about what just happened.

"Let the celebrations begin!"

Tehl wove Sage's arm through his and muttered. "Let's get this over with."

Wading through the crowd of well-wishers was a nightmare. It took forever just to make it to the raised dais where the ceremonial dinner was to be served. Then, dinner passed in a flurry of conversation and courses. Sage ate next to him, conversing with anyone and everyone like a true princess. She listened and empathized with those she spoke to, building a personal connection with each interaction. She made people feel comfortable and important, her conversation a good blend of sense and witty remarks. The cords of a soft and slow tune began, reminding him of their last ceremonial responsibility. Tehl scooted back his chair and stood, holding his hand out to the rebel looking up at him through her lashes. "My lady, will you dance with me?"

"Of course." She placed her napkin on the table and placed her hand in his, rising. Turning to the table she gave them a nod and a smile. "Excuse us".

Tehl lead her down the dais and to the stone dance floor, the stars serving as their backdrop. People emptied the floor and gathered in a circle around them so they were the only dancing couple on the floor. Tehl twirled her once before bringing her into his arms. With practiced ease, he began the twirling steps that had been drilled into him as a child. The crowd smiled and whispered as they pranced and whirled. Tehl looked down, scanning Sage's profile. He was pretty sure he hadn't said more than two words to her since the ceremony. She raised a silent brow in question. Apparently he'd been caught staring. In response he simply said, "It's done."

"Indeed, it is." Her lips twitched.

"What's so funny?"

"You."

"Why?"

"I know it's done. If you'll recall, I was there too."

Tehl snorted and looked over her head, amused at himself as well. "True."

"One word answers, my lord?"

He shrugged. "Are additional words necessary?"

Sage glanced up at him briefly before looking away. "I suppose not, sometimes simplicity is the best." A pause. "The decorations are beautiful."

Tehl blinked at the change in subject. "I am glad you like them."

"It looks like my meadow."

"I wanted you to have at least one thing you'd always wanted tonight."

She gave him a genuine smile, one that reached her eyes. "It means more than you know. I won't forget your kindness."

He cleared his throat, slightly embarrassed. "It was nothing."

"If you say so, my lord."

They finished their dance in comfortable silence, neither feeling the need to fill it. By the time the song drew to a close, Sam was already at his side, ready to sweep away his bride for the next number. After a few hours of dancing, he was done with the night. Tehl thanked his last dance partner and strode toward Sage and her current partner, Zachael. He stopped and sketched a shallow bow.

"If you don't mind, old friend, I am here to retrieve my bride."

Zachael kissed her on the cheek and handed her over to him. Her smile dimmed some at the change in companions but did not disappear completely. Cheering went up as they exited the dance floor together. Tehl guided her to her family and bowed over her hand. "I will see you soon, my lady." Tehl nodded respectfully to her brothers and father before making a quick exit. Swiftly, he made his way to his rooms, thinking about the awkward evening ahead of him.

He jerked to a stop when he opened his door. Every surface was covered with lit candles and a fire blazed in the hearth. Someone had placed sweet treats and a few bottles of spirits on the table between two wingback chairs that sat a comfortable distance from the flames.

Grimacing, Tehl skirted the bed and pulled off his boots. He reached the spirits and poured himself a drink then wandered passed his closet. Frowning, he took a couple steps back and eyed the mass of feminine clothing items now in it. The staff had certainly been busy. He rolled his eyes and downed the alcohol, relishing its burn at the back of his throat. He then plopped into one of the chairs and stared into the flames, mulling over the fact that his wife would arrive soon.

He froze.

His *wife.*

Tehl jumped out of the chair and poured another drink. He had a wife. He was married. There was no reversing what had happened today. For better or worse they were bound forever. The door slammed open and he startled. He spun as Sam, Gav, Rafe, and Sage pushed into the room, all of them shouting. Sam shut the door and latched it while Sage shook off Gavriel and brushed by Rafe to pour herself a drink.

"What in the name of hell?" he barked and stabbed a finger at the rebellion leader. "Why is Rafe in our room?"

Sage glared at him before downing her drink. "Well, Your Highness, the issue is that someone just tried to kill me."

TWENTY·ONE

TEHL

TEHL BROWS FURROWED. DID HE hear her right? He tore his gaze from her face and glanced to the room's other occupants. By the murderous looks he saw on their faces, he must have indeed heard correctly.

"What happened?" he asked firmly but calmly. They'd been expecting something like this, so there was no need to completely lose it.

"I'll tell you what happened," Sam exploded. "An assassin strolled right through the crowd to congratulate our new princess on her marriage and, in front of everyone, attempted to cut her heart out!" Sam's hands shook as he ran them through his hair.

Tehl blinked. Sam never lost his cool. If his brother was upset it had to have been a very close call.

Tehl glanced to the seething brunette beside him, and an image popped into his mind of her lying there on the stone floor, her body in a pool of blood. His stomach soured at the thought.

"If Sage hadn't been carrying one of her daggers she would be dead," Sam added.

The words hung in the air, leaving a sense of darkess on the room. Tehl breathed through his nose, frustrated. He bit out his next question, "Where is he?" He expected an attempt on her life, it was part of being a royal, but it still rankled. How dare someone attack Sage, his wife, a woman under his protection.

"Dead," Sage answered, flatly.

"By whom?"

"His own hand, the coward," Rafe growled.

That grated on Tehl as well. Apparently the man had no honor at all and now they had no way of getting any more information. "Did any of you recognize him?" He pointedly looked to Sage.

"I didn't know him. He wasn't part of the rebellion if that is what you are asking." Sage massaged her temple and stomped over to his chair, plopping herself into it. She scowled in the rebellion leader's direction. "Did you know him?"

"No."

"You're *sure* neither of you knew him?" Gav asked again.

"I never forget faces, and I would have remembered his for a certainty. It was exotic, beautiful even. The planes of his face seemed perfectly cut." Sage interjected. She turned to Sam, "You noted it as well."

His brother nodded. "He was pretty for a man, hardly inconspicuous."

A pair of burning golden eyes met his. "And what of your enemies?"

Tehl studied Rafe. "What enemies? You mean the ones you've incited against me?"

"You can't tell me you don't have enemies of your own?" Sage asked incredulously, pulling his attention from Rafe's glare. "Nobody's perfect, and you're about as companionable as a porcupine. Who have you offended recently?"

"The names would be too long to list," Gav grouched.

"Mmmhmmmm…" the rebel hummed in agreement.

Tehl gave Gavriel a black look. He didn't have great people skills, but he wasn't that bad. A thought occurred to him. He smiled wickedly at Sage. "Now I'm married to you I don't have to worry about that, you can put out all my fires."

Her mouth snapped shut. That silenced her.

"We won't figure anything out tonight. Tomorrow morning we can look into it," Gav reasoned.

"I will reach out to my contacts," Rafe added, inserting himself into the investigation.

Swamp apples, he would never be rid of this man.

Sage yawned and tipped her head back against the chair. "How long do I need to stay here before I sneak back to my rooms?" she mumbled.

All three princes darted glances to each other.

Oh hell.

"Did no one tell her?" Tehl asked, ignoring Rafe's narrowed eyes. How could no one have mentioned anything? And how in the world did it fall on *him* to do so now?

"Tell me what?"

Tehl pinched the bridge of his nose and gestured to the closet, preparing for the huge fight ahead. "Take a look for yourself."

He placed a hand over his mouth, waiting for the explosion soon to come as he watched her heave herself from the chair and onto her feet. She then proceeded to do as he'd told her. She opened the door.

One, two, three...

"What in the bloody hell?" Sage stormed from the closet and to him, scowling. "What is the meaning of those dresses?" she demanded, stabbing a finger to the closet.

Tehl lifted his drink and took a fortifying sip. This wasn't a conversation he really wanted to be having as a group. He faced Sage, but he made sure to track Rafe's reaction in his peripheral. The rebellion leader was unruly at best when it came to Sage. "Exactly what you think it does."

Her eyes narrowed. "I am not staying here."

"It has always been this way. There is not a ruling couple in our history that did not share the same room." Tehl tried to sound as reasonable as possible. Maybe if he showed her the advantages, they could avoid an argument as this was not something he could compromise on, it simply had to be done. "Everything about this ruse will be easier to keep up if you stay here."

Her eyes narrowed so much they were thin slits. "I'll not do it."

Rafe stepped to her side, placing his hand on her back. Tehl arched an eyebrow at him.

"I would listen to the lady." Tehl could detect a touch of malice in Rafe's voice. The rebellion leader was playing with fire, he shouldn't even be in the room and here he was commanding Tehl and touching his wife. This was not heading the direction he'd hoped.

Tehl blew out a breath. *All right*, he thought, *unreasonable it is.*

"In this we have no other choice. Do you think I want to sleep in the same bed as you?"

"She will *not* share your bed," Rafe hissed.

Sage's face turned an alarming shade of red. "Sharing a room doesn't mean sharing a bed."

"No, it does not," Sam said, sounding reasonable. Then he grinned and wiggled his eyebrows. "As a matter of fact I frequently share be—" Sage grabbed a pillow from the bed and launched it at his brother's head.

Sam held up his hands. "Now, now. No need to be feisty. I was just pointing out the differences."

"Enough," she growled, turning her glare from his brother to him. "I promised to marry you, but I never agreed to this. This was not included in our negotiations. I can never sleep knowing you're in the same room."

Tehl scoffed, a little offended. "What do think I will do? Knife you in the middle of the night?"

"Among other things."

Tehl rolled his eyes. "I have no designs on you tonight or any other night. Contrary to your absurd opinions about me, I am absolutely not interested in unwilling women." Tehl threw his hands in the air and stomped to his bed, yanking back the covers. "Listen. There are guards posted outside our door, they will see you if you sneak out so it's ridiculous to keep arguing about this. Tonight, and every other night, I am sleeping in my bed. You are welcome to sleep wherever you wish, be it in the chair, on the floor or somewhere else. But it will be in *this room*. You agreed to this marriage, and this is just a part of what it entails."

He could see her start to fume. "This was thrust upon me, I had no choice in the matter so I didn't actually agree to anything," Sage spat.

"Sage, it's true about our kings and queens sharing the room," Gav added gently.

She held his cousin's gaze for what seemed an eternity and finally spoke. "It seems I once again have no choice in the matter, just as in every other aspect of this mess." She then swung her infuriated gaze back to him. "If you so much as twitch in my direction…"

Her hand flashed and a dull thwack sounded very close to his head. Tehl twisted to find a dagger embedded in the bed poster a scant three inches from his ear. "Did you just throw a knife at me?" he asked, incredulously.

The smug smile the rebellion leader now wore had Tehl fighting the desire not to walk over and punch him in his interfering, smug face.

"That was a warning. You stay in your bed and I will stay in mine." She whirled around and snatched something from the closet before slipping into the bathing room. The clicking of the door was followed by the sound of running water.

"Well," Gav sighed, "that sure went well… "

"I guess the traditional wedding night is out," Sam deadpanned. That pulled a low growl from Rafe.

"Enough," Gavriel chastised, elbowing his brother. "It's well past time we be leaving. If she has nightmares," Gav paused and winced, "*when* she has nightmares watch for her blades and call for me. I'll use the secret passage ways so as not to stir up gossip."

Gossip about their new marriage was the last thing they needed, Tehl thought.

He nodded to them both so Sam bellowed, "We're leaving!" in the direction of the bathing room. Sage burst into the room ,and, when Sam opened his arms, to Tehl's surprise, she walked right into them.

"Thank you," she whispered.

His brother caught his eye and, over the top of her head, flashed a real Sam smile. "Anything for you, darling."

Sage smiled softly. She stepped from of his arms to Gav's, giving him the same treatment. When she reached Rafe, she hesitated a moment before sliding her arms around his middle. At that moment, a spark of jealousy ran through him as he observed the rebellion leader run his hands through her hair. He gritted his teeth when Rafe looked him in the eyes and, maintaining eye contact, kissed her forehead. The man was dangerous. Tehl would have to keep an eye on him just to make sure the lecher didn't steal his wife right out from under him.

Sage pulled away and retreated once again to the bathing room, sparing Tehl only a brief, annoyed glance. When he looked at the other men in the room, they all stared at the door with varying degrees of affection in their eyes. The damn woman had wiggled her way into all of their hearts.

"You better not mess this up," Sam mumbled. "She is worth her weight in gold. I hope you know how to handle something that precious."

"I run a kingdom."

"Women are more difficult."

"You'll not find me brooking argument there."

"You'll be dealing with more than her family if you hurt her," his brother said, eyeing him.

"I will not harm her."

"I'd kill you if you did," Rafe tossed in.

Tehl didn't doubt it.

"You better not," Gav grumbled. "Okay. It is now well past my bedtime and there is still much for me to do before I can even think of sleeping, so I'm going to bid you all goodnight."

Sam rolled his eyes. "Come along, *old man*," he said, exasperated.

The two princes left his room, bickering, while Tehl had a nice little stare off with Rafe. The door closed, the room filled only with the sounds of running water and a crackling fire.

After a few moments, Tehl finally grouched, "Out with it, I haven't got all night." He really was tired. Today had taken a heavy toll on him and he needed to rest.

"She may be your wife, but she is not yours."

Tehl's hackles raised. Their marriage may be a business deal, but that certainly did not mean Rafe could speak of Sage with any sort of possession. "And who pray tell, does she belong to? You?" Tehl asked, holding his eerie gaze. "From what I hear, she has rebuffed you at every turn."

The rebellion leader's eyes turned murderous. "You—"

Tehl held up a hand, cutting him off. "She doesn't belong to either of us," he said frankly. "But legally she is mine, and I will care for and protect her."

"I don't make idle threats. I meant what I said. Do not hurt her."

"I would expect nothing less."

"We have an understanding then?"

"Indeed."

Rafe dipped his chin and stalked from the room.

Tehl grimaced, the rebellion leader was nothing but trouble. For the next while he went about blowing out the ridiculously large amount of candles that had been placed in their chambers. He slipped into a soft pair of sleep pants and sat on the bed, elbows resting on his knees and hands clasped, just thinking.

Not that much had been altered in it but his own chamber felt so different having Sage here. He had moved to these rooms when he became of marrying age, and, until this moment, Tehl never thought about what it would feel like to bring a woman here. When he imagined getting married, he thought that it would be a sedate occasion to some mousy bride eager to do his bidding. Obviously, he could have never imagined that he'd get a coerced bride who wouldn't spit on him if he was burning.

The bathing room door opened, interrupting his thoughts. Steam billowed out, announcing Sage's arrival. Her skin was pink and shiny, her dark hair dripping water onto the white linen shirt she was wearing, making it most-becomingly transparent.

"Keep your eyes to yourself," his new wife barked. She then strode purposefully to the other side of the bed, ripping pillows off it.

Tehl raised brow. "Keep my eyes to myself? Really? That's the best you could come up with?"

She growled at him and yanked the coverlet out from under him, apparently refusing to dignify his comment with a response. She then ripped off her cuffs, slapping them onto the side table, and stormed toward the fire where she began constructing a nest on the floor.

"You really intend to sleep there?"

"I do," Sage sniffed. "It is better than being in the same bed as you." A dagger appeared in her hand, and she pointed it at him. "You stay on your side of the room, and I will stay on mine."

Exhaustion tugged at him. He didn't have the energy to spar with her. Wearily, he ran a hand down his face and returned his gaze to the hostile woman watching him. "I won't argue with you there. Do whatever you like as long as you don't disturb my sleep." Tehl stood and yanked back the remaining sheets and crawled into bed. He stared at the ceiling and listened as Sage shuffled around, mumbling to herself or cursing under her breath every so often. He couldn't help but smile at a few of the black oaths that came out. A docile wife she most certainly was not. At least his life was about to get a bit more interesting.

"Goodnight, Sage."

Her rustling paused. "Goodnight, my lord."

"Tehl," he insisted.

"Tehl," she repeated.

Tehl's eyes snapped open, instantly awake. Darkness weighed down on him blanketing the room. His hand crept toward the dagger hidden under his pillow. What woke him? Tehl's brows knitted when he heard a small whimper. What the devil was that?

He sat up and scanned the room, pausing at the slumbering figure before the fire. The tension drained from his body when he realized it was only the rebel. He grumbled and stashed his dagger, irritated at having been awoken needlessly. A dry chuckle fell from his lips as he settled back into bed. Sage was tiresome even in her sleep.

A sharp cry had him bolting upright. "Sage?"

No response.

Tehl yanked back the covers and hissed when his feet touched the cold stone floor. He strode around the foot of the bed, avoiding pieces of furniture, intent on Sage. He barely made out her features in the dark, illuminated by the dying embers in the hearth. She struggled against the covers knotted around her.

"No!" she shouted and struggled harder. "Don't touch..." She broke off with a cry, tears slipping out the corners of her closed eyes.

Tehl's heart seized. This is what Gav was talking about. Sage was having a nightmare. "Sage, wake up." She thrashed harder and let out a wail he was sure would have the Elite crashing through their door. He sank to his knees, trying to decide the best course of action. Sage was so wrapped up in whatever horror she was experiencing he couldn't get through to her. Gavriel warned him about her weapons. It wouldn't do to get stabbed while attempting to wake her. If, however, he could clamp her arms to her sides, he might be okay. He would not become her pincushion.

Tehl blew out a breath. Here went nothing.

He snatched Sage and pulled her back against his chest. "Wake up, you're dreaming."

A feral cry burst out of her, and she exploded into motion, bucking frantically and throwing her head back, clipping him in the chin. Losing his balance, Tehl landed hard on his butt, his legs hugging her hips. He threw both legs on top of hers, tightened his arms, and pushed his head into the side of her neck to pin her to the ground. Meanwhile he spoke in a soothing voice. "It's a dream, it's just a dream, love," he found himself saying over and over.

Her fighting gave way to teeth rattling shudders and sobbing. He released her legs and rolled up to his feet, standing with Sage hanging in his arms. Tehl shifted her in his arms and carried his broken rebel wife to their bed.

"Shhhh…it's okay. I have you."

He set her in it and stared down at her frightened eyes while she fought her way back from whatever hell held her hostage. Tehl ran his eyes over her shadowed features once more before walking around the bed to sit down himself. Emotions washed over him in waves. Guilt. Sadness. Disgust. Anger. He may not have been her attacker, but, to a certain degree, he still felt responsible, as it was his actions that had set the stage for her to be so taken advantage of and hurt. Sage's defiant face when he'd flung back her hood flashed through his mind followed by the memory of her broken cries before the wedding. Tehl sucked in a ragged breath and scrubbed a hand over his face. The vibrant woman he'd first encountered was a dim remnant of her former self, and he hated that he'd had any part in that. He wasn't sorry that they'd thus far subdued the rebellion, but he did regret the way some of it came about.

"We're never to speak of this," Sage's sleep roughened voice pulled him from his reverie. Tehl looked over his shoulder. In the darkness, he could barely make her out as she lay on her back, staring up at the ceiling. "I am not weak," she insisted.

"I never said you were."

"You were thinking it, I could hear it in your silence. You were pitying me."

Tehl pulled one of his legs beneath him and turned to get a better look at her. "No."

"No? I don't believe you, husband."

Tehl stiffened at the title. It wasn't said in an inflection he remembered his mother using to his father, but as a joke. For a reason he could not quite define, that bothered him. After taking a moment to ponder it, however, he realized it made sense since their marriage was a joke anyway.

"Believe it or not, I was raging at the injustice of what befell you, especially since the burden of guilt is partly on my shoulders," he said heavily, his confession hanging in the air.

Her profile turned his way, studying him. "You may have contributed to the circumstance, but you are not responsible for everyone's actions. I have to take responsibility in my part as well. If I hadn't taken part in treasonous acts, I would never have found myself in that situation in the first place. We must all face what we have done."

He was momentarily shocked by her humility, he couldn't believe she was willing to see, much less speak of, her own burden of guilt in this. It was a surprisingly mature response and he respected her for it. "What you speak is true, but, still, I am sorry for what you have suffered. I dare say I will carry a part of the burden all my life."

"Good."

Tehl winced and dropped his head. He supposed he deserved her cruelty.

"I don't mean it like that. I don't want you to suffer, but I believe if you carry the memory with you always then it will inculcate a lesson into your heart. It will influence the way you rule and how you deal with others. That can be a good thing." Tehl lifted his head, watching her watch him. "I won't ever forget what happened to me, but, one day, I will be able to forgive both you and I, it's just not today."

Tehl nodded. He knew the feeling. Forgiveness could be an elusive thing.

TWENTY-TWO⊙

SAGE

SAGE'S EYES SPRUNG OPEN. SHE blinked at the unfamiliar ceiling. Where was she? Something warm shifted against her side. Sage turned her head to the side and stilled. There was a man in the bed. A half-naked man. She blinked a couple times and then let loose an earth-shattering scream.

As soon as she did so, his eyes flew open and he bolted upright. Sage scrambled backward on her hands, kicking at him as she tried to escape. One of her kicks clipped him on the chin, clacking his teeth together and sending him off the bed. Her whole body trembled as she scrambled to find a weapon of any sort and figure out what was going on. Burning pain seared her hand as she clumsily grabbed the blade of the dagger hidden under the pillow. Ignoring the pain and blood, Sage rolled off the bed and fell into a defensive crouch. How did she end up here? She darted a glance around the room searching for an easy exit. Blast. The only door was on the other side of the bed.

"Stars above, what are you doing, woman?" a familiar voice demanded.

A large hand gripped the edge of the bed and irritated dark blue eyes peeked at her over its edge.

"What was that for?"

After a second, recognition dawned. Tehl. The crown prince. Her husband. Sage pushed her unruly hair out of her face and tried to calm her heart as it tried its best to beat right out of her chest. She scowled at the bed then looked

486

at her abandoned nest on the floor. "Why did you move me?"

A snort pulled her attention back to her husband as he hauled himself from the floor, attempting to untangle himself from the bedding. "Do you not remember?"

Sage stared blankly at his naked chest for a beat before shifting her focus back to the rumpled bed, her brows furrowed. She remembered talking a bath, slipping into bed, and then—suddenly it came crashing back. Muddy-brown eyes, traipsing hands, and pain. Nightmares. She'd had a nightmare. Sage's jaw tightened when she remembered how she had lain in Tehl's arms, crying like a pathetic victim. How scornfully weak he must think her.

Sage's eyes snapped up to find Tehl regarding her evenly. She scrutinized his face, searching for any hint of condescension or pity, but, miraculously, she found none. His eyes wandered down her arm and paused, a flicker of concern on his face. Sage followed his gaze to her crimson stained hand. She blinked. She'd forgotten she'd even done that.

Tehl grabbed the sheet and ripped a strip off, moving around the bed toward her. He halted in front of her and held his hand out. Sage eyed it before unclenching her hand and carefully placed the bloody dagger onto the side table, and, immediately, she felt the pain begin to pulse from the wound. Reluctantly, she laid her hand in his. It had already bled quite a bit, making it look worse than it was, but fortunately it wasn't deep enough to require stitching, however, it would prove to be annoying in the coming weeks.

As he examined her hand, palm up, his calloused hands were surprisingly gentle. Sage winced when he used his fingers to probe the cut, ascertaining its depth, and focused on a soot mark marring the fireplace. An uncomfortable silence filled the room as he wrapped the cloth and bound it. After what seemed like an eternity of awkwardness, he finally said, "All done."

Sage pulled her hand from his grasp and shifted backward, clearing her throat. "Um, sorry about kicking you off the bed."

He took a step back as well and leaned a bare shoulder on a bed poster, crossing his muscular arms against his very bare chest. It irked her that he cut such a nice figure. Sage was no stranger to the male physique; she did, after all, grow up with two brothers and had spent plenty of time training with men. For some reason, however, she was discomfited by it when it came to the crown prince.

"Would you put a shirt on?" she snapped.

"No, I won't. I have slept without a shirt for as long as I can remember and that's not going to change just because I have a wife. If it makes you uncomfortable, don't look." The crown prince turned on his heel and left, entering the bathing room. Just before slamming the door, he called out, "You're lucky I wore pants."

Sage glared at the door a moment but soon left that to examine the room. The bed looked like a wild beast had been let loose on it. Blankets and pillows were strewn about the room, the sheets ripped and blood stained. Feathers decorated the bed, its side-table, and the floor. When did that happen? And how?

A sharp knock at the door had Sage scrambling. She rushed to pick up her nest of blankets and threw them on the bed. No one could know they weren't actually together. She plucked a pillow up and lobbed it at the bed.

No doubt hearing her scrambling around, Tehl yanked open the door, frowning. "What?"

"There's someone at the door!" Sage hissed.

Tehl's eyes widened. "Put a robe on over your clothes."

She dashed into the closet and tugged on the first robe she found. "One moment," she heard the crown prince call out. It was so large the sleeves covered her hands and it dragged on the floor, but it would do.

Sage stepped out of the closet just as Tehl placed the bloody dagger into a drawer. He turned to her and nodded. "Good. My robe is a nice touch."

That's why it was so big. She was an idiot sometimes. He moved to her side and reached for her braid. "What are you doing?" Sage barked, batting his hand away.

"Making it appear like you have been tumbled all night," he growled.

"I can do it!" Speedily, she unwound her braid and ran her fingers through her locks. Sage bent forward and flipped her hair back, tousling it. "How's that?"

The crown prince stepped into her space and speared his fingers through her hair, ruffling it. "There. Now you look tumbled."

She jerked away from him with narrowed eyes and opened her mouth to retort.

"Enter," Tehl called, plopping into a nearby chair, yanking her with him. She fell with a grunt into his lap. Annoyed, she stiffened and tried to get right back up.

"Sit back and relax," his deep voice whispered into her ear. "They are bringing breakfast to a newly married couple. What do they expect to see?"

Sage had no choice but to curl into him as the door opened, admitting one of her ladies-in-waiting and a few servants. A large hand settled on her thigh, and she couldn't help the blush that crept up her cheeks.

"How are you today, my lady?" Lera, a plump serving woman, asked while spreading a feast before them.

"I am well, Lera. Thank you."

Tittering drew her attention to her ladies-in-waiting that she avoided since they had a tendency to gossip and she had no interest in such things. They were glancing from the bed to one another, whispering furtively. Sage's brows furrowed as she tried to figure out what they could possibly find *that* interesting. One of their gazes flickered again to the bed, curiosity evident on their face. Sage glanced to the bed, but she noted nothing worth commenting on. Dismissing it she was about to turn away when her eyes snapped back to the bed in horror.

The blood.

That's why they were staring.

Her cheeks burned at what they must be thinking. Lera noted her preoccupation and looked to the bed, stilling for only a moment. The sweet servant smiled softly, kindness on her face. "Would you like me to draw you a bath? I have lavender. It is wonderful for soothing all sorts of aches and pains."

"Please do," Tehl responded, "for the lady and I."

Humiliation burned her at the knowing glint in Lera's eyes. "Of course, my lord."

Sage blocked out everything and everyone in the room and instead focused on simply appearing comfortable and relaxed. What was she doing here? She rubbed her wrist and blanched. What did she do with her cuffs? She scanned the room frantically, attempting to be subtle in her search. Her heart banged against her ribs when she caught sight of them under the bed. A rough shake pulled her out of her stupor. She blinked and turned to stare at narrowed dark blue eyes. "What?"

"You can get off of me."

Her own eyes narrowed at his tone. "Excuse me?"

"They're gone, you can drop the act."

Sage leapt from his lap and tugged off his robe, tossing it onto the bed with disgust. Her new husband remained seated, relaxed in the chair slouching with his legs splayed in front of him, still without a damn shirt. His blue eyes were thoughtful as he rubbed at his chin, musing.

"I think that went well."

She snorted. "*Hmph*. What part?"

"All of it," the prince gestured to the bed. "I couldn't have planned it any better. In an hour the whole palace will know what ardent lovers we are."

Sage sniggered. "*Ardent* lovers?" she asked, her nose scrunched.

Tehl's lips turned up. "Yes. Ardent lovers."

Sage rolled her eyes and swiped her cuffs from under the bed, plopping down on it. "What do we do now?"

"Our court already knows we aren't leaving for a bonding period like some do, so they'll be expecting us to be holed up here instead for a while."

She stared at him in horror. How long would she have to stay in the same room as him? She didn't think they could survive; one of them would surely murder the other. "How long?"

"Two weeks."

"No."

"Yes."

"I will not be trapped in this room for two weeks. Who will run Aermia?"

"Sam, I imagine."

"You can *not* be serious."

"What would you have me do?"

"One week. I will stay here one week and one week only, not a moment more," she said severely.

"We could get away with one week, I suppose. That would be ideal since I don't relish being stuck in here either."

Sage blew out a breath. "One week."

"One week," Tehl echoed.

The week wasn't as horrid as Sage had imagined. She discovered, to her delight, her new husband felt the need to avoid her as much as she did him. The worst part was being cooped up in a single suite. She read books, practiced, and lounged in the sun on the terrace to pass the time. At one point, she'd become so bored that she convinced Mira to bring her a sewing basket. After hours of trying, and nothing but knotted thread, a wounded finger, and jabs from Tehl to show for it, she finally just threw the blasted thing over the balcony.

Sam popped in a few times with updates on her assassin, or rather, the lack thereof. They could find nothing so far. They had a body but no names or connections. So many times she wished she could go and investigate herself but was always politely reminded that Rafe was looking into it as well and that it was more important that she stayed where she was.

She also missed her family. It was lonely being stuck with just the prince. Gavriel stopped by for a few games of chess but never for very long nor frequently enough to fill her need for company. Sage grew so desperate she even attempted to converse with her husband but he was dense. He couldn't hold a conversation to save his life.

Husband.

She'd never be comfortable with him wearing that title.

Her biggest issue, however, was every night. The crown prince dropped into a deep sleep as soon as his head touched the pillow, whereas Sage would curl up by the fire, staring at the ceiling for hours until she finally succumbed to sleep. She envied his soundless sleep night after night for, inevitably, she would have a nightmare. Thus, every morning, she woke up, not only exhausted, but irritable because the stubborn man wouldn't leave her in the nest on the floor. She hated that every morning she awoke plastered to his warm side.

When Sage woke on the eighth day, she couldn't hold back her excitement. She was free. She shoved her feet into boots and snatched her daggers from their various hiding places. Tehl rolled from the bed and watched her.

"You're chipper this morning." His voice sounded like two rocks being rubbed together.

"We are free of each other." Sage grinned at him in the mirror while she quickly braided her hair.

The crown prince pushed up from the bed and plucked something from her side-table. Sage turned to him when he stopped behind her. Her lips pinched when she saw what he was holding. Her cuffs. Sage held her wrists out to him, keeping her face neutral. She hated them. She shivered when the cold metal kissed her skin. Tehl ran his thumb over one cuff and released her. Sage plastered a bland smile on her face and slipped out the door with a quick goodbye.

The surge of excitement she felt at her newfound freedom added a skip to her step. She ignored the Elite following her and lengthened her stride. Finally, she burst through the doors leading to the practice ring and tilted her face to the sun, basking in its warm embrace.

"You appear mighty satisfied." Sam teased.

Sage's lips twitched. "I am indeed."

"Oh?"

She opened her eyes and peeked at Sam who was lounging against the castle wall. "Married life suits me well."

Sam smiled widely at her with twinkling eyes. "I am inclined to believe you. You're ravishing this morning."

"Always the flatterer," Sage replied, a hand on her hip. "How many women have you said that to?"

Sam clasped his hands over his heart. "You wound me."

"I doubt that. There'd have to be a heart in that chest before I could wound it." Sage left him sputtering.

"I have a heart full of love."

"You love too much," she called over her shoulder.

"There's no such thing!" he insisted.

His feet marched behind hers, chasing her toward the practice courtyard. "It's not so much about quantity as it is quality."

"So you're saying one woman is better than many?"

Sam tugged on her braid and threw his arm over her shoulder.

Sage elbowed him in the stomach and shrugged off his arm. "Better be careful or you might have a horde of women thinking you love them."

Sam's face blanched and she giggled. After patting his arm, she attempted a sympathetic expression. "Don't fret, I'm sure you'll figure out some way to thwart them. After all, I've heard you're an excellent liar."

"Says the pot to the kettle," he mumbled.

"You and I are going to be great friends."

He smiled down at her. "Yes, we are."

TWENTY-THREE

SAGE

THE CROWN PRINCE WAS IN so much trouble.

She'd kill him.

Without so much as a word she blew passed the two guards holding the dungeon doors open. Her footsteps echoed on the stone walls as she descended the steps leading to the dungeon, her jaw clenched.

She had to be wrong. When she had stumbled across a pair of Elite speaking about a woman in the dungeon, Sage had frozen, hardly able to believe her ears. There was another woman being held captive? There was no way Sam and Gav would keep this from her, she had to have heard wrong. Jeffry's head jerked up as she slammed into his office, halting just before his desk.

The old man blinked and steepled his fingers beneath his chin. "Yes?" He leveled an assessing gaze at her. To many, his silver eyes would be off-putting and intimidating, but she'd already known him for quite some time. She was not deterred.

"Where is she?" Sage growled.

"Who?"

So he was going to play dumb. How original. "The woman!" she spat.

Pity filled Jeffry's face. "She's been well taken care of."

A stone settled in her stomach. It was true. Stars above. "That's not what I asked."

He glanced to a soldier stationed in the corner of the room. "Jacque, show the princess to cell nine-twelve."

Dismissing the Keeper, she followed Jacque's wiry form into the labyrinth of hallways which made up the dungeon. How could they keep this from her? She rubbed her arms as chills ran up and down them. The walls seemed to inch closer, the deeper they descended. How she hated this place!

A dirty prisoner caught her eye when he held a limp hand out to her. Old insecurities rose. What did these people do to deserve their sentence? Were they all guilty?

Lost in thought, Sage failed to pay attention to her footing and stumbled, stiffening as a hand wrapped around her bicep. She glanced up into Jacque's angular face with a frown.

"Be careful, my lady. That one is in here for crimes you couldn't imagine. Preys on women and children alike."

All her pity disappeared. Children were to be protected, not preyed upon. Sage bared her teeth at the man and continued to follow Jacque. They turned a final corner and the soldier stopped at a cell at the very end of the hallway.

Her heart fell to the floor when she made out the sleeping prisoner on the other side of the bars.

A woman.

How could they do this?

Sage pushed closer and grasped the bars. She scoured the woman for injuries, but, apart from being loosely shackled to the cell, she looked thus far unharmed. Beneath the dirt, the woman was stunning. Her mocha skin was perfectly smooth, faint swirling patterns somehow etched or painted on it. She had hair so dark it seemed to soak up any surrounding light.

"How long has she been here?" Sage croaked. She wet her lips waiting for the guard's answer.

"I would say almost three months. They brought her in about the time you were taken to the healer."

Bile crept up her throat.

Three months.

They had kept her in here for three bloody months. Sage pulled in a deep breath through her nose, trying to keep from heaving. All she could see was herself hanging above the grate, bleeding. The pain. The terror. The iron bit into her palms, but she didn't feel it. The sensation was lost in the memory.

"My lady?"

Sage blinked and shook away the memories. She turned to Jacque. "What?"

He hesitated for a moment. "Are you all right?" he asked gruffly, jerking his chin toward her face.

Sage lifted her hand to her forehead and followed the bar's impressions down her cheek, discovering it was wet. She hadn't even realized she'd been crying. Sage scrubbed her face with her arm and dismissed the guard's concern, choosing to focus on the cell and its occupant.

The prisoner had woken, and she stared at them with midnight eyes so dark it looked like she had no pupil. The perfect symmetry of her face struck Sage as odd and then the breath in her lungs froze. What had the princes done?

A Scythian.

She had seen few Scythians growing up. The ones who sought refuge in Aermia tended to live in relative solitude, but when she did come across them, she had always admired their beauty, but this woman looked like none she'd ever encountered. She was unearthly, as if her features had been carved rather than born of flesh. Sage suppressed a shiver. In a way, the woman probably was. She didn't doubt for a second that this woman was one of the 'Flawless' Scythia manipulated into existence.

Sage watched the woman watch her. "What's your name?"

The woman cocked her head. "I have been asked many questions since I have arrived here, but none of them have been in regard to my name." She spoke with a faint, lilting accent. "Why would you ask me such a thing?"

Sage shrugged. "It's fairly standard practice when meeting a new person to ask their name. You're a person, aren't you?"

The Scythian woman let out a short, harsh laugh. "I am indeed." She lifted her wrists and rattled her chains. "But in here I am little more than wasted space."

"I doubt that."

"Why are you here, princess?"

Sage regarded the woman with interest. She knew more than a prisoner should know. Interesting. "You know who I am?"

The prisoner waved her hand. "I'll not answer your questions. Did the commander send you? Did he think a woman would goad me into speaking? Have the last three months taught him nothing?" She lifted her chin and looked at Sage with haughty eyes. "I am unbreakable."

"No one is unbreakable." Everyone had a weakness.

"Lies." She scanned Sage from head to toe. "You are a close companion to the lie. Your new nuptials are not as perfect as everyone believes."

Sage kept her expression blank as her mind spun. The only ones who knew about their agreement were the Circle and the Crown's advisors. How did this woman have that information? Was she guessing? Or had someone passed it along to her? Either way boded ill. The question was, did they have a traitor or a spy?

This was nothing like what she had expected to find. She thought she'd encounter a broken woman in need of care, but what she found was a woman strong enough not only to converse but to play at words and toss out threats. She'd bet her best hat the woman was a spy. She smiled and crossed her arms, she knew how to deal with spies. Lie. Believe the lie.

"I love my husband."

The woman snorted. "Indeed. You love him like you love a snake in your bed." A sly smile appeared on the woman's face. "You're good. Your façade at the moment is flawless but that is also your tell." Her eyes slid to the guard, hovering just behind Sage's back. "It won't be long now."

Sage refused to inquire further for she wouldn't rise to the bait, as that was what it was. Time to throw her off guard.

"Are they feeding you?"

Confusion wrinkled the woman's brow at the change in subject. "Yes."

"You're not sick? Or wounded?"

"No." She jiggled her wrists. "I have sores but nothing life threatening." Her eyes narrowed. "What is your angle? Are you going to befriend me? Attempt to have me betray my people? What do you want?"

Sage squatted in front of the bars to better look her in the eye. "Nothing."

The woman froze and suspicion filled her gaze. "Nothing? Likely story. No one wants nothing."

Sage smiled sadly. "What a bleak world view." Sage shook her head. "In truth, all I want is for you to be healthy."

"I don't trust you."

Sage sniggered. "And I you, but that doesn't mean I want you to suffer."

Silence.

The woman scrutinized her for long minutes. "You mean that." The woman squinted at her, obviously baffled. "I am your enemy."

"You have done nothing to me. Have you hurt any of my loved ones?"

"No."

"Then I harbor no ill against you."

The woman lunged toward the bars, chains jerking her back a touch. Sage was careful not to flinch; instead, she simply watched the woman who was now a mere hair's breadth away.

"You're dangerous," the woman whispered.

"Indeed."

A sharp smile flitted across the prisoner's face. "I like you, so I will tell you a secret."

"I don't want a secret. I would like your name."

The woman brushed aside her comment without breaking their stare. "Darkness approaches your land. You think you understand its magnitude…" Her eyes unfocused. "But you do not. It is like nothing you have ever seen." She focused back on Sage. "Prepare yourself. It will not be stopped, and there will be war, the likes of which will put the Nagalian Purge to shame. Prepare yourself now or you will all die."

Sage pushed aside the spike of fear she felt at this revelation. It was not so much the words but the way the woman seemed to feel about them as she said them. She hid it well, but there, at the end, fear had seeped through for she had not been able to stop her voice from quivering when she spoke of all their deaths. Sage was an expert at hiding fear. She had to do it every day when someone touched her unexpectedly or surprised her. Whatever was coming terrified this warrior woman.

"Why tell me this? Why lose the element of surprise?" Tactically, it made no sense to share such information.

"No one likes an easy fight and…" The Scythian hesitated. "The strong deserve to live. You are built from strength. You wear it like armor."

Sage tilted her head. "I believe you and I are alike in that way."

"Indeed, princess."

"Sage."

"Your visit has been interesting, Sage."

"Likewise." Sage stood and began walking away.

"And Sage?"

Sage peered over her shoulder.

"My name is Blaise."

Sage smiled and nodded before continuing. A name. She counted that a success.

Jacque took the lead, making their way out of the maze of cells. When Jeffry came into view, she slapped a hand against his desk.

"Is she being given food?"

Jeffry eyed her hand and brushed it off his documents. "She's given rations and cared for by no one but myself. She has not been harmed."

Not like her.

Sage jerked her arm back and closed her hand into fist. "Are they interrogating her?"

"One of the princes has been here every week since she was first imprisoned."

That was at least twelve times. "Excuse me, Jeffry. It seems I have some business I need to take care of."

Sage sprinted up the stairs and burst into the courtyard, startling a few doves pecking the ground. She stalked into the palace, ready to tear someone's head off. Demari's eyes widened when she stalked over to him. "Where's the crown prince?"

"In the war room," the royal steward answered.

Sage nodded and stormed through the castle toward the war room, irritated even further. She should have been invited. Were they keeping her from other meetings as well? What else was she being kept in the dark about? Did they think her merely ornamental? If so, they had another thing coming; she was not a pretty thing the prince could take out when he wanted and then shelf when he felt she wasn't useful. The closer she got to the war room, the more she fumed. The whole reason for their marriage was for her to check his power. Was this the first war meeting since their marriage? She doubted it.

How many had she missed so far?

Sage smirked when she finally caught sight of the doors. They weren't prepared for the storm they had coming.

TWENTY-FOUR

TEHL

"WHERE IS SHE? SHE'S YOUR consort, your check to power. Why isn't she here to represent us?"

Tehl pinched the bridge of his nose. This was their third meeting since adding the rebellion leader and it wasn't going well. They rarely agreed and it usually ended in them arguing with one another until he shouted over them all.

He lifted his head and glared. "I agreed to make her my wife and consort, but I never agreed to her sitting in on the war council." That shut the little rebellion weasel up.

"The attacks along the border have stopped," Zachael put in, but he said it like it wasn't a good thing.

"That's a good thing, right?" William asked.

"No," Rafe's deep voice rumbled. "It means they've focused on something else. Something we know nothing about. So now we're blind."

The group quieted.

"Have you no spies in Scythia?"

Sam stiffened and sat forward at the question. "No, not at the moment. I have sent many but, as of yet, none have returned"

"None? How many have you sent?"

"Twelve."

Gasps and a few curses echoed around him.

"We need to find out what they're planning," Rafe stated, but, before he could continue, the double doors were shoved open, slamming against the walls, and through them sauntered Tehl's wife, as if she owned the place. Tehl caught her eye and swore to himself. The furious glint in her eyes did not bode well for him.

She looked around the room. "Good afternoon, gentlemen. Have I interrupted anything?"

Tehl jerked his chin to the two guards accompanying her. They closed the doors while she smiled as his council scrambled out of their chairs to bow.

His eyes narrowed when Rafe stood, kissed her hand, and whispered something in her ear that made her smile. Zachael and Garreth tossed him questioning glances. He shrugged; he didn't like the exchange anymore than they did. He liked it even less when she lifted onto her toes and kissed the corner of Rafe's mouth while watching the table of men. When she turned away, she didn't catch the heat in Rafe's gaze as he eyed her covetously, but Tehl did and he didn't like it. It was true that many men admired his wife, she was after all a beauty, but it was different with Rafe and her actions certainly weren't helping. She was playing with fire, but why?

Sage walked up to Sam and patted him on the cheek a bit harder than was friendly.

"Always the sneaky one, aren't you, brother?"

Sam's brows furrowed at her mocking tone.

Sage skirted around Sam and moved next to his seat. Tehl about choked on his tongue when she leaned down and smacked a loud kiss against his mouth before ruffling his hair. "Hello, husband of mine."

Tehl scrutinized her. Something was definitely wrong.

She plopped down onto the arm of his chair and waved to the group of men. "By all means, continue."

The council members were obviously taken by surprise, some gaping while others watched her through narrowed eyes, no doubt attempting to figure out her angle.

Rafe coughed, eyes twinkling, obviously enjoying her show.

Bloody mischief-maker.

"We were discussing the need for information on Scythia," the rebellion leader supplied.

"Indeed." Sage pulled out a wickedly sharp dagger and, somehow, produced an apple out of thin air.

Where the hell did the apple come from? How did she keep doing that?

She sliced a piece, stabbed it with the blade, and held it out to him. "Hungry?"

Tehl's brows lowered in confusion. "No... I am not," he drew out the words, trying to make sense of her odd behavior. What was she up to?

She shrugged. "Suit yourself." His wife crunched into the apple and gestured with the knife. "So, you need information?"

"Yes," Sam drawled, placing his hands behind his head.

"Perfect. Especially since I have some and you might find it fairly useful."

Suddenly, she had every man at the table leaning forward, both suspicious and eager. She continued to snack on her apple, studiously ignoring them.

Information? Tehl placed a hand on her thigh to get her attention. She stared at it for a beat before placing her dagger against his hand and pushing it off. Point taken. Don't touch her leg.

She grinned at him before biting down on the apple with a loud crunch and smacking her lips.

Tehl twitched. If she smacked her lips in his ear one more time he'd push her off his chair. He hated people chewing in his ear.

"Are you going to tell us your information?" Jaren snapped. "Or just dangle the promise of it in front of us all day?"

Half the table stiffened. The pompous windbag didn't seem to notice, or if he did, he didn't care. No matter how it came about, she was now a princess of Aermia and therefore ought to have been accorded due respect.

"Watch your tone, old man," Tehl warned.

Jaren scowled and his face reddened so much he was almost purple.

"Is he going to explode?" Sage whispered loudly.

Several chuckles, poorly masked as coughs, had Jaren glaring round the table as Tehl held in a groan. Why today? Did she always have to be a thorn in his side?

Abruptly, Sage pushed from his chair and sat on the table's edge, swinging one leg. "As much as I would like to keep you in suspense, Jaren, I have much to do. So," she paused tracing the grain of the table with her blade. "Would it interest you if I told you Scythia will invade soon?"

"That's nothing new, Scythia has been a threat for some time," Garreth stated. "We've suspected invasion for awhile now."

"True." Sage locked eyes with Garreth. "But I collected information that confirms they plan to move against Aermia, and that it will be soon." Sage dropped her eyes and continued to trace the grain. "I have it on good authority that the invasion will be on a scale we have not previously anticipated. It will make the Nagalian Purge look like child's play."

The room stilled, and Tehl's stomach soured.

The Nagalian Purge was the worst crime ever committed within living memory. Two entire races, Nagalian and Dragon, destroyed at the behest of a single nation. Women and children were not spared and every aspect of their cities and culture were reduced to rubble before the surrounding nations even heard of Scythia's betrayal. Then, the warlord had claimed it was necessary to purge the world of the Nagalians and their 'undesirable' and 'debased' ability to communicate with the draconian species.

It wasn't purification. It was genocide.

"Where did you come by such information?" Garreth probed. "I wasn't aware the rebellion had spies in Scythia."

"We don't," Rafe replied while watching Sage.

"You don't know?" Sage lifted her face and took in the council's expression before throwing her head back, roaring with laughter.

Now was not the time for laughter. "Love, could you get to the point?" Tehl growled.

Her head snapped to him and all laughter cut off. "You don't need to use such endearments here my lord. Remember that all these men were witnesses of my sale."

Tehl blinked. He had called her that in public so many times this last month that it now came out naturally. He didn't even think about it. "It wasn't deliberate."

She waved a hand at him, that malicious glint returning to her eye. "It's nothing, but if you insist on using pet names..."

Tehl stiffened and her smiled widened. "I think I will go with *pookie*."

He grimaced.

No. Not now. Not ever.

"Not so fun is it?"

Tehl released an exasperated breath. This was so not the time. Patience, he needed patience.

Sage dismissed him and turned to the table. "Let's expose some secrets, shall we? Pookie, here—" She hitched a thumb over her shoulder at him. "—has been hiding things."

Tehl glanced at Sam and Gav wondering what the hell what going on.

"He's had this information for months."

Tehl's nose crinkled in confusion. He glanced to Sam and Gav who were wearing the same expression.

"What are you talking about?"

She smirked at him over her shoulder. "Imagine my surprise when I discovered the Crown was keeping another woman chained to the dungeon's floor."

His heart sped up. Damn it.

"A Scythian woman."

Gasps filled the room.

"What?" Lelbiel hissed.

Sage's smile turned triumphant just before she turned to Lelbiel, face serious. "You heard me. From the looks on your faces, I can tell you have been kept ignorant of this fact too, just as was I."

"Is this true?" Zachael asked.

"Yes, but she has been useless," Sam interjected. "We have interrogated her for almost three months, but we have gained absolutely nothing. Unless she provided us with any new intelligence, she wasn't noteworthy to the council."

"We still should have known," William commented.

"It wasn't for you to decide," Tehl stated. "Her capture didn't affect you in any way unless she had information to share with us. Which she didn't." Tehl stared at the back of the rebel woman's head. "She didn't feed us lies, as you did, she gave us silence. There was only so much we could do. Her experience has been completely different from yours."

His wife stilled, and his advisors quieted at whatever look was on her face.

Slowly, she turned toward him and spoke, her voice indignant. "So she should be thankful she's been chained to the floor in a tiny dirty cell for ninety days? That's better than what I suffered at your hands?"

He squinted at her trying to see the trap she was weaving. "She made the choice to attack Silva, leaving children without parents and burning homes, so these are simply the consequences of her own actions. She struck first."

"That makes it okay to strike back? To hurt her?"

"She has never been hurt. She's been fed, clothed, and well taken care of. She hardly has reason to complain, all we've asked for is her cooperation. The information she has could save hundreds if not thousands of lives."

"Not that it matters," Sam added. "She's not given us a bloody thing, so it's turned out to be a useless gamble."

"You're more morally corrupt than I thought. Basic human needs are not a privilege, not something to be rewarded, or they shouldn't be," she said softly before pinning Sam with her gaze. "And she's not useless. I spoke with Blaise today."

"Blaise?" Sam scooted forward with excitement. "She gave you her name? She's hardly spoken a word these three months past. What did you do? We've tried everything."

"Not everything obviously. If you had you'd already have known that a little human kindness goes a long way. People don't like to be manipulated, Spymaster." Sage stared his brother down. "They like to be treated as fellow humans and not just assets." A pause. "They are *people*, not things to be used and tossed away, a lesson it seems you haven't learned yet."

Sam flinched and dropped his eyes looking upset. "She's a prisoner of war, Sage. She made her choice when she attacked Aermia."

Her lips pursed, but she didn't argue.

Tehl frowned. Now was neither the time nor the place for moral lessons. It was a war meeting for God's sake and she needed to get off her high horse. This did nothing for the unification of the council, and it was high time for her show to end. She'd made her point. "Are you about done?"

Sage turned placing her boots on his knees and leaned forward. "Not yet, but almost. I don't take kindly to lies of omission, nor do I care to be manipulated. If you think the Scythians are dangerous then you have never been on my bad side."

"Duly noted."

Her eyes narrowed. "I know several of these meetings have happened and yet this is the first one I've been to. I am not your errand boy, your steward, or even your wife. I am your consort, your balance, your judge, and your fellow in arms. Do not think to exclude me." Her hair had fallen around her face framing her flushed cheeks and fiery eyes.

For one moment, he let himself admire her wild beauty. He admitted to himself that her inner fire was appealing. A life with her could actually be enjoyable one day if they could be true comrades in arms, but, until then, it was fight or die. She could have her say but making a scene was not acceptable.

Tehl placed his palms on either side of her thighs and leaned into her space, their noses touching. "I'll make sure you're included but just because we have an alliance and a document that states we are bound, it doesn't mean you are privy to everything that happens in *my* kingdom."

"I understand." A smile flitted across her mouth. "But just because we have an alliance and a document that states we are bound, it doesn't mean you can order me around and exclude me from matters of *our* kingdom."

Stubborn wench. She never made anything easy.

His nose twitched. Cinnamon.

Tehl tipped forward, his nose against her jaw and breathed in. The blasted cinnamon. He loved that smell. A month of sharing a room with her and it permeated everything. Even his clothes smelled like her some days.

She jerked back and crossed her arms. "I am not your mistress, either."

That startled a laugh out of him as he sat back in his chair. "Indeed, you are not."

"As long as we understand each other."

"You're my wife." Her face soured. She didn't like that reminder.

"In name only."

"Not for long." Tehl barely held in the snigger at how her whole body stiffened.

"As long as I say."

"You don't have forever."

"Drop dead."

"Maybe you'll get lucky."

"If only," she muttered.

Tehl studied her. She was a giant pain in his ass, but she wasn't without virtues. As long as she used good sense, Aermia could well benefit from that fire of hers.

Her lips turned down. "What?"

"I think you have the potential to be exactly what Aermia needs."

Her eyebrows rose. "Remember that the next time you try to hide something from me." She swung around and stood on the table.

Tehl rolled his eyes as she strode down it, everyone's eyes on her. So dramatic.

She paused at the end and eyed the group with a grin. "Never underestimate women, gentlemen, especially when provoked."

Rafe stood and held his hand out to her. She ignored him and smiled at Zachael, who stood and offered his hand. Sage accepted and jumped down from the table, then waltzed to the empty chair next to William and flopped into it, lacing her hands across her stomach. "Well, that's taken care of. So where were we gentlemen? What's on the agenda today?"

Silence descended as all the men in the room stared at her, some annoyed, some condescending, and others a bit awed. Tehl cocked his head and watched Rafe stew at the vexing creature his wife was. Seemed she didn't just get under his skin but the rebellion leader's as well.

One by one, his advisers looked back at him.

"Your hands are full with that one," Jaren remarked, eyeing Sage as she fluttered her fingers at him.

Tehl rolled his neck and stared at the ceiling. "You have no idea."

"I heard that."

Tehl tipped his head forward, one side of his mouth lifting. "You were supposed to."

Mason coughed and arched his brows. "Now that we all understand your theatrical skills, we are still anxiously awaiting more information on the Scythian woman."

Her careless smile fell from her face as she straightened in her chair. "There isn't much to tell. She revealed to me that Scythia was coming, time was short, and that we needed to prepare ourselves."

"Did she give you any details, anything specific? Anything more helpful?" Zane asked.

Sage stared at him drolly. "Why yes, she handed over a detailed plan while we were braiding each other's hair."

"Why would she warn us?" Zachael questioned.

"Scythia is founded on the ideal of perfectionk, on achieving the perfect warrior, love for battle. She warned us so that the battle would be more difficult for them, thus the win more satisfying," Lelbiel explained.

"That makes no sense," Garreth argued.

"Neither did the eradication of the Nagalians in their pursuit of perfection, yet it happened," Rafe pointed out.

"She could be lying. How do we know the information is trustworthy?" Jaren inquired.

"She could be, and we don't, but are we willing to take that chance?" Gav asked.

"We treat this like the threat it is," Tehl stated. He cut his attention to his wife. "Can you get her to speak with you again?"

"Yes."

He turned to his brother. "Sam, will you collaborate with Sage?"

"That won't work," Sage cut in. "She doesn't trust any of you, and certainly not the man who has been interrogating her for the last three months. I need someone else."

"I'll join you."

Tehl glanced at Rafe, his look not quite friendly. "What do you plan to do?"

"Sage and I work well together. We'll figure it out."

Turning to Sage, Tehl met her eyes. "Does that work for you?" It was her choice now.

Her lips thinned, and she shot Rafe a look, but nodded. "Rafe is the best at what he does. If there's anyone who could secure her help, it would be him."

"It's settled then." Tehl's gaze swept the table. "You all have your assignments. We'll meet here in three days to discuss our progress and any other concerns. I have things I need to attend to. Good day." With the dismissal, his advisors filed out of the room.

Closing his eyes, Tehl listened to the murmuring voices of the councilors drift farther away, though neither his brother nor cousin made move to rise, both choosing to remain in their chairs. Tehl heard the door close and the sound of footsteps approaching. One guess as to who that was. He snorted and opened his eyes as Sage kissed Gav on the cheek and sat next to him.

"What about my kiss?" Sam complained.

Sage pierced him with a look. "I am so angry at you right now, Samuel, I don't even want to see your face."

"What did I do?"

"Don't play stupid. You could have come to me with this. You know I would have helped you with her. Yet you stayed silent."

Sam pursed his lips.

His wife rubbed her temples. "But I have a bigger issue to deal with than my anger at you." She peeked at him. "She knows we aren't a love match, Tehl."

Tehl jerked back. "How?"

She shrugged. "I don't know. The best I can figure out is that someone in this room is a traitor or a spy."

Gav blanched. "What led you to that conclusion? There were many in the room when the treaty was negotiated that are not present here."

Sam swore. "She's right. The Scythian woman has been in our dungeon since before the Midsummer Festival. The only ones who both have access to the dungeon *and* know about the treaty are those serving on the council."

"So there's a spy then," Gav growled.

"Yes," Sage replied.

"If it's not one thing, it's another," Tehl grouched.

"Such is the life of ruling," Sage stated.

"Indeed. Welcome to the rest of your life."

TWENTY-FÎVE

SAGE

THE REST OF HER BLOODY life.

Sage stared blankly at the princes of Aermia. It truly sunk in for the first time.

It was forever.

Here.

With *him*.

Her body flashed hot and cold.

The crown prince's smile fell, his brow furrowing. "Are you all right?"

His distorted voice reached her ears as pinpricks of light danced across her vision. Stars above, she was going to pass out.

"Sage!"

Sage blinked and jerked her head toward Gav. "What?"

Her friend looked at her with concern. "Are you all right? The color in your face drained, and you swayed."

She pasted on a weak smile and waved away his concern. "It's nothing. I skipped lunch, and all I have eaten is that apple. I am starving, I need meat." Male grumbles of understanding sounded as they accepted her excuse. Carefully, Sage met Tehl's eyes. "Why did you keep me in the dark?"

"I didn't think it was necessary. She had nothing to do with you." The crown prince shrugged. "You've had many new duties and burdens you've taken on since we wed. You didn't need this one on your shoulders too."

She gritted her teeth and sucked in a deep breath. Patience. She needed patience or she'd knock his head off. "And you're the one who gets to decide that for me?"

"It's a trap, brother. Don't answer that question," Sam whispered out of the corner of his mouth.

Tehl glanced to his brother. "I am the crown prince," he said slowly before looking at her. "And acting sovereign of Aermia, not to mention your husband, so yes. I do get to decide."

Sage blew out a breath and clenched the arms of her chair.

"Bad choice," Sam sniggered.

She glared at Sam who promptly turned his snigger into a cough. She turned her neck and stared at Gav attempting to gather every last thread of her control. "I will kill him. That's all there is. How can anyone expect me to spend my life with that blundering offensive oaf?"

Gav smiled at her. "He's what I like to refer to as a very smart-dumb person." A growl from Gavriel's right made his smile widen. "He's not *so* bad. Emma and I used to argue all the time, and we grew up together. You've only known each other a handful of months. You need to keep in mind no one is perfect, Sage, including yourself."

Her lips thinned at the gentle chastisement. Grudgingly, she admitted to herself that Gav was right, but it still didn't excuse the words that came out of Tehl's mouth. "Agreed, no one is perfect, but I am not the one in the wrong this time." Sage looked at her clenched hands and tried to loosen her grip. Gav's large hand came into view and squeezed her hand once.

"What he said has merit."

Sage whipped her face toward Gav. He was taking the crown prince's side?

Gav held his hands up at the hostile expression on her face. "Before you bite my head off, just listen. There was truth in his words, what you're upset with is how he said it, which makes sense because you and he are different. Tehl doesn't see why what he said could be offensive because he was being truthful. You need to explain why it made you angry or he won't understand."

"I am still here," the crown prince cut in.

Sage stared at Gav wishing to bang her head against the wall. "Why me?"

she moaned.

His lips twitched as he held back a laugh. "Because you're not the emotionally stunted one."

Sage narrowed her eyes at him and turned her attention to the irritated prince glaring at her. She needed to speak to him like a child. "Do you like to have your opinions acknowledged?"

He squinted for a moment before answering. "Yes."

"Do you like controlling choices that will affect your life?"

"Yes."

"Do you enjoy being belittled?"

"No."

"Do you like being patronized?"

"No."

"That's how your statement made me feel, like I am ignorant and don't understand what's best for myself." Sage paused, noting how his forehead wrinkled in thought. "You don't know me, you don't know what I can or cannot handle. Don't presume to run my life because you are the crown prince. And, as far as we're both concerned, our marriage is a piece of paper, but if we had a real marriage that would mean a partnership, a team, not a man ruling over a woman. I am here to solidify our kingdom, and I can't do that if you don't include me in things that are important."

His eyes dipped to the table before meeting hers again. "I understand."

Sage arched a brow. "Do you?"

"You don't want to me to tell you what to do."

"That's not what I am saying. I want you to speak with me before you make a decision that concerns me."

"Did it occur to you I said nothing because of the situation? Because it was similar to something you experienced, and I—" He paused, running a hand through his hair. "I didn't want it to trouble you."

She straightened in her chair. If he was trying to say he kept the Scythian woman from her to spare her any trauma he had to be lying, but, for the sake of the argument, she would entertain the idea. "If that was the case, you could have just asked and I would have answered."

He scoffed. "Because you're so approachable and reasonable."

She barked out a laugh. "Mmmhmm.. because you've given me so many reasons to be courteous to you."

Sam rolled his eyes.

"Don't you roll your eyes!" Sage stabbed a finger at him. "Think of the information we could have had by now if I had been made aware a month ago."

"*Could* have," Sam emphasized.

Sage smirked. "In a half hour on my first day I received more information from her than you have in the last three months." That snapped the spymaster's mouth shut. Sage threw her hands up. "And why in God's name would you pair me with Rafe?"

"I left the decision in your hands," Tehl barked, "exactly like you just asked me to."

"I was put on the spot in front of your war council, what was I supposed to do?"

"Say no."

"Men," Sage muttered, "you understand nothing."

"It seemed like you enjoyed the spotlight, what with the performance you put on. I thought you would give Jaren a fit."

That brought a smile to her lips. "If you hadn't excluded me from the meeting, which is a violation of the treaty I might remind you, I wouldn't have had to do so."

"Children, children," Sam sang.

"Shut up, Sam," both of them snarled, at the same time.

Sage paused, meeting Tehl's eyes. His eyes crinkled and the corners of his mouth hitched up. Suddenly Sage had to purse her lips just to keep the laughter from spilling out. When Gav gurgled next to her, trying to keep his own humor in check, that was the end of it. All of them burst into laughter, and the tension melted away. Sage felt a lightness she'd not experienced in a while. Shaking her head, she pushed back from the table, still chuckling, and rubbed her forehead. "Well, that is as good a note as any to depart on. It seems I have to go and make plans with Rafe." Sage made a face.

"Do you need assistance?" Sam asked, wiping the corner of his eye and standing.

"No, you nosy thing, I have it handled." Sage waved his forlorn look away and strode toward the door.

"We have a dinner party tonight. It's a dressing-up affair."

Sage smiled at Tehl's grumpy tone. He hated court almost as much as she did. She schooled her features and peeked over her shoulder.

"Eight o'clock?"

He nodded.

"Will there be dancing?"

Sage had to smother another smile at the grim face he wore as he nodded a second time. She turned back to the door and reached for the handle and said, "I'll be sure to wear my dancing shoes." His responding groan brought a full-blown smile to her face. At least he would be as miserable as she was.

When she'd quit the room, the first thing she spotted was Rafe, and, immediately, the smile left her face and tension crept back into her muscles.

He pushed off the wall and scanned her from head to toe. "Little one."

Pausing in front of him, she arched a brow. "That's not the proper way to address a princess." Sage knew it was petty, but she didn't want him acting familiar with her. She wouldn't allow herself to be sucked back into a friendship with him. All he did was ruin people.

She watched with satisfaction as his jaw tightened for a moment. "My lady," he growled through gritted teeth.

Sage nodded to him with a smug grin, walking around him and down the airy hallway. She ignored the prickling sensation between her shoulders; she may not have heard him following her, but that didn't mean he wasn't there. He moved with stealthy feline grace. As she reached the stairs, a large hand gently wrapped around her bicep. Sage stared at the hand and slowly peered up at the large man with raised brows. "Yes?"

He cocked his head then released her, offering his arm. "My lady?"

Her eyes narrowed on him. The surrounding Guard shifted uncomfortably as she stared Rafe down. It was a trap. If she didn't take it, she'd look petty but if she did, he would have control.

"It's not a problem to be solved, Sage, it's an offering."

She bit her lip and hesitantly slipped her arm into his. They were both silent as they descended the stairs. Even when they reached the bottom, he didn't release her but guided her through the palace like it was his own home.

Inwardly, she rolled her eyes. No doubt he had been doing his fair share of snooping in the last month. He probably did know it as well as his home.

"I am curious to meet this Scythian woman."

Sage looked at him through the corner of her eye. "I just bet."

"I would like to meet her today."

"No."

"Why not?"

Why not? Because he was dangerous. Rafe wasn't even Aermian. She didn't even know what he was really doing in their country. How could she trust his motives? She couldn't. He was a liar, a fake. Sage felt him staring at her as he tried to figure her out, to read her. She kept her face blank.

"I taught you that mask, little one," he whispered. "You cannot hide from me."

Her teeth ground together for a moment before she answered. "I don't trust you."

He sucked in a breath. "Did you not agree to my help before the war council?"

Sage let a smile play on her lips. "I did, but I did not say in what capacity."

"Oh?"

She halted and looked into Rafe's familiar amber eyes. "I neither need your help nor want it. You cornered me in the meeting, and I didn't appreciate it. You forced my hand."

He shrugged a shoulder with a smirk. "I am a spy, little one, it's what I do."

Sage returned his smirk with one of her own—but hers had an edge. "Indeed, but as you often taught me, the devil's in the details. I never said in what way I would work with you." Her smile turned smug as his faded. "I find myself in need of a bodyguard that can blend into the crowd."

"You want me to be your bodyguard?"

"Yes, unseen, unheard. Zachael and the rest of the men would rip into me if I disappeared into the city without an escort but—" Sage slapped his chest, "—with your protection that takes care of that little detail, thus negating the necessity for a military escort. Meanwhile, I can go and retrieve my real helper."

"Indeed. Might that person have magenta eyes?"

Sage smiled brightly at him. "Indeed. What a lucky guess." She turned her back to him and sauntered toward the doors. Sage flipped her hair and called over her shoulder. "Don't forget a cloak, at the moment you practically scream 'see me'." His grumbling about cheeky women made her smile widen. She couldn't wait to see Lilja.

TWENTY-SIX

SAGE

SAGE SPRINTED DOWN THE HALLS, her boots echoing on the marble floor. She was running late. Adjusting the delicate package in her arms, Sage veered to the right, heading toward the infirmary. Hopefully, Mira was still there.

She rushed into the room, slamming the door back. The look on Mira's startled face was priceless as she dropped the sheet she was folding.

"Sage Ramses, what are you are doing?"

Sage halted in front of her friend and pulled her into a quick hug before Mira pushed back and scolded again.

"Where have you been? Sam dropped by looking for you. He questioned me until I finally booted him out of my space. Aren't you supposed to be at dinner?" Mira's gaze flickered to Sage's hair. "Good grief. What happened to your hair?"

Sage blinked at the rapid succession of questions fired at her. "I visited Lilja." She pointed to her crazy hair. "Lilja is what happened to my hair, and, yes, I should be at dinner which is why I am here."

"That makes no sense."

"Yes, it does." Sage huffed. "My ladies-in-waiting will take far too long to get ready for dinner. The crown prince will be as ornery as a badger by this point, so I need someone who can help me tame this beast." She gestured again to her hair. "And quickly."

Mira threw her head back and laughed. "There's no helping that mane."

"Please?" Sage pleaded, batting her eyelashes. "I'll hand over what Lilja sent home for you, if you help me."

The healer perked up, intrigued. "What did she send?"

Sage took a step back and swung the parcel before her. "Fix my hair, and you'll find out."

"You drive a hard bargain. But I suppose I accept," Mira smiled as she moved over to a desk. She peeked up as she dug around in one of its drawers. "You know, I would have helped you without a bribe."

"Just as I would have given you Lilja's gift without your help," Sage retorted, and plopped onto a cot.

Mira yanked a brush out of the drawer and rushed to her side. "This might hurt."

She winced. "I know."

Mira began the painstaking process of untangling Sage's salt-encrusted hair. "You smell like seaweed."

"I know."

"You look like seaweed too."

She reached around and smacked Mira's hip. "I know."

"Will you tell me what Lilja sent? I'm dying here."

"Just some seaweed and herbs."

Mira stilled for a moment. "Sea herbs?"

Sage smiled at the excitement in her friend's voice and nodded. "Sea herbs."

Mira let out a little yip and spun in a circle before attacking her hair with the brush again. "I can't believe she was willing to part with some. Sea herbs are so hard to harvest that they're extremely hard to come by, not to mention expensive. It must be because you're living here now."

"I doubt that's the case," Sage replied with a soft smile. "Lilja trusts you. You are not only skilled but a very caring healer. I'm sure it had nothing to do with me and everything to do with your own kindness."

Mira said nothing for a moment as she began to braid above sage's ear. "Thank you."

"We've been through this: there's nothing to thank me for."

"You've done more than you could've known." Mira tied off the left braid and began on the right. "Before I met you, I thought about pursuing something other than healing. I was so tired of the slurs from men and the vicious comments from other women regarding my profession. The things they would say about Jacob and I…it was disgusting." Mira's voice hardened. "I am his daughter, blood or no blood. It abhors me how people speak of us."

Sage closed her eyes as Mira's fingers worked through her hair. "I'm sorry. People can be cruel, especially when they don't understand something."

Her friend sighed. "I was tired. All I wanted was peace, and to work with my father in the infirmary, to just do what I love. I saw that it hurt Jacob every time someone spouted off something ignorant. I didn't want him punished for my choices so I was very close to giving it all up, both for his sake and mine, but then I met you."

Sage's eyes popped open, and she stilled Mira's hand while twisting around. Mira met her gaze, her face full of so much affection that her heart squeezed. In the most unlikely of places, Sage had found true friendship, a sisterly companion she'd forever cherish.

"Even at your weakest, despite the pain, you worked through it so you'd be stronger. Each nightmare could have kept you cowering in your bed, but you didn't allow them to overwhelm you, you kept pushing forward. Watching you deal with your demons gave me the motivation to face mine and not let the actions and opinions of others steal the joy in my life."

Sage swallowed against the lump forming in her throat. She was so fortunate to have Mira in her life. The woman's heart held more love, compassion, and kindness than anyone she had ever known.

Sage lifted Mira's hand up and kissed the back of it. "You're a gem, Mira."

The healer brushed aside her comment and kissed her on the crown of her head. "The feeling's mutual dear."

Sage twisted back around with a smile.

Mira spat into a bin. "Blech. Even your hair tastes like seaweed."

Sage laughed.

"Time to get you out of here." Mira piled the remaining loose hair high on the back of Sage's head, pinning it and then wrapping the braid around the updo. "Done."

Sage murmured her thanks as she leapt up and opened the package. Deep purple fabric slithered out that Sage couldn't help but caress. Mira halted by her side and Sage absently passed the healer her herbs, her eyes never leaving the exquisite fabric.

"Where did Lilja find that?" Mira asked in awe, hugging her herbs close to her chest.

"I stopped asking since she never gives me a straight answer."

"Sounds like Lilja." Mira plucked the fabric from the cot, her eyes rounding. "How do you wear it?"

Sage smiled. "Just wait and see."

After many knots, curses, and giggles, Sage was ready to go. The process had proved more complicated than anticipated, but she was finally done. Sage brushed her hands along the eggplant silk once more. "Well? What do you think?"

"What do I think? Everyone will stare at you for it looks exquisite. It resembles a dress, yet there are no seams, laces, or buttons." Mira shook her head, bewildered. "It's both fascinating and confusing. I'm still not sure how we figured out how to tie that thing together, and I'm sure I couldn't figure it out again if I tried. "

"Let's chalk it up to exquisite craftsmanship." Sage swept the fabric to the side and hugged Mira before hustling to the door. "Thanks for your help, I owe you."

"Yes, you do. How about you get Lilja to cough up another one of those dresses for me but in blue?"

"I can do that." Sage sniggered and paused at the door, craning her neck to look at her friend. "You sure you don't want to quit being a healer to be a lady-in-waiting? I hear there's a position open. Surely, it would be better than working here. I mean, just think of your reputation!" Sage widened her eyes dramatically.

Mira picked up a sheet and tossed it at her. "Get out of here, wench."

Sage laughed as she departed, calling out, "Your wish is my command, harpy."

Her smiled widened at Mira's fading cackle. It felt good to laugh. She picked up her skirts and sprinted to the dining hall taking care not to wrinkle the material. She winced when she heard music drifting down the hall. Swamp apples, they had already started dining. She was *so* late. Tehl would not be in a good mood.

She paused in the shadows just outside the door to arrange her dress, squaring her shoulders. Time to put on a good show for the court.

Sage tipped her chin up and adopted a careless air as she glided into the hall, the silky fabric gliding with her as she moved across the smooth marble floor. Sam spotted her first, arched a brow, and sent her a look as if to say *you're in trouble.* Sage forced herself to stay relaxed, holding her smile instead of sticking her tongue out at him, like she wanted to. She puffed out a laugh. He would, no doubt, figure out a way to crack a joke about how the gesture was somehow provocative.

Tehl noted the direction of his brother's attention and finally spotted her. Sage widened her smile in what she hoped looked like delight. Leisurely, the crown prince stood and moved down the stairs from the dais, wearing his full court smile. Oh boy. He was definitely *not* happy. Her afternoon with Lilja had been so fantastic and now he would surely ruin it. She forced her feet forward and dipped into a curtsey when he reached her. "My lord."

His large hand slipped into hers and lifted her. "My lady," he rumbled deeply, placing a kiss on her cheek. "What in the hell are you wearing, and where have you been?" he hissed in her ear before pulling back, his smile still in place.

Sage snuggled up to him and peered up into his face. "I got caught up."

"Obviously."

"Sorry."

He eyed her dress once more and scowled briefly before once again schooling his features into something more pleasant. Tehl placed her hand on his arm and turned, guiding them both toward the dais. He blew out a breath and glanced at her from the corner of his eye. "Did you have to wear that?"

Sage dropped her eyes to her dress with a faux smile like he complimented her. "What's wrong with my dress?" she murmured.

"It leaves nothing to the imagination."

Sage bit the inside of her cheek to keep herself from biting out a nasty retort. Most of the women of court were dressed much more scantily. "I am completely covered." And she really was, save a small keyhole on her back. The dang thing didn't even have a slit. "I've worn much more revealing dresses than this."

Tehl helped her up the stairs and pulled her chair out. Sage sat and eyed him as he seated himself.

"What?" he muttered.

"What's so immodest about it?" she asked softly.

"It's not what it covers." His eyes roved down her body and snapped back to her face. "It's how it fits."

"It was a gift from Lilja, and it's lovely." The purple complimented her hair, skin, and eyes. It flowed over her curves and onto the floor, neither too tight nor too loose, just fitted.

The crown prince snorted. "Of course, it was," he muttered underneath his breath. "I agree it is lovely, but it's enticing."

Sage blinked. Did he just compliment her? "And that's a bad thing?"

He blew out a breath. "My problem is that every other man is intrigued by the knots tying your dress." Tehl shifted looking uncomfortable.

"Why would they be interested in my knots?" Sage asked, playing stupid.

His eyes narrowed. "You know what I am talking about."

A smile played on her lips. "I'm sure I have no idea what you mean." Sage wanted to cheer when his nostrils flared.

"Every man is wondering if they tugged just right if it would come undone," he gritted out.

"Oh," Sage fake-gasped, though his obvious embarrassment had her bursting inside with mirth. She stifled a laugh.

"Oh indeed," Tehl growled. "I bet the rotten bastards will all vie to dance with you tonight."

Sage took pity on him and patted his hand. "It would take a lot more than that to get this to come undone. Mira spent a half-hour wrapping me in it."

Tehl plucked a grape from his plate and leaned back into his chair with a grin. "I bet you loved that."

Sage rolled her eyes and snagged a piece of cheese from her own plate. "I swear she was slow on purpose."

The crown prince shrugged one shoulder. "It's a possibility. She has a vengeful streak, that one. Have you done anything to vex her recently?"

"Too many things."

"Enough flirting you two," Sam teased from across the table. "It's bad enough I have to deal with it every day. I don't need to experience it at the table as well."

Good-natured laughs surrounded them. "Leave them alone, they've only been married a month."

Sage dipped her head like she was embarrassed to cover her humor. This was the game they played. Little pieces of truth mixed with deceptions so no one suspected what they were really about. The laughing faded and dinner resumed with soft chatter and the tinkling of silverware.

Over the last month, she and the crown prince had finally settled into a routine of sorts for dinner. They didn't say too much unless others engaged them and that suited them both very well. They stole small touches during the meal that weren't so stolen with many eyes on them. Each of these things was, of course, meaningless to them personally, only a deception to please the people surrounding them.

That evening, Sage chatted a little with the gentleman next to her who looked old enough she feared he might keel over at any moment. When the music changed, Sage met Tehl's eyes. This was always the hardest part for them. She loved to dance, and the crown prince could dance, but they weren't comfortable dancing with each other. It was still hard for them to pretend to enjoy being in each other's arms.

Tehl stood and offered his hand, and Sage slipped into her love struck persona as she accepted his hand. He led her down the stairs to the floor and stiffly pulled her into his arms. They began a slow swirling dance, and she smiled at the couples that whirled past, speaking to him from the corner of her mouth. "You're too rigid, you need to soften."

"Said no woman ever."

Her gaze flew to his and she stumbled a step. His face had not changed but she could just detect some humor in the crinkling of his eyes. "You've been spending too much time with your brother."

A smirk lifted the corners of his mouth, and his eyes flashed down to hers for a moment. "Or yours."

"What?" she asked stupidly. "When did you see my brothers? I haven't seen Zeke and Seb in a good two weeks."

"They had a shipment that needed to be dropped off."

"And they sought you out?" Sage questioned.

"No, I saw them and invited them for a pint."

"A pint?" she echoed. Who was this man and what did he do with her cantankerous husband?

He grinned. "You said that out loud."

That mortified her a bit but she shook her head and focused back on the surrounding crowd. "I still can't believe they didn't come and see me."

"Don't worry, you're still their favorite. I think they had a drink with me only so they could interrogate me for your father."

Now *that* sounded like something her brothers would do. "And?"

He shrugged. "The typical you-hurt-my-sister-and-I'll-kill-you threats, and then they left."

Sage chuckled. "I love those men."

"Of course you would, they're as bloodthirsty as you are."

"Very funny."

Tehl halted at the end of the song and bowed over her fingers. "Thank God it's over," he whispered against her skin.

Sage winked. "You think that now. By the end of the night, you will wish you were still dancing with me." His grimace made her chuckle as Sam sidled next to her.

"May I have the next dance, my charming sister?"

Sage avoided his gaze and scanned the group of women eyeing him. "You have a group ready and willing to be your partner."

"Yep, but I want to dance with you, sis."

"Why do you feel the need to subject me to your company?" she grumbled. In truth, she was still angry with him.

"Because they're empty-headed fools, and I prefer your company."

He wasn't giving her much of a choice. She placed her hand in his and scrutinized her brother-in-law. He had said it without a single drop of irony.

Sam pulled her into a slow glide, and they twisted between couples.

"Truly?"

He looked down at her, his face serious. "Yes." He pursed his lips before continuing. "I am sorry for earlier."

The prisoner. Good. He should be.

Turning away from Sam, she watched Tehl parade a star struck young brunette across the floor, who looked as if all her dreams had come true. At least someone was enjoying his grumpy company.

"Sage. I'm sorry."

She peered up at the spymaster and noted true remorse in his eyes. He *really* was upset, it wasn't a ploy or a joke.

"I am angry that you didn't tell me. Out of everyone, Sam, *everyone*, you know I would have been your best asset to retrieve information. We could have spared her some suffering." Sage huffed out a breath while holding on the threads of her serene mask. "And much to my chagrin, I am also a little hurt you didn't *want* to seek my help." She dropped her eyes, staring now at his chin.

Sam pulled her closer and kissed her forehead.

"You're never an asset. I learned much when dealing with you. That's why I didn't seek you out, I wanted you to feel at home here and not like a tool we married into the family to utilize whenever the need arose."

"Careful there," Sage chastised, scanning the people watching them, "or people might think you have a heart."

"Take that back."

She smiled and glanced up into Sam's face. "Never. I know others don't see it, including your family sometimes, but I do. I can spot a mask a mile away, and you, my friend, are rarely genuine, but when you are, I see the good man you hide behind this rake persona."

His gaze sharpened for a brief moment as he scrutinized her face but it quickly faded back to his usual look of casual interest. "You, my dear sister, see far too much."

"And you, my dear brother, hide far too much."

"Touché."

When their dance ended, she was passed from one man to the next for much of the evening, and, as it wore on, each dance and conversation seemed more tedious than the next. Her only reprieve were the dances she took with those on the war council. They knew her and her situation so she didn't have to be fake with them.

Zachael was quick on his feet. Sage should have figured, he was a weapons master, after all. Her dance with William was full of stories and tales, and, by the time she finished dancing with Garreth, her belly hurt from laughing so hard.

She was about to call it a night when a Sae tune began playing. Sage closed her eyes and swayed to the music. The Sae was a dance that was loosely based on myths of the Sirenidae. It was supposed to romanticize the lure and capture of her prey.

"May I have this dance?" rumbled a deep voice she would know anywhere.

Sage turned and stared into liquid golden eyes. That sneaky bastard, leave it to him to corner her before everyone so she couldn't refuse. She bared her teeth at him in what could be called a smile but was actually a warning. "I would be delighted."

Slowly, Sage glided backward, swaying her hips and twisting her arms above her head, keeping her eyes on Rafe as he prowled toward her like the hunter, not the prey. He clasped his large hands around her wrists like shackles and spun her around so her back pressed against his chest. She gritted her teeth, irritated that of all the dances, she had to dance the Sae with Rafe, and that he was taking liberties he had no right to take.

Everything about the Sae was meant to depict temptation without much actual physical contact, only the hands and wrists. Sage spun underneath his arm and slid around his back to his other side. His hand caught hers deftly and reeled her in, his arms crossed in front of her, holding her hostage.

Sage looked across the sea of dancing people and locked eyes with Caeja, a manipulative but beautiful young woman who had no problem making it known she was open to being the crown prince's mistress. The vile woman smiled smugly and draped herself against Tehl. So much for only the wrists and hands. She too seemed to take liberties.

Tehl frowned and maneuvered her into a different position that made Sage smile, not because he moved her but because he must have been even more uncomfortable than she was at the moment.

She slid her foot to the side and slipped to the floor, Rafe holding her hands above her head. He spun her once before yanking her to her feet, once again lifting her hands and drawing an arch with their limbs, leaving them face-to-face. "You look stunning, little one, like a true Sirenidae. You have never been more beautiful."

Her mood soured. He didn't have the right to say those words to her. "Not another word," she hissed while twisting side to side in front of him.

"Am I not allowed to pay my mate a compliment?"

Anger burned through her. Had he lost his mind?

Sage forced her smile to stay firmly on her face. "I am not your mate! If anything, I'm Tehl's mate," she tossed over her shoulder while Rafe continued to spin her. The music crescendoed, signaling the end of the song where the male counterpart thought he had captured his woman. Relief cooled some of her anger. At least the song was almost over.

Rafe pulled her close, their chests not quite touching, and swayed with her, his hands resting on her hips. Ever so carefully, Sage ran a finger across his chest and swooped under his arm to run her hand along his shoulder and then neck. The music stopped. All the men were considered dead. The Sirenidae captured their prey.

The rebellion leader spun, eyes filled with something hot that she deliberately ignored. Sage curtsied to him and excused herself. Not the time to dawdle. Her neck prickled as she bustled out of the dining hall so she glanced over her shoulder, locking eyes with Rafe. She frowned as his lips tugged up into a smug grin.

Arrogant man. Foolish man.

What was going on with him? He was acting out of character. Sage brushed the thoughts aside for another time; she had to make her escape. A bath was in her immediate future.

TWENTY-SEVEN

SAGE

SAGE TOOK THE SERVANTS HALLWAYS to avoid unwanted company, enjoying her solitude. Every so often, she stumbled upon couples in shadowy corners whereupon she would roll her eyes. It was surprising how many trysts she'd interrupted. You'd think they were more capable of finding seclusion.

She swung around a corner and paused to scrutinize the couple in the shadows. She blinked. Stars above, *really*? Familiar blond curls and wide shoulders. Sam.

She hesitated for a moment not knowing if she should startle them or backup and pretend she never came upon the embrace. After a moment, she backed into another alcove to watch. Who was Sam with? Some kind of redhead.

Sage cocked her head and watched with interest. Something wasn't quite right. Her eyes narrowed. For all the world they looked to be lovers, but something was off. There wasn't heat in the manner of his hold on the woman. And the redhead did not seem to behave in a passionate daze, rather her stance and expression demonstrated alertness and intelligence to the trained eye.

Interesting.

The woman leaned forward, whispering in his ear while scanning their surroundings. Sam slipped a hand up her side and plucked a small folded parchment from her skirts. It was naught but a little cream blur before it was gone, but she'd seen it. An idea took root in her head and she smiled. Could she be right? Time to test her theory.

Purposely she stomped her feet and immediately Sam reacted by kissing the woman and pulling her flush against him. Sage burst around the corner and paused, as if she'd been surprised by their appearance. The woman's eyes widened when she saw Sage, and she jerked back from Sam, seemingly scandalized. Sam peered over his shoulder and smiled at her lazily. "Sister, what a pleasure."

What a damn liar.

She shook her head and moved forward while the woman smoothed her skirt, whispering something in Sam's ear before dropping her head and brushing by Sage.

"You have something," Sage pointed to the pink smear on Sam's face.

He smiled and wiped at his face. "Did I get it?"

"Mmmhmm…" Sage stared after the redhead who was now bustling down the hall. "She was lovely."

"Indeed. Her body," Sam groaned, and then frowned playfully. "You scared her off you know. Now you owe me a date."

She snorted and turned back to the spymaster. "I'm sure you are more than capable of finding your own."

His grin turned rakish. "Many."

"Don't be crass," Sage chided. "Well, I am off to sleep. Are you off to find your bed as well?" she asked as she turned to walk away, leaving her trap open.

"Indeed, but, hopefully, I won't have to do so alone."

Sage smiled smugly. Trap set. "Somehow I think you will."

"Why would you say such a thing? You're trying to curse my good luck."

"I don't think luck has anything to do with it."

His voice trailed behind her. "Thank you. I too like to think my good looks have something to do with it."

"Now, now." Sage *tsked*. "You're getting ahead of yourself. You and I are alike. We don't leave things to chance. We plan and plot."

"What does that have to do with anything?" Sam asked.

"She was pretty, I'll give her that, but next time, find a better actress."

Sage held her breath.

Silence.

Wait for it.

Her smile widened when rapidly thudding boots started chasing her. He reached her side, but Sage kept her eyes ahead, ignoring his burning gaze. Sam cut in front of her and stopped. She halted, her skirts swishing around her feet. "Well?" she questioned.

His deep blue eyes ran over her like he was trying to see her secrets, to figure out what she knew. "Blye is a companion of mine, we have a unique relationship."

"I can see that. What sort of relationship exactly?" she probed.

"One too scandalous for your virgin ears."

"I'm not so innocent."

Sam scoffed. "I can spot them from far away. You have *that* sort of innocence written all over you."

"I'm not the only one."

The spymaster smirked. "I'm not sure what you mean, but if you need any lessons in seduction, I'll be your teacher."

Sage grimaced. "That sounded creepy."

Sam wrinkled his nose. "Oh, God, no. Not like that."

She smiled and stepped up to her brother-in-law, tipping her face up to stare into his eyes. "The funny thing is, Sam." She lifted her hand up and stroked his cheek tenderly. "Your words and action may be right, but it's the eyes that tell the truth." Sage lifted onto her toes and stared down the hall while whispering in his ear. "You're a master, but your lady? She gave herself away. Maybe you should have instructed her better."

She stepped back and moved to depart when he caught her arm.

"You are trouble."

"You already knew that."

"You see too much."

"You already knew that."

His eyes were hard as he studied her. "How?"

"Anyone with eyes could see it."

He scoffed and glanced around. "Not true."

"Will you tell me the truth?"

No response. A little disappointed, she pushed around him. "Goodnight, Sam."

A growl.

"Not here."

Sam pulled on her arm, guiding her down the hallway and up a set of stairs she'd never seen before that seemed to head in the direction of the royal wing. Sage filed its location away. One could never have too many escape routes.

He moved her to a shadowy alcove behind a tapestry and she gaped. How many times had she walked passed it and never guessed what was here? Sage shook her head and leaned against the wall, jerking slightly when part of her bare back touched the cold stone.

The alcove was just big enough for Sam to pace. He would grumble, look at her, open his mouth, and then close it as he began to pace again.

Sage yawned and waved her hand. "Are you going to start any time soon?"

"Wait a damn minute, woman. I am trying to figure out how to start."

Sage pushed off the wall and placed a hand on his arm to stop the pacing. "Then let me begin."

He looked down at her and nodded before taking her space against the wall.

"Your spies are women." Sage watched as he tensed, looked around, and reluctantly nodded. A laugh burst out of her at the uncomfortable look he wore. "It's brilliant, Sam. No one would suspect a table wench, a baker's wife, a washerwoman, or a lady of court was dealing in secrets."

"How?" he asked, the muscle in his jaw ticking.

"She wasn't that good of an actress. There was too much awareness in her eyes for it to be a tryst."

Sam cursed and ran a hand through his tangled locks before stabbing a finger at her. "You, you are a troublesome wench."

She grinned. "If you had trained your woman better than she wouldn't have given you away. Most people wouldn't have noticed but anyone with extensive training or experience would have known her as a fake."

"No one in years has ever guessed—" He broke off, swallowing hard.

Sage stepped closer and squeezed his hand. When his eyes met hers, she gave him a genuine smile. "I don't know how your brother and cousin haven't seen through your womanizing disguise but I understand the weight that secrets can have on a person. When you wear the persona so long you're not sure what's really you and what's the mask."

His mouth thinned, but he said nothing.

Sage kept from looking away as Sam stared at her, so many emotions rippling across his face in rapid succession.

"I'll be the person to remind you," Sage offered.

"It's been a long time since I've had that," he whispered.

The longing and vulnerability she heard in his voice made her do something she rarely did with Sam. She hugged him. He was warm and smelled spicy. When her anxiety grew, she pulled back and stepped out of his arms.

"I also want to train the women."

Sam blinked at her then sniggered. "Well, you don't take very long to assert yourself in other people's business now do you?"

"You need me. Between your experience and mine we could make your spies unparalleled in their field."

His eyes glittered with excitement. "I've wanted you to work for me since the beginning."

Sage scoffed. "I will not work for you but with you. We'll be equals, partners."

"There can only be one spymaster."

"There can only be one spymistress." she retorted.

Sam grinned at her. "Spymistress, huh?"

She grinned back. "Spymistress."

She would finally have something of her own again. Something she chose. Something she wanted.

"I guess it's settled then." He pushed off the wall and held his hand out to her. "To the future of intelligence gathering."

"To mischief and information."

"I like the way you think." Sam held his arm out to her. "Oh, spymistress of mine, I would like to accompany you back to your room."

Sage faked a gasp. "You don't have designs on my virtue do you?"

"Never, fair maiden. Too many men have designs on it already. It's getting kind of crowded, and I wouldn't survive the fight for dominance."

An uncharacteristic giggle slipped out that gave way to a carefree belly laugh as she took his arm and began walking toward her chamber. "No doubt you'd figure out how to turn the men against each other and run off with me."

"I'm a lover not a fighter."

Sam peeked out from behind the tapestry and waved her out. He settled the fabric and led her around the corner. Sage smiled at the guards standing outside her door. She frowned as she took in their expression. Garreth looked down right angry.

"Garreth," Sam greeted. "What's with the grumpy face?"

The Elite eyed Sam and then focused on her with an apology in his eyes. What was wrong?

"Are you all right?" Sage reached out to touch his arm but froze when a faint sound reached her ears from her room.

A giggle.

She glanced at Sam who was burning a hole into the door with his eyes.

Stars above. Really?

She took a step forward and placed her hand on the door.

"My lady," Garreth sighed. "Sage, walk away."

She gritted her teeth and pushed the door open, stepping inside.

There on her bed, tangled together, were the crown prince and Caeja. Her heart beat heavy in her chest as the smug woman smiled and squeezed Tehl's muscled bicep. Sage pulled her gaze from the clawed hand gripping the prince to his blue eyes filled with hostility.

She jerked straight and backed out, her gut churning. "Excuse me for the interruption."

Sage paused for a moment realizing that a woman in love wouldn't walk away. She squeezed her eyes shut, morphing her face into anger and spun toward the door.

"Sage, I…"

Sage peered over her shoulder at the two. "Save it. You disgust me. I'm done."

She slammed the door shut behind her. That was…odd. Her eyes burned a little. What was wrong with her?

Sage looked up to find both Sam and Garreth were looking at her in concern. Oh no, did she muck it up? Stepping away from the door, Sage looked between them. "That was convincing, right?"

"What now?" Garreth asked, confusion wrinkling his brows.

"Sage wants to know if her performance was good enough to fool the whore in there with my brother," Sam growled.

The Elite blinked. "You're pretending to be upset?"

"Yes," Sage drew out.

"You're not upset by what you saw?" Garreth nodded at the door.

"No," she said slowly, ignoring the betrayal churning inside her. "Why would I?"

"Because he's your husband, and what he is doing is wrong."

"Technically, I was sold to the Crown. I could have the marriage annulled if I wanted. It's not real." Her heart pinched; they weren't a married couple in the normal sense but she still thought they would be respectful of each other.

A crash and a loud bellow was her cue to leave. Sage backed away from the two men and shrugged. "Let the prince know I'll stay somewhere else tonight, but I will be back by morning before the servants arrive. Make sure his guest is gone by then. Garreth?"

He shook himself and met her eyes. "Yes?"

"Are you going to be guarding through the night?"

"Yes."

"Make sure no one notices her exit, please."

She paused when Sam started in her direction. He placed both of his hands on her cheeks and searched her eyes. "This isn't right, even if you feel like your marriage isn't real. There were oaths." He dropped his hand and touched her cuff. "You wear his cuffs."

"Not by choice," she said lightly pulling his hands from her face. "Don't worry about me," Sage wiggled her eyebrows playfully, "I am the spymistress, I wear many masks, hurt isn't one of them, but I ought to be going. We'll speak more tomorrow."

His lips thinned, but he didn't stop her from walking away. Her joking manner dropped and her lips quivered. Even if they weren't a real couple, no one liked feeling worthless and betrayed.

TWENTY-EIGHT

TEHL

"GET OUT!" TEHL GROWLED AS he shoved the treacherous woman off of him. She stumbled to her feet, looking shocked. He cursed loudly and glared at her.

"Are you deaf? I said get out."

Caeja jerked back a step, tripping on her garish red dress. "But I thought…"

"You thought wrong."

She blinked. "But you invited me to your rooms, and we danced the Sae."

Tehl didn't quite remember it like that. "No," he said slowly, "you are my wife's lady-in-waiting, and you offered to help her undress."

At his statement, a seductive smile replaced the uncertainty. Caeja held her hands out in innocence and took a step forward. The innocence was as fake as she was.

"Well, she wasn't here, so I wanted to lend a hand," she purred.

He snarled, and she froze. In no way, had he given her the impression she was welcome in his bed. He was a married man for heaven's sake, and for all intents and purposes, he was in love.

"I love my wife," Tehl stated.

Caeja barked out a sharp laugh crossing her arms. "If you love her, I'll eat my own hat."

Tehl frowned as she drew shapes on the bed with her finger. He wished she would stop doing that. It was creepy.

"I am not blind, I know when a man is enthralled with one woman."

Her eyes traveled from the bed and met his.

"And you, my dear prince, are not that man. The Methian prince on the other hand…" She *tsked*. "Well let's just say he has an issue with covetousness."

Tehl's eyes narrowed to slits. So he wasn't the only one who took notice. The heated exchange between Rafe and Sage during the Sae was plain for all to see. The small, jealous part of him had reared its ugly head as he had observed their dance. Sage was alive in Rafe's arms. He detected the loathing but there was also something else there. And she hadn't responded to him like that, ever. Was it an act? Was it hate? Or was it something more? He still didn't know.

When she'd excused herself, the rebellion leader had discreetly followed her. Tehl decided to call it a night and see what his troublesome little wife was up to, but Caeja had managed to come along.

"I am here for you if you need anything."

He snapped back to the disgusting woman who was still somehow standing in his room. Tehl had dealt with her flirting and blatant advances for years, but now it would end. He was tired of it.

It saddened him to remember the girl she used to be growing up. She'd been a wonderful person, but somewhere along the way she'd become a power-mongering harpy. Maybe if someone spoke frankly to her, it would snap her out of her ways.

He drew in a deep breath and stared her down. "Caeja, this needs to stop. As a girl you were precocious, kind, and funny." Her smile widened, and she batted her lashes. "But now all you are is an insipid, shallow wench."

Her smile dropped. "Excuse me?"

"What made you this way?"

Silence.

"Caeja, you need to change. If you act the whore, men will treat you that way."

"You don't know a damn thing about me!" Caeja hissed, rage sparkling in her eyes.

"You're right, and I don't care to." He winced. That was a little harsh but he continued on. "I would be remiss if I didn't straighten you out while I have the chance."

"You're not my father, how dare you speak to me in such a way!"

"You're right, I am not, but I am your crown prince and acting ruler. Remember who you are speaking to." Her eyes dropped to the floor. "Where are your morals, Caeja? You were raised better than this. Your father may be a ruthless man, but he would never wish this type of life on you. Have you forgotten what's right and wrong?" Tehl gestured to her dress. "What are you even wearing? What kind of attention are you trying to attract? You're barely covered. What happened to modesty? You've thrown yourself at me without any thought to your future. Don't you desire a family? A husband who loves you?"

Her lips quivered for a moment before she pressed them together so tightly they turned white. "Yes."

"Then take a good look at yourself, and change, or you'll find yourself in a place you don't want to be." Tehl ran a hand through his dark locks staring at the plush rug beneath his boots. "Now, leave me."

Tehl lifted his head when the swish of her grown signaled her exit.

He needed to find his wife and explain. It had taken a while, but he was beginning to read little things about Sage, and she had been genuinely shocked finding them. She'd recovered well, but he had sensed emotion.

Tehl waited a minute and then pushed off the bed, striding to the door. He wrenched it open and halted at the sight of Sam casually leaning against the far wall.

"Where's Sage?" He looked left then right, nodding to Garreth who jerked his chin up at him in a stiff way.

Hell. Even Garreth was pissed at him.

He spun back to Sam and noted his brother hadn't moved or spoken. Usually he had too much to say. "Where is she?"

Sam shrugged. "I don't know."

"Sam, you keep track of everyone. You're a better liar than that."

Another shrug.

Tehl rolled his eyes. "No comment."

Anger crossed Sam's face surprising him.

"She needs to be alone."

"I need to explain."

"Well, that's for damn sure," Sam snapped.

"Nothing happened." Tehl's fists closed and his jaw clenched. "Caeja instigated it and tricked me."

"Now that sounds like Caeja."

His brother pushed off the wall and strode toward him.

"What I don't understand is the amount of time you spent with her after Sage barged in on you." Sam jabbed him in shoulder. "Are you so stupid to risk everything for *Caeja?*"

"We were talking," Tehl said.

"Is that what they're calling it these day?" Sam snorted. "I know a tumbled woman when I see one."

"She looked tumbled because I shoved her off the bed! Do you really think I am capable of being that callous? We're not a love match but do you think I'd so readily disrespect my wife and my standards?!"

Sam searched his face and visibly relaxed. "You're not a very good liar, and you're one of the most loyal people I know. I should have figured. I am glad I won't have to defend Sage's honor by kicking your ass."

His brother believed him. Tehl let loose a deep breath. "Do you really not know where Sage is?"

"She disappeared right after she walked in on you." His brother's lips thinned. "Rafe sauntered by a few minutes ago."

Tehl straightened at that. The rebellion leader was always lurking. "He was in the royal wing?"

Sam rolled his eyes. "The rebellion leader is everywhere. I doubt there is any place we could keep him out of. He moves like a ghost. I am a little envious sometimes, I'll admit."

That's all he needed, Rafe finding Sage while she was upset at him. After the rough day they'd had… One thing was clear: he needed to find her because the rebellion leader wasn't playing by the rules.

"It's like he doesn't understand that she is taken." Tehl found himself saying. "Doesn't anyone have any respect these days? Sage is a married woman, and I am a married man."

"You might want to speak about that with your bride, then," Garreth piped in.

Tehl craned his neck to look at the Elite. "What do you mean by that? Has she been unfaithful?" The words burned in his mouth as he said them.

Garreth's eyes rounded as he shook his head emphatically no. "No, that's not what I meant. What I meant is that she doesn't consider herself in a real marriage."

"It's real."

"Is it?"

"It's not fake, we share a room every night." Tehl pointed to the cuffs on his biceps. "I am wearing her damn cuffs. What could be more real than that?"

Garreth held up his hands. "I am just repeating what she has previously said. Sage is of the mind that she's been sold, and that she can annul whenever she wants."

"What?" She wanted an annulment? Not in his lifetime. "Like hell that will happen. Plus, there's no one who'd examine her for innocence without my say so."

"Mira," Sam breathed.

Tehl froze. Mira, of course, the blond healer wouldn't care what he threatened her with if she wanted to help Sage. "I need to go." Stars above, why did everything feel so unsecure all of a sudden?

Sam slapped him on the shoulder as he stormed by. "I'll look for her too."

Tehl tossed his thanks over his shoulder before searching all the places he could think of where his little wife liked to disappear to.

Nothing.

He rushed up a stairway and spotted Rafe walking toward him. Tehl swerved and intersected Rafe's path. "Have you seen, Sage?"

Rafe's golden eyes studied him for a moment before answering. "No, I've not seen her since our dance."

Tehl fought back a growl at the memory of how the other man had looked at Sage. "If you see her, tell her I am looking for her, will you?"

Rafe nodded.

"I also don't appreciate uninvited guests in the royal wing. Especially ones looking for *my* wife late at night."

Every drop of civility Rafe held disappeared. "She's your nothing."

He said it simply like it was the truth.

Tehl bared his teeth. "That's where you're wrong." He tapped his cuff. "She's now my everything." Tehl ignored the growl that rumbled out of the dangerous man. "Your covetousness and blatant disregard for the sanctity of marriage tonight could cause the death of many. Sage and I are working as partners the best we can to protect Aermia, and you're just making it difficult." He stepped toe to toe with Rafe, their noses almost touching. "So I'll say it again, stay away from my wife."

Rafe's eyes hardened. "You will *never* deserve her."

Tehl nodded. He may not have been in love with Sage but he did see her worth. "Maybe you're right, but I am thankful you drove her into my home."

He dipped his chin and stalked around the rebellion leader to the grand staircase. Hopefully, he had talked some sense into the man. Tehl snorted. Doubtful. The man was as stubborn as he himself was.

Tehl reached the royal wing, irritated that Sage had disappeared. As he wandered down the hall, firelight flickered underneath a door casting wispy ropes of dancing light on the dark carpets. He followed the light to the door.

A smile.

Sage's old room.

He'd found her.

TWENTY-NINE

TEHL

HE PULLED IN A DEEP breath through his nose and knocked. Time to prepare for battle.

Silence.

No way. She wasn't going to ignore him. They were going to talk. Tehl pushed open the door and stepped inside.

"Sam, do you ever wait for an invitation—" Sage swung out of the bathing room wearing a playful scowl that dropped at the sight of him.

Tehl clicked the door shut and gaped. She'd changed out of her Sirenidae dress into a long silk nightgown. Tehl scanned her from head to toe. Stars above, she was a lovely woman. His mood soured. A lovely troublesome wench. But even that thought didn't tear his eyes from her. He hadn't seen her in anything like that since they'd been married. Each night she went to bed in her linen shirt and leather pants armed to the teeth with weapons.

"You're wearing a nightgown," he said stupidly.

Her scowl returned. A real one. Great.

"Thank you for stating the obvious. I wasn't expecting any guests. Give me a moment." She spun and disappeared into the bathing room.

"You called me Sam when I walked in." Tehl pointed out as he strode farther into her room. He paused by the fire, enjoying the warmth wrapping around him. "Obviously, you were expecting some company."

542

"Sam's harmless," she hollered.

What a crock. "Are we still speaking about the same person?"

"He doesn't have any design on my virtue," came her muffled reply.

"Sam has a design on every woman's virtue." His tone was full of disgust. His brother's questionable pastimes bothered him. "Anyone who thinks differently is foolish."

The door swung open revealing Sage in her typical nighttime attire, leather and linen. For a moment, he thought it was a pity she'd discarded the nightgown, but he shook his head and focused on what needed to be said. "We need to talk."

She paused at the dressing table and pulled a brush through her tangled hair which left transparent wet spots on her shirt.

"What about, my lord?"

Damn it, she was using formalities. One thing he had picked up living with her is that when she wanted to distance herself from someone, she was overly formal.

"I want to speak about what you witnessed earlier. I need to apologize."

Her brushstrokes stopped, and she met his eyes. "There's nothing to apologize for. We don't love each other, and it's not my place to judge you." She turned from him and began yanking the brush through her hair. "Is that all?"

Tehl's brow wrinkled in confusion. He explained nothing. Sage believed he had broken his marriage vows and yet she acted like it was something as common as stepping on someone's toes. That it wasn't a grievous sin against her. He'd have been angry if he had caught her in that position.

"So you're not upset that another woman was in our bed?" Tehl waited to see if she would pick up the bait. She said more when she was angry. It lit her up.

"No, technically it's not even my bed, it's yours."

"But I am bound to you," he prodded, trying to get some read on her.

"A written piece of paper, some words, and silver does not constitute a marriage."

Now that was a damn lie. Her words ignited his anger. How could she be so callous about marriage vows? "Do you remember what we agreed upon before we were betrothed?" Tehl asked meeting her eyes in the mirror.

She nodded.

"Have you up held them?"

Carefully, she set down the brush and watched him in the mirror. "I have," she ground out. "And I find it unfair that since you have broken yours, you now question mine." Sage placed her hands on the dresser not losing eye contact. "Have I not been a good wife?"

"Yes."

"Have I not shouldered the responsibilities you heaped upon me without a single complaint until today?"

"Yes."

"Have I not given all to keep your kingdom together?"

"Yes."

"Then how dare you question my morals."

Well, hell. That's not what he meant at all. Tehl took a couple of cautious steps until he stood behind her, placing his hands on her rigid shoulders. "It was not my intention to accuse you of anything. My purpose for seeking you out was to clear the air."

She dropped his gaze to stare at the brush. "Well, you sufficiently cleared the air. Thank you for coming to apologize, but it isn't necessary. Now, if you'll excuse me, I am heading to bed. I'll make sure to sneak back into the suite before the servants come to greet us."

"You'll be sleeping in our room." They would not go to bed angry with each other. His mother always said never go to sleep provoked but to make peace, and he planned to.

Her head snapped up, her eyes glittering with true emotion for the first time. "I may brush aside what you do but that does not mean I will sleep in a bed that smells of another woman. I have more self-respect than that."

Sometimes, he laughed at the oddest times, and this was one of those times.

Her eyes narrowed, and she jerked out of his grasp, rounding the bed and yanking back the covers. "Don't you dare laugh at me."

"I'm sorry, I'm not laughing at you," he wheezed. "It's the situation. You haven't let me speak. You've twisted everything around." Tehl watched her whack the pillows. "Sage."

She ignored him and smoothed the sheets.

"Sage."

"What?" she yelled, her chest heaving.

"I didn't sleep with her."

She whipped out a dagger and stabbed the air with it. "Don't lie to me. I saw what happened with my own eyes. I'm not a fool. I'm a fake but no fool."

"Caeja is a snake."

"On that we can agree," she huffed.

"I swear to you on my mother's memory she did not come to our room for that purpose."

Sage paused in making the bed before sitting on the smooth sheet to stare at him. "Then what happened? She was all over you during the Sae." His wife shrugged. "She's beautiful."

Now it was his turn to scowl. He vividly remembered the rebellion leader taking liberties. "I am not the only one who needs scolding about dancing with another."

His wife rolled her eyes. "I can't even stand the sight of Rafe at the moment. Are you sure you can see properly?"

"I know what I saw, it might not have been you, but the rebellion leader..."

"Rafe is just being Rafe."

Tehl shook his head. They could argue this for hours. "We're getting off topic. Caeja only came to our room so she could help you out of your dress, but when you weren't there she tried to seduce me."

A choked sound came from her throat.

He squinted at her blank face. "Your blank face shows me more than you know. You doubt me, I get it, but this is what happened. She had her damn dress pulled so low she tripped on the skirt and slammed into me. We ended up sprawled across the bed." Tehl cleared his throat when Sage's face cracked, and she sniggered. "When I booted her from our suite, she tripped on her skirt and about brained herself against the wall, again." Tehl sighed. "I don't want her. Ever."

Sage eyed him in the quiet of the room. "I believe you."

He blew out a breath, surprised by how much her answer calmed him. "Thank you."

"But I am still not sleeping in there 'til the bed sheets are changed tomorrow. The whole room reeked like roses." Sage's nose wrinkled up in distaste. "I'm staying here."

"I hate roses."

Sage gasped. "You hate roses?"

"Well, not the flowers, just her perfume. It gives me a headache. If you're staying here, then so am I."

Her eyes narrowed. "This is my room."

Tehl sauntered to the other side of the bed and flipped back the covers. "It's mine."

"It's your father's," she countered. "He gave it to me, now out!"

"A technicality. Plus, my father always said you sleep with your wife no matter what. You never let the sun set when you're upset with each other."

"I thought your mother said that."

"They both believed it true."

Her lips pursed. "Fine. Sleep on the floor."

He pulled off his boots and unbuttoned his vest, tossing it next to his boots before plopping onto the bed. "If I'm in my own home, I don't sleep on the floor."

"Then I'll sleep on the floor."

"Stars above," he growled. "When's the last time you had a good night sleep and woke up without an aching back?"

Silence.

Tehl closed his eyes. "I would like a full night of sleep. I'll just end up moving you in the middle of the night after you experience a nightmare. Save us both some time and sleep; get in the damn bed." He cracked an eye and peeked at her. The anger and fear warring on her face softened him. She was a warrior. Stronger than she knew. "I'll sleep on top of the covers."

Uncertainty still showed in the way she stood.

Time for a different tactic. "What are you afraid of?" She never backed down when challenged.

Her jaw tightened before she stormed around the room, blowing out each of the lanterns and candles. Tehl spied on her through slit lids as she hovered by the side of the bed before making her mind up and slipping in. A smile spread on his face when he closed his eyes. They had survived today and they would survive tomorrow. Tehl jerked upward when a large pillow slapped him in the face.

Sage smiled innocently at him.

"Sorry, I didn't see you there."

His eyes narrowed. Devious wench. Lying down, he watched her build a pillow wall down the entire length of the bed, except for where their heads would rest. Nodding, she lay down and stared at him.

"Don't try anything or I'll stab you."

He couldn't help rolling his eyes. "Like I haven't heard that before."

She nodded and closed her eyes. Tehl's gaze traced over her arching brows, long lashes, full lips, and high cheekbones. It would have been easier if he had been married to a hag.

"Would you stop watching me?" she muttered.

"Sorry," he mumbled, still looking at her.

"If you were sorry you would stop it."

Tehl nodded even though she couldn't see him and turned on to his back. He thus far had found their marriage surprisingly entertaining, and he was finding it more intriguing by the day. "I really am sorry for any pain our misunderstanding I caused you."

"You didn't hurt me."

His brows furrowed. "It didn't bother you at all?" He turned his head to look at her. "If it had been you in my position, it would have bothered me."

Sage blinked her eyes open and gazed at him. "It didn't hurt me but I did feel disrespected." She swallowed. "And lacking."

That surprised him. "You're not lacking, that's why I was staring. You may be annoying, but you're also beautiful."

Her eyes crinkled before she laughed. "Tehl, you have a horrible way with words."

"I know."

"And atrocious manners."

"I know."

"But a loyal heart."

He blinked. Sage had said something nice to him. "Thank you."

"Now, stop talking and go to sleep, it's been a long day."

Tehl turned to stare at the ceiling. "You have a brave heart."

The fire crackled, and, it was so quiet, he was sure she didn't hear him. It wasn't until he had just about drifted off, that he heard a soft thank you. Tehl smiled. They would make it through the mess of their lives.

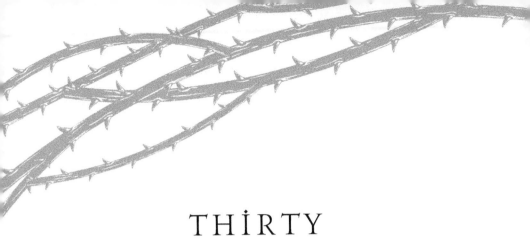

THIRTY

SAGE

❧

FINGERS AND STEEL TRAINED ALONG *her skin, pain kissing her all over. "I will break you…"*

Sage jerked away and blinked, her breath sawing in and out of her chest. Frantically, she searched the room for the monster that lurked in her dreams. The room was dark, except for the glowing embers of the fire. She gulped a deep breath of cool air and tore the covers back, swinging her feet to the side of the bed.

It was just a dream, Sage. He's not here. You're okay.

"Sage?" a deep voice rumbled.

She jumped, her hand going for her dagger before she remembered who was next to her. The crown prince. Tehl. It was just Tehl. Sage craned her neck and peeked at him over her shoulder as he stared at her, half asleep, his hair messily tossed across his forehead. Her panic loosened at the sight of him. He wouldn't hurt her and Tehl slept with as many weapons as she did. No one would be able to get past the two of them together.

"Go back to sleep, my lord. It's nothing."

"You sure?"

"Yes."

The crown prince nodded and rustled around in his blanket before falling back asleep with deep, measured breaths. Sage stared at him for a moment, jealous that he'd fallen asleep so quickly. Part of her wanted to whack him in the face with a pillow again and pretend to sleep so that when he jerked awake, he wouldn't know it was she that disturbed his sleep. She stared at him for a beat longer, feeling restless, before deciding to go for a walk.

She slipped on her boots and silently slipped out the door, startling Garreth. When he'd recovered, he raised a brow in question.

"I couldn't sleep. I need to walk." Sage paused, her brow furrowed in confusion. "How did you know where—"

"We always know where the crown prince is."

"That sounds…tedious."

A silly smile turned the corners of his mouth up. "Sometimes."

Garreth turned and whispered to the other Elite posted by the door and walked to her side. "If you'll allow me, I'll escort you."

She wanted to argue, but she also understood it wasn't really a request. Royalty required protection and she was now considered royal. She'd spent time with Garreth in training, so he wasn't a complete stranger, and at least he knew how to be silent. He was almost as sneaky as she and Sam were. Sage nodded curtly and spun on her heel, heading to the hidden room the king had shown her to when she first arrived. He hadn't visited her in a while but today she'd make sure to track him down for some tea or a walk.

Sage pushed into the suite, Garreth on her heels. She paused, waiting for him to close the door, and then hastened to the bookcase. Her eyes searched in the dim light to find the silver leafed book. She pressed firmly on its spine until a faint click sounded and the bookcase rolled to the side, revealing the hidden doorway.

"Stars above, how long have you known about that?" Garreth breathed.

A grin touched her lips at the censure in his voice. "The king showed me when I was being held here." She ignored his cursing and began to descend the dark stone stairwell. "Be a darling and light a lantern. It's pitch dark in here, and I would prefer not to break my neck or have to explain why you broke yours."

He grumbled behind her but soon enough was stepping behind her with a soft light. "I'm not too comfortable with this. The stones are slick as snot, my lady."

Sage waved off his concern and descended the spiraling staircase. It was slow going, but it brought her a measure of peace. When the sound of thundering waves echoed up the stairs, she felt a spark of excitement. "We're close," she said, gleefully.

When they rounded the last corner, Garreth's sharp breath of awe warmed her. He found the sea cave as beautiful as she did.

"It's lovely isn't it?" she asked as she stepped over a porous rock, running her finger over a starfish.

"It's wondrous."

"Indeed."

When they reached the mouth of the cave, Sage sat down in the sand that had turned silver by the light of the waning moon. She pulled her boots and socks off, enjoying the feel of the sand between her toes. Garreth followed her lead, placing his boots and the lantern off to one side. Once he finished doing so, she meandered down to the beach, savoring the feel of the cool breeze as it ruffled her hair. She listened to the crashing waves and entertained herself, discovering small treasures the ocean had deposited on the beach, curling her linen shirt up to contain them. When her makeshift sack was filled, along with the Elite's hand, she decided it was time to return. Her restlessness had faded, as had the memory of her nightmare, so fatigue weighed heavily upon her.

When they arrived at the cavern's mouth, Sage carefully placed her treasures in the sand so she could pull on her boots. She shuddered when she remembered how she'd previously been forced to walk through the slime since she hadn't any shoes. Never again. She eyed her treasures and then the cave.

Garreth rolled his eyes. "You'll break your neck if you try to haul all of that up the stairs. Leave it for now."

"But..." Sage glanced at the sea loot longingly.

He sighed. "Fine, I'll carry them."

Sage beamed. "Thank you."

"Yeah, yeah. I'm supposed to be an Elite, and yet I find myself a glorified beast of burden," he grumbled some more as he collected her shells and sea glass, this time using his own tunic front.

As they began the long ascent, Sage thought about her quiet companion. Their entire walk had been comfortable. She appreciated the quiet, the peace. It was times like these that she realized just how skewed her perception had been of the Crown and those loyal to it. She'd found true friendship in places she never expected. Sage peeked over her right shoulder at Garreth, smiling. "Thank you for coming with me," she said simply.

The happy smile which lit up his face and eyes was the perfect ending to their walk. "My pleasure."

Sage's smile widened as she weaved back through the cave, approaching the stairs. She eyed the stone steps with distaste and groaned, remembering the long trek ahead of her. "All those stairs to hike up, how miserable."

A snigger sounded behind her. "You're the one who chose to come down here. Didn't you account for the trek back?"

She sniffed. *Now* he decided to have something to say. Sage blew out a breath and took the first step up the endless staircase. After a few flights of stairs, her legs burned and her lungs labored. She really needed to train more. The further they trudged, the more Sage questioned her sanity. Why in the world did she decide to come down to the beach? She paused as something plinked against the stone behind her. "Everything okay?" she asked looking over her shoulder.

Garreth was struggling to hold onto all of her sea treasures and the lantern. He glanced up at her. "Actually, no. Could you hold the lantern for a moment while I adjust your loot? I will lose all of them if I don't figure out a different way to hold them."

She carefully spun on the step and took the lantern from him, trying to hide her grin as the highly trained soldier fumbled with the dainty shells. "And here I thought the Elite could do anything with ease," she teased.

He snorted while he adjusted his hold on her treasures and his tunic. "That sounds like propaganda from Sam."

Sage chuckled as she turned and lifted the lantern to one of the darkened hallways. "Indeed." The darkness was so thick she could only see a few feet down them. There were so many hidden passageways in the castles. It would take her years to explore them all. "I wonder where this one leads," she mused out loud. "Eventually, I would like to explore them all. Do you know where it goes?" she asked, hitching a thumb over her shoulder.

He lifted his head from arranging the shells wearing a teasing smile that quickly shifted to horror.

"Sa—" was all she caught as pain exploded in her head. Spots of light and dark danced across her vision, and the world spun around her. She blinked once and the last thing she saw was Garreth exploding into action while her treasures flew through the air. Then she knew only darkness.

Something was thundering, and the pain in her head pulsed with the sound. Where was she? And why did everything hurt? Sage groaned, wishing the pounding in her skull would stop. Groggily, she lifted her head and slit her eyes only to slam them shut as bright light brought on another wave of pain.

Suddenly, the pounding made sense. A horse. She was on a horse.

Her stomach lurched as the horse's speed increased, aggravating her head. How did she hurt her head? Why was she on a horse? She couldn't remember anything.

"You awake, consort?" a familiar voice sneered.

Her breath froze in her lungs and her entire body locked up.

No. It couldn't be.

The arm around her waist tightened and warm breath dampened her neck. "I know you're awake. You can't hide from me, love."

Bile burned her throat and panic clawed at her chest.

No, no, no, no, NO!

"Yes, yes, yes," the deep voice crooned in her ear. "Your training is slipping. I know exactly what you're thinking. Now look at me."

Her body trembled, and she squeezed her eyes tighter closed.

"Defiant to the end?" the monster mused. "Well. He will relish breaking you."

Stop being the victim. Don't let him take you without a fight.

She blew out the breath she'd been holding, hyper-aware of his arm below her breasts.

Open your eyes, Sage. Open them!

She turned her neck and forced them open to stare into ordinary mud-brown ones.

Rhys.

A sinister smile curled his lips. "Hello there, love. Shall we play a game?"

CONTINUE THE SERIES WITH

QUEEN
◈— OF —◈
MONSTERS AND MADNESS

ABOUT THE AUTHOR

Thank you for reading *Kingdom of Rebels and Thorns*. I hope you enjoyed it!

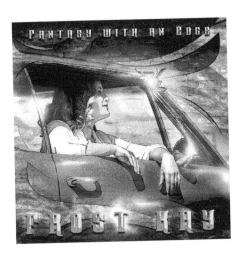

If you'd like to know more about me, my books, or to connect with me online, you can visit my webpage WWW.FROSTKAY.NET or join my facebook group FROST FIENDS!

From bookworm to bookworm: reviews are important. Reviews can help readers find books, and I am grateful for all honest reviews. Thank you for taking the time to let others know what you've read, and what you thought. Just remember, they don't have to be long or epic, just honest.

CPSIA information can be obtained
at www.ICGtesting.com
Printed in the USA
LVHW092045110222
710781LV00024B/724/J